'A ... ...oving, compelling story, brilliantly im...
Conn...

'A ... ...oughly good read . . . vividly imagined . . . elegant, lively ...
Sunday Telegraph

'... ... undertaking, *Romanitas* creates a fascinating world that
... ... contemporary in tone, and yet about as far removed from
... ...orld we live in as it is possible to imagine. McDougall's
... ...g style is fresh and light and the involving story ensures
... ... gobble up the four hundred pages in no time, staying eager
... ... out how the remainder of the trilogy unfolds'
Dreamwatch

'... ...triguing debut novel . . . the plot of *Romanitas* gripped me
... ...ept the pages turning. McDougall's setting is original . . .
... ...ternate history feels well researched and believeable'
Starburst

Also by Sophia McDougall from Gollancz:

Romanitas
Rome Burning

SAVAGE CITY

SOPHIA McDOUGALL

The right of Sophia McDougall to be identified as the
author of this work has been asserted by her in accordance
with the Copyright, Designs and Patents Act 1988.

First published in Great Britain in 2011 by
Gollancz
An imprint of the Orion Publishing Group
Orion House, 5 Upper St Martin's Lane,
London WC2H 9EA
An Hachette UK Company

This edition published in Great Britain in 2012 by Gollancz

1 3 5 7 9 10 8 6 4 2

A CIP catalogue record for this book
is available from the British Library

ISBN 978 0 575 09638 7

Typeset at The Spartan Press Ltd,
Lymington, Hants

Printed and bound in Great Britain by
Clays Ltd, St Ives plc

The Orion Publishing Group's policy is to use papers that
are natural, renewable and recyclable products and made
from wood grown in sustainable forests. The logging and
manufacturing processes are expected to conform to the
environmental regulations of the country of origin.

www.romanitas.com
www.orionbooks.co.uk

To my family

[CONTENTS]

THE MAP OF THE WORLD

Hyouden

Souko

Yukimiji

Aokusahara

Iwatougen

TOKOGANE
(Roman-Nionian shared territory)

VENDATIA

ABENACIA

THULE MAIOR

THULE MINOR

Nova Dgva

Colonia
Vincia

Enkono

LACOTA

Sorasanmiyaku

ARCANSA

Cayarta

Mixigana

Stadacona

ALGONQUIANA

GOTHIA

BRITANNIA

London

GERMANIA

Moguntiacum

RHAETIA

PANNONIA

GAUL

Savaria

DALMAT

ANASASIA

Sievibacum

Cathocia

Augusta
Tuiscorum

Lugdunum
Convenarum

ITALIA

Tarraco

Rome

HISPANIA

MEXICA

CALUSA

Carthage

TRIPOLITANIA

Tecesta

TERRANOVA

Cinitisia
(Roman-Nionian shared territory)

Lepcia
Magna

Tenaclanum

MAURETANIA

Garama

LIBYA

MASAESYLIA

GAETULIA

MAIA

Asantium

Daura

Bacata

ARAVACIA

TUPIA

Caesarea
Incarum

Xavantium

ARAUCANIA

GARANIA

Diaquitia

HARPEIA

IN

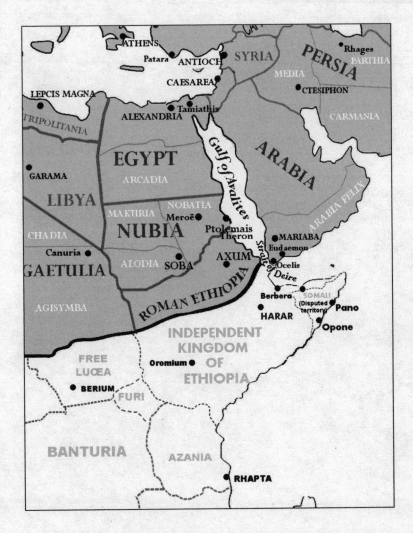

ROMAN AND INDEPENDENT AFRICA, AND THE NEAR EAST

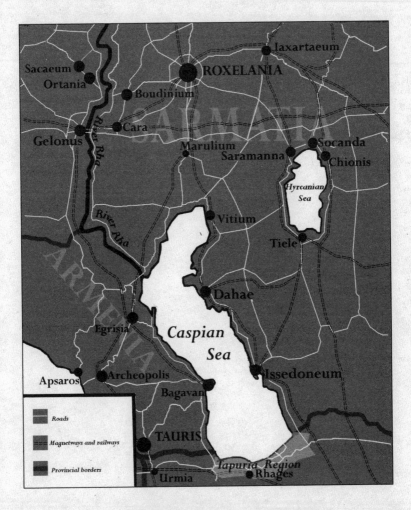

MAJOR ROUTES IN THE RHA REGION
(Venedia, Sarmatia, Armenia and Persia)

[RECENT HISTORY]

CE	AUC	
1943	2697	Titus Novius **Faustus** born in Rome.
1949	2702	Lucius Novius Faustus born in Rome. Prince Atsuhito, later the **Go-natoku Emperor**, born in Cynoto.
1957	2710	**Delir** born in Aspadana, Persia.
1958	2711	Tertius Novius Faustus, later **'Leo'**, born in Rome.
1962	2715	**Ziye** born in Shandong province, Sina.
1969	2722	Titus marries Julia Sabina.
1971	2724	Novia Faustina (**'Makaria'**) born to Titus Novius Faustus and Julia Sabina. Ziye is sold into slavery, and begins intensive training in martial arts.
1975	2728	Prince Atsuhito succeeds to the Chrysanthemum Throne of the Nionian Empire.
1977	2730	Lucius marries **Drusilla Terentia**. Caius **Varius** Ischyrion born in Rome.
1979	2732	**Drusus** Novius Faustus born to Lucius Novius Faustus and Drusilla Terentia. Ziye debuts as a gladiatrix in the Roman Empire.
1981	2734	Lucius succumbs to hereditary madness – the Novian Curse.
1982	2735	Gaius Novius Faustus Rixa dies. Titus succeeds as Emperor of Rome. Tertius Novius posted to central Terranova.

He quells an Aztec uprising and his courage gains him the agnomen 'Leo'. He is hailed as hero, but sees hundreds of previously free Aztecs enslaved and is shocked by the experience.

1983	2736	Faustus divorces Julia. **Princess Noriko** born to the Go-natoku Emperor and Empress Reishi in Cynoto.
1984	2738	Leo marries **Clodia Aurelia**. With Senatorial approval, Faustus names Leo as Caesar and Imperial heir. **Dama** born to unknown slave parents in Rome. Clodia's disgust at slavery crystallises Leo's own doubts, and he plans to abolish slavery on succeeding to the throne.
1985	2739	**Prince Tadahito** born to the Go-natoku Emperor and Lady Akiyama.
1988	2741	**Marcus Novius Faustus Leo** born to Leo and Clodia in Tusculum. **Sulien** born to a slave mother and free father in London.
1989	2742	**Una** born to a slave mother and free father in London. **Princes Kaneharu** and **Takanari** born to Empress Reishi and Lady Himura respectively.
1990	2743	**Lal** born to Delir and his wife in Aspadana.
1996	2749	Sulien and Una's father dies. Under the terms of his will, they and their mother are freed. She, however, is unable to support herself or adjust to freedom and allows her children to be sold again to Rufius, the owner of an eating house.

1997	2750	The children are separated when Rufius sells Una off. Little is known about her history between this point and the autumn of 2757 AUC.
1998	2751	Sulien's healing ability manifests and he is sold to a wealthy London doctor called Catavignus. Catavignus treats Sulien almost as a son, but attempts to locate his sister are unsuccessful.
2000	2753	Faustus marries Tullia 'Tulliola' Marciana. Varius begins working for Leo as a cubicularius, or private secretary. Dama murders three citizens he held responsible for the death of a fellow-slave, and is crucified. Delir, a Persian merchant travelling through Rome, sees the dying boy from his car and rescues him. Dama survives, though he is left with disabilities and continuing pain. Now a fugitive, his own citizenship and that of his daughter Lal having been rescinded, Delir establishes a secret refuge for fugitive slaves in the gorge of Holzarta, near the Vascone village of Athabia in the Pyrenees. Ziye escapes slavery and arrives at the slave refuge.
2002	2755	Varius marries Gemella, a cousin of Clodia's. Drusus visits the Sibyl at Delphi.
2003	2756	Leo and Clodia make contact with Delir and donate money to his slave refuge.
2004	2757	Sulien begins an affair with Catavignus' daughter, Tancorix. Her mother catches them in bed together. Sulien is convicted of raping a citizen's daughter and sentenced to crucifixion.

Leo and Clodia secretly visit Delir in the Pyrenees.

Leo and Clodia are killed in a car crash in the Gallic Alps.

On the day of the state funeral, Una escapes her owners and sets off to rescue her brother from a prison ferry on the Thames. The pair flee into Gaul. Using her ability to perceive the thoughts of others, Una supports them by working as a fortune-teller.

Varius and Gemella tell Marcus their suspicions concerning his parents' deaths – and their belief that his life, too, is in danger from an anti-abolitionist conspiracy.

Gemella dies by poisoning in an assassination attempt on Marcus. Varius sends Marcus into hiding, instructing him to make his way to Delir's refuge in the Pyrenees.

Varius attempts to reach Emperor Faustus to tell him of the conspiracy and the reasons for Marcus' disappearance. However before he can do so the conspirators realise the threat he poses; he is intercepted by Cleomenes, attempting suicide during the arrest.

Agents of the conspiracy attempt to force him to reveal Marcus' location. Gabinius, a construction magnate, eventually succeeds after threatening to kill Gemella's younger sister.

Una and Sulien meet Marcus in Tolosa, and decide to turn him in and claim the reward, and freedom. Realising their intentions, he persuades them to accompany him to the Pyrenees instead. Once there, Sulien is able to reduce Dama's disabilities and pain.

After attempts to penetrate Holzarta and kill Marcus fail, Gabinius and the other conspirators decide to draw him out of Holzarta by charging Varius with Marcus' and Gemella's murders. Marcus successfully avoids the agents sent to kill him and reaches Rome. He reveals himself and the existence of the conspiracy in public, but, before the Emperor can speak with him privately, the conspirators drug him in order to convince Faustus that his nephew has succumbed to the family curse of madness.

Una and Sulien follow Marcus to Rome. Dama and Cleomenes assist them in rescuing Marcus from the Galenian Sanctuary, but Dama disappears afterwards. Una, Sulien and Cleomenes take Marcus to the Palace where Una identifies Tulliola as a member of the conspiracy.

Marcus is named as Faustus' heir.

Gabinius is shot dead attempting to escape arrest.

The inhabitants of Holzarta have been forced to flee after conspiracy agents raid the camp.

Sulien and Una are granted freedom by Emperor Faustus. Their new citizens' names are adapted from the Imperial nomen: **Noviana** and **Novianus**.

Tancorix has been married to a much older man and is pregnant by him; however she comes to Rome in order to exonerate Sulien and then stays there.

Drusus meets Tulliola in custody – the pair were lovers in secret for years. He kills her to prevent her revealing his involvement in the conspiracy.

2005	2758	Varius establishes the slave clinic planned by Leo and Clodia in Transtiberina, and Sulien begins working there.

Varius establishes the slave clinic planned by Leo and Clodia in Transtiberina, and Sulien begins working there.

Tancorix gives birth to a daughter, Xanthe.

Marcus begins studies at the Academy in Athens.

Delir, Lal and Ziye settle in Jiangning, Sina.

| 2006 | 2759 | Tensions increase between Rome and Nionia. Nionian Ambassadors are expelled from Rome. |
| 2007 | 2760 | A series of unexplained fires cause damage across the Roman Empire. A skirmish between Nionian and Roman troops over the Great Wall of Terranova escalates into a massacre and the two Empires are pushed to the brink of war. Emperor Faustus suffers an incapacitating stroke. |

Marcus and Una, now lovers, return from Greece to Rome, so that Marcus can take over as Regent.

Drusus visits the Sibyl at Delphi for a second time, receiving a repetition and elaboration of the original prophecy. Faustus asks him to assist Marcus as an advisor, but on his return to Rome, Una identifies him as a member of the conspiracy against Marcus and Tulliola's murderer. Drusus attempts to kill Una before she can reveal this, but fails.

Varius, now working as Marcus' advisor, and Una travel with Marcus to Sina for peace talks with Prince Tadahito and other Nionian nobles.

General Salvius, persuaded that Drusus has been unjustly accused, has him released from prison. Drusus convinces Faustus too that he is the victim of a plot by Una and Varius, who he claims are manipulating Marcus for their own ends.

Faustus summons Marcus home and Drusus arrives in Sina to take his place as Regent. Fearing that Drusus will have Una and Varius tortured or killed, Marcus persuades Tadahito to take them into Nionian custody. At the same time, **Kato Masaru**, Lord of Tokogane, is assassinated.

From Nionian custody, Una and Varius work

to avoid an immediate outbreak of war, with assistance from Noriko and the Sinoan **Empress Jun Shen**.

Empress Jun Shen orders a crackdown on Roman immigrants in Sina, forcing Delir, Ziye and Lal to flee. Delir and Ziye are nevertheless arrested, leaving Lal behind. Drusus learns of Lal's presence in Sina through a letter to Una; he hopes to be able to extract testimony from a former resident of the inherently criminal slave refuge to discredit Una and, through her, Marcus. His agents search for Lal and eventually capture her; however, she is rescued by Dama, who conveys her to Una.

Unable to decide which of his nephews to believe, Faustus orders them to share power between them. Marcus, however, returns to Bianjing, attacks Drusus, almost kills him, and then marginalises him by sending him to govern Canaria.

Marcus is now under pressure to marry Noriko to rescue the peace negotiations. Una leaves him, taking Lal with her.

On the day of Marcus and Noriko's wedding, Dama appears on Una's doorstep and invites her to join him in a campaign of rescues of slaves and rebellion against slave-holding Rome. She joins him at a farm near Rome, actually a revolutionary base.

She contacts her brother from the farm. Sulien, however, has recognised that Dama is behind the fires, many of which were mass-rescues of slaves. He also had Lord Kato assassinated and stole explosives from Veii Arms Factory – he is trying to foment a world war.

Realising what Una now knows, Dama imprisons her at the farm and abducts Sulien and Lal. Sulien and Lal eventually escape, revealing Dama's role in events – but not before Dama has perpetrated another attack in Tokogane, this time killing seventeen hundred people. Again, war seems inevitable, but Marcus and Noriko just succeed in preventing it.

Dama allows Una to leave, and disappears. Distraught at what Dama has become, but unable to bear the possibility that, on arrest, he will be handed over to the Nionians and crucified, Delir finds him at Holzarta and convinces him to accompany him into voluntary imprisonment on a remote island off the coast of Caledonia. His plans in ruins, Dama tolerates captivity and penance for some months, but eventually wades away into the sea. He barely survives, but is picked up by fishermen and once again vanishes.

2008	2761	Now largely recovered, Faustus resumes his duties as Emperor. Games are held to celebrate. All the Imperial Family are in attendance.

Una sees Dama in the street nearby but is unable to stop him; Dama attacks the Colosseum setting off an explosion right over the Imperial Box, before falling to his death.

For what do we see that is so wretched, so lonely, that one would not think it worse to live always trembling in fear of fires and falling houses, and all the thousand perils of the savage city . . . ?

Juvenal, *Satire 3*

'Wait,' she repeated, and then, on one breath, dying away to a garbled mutter, '*What you want it will be you the last one Novius it will come Emperor of Rome you.*'

Then he thought she was beginning to say his name again: 'Novius.' And she did say it, many times, but she no longer seemed to mean it as a name, *novii, novissimi – newer, newest.*

'*The new,*' she said, a loud voice droning from deep within her chest. '*The newer newest. The newly come, no Novian but one. The newer branch of Novian stem. No Novian but another comes to ruin you. Save yourself from that, if you think you can.*'

The Sibyl at Delphi, to Drusus Novius, Summer 2760 AUC

CORONATION

It might have been falling rather than running. Una didn't feel the ground under her feet, her body was loose and tumbling, as if some force other than her own will hurled it forward through the rain, past oncoming cars she didn't see. The gash on the back of her head seeped blood, warm under her cold hair.

Then the sound came: the grey sky rattled like a metal door slammed shut. The glass roof of the Colosseum cracked open like a shell, hatching fire and smoke into the wet air. For a second the belt of screens above the arches showed what was inside – flame, and debris falling – then they went dark. Una lurched forward on the wet paving, putting down one hand to keep from falling, and ran on, as if there were still time to stop it.

The noise collapsed into voices screaming, and the mass of people jostling around the Colosseum began to hurtle apart, skidding across the ground like drops of water on heated metal. At first Una, running the wrong way, towards the scattering glass and the flag of smoke overhead, scarcely noticed them. Then the shouts of horror began to hit her like flung stones and she realised she was charging against an oncoming riot, the front line of a panicked army sixty thousand strong.

Head down, she threaded and dodged, then collided hard and fought to keep her balance as she was carried backwards a few paces. She heard her own cry of shock loud and strange, as if it came from somewhere else, beside or behind her.

Closer to the arena, the crowd was thicker still; the narrow, wavering ways forward closing up ahead of her as more people spilled from the eighty gates. *So many*, each one of them too solid and real, stamping themselves on her in jarring, colourful focus: plump lips stretched wide in horror; two brown moles on a flushed wet cheek; a long-haired little boy, wailing, astride a man's shoulders. Gritting her teeth, Una tried to tack sideways across the flow, battering herself against straining ribs and elbows, until she was able to stretch out and grasp the counter of a deserted souvenir stall. No way of getting any further yet.

Other people's fright and shock roared through her brain like a landslide, until something gave way beneath it and left her in throbbing silence as if her eardrums had ruptured.

She clutched the stand, anchoring herself against the current, feeling the frame of the stall buffeted by the weight of people behind. She looked down at the fallen plaster figurines around her feet, promising Dama in her head: I'll kill you.

No. Dama had not survived this, or would not by long. She'd known that as soon as she'd seen him in the street. And what did she care what happened to him now? What did anything matter, as long as she could force her way inside to find that Marcus was not dead in there, under that dark wing of smoke.

Inside the Colosseum, something else broke away and fell. There was another gush of screaming. Una's vision blurred again as faintness flooded her injured head and the hand she tried to lift to the wound on her scalp sank limply to her side. She doubled over the counter, staring at an ink mark on its surface, mouthing, 'Marcus—'

Cold rain, scattering over his face, falling for a long time. He shivered, but it didn't occur to him to move, or that there was anything to do but wait – no, not *wait*, for he had no sense of any end to this – *remain*, then, on the edge of the cold and weight, and something else—

'Marcus.'

The fact that he badly wanted that to be Una's voice, and knew it was not, caused panic to shrill somewhere in him. Why was it so important that she should be here? He turned his head, facing the sky. Raindrops slid into his hair as noise swept over him, cars crashing, lightning splitting old trees.

His voice came out careful, shallow, saving the breath: 'Makaria.'

'It's all right. It'll be all right.'

Some of the weight on him was lifted away and streaks of pain came rolling up from waist to throat – not too bad yet, slow and secondhand, like echoes. They had been in an accident, then. 'What happened?'

'I— I don't know— There was an explosion on the roof.'

It was strange, because he had the impression that he was looking up the blank sides of steep cliffs from the dry base of a ravine, but he realised his eyes were still shut. He opened them with a long, sleepy effort and saw the smoke-stained sky, wavering above a jagged rim of blackened glass.

'I remember now,' he said.

He was lying on the wet stone at the base of the marble seat, near the front of the Imperial box; the silk carpet had been scraped back by his fall. The enclosure had been smashed into a caved-in heap; several of the columns around the box were down, the bullet proof screens between them crushed inwards. Stained glass dust and lumps of charred metal and masonry were strewn all round him.

The dust had powdered Makaria's hair grey, aging her. There was a scattering of little cuts on her dirt-streaked face, and she was pressing a hand to her shoulder, grimacing; otherwise she didn't seem seriously hurt. Marcus could hear cries, sense heaving motion outside the box, but he couldn't see anyone else.

He thought, Dama must have done this, and tried to pull himself up.

Makaria said hurriedly, 'No, don't move,' but it was too late: he'd barely lifted his head, barely glimpsed more than the flood of red he was lying in, when the pain sprang, astonishingly, crouched on him like an animal and held him pinned down and rigid so that not even a cry could get free. His head dropped back, but the pain hung onto him, obliterating so much that he could not even have said where he was hurt – he scarcely remembered who it was lying here in its grip, helplessly imploring it to stop.

3

Broken edges of glass or bone, cutting in— *Stop, oh please, stop . . .*

Makaria was holding his hand, and even that, to be touched at all, lent the pain its small weight. Everything roiled, and a chilly flush of sweat filmed over his skin; his body couldn't bear any more feeling. He couldn't speak to tell her to let go.

It retreated grudgingly, and not far enough. Struggling against the need to gasp down air, he rationed himself to small, inadequate wisps of breath, stolen from the top of his lungs, trying to stir whatever was piercing him as little as possible. Makaria went on thumbing the back of his hand and that was better, too. The roaring in his head had subsided, and he became aware that she was shouting for help, and he thought dizzily: *Is anyone else alive in here?*

Yes, there was a groan from somewhere to his right, and someone else was pushing his way through the wreckage behind him. It occurred to Marcus that he couldn't hear Drusus, or his uncle, or his wife.

He whispered Noriko's name, and Makaria soothed him, 'No, no, she went out just before, do you remember?'

He didn't, not really, but he couldn't think about that any further, for now he realised what he had seen. A great broken strut from the roof had fallen into the box and was lying precariously propped against the low wall at the base of the ruined screens, pointing away into space. And the twisted end of it was resting on his legs. His knees and shins must be crushed under the weight. Sickness kneaded into him just at the thought of it. But below the waist, the pain blurred into a dull electric tingling, and he couldn't feel it.

He thought that perhaps he should be grateful for that, but his heart sped unsteadily, and he shivered again.

He heard the short buzz of a radio, and someone muttering a low stream of instructions into it. The Praetorian drew closer slowly and, with a grunt of pain, lowered himself awkwardly to kneel beside Makaria.

'Help is coming, my Lady.'

'No, you must do something to help him now,' ordered Makaria, and Marcus could hear the shrill quiver in her voice that she hadn't allowed herself when talking to him. He had closed his eyes against the wheeling air; he heaved them open again now in slow, irritable protest. They should remember he was still conscious, still there.

The Praetorian's face swung over Marcus, large and blurred and, when it shifted into abrupt focus, briefly frightened. Then the hesitation passed and he placed dispassionate, courteous fingers over the pulse in Marcus' throat, showing no reaction to whatever it told him, and began carefully sweeping the shale of glass and metal off his body.

Marcus spent a little while collecting his strength to make the words clear, and to bear the pain in his chest, then he announced, 'I think my back's broken.' He felt distantly pleased at how calmly he had said it, but Makaria's face twisted in anguish, and his mind began a horrified, uncontrolled babbling: *if I can't walk, if I can't . . .*

Better that than dying, he thought, as another flux of cold pulsed through him and into the shadowed air. The man was slicing open his tunic, the wet cloth snagging on points of glass lodged in wounds he couldn't see. Sparks of pain shot through the dark and the chill, and he remembered thinking, in that first onslaught, not only *please stop*, but *please let me die*. A detached wonder at the memory came over him: did it take so little, was it so easy to come to that?

The fear changed, oddly. It was like the numb half of his body, still there, pressing evidence of how hurt he was, yet somehow separated from him.

Now he could feel the bloodied rain trickling over his exposed skin. He looked away from Makaria and murmured, 'Maybe Sulien—?'

Makaria seized on this with too much eagerness. 'Yes! Tell them to find Novianus Sulien.'

The Praetorian relayed this into his radio. He had stripped off his uniform jacket and began hacking out the lining. Marcus felt him holding the bunched fabric against a gash under his ribs, trying not to press something sharp fixed there, but pain gripped again. Marcus bucked involuntarily against it, and this time as the muscles tightened and edges shifted again, it rushed him away into the dark, almost before he had time to feel the shock of it.

Come on. Wake up. Don't be so lazy. You know what'll happen if you don't. Come on, do it.

'Marcus!' Makaria's stern, raw-edged voice was just short of a shout. 'Come on, Marcus. You've got to talk to us, wake up.'

It was only what he was already telling himself. Sleep lapped at him with such soft insistence that he was really not sure he had any choice in the matter, while his mind screamed incredulously at him: *Aren't you even going to try? Are you going to give in as easily as that?* He thought of Una again with another stirring of desperation, and now it began to sound like her voice in his head, loud and furious. *Wake up, wake up.*

He struggled to find a way of responding and thought at last, she wouldn't do this. Una would open her eyes.

He prised up his eyelids, stiff as rusted hinges. It took another effort to see anything, to search for Makaria's face, even with them open. He was surprised by the soft weight of damp fabric lying over him now, carefully wadded in around him. A different Praetorian, this one with blood in his hair and a glassy look in his eyes, was crouched over him, holding his jacket over his head as a rough awning to keep the rain off Marcus' face. He couldn't see the first man. He was so grateful not to be so cold.

He could feel Makaria was still holding the bundle of cloth against the wound below his ribs. He grimaced up at the dark tent of the Praetorian's jacket. He didn't think the improvised dressing could be making much difference, and it felt strange, his cousin's hand on his wet, bloody skin – too intimate, wrong.

'Marcus. Marcus,' repeated Makaria.

His mouth was dry; he parted his lips as a string of water drops slipped onto them from the small canopy above. He moved

6

them, realised he hadn't produced any sound, and tried again: 'I'm here.'

Makaria sighed and grinned at him, her mouth tight. 'They're coming. They can't . . . they can't get through yet. The stairs down to the passage are blocked. But they're coming. And they're looking for Sulien; they'll bring him here. It won't be long, don't worry.'

'I'm not,' he said.

It crossed his mind that he didn't want Sulien to see him like this, so weak, and needing his help so badly. They did not know each other as well as they once had, but Sulien would forget that when he saw him. He would be too fervently sorry to do anything else, Marcus knew that. It wasn't the way it should be.

He heard the first Praetorian saying, 'Madam, even if we could move this by ourselves—'

He must be kneeling by the beam that was lying on his legs. 'Talk to me,' said Marcus, breathless, trying to get a little more strength into his voice.

There was a pause and the Praetorian shuffled slowly closer. 'I'm sorry, Sir,' he began.

'Your Majesty,' corrected Makaria, in an odd, blunt voice.

Marcus blinked through a suspended second of incomprehension. Then, instinctively, he tried to tip his head back to see where Faustus was. Dizziness swayed his vision again, but he managed, 'He's dead?'

Makaria's free hand found his again and gripped, and her eyes flicked down to his face, then back to the Praetorian. 'Your Majesty,' she repeated. 'You are addressing the Emperor.'

Sulien sprawled peevishly for a little while after Lal had gone, then pulled himself up with a sigh. 'We're not married,' she'd said. 'It's wrong.' Closing the door on the rumpled bedroom, it occurred to him sourly that if this had only struck her while already in his arms and in his bed, her sudden principles shouldn't be impossible to undermine. But that thought discomfited him somehow, and all at once he wanted to stop thinking about her at all. He went into the living room and tried to see his belongings as if she had never been here, as if he didn't even know her.

It was summer, and a holiday, and it was depressing to be suddenly alone in a silent flat with the rain beating against the windows. Sulien tried to remember what each of his friends was doing, working out how long it would take him to get to somewhere better. He felt a brief, defiant desire to go in immediate search of a more accommodating girl— But no, he didn't want to think about that yet either.

He turned on the longvision, to make a bit of noise, and remembered as he did it that there would be nothing on but the Games. His hand hovered over the button, caught between aversion and fascination: Marcus would be there, of course.

Nothing appeared on the screen but the Imperial Eagle and motto against a background of dark blue. A vapidly solemn piece of horn music sounded, and after a moment a slow male voice, sonorous and faintly sing-song, promised more information as soon as it was available; meanwhile the people of Rome were to remain calm and keep inside and away from the windows.

For a minute or two, Sulien stood where he was, staring obediently at the longvision and waiting for an explanation. The music came to an end and was replaced by another dully martial tune, and the message was replayed, exactly as before. After a little while, five-year-old footage of a rally in celebration of Faustus' sixtieth birthday began to roll under the continuing music. Sulien had already strayed in frustration to the prohibited windows. He dug his fingers into the skin of his left wrist as he looked for smoke in the sky.

Finally he turned back to the longvision, scoffing aloud, 'Why don't you just *tell* us?'

His stupid keys slowed him down – they'd fallen under a backpack. He was halfway down the stairs when he realised that he didn't need anyone to tell him what had happened, not really . . . it was only a question of where, and how bad it was, and whether anyone he knew—

He began to think: Where's Una—? But he snapped off the

8

thought as soon as it sprouted: *No.* Out of all the millions of people in Rome, why should anything have happened to her?

He remembered smoke, dry and velvety in his lungs, and a column of noise burning in the air, and then he couldn't get it out of his head – *Dama.* He closed his eyes, unable to think anything beyond, *Oh no.*

There was a man with a dog going past the steps of his building, but he couldn't tell Sulien anything – didn't even know something had happened. 'There's a warning on the longvision,' explained Sulien hurriedly, running downhill towards the little forum around the Temple of Minerva.

The order to stay inside carried enough weight to make him feel exposed now, and unpleasantly conscious of noticing places to take cover, glancing from time to time at the windows overhead and at the empty clouds. He shook his head at himself in annoyance – this was Transtiberina, just creepers and lame dogs and graffiti – what was there to attack?

There was a small, speechless crowd of twenty or so in the forum, sheltering under awnings and staring, appalled, at the public longvision over the temple. Sulien looked up to see if anything had changed, but no, the same dreary music was playing and the message, a little distorted here, began again.

He asked, 'What's happened?' He was vaguely aware of having directed the question towards a girl he liked the look of: a shawl draped over her heaped, curly hair, full breasts, and arms showing brown and rounded where her sleeves fell away. Her small hands were cupped around her mouth in shock.

She turned to him. 'They've bombed the Colosseum!' she said, her voice sounding loud and outraged in the shared silence.

The way she phrased it made him ask automatically, 'Who?'

'I don't know— The Nionians!'

No, he knew, not them. 'When?'

'You shouldn't be out here, love,' someone said to the girl, 'that's what it says.'

She shook her head, almost crossly. 'We haven't got a

longvision at home.' Her eyes had already returned to the impassive screen. No one else had looked away.

Sulien's shoulders moved in a kind of tense, angry shrug as impatience and fear hummed through him, beginning to warm his chilled blood. 'Were you watching the Games? When was this?'

'Only about ten minutes ago,' said the man who'd warned the girl, quietly. 'Something blew up – we saw that. Then it went black. Then this started.'

Involuntarily, Sulien looked at the marching people on the screen for some kind of assistance, and then the opposite way, towards the Colosseum. 'My friend's there,' he said to the little crowd, not knowing why he needed to tell them that; it wasn't as if they could help him. He turned and sprinted back towards his building, coming up with almost as many reasons why this might not be that bad as it took him strides to reach it. He was composing the announcements on longvision and in the newssheets while driving his long body as fast as it could go. *A miracle*, he thought, grimly; *it looked bad, but in the end no one was seriously hurt. Marcus Novius Faustus Leo said* . . . No, that felt like bad luck; he wouldn't go as far as imagining that part.

But in any case, even failing that, he could help, he knew he could.

He was glad it had never been worth having a car in Rome, with its trams and dense traffic and work only a short walk away. But he had a fast electric trirota, good for the narrow streets of Transtiberina and for slicing through Roman gridlocks, and it was heavily chained up by his apartment block. Sulien's hands trembled a little as he dragged the chain free and let it fall; he noticed that, promised it to himself as a memory for later, when this was all safely over. *I was so worried*, he thought, practising the past tense. Maybe he'd even tell Marcus that: *You had me scared, you bastard*. He hauled the machine upright, headed it east.

*

The deluge of people had begun to thin out a little. Una pushed off like a swimmer, heading towards the walls. She could see vigiles and medics now, cutting through the crowd, and she tried to shove her way through towards them, to get into their wake. For a moment she was held almost motionless and trapped, a few feet from the nearest archway, then at last the pressure broke and she was able to duck inside.

The passage was crammed and heaving. Una reached the wall and flattened herself against it, her arms spread against the posters covering the stone, her stomach pulled taut, her breath held rigid in her chest. She inched along sideways: the air tasted soiled. Crushed between bodies too close to see, she could hardly breathe. She swallowed, feeling sweat on her face and that faintness gathering dangerously in her head again. For a while the physical discomfort and effort of remaining conscious and moving required so much of her attention that it was almost a relief: there was no space to think of Marcus.

Then she scraped out of the bottleneck into the inner causeway. The Colosseum was full of voices, warped in the curved space: weeping, and calls for help, and cries to different gods. The crowd was still dense, but fluctuating, and Una ran, shoving her way blindly and ruthlessly into the stands.

At first the amphitheatre looked almost empty of people. The bare slopes of seating were startlingly decked with colour: red and yellow cartons, and wrappers everywhere, like petals on a hillside. But in reality there were still hundreds of people – thousands even, limping down the staircases, clinging together, stretched out on the seats and in the walkways. And there were bodies lying where they had been trampled or heaped in the aisles nearest to the arena, faces red, mouths dragged open.

And the black wound gouged into the roof gaped over the remains of the Imperial box, hardly recognisable in the wreckage that spread around it down into the arena. Sheets and flakes of glass, long spars of metal and slabs of broken stone scattered everywhere. And the vigiles were coursing in now, carrying ladders and stretchers.

Already running, climbing, Una called, 'Marcus.' The space swallowed up her cry. And it was such an ordinary name, anyone here might have called it to any of the injured or dead men and boys.

Cautiously, Makaria let go of the wad of cloth she'd been pressing against Marcus' side. The warm trickle of blood under her fingers seemed to have stopped, but his breath was coming in sharp, quiet gasps now, and his lips were turning a deep bruise-blue under dried-out skin. His eyes were fixed somewhere on the grey distance. Makaria touched his cold forehead, began stroking the dust and crumbs of glass out of his hair.

Marcus looked quickly at her, at her moving hand as it slid over his temple into his hair, and the muscles of his face tensed strangely, eyes suddenly alive and keen, as if somehow catching her out. Then they drifted out of focus again and he whispered, 'I'm sorry.'

'Why?' Makaria crooned, still smoothing the fair hair, mindlessly gentle, hearing her voice soft and high and scarcely like her own at all.

'Your father.'

Self-conscious now, she fumbled for something to say. 'I'm glad that . . . that you're Emperor now, and—'

Marcus' eyes squeezed suddenly shut and Makaria leaned forward apprehensively, knowing she must not let him fall asleep – but before she could say anything, his face twitched sharply, a humourless, sardonic jerk, and he repeated indistinctly, 'Emperor.'

Makaria stared down at him letting her fingers trail over his hair for another moment, then lifted her hand, rising onto her knees. 'Wait a minute,' she said, 'I'm coming back.'

Marcus gasped thinly at the wet sky.

'I'm coming back, I'm coming back,' she promised. It was a relief to turn away from him for a second, not to look at that face. The wound she'd staunched was only one of several, and the Praetorian had said he was probably bleeding inside. A coil of

12

effort, knotted from throat to gut, spiralled loose through her and Makaria stumbled back through the detritus towards her father's body, shaking as she absently wiped the tears and grimy rain from her face.

Faustus was still sitting slumped heavily on the high seat, his head hanging forward, the hunk of masonry that had killed him lying harmlessly at his feet. The gold wreath had dragged his hair askew when it had been struck off onto the cushions beside him. Makaria released a quiet breath as she stood and looked at him. He looked at once pitifully frail and solid, hard to shift. She was glad he hadn't been knocked to the ground.

She picked up the wreath and muttered, 'Sorry, Daddy.'

His dust-covered hand, when she lifted it and slid off the Imperial ring, was warmer than Marcus' had been.

Marcus had no sense of how long she was gone; he almost forgot that she had been beside him. The men went on dutifully talking to him, keeping him from letting his eyes close, but the patch of stone he was lying on was speeding through space, and the pain mattered less now; it had been a while since he'd thought of trying to stave it off. And he was aware of his heart, a knot in a rope cold hands were pulling, running taut into the distance, every beat a long tug.

Before, under the intact roof, he had been waiting to see Una, willing the hours to pass, the day to end. It was not Una's name, or her image, or any one memory of her that possessed him now, but a terrible intensification of waiting for her.

No, no, he thought, trying to find some different way of trying. He should be doing something, not just lying here.

Then Makaria was there again, taking his hand and talking urgently, not to him but to the Praetorian. 'You're a witness, you're representing the Roman Army, all right? I need you to say what I tell you.'

He knew it was important to pay attention, not to wish for quiet and rest, but it was so hard to bother himself with whatever she was doing. He tried, and moaned, more with exhaustion than with pain.

'Marcus! Listen to me, Marcus. Do you promise to govern Rome and her Empire, on behalf of the People and the Senate?'

The thing she was trying to prop against his head – that must be the Imperial wreath. He panted a laugh, or as near to it as was bearable. 'Doesn't count,' he said.

'Yes, it does,' she insisted quietly. 'It does.'

Marcus was silent. The cold deepened. Now he did remember and wished for the warmth of Una's body against his, her breath against his cheek, her weight, held briefly off the ground in his arms, so close to tangible it might have been the beginning of a dream, or really happening. 'All right,' he answered, finally. 'All right, yes, I promise.'

'Do you promise to – to defend the rights of the Roman people established in custom and law?'

He'd heard these words once before, a year ago, flying back over the sea towards Rome. Makaria might not be word-perfect, and sometimes he couldn't keep his mind from sliding away from what she was saying, but her tone and the pressure on his hand prompted him to murmur, each time, 'Yes.' If this was anything more than a macabre game they were playing, it was near enough, probably; it was clear what was meant. And if it wasn't, then it didn't matter.

'Now, you must say, "The Roman Army—"'

'The Roman Army acclaims you as Caesar and Emperor, and implores the gods to grant you health and victory,' finished the Praetorian, soberly. Makaria pushed the ring onto Marcus' finger, then clasped his hand again, holding it there.

'I will . . .' What was it he was supposed to say? He sighed, searching for it, slowly mumbling out the words, 'I will perform what I have promised . . . in the name of the gods.'

'There,' breathed Makaria, bowing her head.

The ring of office was loose, as it had been the first time he'd worn it as Regent, not like the months afterwards when it had fitted his index finger so closely he scarcely felt its weight as

14

separate from his body, grafting authority onto him, and still there had been so much he couldn't do. And now?

'Then I say that . . . Then I . . .' How had he imagined this happening when the time finally came? What words had he been going to use? For of course he had thought about it, over the years, weighing different phrases that had sounded good, enough to string something simple together, at least . . . 'Slavery is to be abolished,' he said, 'everywhere in the Empire.'

Makaria nodded. 'All right.'

He didn't quite like the way that sounded, too mild and soft, as if she were only humouring him and it didn't matter what he said. He urged, 'Write it, write it down.'

Makaria looked anxiously round at the ruins, letting out a small grunt of powerlessness, but the Praetorian felt in the ragged remains of the jacket he'd laid over Marcus and handed her a little pad and a pen.

'From now,' Marcus rasped out as she wrote. 'From right now.'

She folded his fingers around the pen and guided it through the shapes of his long name.

Marcus felt a thin flow of relief, and with it, some slight remaining strength suddenly spilling out of him. What little force of his own had been in the hand that held the pen lapsed away.

Makaria bent closer, pale stripes of tears on her face. 'Look, Marcus— Don't just— I can hear them coming, I can *see* them. Just keep listening to me, just wait a little longer, you'll be fine . . .'

Marcus said, 'You wouldn't have done this if you thought that,' and then realised dimly that he hadn't said it, hadn't spoken at all. It didn't seem worth the effort of trying again, only to say that.

He turned slow eyes up to the punctured roof again. The Colosseum had been built for people to die in. That thought should have been chilling, but somehow it was not, it almost comforted him in the solitude that crept through him inch by inch, for all that Makaria hadn't let go of his hand.

Then the medics did climb in, on ladders propped against the walls of the box, over the wreckage of the screens. The colours of their uniforms flashed around Marcus indistinctly, like wings. Then there were fingers on his throat again, and pain and cold hollowing him out. So many people, so much noise and movement filling the place, piling over him, that Marcus felt himself recede, helplessly, to make room for them.

Something he should have made sure of, something forgotten and terrible scratched like a rat in a wall at the edge of his mind, requiring him to try, reluctantly, to remember.

Makaria, further away from him now, repeated his name: 'Marcus. Marcus.'

From this approach, the Colosseum looked unscathed, but he'd seen ambulances and vigile vehicles swerving through crosscurrents of a loose, complex mass of people spreading down the broad street, under the mirrory surfaces of the courts and temples of the Sacred Way, limping and pushing along in the rain.

They were turning back cars on the Sublician Bridge, but Sulien, half-guiltily, slid the trirota out of the choked traffic and between the tight-faced officers before they could decide it was worth stopping him. He swung straight from the saddle into a run, leaving the trirota by a Praetorian car at the end of the Sacred Way.

There was already a short, tidy line of corpses under plastic sheeting outside the Colosseum, and a rough cordon of vigile officers around it. Sulien ran up, feeling hastily in his pockets for identity papers, wishing he'd brought his pass from the clinic.

'Move back, move back.'

'My name's Novianus Sulien; I—'

'Move back,' repeated the nearest officer, in a kind of blank, droned-out bark, not hearing anything.

'No, I can *help*, my name's Novianus Sulien. I'm a friend of Marcus Novius a—'

Under the helmet, the man's face flinched into alertness, becoming individual and, briefly, naked with feeling. 'Novianus

Sulien?' He let out his breath in a tense sigh that made Sulien's stomach clench in apprehension. 'Come with me.' He seized Sulien's arm and pulled him past the line, hurrying him towards the Colosseum as if he'd proposed running away rather than entering.

An aching quiver throbbed up through his bones, shaking the pain awake. Marcus couldn't understand it for a while, then, distantly, he connected the vibration to the sound of metal grinding and realised they had begun cutting through the beam pinning down his deadened legs. They'd fixed a tube in his arm and there was something cold pouring in. It was strange how intrusively close yet separate from him all this activity seemed, like hammering or laughter in an adjoining room.

And they were moving through the rubble behind him, lifting someone on a stretcher, carrying him away—

Horror raked into Marcus, almost indistinguishable from the physical pain. He stiffened and tried instinctively to brace a hand against the ground and lift himself, but everything was failing, his mouth was opening and failing to make a sound . . .

'Give him something, he's in pain,' ordered Makaria wretchedly.

That was true enough, but it was worse, terrifying, that he couldn't make himself understood. He rolled his head, trying to swallow, to get his throat to work, and managed to choke out some mangled approximation of the syllables he wanted, then, clearer, 'Drusus. Drusus – is he alive?'

Makaria looked over her shoulder. Drusus had been lying under a crumpled panel of bullet proof glass, but he had been irrelevant to her. She could not see him now, hidden between the men who were passing the stretcher down into the excavated passage, out of sight, but they were not moving as if they were handling a corpse.

'I don't know,' she said, 'yes, I think maybe—'

Marcus tried to twist again, fighting uselessly against his unresponsive body. 'Not him— Don't let— Not Drusus.'

17

Makaria leant in between the medics, trying to hear. 'What? What is it, Marcus?'

'Succession.'

'Oh, Marcus—'

He struggled to find a clear place in the pain and murkiness to think clearly, just for a few seconds. Varius, he wanted to say, and the thought of how shocked Varius would be, hearing that, made his lips twitch with bleak amusement. He thought, but you'd make a good Emperor, Varius. Except that he wouldn't have the chance. Anyone Marcus named outside the remnants of the dynasty would need an existing stock of power and prominence to have any chance of holding the throne. Drusus had his name, and the nominal status as joint regent Faustus had given him. Salvius had the army. Varius had neither of these things, and Marcus would guarantee his murder just by saying his name.

He had scarcely any choice. It would be Drusus or Salvius.

'Salvius,' he croaked roughly. 'Has to be.'

He wasn't sure if Makaria answered that. His breathing sounded startlingly loud now, and he had no control over it any more; the pain from his broken ribs pulled through him with every breath, still violent and yet dissolving, splintering apart. So recognisable, this *tug*, like a word whose meaning he'd only briefly forgotten.

The dull juddering ground on. He wanted to curl up on his side, hiding from it, and he didn't want Una to think he hadn't resisted, that he wouldn't have given anything or borne anything to see her again, if there had been any way, any strength left in him. He made another long effort to speak, and heard his voice stutter unexpectedly into motion, though he didn't seem to have chosen the words: 'I can't— I'm sorry—'

'You have nothing to be sorry for.'

Makaria's voice, falling in from somewhere as remote as snow-flakes, but it wasn't her he was talking to. He said, surprised at hearing himself again, 'I tried.' He could feel the hectic motion of the people crowding over him, their hands on him, and yet it was as if they were beating against an impenetrable surface to reach him, as if he'd slipped through the marble floor and they hadn't realised it.

The pale oval of sky darkened, pulsed white, spread. An intense sweetness of relief overwhelmed him as even the pain finally shivered into nothing. He couldn't breathe, and he was aware of his body straining desperately for the unreachable air, but oh, mercifully, the struggle barely touched him, did not hold him, although he was glad when it stopped. He couldn't feel anyone near him any longer; no one else was there.

The world held, transparent as ice for another instant, before it thawed and broke – so easily, with such simplicity, that if any words had remained he would have called it beautiful.

No one noticed Una on the medics' ladder until she had almost reached the top, scaling it in one breathless rush. Then the vigiles closed ranks at the parapet of the box, shouting, 'Get down, get down!' Two of them below rushed for her, one aiming a gun – and Una couldn't take that in, it was just a little thing in the man's hand. She clung onto the ladder, unable to explain herself, only stammering, 'Please, please—'

Then Makaria appeared, filthy and exhausted, at the wall of the box. She raised a hand and ordered, 'Let her through.'

Una didn't know how she came to be on her hands and knees, bending over Marcus as if she'd been dropped there. Between the ladder and here had been nothing except a kind of dazzled after-image of Marcus on the far side of the ruined box, dead on the ground – but she hadn't seen that, she didn't remember it.

She said his name again, and the claw-sharp catch of expectation was the same each time she repeated it; she couldn't stop. She ran a hand up over his face, not gently, as if there were something there that could be wiped away. The sweep of her palm tipped his head back a little, and though she knew she'd caused the movement, it was stupidly arresting to her: it looked like a drowsy stirring out of sleep, as if his eyes were about to blink open. She took his face in both hands, shook it. *Absurd.* She did it again.

No one was doing anything; even the men who had been cutting away the terrible length of steel that lay on Marcus' legs were just standing there looking at her. Una turned on them, shaken by how furious she was. 'Why have you stopped?' She heard her voice as it would sound to another person, loud and raw and irrational; she tried to make it more controlled, but the mad voice babbled, 'Please don't stop, please do something, oh God—'

They didn't move. Someone said something.

She made a sound that horrified her, because she had no warning it was coming, and because the meaning of it was unmistakable. Her hands moved over Marcus' throat, chest, searching for something to put right. 'Marcus, come on, you can't— Marcus . . .'

Then time crumpled in on itself again and now she was lying half-across him, her face buried into his neck. But this wasn't an embrace, that wasn't the point: if there was any life left to be detected, however faint, she must be close enough to find it. But she couldn't feel anything except his chilly blood soaking her clothes and his broken ribs shifting beneath her; the weight of her body would have caused him agony, if—

Sulien raced up the steps from the passage into the wet daylight and Una was lying among the wreckage covered in blood. So different – and so much worse than anything he'd expected – that cold crashed over him before the queasy slide from horror to relief to horror again as he understood.

And Una jolted upright, her face lit with dreadful hope, crying, 'Sulien! Sulien, do something, please, please . . .'

'Oh, no,' murmured Sulien helplessly, closing his eyes and not wanting to open them. Something in him curled up, went into hiding. He began weakly, 'Una, I—'

She had started crying raggedly, even as he opened his mouth, and before he could finish she was begging, almost in a scream, 'Please try! Please just *try*!'

Don't do it, anything except that, Sulien warned himself. For his own sake he wanted to go to Marcus, touch him, make himself understand what had happened. But it would be better not to go near him if doing so would let Una convince herself there was any doubt. To *pretend* to try – which was all it could be – would be horrible, a betrayal of all three of them.

But she kept pleading, and he couldn't bear it, and a kind of shifty, two-faced optimism reared in his mind, that maybe he was somehow wrong, perhaps it wasn't too late, even now . . .

He couldn't help himself. He stepped forward and knelt down beside Marcus, and at once Una sprang to her feet and stood back, out of his way, and it was easier to look at Marcus' still face than to look at her, so he did that with the first spasm of true self-revulsion he'd ever felt in his life.

Tears filled his eyes almost at once. He blinked and exhaled hard, laid a hand on Marcus' chest for scarcely a second and pulled it back to drag his fist across his eyes.

All right, he told himself, not realising he was mouthing the words, and closed his eyes. He rested his hand over Marcus' heart again. Nothing, nothing. Sulien tried to make himself believe that if an electric flicker could only stir it – for the first time in what must be several minutes – there was enough blood left in its hollows or in the quiet veins to start flowing again . . .

But there was not, and nothing happened, and he thought of pressing down brutally on Marcus' chest just for the sake of doing something. The ribs were too badly broken, so, quickly, before he could think about it, he bent his head over Marcus and breathed into his mouth.

The air sighed out passively, and he saw now that Marcus' eyes were not quite closed; a motionless crescent of white and slate-blue showed under the eyelashes: a cold, faintly critical stare.

One of the medics said quietly, 'We've tried that.'

Sulien knew that, and he tried again anyway, though he could barely manage a steady breath himself. The tears spilled out again and he lifted his face, letting his hand fall onto Marcus' cheek in a glancing caress, and blurted, 'Una, please, I'm sorry.'

Una gasped in a scraping breath and Sulien braced himself to hear her pleading, or crying again. Instead, her body stiffened and her lips closed without releasing anything. She stopped crying, and her face emptied, slowly and utterly. Her eyes lowered slowly from Sulien's face to Marcus'. Her hands, knotted in tight fists, fell slack. She turned away.

Sulien sagged, shuddering, feeling a brief, desolate relief. For the first time he noticed the Imperial wreath lying beside Marcus' head where it had fallen, and the ring loose on his finger. He turned to Makaria, slumped on one of the incongruously intact marble seats, her forehead resting on her hand, and she met his eyes in numb confirmation.

Sulien looked back at Marcus and those gold things, and his throat burned; he pressed the heel of his hand into each eye. The wreath shouldn't just lie there, he thought, and reached for it, first meaning to put it back on Marcus' head – but it would have slipped off again when they lifted him. So instead he laid it on Marcus' breast, and, as he let it go, he felt how strange it was that he should ever have touched it. It was heavier than he had expected.

He stood up, wondering how he could be so tired after having done nothing at all.

Makaria gestured, and the men began cutting through the metal rods again. She stopped Sulien as he started to pick his way towards Una and held something out.

'Look,' she said. She handed him a folded sheet of notepaper, dimpled with rainwater and coloured with blood.

Sulien read disjointedly down to the pitiful scrawled signature, which made him shut his eyes and moan, 'Oh, *gods*.'

Una took it from him silently and stared at it for a few seconds, as if trying to make sense of a foreign language. Then she began to shake breathlessly and sob again, pressing one hand over the name for a second as if trying to feel Marcus in the writing. Then Sulien was reaching for her, imploring, 'Don't, please don't—' as she darted past him, back towards Marcus' body.

Una pulled roughly free of his hand as he caught at her shoulder, but came to a standstill a few feet from Marcus. 'I wanted to look at him, that's all,' she said, in a flat, almost normal voice.

She looked down to the paper in her hands and began straightening out the creases she had made. Stiffly she handed it back to Makaria. 'Is this going to happen?' she demanded. 'Who'll make this happen?'

'I don't know,' said Makaria. 'I'll try. I will try.'

Una's mouth quirked bitterly, then her face went blank again.

Sulien stammered, reluctantly, 'Who's—? Who's going to be . . . ?'

'Salvius,' said Makaria. 'He said Salvius.'

Sulien found that though he'd asked, for now he barely cared who the Emperor would be – except that to think of Marcus, lying there in agony and knowing what was coming, and still planning, for afterwards . . .

There was a sharp *whirr* and a clang of metal as at last the vigiles finished cutting through the beam. Sulien watched as two of them strained to lift the remaining section and let it fall on the paving beside the body, the sound loud and ugly as it struck the stone. Una did not look, but flinched, hard.

Makaria suggested quietly, 'Perhaps you should go home.' She added, 'Thank you.'

'Don't say that,' muttered Sulien, reaching to put his arm round Una, who started moving briskly before he could touch her.

He hurried after her. The cut-glass lamps in the passage had gone out, leaving dim emergency lighting coating the frescoed walls like disinfectant. Ahead, Una was a colourless shadow, walking unsteadily but very fast, her head down and her hair hanging forward. Even when Sulien caught up with her he couldn't see her face.

Without looking up she murmured, very quietly, 'You ought to stay.'

'What?'

Una gestured blankly at the wall. 'Could help people.'

'Oh . . .' Sulien slowed, hampered by a moment of tired, half-incredulous guilt, then shook his head and strode on. 'I'm not going to leave you alone.'

23

'I'm better on my own,' said Una in a chilly, remote voice.

Sulien tried to stifle an unexpected and unreasoning sting of hurt.

Una sighed, and he could see the effort when she turned her face towards him. More softly, she said, 'I'll meet you later.'

'No, Una—'

'I'll wait for you at the bridge.'

Sulien began to feel an urgent dread of letting her out of his sight. He was afraid to examine it too closely. 'There are other doctors. Let's just go home and—' And what? he thought. What would they ever do?

'You're different. There's too many people hurt.'

'I don't care.'

'Yes, you do,' Una said, still distant, but certain.

Sulien felt strangely unnerved by this, as automatic trust, that of course she must be right about him, jostled alongside a disconcerted conviction that no, he'd been telling the plain truth: he didn't care. But he couldn't muster any argument that would stand up.

'An hour,' he said, unhappily. 'I'm not— I won't stay any longer than that.'

Una said nothing, just walked even faster than before, and when they reached the gates and shuffled through the scrum of Praetorians and vigiles into the crowd beyond, he lost her immediately.

In the ambulance, Drusus kicked into consciousness as if out of a nightmare. A bright crest of pain burned on his head, and more studs of pain were scattered across his back and along his arm. Gasping, he asked, 'What happened to me?'

Someone tried to hold him down, hushing him. 'Try to keep still.'

'I'm all right, somebody tell me—'

'Let us make sure of that before we worry about anything else, all right, sir?'

'No, I have to— I have to—' He had a sense of electric urgency so strong it was almost terror, and it shouted in his throbbing head: *Now, now!* as he repeated, 'What happened?'

But he began to remember: an explosion overhead, a cataract of glass pouring in, like the understanding that had struck the very moment before: *glass on the ground* . . .

He knew his left arm was broken, he recognised the sensation of bone grating on bone when he moved it. Something was wrong with his knee. His right hand came away from his face coated in half-clotted blood. His skin was cold. But he remembered the heat of the chamber beneath the temple, at Delphi.

It could have been worse. He'd known worse.

'My family?' he asked, tentatively, hearing his voice shake. He *was* afraid, of not being ready, and he could recognise this as a terrible day, even if it meant the resurrection of his hopes.

No one would tell him. But with this flood of adrenalin in his veins, Drusus began to think he already knew.

SUCCESSION

Salvius and his family were also at the Games. His son Decimus was sitting beside him and when the bomb went off Salvius hurled himself down on top of the boy as instantaneously as if he'd been expecting it. Noise bulldozed across the Colosseum; his daughters' screams were the closest, spraying forward on the explosion's surge, and Salvius had reacted so fast it took him a moment to remember the orange flash somewhere on the left of his field of vision. He heard the roof groan, then a sequence of heavy impacts pounding across the arena, and he tensed over his son as shrapnel rattled down into the seats. Decimus felt sparrow-fragile against him, his heart racing beneath ribs narrower than Salvius' fingers. Salvius shouted, 'Stay down,' as sharp fragments bounced from marble and brick and sprayed like handfuls of pebbles on his back.

It slowed and stopped. Salvius raised himself, keeping Decimus down. His wife, curled on the paving next to him, was cautiously lifting her head, and Salvilla, their youngest girl, was clinging to her, beginning to cry. 'Come on, you're not hurt,' he said gruffly, checking her over with a glance. Letting go of his son, he looked for his three elder daughters and their husbands, who had been seated behind him, calling, 'Is anyone hurt?'

No one had worse than shallow cuts. Salvius looked across the arena – and saw the wreck of the Imperial box, the devastation around it. 'Gods above,' he whispered.

They were in the best seats, almost at the base of the terraces. Salvius looked back and up the slopes of seating to see the aisles overflowing and a landslide of people bearing down on them. Around the shaft of rain that hung above the arena, the roof shuddered and strained. He pulled his wife and Salvilla to their feet and turned to his eldest son-in-law. 'Into a line, quickly. Magnus, lead the women out, Fulvius and Albus on either side. I'll be behind you.'

The pressure was building on all sides as nobles and senators pushed and shoved, and Salvius, aware of the weapon at his side but not yet reaching for it, turned and snarled, 'Are you Romans? Will you disgrace yourselves? Keep steady.' He realised with a swell of mingled pride and exasperation that little Decimus was trying to struggle towards the back of the column, to Salvius' side, face alight with the desire to prove himself. Salvius shoved him forward, growling, 'With your mother.'

The worst moment came when they were almost outside, the crowd oozing slowly through one of the archways, when he lost sight of Decimus beneath the heads of the mob, and he couldn't hear any response above the din when he called his name. But when finally he reached the open air, the crowd pulsing around him, he saw the little column of his family, still moving ahead: all there, and together.

Salvius scanned the sky and rooftops as his family hurried through. To his relief the rank of Patrician cars was still waiting at the Sacred Way entrance, behind the gathering ambulances and vigile vans. Salvius could see his driver standing outside their vehicle, staring in horror at the oncoming crowd. His expression lifted a little when he saw Salvius.

Salvilla was still weeping and sniffing, but Salvia Prima already had an arm round her little sister and was murmuring, 'Now, then, don't give the swine the satisfaction. You'll make everyone think it's worse than it is.'

'What about Philia and Lysander and Psyche?' quavered Salvilla. The family had taken some of the household staff to the Games; of course they'd been seated in the uppermost tiers with the other slaves.

'They'll be fine,' said Salvius firmly. 'It will just take them a little longer to get out, that's all.'

'It was over the Imperial box,' said Magnus, quietly.

Salvius turned to watch a convoy of ambulances and Praetorian cars slide through the crowd and round the Colosseum, towards the private entrance the Imperial family used. He felt an unbidden rush of hope, followed by an immediate backwash of guilt. May they all be safe, he thought conscientiously.

But he couldn't believe that no one in that box had been hurt, and even at the best, there were steps that had to be taken at once, and it was clearly impossible the Emperor would be able to do so.

He kissed his daughters briskly. 'Go home as fast as you can,' he said. 'I have to get to work.'

'Will there have to be martial law?' asked Decimus passionately, climbing into the car.

Salvius laughed. 'In some form, probably. You be good.'

And minutes later, in the strategy room at the Palace, Salvius did indeed place all military units in the Empire on high alert, order curfews in all the major cities, cancel all public gatherings and start patrols in Rome's streets and airspace. After he'd deployed infantry around the Palace, the Senate buildings and the various Fora, General Turnus asked uneasily, 'Is it certain we have the authority for this?'

'If the Emperor is unhappy with anything, of course he will countermand it,' answered Salvius, ignoring a moment of uncomfortable disingenuousness.

From the other side of the room Memmius Quentin called out in a kind of frustrated howl, 'Do we have any word on the Family yet?'

And Glycon was suddenly at Salvius' elbow. Salvius hadn't noticed him enter the room; the cubicularius always moved so unobtrusively, even amid all this noise and motion. But up close he was unexpectedly dramatic, his face pale and damp-skinned, his limp hair dishevelled, his eyes bloodshot and sunken.

He said thickly, without elaboration, 'The Imperial Office.'

Makaria was standing beside her father's desk. Her arm was in a sling, and though the dust from the Colosseum had been washed from her face, her hair was still thick with it, and it was hard to imagine what her filthy clothes must have looked like when she had first put them on. Salvius was not sure whom he'd expected to find in the painted garden. She looked startling and ominous here, like the spirit of someone walled up alive. But she stood as upright as a soldier, and Salvius felt an odd stirring of pride, a faint, vicarious echo of what he'd felt for Decimus and Salvia outside the Colosseum.

She cleared her throat, and said, 'My father and my cousin— my cousin, Marcus, were killed today.' And it was clear she was trying to keep her voice steady, but it twisted away from her and she had to catch her hand to her face.

'Oh—!' Salvius was simply and wholeheartedly horrified. He even had an immediate impulse to put his arms round her, which was unthinkable. 'Madam, I'm so sorry—'

Makaria shook her head several times, and breathed deep before continuing, 'My father was . . . he was killed outright. Marcus wasn't. He— He . . . I put the ring and the wreath on him. He knew what was going on. He was Emperor. Marcus named you as his heir.'

No shock of battle, no unexpected success had ever robbed Salvius so completely of himself. At first it was almost a mercy that he did not know what to do or say, because that kept him in place, looking at her gravely and quite unable to stir, when otherwise he might have been – what? Lifted into the air, while this riot of incredulous excitement and bafflement pealed through him and bells deafened him?

It had reached and passed the point when he must respond and all he could manage was, cautiously, 'You are quite sure . . . quite certain that was his intention?'

'You don't imagine I would hand away my family's birthright if I were in any doubt?'

'Were there other witnesses?'

'Some of the guards. The medics. Yes.'

Salvius felt the continued pulse of delight, utterly unseemly in the circumstances, throbbing through the ringing of something

29

he refused to name as fear. It was not that he had any sense that he was not fitted to be Emperor, nor that he'd never contemplated it. For a long time he had believed he would do better than Faustus or Leo, or, in recent years, Marcus himself. As the crisis with Nionia drew in, he had nursed something between hope and dread that one day it might be necessary – *justified* – to take power himself. Only if it were justified, he had always told himself, uneasily; only if Rome were in danger and someone had to act. But that Marcus, who had fair reason not to like or trust him, should have given this to him, in the last moments of his life . . . What was he supposed to do, right now, stranded so far outside the margins of what he'd considered possible?

And Faustus' daughter was standing there in tears, and he thought of charming, ambitious, infuriating Leo, four years dead, and now his only son – the line gone, over.

He said, 'I would never have wanted this.'

Makaria rolled her eyes and said with a damp, laughing snort somewhere in the back of her voice, 'Salvius, spare me.'

'Not like this,' said Salvius softly.

She struggled visibly against another spasm of crying and remarked, 'I'm not altogether certain what happens next.'

'Everything must be done properly,' he said in a firm, reassuring tone. But what did that mean? There had been no such transition in more than two hundred years. He added, pressing any note of experiment or hesitation out of his voice, 'I shall call a session of the Senate for tomorrow.'

Makaria squared her shoulders. 'Listen, Salvius. You know Marcus was no friend of yours; it must be obvious to you he named you only to keep my other cousin off the throne. And I don't know yet how badly Drusus was hurt. I don't think he's dead. Marcus would want me to warn you: Drusus is very dangerous. You must secure your position. You must be careful.'

Salvius remembered Drusus bloodied and piteous on the floor at Marcus' feet with a vague after-twinge of distaste and disappointment. *No substance to that man*, he thought. And if Drusus wasn't the leader Salvius had once hoped for, surely he wasn't the monster Marcus had made out either. Nevertheless, Salvius could see that Drusus might be a threat in the coming months, if he garnered much support in the Senate, or worse, the army. If Drusus' injuries were not so serious as to keep him away from the Senate tomorrow, Salvius would have to let him speak, but he could make sure the army knew at once who was the legitimate Emperor.

He said, 'Thank you.'

'There's something else,' said Makaria, brusquely unfolding something and holding it out to him.

To be handed a crumpled, dirty sheet of notepaper seemed incongruous to Salvius, but he scanned it, and felt his eyebrows shift upwards as the words resolved themselves into outrageous sense. He said, entirely certain, 'It's impossible.'

Makaria lifted it curtly from his fingers, folded it up again and tucked it out of sight. 'Then I shall keep it for now, if you don't mind.'

'Of course,' said Salvius, at once relieved and mildly annoyed.

Her mouth pulled into a stretched, miserable smile, and her eyes started filling again. 'I have to . . . to see to my father. I suppose we will have to talk more later. You . . . Well, you can do whatever you want now. '

Left alone, Salvius looked around at the calm splendour of the Imperial office and tried out the thought that it was his. He laid a hand cautiously on the desk and, breathlessly, guiltily, laughed. Decimus came into his mind again, this time as a future Emperor, and it brought another rush of elation and unease. Hastily he straightened his face and put the thought aside. Rome had been attacked, whether by Nionia, or by Roman anarchists, or some conspiracy of both; his first efforts must be to defend the Empire. He went back to the Strategy Room, and to work.

In the doorway behind the doctor, from whom Drusus had at last succeeded in extracting the truth, a nurse with no good reason to be there was standing and crying. Drusus looked at her curiously, and felt water suddenly sliding out of his own eyes. He was startled, because he hadn't consciously made any decision to do that – although it was good, it would look right. And a moment later he knew that this feeling was not crude excitement, nor hypocritical grief, but awe, breaking across him like a sunrise.

'Where are they? Are they here?' he whispered.

'No . . . I am afraid they had passed away before they could be moved. They were taken back to the Palace, I am sure,' the doctor said.

'I must go there,' Drusus said, standing up, and cursed as the movement dragged at the lines of stitches. His knee burned under his weight. He gasped and waited the pain out. As soon as it began to fade he pulled off the sling they'd put on his arm. 'You have to help me. The people will need to see the Emperor strong at such a time.'

The doctor blinked at the word 'Emperor' but said, 'You're hurt, Sir, you're not ready to leave.'

'I'm not dying. It can wait.' He ran his hand gingerly over his face and wished for a mirror. 'You can put some kind of splint on my arm, so long as you can do it fast and it's nothing that shows.'

He had them call for a car, a couple of slaves and a change of clothes – formal, he specified, something like what he'd worn to the Colosseum – from his house on the Caelian Hill. He supposed he had better speak to his father, to let him know he was alive, and was both amused and angry to find that Lucius had no idea anything had happened. He rejected the wheelchair they tried to insist he use to get him to the lobby and hobbled there resentfully, panting through clenched teeth.

The lobby was half-full of Praetorians. He had no idea where his own escort was, not that he was sorry to be away from them – they had all been Marcus' spies. These soldiers looked awkward as Drusus came limping in among them, drawing up his wounded body to stand as tall as he could. As they shuffled uncomfortably, one of them, who must have been the squad leader, bowed and said softly, 'Please accept our condolences, Sir.'

Drusus took a breath, bracing himself for this first test, and looked the soldier calmly in the face as he corrected him, 'Your Majesty.'

There was a silence, and Drusus felt his heartbeat stammer in terror, and the man actually blushed and mumbled something inarticulate about Salvius before starting again, carefully, 'We have been told that the late Emperor Marcus Novius chose General Salvius . . .'

They all looked apprehensive; they were watching him to see what he would do; he was watching himself for the same thing. And he found that that there was no need to be angry or alarmed at all. He said, quite mildly, 'Really?' and turned away from them, back the way he had come. He caught the wrist of the nearest nurse and smiled at her, earnestly and sadly. 'I need to see a longvision.'

Part of Sulien was incredulous he'd stayed even this long, just because Una had told him to. Where was she? How could he have let her go off by herself? He pressed the torn edges of a wound together and thought, *She won't be there . . . She's gone . . . she won't be there.* He could not seem to think anything else; sometimes the words came almost as a matter-of-fact observation, just one of those things; sometimes as a frantic shriek hurling against the walls of his skull. He forgot each injured person the moment he'd finished with them, wasn't even sure how many there had been. Though he moved from one bleeding body to the next, and was dimly aware that for a moment at least he must have been able to concentrate on them, neither they nor their need of him seemed real. When he touched them, they were only solid enough to press the feel of Marcus' cold skin deeper into his own.

And though it felt as if it had been so much longer, the hour still wasn't up. He knew that, and ran out of the Colosseum anyway.

The rain had stopped and outside was a stunned, unnatural

calm, the streets emptier than Sulien had ever seen them. Soldiers moved around quietly; a flight of pigeons scythed down over the street. He ran down the middle of the Sacred Way, past an oncoming Praetorian van that seemed to drift past slow as a pleasure-boat. He'd thought it would be better to find Una first and then go back for the trirota, but he was already too tired to sustain a good pace, instead pushing himself on breathlessly in painful fits and starts. For a moment he observed himself clinic-ally, as if from a distance, as a living thing, warm and in motion and desperate. She'd said the bridge, and he'd assumed she meant the Sublician, but if she expected to go to her flat rather than his, then she would have gone to the Aemilian. The possibility of choosing the wrong one loomed like a disaster, though at no point did he name to himself what he feared might happen beyond repeating wretchedly, *she won't be there*. Instead he found himself thinking of the door of the cell on the prison-ferry opening, Una's impossible arrival, after seven years not knowing where she was. He didn't like the idea of her waiting on a bridge at all.

Beyond the Praetorian cordon around the Colosseum the streets were crowded again, but there were no cars moving; people were all on foot, slowly walking home. Sulien ploughed through onto the bridge, plunged restlessly back and forth, his breath catching jaggedly in his throat. He could see over most people's heads, but he couldn't find her, and he wasn't going to because she wasn't there—

'Sulien.' Her voice was barely raised – she was just a few feet away, and lower than he'd thought to look.

She was sitting on the pavement, her knees loosely drawn up and her back against the parapet, like the beggars crouched further along the bridge. One hand rose in pallid greeting. Some-how he'd forgotten that she was painted in Marcus' blood, clothed in it.

Sulien stared at her, feeling scoured, wiped blank with relief.

He moved towards her and she levered herself up gracelessly and started walking away over the bridge.

'There's— The trirota's back that way,' said Sulien, apologetically.

Una turned obediently and came back without comment. She gathered speed as she approached, overtook him without looking at him. As she did so he saw the stripe of dark blood on the back of her head – he might not have noticed it, realised it was her own, except she stumbled slightly as he saw it, swayed dizzily, and propped herself against the low wall of the bridge.

'You hit your head.' He was almost relieved to see it – something reparable. He reached out towards her, saying 'Let me see.'

Una swerved, throwing up one hand to bat away his, the motion strangely fluent, like a rehearsed dance step. 'Leave it.'

'You're concussed,' protested Sulien, after a moment's baffled alarm, not managing to find a more helpful tone than exasperation.

'Yes,' said Una, a thin smear of sarcasm across a voice otherwise bare as a slab of metal, 'and it'll get better. What's the point in . . . ?' But she let the sentence drop away unfinished, losing interest in it.

'How'd it happen?' Sulien insisted, thinking of the mass of people that had erupted out of the Colosseum over the hard ground.

They had reached the east bank again. Una's rapid, irregular march shuddered to a halt. She looked up at him, not for long, but for the first time since she'd understood Marcus was dead, and so horribly unguarded that Sulien didn't want to look back at her; it was as if a knife had been dragged across her face.

She said, 'Dama.'

For a moment he thought she was telling him what he already knew – who was responsible for the bomb – then, inwardly pleading that the answer would be no, he asked, 'You saw him? He did this?'

Una nodded jerkily, too hard, a slow, sticky spill of pain spreading through her head. She felt her arm rise, almost of its

35

own accord, in a helpless gesture towards the Colosseum and heard herself beginning in a whimper, 'I . . .' *I couldn't stop him*, she must have been going to say, and that struck her as the most redundant statement that could be imagined: as if her inability to stop Dama had not been amply demonstrated to everybody. Sulien clamped one enormously heavy hand on her shoulder, pivoting towards the Colosseum with a little gasp of rage.

She whispered, shivering, 'I think he's dead,' because she knew Sulien wanted to kill Dama. She knew it from the look on his face and the way his free hand had squeezed into a fist, not because she could hear him thinking it. Her mind was still clenched up, containing no thoughts but her own. If she closed her eyes it might almost be as if Sulien wasn't there, if he would only let go of her and stop breathing so loudly.

But instead Sulien dragged her off-balance against his chest, making her head ring and throb again. She thought, *Haven't I done enough for you already, can't you just leave me alone?* and said in a low, ugly rumble, 'I said get off me, Sulien.'

Neither of them had said anything more. Riding back over the bridge later, he thought he could just feel the movement of her breath at his back, her arms round his waist light and loose as a circle sketched in pencil. He drove as slowly as he could.

As Drusus entered the Palace a group of servants hurried to meet him and tried to prop him up. His own slaves had done the same thing as he got out of the car, and as then, Drusus waved them all off, but he had to lean against the wall of the atrium to take the weight off his leg. He cradled his arm against his chest, anxious now that he looked vulnerable and there was nothing more he could do to disguise it. He gasped, 'Where's my cousin?'

One of them said, 'Come in and rest while I send someone to find her.'

'No,' panted Drusus, somehow reluctant to voice clearly what he meant, 'no. Please.' The servant looked startled and Drusus himself didn't know why he sounded so diffident; he knew his only chance was to act fast and decisively. 'Marcus. I have to see Marcus.'

The room was dim, and incense was burning, the soft weight of amber and myrrh in the air sharpened by the resiny green scent of the branches of olive and laurel that lay around Marcus, over the robes of Imperial purple in which his body had been dressed. Of course there was no trace of blood or dust now. His pale hands were folded over the cloth-of-gold spread over his lower body. His smooth hair and the wreath resting on his breast gleamed dark gold in the half-light, and white roses and poppies shone like candle flames against the dark silk and the green leaves. From this distance and in this light Drusus could not see the cuts on his cousin's face; he could see only that Marcus looked tranquil, and Roman, and beautiful, and that feeling of reverence and rightness welled through him, pure and golden again. And yet the silent tableau looked strange to him too, for Marcus had not been laid on a bier but on a mat of pale silk on the floor, and Noriko was kneeling motionless beside him.

He had met her for the first time just that morning, and had been struck at how Roman she had looked with her dark hair heaped up in curls, almost like Tulliola. And now she looked absolutely foreign, folded into that odd, composed posture on the floor, her loose hair combed out straight and falling over the long square sleeves of the pale Nionian gown she wore to spread and pool behind her.

She said quietly, 'I hope I have done right for him.'

'Yes,' said Drusus in a whisper from the doorway. He could not move into the room and disturb the depth of the hush, not yet, could not intrude the evidence of violence he carried in his own damaged body. 'Everything is right.'

She looked up quickly and stared at him for a few seconds, her expression stiffening a little. Drusus watched her face, interested by the change, though unconcerned with what it meant.

'You are hurt too.'

Drusus shook his head. 'It doesn't matter.'

37

Noriko accepted this without reply. She slumped very slightly, her hair trailing forward over Marcus' wrist.

Drusus realised vaguely that the construction of this quiet, clean beauty must have been prolonged and difficult, and could only just have been finished. He asked, gently, 'May I have a moment alone with him?'

Noriko tensed again, crouching forward over Marcus' body, but she said, 'Of course.' Looking down at Marcus' face she laid one hand over his and gripped, quickly, biting her lip.

Then she rose, and as she passed Drusus he said lightly, 'You weren't there, were you?'

Noriko answered only with a polite bow of the head. But her sleeve brushed against him. She was trembling.

Drusus did not move for a moment, letting the stillness flow back into the room. There was no one there to see him, but he had never been so conscious of what looked right. He advanced slowly, barely breathing, because it would have looked wrong to rush, to grab; he tried to suppress his limp, because it would have looked wrong to be awkward; he was solemn, because it would have looked wrong to be anything else. He was anxiously aware that he too would have to kneel down, and he was afraid he might not be able to do it without falling; certainly it would hurt.

At Marcus' side, after staring down in fascination for a moment, he braced himself and tried to lower himself to the floor. Pain lashed up his body like a snake and for a moment he lost all awareness of anything but the blind effort of forcing himself through it. He would not relinquish control to it. And, as he'd feared, he couldn't hold himself up; he stumbled and instinctively put down his left hand so the broken bones took his weight and he crumpled sideways, barely saving himself from falling onto Marcus' body. He hissed in frustration and shame and pulled himself up awkwardly onto his knees. Curled protectively over his arm, he let his breathing steady and the echoes of the cry he hadn't been able to suppress die away.

He'd knocked aside a spray of laurel. He put it back, carefully. Now he could see the clean, bloodless gashes. Drusus raised a hand to his own face and touched the stitched cuts, then ran a fingertip along the cold outline of a wound on Marcus' cheek.

'Marcus,' he whispered finally, breathless, 'Marcus, I'm sorry. Because the Sibyl told me this would happen, and if I'd understood I could have been patient, I could have let you be. I didn't know.' Still he didn't stir, crouching low over Marcus, eyes fixed on his impassive face, knowing there was something else that needed saying. He flexed the hand Marcus had smashed, months ago. His bones cracked and ringing once again, it was easy to remember lying powerless at his cousin's feet. At last he added, 'And I forgive you.'

He lifted the wreath very slowly in both hands, and in a strange way he was glad his arm was broken, because it seemed right that this should hurt him, as he raised it to his own head. His eyes closed against the pain, and stayed shut as he felt the unfamiliar weight settle over his hair, the metal cool against his forehead. He released a long breath, almost a moan, as if something clenched in his lungs all his life could be expelled at last into the air. Then he took Marcus' hand, finding the fingers chilly but not yet rigid, and the ring slid off easily. It was loose on his own finger too.

He laid Marcus' hands back, one over the other, and clasped them both as a kind of farewell, because of how it had looked when Noriko had done it. As he did so he noticed something that didn't belong: under the folds of the robe, where it closed at Marcus' breast, there was something made of cheap-looking dark blue wool lying against his skin. It had been hidden by the wreath. It looked strange and unfitting to Drusus, but it must have been placed there with some meaning that did not concern him and he did not touch it.

He gritted his teeth, wincing as he got to his feet, but it was easier to rise than it had been to bend down.

Hesitantly, Sulien turned on the longvision. Of all things, they were showing a pink-and-white legion of girls performing some traditional dance in Fennia before smiling officials: a celebration

39

in honour of Faustus' recovery that was, apparently, still going on. Meanwhile a rolling subtitle across the bottom of the screen admitted that there had been an incident at the Colosseum, and that General Salvius had called a session of the Senate for early tomorrow, after which there would be a further announcement. Citizens in Rome should listen for instructions from the Praetorians or vigiles. Una lifted her head a little from the table-top and stared; the music jigged briskly and Sulien turned it off.

Una pressed her cheek back against the surface of the table. She was gripping the edge of it with both hands, as if she thought she could drive her fingers right through if she kept at it long enough. Her lips were pulled back a little, showing the teeth, her eyes wide and red, like a dead fox's. The bloodstains all over her glared darker as the rainwater dried and Sulien suggested cautiously, 'Do you want . . . Do you want to change your clothes?'

Una shrank back slightly in the chair and looked up, her expression changing slowly from uncomprehending to almost pleading. She whispered, 'Later.'

Of course the feeling of Marcus' blood against her skin was unbearable, of course she knew she would have to wash it away like so much dirt, put on clean clothes, equip herself to meet the advance of the next day, the next minute even— but oh, she could not begin yet. The time that had passed was so short that she could hardly believe it was not possible to smash a way back through to the moment she'd seen Dama in the street, to try again.

And now she couldn't tear her attention from the blood, as horrifying as if she'd only just realised it was there. She stood up, the chair skidding back across the floor, and she could hardly tell if she was trying to breathe, or trying not to breathe. Either way she felt it might have been easier if she could have hurt something, and Sulien loomed there mournfully, his anxious face sweet and oppressive, he seemed to sway like a mast in front of her, as the whole room rolled indistinctly, as if at sea.

'Don't,' she gasped pre-emptively, lurching away from him, out of the room.

Sulien went after her as far as the short flight of stairs up to the two bedrooms, moving carefully, placing his feet as quietly as he could. He sat there, a few steps down from the landing, his forehead pressed into his hands, hoping he wasn't waiting for anything. He could hear her moving about restlessly. He flinched at the noises – the thud of something hitting the wall or floor, and at the dreadful sobbing, like a long, hitching attempt at a scream without enough breath for it – but forced himself to remain still, letting it go on and on. After some minutes he closed his eyes and made his thoughts diffuse, monitoring Una's cries on the edge of his attention, falling into the forgiving blankness at the centre.

There was a shriek, and the sound of glass breaking. Sulien sprang up the remaining steps, through the door and into the middle of the dark bedroom in a few strides, overcharged with fear and readiness.

A cool gust of fresh, damp air flowed across the room. Una, silent now, was standing by the window and surveying the damage with a taken-aback, interested look on her face. Her arms were gloved to the elbow in blood, fins of glass standing out of the flesh. Her scarlet fists were still clenched. She turned with a look of slightly embarrassed surprise at Sulien and raised one shoulder in a tiny, nonplussed shrug.

'Oh . . . *Fuck*, Una,' breathed Sulien, running his hands over his face.

'It's all right,' said Una knowledgeably, calmly, stuttering a little. And yet again when Sulien approached, she drew back.

'Are you going to walk around with glass in your arms for the rest of your life?' asked Sulien, hearing a shrill tremor of hysteria in his own voice.

Una found it remarkable that she could have acted so violently without any awareness of what she was doing until it was over. The pain was far more intense than she would have expected, and fascinating, a glittering red lattice she could almost see in the air around her.

She backed a few unsteady steps away from Sulien and

41

explained reasonably, 'Let me have some water and towels and I can do it myself.' She looked down and plucked curiously at a quill of glass lodged in her wrist. It snagged on the underside of the skin.

'Stop it! Gods, stop it!' shouted Sulien, terrified, hideously aware of how close the sharp edge was to the artery, and rushed forward, closing the gap between them whether she liked it or not. He grabbed her hands and forced them to her sides.

Una's detachment winked out in an instant; she let out a cry of rage and struggled savagely, weeping, elbowing him and twisting until he felt her blood running over his hands and let go, afraid of doing worse harm by holding on.

Released, Una's hands flew up and struck at him wildly before she limped away to huddle against the wall, panting.

'What are you doing, Una?' said Sulien helplessly. He felt tears starting again, and pleaded, 'I got there as fast as I could – you know that, don't you? If there was anything I could have done, I— You *can't* blame me; it's not fair.'

Una gave a scoffing, worn-out laugh, her face still curtained off within her blood-tipped hair. 'I know. I don't. For God's sake.'

It was strange that somewhere far off he could feel so much relief at that, while he was still so unnerved and frantic. Voicing the idea of his own guilt, even to deny it, had somehow given it form and weight. 'Then come on, come here—'

But she didn't move except to turn her head against the wall and moan, 'Can't you let me have a second by myself?'

'Like this? Of course I can't,' said Sulien. 'What have I done? Why are you so angry with me?'

Una looked up sharply, the motion like the snarl of something baited and attacked. 'Because I can't *leave* you here, can I?'

For a second Sulien stared at her blankly, but when comprehension did come, and too quickly, it was strangely neutral and businesslike, even when, the next moment, Una staggered forward to sit crumpled on the bed, and cried, 'But I can't do it, Sulien, I'm sorry, I can't— *Marcus*— I can't—'

'All right,' said Sulien harshly, crossing to her again and this time crouching in front of her, 'you sit there, and you don't move, you hear me? You don't touch anything. I'm going to call the clinic, see if someone can bring round some bandages, suture needles . . . You just sit there.'

Una went on crying, almost but not quite oblivious to him, a little quieter now. More gently he said, 'You can do it, but not by yourself, all right? We'll do it together. I won't do anything you don't want me to do, I promise.'

She met his eyes briefly, as close to assent as he was likely to get, and so he retreated, hesitantly, dreading the moment of actually turning his back on her. Once outside the room he vaulted down the stairs into the living room, ran to the long-dictor and punched in the clinic's code with shaking fingers.

It had occurred to him that she had shown no sign of knowing anything he was thinking for a while. Surely she could not, not in this state.

The conversation took longer than he liked because they wanted him to come in and help with the influx of wounded from the Colosseum. Sulien was quickly reduced to panicked begging under his breath for what he wanted as he dragged the longdictor across the room, fearfully listening for any sound from upstairs.

But she was still sitting on the bed when he came back into the room, with her arms resting passively on her knees, eyeing the blades of glass and the slashed flesh with a more settled despair. She was shuddering even more noticeably now.

Sulien lowered himself cautiously to the floor in front of her again, murmuring, 'Should be a few minutes.' In the meantime, all he could think to do was try and fold himself up as small as possible on the floor, to be somehow less conspicuous and provocative.

Una stayed where she was for now, but the lull felt temporary. The cuts were plainly hurting more now the first shock had faded; he could see her muscles tensing as she shifted on the bed, and her breath was growing louder and less steady. *Oh hurry*, Sulien silently begged the assistant from the clinic. Una was looking at him now from time to time, a furtive, kidnapped look: half wretchedness at being trapped and half stealthy assessment of the prospects of escape.

And then he had to leave her again to answer the door at last and gabble hasty thanks to the tired girl who'd brought the supplies: only a minute or two, hardly enough for what needed doing, but plenty of time for some further terrible thing to happen.

Una was on the floor when he came back this time, clenched in an agonised knot. She jolted up warily as he drew near. Sulien knelt beside her and started laying things out – tweezers, dressings, a bowl of boiled water. He brought a lamp over from beside the bed. He began, unable to help a slightly too jaunty, slightly exaggerated professional manner: 'Let's start with your hands, then. At least you didn't break any bones.' He pushed the wet, tattered sleeve further up her arm to get it out of the way and put a wad of wet gauze into her left hand. 'You clean it up so we can see what we're doing.'

Una's taut shoulders relaxed slightly and she said, 'Thank you.'

Sulien sighed, and stabbed the syringe he'd hidden from her into her arm, pushed her over onto her side and held her down without too much difficulty as he finished pressing the fluid in.

She scrambled up as soon as he let go, gasping, outraged.

Sulien slumped back against the foot of the bed and just watched her, waiting.

'What—? What have you done?' she demanded, incredulous.

Sulien didn't even bother to answer immediately; he felt boundlessly exhausted, and he couldn't see much point in a conversation now. 'You know what I've done,' he said. 'You need it.'

Una knocked the bowl over as she headed for the door, casting about clumsily for some kind of impossible escape from the encroaching softness that was already pulling the ground away, dragging at her eyelids, weighting her limbs. 'You lying bastard,' she said thickly.

Sulien looked up at her with weary patience that made her nerves ring with betrayal, and then rose slowly to his feet, in obvious preparation to catch her when the drug had completed its work, on the correct assumption that she wasn't going to lie down of her own accord. She had a furious impulse to see if she couldn't reach the top of the stairs before he could get to her, and was even more maddened by the thin tether of self-control that kept her from trying. 'You and Dama,' she gasped, 'knocking me out—'

'I'm sorry,' whispered Sulien.

Una glared at him, and muttered bitterly and accurately, 'No you're not,' and toppled forward.

The relief was so strong as to make everything, even Una's fall, look slow and languid. Sulien caught her awkwardly but easily enough and brought her down onto the bed so that they were sitting side by side, Una propped against him, her head limp on his shoulder. He sat there, his arm around her, staring at a knot in the wood of a wardrobe standing against the opposite wall, and could not move. He didn't want to look at Una; he wished there were a way of getting out of the room without having to do that again.

'Marcus,' he said aloud, into the quiet room, 'please.'

He eased Una around and down onto the bed. Her eyelids strained half-open and she made a cramped, angry motion, as if to raise herself, before her hands fell helplessly still and her face smoothed again. Sulien watched in bewilderment, almost a kind of admiration. She couldn't possibly want to be awake, so what was this effort for? Could anyone be as vengefully perverse as that, even Una?

He went out and refilled the bowl with water, picked up the rest of the things from the clinic and got to work on her arms. It was good to have the tweezers and scalpel to slide out the glass slivers, though he didn't need the suture kit to close the skin. But it took a long, messy time, longer because he was dizzy with tiredness now. And there was still the injury to her head.

She looked as if she'd been murdered. He hated to think of her sleeping in the blood, waking up to this tomorrow, but the idea of undressing his sister, having already drugged her unconscious, made him squeamish. Maybe if another girl did it? He tried to think through all the girls and women he knew nearby. Lal was the right person, really – Una might not mind so much if it was Lal. She had looked after Lal when she was ill; there would be a kind of reciprocity. But of course he couldn't ask Lal; he could not call her back to the very same flat in which he had been trying to coax her to give up her virginity only a few hours ago, and where now there was blood everywhere. And Lal would have her own family to deal with when they heard this. He wondered if they knew yet that Marcus was dead, whether they'd guessed it from what was on the longvision; if you could, if you hadn't been there.

To his own surprise, for it was years since even the idea of her had occurred to him, he found himself thinking angrily that their mother was probably still somewhere in London; there was no reason to think she was dead. Perhaps she had been watching the Games on longvision and had seen the explosion. She would not know it had anything to do with her children. She was doing something right at this moment and it wasn't looking after her daughter, or helping him. He tried, more aggressively than wistfully, to pull up a single solid memory of her, and could not find anything there. What was wrong with him? How was it that he had always forgotten so much? In what little he could remember from that time, Una was always the only other person there. He had accidentally knocked her down the stairs – he had been so horrified; her hair had been full of blood then, too.

He rubbed away the new tears that came at that thought. He had to decide what to do about Una's clothes. Una wouldn't want them to be taken off, however Sulien went about it. It would be a second intrusion after what he'd already done with the needle. There was no vital reason to force anything more on her.

So he cleaned the last traces of blood off her arms and her face, and tried to get as much as he could out of her hair, then dragged

46

a blanket up to her chin, as much to cover up the mess as to keep her warm.

Of course, there was a lot of blood on his own clothes – Una's and Marcus' and any number of strangers', all mixed and all over him.

There was a communal bathing block under his building. Sulien skipped most of the stages of a good bath and headed straight for the warm fountain in the centre of the caldarium. He tried not to look at the reddened water as it ran off him. Scrubbing his hair, he set to working out in his mind how to be organised and systematic now: how to clear up the smear on the wall where Una had leant, and the crescent of blood drops between the window and the bed, collect the broken glass; in what order he would do these things. It was how Una would have acted in his position. But the plan unravelled into unexpectedly strong irritation that she'd broken the window, which was his, after all, and now he'd have to get it fixed. Back in the flat, he got only as far as sweeping the bloody glass into a little heap by the wall before wandering back into the kitchen and forgetting about it.

He poured a drink and let the longvision play, not watching it. He found himself wondering again who would know what had happened, who else would be beginning to grieve for somebody. He thought of Varius then, with a sting of sympathetic pain, and decided that someone from the Palace would have told him by now, surely.

And suddenly it occurred to him that it might not be a question of telling Varius; he might have been there himself, might have been hurt, or killed.

He groaned quietly, in protest. No, Varius wouldn't have wanted to go to the Games, he reasoned. Except that he was Marcus' advisor, his friend – perhaps he'd kept him company. He might have been carried out of the box before Sulien arrived. Or perhaps he would not have been in the box itself, but somewhere nearby . . .

Sulien knocked back the rest of his drink, and called Varius' flat. He fidgeted as he waited, half-hoping that Varius would not answer, because he did not know what he was going to say if he did.

Varius did not answer. Sulien left it for a few restless minutes and tried again. This time the line was busy, as it was on all his attempts afterwards. He was reassured at first, before he realised it might be that others were trying to reach Varius too. He closed his eyes and thought longingly, *I don't have to do anything more today. I can't.*

But he wasn't going to get away with that; he couldn't shut out the possibility that Varius, who had dragged him out of the fire at Veii, might need his help as badly as Marcus had, and Sulien was, again, leaving it too late. And even if he was safe, Sulien was growing increasingly certain that he should be the one to tell him about Marcus – or at least *say* something to him, be there for a while, if Varius had already heard.

Hesitantly, he picked up the longdictor circlet again, tried Varius once more, just in case, and then called Tancorix. She sounded frightened and excitable. 'Sulien! Are you all right, have you heard about the Colosseum? Calliope was there and—'

'Yes,' interrupted Sulien baldly. 'Marcus died.'

There was a confused pause. 'Marcus Novius?'

At least she would not be personally hurt; she had never met Marcus. So Sulien did not listen to whatever she said next but rested through it, just waiting for her to finish speaking. 'Can you come here?' he asked. 'I have to go somewhere and I can't leave Una alone.'

The basilica housing the Department of Information was only a couple of hundred yards from the gates of the Palace, closer still to the Colosseum. Drusus' car pulled up outside and he said to one of his slaves, 'Go ahead and tell them the Emperor is coming.'

He closed his eyes, feeling fear thrill through him once more, heady and pure and almost sweet, like a ringing high note of a song. Here again he might be on the point of walking into humiliation, failure – perhaps even death, if Salvius had discovered where he was and what he was doing. He had walked out of the Palace as soon as the wreath was on his head, pausing only to study himself with elation and unease in a mirror he passed. But they had bowed, everyone who saw him – just servants, but it meant that he did not look an impostor, he did not look ridiculous. It meant that people could understand he was showing them the truth.

His slaves opened the doors for him. The atrium was full of startled, uncertain people, hastily gathered, some still hurrying in at the back, and they all bowed at the sight of him. He saw bewilderment and shock on many of their faces as they bent forward. But they did it, regardless. Drusus felt their attention flow into his bloodstream like a painkiller and held himself up straight with greater ease.

He said, 'If you were not already aware of what has happened today, of what Rome has lost, then my presence here must make it all too plain. I wish I were meeting you in other circumstances. But we must show the cowards who did this how strong we remain. I need a longvision crew at once. And I need you to be ready to clear the airwaves.'

Varius witnessed nothing stranger than heavy traffic as he drove back into Rome. He didn't speak to anyone on the way into his flat, could see nothing from his window but rain over the Aventine streets. He had stood in the rain at Gemella's grave for some time, but his drenched clothes had partly dried in the car. He flicked on the longvision while he tried to decide whether it was still worth changing, but did not really look at it for a while. Militantly cheerful music and a voice droning on about the patriotism and commitment of the women dancing to it filled the flat and Varius only noticed the message on the screen when the sound had grown irritating enough for him to make the effort to turn it off.

An incident at the Colosseum. Salvius had called a session of the Senate. Varius felt his waterlogged clothes suddenly icy and heavy on his skin, even before he'd made conscious sense of what he was reading.

There was a scale of possibility, and a number of plausible culprits, but he already knew the nature of what had happened. *Not Marcus*, he thought fervently, knowing that it was; it had to be: Salvius would not be calling sessions of the Senate if either Marcus or Faustus were in any position to do the same thing.

He might only be hurt – only seriously hurt—

Already he was entering the code for the Palace into the long-dictor. For a long while he could not get any answer at all, swearing and pleading into the longdictor's oblivious buzz. The lines must be jammed. He tried a different code, and this time managed to speak briefly to a shaken young man in the Palace main exchange who was unable to tell him anything more than what was being repeated on the longvision, and whose attempt to put Varius through to Glycon's office produced only a dead connection.

Somewhere outside he heard the siren of a military vehicle, a muffled loudspeaker. He thought, whatever has happened, perhaps it is Salvius' work; perhaps this is a coup. For a moment he hoped passionately that it was, because it was possible in that case that Marcus might not have been physically harmed, at least not yet, and perhaps something could still be done.

The next moment he was frightened at having even thought that, as if hoping inadvertently for the wrong thing could wreck any chance of good news. He tried again, and this time managed to extract the information that members of the Imperial family had been injured, someone had been taken to hospital . . . Then there was another long period of standstill which suddenly he could no longer tolerate, and he tugged off the longdictor circlet and rushed out of the flat.

As he started down the last flight of stairs, he saw Sulien entering the lobby below. He stopped dead as Sulien looked up at him tremulously. He was taking a breath to try and say something, and his eyes were red, his skin white and blotchy. It could not have been more obvious what had happened.

Sulien had no idea what he looked like, and so he was unnerved when Varius took one look at him, said, '*No,*' and sat down on the staircase, staring straight ahead, one hand still tight on the banister.

Sulien ran up the stairs and sat beside him. 'I'm so sorry,' he said, and put his arm around Varius' shoulders. Varius dropped his head without seeming either to hear or feel him, and with a flicker of self-pitying frustration Sulien wondered why he was stuck with these people who wouldn't take any comfort from being touched, even when there was nothing else. At least Varius was alive, as Sulien had half-convinced himself he wouldn't be.

Finally he heard Varius say indistinctly, 'Drusus?'

'No. No, it wasn't him. It was Dama. There was a bomb on the roof . . . it was Dama. He was killed too, probably.'

Varius' last memory of Marcus was only a few hours old. It rushed at him now, and though there was no possibility of holding it off, he was wholly occupied in trying to deflect the full power of it. If he pictured Marcus now, talking to him, vital and younger than bore thinking of, he would say this couldn't be true, he would ask if there could have been a mistake. The urge to do so was already rising, cutting off his breath. He should – *he did* – know better than that, and he knew he couldn't stand to hear the truth repeated. He gasped a little, shutting his eyes under the force of the thought that he should have been with Marcus at the Colosseum, Marcus had wanted him there.

He whispered, 'Were they all – were all of them—?'

'No. Lady Novia had her shoulder broken, I think. They took Drusus to hospital. I don't know what was wrong with him.' Sulien hesitated. 'The Emperor – the *other*— Emperor Titus must have— He must have gone first, because the ring, because Marcus was . . .'

Varius looked at him finally, distracted. He muttered, 'What?' then, flatly, before Sulien could answer, 'Emperor.'

'He said to end slavery. He did that,' urged Sulien, hoping there was some consolation in that somewhere, if not yet. 'He didn't forget, even when . . .'

Varius hitched in another breath, and stood up. He gazed down the stairs with a look of dangerous, unearthed energy, then turned purposefully and raced back up towards his flat.

Sulien rubbed his tired eyes and followed. Varius hadn't locked the door and Sulien was in time to see him meditatively weighing a kitchen-knife in his hand before tucking it inside his jacket.

'Varius?' asked Sulien cautiously as Varius pushed past him, 'what are you doing?'

'You can go home,' ordered Varius, making for the stairs again. He paused on the landing and looked back at Sulien. Confusion cleared on his face, as if he had reminded himself, with some difficulty, who Sulien was. He said, 'Thank you for coming,' and set off.

'What's that knife for?' Sulien persisted, going after him, helplessly producing much the same friendly, humouring tone he'd used on Una earlier.

Varius slowed a little and looked at him warily, as if not intending to reply, then as he hurried out into the street he said shortly, 'Drusus.'

Sulien made a sound like a laugh, though not because there was anything funny about it. 'It wasn't him. I told you,' he managed after a moment, but Varius strode on, apparently uninterested in that. Sulien sped up to keep beside him and said, more loudly, 'He's not going to be Emperor—'

'No,' agreed Varius, 'he's not.'

Noriko came running to meet Makaria as she trailed like a sleepwalker back from the Palace baths towards her rooms, a few maidservants in tow. 'Drusus is here,' Noriko said, exhaustion and anxiety blurring the Latin words. 'He has come to the Palace.'

Makaria grimaced unconsciously at having to make the effort to understand what she had heard, then ran a hand through her damp hair. 'Where is he? What was he doing?'

'I don't know. I came to look for you at once. He wished to see . . . my husband's body. I am sure it is his right; I could not stop him, could I? But I have been told such things of him . . .'

Makaria straightened grimly. 'Come with me.'

Salvius had returned to the Imperial Office. He still felt a little tentative about using it, but it was the best place for the discussion he needed to have.

'Only a month ago you were telling me the Onager was nearly ready. You said you were within striking distance of producing a deployable weapon.'

The scientist shifted uncomfortably in his seat. 'Well, yes, we are certainly on the right track, and I think we've made very fast progress, considering how limited our data was at the beginning, and the head start the Nionians had on us . . .'

'But now you say it doesn't work.'

'It will work,' claimed the scientist cautiously.

'Vonones, Rome may be at war. We need to be able to win, with or without one of these things, but I have to know which it's going to be.'

Vonones hunched over a little, unhappily studying his hands. He muttered, 'I think— I didn't mean to create the impression— That is, we have definitely made significant breakthroughs, but when I said we were approaching success I didn't mean—'

Salvius sighed. 'How long?'

'I feel we're very close, but obviously with experiments of this nature it's impossible to predict the precise timing of results . . .'

'How long?' Salvius repeated.

Vonones sighed in turn, spread his palms in his lap and returned to his intense scrutiny of them. He answered, at last, 'Maybe another year?'

Makaria and Noriko burst into the room. An official at the door had been trying to make them wait until Makaria, sounding so like her father that a shiver played over Salvius' flesh, barked out, 'It's still my family's house, damn it!'

Vonones got to his feet, startled.

53

'You can go,' Salvius told him, rising also.

Makaria ignored Vonones. 'My cousin is here, or he was a moment ago, Noriko tells me.' She struck Noriko's shoulder for emphasis. Noriko managed a weak nod in confirmation. At Marcus' side she had had a sense of order that was steadying, if not comforting. The clothes she had put on to watch over him had helped her sculpt a view of herself as Marcus' widow, doing for him what women had always done for their dead. Away from him her mourning clothes were outlandish and out-of-place, and everything was rushing at terrible speed. She wanted to be in her own country, to lie down on any bed or any floor there and weep for confused grief and pity. She wanted her mother.

But Makaria, though she had clearly been heading for bed and wore only a loose gown over bare flushed skin, was unembarrassed and fierce: 'I *warned* you. What are you doing about it?'

Salvius hesitated, alarmed for a moment, then hastily clearing the unacceptable feeling away. 'Of course he has every right to come here . . .'

'Salvius! He's not here to pay his respects, he's here to *do* something – and whatever it is, you need to stop it.'

Salvius bristled at being lectured – by a woman, in front of others – but he turned to the longdictor on the desk. He told Glycon, 'Apparently Drusus Novius is well enough to be out of hospital. I'd like to see him here urgently.'

But he only felt the beginnings of real unease when it became clear that Drusus had left the Palace almost as soon as he'd arrived, and he had not gone to his house on the Caelian. 'Come on, find him,' he urged the aides who'd begun filing in without any news of where Drusus was. He was starting to pace a little round the room. 'Try the Capitol.'

He tried to think where else Drusus might go if, as Makaria was so certain, he was somehow attempting to seize power. Some kind of military base would be the most dangerous possibility – but Salvius had already made the military aware of his own claim, and surely Drusus had never had any serious ties with the army beyond the alliance he had once had with Salvius himself – nothing that could threaten him.

The door flew open as if blown and Glycon almost fell into the room. He stopped, trembling, staring at Salvius, and said, almost with deliberate rudeness, 'You'd better see the longvision.'

Drusus put his good hand to his face again. He had been meaning to ask for make-up, fretting about keeping the worse side partly out of shot. But he could not afford to waste time, and his sense of the import his injuries carried was changing. He straightened the pallium draped around his shoulders and faced the cameras full-on.

The smashed hole in the roof of the Colosseum glowed behind Drusus' head like an extension of the wreath he wore. He stood on a slab, part of the fallen wreckage, raised above the small audience of Praetorians and vigiles still working in the ruins whom he had gathered to listen to him speak. They were still uneasy and uncertain, but the presence of the longvision crew had acted as if to corroborate the wreath and the ring and his complete expectation of being obeyed.

He had told them to place cameras outside, too; it was important that it should be completely clear where this had happened, in the heart of Rome.

Without knowing or needing to know precisely what he was going to say, he began to speak.

'My friends,' said Drusus, on tens of millions of screens, across millions of square miles, 'how can I begin? What can I say to you when the sight before you tells of more grief than I can put into words? For the last few hours you have been waiting for news, knowing that something was wrong. Perhaps you do not need to be told the truth; perhaps you were one of those citizens from across the Empire who had gathered in the Colosseum to celebrate my uncle's reign; perhaps you were here with me in the Colosseum when the bomb went off, and in that case you and I survived this vicious attack together. I have to tell you that my uncle, the Emperor Titus Novius Faustus Augustus, and my cousin Marcus Novius Caesar did not.

'They were murdered beside me, they who worked so tirelessly for peace. I know that even in the first shock of grief and outrage, you will not be afraid, because you are Romans. I know you demand revenge. You will have it. If it is a terrible duty to tell you of our loss, and of Nionia's betrayal, it is worse to have to say that there are a few among us who have acted to shame Rome while our soldiers, doctors and ordinary citizens were giving of their best, to honour her. There is a destructive fraternity, criminals and escaped slaves, who have attacked innocent citizens before now, and they may have been the weapon Nionia wielded against us. And there are those – like General Salvius – who have either colluded with the perpetrators or at best, exploited this crime to further their own ambitions. The full truth will be known; the guilty will be dealt with swiftly, and the dead will be mourned. But my first act as Emperor will be to grant a special donative to our armed forces, including the Praetorians and vigiles, for they richly deserve it for the brave and selfless work they have done today, and the work they will do in bringing our enemies to justice in the future.

'You can see my face. There is no hiding that, like Rome herself, I have been wounded, and like Rome, I am still here. Romans, if you are in this great city I want you to come to me now. On this terrible day, let me see that you will stand with me against anyone who dares provoke you! Don't hesitate – I want to meet you now, in our grief and in our determination. And if you are in the smallest village in the furthest province of our Empire, still I want you come out into the streets, together, and show the world what a mistake it is to make an enemy of you.'

For a second after he finished speaking Drusus felt something like a ringing in his ears, then numbness, silence. He stepped down not quite steadily from the rubble and only as he felt the Praetorians' hands on his back, holding him up, did he really understand that they were applauding.

'Thank you,' he said, 'thank you.' He smiled. He wanted to

collapse into the excitement he had created, but there were still things to be done. 'I'm afraid I have more work for you. There are people I need arrested.'

Noriko said tentatively, 'But he cannot do that.'

'Get it off,' ordered Salvius, hoarsely.

'But he is not Emperor,' protested Noriko more loudly. She and Makaria were gripping each other's hands. 'He cannot make it true just by saying it in front of a camera.'

'Tell them to pull it now,' bellowed Salvius.

Glycon breathed out a laugh. 'I have. Of course I have! They say they cannot act against the Emperor's orders.'

Outside, coming from the north, they heard a faint roar, like a high wind in far-off trees: many raised voices already gathering in one cry.

Sulien speechlessly kept pace with Varius for a little while. Part of him expected Varius to realise any minute what he was doing and stop. But he did not; Sulien knew, really, that he wouldn't.

'I— I really don't think this is a good idea,' he tried.

'It's a preventative measure,' said Varius. 'If Marcus isn't there to control him then he could— He will—' His voice tripped at Marcus' name and it fell away. But he kept walking, and already they were close to his car.

Sulien stepped in front of him, trying to block his path. 'You can't. You're not thinking. The Emperor was just killed. The army's crawling over everything; the Praetorians— No one's going to let you near Drusus with a knife, not after this.'

Varius stopped. 'He won't let me near him if I give him any time to recover. But today, why should anyone stop me? I'm Marcus' senior advisor. If Drusus is hurt, if he's in hospital, I might be able to get to him.'

'You try it and you're just going to get shot.'

Varius said nothing, and his expression barely changed: just a bleak drift in the focus of his eyes, a catch at the mouth towards a smile, gone at once.

But Sulien froze, seeing it, and Varius shouldered past him again.

'Oh, come on, Varius, no,' begged Sulien, grabbing at him. 'You're not trying to— Marcus is gone already, don't you think that's enough?'

Varius shook him off and reached for the door of his car, and Sulien tackled him against it, pinning him there, saying desperately, 'Listen, listen! I understand; maybe it would be worth it— I would let you— I would let you, if I thought you could do it, all right? But you can't. You won't. Maybe you don't mind being killed, but you don't want it to be for nothing, do you?'

Varius had started to push him away, but at that he shook and went slack against the car. Eventually he said, 'You should go back to Una.'

'Yes, I should! But I won't until I know you're not doing this!'

But Varius' gaze slipped away from him again and he shook his head, regretfully. He said softly, 'It's all I can think of to do,' and struck out, punching Sulien's stomach while making a messy attempt to kick his feet from under him. Sulien tried to hang on to him and managed not to lose his footing altogether, but Varius needed only a moment of separation between them to wrench himself free and slide into the car. Sulien limped a little way after it as it moved away, uselessly calling Varius' name, then after a second of irresolution, he swung round and stumbled back towards his trirota parked outside Varius' building, deciding that he'd have to follow. At least he knew where Varius would be heading—

A Praetorian on a trirota swerved down into the street and alongside him loud and fast enough that Sulien glanced round but ran on, unconcerned, and did not imagine for a moment that the running footsteps were anything to do with him until suddenly he was on the ground with a man's weight across his back and words like 'treason' were being shouted in his ear.

Sulien gasped, 'What?' and struggled reflexively, not so much to escape as to see the man's face. Then he registered the gun pressed against the back of his neck, and the Praetorian kneeling on him broke from babbling excitedly into his radio to scream at Sulien not to move, to keep his hands flat on the ground . . .

He could hear – almost feel, through the paving – someone racing towards them: the backup the Praetorian had been calling for—? And then there was a further impact above him – someone else piling on – but the Praetorian was knocked sideways, uttering a choked cry, and Sulien felt the gun slither loose over his shoulder, and that was blood, splashing onto his back—

Sulien scrambled up from underneath the man. Varius' knife was still in the Praetorian's side and Varius himself was standing there, his face dulling as the ferocity faded and his hands had dropped numbly to his sides. There was a second or more of mutual shock, Sulien staring at Varius and at the man on the ground, all three of them immobile and gasping. But he heard the sirens approaching when Varius clearly did not.

At their feet, the soldier stopped breathing.

Sulien said, 'Come on,' and pulled at Varius' arm to make him move, dragging him back up the road. Somehow he managed to get them both into Varius' car, Varius silent and inert in the seat beside him as Sulien drove.

The man on the trirota had been the first arrival, speeding ahead of the Praetorian cars closing in on Varius' building. And if they were here, and if they could recognise him so instantly, then they were or would be at his home too, breaking the door down, charging into the room where he'd left Una helplessly asleep.

'What do you want me to do?' said the commander of the Palace detail of the Praetorian Guard, 'tell them to fire on Roman citizens mourning their Emperor? They're not criminals. They're not doing anything wrong.' His voice was taut with restrained panic and barely disguised contempt.

Salvius had not been spoken to in such a tone in decades. He struggled to ignore the sickness twisting in his gut, the dampness invading his scalp and armpits. He silenced the shamefaced, furtive thought of flight before he had to notice it. But even convincing himself his only feeling was fury, he still had no proper action into which to direct it. 'I want you to remember to whom you're speaking,' he managed, his throat dry. 'And contain the crowd. Just set up a perimeter; keep them where they are.'

The commander stared at Salvius, making a decision. He shrugged. 'I can try, I suppose. But I'm not sure anyone else is going to listen to an order that comes from you. Sir.'

Sulien took one winding detour round a section of the Aventine in the hope of throwing off any pursuit, but then, panicked, sped straight towards Transtiberina. He didn't think the Praetorians had seen him drive away, but it really made no difference whether they were right behind him or already there, waiting for him; all he could do was try and get home as fast as he could. He was far too agitated to think of any other choice. He didn't know why the streets were filling up with vehicles and people, all streaming purposefully towards the centre, but though the sudden weight of traffic provided some kind of cover, and would make it almost as hard for the Praetorians to move through as it was for him, Sulien only really cared that it was slowing him down. At Transtiberina, so many people came flooding down the Janiculum Hill that he could barely move at all. They were on foot, some of them were carrying little flags and standards, the kind of thing they'd have taken to the Games earlier that day, and Sulien felt a faint chill as they strode past. He shook it off, and decided he'd get to Una faster running.

'Varius, you have to drive the rest of the way.' He shook Varius' shoulder. 'Varius!'

Varius turned, barely seeing him, and Sulien climbed out of the car without being entirely sure Varius was going to move into his place.

He knocked some of the fervent, marching people out of his way as he ran, feeling a brief, irrelevant residue of embarrassment. He couldn't see any Praetorian cars. He'd left Tancorix there too – and she'd come with one of her lovers, and her little daughter. He

60

slammed into his building, glanced at the lift and then, panting, took the stairs two at a time.

And he stopped, a few steps down from his landing, fixed in place, unable to fill his lungs, or blink.

His door had been knocked flat and was lying over the threshold like a gangplank into his home. After a while Sulien stepped across it, feeling it tilt under his weight, and crept soundlessly through the living room past the overturned furniture, as if Una might still be sleeping quietly in the bed, even with all the doors in the place flung open around her.

He got as far as the doorway of the empty room and then found himself on his knees, looking stupidly at the bed. Well, all right, here he was on the floor, breathing hard, but it was not so much now that he could not move, as that as long as he did not, it would be possible to prolong this incapacity to think or feel anything, or to reproach himself for what he'd done.

'Sulien? Sulien—'

He started, as if the hand that touched his shoulder were made of ice. Tancorix stood there bafflingly, like a hallucination.

'It's all right,' said Tancorix. 'She's here. She's upstairs.'

She led him up to the floor above. The front door was open a crack and Arria, the old lady who lived there alone, was peering warily through it. She beckoned Sulien and Tancorix in with a little gasp of some feeling that contained anger, sympathy and bewildered excitement all at once. Sulien knew nearly everyone in his building, at least slightly; he had helped Arria with the arthritis in her hands, and half-remembered some lengthy complaint about her daughters' marriages.

'Sulien!' she exclaimed, 'all these people charging in – can you tell me what this is all about?'

Sulien opened his mouth to try, and said, 'No.'

Tancorix's lover cast a tense, put-upon glance at Sulien as he laid Una down on Arria's bed. 'Blind gods,' he muttered, sitting down on the end of it.

From within the large built-in wardrobe, Xanthe looked out at Sulien and said, 'We were hiding.'

Sulien went and stared down at Una's calm face. The wall by the bed felt like a tempting place to go to sleep as he leant against it.

'Bassus saw Drusus Novius on the longvision saying he's Emperor,' said Tancorix quietly. 'And then I heard sirens, and I looked out of the window and I could see the vans coming. And I thought . . . I was sure . . .'

Sulien forgot the splash of blood on his shoulder and hugged her tight; he might even have kissed her if Bassus hadn't been there.

'Did they come in?' he asked at last, hoarsely.

'Just came banging on the door,' Arria said, 'asking if I'd seen either of you. It's not hard to make young people think you're too stupid to bother with.'

'Thank you.'

'Well, it was too late to have second thoughts, wasn't it? With them all in here,' Arria complained. 'Your sister's really all right? She looks terrible.'

'Yes,' he said, although he was again reluctant to look at Una. 'Can I use your longdictor?'

Lal answered. He'd hoped he wouldn't have to speak to her, although the prospect of talking to Delir wasn't much easier to face. 'Sulien,' she whispered, and for a second or two they listened to each other's unsteady breathing, both trying to work out how to negotiate the incompatibility between the way they had parted and this.

After a moment, Sulien said, 'You've seen the longvision.'

'Yes,' she answered, in a halting, makeshift voice. 'It's not— There's no way it could be wrong? He couldn't be . . . lying, somehow? About Marcus?'

'No. Not about that.'

'Oh God,' she said, muffled. 'Oh God. Marcus.' She was probably crying, he thought, although very softly, trying not to let him hear. There was a desolate exclamation of horror in the background, then Lal whispered, 'And it was Dama?'

'Yes. I'm . . . I'm sorry. Look, I haven't got a lot of time; let me talk to Delir.' He could hear the longdictor change hands, but Delir didn't speak. 'Delir?' said Sulien, and waited a moment before beginning to explain, trying to be clear and practical: 'Delir, we've got to get out. Varius and I were just nearly arrested, and they've raided my flat. You'll have to decide what to do. I don't know if he's going after all Marcus' friends or if it's just us. But . . . you should know.'

The quiet persisted so long that Sulien repeated Delir's name, impatiently, and at last Delir answered in a winded breath, 'Sulien, I'm so sorry.' And it was obvious at once that this was not simple condolence.

Sulien felt a slow-moving, insidious shock. He had not connected Delir with what had happened, other than as a possible casualty, and a possible source of help. There had been too much else to think of; it had not occurred to him to remember how Dama had come to be free to kill anyone. He shrank from Delir's guilt, but as he tried to find some way, however flimsy, of telling him not to blame himself, the memory of Marcus' face, the touch of his cold lips interceded – as clear and immediate as if Sulien were still there, leaning over him in the broken box. And that faint taste: not only blood, but also the emptiness into which his own breath had vanished.

Sulien shook his head, and spent a long time trying to speak. In the end he could only manage, stiffly, 'Yes.' He cleared his throat to break the pause that followed, mumbled, 'Well. I thought you might know somewhere we could go, for tonight at least. I don't know where . . . and I've got Una and Varius with me.'

The paralysed silence on the line continued for a while, but eventually Delir spoke and Sulien decided he didn't have to notice anything in his voice but the information: 'There's a place at Lavinium.'

Sulien wrote down the directions, then pulled the small weight of the longdictor circlet off his head as quickly as he could.

'You should get over the river,' he said to Tancorix and Bassus.

'Go along with the rest of them, cheer for him, if that's what they're all doing, and make sure they see you there.'

Xanthe launched into a string of questions that all began, 'Why—?'

Sulien couldn't count how many times he'd thanked them all before he was finished. Arria and Bassus remained understandably nervous, even a little suspicious, but Tancorix, sitting with Xanthe in her lap, was calm, her tired face strangely relaxed. She said, 'It makes up for what I let happen when we were younger, doesn't it?'

Sulien turned to her, rubbed his face in weary surprise. 'I didn't— That didn't need . . .'

Tancorix looked at him steadily, eyebrows a little raised. She smiled.

Sulien went back into the bedroom and lifted Una off the bed. He had only picked her up once before, a year or two ago – for a joke, and to show how easily he could do it. But she hadn't liked that, and he didn't like doing it now. Her limp body felt horridly insubstantial in his arms: too light, too easily broken or removed.

The building was quiet. Most of his neighbours who'd been inside must have gone out in answer to Drusus' call. Still he felt raw and exposed, creeping down the stairs with Una clutched against him – though surely his neighbours wouldn't just turn him in if they saw him, whatever the Praetorians had told them? But he should have covered up the blood with something.

He hesitated when he reached his own floor, crouching on the steps as he settled Una more firmly in his arms and eyeing the doorway of his flat, thinking of what he could salvage, but afraid of taking Una in and being trapped there.

Varius came up the stairs looking for him, moving slowly, as if he were drugged. In that first second of seeing them, he plainly thought that Sulien was holding Una's corpse and he stumbled back, horrified out of the stupor that had held him since he'd stabbed the Praetorian. He gasped, 'Gods—! Una—'

'She's fine,' Sulien said hastily, wishing he'd made a different

64

decision about Una's clothes. 'She put her fists through a window. A lot of cuts, that's all. I gave her a sedative.'

Varius nodded jerkily, but he continued to shudder, too many coiled loops of shock beginning to unwind at once.

'Look,' said Sulien, loading Una unceremoniously into his arms, 'you get her into the car. You look after her. I'm going to get some things from the flat.' Aside from the practical reasons for this, he hoped it might make Varius hold together a little longer. And part of him knew he was glad of an excuse to get Una's motionless body away from him for a while.

It felt strange to be giving Varius orders, but it worked, at least to the extent that Varius didn't actually collapse and managed to hold Una up, although not very steadily. Sulien went to the door of the flat, reached inside and grabbed a winter coat hanging there. He draped it over Una. 'If anyone stops you, say you're taking her to a hospital; she was at the Colosseum and knocked her head. We thought she was all right, but she just passed out, a minute ago.'

'We can't keep using my car,' Varius said, sounding quite dispassionate, more like himself.

Sulien, down to the last scrapings of self-control himself, moaned through his teeth. Anyone who lent them a car would be taking far too much of a risk. 'It'll be all right for tonight, won't it? It'll have to be, we can't— I don't know how to steal one, I can't think of—'

'Nor can I,' admitted Varius, and gave a misshapen smile. 'Just a murderer, not a thief.'

'Varius—' began Sulien.

Varius shook his head impatiently, forestalling anything Sulien might say – or trying to clear away the thought – and muttered, 'I suppose they can't have a checkpoint on every road out of the city, not yet,' and carried Una away.

Sulien began picking through the mess, snatching up things almost at random until he was no longer able to ignore certain facts: that anything left behind now would be lost for ever, that he would never see the window mended, or sleep in his own bed again. He felt a choking impulse to search more carefully, choose more sentimentally. What about presents Marcus had given him, or books borrowed and now unreturnable? How could he just leave them here? But he hadn't even found a change of clothes for Una yet, and he couldn't very well drag a leather shield from Ethiopia wherever they were ultimately going, unless he was planning on selling it. He picked up a bag of pulmentum from the kitchen and thought, I can't live like this again.

Drusus allowed the crowd to support him – indeed, by now, held in a huge, fierce embrace, he had little choice in the matter. Girls' hands, daring and protective, stroked his injured cheek. He saw a thrill blaze in people's faces as they reached to clasp his hands, touch his clothes. It was electrifying, but there was terror and distaste in it too; he had always been kept at a safe distance from this human welter, and now he was surrounded, engulfed, and he could smell their breath and sweat; he could be crushed, or torn to pieces.

He led them from the Colosseum towards the Palace, leaning without shame now on the Praetorians and vigiles who had joined him, until they wanted to hoist him up onto their shoulders, and he let them do that too.

Salvius sat hunched over the desk in the Imperial Office, alone, his fists pressed against his temples, his eyes shut. The roar outside was very close now, and he could hear occasional peals of gunfire, too: the duped, the faithless soldiers, anyone else who'd got hold of a gun, they were all firing at the sky. Only at the sky, for the moment. *Come on*, he urged himself, as his heart raced and blackness danced behind his eyelids, *face it. Make a decision and act.*

Moving swiftly as if making some necessary cut in his own flesh – to produce some blood for an oath, perhaps, or to cut out poisoned tissue – he lifted the longdictor circlet and called his wife. He had not spoken to her before, to say that he was to be Emperor; he was glad of that much now.

'My dear,' he said, and his heart sank at how calmly affectionate her greeting was. She could not have seen the longvision. That he should want his wife to hear his name ruined! But it was hard to have to bear the whole weight of this explanation alone. 'Something's happened,' he said, inadequately.

'What is it?' she asked, of course. 'Is something wrong?'

Salvius cleared his throat. 'You have to be a good girl and not panic. Take Decimus and Salvilla out of the house, as far as you can, and stay out. Take what you can, but be quick. Don't go to your sister's or to any of our friends, at least not until things have settled down. And don't use your real name to anyone. And you need to tell the girls and their husbands to do the same.'

There was no reply, and it went on so long he almost wondered if something had gone wrong with the line. He repeated, 'My dear?'

'Salvius? What—?'

'There isn't much time, and in any case you may find it hard to understand.' Perhaps he would have done better to speak to Magnus, his eldest son-in-law, first – he would be head of the family, after all, until Decimus came of age, and it would be easier to tell a man. But it hadn't occurred to him to do that, not after thirty years and barely a cross word between them.

And she had had little practice questioning him; she began it now, timidly, inexpertly: 'But I— I have to— Salvius, you can't say such terrible things and then not explain.'

Salvius exhaled heavily, then began to speak, pretending to himself there was no one listening to the facts as he set them out – it wasn't so hard, that way: 'I'm in the Palace. I'm surrounded. The people— The people have been deceived. I don't have a great many options. I doubt I can get out. And in any case, you know I'm not one to turn my back on a fight. And I don't mean to give in without one, but—'

This time he could hear a rough flutter of breath on the other end of the line which grew into a kind of hissing wail: 'How am I supposed to tell the children a thing like that? How can I do any of it? You can't leave me to do— You can't leave me by myself! If things are that bad you have to come home and help me!'

'I wish I could,' said Salvius, awkwardly. 'You should . . . You should have Philia pack a bag while you call the girls.' Or was Philia still missing? Well, he couldn't think about that now.

'But everyone's here – Albus and Magnus and all the girls. No, Salvius, this is—'

Salvius clenched his teeth, growing cold. Of course they would have been in no hurry to go their separate ways after the bomb. Such a large and easy target, then! 'Then it's even more important that you hurry. And I'm afraid you'll have to separate for now – just for now. You can't lie low if you're all together.'

'What have you done?' she keened. 'What have you got us into?'

'It isn't my fault,' whispered Salvius, hearing his voice catch and despising himself for it. He added involuntarily, 'You won't believe anything hard you hear of me, will you?'

'Oh, my darling, of course not,' she retorted at once, and fell quiet.

Salvius closed his eyes again, and felt somehow sure she was doing the same, both of them pressing against the dark as if against different sides of the same wall.

She asked, in quite a different voice, 'Do you want to say anything to the children?'

He wanted to, desperately, and couldn't bear it. 'I'd rather know you were safely on your way,' he said, affecting nonchalance. 'Tell them all to be brave.'

Afterwards, he had the commander bring him as many guns and as much ammunition as he could lay his hands on. Salvius had also said, 'And as many men as are willing to fight,' but the man came back alone, laid the weapons formally in Salvius' arms and then stepped back. 'I'm not dying with you. Sir.'

Salvius glowered, certain the commander had not even tried to rally the guard. Salvius could try it himself; he could shoot the commander on the spot for desertion, come to that.

But instead he said, 'Fair enough,' and walked away.

He made his way towards the main stairs of the Palace and the approaching noise. There was such a clash going on just below the surface of his mind, not over what to do, but how to think. These last minutes would be bearable if he did not think of his family, of how desperately ill-equipped for flight they were; if he did not curse himself for ever having trusted Drusus. He was good at narrowing the focus of his mind when he needed to, leaving what was personal outside.

He could do it even now. But wasn't that useful, necessary singlemindedness a kind of lie, if carried right to the end? Was it enough to face what was rushing to meet him up the stairs? Should he be able to face worse, in imagination, at the same time?

Without resolving this, he broke into a charge, raising the gun.

They carried Drusus into the Palace. The front line had swept ahead of him and in through the doors, unchecked – Salvius was already dead, lying sprawled headlong on the staircase, and the place was in such bubbling uproar that Drusus did not see him immediately. The Praetorians set Drusus down, not sure where further to take him, and watched expectantly as he hobbled forward a few steps. He too was at a momentary loss for what to do next.

First he saw the corpses lying at the foot of the stairs, and felt the more violent mood in the air now. Then he glimpsed Salvius' pale head on the marble.

'Help me,' he said, limping towards the staircase. He climbed painfully and stood above Salvius' corpse, preparing to speak again.

Bliss at his success would come later. For now he must be sure that the fierce excitement that had brought so many people here did not crumble away. He would thank them. He would ask them to stay and celebrate a first blow struck against Rome's enemies. He was aware that he had promised a lot to purchase this, and it would cost a lot to keep it: a party now, then the donatives to the army, and then the war.

'Sulien,' whispered Varius, in the back seat. His voice had no weight, no tone. It was the first time either of them had spoken in more than an hour. They were somewhere to the west of Ferentum, still only a handful of miles from the outskirts of Rome. Sulien had been avoiding the Via Laurentina, moving south along the quietest roads he could find. Several times they had heard sirens whining close by, but not for them yet.

Warily, Sulien looked back, and was startled at how carefully Varius was holding Una: her head was supported on his arm, safe from knocking against anything hard, her body cradled with an automatic tenderness that Sulien found strangely painful to witness. But the coat had slipped or been folded down and Varius was examining the bloodstains on her clothes by the flat blue glow from the streetlights, his face calm, studious. 'All this blood,' he continued, 'it looks as if she was lying in it. There's too much, it's not right if it was just from the window.'

Sulien paid fierce attention to the rain-slicked road, watching for a left turn. His shoulders were stiffening. Outside the car there had been nothing but damp fields of corn for so long; everything looked the same in the dusk. Perhaps he had gone the wrong way.

'Was she at the Colosseum?' Varius persisted, hesitant but relentless. 'Is this . . . ? Is this someone else's blood?'

Sulien glared into the dark spray, hunching over the car's controls. He felt powerlessly resentful of Varius, for the flush of muddled guilt that heated his flesh, for extracting information from Sulien that would only hurt him. It seemed unreasonable that Sulien should have to be involved in any more of that. He didn't want to hear Varius react, the way his breath would change, even if he didn't say anything.

'Yes,' he confirmed shortly. 'It's his.'

Varius closed his eyes, and felt tears slide from beneath the lids, leaving the surfaces raw, although no more moisture came.

Turning his head away from Una, he looked out at the quiet fields and the glow of Rome on the horizon, and though he didn't know where they were heading, and scarcely remembered the journey so far, he knew more or less where they were. They couldn't be much above two miles from Tusculum, Marcus' home. Varius had met Gemella in that house, and Marcus, who must have been thirteen back then . . . Wasn't there some way not to think of what had become of everyone he'd known there? Leo, Clodia, Gemella, Marcus . . .

Ordering – begging – himself not to do it, he closed his fingers around a darkened fold of cloth at Una's shoulder – the blood was powdery against his fingertips, blue-black in the light – and curled his hand into a fist around it, as if he couldn't let go of it.

Lavinium was a faded seaside town, half-absorbed into the bigger resort of Antium and surviving listlessly on the overflow of Antium's tourist trade. There were a lot of Eagles, fitfully fluorescent in red or blue on shop fronts or guest-house roofs, and not much else to show for the fact that this was supposed to be where Aeneas had landed. Sulien nosed the car back and forth in frustration along a strip of small villas and shabby gambling halls before finding the gritty track that led north through the dark pines that edged the coast.

There was a small, disorderly row of holiday cabins on the beach, thirty or so, between the rough dunes and the sea. The fourth from the end, Delir had said. Sulien eyed the lights in the other huts anxiously as he drove past. It was still summer, and at least a third of them looked occupied, though no one was out in the soft rain to see them now.

He stepped out onto the damp sand. The sea and the wind in the pines sounded boomingly loud, and his skin tightened in subdued panic, as if inside the car he'd been safe.

'I'll find the key,' he said to Varius, although Delir hadn't been very clear about where it was supposed to be, and it was so dark, and maybe there wasn't a key at all. Varius let him fumble around for a while, sitting passively in the back as if the journey wasn't over yet, but then he climbed out of the car to join him, circling the cabin without speaking, patting along window ledges and on top of lintels. Sulien tried to ignore a pull of tension at leaving Una lying alone and out of his sight on the seat, even as close as she was.

'Here,' said Varius, finally. The key was under one of a stack of concrete bricks by the steps, left over from laying the foundations, perhaps.

The floor was coated with sand and the air smelled slightly stale, dust tinged with salt. Sulien's head skimmed against the ceiling and he could almost have touched the opposite walls with outstretched hands. There wasn't any electric lighting, but Sulien found a gas lantern hanging by the door. There was a sink, and a tiny stove. Varius and Sulien carried Una in between them, clumsy now, and put her down on what seemed to be the only bed. Sulien dropped the heap of things from his flat in the middle of the floor, dragged a flimsy folding chair across to beside the bed and sat there, his head tipped back against the wall.

Varius didn't sit down. 'I'll get rid of the car.'

Sulien just nodded, too tired to ask any questions. But as Varius pushed open the door he began, 'I haven't thanked you—'

'For killing that man?' asked Varius, his voice uneven. His shoulders moved in something between a shrug and flinch, and he said gently, 'Don't.'

Sulien sat there as the noise of the car faded. The rhythm of the sea's hiss matched Una's quiet breath on the bed, steady, continuing. For a while he couldn't be bothered to do anything about how hungry he was, but eventually he tipped himself wearily onto his knees to rummage through the bundle on the floor. He ate some bread, still crouched there, then got up and drank some water straight from the tap because he didn't feel like looking for anything else.

Belatedly he realised that he did not know if Varius intended to come back, let alone how he would do it.

There must be at least a roll-up mattress or something, perhaps under the bed, or in one of the cupboards, but he only thought of that when he was already lying beside Una, awkwardly curled so his feet wouldn't hang off the end of the bed, and by then he couldn't have moved.

He came close to waking early, as dawn was pushing in callously through the skimpy curtains, but Una was still motionless at his back and he thought at once, *No*, and rolled over onto his face, burying himself wilfully in sleep, hiding.

Decimus understood what was happening; at least, he understood enough. They were under attack, and there hadn't been enough time to evacuate. His mother and the slaves were still running from room to room grabbing clothes and crying, though his eldest sister and her husband had kissed him and run out to their car. But there was a tide of noise breaking against the villa's gates, and then the lights of military trucks flooded the windows.

Salvilla shrieked and grabbed his hand, pulling him towards the back of the house. *But they'd have the house surrounded.* He tried to tell her that, but she didn't listen, and so he pulled free and ran back into the atrium, darting through as the soldiers kicked in the door and burst into his father's study. The chest where the guns were kept was locked, but it had never been any secret where the key was, because his father trusted him. Decimus opened the chest, took out the pistol he'd used for target practice and loaded it. He'd never fired it at a person before, but that was what it was for, that was the point of learning how to use it. His father had made sure he understood that, even when he was firing toy guns at his friends. His hands shook a little, and they were damp around the wooden handgrip, which was strange, because he really wasn't frightened. He hoped that would be completely clear. There was a strange ringing feeling instead, humming all through him as if his body were a metal bell. His senses were alive, leaving too little room to think, and no need.

He slipped back into the atrium, quietly, aimed at the head of the Praetorian who was wrestling his sister Secunda towards the

73

door, and fired. The gun sounded louder than usual, fired indoors. His aim was perfect, and for a second he felt an eruption of triumph. But at the same time incomprehension hit him, more jarring than the noise of the shot, leaving him dizzy. It wasn't so much the blood or the collapse – it was the man's uniform; these were *Roman* soldiers he had to fight, who had come to kill them, not Nionians or separatists or even mutinying slaves, and if he was not on their side then there was no solid ground left on which to stand.

But all the same his hand had moved as if by itself, aiming the gun again, and he shot another of them, and before they could react, he'd dodged inside the doorway of the room through which Salvilla had fled, guarding the way. And he killed two more of them before they could get close enough to shoot him – the only one of the family to die in the house.

EXUVIAE

Climbing out of the car, Varius glanced up into the dark eye of a security camera and felt like staring straight at it, letting it take a good look at him. But of course that wasn't how a man trying to hide would act, so he lowered his face and set off towards the port. There was no boat waiting for him, or any of them, but there could have been. The vigiles would find the car and the footage in a day or two, and if it wasn't already over by then, they would waste some time thinking he, at least, and maybe all three of them, were somewhere across the water, anywhere.

The tideless sea lapped black beside Varius' feet. All he had to do was work his way along its edge, no risk of getting lost, between the pale glow of the coastal road and the red and white lights of freighters and cruisers, pegged out along the horizon, sliding over.

Perhaps it was not guilt he felt over the Praetorian he'd killed; he might not have been thinking very clearly, but even so, his judgement of what would have happened to Sulien had been right. He supposed he would not have undone it. But he could feel, lodged within him, a splinter of the aching space into which the man had vanished, which had been too close and huge already.

He'd been walking for hours, and had left Ostia a long way behind now. The black sky was deeper, wider, without its tired, blank light. Sometimes Varius whispered as he walked, without realising he was doing it, half-formed, frantic apologies and pleas on the edge of his breath. And then he said, loud enough to hear himself this time, 'Not you too.' And hearing it he stopped, as if he'd caught himself doing something ridiculous, and it was not speaking into thin air, but walking along for however many miles in the middle of the night, as if there were somewhere he could get to that would be any better than here. So he sat down and let his eyes rest on the sea for a moment, but then even the dark water was too difficult to look at and he shut his eyes and lay back on the sand.

His body hurt, as if in a kind of protest against itself, blood and breath resisting their own healthy, unreasonable flow – a not entirely unfamiliar feeling. He asked, 'What can I do now?' – aloud or not, he didn't know, but a whimper either way.

Something, answered a whisper in his mind. Varius let the word repeat, a little stronger this time, and the voice was Gemella's. And that was just imagination, he knew, not a re-union, nor really a message. And 'something' was not much of a resolution, and not a comfort at all. Still, he lay there, quiet and listening, almost as if there were something to hear.

Of course he heard only the sea scuffing at the sand, and himself, getting his breath back. He was more tired than he'd realised. He didn't want to stand up. But after a while, and almost without knowing why, he did so, feeling sand scattering inside his clothes. And soon, as he walked through the morning, he grew too thirsty and too worn out to think at all, which made the long walk easier.

Una lurched through dreams and couldn't wake from them, encased in warm, unyielding layers of sleep. She dreamed, not of Marcus, but of a hairless old man cowering in the dark beneath the dome of a cave, clutching her hand to his cracked brown scalp, pleading, 'Comfort me, comfort me.' Una struggled impotently to free herself, panting with terror, for she could not bear to hear him and her hand was trapped in his as if they were nailed together. But as she finally managed the horrified sound that awakened her, she forgot the dream instantly, and she knew the cry scraping out of her wasn't for a nightmare but for Marcus, Marcus lying there with nothing moving behind his smashed ribs and his dried blood still all over her.

Almost before her eyes were open she had backed up against

the headboard of the strange bed, clinging to it and screaming again in panic because she knew that she had been drugged, taken somewhere—

'Shh, please, Una. Una! There are people here, they'll hear you – *quiet* – quiet!'

Una let out another cry anyway, and then stopped, gasping, staring wildly at the terrible pale curtains, the sunlight on the wooden floor, at Sulien. He was kneeling beside her on the bed, hissing at her desperately, and his face was still crumpled with sleep and his hair was sticking up in ridiculous dandelion-like tufts. Una relaxed without realising it while her face settled into a disgusted scowl.

Sulien shuffled back from her and sat hunched on the far corner. Una swung her legs over the edge of the bed, facing away from him, and began trying to deduce as much of what had happened with as little recourse to him as possible.

'Had to get away,' she concluded, in a low, grudging voice, trying to flatten any questioning note out of it.

Sulien confirmed quietly. 'Yes.'

After a second's silence, Una shrugged lopsidedly and muttered, 'Oh well.' It was not as though she had ever thought safety in Rome was guaranteed to last forever. But she heard Sulien make a little grunt – an incredulous, slightly pained sound – and she ignored it. She eyed the blue sky showing between the curtains, listened distrustfully to the sea and added, 'West coast.'

Sulien sighed. 'Lavinium.'

Una frowned, beginning to work out how he would have found this place, considering Delir, and then flicked that line of thought away, irritably – they were here now, it didn't matter. She said heavily, 'Salvius doesn't have any reason to go after us. Drusus is Emperor.'

'I don't know how . . .' began Sulien, almost apologetically.

Una's shoulders rolled in a defeated slump. She looked down at her clothes and then contracted, as if shrinking from within them. She sank quietly back down onto the bed and curled on her

77

side, pressing her face against the musty blanket. She whispered, 'Everything we did . . .'

Sulien, very hesitantly, laid his hand over hers and Una's one visible eye looked up at him blankly, as if bemused as to what he was doing.

'I have to get this off,' she said in the same little voice, without moving.

Sulien nodded and stood up, looking for something to do. He started to talk, busily: 'I've got some of your clothes; I think they'll do for now. The water's cold, but there's a stove, I'll—'

'I can see there's a stove,' snapped Una, suddenly sitting up, then drooping again at once. 'Just go outside.'

Sulien trailed a pale, doleful look back at her, and Una twitched in exasperation. Left alone, she sat for a moment longer, motionless on the edge of the bed, tensing like an athlete before a race. Yes, she could heat some water; there would be some kind of bowl or tub somewhere. But when she stood up she began yanking off her clothes at once, violently pulling open buttons and clasps, teeth clenched. A set of keys and the plastic wallet containing her identity papers skidded across the floor. The blood had soaked through to her underwear, to her *skin*: dark, mottled patches were flaking away. She couldn't touch it; she couldn't watch it turn liquid again on her skin, fall in drops on the floor to be wiped away. Una sobbed tearlessly, elbowing out of the last loop of fabric and dropping into a crouch beside the heap of clothes, fists pressed against her face.

The morning was perversely beautiful, after the wet dinginess of the day before. There were still only a few people out on the beach. Sulien sat on the sand, unsettled by the warmth and the sparks of light on the sea, as wrong as the flush and glitter of fever. The sky was a brash, swaggering blue, and his flesh felt heavy and constrictive underneath it, like badly chosen clothes. He wondered where Varius was, and regretted that he had not come back; he wished someone older were there. The door of the hut banged open behind him and Una strode out, wearing one of his tunics which barely covered the rusty stains on her bare throat and legs. She marched past him without a look, down the beach, into the sea. Sulien started up nervously, dithering on the waterline as Una kept going – stamping forwards as if to settle an argument with someone waiting for her there in the water, a long way out.

She wanted a cold shock, to be suddenly out of her depth, but the water was warm and shallow, nothing like the Thames. While it was still barely up to her waist, Una threw herself forward impatiently and began to swim. She carved fiercely through the water, as fast as she could, trying to outpace what was floating off her skin. But her feet still trailed on the bottom when she put them down; she would have to go a long way further to reach deep water, out along the white trail of flaking light towards the horizon. She could feel the energy, coiled ready in her muscles. She ducked below the bright surface, arms wrapped round herself. *Oh, where are you?* she whispered into the water, and waited there, letting the pressure build in her head and chest towards a choice that she didn't really have.

So she came up and saw that Sulien was standing exactly where she'd left him, featureless in the light, but the tension obvious from here.

She swam back.

Sulien came back into the hut later and found her dressed in the clothes he'd brought for her, sitting on the floor by a bowl of water, staring at the heap of bloody cloth.

'I can't remember how you did it,' she remarked.

Sulien leaned over and poked the place on her arm where he'd jabbed in the needle, finding that this time he felt neither like apologising nor justifying it. Una flinched and glowered. She said very clearly, 'You can't ever do that to me again.'

'I wasn't planning to.'

Una raised her head, deliberately meeting his eyes. 'I mean it.'

Sulien looked back without giving any further guarantee of

compliance. *And what if I do*, he felt tempted to ask, despite what had happened, *what if you're in that state again?* But he held back, or did not quite dare, and if there was a specific threat, she didn't say what it was.

They stared at each other, neither promising anything.

'All right,' Una said finally, shrugging again. But she studied the web of pink lines on her arms, which might have been a month old, might never have been deep. 'I can't remember doing this.'

'Would you want to?' asked Sulien, wondering.

'Yes,' said Una instantly, with such unqualified stubbornness that Sulien let out a little puff of laughter, startling himself.

But Una's gaze had already slipped back to Marcus' blood, her face softening into helplessness.

Sulien bent down and began to pick up and fold the clothes. 'I think we should burn these,' he said quietly. Una nodded, a pale flicker of gratitude crossing her face.

He was searching for something unremarkable in which to bundle the clothes so the stains were hidden, when Una stiffened, lifting her head sharply to stare at the door, a look of incredulous attention on her face. She whispered, 'Varius . . . ?'

She got to her feet. Sulien froze for an instant, and then hurled open the door.

Varius was stumbling heavily up the steps, eyes barely open, scarcely able to lift his feet from one step to the next. Sulien started forward on a strange little thrill of relief and dismay, reaching to help him. Varius speechlessly accepted Sulien as a convenient upright surface from which to push his way forward, staggered to the sink and began gulping water, gasping between swallows.

'I thought you weren't coming back!' cried Sulien.

'I shouldn't have, really,' said Varius, collapsing onto the edge of the bed and leaning his forehead against his wet hands.

'Where did you—?'

'Ostia.'

'That's twenty miles!'

Varius made a sort of laugh deep in his throat, as if to say yes, it certainly was.

'Varius,' said Una again. Sulien heard the shake in her voice and saw that the shock of Varius' appearance had been enough to jolt her back almost to the point of tears. She took a step towards Varius, who looked up at her, raising an almost identical look of desolation to meet hers, compassion the only shade of difference.

He reached and took hold of her hand and Una gripped back with brief, surprising force, then drew away and walked out of the cabin.

Sulien located the remaining bread, lying amidst a pile of other things from the night before. 'Here,' he said.

Varius took it slowly, but he'd noticed the bundle of clothes Sulien had put down.

Sulien was already too familiar with that arrested look, the failure to turn the eyes to anything else.

'Need to get rid of that,' Varius said, neutrally.

'We're going to burn it. Look, I thought we could do it . . . properly. Do you want to come with us? We were going to do it now, but we could wait for you—'

Varius understood what Sulien was offering: not just the disposal of evidence but a kind of funeral. But it seemed so pitiful, to be reduced to that, a camp fire on a beach, like children with a dead pet. 'No,' he said, rather coldly, moving away a little.

Sulien left him alone and went after Una.

They made the fire in the stretch of pine wood between the beach and the road, away from the holidaymakers beginning to emerge onto the sand. Una felt, in a marginal way, pleased at how straightforwardly and smoothly they worked on this together, choosing the space, sweeping it clear and level, setting out a circular hearth of stones, collecting a heap of sticks. They handed things from one to the other quietly, speaking only to issue and accept small instructions – 'break that one, put it there' – as if this were a practised, daily routine. Well, it almost had been once; Una laid the last piece of kindling, watched Sulien light it and drove her fingers into the dust at the memory of the three of them, crouched by fires lit for warmth in other woods.

They sat on the sandy ground and watched: the wood caught easily enough, but the clothes burned slowly, drenching black, flaking red. Una, otherwise unmoving, worried a fistful of sand until the fire rose higher and the clothes began to fall into unrecognisability. A few dark scraps floated away into the warm air. She'd unthinkingly stuffed her freedwoman's identity papers into the pocket of the clothes she was wearing now; she pulled them out and unfolded them. She studied the summary of her rights around her own mistrustful face, read out the name 'Noviana Una' aloud, in a rough, experimental voice, and flicked the papers quickly into the fire. She looked over at Sulien, who reached for his own papers and laid them beside hers, as carefully as the heat would allow.

They tried to hide it, afterwards, swept the sand back into place, scattered the stones. There were more people on the beach now, children galloping in and out of the surf, and adults standing in dazed clusters outside the cabins, unsure what to do. The news was still spreading. Una shrank from the sight of them and fled towards the hut. Varius had left the door slightly open; Sulien peered in and saw him lying with his arm over his face against the light, and crept back, carefully.

'We're going to eat something now,' he told Una firmly, forestalling resistance, but she only nodded dully. She had retreated into the corner of space between the pile of bricks and the wall of the hut, leaning her head against the warming concrete. Sulien, fighting off a pang of unease, left her there, found a stall at the base of the road leading up to the town and bought a bag of greasy little fried cakes.

'We should use what we have first. Don't go and buy things we don't need,' complained Una when he came back.

'Well, Varius is asleep in there,' said Sulien, as if that made entry into the hut and the preparation of food physically impossible, 'and we're not going to live or die on ten denarii.'

'It adds up. And it isn't only the money, it's people seeing you. We'll have to . . . we'll have to—' And the multitude of things they would have to do swelled in her mind without form or order, turning her dizzy, and she couldn't speak.

'Eat,' supplied Sulien.

Doggedly Una obeyed, and to avoid being coaxed through every mouthful she forced down everything he handed her, though what little hunger she'd been aware of disappeared almost once.

'You'd better tell me everything that happened,' she said at last, screwing up the empty bag.

She listened to the first part of it without any comment, only grimaced a little to think how helpless she had been, put down and passed about and collected like a suitcase. But when he came to the arrest and Varius' intervention she lifted her head to stare at him in quiet shock, then cast a distressed glance towards the cabin and Varius. 'Those bastards,' she muttered. 'I can't . . .'

Sulien could only remind her softly, 'We got away.'

'We don't even know what he wants!' exclaimed Una with abrupt force.

'I thought it was pretty clear what he wants,' said Sulien grimly.

'But it's not. Is it just us three? And is it the same for all of us? Is it anyone who's close to Marcus, or . . .' Her voice sank, grew tentative: 'He used to . . . He hates me, because I was the one who found out about him, I told Marcus what he'd done . . .'

Sulien tightened his mouth uneasily, feeling the conversation tilt towards something he didn't want spoken, even considered. 'Why does it matter? He's after us; we get out of the way. That much isn't complicated.'

'It does matter,' argued Una. 'We might be able to guess how far he'll chase us, and for how long. And if we knew whether he was targeting one of us more than the others, we might have some kind of options.'

Sulien scowled. 'Well, we don't know. And it doesn't matter.'

Una looked away. 'How do you get to the town?' she asked, after a pause. 'We need a longvision. See how bad it is.'

'Fine,' said Sulien. 'Let's go.'

Una shook her head dubiously. 'I don't know. If they're showing pictures of us together in the forum . . . then we shouldn't be there at the same time.' Sulien's mouth pulled sideways, and Una sighed. 'Or you can go and I'll stay! Either way, I'll be back here. I'm not going to just . . . You seem to think I'm going to vanish. I won't.'

'You still don't remember what happened yesterday?' muttered Sulien, with a quick, faintly barbed look down at her arms.

Una scowled and moved in an angry jerk, as if she were about to spring up, but she didn't complete it, and her face gradually slipped back into such bleakness that Sulien regretted saying anything. She folded her arms. 'No more of that,' she said. 'Had my fun. Anyway, you can't spend every second with me and there are things that need doing. I might as well make a start.'

Later, when he was striding down the strip of gambling halls looking for her, Sulien found that there were indeed pictures of the three of them showing regularly on Lavinium's public long-visions. He couldn't ask anyone if they'd seen her. Varius, who had rolled off the bed groaning just when Sulien was on the point of waking him, was searching the north side of the town, though with an air of humouring him. He hadn't appeared very concerned, which might have been just because he was too tired and numb to worry much about anything.

And when, after an hour and a half of this, Sulien went back to check the hut and found her there, he felt for a second of almost joyous fury that he wished she hadn't come back, that he wanted nothing more to do with her. He might have shouted it at her, except for the distracting shock of her appearance. Her hair was wet again, and a different colour – a much darker brown than its natural pale dun. Much of the mess had been cleared away and a couple of plastic bags were spread over the small table, on which stood a pot of dye beside a pan of water, spreading a chemical reek into the air. She'd plainly tried to be careful but there was a faint purplish stain banded around her hairline, and dark smears on the plastic and on her fingertips. A bag she hadn't had before hung from a chair.

'Sorry,' she said, as Sulien entered and drew in a loud, indignant breath and tried to decide what to do with it.

Varius was back too, sitting with his legs stretched out on the bed and his back against the wall, eyes half closed. He and Una had a silent air of sad companionship that incensed Sulien even more.

'For fuck's sake—' Sulien knocked a hand, half by accident, into the too-close wall.

Una stifled a little start, which dragged an irritating twinge of premature remorse from him.

'I'm sorry,' she repeated, 'I didn't—'

'Aren't things bad enough for you yet? Or are they just not bad enough for me?' Varius was impassively waiting this out, not interfering, and Sulien felt discomfited that this was happening in front of him, though it wasn't enough to stop him: 'Don't you ever think of anyone else? It's so fucking selfish!'

'Look,' said Una, irritably, guilty patience already beginning to evaporate, 'do you want to know what I was doing or not?'

Sulien laughed, hard. 'I don't know if I do.'

He turned away a little, and Una sat down with an exasperated sigh. A sullen quiet fell between them. But Sulien had no realistic retreat available beyond silence, and so after a while Una sighed again and said, 'The longvision's near the station.'

'I know.'

'I didn't think of it when I went out, all right? Or I would have said. But there was a train leaving when I got there . . . they don't run that often and if I'd come back and told you first we might have had to wait till tomorrow. And by then it would be even more dangerous, with those pictures everywhere. I might not have had another chance.'

'For what?' groaned Sulien, resentful at having any response dragged out of him.

Una was already reaching into the bag; she set out a number of bottles of what seemed to be bathing oil on the table. 'I had a locker in a bathhouse in the Aventine,' she explained, quietly, 'not in my real name, of course. That's where I went.' She fished inside the neck of one and drew out sheaves of money, twisted off the stopper of another bottle and pulled out more.

Sulien stared at the money, moved across and sat down opposite her almost without realising he was doing it. He whispered, 'How long have you—?'

'Two years,' replied Una, 'maybe two and a half.'

Sulien breathed out a wordless question, and Varius, coming over to the table, answered it: 'In case this happened.'

Una's face crumpled, and she shook her head. 'Not this. Not *this*. In case we ever needed to leave, but I thought he'd be with us; I never meant in case he died . . .'

'You never told me this,' said Sulien, his voice still soft.

'I didn't tell anyone. I didn't tell him.'

'Why not?'

'If it wasn't secret it wasn't safe,' said Una, mechanically, then blinked in distress and shook her head again. 'I needed it. I couldn't help it – I didn't like it; I didn't like the way I had to have it there. So I didn't want anyone to know. And you would have said – *he* would have said – we're safe now, you shouldn't keep your money somewhere like that – shouldn't have to do these things any more. And I don't know, maybe then I wouldn't have done it, or I would have got rid of it. And I needed it, even though I thought it was a stupid thing. I mean, I hoped it was.' Her face went dull. She ran a thumb critically over the edge of a roll of notes. 'I should have put more in,' she said.

'Well,' muttered Sulien, after a moment, for want of anything else to say. 'Well done.'

Una pushed her hair away from her face and straightened her back, one hand on the money. 'Tadahito knows us,' she said, looking from Sulien to Varius. 'I think he would give us asylum . . . if we could make it there.'

Sulien felt a pang of vertigo at the distance and the otherness of Nionia, cringed away from imagining either the attempt or its success. 'There's got to be somewhere in the Empire, somewhere quiet we could—'

Una shook her head. 'We're the first thing Drusus thought of on the day he got everything he ever wanted.'

Incongruously, Varius laughed. When they looked at him, he said, 'It sounds like true love, when you put it like that.'

'Well, it means he's not going to forget about us any time soon,' said Una. 'You know how much work it is staying hidden. And it's not just us we have to worry about – there's everyone who has ever had anything to do with us. Whoever owns this place. This way there's only the journey, and then we wouldn't have to hide any more. And I don't think I can face more than that. Not a whole life . . .'

Once again strength seemed to leave her suddenly. She leant over the money on the table, sinking her head in her hands.

Varius pulled back the hand that lay nearest the money as if bowing out of a game of dice. 'This is yours and Sulien's,' he said. 'You'll need all of it.'

'Don't be stupid, Varius!' said Una, almost disgusted. 'What do you think we are? It's too late for any of us to just . . . Why didn't you let them arrest Sulien – why did you even let us use the car – if you wanted that?'

'It's not only that,' said Varius. 'Just look at us: you can dye your hair, but we can't any of us change our skin colour, can we? I'm more than ten years older than the pair of you. You don't get many groups that look like us travelling across country – even back in Rome we're not the most everyday set of people, are we? So whatever we do, we'll have to separate.'

'Not us,' said Sulien, too fast even to think about it, glancing at Una who agreed, 'No.'

'No, not you two,' said Varius, with a twitch of a smile, 'but the three of us together, we're too memorable. That's why I should have stayed away. But I wanted to see you were safe, before . . . I wanted to see you.'

'Well, you could travel on your own,' said Sulien reluctantly, 'but we could still – I mean, we could agree towns along the way

87

where we could meet. Or just look each other up when we get there, I guess. If we're going to do this.'

'But I'm not,' said Varius, and there was a surprising brightness in his face. 'I don't want to leave Rome. I'll go where I have to, but I'm not giving up. I don't have any kind of plan, and this is no place to start, but I'm still going to try and stop Drusus. Something has to come of everything Marcus did – and everything we did. I want to do something so that won't be wasted.'

Sulien was touched and impressed by this. But as Una looked at Varius the sadness in her face only seemed to deepen and grow strangely gentle. She told him quietly, 'It is wasted.'

Varius shook his head fiercely, his eyes wide and shining. 'No. I don't believe that. I won't let it be.'

Una painted the remaining dye into Sulien's hair and they studied the results with dissatisfaction. The change was less dramatic in his case, as his hair had been darker to begin with, but with that difference in colouring erased they looked more obviously like brother and sister than they had before. They were both startled to notice resemblances in the contours of their faces that seemed new, as if freshly stamped.

'Hmm,' said Una, running her fingers uneasily over her upper lip, as if she could tweak it into a different shape.

'It's a start. I'll stop shaving for a while,' said Sulien. 'Your eyebrows look weird.'

Una shrugged. 'I can't use the dye on them; I haven't got anything small enough to do it with.'

'I didn't mean just now,' gibed Sulien, as a kind of experiment. Una did smile, but too slowly, having to work out what was required of her and how to do it. Not that he'd expected much more. 'Lal might be able to make us new identity papers,' he said, and then, 'Una – maybe Varius is right, maybe there's something we could do, something more than running away. Wouldn't it be better? Don't you want to?' Almost under his breath, he added, 'For Marcus . . .'

Una moved away. Varius was asleep again, the bedroll they'd

found filling much of the floor. She stepped around him carefully, sat on the bed and subjected him to a faintly chilling appraisal, sympathetic but detached, certain.

'He's going to die,' she said, quietly, so as not to wake him, such a sure, authoritative prognosis that Sulien's gaze jumped to Varius with swift horror, as if expecting to see fatal injuries and blood seeping through the blankets.

'He wanted to kill Drusus yesterday,' continued Una, 'what's changed? What else can he try to do? Maybe now he'll take a year over it, but it'll come to the same thing. And so he'll try, and they'll kill him. And even if he could do it, what good would it do?'

'No,' said Sulien, confusedly, moving a little closer to Varius as if to shield him from something. 'No. If that's what he's planning – well, Drusus would be gone, that's—'

'He wouldn't be gone – not in a way that meant anything. It wouldn't put right anything he'd begun. And Rome would fall in love with the memory of him, and who is there to follow? None of what we tried for – what we tried so *hard* for – will happen, anyway.' She looked down at Varius again, who was lying with near-unnatural tidiness on his back, arms at his sides, composed and still. Her voice was almost a caress, regretful and final: 'He just wants revenge for Marcus, and the right person isn't even alive. And he doesn't want to see . . . any of this. Soon he won't have to.'

Sulien's eyes recoiled from Varius, who seemed changed, as if Una had been chanting a spell over him, left fragile and not even older in any reassuring way, if you imagined him setting off to die at thirty-one or two, if you imagined looking back on it. He said, 'Then we should . . . I'll talk to him.'

'Why? He knows what he wants. Leave him alone,' said Una.

Sulien stared, waiting to see if that made any sense that didn't horrify him. 'No,' he said.

And he tried, because he couldn't stop seeing a kind of doomed halo around Varius now; he felt it like a low rumble in the air, all through the long night while Una shook and ground her teeth and cried in her sleep beside him. But in the morning, no matter how baldly he tried to say it, the point kept slipping out of his grasp. The trouble was that Varius did not have a definite plan to be talked out of or persuaded to change. He kept agreeing, almost cheerfully, that yes, targeting Drusus might be part of it, and of course it would be dangerous.

Sulien could only implore, as Varius moved away from him, 'Please be careful, whatever you decide to do,' which people must have said countless times since the beginning of the world without it ever doing any good.

But Varius turned back and looked at him and said, 'Listen, your sister's right,' which seemed to Sulien a surprising admission for a moment, but that wasn't what Varius meant: 'We're the first thing Drusus thought of. He doesn't think it's hopeless: he thinks we could accomplish something – otherwise we'd still be at home. I think we should have as good an opinion of ourselves as he does.'

We, he'd said, and Sulien felt another tug of willingness and hope. But he looked past Varius at Una, sitting pale and tense on the steps of the hut, remembered how she'd moaned in the night, 'Please try,' and thought he should be grateful she was willing not to fling herself alongside Varius, towards the risk.

[IV]

MANOEUVRES

Early in the morning, the soldiers broke open the doors and knocked down the barricades Makaria and Noriko had built within the chamber where Marcus' body lay. Makaria stood facing them squarely, white with exhaustion but upright and rigid. One arm was tight around Noriko, pressing the dark head against her shoulder, and the other hand held a pistol, levelled at the incoming men.

'My Lady,' said the commander, edging towards her, 'no more need for that now.'

'Isn't there?' asked Makaria, tightly. She knew the man, of course, and blinked, trying to stow that recognition somewhere out of her way.

'Lady,' repeated the commander, carefully, 'it's been a bad enough night.'

'Please,' moaned Noriko, into Makaria's taut shoulder, certain that if Makaria fired a shot into whatever half-formed order had been restored outside, it was as good as suicide. It might still be the right thing to do, but she couldn't work that out; she could not muster anything but dread. She felt Makaria tense very subtly; the Praetorian might not have seen it, even as close as he was now.

Makaria placed the pistol crisply into his outstretched hand. 'It has,' she agreed. She folded her freed arm over Noriko, patting her in a brisk, stoical way, while closing her eyes in anguish and lowering her face to press her cheek against Noriko's forehead. Noriko made a convulsive effort to straighten, to sustain a fair share of the embrace, not just to cower in Makaria's arms.

Only when assured it was safe did Drusus limp in, leaning resentfully on a Praetorian's shoulder. He looked from the fallen barricade to Marcus' body, understanding they had not only been defending themselves. 'What did you think I was going to do?' he asked, disgusted. His arm and knee hurt almost enough to keep him from caring about anything else; he could not stay on his feet much longer, and a low panic was sneaking its way below the surface of his mind: he wasn't sure how he would know when it was safe to lie down.

The two women clung to each other and stared at him, mute and hostile.

'Let go of each other,' insisted Drusus. He cast another uneasy look at Marcus' body, which had changed subtly during the night, becoming impossible to mistake for a living person. He sincerely felt that Noriko and Makaria had violated the stillness of this place, stained what had happened here between Marcus and himself. He announced, louder than was necessary, wanting this action to be witnessed, yet angry that he was defending himself, 'I will give him a funeral worthy of him – he will have all the honours fitting for a Novian.'

'An Emperor,' said Makaria, recklessly.

A scowl slammed across Drusus' face. 'I said get away from each other,' he snapped. 'Take the Princess to her rooms,' he ordered the soldiers. 'Lady Novia will come with me.'

At the head of a little escort of Praetorians, he led Makaria out to the main atrium of the Palace. Makaria believed he had brought her this way to warn or frighten her with the sight of Salvius' corpse, still lying sprawled on the stairs, and the blood and broken glass everywhere. And she was afraid of being killed; it almost surprised her, after all she had witnessed and lost in the last twenty-four hours, how greedily eager she was to go on living. But she had heard the gunfire, and she had scrounged scraps of sleep in the same room as Marcus' body. She had known Salvius must be dead, so there was no further shock in seeing it now. She looked at him briefly and sadly and then back at Drusus, holding herself reasonably steady, she thought. She was aware that bursting into tears and abasing herself might please him, might even save her, and in theory she was in favour of doing anything necessary. But she could not actually bring herself to it, even afraid as she was.

Drusus stopped at the foot of the stairs, looking at her for a while, as if waiting for something – a reaction from her, maybe, or some return of energy and excitement in himself. 'You will remain in Rome to attend the funerals, because it is right that people see you there,' he told her at last. 'You will not leave your quarters at any other time. Then you will return to Siphnos, and you will stay there, unless I have you brought to me. And you will not receive any messages or visitors I have not approved.'

Makaria nodded coolly, as if this was only to be expected, although her eardrums were booming with her pulse and her fingertips tingled icily. 'Let Noriko come with me, then,' she said, unable to plead for that either, almost just suggesting it.

'I am not going to leave her to your influence. You are not to be trusted,' said Drusus in a low voice. 'And if you have people you value back on that island of yours you will be careful how you behave during this time.' He met her eyes. 'You should consider yourself very lucky indeed.'

Makaria could not answer that, because she agreed with him. Later, hugging herself tearlessly in a chair in her locked room, she reflected that she had not said or done anything particularly clever, but at least she had forborne from thanking him. Heaven help her, but to be allowed to go home, and to be spared any further part in events, was, for now at least, an incredible privilege, a stroke of undeserved grace.

But she could feel the folded edges of the letter she had helped Marcus write, hidden inside her clothes and prickling against her skin. Not a letter – it was his will, really. And if she could think of nothing else to do with it, she could at least plot how to keep it safe.

'I want you to be able to contact me,' said Varius. It was early evening, and they were on a small road through the fields outside Ardea, leading away into hot green hills. The lime-coloured lights of fireflies were pulsing on, off, on, through the grass:

small optimistic signals. Una tried not to see them; they were part of the world's dreadful avalanche of detail, which poured on, ignoring the gouged space in the world where Marcus had been.

They had persuaded Varius to accept a little of the money from the bathhouse locker, and they had each acquired a change of clothes. Varius and Sulien both had a few days' growth of beard. Una had darkened and thickened her eyebrows with make-up, and the dye in her hair and Sulien's had softened a little, looking less stark and artificial. For now, this was all they could do to disguise themselves, and it felt like very little to hide behind, a thin, shivering skin between themselves and the pictures of them glaring out of every forum, and the terrible things that by now they were said to have done.

Varius handed Una an advertising magazine he'd bought in the town. 'I want to know that you're safe. If you make it out of the Empire, you can put a notice in that.' Una noticed with vague approval that he had not said *when*. Varius explained, 'It's got a message service. If you're in trouble – if you need my help, you can use that and I'll answer. I'll look for the name L. Soterius. Make the cognomen Clarus if you're all right, and Ater if something's wrong.'

Una nodded, but it was difficult to concentrate on something she was so sure was not going to happen. Beside her, Sulien sucked in an unhappy breath.

Varius read their faces and said, 'You'll know if something's happened to me – it'll be on longvision.'

'We could say we're selling a slave,' suggested Una drearily, looking at the section of the magazine that carried such advertisements.

Sulien sighed and took it off her. 'We'll say a tropical fishtank.'

'All right,' said Varius with a half-smile, and he paused. 'I might look for Delir.'

'I think they'll have gone— No, they're bound to have,' said Sulien, trying to quiet a sick flutter at the thought of Delir's devastated voice on the longdictor, while Lal's lost touch flared suddenly over his skin.

'They might not have left Rome,' said Una. 'They had more time. And Delir's Persian, Zeya's Sinoan, and she's got the scars on her face . . . they wouldn't stand out so much together if they stayed in the city.'

'They'll have made themselves hard to find. And you shouldn't try; it's too dangerous, for you and for them.'

'I'll be careful,' promised Varius, unsatisfyingly.

Una wanted to say: Better get it over with quickly, Varius, make sure they have to shoot you on the spot, and do it soon, don't let them drag it out. And as she subdued that impulse, for courtesy's sake, another sprang up unexpectedly: an urge to plead, Don't go, stay with us, because we need your help already. But instead she made herself mumble weakly, 'Good luck.'

Varius hesitated, and placed a hand on her shoulder to draw her a little distance from Sulien. 'Una, when we were in Bianjing, when Marcus left us there . . . do you remember what he said to you?'

Una stared carefully at a dried-out fencing post to one side of him, avoiding his face. She didn't want to have to spend the last time she saw him tamping down irritation with him, and it was unfair of him to force her to do it. But it was a ridiculous question. She would hardly have forgotten – although she could only just stand to skim over the cutting edges of the memory. 'If I never see you again,' she had cried out, and Marcus had answered—

But she and Sulien had ground to cover; she couldn't drop down into the dust and howl, which was all she would be able to do if she let herself remember in detail. She knew Varius only wanted to be kind. She said, tight-lipped, 'Yes.'

'I know it doesn't help now,' said Varius, 'but later it might.'

Una nodded slightly, to please him. For another moment she had to struggle to stand firm, not to cry out under Varius' soft look at her. Then, to her relief, he went and patted Sulien's arm with awkward warmth. 'You got us out,' he said.

Sulien pulled him back and embraced him briefly, with a rather obvious and final air of making sure he would not have anything to regret. They went through another round of 'Good lucks' and Varius shouldered his bag and walked away.

Later, reaching into the pack for a map as he crossed a field beside the Pontine Road, he discovered the heavy bundle of cash Una had left there, and the terse note wrapped around it.

Una and Sulien reached another coast that night, flying across Samnium in a cramped, dirty train. Una didn't like being trapped like this, under electric light with so many people, but at least they had the protection of adult respectability now: she'd strapped a round pillow under the long, matronly dress; they pretended, queasily, to be a young married couple. The curve at her waist drew attention away from her face, at least, though the drawback was that it encouraged people to talk to them, even to try and touch her.

Turned loose into the dark at Aternum, they were drawn as if by gravity into the large crowd below the public longvision in the forum, by the sea. The footage playing had been taken from a volucer cockpit: pale missiles flowed through the evening sky over the Promethean Ocean, leaping like dolphins and diving down onto Yuuhigawa.

For a while, a grave, frightened silence held around Una and Sulien. Then, as a splash of fire blazed close to the camera, someone uttered a wild, barely celebratory cry, and from that an angry cheer began to spread.

Varius gripped the barrier set out along the Via Triumphalis. As the cortège bearing Marcus' body approached, the weight of the crowd behind pushed gently, at once forcing him off balance and propping him up. He could see Marcus' face, quite clearly – and he tried to keep his eyes on it as long as he could, until the soldiers had carried the bier past him and towards the Forum, out of sight. But he could not, quite; his vision warped and blurred and once he had ducked his head to wipe his eyes he couldn't bring himself to look back.

There were Praetorians and vigiles everywhere – Drusus himself could have looked out of the window of his slow-moving armoured car and seen him – but Varius felt strangely safe, even though he hadn't meant to get so recklessly close to the procession. They would not expect him here, and he was one of so many faces.

It was strange; when Leo and Clodia had died the glut of public mourning had irked and embarrassed him – what business had people to cry and make fools of themselves for someone they had never met? But now, dissolved into this crowd which stretched back from the route of the cortège for so many streets, he felt grateful to them for their company. He was so fond of this fat woman, crying beside him, who looked up at his face with blind fellow-feeling and clutched his hand. How sweet that she cared about people she didn't know – Marcus and Faustus, and himself – even if only temporarily. He spoke to her, choking out, 'This shouldn't be happening,' and she shook her head sorrowfully and answered, 'I know.'

She didn't know about the gun he carried under his jacket, just in case. But he hadn't had much expectation of a chance to use it. After what had happened at the Colosseum, it was no surprise that Drusus was not walking behind the cortège this time, as he and Marcus had at the last Imperial funeral. And he would be safe, delivering his oration in the Julian Forum; it was closed to all but appointed guests, with a heavy Praetorian cordon blocking every entrance.

Still Varius tried to pay attention, noted the car that had been chosen, counted the number of guards who walked beside it, tried to memorise every detail that he could, in case it revealed some weak point later.

Helplessness caught him, and he told himself that for the moment he was only compiling information; he didn't have to know what to do with it yet.

The centre of Rome was laminated with even more giant

screens than usual, so that Drusus' speech should reach all the thousands of mourners in the streets. Varius had only to lift his head to watch Drusus get out of the car and walk up to the Rostra. Already he moved with only a trace of a limp, although the bruises on his face were still vivid. Instead of the ceremonial black toga Varius had expected, he was dressed in military uniform with a black pallium draped across the breastplate, and the wreath bright on his head.

Varius, who had tried to prepare himself to bear the sight of Drusus victorious at Marcus' funeral, was breathtaken with disgust.

Behind Drusus, Makaria, pale and dull-eyed, was flanked by ladies-in-waiting. Noriko was absent. Varius, who had seen a pack of furious Romans burning the Nionian Sun on the steps of the deserted Embassy only that morning, understood why. He still tried to observe and remember; he willed the camera to linger on the audience of aristocrats and generals so that he could see who had been placed closest to the front, who was not there.

But as soon as Drusus began to speak of the attack on Yuuhi-gawa, Varius knew he couldn't stand to listen to him. Around him, people were gazing up at Drusus with a sort of longing, and Varius' fusion with them was lost. He was a malign, disenfranchised presence here, not one of them. He pushed his way to the back, tolerance for the cramped density of the crowd fraying quickly now, dodged down the first turning, past the shuttered bookshops on the Vicus Sandaliarius, but with all the screens, and the speakers turned up so loud, he had to hurry a long way before he could leave Drusus' voice behind. It waylaid him at every street corner: 'Rome will find comfort in justice, and in the courage of her soldiers . . .'

At last, at the edge of the Subura, it was out of earshot, and the streets were empty; as everyone had drained in towards the centre, like blood to the body's core. Varius lowered himself to the ground, sitting against a wall like a tramp. He had been there; that was all he really wanted. And there was a measure of solace in the thought that Drusus had no idea how close he'd been, how close he still was.

The wall was patched with torn posters and graffiti, a lot of new scribbled curses and hysterical slogans against Nionia. Varius got up and moved along the wall, looking for a space that was clear, but not too clear, where an extra word would neither stand out too much, nor be swallowed completely by the surrounding clutter of letters. He took a lump of chalk from his pocket, checked around, and wrote ATHABIA on the brick. As soon as he'd done it a self-conscious flush of sweat rose to his face and for a moment his impulse was to rub it out: it looked so stark and obvious, surely the vigiles would see it at once and recognise it for what it was.

It could have been a woman's name. He hesitated, then drew a heart around it, framing it, disguising it.

He began to walk again, with no destination in mind, fingers still closed around the chalk in his pocket.

Drusilla flinched as she entered the ballroom and a herald cried, 'The most august Lady Drusilla Terentia, the Emperor's honoured mother!'

The music died for a moment and the couples on the dance floor broke into polite applause. Drusilla felt her face blaze. She made her way stiffly down the staircase, as if afraid of falling.

Drusus was coming to meet her, his face brilliant with eagerness and aggressive pride. 'Well, Mother, here we are!' he exclaimed almost wildly as he bent and kissed her cheek.

Drusilla embraced him a little clumsily, hissing to him as they separated, 'I didn't want my name called out like that. It's not right for a woman's name to be shouted about in public.'

'Mother,' said Drusus, at once exasperated and faintly pleading, 'you are the most honoured matron in the Empire. Isn't that what you always wanted?'

Drusilla pursed her lips.

Drusus patted her hand coaxingly. 'It's perfectly right for you to be lauded as you deserve.'

Grudgingly, Drusilla smiled. 'Well,' she said, 'congratulations.'

Drusus pressed her hand again, and an incredulous smile hovered at his lips. 'It doesn't feel real,' he murmured.

'You've been very lucky,' she said.

Drusus scowled. 'Luck— It's not a matter of *luck*. That's no way to speak about it. The Empire is in mourning. This is the gravest of all responsibilities.' The musicians struck up again. He sighed and offered her his arm. 'Would you like to dance this with me, Mother?'

'You know I never dance,' said Drusilla. 'I don't like fuss.'

'Mother, now of all times—!'

Drusilla turned to survey the dancers with an air of suspicion. The ball's splendour was carefully restrained, so as not to jar with the recent tragedy. There were military standards ranked around the walls, and wreaths of laurel branches hanging from the gallery, but no flowers, and the music had a martial urgency to it. Many of the men, like Drusus, were in ceremonial uniform; the women's dresses shone darkly, deep indigo, pine green.

'Are you going to marry any of these women?' Drusilla asked sharply.

Drusus sighed again. 'I cannot tell whether you wish me to say yes or no to that.'

'It's not right for the Emperor to be unmarried. Your cousin was married, and he was younger than you.'

'Indeed.'

'Though it wasn't what you could call a *proper* marriage, not with that foreign girl. And look what came of *that*. What are you going to do with her?'

'I will do what's right,' said Drusus.

'I hope so. She must have been mixed up in what happened; the people will expect her to pay for it.'

Drusus said nothing for a while. 'Father will be moving in here soon,' he remarked after a while with artificial casualness, and Drusilla tensed. She hated any direct reminder of her marriage, of Lucius' existence. 'He's been quite well, lately, you'll be glad to hear. And it's not as if there's any shortage of room for him. Of course, you're welcome here too. It is not really right for the Emperor's mother to live outside her son's guardianship, is it? And the people would appreciate an example of family unity at such a dark time.'

'You know very well that's impossible,' said Drusilla, tight-lipped.

'Ah, well. I try to be a good son,' said Drusus, and went forward to take a senator's daughter by the hand and whirl her into the next dance.

The Empress Jun Shen examined the new Roman Emperor on the jade-framed yuan-shi screen in her audience chamber. She saw how his new dark uniform suited him, how handsome and noble he looked, and at the same time she thought he looked like a little boy dressed up. In the latter aspect she found him more frightening.

She said, 'But you were attacked by a group of anarchists from within your own Empire who have been trying to provoke a war for over a year. Do you not hesitate at all to give your enemies precisely what they want?' She waited for Weigi to finish trans-lating.

Drusus replied calmly, 'No one believes a gang of slaves could have succeeded without both Nionian sponsorship and inside help.'

The Empress grunted. 'If they are going by your speeches, I suppose they don't.'

Drusus smiled tightly. 'I have done my best to keep the Roman people informed. If you have been listening to my speeches, you can need no further explanation from me.'

'And I see that you have grown no fonder of your cousin's advisor or his concubine since I last saw you.' She remembered them in their temporary prison in the Nionian quarters, the young girl tense and urgent, warning her what Drusus would do to Sina in a war . . .

'They were traitors then and they're traitors now. If my cousin had realised that he might still be alive.'

'Even the girl's brother?' added Jun Shen.

'It's not a mere matter of association, your Majesty, I promise you that. They all had ties to my cousin's killer.'

Jun Shen leaned forward, her scented armour of clothes stiff around her, fringes of petals and beads drooping against her forehead. 'Perhaps you will not object if a much older sovereign suggests you reconsider your course? I saw how hard all sides worked to avoid this. You, I think, had other concerns at the time. But it is a pity if it is all to be thrown away. You have knocked over a lot of buildings in Yuuhigawa; I think there are Roman towns in Anasasia and Arcansa already paying for it. Must it go further than that?'

'Yes, it must,' said Drusus, quietly. 'I am acting from necessity.'

And Jun Shen studied his face, radiant and terrified under the fading bruises, and thought, *Yes, that much is true, for him it really is necessary.* More truculently than mournfully, she considered and rejected the wish that history could have waited until after she was dead to produce him. She did not like to think of her ministers or her grandchildren attempting to handle this.

Drusus finished, 'And Roman forces will need the freedom to cross Sinoan territory.'

Jun Shen sucked in her lips. 'What am I to say when Nionia requests the same thing? I am not having my lands become a battleground.'

'We will not be coming as your enemies, Madam.'

'On the contrary,' said Jun Shen, 'any force entering my lands without my permission will have made itself my enemy.'

Drusus stiffened. 'You would have to take responsibility for the consequences of resistance.'

'Yes. But I prefer to have no part of this, your Majesty. I think you should be glad of that. You've already gone looking for one fight; it would not be wise to take on another.'

Drusus stared palely out of the screen at her, which then, without warning, flashed and went dark. Jun Shen raised her eyebrows and settled back on her throne with a quiet groan. She lowered her chin to the mail of necklaces on her chest and remained silent for several minutes, thinking.

She looked up at last, to see the alarm on the faces of her interpreter and attendants. 'He won't do it,' she said to them, 'not yet, anyway.' But she felt her heart still bobbing rapidly against her thinning bones, under the solid weight of pearl and amethyst.

Drusus looked around at his generals in the Strategy Room and said, 'Well, let's rest a little. We'll talk more of this later.'

The fury and panic faded almost too quickly, soaking away into the maps of the world that covered the walls. Had he really just had a conversation in which the future of a billion lives had been shaped? He was left fretfully stranded between excitement and a feeling of puzzled doubt that anything was really happening, that he was truly Emperor, that the little dots on the maps meant something true.

He looked at the outline of the coast of Greece, where Siphnos was an invisible speck, Makaria already fixed there, definite. But the world's slippery surface stretched away, without even a ripple to show where Sulien and Una and Varius had hidden themselves.

It would have been foolish to completely ignore the risk that existed as long as Varius was alive, but Drusus felt only a patient, businesslike level of concern on his account. But that Una and Sulien had escaped with him, despite how swiftly Drusus had moved, that felt like something worse than bad luck: another uncanny sign of what they were, what they were *meant* for. Ruin, the Sibyl had warned him, and he repeated to himself the borrowed names that had allowed him to understand, names that wound tight around his own: Noviana, Novianus.

Walking meditatively through the Palace, he found he was heading towards Noriko's quarters. Why not, he thought, turned up the shallow flight of stairs towards her door and had the guards unlock it.

He had let her keep the apartments Marcus had used when he stayed in the Palace, which were extensive and beautiful. She had everything she could reasonably want. She was not trapped indoors, for there was a wide balcony looking over the gardens. So he did not think she could have suffered much from having to stay there.

Much of the furniture had been cleared away. He found Noriko by the open doors to the balcony with her waiting women, all of them in that strange kneeling posture again, though this time their clothes were largely Roman in style. But quiet Nionian music was playing, and Noriko's ladies were combing out her hair, trimming away tiny frayed sections of individual strands with slow, practised hands. All three women's faces were still, as if in a shared trance of boredom and unhappiness. As they saw him their eyes widened and they all rose as hastily as their sheets of hair would allow. Drusus almost wished he could press a button to replay this response, it was so pretty, like the fanning tails of frightened pigeons.

'I came to see how you are,' he said.

Noriko didn't lift her eyes from the floor. Eventually she murmured, rather indistinctly, 'I am well.'

'Good,' said Drusus. He gestured to the women, who looked from him to Noriko in startled dismay and then, reluctantly, left the room.

Noriko cast a nervous glance after them but straightened her back and raised her head. 'I'm glad you are here,' she said resolutely. 'I wished to speak to you.'

Drusus nodded permission, while allowing himself a mild, sensuous pleasure in her proximity, only half attending to what she had to say.

'I have not been allowed to leave these rooms,' said Noriko, in a low voice, 'because I was not there when . . . You have been making everyone think that my country . . .' She took a small step back from him; the balcony was behind her and there was

104

not much space into which she could move. 'You have accused me, because I left the Colosseum . . .' She glanced at the long-vision, then said, 'Are you going to put me on trial?'

'Was there a signal of some kind?' asked Drusus, kindly, almost as if he would be prepared to sympathise if she said there was. 'Had you been warned beforehand?'

'No!' cried Noriko, 'of course not! Why would I ever have come here, if—? He was my *husband*. Our marriage was supposed to bring peace. If I had known what would happen, I would have protected him; I would have prevented this.'

'Very well, then,' said Drusus, easily. 'I'll believe you had nothing to do with it.'

Noriko blinked, baffled. 'Thank you,' she managed at last, her voice strained. 'Then I would ask you to let me go home. I would like to . . . I would like to mourn for my husband there.'

'You are at home,' said Drusus. 'You married into this family. You are part of it. Of course I cannot let you defect to our enemies in a time of war.'

Noriko, who had retreated until her back was pressed right against the balustrade over the gardens, lifted her hands in a kind of cramped despair. 'But I have no purpose here any more. You have made your people think I am a murderess; you are trying to destroy my country. How can I stay here?'

'It's true that it isn't safe for you to be seen in public now. And it's a shame you couldn't come to the funeral, I know. I think the best thing is to let people forget you. It won't take so long, believe me.'

Noriko lowered her head again. 'What are you going to do with me?'

'I will protect you,' said Drusus. He was leaning against the jamb of the balcony doors, not touching her at all.

Cleomenes was walking back along the Tiber towards head-quarters when a drunk stumbled into him and nearly fell at his feet. He dragged at Cleomenes' jacket before lurching away towards a gang of other tramps on the bridge. Scowling, half-inclined to go after the man and arrest him for something or other, Cleomenes tugged his jacket straight – and found the folded sheet of paper that had been thrust beneath it. He opened it immediately with unthinking professional interest, and felt the blood light up in his cheeks like a neon hoarding.

He screwed the paper up tight, buried it in his pocket. He spent the rest of the day feeling that his colleagues could read its contents on his face, that he would be forced to produce it and be arrested. He burnt it when he got home, disguising even that as part of an impromptu offering to the household gods, in case his wife should be endangered by knowing; in case, somehow, he was being watched here.

After that, he meant to forget it, but fear that it would happen again, and gathering indignation at how he'd been compromised, sent him to an underpass outside a sprawling tram station in the Ciconiae just before midnight. It was a natural stop on his route home, although he'd had to manufacture a lot of unnecessary paperwork to explain why he was travelling so late, in case anyone was paying attention.

'Damn you, don't ever try anything like that again,' he began at once. 'You stay away from me, for both our sakes. Don't you think they're watching me? They know I was mixed up with you and those kids. They're just waiting for something like this. The longdictor's tapped, I'm sure of that. And they're keeping me away from anything big at work – I know they're checking I'm not poking into anything. Half the time I think they're following me. Gods,' he finished, deflated, as the sour yellowish light caught Varius' face, 'you look terrible.'

'I'm supposed to,' said Varius.

'Got yourself beaten up?' said Cleomenes, still with an air of harassed disapproval.

'I've been in a fight,' Varius corrected him, with mild, irrelevant pride. He'd found that a degree of violence was inescapable, living the way he was, and he felt he'd done reasonably well, considering.

'Why don't you just get out of the country while you still can, Varius?' pleaded Cleomenes, 'because it's going to get harder, I'll tell you that much. They're bringing in these new identity papers; they're tightening up all the borders – and it's mostly because of you.'

'I have things to do,' said Varius.

Cleomenes studied him curiously, and something, perhaps the way Varius held himself, prompted him to grasp Varius angrily, push him against the wall and pat down his clothes until he found the gun, strapped against his side.

'Jove!' He backed away until the width of the underpass was between them and looked nervously at the steps leading up to the dark street. 'Don't tell me what that's for,' he said adamantly.

'You know, Cleomenes.'

'Well, I'm going to forget I know. And that's the only way I can help you. Gods, what are you expecting from me? Because I can't— I can't. I've got a kid now. Do you know what happened to Salvius' family?'

Varius nodded grimly. 'Yes, I do. I went to his house. New people in there already. Everyone's behaving as if Salvius was never there.'

Cleomenes was slightly taken aback. 'I don't know if they're expecting people not to notice . . .'

Tiredness was pooling in the bruised hollows of Varius' face, as if he was standing in an invisible rain. He shook his head. 'They want people to know and not know at the same time.'

'A terrible thing,' muttered Cleomenes, uncomfortably, 'all of this.'

'But there's nothing you can do about it?' asked Varius lightly. 'Are you sure that's why you came here?'

'Yes,' said Cleomenes firmly, but added, 'What did you want me to do?'

Varius smiled. 'You've already told me about the borders; and I think you'd have said if they knew where to look for my friends. Or me.'

Cleomenes restrained himself from asking about Sulien and

Una, despite his real concern for them. *I won't know anything more about this*, he thought. 'I'm thinking of leaving the vigiles anyway,' he said gloomily, 'getting away from this place. Maybe I should have done it years ago.'

'Don't do that, not yet. Just stay in touch with me, for now. Help me find a better way I can contact you.'

'And then what? Pass you information? Feed them false leads?'

Varius was silent for a moment and then said, 'Yes.'

'Well, it's not going to happen.' But again, quite against his first intentions, he found himself qualifying this: 'If you change your mind, I'll help you get away. If you get yourself into trouble . . . well, most likely there'll be nothing I can do about it, but if there is, then I will. But I won't help you with that—' And he gestured at Varius' side, where the gun was hidden.

Varius said nothing.

Wincing again at the state of him, Cleomenes finished gruffly, 'Do you need money?'

Varius shook his head. Una's note had advised him to divide the money into caches and hide them around the city, not to keep much on him. He guessed that she had learned to do this herself, in London, years ago. Perhaps he was not quite so adept at finding hiding places; one hoard at least had been found and raided, but there was still a lot left. 'I'm not as badly off as I look. I've got other reasons for this. But thank you.'

After they parted, riding back towards the centre of Rome, Varius inked the words LOOKING FOR YOU ATHABIA onto the back of a seat on a late-night tram. He had begun to add such messages to the bare name in the last few weeks: ATHABIA WHERE ARE YOU? and, most importantly, ATHABIA MEET ME, TRAJAN'S FORUM. A pillar by the Clivus Cinnae; a shop wall in the Field of Mars; an arch on the western approach to Vatican Fields Station.

He could not use the word Holzarta; that was too blatant; he was sure that would be remembered. Athabia, the name of the village where he'd sent Marcus, where Delir's people had met him, was dangerous in itself, but it was the only possible point of reference between Delir, whom he had never met, and himself. He was trying to make it just ubiquitous enough that it would be glaringly conspicuous to someone who knew the name, while scarcely visible to anyone else.

But he dared not put a date, or even a time, in case he'd gone too far and made anyone else curious, and he'd deliberately chosen a large, busy place where meeting anyone would inevitably be difficult. Even so, when he first went he half-expected to find every vigile officer in the city – or alternatively, every pimp looking for a client – waiting for him. He sat hunched in the corner of the forum, one of a row of beggars, and watched for someone trying not to look as if they were searching for someone; someone filtering cautiously through the crowd; someone who, like him, didn't stray too far from the possible routes of escape.

There were advantages to begging: it allowed him to sit and watch, excused him the duty of appearing to have somewhere to go. But beggars were city landmarks in their own minor way, and most of them had missing or withered limbs, blind eyes, cratered skulls. Varius, feeling self-conscious and absurd in having nothing wrong with him, had tipped half a bottle of methousia over his clothes and tried to cultivate a ravaged shake: a reason for being there that simultaneously repelled sympathetic attention. He was not given much money, and he remained nervous among the other residents of the streets; he thought they sensed something false about him, in the half-heartedness of his requests for change, in his caginess when he could not avoid speaking to them.

His appearance was changing, deteriorating steadily, and that was, in one way, good. But it was not an adaptable disguise; it was inevitable that the vigiles would be vaguely conscious of him, and as time went on it would be harder to melt anonymously into the crowd.

Indeed, from most perspectives, he was taking ridiculous risks. He had not told Cleomenes that sometimes he slept in a doorway just a hundred yards from the vigiles' headquarters. Having thought, once, *they won't expect me to be so close*, now he made a strategy of it. He followed Drusus to every public appearance, staying as close as he could get, studying the behaviour of the guards while watching for his chance. He got a foolhardy exhilaration from being right in front of them and getting away with it, though he knew this was not a feeling to be trusted.

Sometimes it struck him that all this – skulking around the city, writing coded messages on walls and plotting to bring down the government– seemed like fairly unmistakable symptoms: *cracked*, he thought wisely, as if of someone else. *Too much for him. Finished up a lunatic on the streets, let that be a lesson to you.* But he did not take the idea seriously, he supposed, since whenever it occurred to him, it was with a little hiccough of amusement. He thought of Lucius, Marcus' uncle, who had found safety and freedom in madness, and he laughed to himself, sitting on a mat of pages torn from the advertising magazine, under the colonnade in Trajan's Forum.

But of course, that brought his mind back to Marcus, whose death was a terrible light by which Varius saw anything he might try to do, any meaning he'd thought there was in living like this, scraped down to bare bone. And wherever he was, he would start moving, trying to outpace the loss and the guilt. After his release from prison, grieving for Gemella, he had walked through Rome like this for hours, busy and hunted, the pace wearing smooth the edge of his thoughts. He fell back into it now almost without thinking, but there was a difference: though he rarely picked a route in advance, he was not aimless, and he was more daring, traversing unfamiliar streets, and flights of steps, trespassing in gardens and on the roofs of tower-blocks. He was learning the city meticulously, like a language: the grammar and history, all its unexpected connections and odd possibilities. He longed to be able to make notes; it would have helped him think, but of course such a document would be far too great a liability. Instead he memorised the locations of unlocked service doors and scaffolds. Once the barriers had been cleared away and the Praetorians had gone, he would go back to the fora where Drusus had addressed the carefully managed crowd and study the buildings which overlooked the Rostra . . .

He had to be careful around the Palace; he avoided the areas where he'd lived or worked, for fear of running into someone that he knew. Sometimes, though, he sometimes wished one of his parents would see him sitting in Trajan's Forum; that somehow he'd be able to communicate something, just with a look. He felt wretched to think of them: they weren't young, and he was so close, and doing nothing to comfort them, when they'd already been through enough on his account. But he could think of no way to contact them without putting them in worse danger. Their mail would be being read, their longdictor tapped, probably even their house bugged, in which case any implication that they had heard from him would be fatal. And what could he have said? He imagined a bald, one-line note: *I am alive.* He could hardly say he was safe, or that he would come back.

And in the end he could only remind himself that they had the same unsatisfactory source of reassurance that he had when he worried for Una and Sulien: the longvision that repeated daily that they were all three still wanted, still not found.

Varius revisited his *Athabia* messages sometimes, in his solitary patrols of the city, half-hoping he might find some reply scrawled beside them. He never had, but lately some of them had been scrubbed off. It might mean nothing.

There was a woman sitting on a bench in Trajan's Forum, whom he was sure he'd seen there before, doing precisely what she was doing now. He remembered the flowered headscarf, and the long dark hair escaping from it. Otherwise her clothes were unremarkable, if rather heavy for the weather. He hadn't been looking for a woman, but he found himself watching her carefully. She had unfolded a large tourist's map in front of her and seemed to be puzzling over it, but Varius could almost have sworn that she was scanning the forum from behind it. Certainly she had been holding it stiffly for a long time, without apparently making any progress towards finding whatever she was looking for.

And now she had got up and was striding towards his corner. Varius gave no signal in response except to keep watching her, and to allow the dulled, vacant expression to slip off his face. A small thrill of paranoia went through him – she could be an agent for the vigiles; this could be the end of it – as she leaned forward to hand him a coin and hissed, 'It's you, isn't it? Why are you doing it? What do you want?'

Varius looked up without speaking, saw the scars under the thick make-up, the Sinoan features the scarf and the long wig obscured.

She glanced around. 'I'll meet you on the corner of Vicus Blandianus,' she muttered.

'Fifteen minutes,' he agreed.

'Was he someone from the camp?' asked Lal. They were standing close together by a skip against the wall, both watching the opening of the narrow street.

'I didn't recognise him,' answered Ziye. 'He could have been from before my time.'

'I might know him, then.'

'You were a little girl,' said Ziye impatiently, looking at her, grimacing with guilty irritation. They'd been through this argument a number of times, but still she repeated, 'You really shouldn't be here. Please go and wait at home. Let me deal with it.'

'I want to see who it is,' repeated Lal. 'It doesn't sound like he's with the vigiles.'

The man rounded the corner into the narrow street and Ziye met him with a cold glare. 'Well, we're here,' she said, as he approached. 'Who are you?'

He did look like a new arrival in Holzarta: battered and dirty, and moving rather gingerly. But Lal, staring at him and trying in her imagination to peel back the rough beard and dishevelled hair, to erase the faint swelling around his eye, said in a cautious whisper, 'Varius.'

Ziye looked him over again to confirm it and sighed. 'I see.'

It had begun to rain. They retreated to a little caupona in the Subura, squalid enough for Varius to enter unremarked. They sat hunched distrustfully over beakers of rough red wine and kept their voices low beneath the deep, harsh music of a hydraulis, blaring over the speakers.

'What are you thinking, writing those things all over town? If anyone just looks up that name, if they followed you—'

'I'm sorry. I didn't have any other way to contact you.'

'We have only come to tell you to stop,' said Ziye.

'No we haven't,' contradicted Lal, quietly, looking at him. 'You want help with something.'

'I want to stop Drusus,' said Varius.

Ziye snorted bleakly, but Lal said at once, 'What can we do?'

'You mean kill him,' said Ziye, and without exactly being shocked at this, Lal felt suddenly as if the conversation had slipped out of reality into a scene from a longvision play, or a dream; it was just not possible that they could be sitting there discussing such a thing.

'Delir had a whole network of people who were against slavery – who were prepared to help slaves,' he said. 'There must have been hundreds; people like that aren't going to support Drusus. If they helped you, perhaps they would help me. I want to know who they are.'

Ziye shook her head. 'What do you think they can do? Most of them used to be slaves themselves. Don't you think if any of them had any power, things would have been different? That's why we needed Marcus.'

Varius flinched. 'I know,' he said, 'but if there are people who are willing to try to help, then I need to know. I have to think about what would happen afterwards . . . if I were successful . . .'

Ziye looked at him, grimly pursing her lips, and thought, as Una had, *He's not planning to live very long.* She said wearily, 'Delir won't be very eager to interfere again, not after Dama.'

It was hard to imagine Delir being eager to do anything: his despair and guilt filled their one room like many stacks of heavy boxes. Ziye had barely forgiven him herself, for leaving them – she did not even particularly want to, but did not seem to want to leave him either. It was dreadful to see him like this.

'I'll talk to him about it,' promised Lal, and it still felt as if she were watching a character in a play, but one she hoped was involved in a particular story, heading towards a good ending. 'And if I can help you—' *to assassinate the Emperor*, she finished to herself, dazed, and shivered at the thought that it was not impossible, for Dama had done it.

'You'll do as you're told,' retorted Ziye.

'Well, I could make more identity papers,' said Lal. 'I know these new ones are going to be more difficult, but I can try.'

'Could you make other things?' asked Varius instantly. 'Security passes, things like that?'

'Perhaps – I don't know if I could get the materials.' She looked down at the stained tabletop and added diffidently, 'Sulien and Una aren't with you, are they?'

'No. And it's better if I don't tell you where they've gone.'

'I could have made papers for them,' she said sadly.

'They wanted to leave as fast as they could,' he said, 'and I don't know if papers would help them, the way they'll be living for a while.'

Lal had not really expected otherwise, but it had been difficult not to hope the messages sown across the city might mean she would see them again.

'You were a gladiatrix, weren't you?' Varius asked Ziye. 'Didn't you fight at the Colosseum? I think I remember hearing about it when I was a student. Though you weren't called Ziye, then.'

To Lal's surprise, the look on Ziye's face was almost one of nostalgia, even though her body had stiffened slightly and her fingers had tightened on her cup. 'Hm, yes. That was a long time ago.'

'How well do you remember it?'

'The match?'

'The Colosseum – the way it works. The parts below the arena . . .'

Ziye, staring at him with eyebrows raised, her mouth half-open, shook her head incredulously.

'They'll open it again, eventually. And he'll be there.'

'And you really think that after what happened there you'll be able to get in and' – despite the scathing conviction in her voice she hesitated for a moment, then retreated to euphemism – '*do* anything?'

'It's just information,' said Varius, shrugging. 'Information is never wasted.'

Ziye snorted, a brief, desperate laugh. 'So, really you are just trying to further your education.'

Varius laughed too. 'That's it, yes.'

'Well, I used to teach!' said Ziye, with the same hopeless amusement.

'Then come with me. I'm going there now.'

Ziye stopped laughing. 'You must be insane,' she said flatly.

'We'll be as safe there as here,' said Varius.

It had been almost two months since the explosion. Two cranes scissored in the sky above the scaffolding bracing the side of the Colosseum. Most of the entrances were closed, but on the south side a milling line of visitors was allowed into a cordoned-off section of the stands to lay flowers, or light incense, at a temporary shrine to Faustus, who had, like most of his ancestors, been declared a god.

The shrine looked pitiful to Lal; the flowers were not being cleared away often enough and the fresh ones were scattered between limp heaps of plastic wrapping and rotting stems. She was glad Marcus hadn't been given the same honour.

In the arena, the wreckage was gone, and the remains of the roof had been stabilised, but the work seemed to be moving slowly: the break still yawned open overhead, wider than before, as sections had fallen or been taken down.

Varius had resumed his alcoholic, shuffling gait. Lal and Ziye tried to give the impression they were standing close to him only by chance, speaking to him only to urge him to go away.

'Well,' muttered Ziye, fatalistically, eyeing the few bored Praetorians manning the cordons, 'there are two levels underground. Most of the prisoners' cells are on the lowest floor, there, you see where the lift-shafts come up? Many of the gladiators stay at the Ludus Magnus, of course; there's a tunnel underground connecting to it over there, and there's a waiting area before we'd come in through the east gate. There's another tunnel leading off to the vivarium, where they keep the arena hounds and any other animals they've got for the show. There's an emergency clinic on the other side, near the Victory Gate. And there's a morgue. I don't see the use of this.'

'What about storerooms?' asked Varius. But his gaze was pulled across the arena towards what remained of the Imperial box, now stripped down to a bare platform above the stands, and all three of them fell silent.

'Do you know how I recognised you?' whispered Lal. 'It wasn't from what's on the longvision now; it was from when Marcus was with us in Holzarta and they were using you to try and trap him. They were saying all these things about you, and they showed this picture of you, and I remember he said to me that even if you'd tell him to stay, he had to go back for you.'

Varius lowered his head, pulling in a sharp breath, which caught in his chest. He said, 'I wish I'd been here.'

Lal looked up at the broad tract of sky above the box, wet as on the day the glass that framed it had been broken. She said, 'You're here now.'

From a redoubt above a beach south of Moulmein, Tadahito and his brothers looked out through field-glasses over the Bay of Bengala as rockets curved like quick lines of bright stitching across the sky. Between the destroyers and beyond the smoke the giant hovercraft carriers crawled like black slugs. They had taken the Angaman Islands just the day before.

'Come on, come on,' breathed Prince Takanari, but the volucer he had been watching darting and stabbing at the destroyers burst apart in a gust of fire, while the hoverships still squatted there on the sea.

The redoubt shook as the launchers fired again and distant explosions flashed on the water. Beside the princes, Lord Daw was trembling with grief and shame. 'Your Highnesses, I wish I could have shown you something better than this,' he said, close to tears.

'It isn't your fault,' murmured Tadahito.

'It isn't over yet,' offered Prince Kaneharu, awkwardly soothing. Tadahito could tell he was deeply embarrassed by the governor's distress, almost more concerned with that than with the losing battle out at sea. Kaneharu and Takanari were both nineteen, not twins, but born to different mothers in the same year. This was the first time either of them had left Nionia.

Down on the beach another missile punched into the ground, the noise bruising their ears, even from here.

'You must leave,' said Lord Daw wretchedly.

'No, no,' said Takanari, almost stammering with urgency, 'we came here to help defend Bamashu. We can bring in more airpower, we can fight—'

'Brother,' warned Tadahito quietly. He bowed to Lord Daw. 'Unfortunately you are right. I'm sorry.'

There was no way to dignify the hurry into the volucer. Tadahito tried to pretend he did not feel the shame of it, as the others too obviously did. The aircraft swung north for a moment so that they caught sight once more of the Roman ships, already much closer to the ploughed-up beach, hurling fire towards the shore as a drove of Nionian volucers plunged forward to meet them – then the princes were over quiet green rice fields and forest, safe.

'We shouldn't leave them,' said Takanari in a low voice.

'I know,' said Tadahito, 'but we would be killed along with those poor people. And our lives are not our own.'

'But we're not going to just abandon Bamashu?' protested Kaneharu. He was full brother to Noriko and the earnest gravity in his face at present brought out the resemblance. Tadahito noticed it with a tug of anxiety and regret. All three of them were largely avoiding speaking about her.

'We just have,' said Tadahito, and they both looked devastated. They were only a little younger than Marcus had been, and there were fewer than five years between them and Tadahito himself, but they seemed to Tadahito far too young to be there. It was as if the death of his closest peer on the Roman side had aged him, somehow jolted him up a generation.

'For now,' he added, chiefly to comfort them, but he looked down at the countryside they were leaving and thought grimly of the weapon Kato had not lived to see perfected.

[v]

BORDERS

Una took an experimental step off the riverbank. A fine layer of snow crunched under her boots, but beneath that the ice already felt solid, hard as the earth under the frozen grass behind her. Ahead, broad veins of black water, cold enough to stop a heart in a minute, still carved between the floes of greyer, looser ice, heaving lumps of it down the Rha. But it would all be white soon, land and sky and water one clean, colourless plain. It was impossible to believe, as the wind from the steppe scoured her face, that back in Rome it was only autumn, and might even still be warm. Una's memory spasmed; there were muscles in the mind she had to keep tightening to hold the months in focus, or else the shock would strike, new and raw, and the last thing she would remember seeing was Marcus' dead face, or Dama, horrified and luminous in the rain, or both at once. None of it can have happened yet, she thought, taking another little step, holding in the impulse to race forward, seize Dama again, to kill him, stop him, undo it all. *Not unless I'm too slow, if I'm not strong enough . . .*

She shook her head hard, which did nothing to shift the thwarted urgency, or the weariness that dragged at her, and didn't get her moving back onto the bank and on her way. Except that after a while she found she was somehow doing it anyway. Maybe I really did knock my head harder than I thought, she thought, mouth twisting, feeling the smile hang oddly on her face, like something caught on a nail.

She'd left the car behind a screen of frozen trees, not far away. As she approached it, she saw something strange in the sky: a pale sphere with a faint, silvery sheen to it, drifting high on the wind. A balloon. Then two or three more, floating north and west, then a loose, silent string of them, bowling across the sky like huge bubbles, or mercury drops. It was difficult to judge how far away they were, and how large – she guessed at least six feet across. She knew they must be something to do with the war, but were they surveillance devices, weapons, some kind of experiment? These possibilities occurred to her unprompted, and she made no effort to sort and choose between them; she could scarcely even summon much interest in which side they belonged to. They were eerie and beautiful, like multiple untethered moons, and once the milky sky swallowed them again, Una almost forgot she had seen them.

She took off her clumsy gloves as she climbed inside the car and the controls stung her hands with cold. Una gripped harder, gritting her teeth, until the action and the pain reminded her of Dama again. It had been riding as a passenger in Dama's car the year before that had finally prompted her to learn to drive. The grey car whined warningly; it had been bought as cheaply and secretly as possible, just inside Venedia: it wasn't made for this tyrannical cold, though it had brought them two thousand miles, all the way to the edge of Sarmatia without having to cross a border. They'd slipped from Italy into Rhaetia, and Rhaetia into Germania easily enough, but by the time they approached Venedia things had changed. There was little free traffic on unwatched roads, and there were patrols out in the woods; the vigiles were even building fences. They'd had to slow down, feeling their way. And now they were waiting for the river to harden, erasing the border between Venedia and Sarmatia.

Una was the only thing moving over the snow, and the thick clothes padded her in another layer of anonymity; she could be anyone, from a distance even her sex was not obvious. The whiteness around her might have come from the old daydreams with which she had always quieted herself when very angry or unhappy. Now, unfolded out across the real landscape, the emptiness still drew her, but it unnerved her too. She felt watched and exposed as well as hidden – a dark, punishable word on a white page. Driving past a distant cluster of cottages, bleached with snow and barely visible against the sky, she felt a muted tug of longing – for they looked so safe, so ignored by the world. But a pair of strangers would meet a blaze of attention, and though the vigiles could never patrol every inch of the freezing river, all the obvious crossings, the port cities and bridges were bristling with them, manning new barriers and checking the papers of anything that moved.

So she drove instead into the outskirts of a drab, medium-sized town twenty miles or so west of the Rha. Perhaps even this dismal place was too small, its population too sparse to offer any shelter. The streets were almost empty, greying ice-sludge giving way to fresh stretches of undisturbed snow. Everything seemed to be shut up, closed either for the winter or for good. The sight of Sulien, waiting for her by the tram station, dismayed her: How obvious, how wrong for the place he looked. He was slouched, in a transparent attempt to disguise his too-well-documented height, and though he was as heavily wrapped-up as she was, he seemed more persecuted by the cold. He was stamping from foot to foot, his breath extravagantly white in the air, and shivering visibly, even from here.

He collapsed into the seat beside her, folding himself awkwardly to sink down as low as he could. He didn't speak as she drove out of the town again, just lay there shuddering morosely, waiting to warm up. Finally he moaned something that ended '—*hate* this fucking place—!'

'You all right?' inquired Una briskly.

Sulien huffed a loud, miserable breath and thrust a torn sheet of paper onto her lap.

She glanced down: their pictures, and red print howling *Who's standing next to YOU? Be vigilant – especially if you live near a border!* The reward had been raised again. That was almost all. There had been quite a complicated narrative at one point, but gradually the details had dropped away, and once the effort to buckle mismatched facts together had relaxed, the case against them seemed somehow the more compelling. There was a fierce complicity implied now between the reader and the authority that addressed them, growing stronger as the number of words had shrunk. Only a few remained now, like 'murder', 'treason' and, sometimes, 'witch'.

Una shrugged, resigned. 'Many of them?'

'Well, too many to pull down the lot.'

'We can try somewhere further back if you want. Or we can sleep in the car again tonight.'

'Gods, no,' interrupted Sulien fervently, cringing from the memory of lying cramped and shivering beneath every blanket and piece of clothing they possessed, while the snow piled down on the roof. They'd never been more than half-asleep, but in the morning they were so dazed with cold they could scarcely wake.

'And we're going to need people who know the ice.'

'Well, there's only one guest house that I can find that's open. I think most of them shut for winter. And I don't think there's anyone else staying there, so they're going to ask what I'm doing here, that's for sure.' He sighed, looking at the crumpled poster again. 'You really don't think they know we're here?'

'No. It's just a border thing, like it says. But this is why we need not to be seen together.' And why she'd been scouting another town about fifteen miles away.

Sulien nodded grudgingly. 'If I'm not there and something happens . . .'

'Then at least they won't get both of us,' said Una.

Sulien's face looked pinched and hurt, not only from the cold, or even the fear of capture.

'You've just got to get used to it,' Una advised. 'That's not you they're talking about. It's someone else.'

Sulien laughed humourlessly. 'Well, he looks a lot like me.' He rubbed his jaw – the beard was quite dense and full now – and muttered, 'Me the way I'm supposed to look, anyway.'

'Oh, you look *fine* – how can you still care?' exclaimed Una, even though she knew. The sheer cold was gradually eroding Sulien's stubborn resentment of the beard, but he still clung on to the scrap of vanity as best he could, as if to give it up would be a kind of defeat.

Sulien managed a short-lived grin. The shivering had steadied to a spasmodic judder, but it hadn't really stopped. They were out in the bare countryside now, and the emptiness leaned in on them again, like a pack of eavesdroppers in a crowded train. There was nowhere to go, and nowhere to hide. A single car heading towards them reduced them both to silence, which lasted well after it had passed.

'Have you got somewhere to stay?' Sulien asked at last.

'I think so. Same kind of place – you were right; hardly anything's open.'

'So,' began Sulien, 'what are you doing here in this frozen shithole all alone, young woman? And what accent is that? And is that car really yours? And don't you know you should be careful by yourself?' He'd put on a different, slightly jocular voice, but towards the end he slipped out of it into stark worry. A girl alone and out of place was even surer to draw attention than he was, and they'd be lucky if that was all.

Una shifted her grip on the controls, softened the set of her shoulders and widened her eyes, regarding the road ahead with a look of humble sincerity and wistfulness. 'Well, I'm from Fennia, but my grandfather was born near here,' she said. 'Oh, he was a character! He used to tell these stories—! So I've always felt like this was home in a way, you know? I've got cousins down in Gelonus – I've got a new job there, teaching – but it doesn't start for another two weeks and my landlady needed my room back, so I thought, this was my chance to see what it's like here, to see Grandpa's home—'

'But it's like *nothing*,' objected Sulien, looking out resentfully at the snow.

'Oh, yes, I wish I could have seen it in the summer!' agreed Una enthusiastically, practically cooing now. 'It was the countryside Grandpa really loved, the fields in the sunshine – they must be beautiful, aren't they? And the Rha too? But oh, he had his stories about winter too – he even said when the Rha was frozen he used to drive *right across the ice to Sarmatia* – you don't think that could really be *true*, do you?' She looked at Sulien as if he could answer, eyes comically agape with innocent incredulity.

Sulien shook his head and laughed, and felt an odd little pang of happiness, taut with the anticipation of its own end. He was sure of the change that was due on Una's face now, the act dropped, and something more gone with it. He looked away, not wanting to see the white, calcified exhaustion, how much older she'd look. Every time they faced another border, the effort stirred up some life in her, but not only did it not last, it left her more depleted than before.

He tried not to think about it, in case she could feel his thoughts as extra weight. 'We need new tyres on this thing if it's going any further,' he said after a while, to break the silence.

'You don't sound like a Roman any more,' Una remarked suddenly. 'You sound like me.'

'Oh,' said Sulien, taken aback, trying to recall the vowels and stresses of the words he'd just pronounced. He felt as if something between them was reinforced, and at the same time, there was a confused sense of loss. 'Well . . . it doesn't make much difference; they've never said anything about our accents . . .'

'I knew it would happen if you were stuck with me long enough. You should try and pick up the accent here,' suggested Una distantly. 'It's a talent, really. You should use it.'

'Smugglers do it,' said the landlady, unsmilingly. 'And they go through, sometimes. Serves them right.'

They were sitting close to the stove in the kitchen, the one reliably warm room in the guest house. The air outside huffed and sucked at the dusty shutters, so that they groaned against their fastenings then banged in their frames, and ribbons of cold floated through the room. It was only early evening, but it had barely got light all that day.

'Oh, he wasn't a smuggler!' said Una, hitching up her eyebrows in artificial shock. 'No, no, he was a little wild, but . . . oh no! There was a girl he liked on the other side.' She felt she was getting dangerously close to overacting, making this character too much the caricature she'd sketched for Sulien. But she had hoped that a display of naïveté would prompt the woman to linger on the subject without the need for too many direct questions, and in any case, she had no more subtlety to give to this. She could still devise the lies needed to probe and parry, but her body, her face resisted, ached at each false word and gesture.

'If you say so,' sniffed the woman. 'It would take more than that to get me trying it. You can see it's not the same colour all over – darker here and lighter there; that's where there's thinner parts and thicker parts. I,' she repeated with stern satisfaction, 'would not try it.'

Una made herself assess the effect she was having; the landlady had already begun to find her slightly irritating, and – still a long way beneath that – to sense something unplaceably strange or wrong about her. But she was bored and sullenly curious in her deserted guest-house, whose grimy, flaking rooms sobbed and groaned to themselves as the wind punched at the walls, so she talked to Una all the same. Her name, there on the taverna's sign, was Vituriga, though she had not invited Una to use it. She was a large, raw-boned woman in her late fifties, and she had that same air of embattled fatalism as everyone Una had seen in this town. Maybe in summer it was different.

'Are you coming down with something?' she demanded abruptly, like an accusation. 'You don't look very well. And you got up very late today.'

Una dragged her mouth into a smile, barely suppressing the trembling behind it. She'd dreamt of Marcus again the night before, the worst kind of dream, worse than the ones in which he was always dying. They had been in a library and Marcus was reaching for a history book and urging her to read it. He was excited, animated, and Una said, 'Of course I'll read a book you wrote,' although the book was old when she looked at it, battered and waterstained, and Marcus wasn't handling it carefully; pages were shifting loose. There was nothing strange about his presence at first; it was some time before Una remembered and clutched him whispering, 'You can't imagine what it was like. You can't.' And she knew it was a dream as his arms closed round her and she woke under the dusty blankets in the cold room, pressing her face against the flat pillow to stifle the wail butting against her teeth, longing for morning not to happen.

For a moment she had such a strong impulse to smash her cup against the woman's face that she couldn't speak, then she said, 'Well, I'm sure they're going to keep me busy down in Gelonus, might as well get my lie-ins while I can.'

'You don't look up to it. I hope it's not infectious,' said the landlady, sourly.

'I hitched here,' said Sulien, shrugging, 'looking for work, doing a bit of everything.' He was trying to mould his accent to those around him as Una had advised, feeling foolish, afraid a conscious effort might wreck this knack she insisted he had. He didn't know whether or not it was working; at least no one had said anything so far. He knew he was better at lying than he had once been, yet he still felt not only faintly amazed but distressed when he said these things and people believed them, didn't see who he really was.

The patrons of the small bar were all male, and Sulien was by far the youngest there. It occurred to him, with a twist of unease, that he'd scarcely seen a man close to his own age since arriving in town.

'There aren't any jobs,' scoffed a man with heavy eyebrows and a face chapped red by the cold. 'Lads round here, they used to go into the factories, but now those places all run on slaves. They've got a load of Nionians in from Terranova.'

Sulien, stricken, felt his face drop and tried to adapt it into a sympathetic nod. *Oh, Marcus*, he thought. He took a swig of his drink, trying not to wince at the unfamiliar taste of fermented milk and sugar – the wine was shockingly expensive – and let his gaze sink to hide his eyes. For a moment he thought of Varius too, and wondered if he still believed there was anything to be salvaged from all that sacrifice and work.

'There is work,' said another man, sharply. Sulien turned to him with a questioning look but the man didn't smile back. He was looking him over critically. 'They could use a young man like you in the army.'

Sulien spread his hands. 'Oh, I think they're better off without me. I'm not cut out for that,' he said, lazing back in his chair with a self-deprecatory grin, trying to look the picture of fecklessness.

Three days before they'd fled down the first side-road they could find to get away from a long convoy of military trucks heading towards Gelonus and the border, like them.

The man muttered something in a proud, censorious hiss; all Sulien caught was, '—*my* son—'

The other men sighed and grunted uncomfortably, and Sulien paid for more drinks to smooth the mood and tried to ease the conversation round to fishing on the Rha, and the places where the ice was thickest.

It wasn't a dream that woke Una that night. She lay still, frozen with the usual dread of daylight, listening for the next swell of a noise she couldn't quite remember. It wasn't morning, she understood first, with relief. The sound couldn't have been thunder in this cold, she realised next. And there was no rain, and the wind had dropped.

The next explosion must have been some distance away, for it sounded strangely soft, a padded beat on a kettledrum, or heavy feet pacing up carpeted stairs. She closed her eyes for a moment, then there was a much louder boom, the shriek of windows bursting, the long howl of some alarm.

Dama, out of reach, too far ahead at the Colosseum. The sound of what he had done ploughing up the air . . .

How widely are they falling? thought Una as the room shivered, on this one town, into the bare land around it, as far as the scattered villages, the next town, Sulien? She grasped the thought, using it to force herself to move; she swung grimly out of bed, hissing at the cold, and groped for her coat, thrust her feet into her shoes.

The landlady, barefoot and wearing only her nightgown, came running along the landing and clutched at Una briefly before racing down the stairs and flinging open the door to the street. Then she shrank back, and for a bizarre moment that seemed longer than it could really have been, Una watched her running back and forth between the door and the foot of the stairs repeating mechanically, 'Oh no, oh no, oh no,' before sinking into a keening heap on the floor.

Una moved past her, into the flood of cold air, and closed the door most of the way. She peered out through the gap. At first she saw nothing, though she could smell something burning nearby, felt a velvety strand of smoke slide over her freezing skin. Raised voices sounded from further up the street; she heard unsteady, sliding footsteps on the icy road. But there was barely any light outside, and the sky was black and silent, unstirred by the beat of volucer wings—

Then sound struck again, like a crack parting the dark air, and fire lit up the street. Una was jolted back, clutching at the doorframe, her head ringing, but she had seen the red light break in reflected crescents on two silvery globes hanging low in the air: the balloons were sinking to earth like dandelion seeds, gently planting their loads of explosives on rooftops and vehicles, and the frozen ground.

Una retreated, teeth chattering, unsure if she was shaking from the cold or a belated flood of adrenalin. *How far?* she thought again, and wanted to hurtle out to the car and speed to Sulien. *Steady now*, she told herself: stupid to go running under a bomb when she had no solid reason to think he was in worse trouble than she was. And with a jab of spite at herself, she thought: *and what could you do if he is?*

'Come on,' she said to the landlady, 'not here.' She dragged the woman by her elbow, and hurried her back into the kitchen. The guest house was quivering from the impacts around it, but it was still larger and sturdier than most of the other buildings on the street. She doubted they'd do better to search for shelter outside.

She thought there must be a larder in the kitchen, though she hadn't seen the door opened before, and yes, here it was: on the side of the house that faced away from the wind, and the one high window was very small; it would have to do. There were boxes and heavy jars of some kind under a counter, and Una began dragging them out of the way. The landlady had recovered enough to help a little. Una left her and ran impatiently back to the front door.

Fire was spilling from a hole in the roof of the house at the end of the street, and by its light she could see that a wall of an upper room had been removed with strange neatness, as if a curtain had been raised. And there were more people outside now, gasping and staggering around. A young woman gripping the hand of a girl of about six had come to a dazed stop near the guest house; another child was clamped awkwardly to her hip, and all three were in the same rushed, half-dressed state as Una herself. There was a smear of blood on the woman's cheek and she was looking about, her face taut with bewilderment.

'In here,' Una called to them.

There wasn't room to shut the larder door with all five of them packed in. Bottles were rattling overhead, and they had the singed taste of the air in their mouths. The larder was cold; they needed the shared warmth of their cramped bodies. And slowly the other two women started to talk, swapping terse condemnations of the Nionians before moving on to a far more ordinary conversation about unreliable handymen, distracting each other. But now she had nothing more to do but wait, Una began to find the closeness oppressive, as if surfaces of her self were being ground away by the contact.

Somewhere several streets away, just at the limit of what she could sense, someone was trapped under a weight of wood and fire. It came abruptly, a flaring of incredulous red inside her skull: someone else's skin burning, someone else who couldn't breathe. Una stiffened and turned her head away, making a swift, brutal effort not to see or hear it any more, but for a moment she seemed to have lost the knack of disentangling herself, wasn't safe within herself in time as the mind in the distance collapsed away, with an awful quiver of relief, peace.

Oh, God, please— Una thought.

There was no reason for it to end at daylight, and no way to be certain it had stopped. There was no squad of aircraft overhead that might be shot down or have to fly home, only the currents in the air.

But when it had been quiet for half an hour or so, they emerged stiffly to find glass and melted snow sprayed across the discoloured carpets. It was still dark outside, the alarm still sounding. The landlady tried the lights while Una was almost pleased to find the longdictor dead, as it gave her the excuse she needed: 'I'm going to find a working longdictor; I have to talk to my family.'

'They won't be worried yet, you'll just wake them up,' protested the landlady dolefully, and Una could see she'd hoped for help with the damage.

'I have to talk to them,' insisted Una, hurrying up the stairs to finish dressing, not listening to the woman from the street who was trying to thank her.

Dawn was just filtering like a pale sediment into the winter sky, as she drove. She saw a few dark craters spoiling the snow on the steppe-land, and there were more vehicles on the road, more people to see her. But on the face of it, the other town seemed unscathed, though all its lights were out. Una relaxed a little. It was hours before the time at which she and Sulien had agreed to meet. She could just drive past his guest house, she thought, make sure the roof was still on. She wouldn't even have to see him to know he was safe. But before she reached the first turn off the main road through the town, there he was, striding along the roadside, scanning the traffic. The moment he saw the car he flung a long arm into the air and started waving urgently, as if she wouldn't have noticed him.

'People can see you,' she hissed furiously as he tumbled into the car, gripped her arm. But he wasn't listening, he was examining her as if she might be missing a limb; the fact that she was here and snapping at him not enough to reassure him yet.

He let go and hunched over in the seat, breathing out fiercely, and Una thought, with a dull pulse of remorse and exhaustion, I have to do better, I have to. She said, 'I'm fine. I'm fine. Didn't get any sleep, that's all. None of them landed here?'

Sulien shook his head. 'We heard them. But the power's out. And the longdictors.'

'I know.'

'Was it bad?'

'No. No,' insisted Una, with all the softness she could muster, 'just noise.'

'Have you heard about Bamaria?' Sulien asked, a sore, anxious scratch in his voice. 'It's gone. We've— The Romans have taken it.'

That was where they had been heading: the sliver of Nionian territory closest to the eastern tip of the Empire. The first place, they'd thought, where they could walk into a magistrate's office or a Samurae hall and state their real names.

'Oh,' Una said, blankly.

Sulien waited for something more. When she only turned the car out towards the steppe again, he found himself prompting almost shrilly, 'So what are we going to do?' and felt ashamed immediately afterwards; he had a mind of his own, so why was he behaving as if, even now, she should settle everything for them both? He hadn't meant that – but she should have had something to say, surely; she should have started dissecting what it meant to them.

'We need the maps,' he supplied, anxiously. It didn't matter, after all, which one of them said these things, as long as they were said. 'We need to work out how far the money will go.'

Una gave him a taut parody of a smile and said, 'All right.'

The dark tracks of water had frozen over in the night, streaks of a fine greyish film of ice, like seams in unpolished marble.

Another few days and they could probably walk across, thought Sulien, while Una searched dutifully for the sheaf of maps in the drawer under the seat.

'Maybe they'll say more about what's happening there when the power's back on,' he said, dubiously. 'Where the . . . the front is. But I don't know. Well, we were going to have to go through Sinoan territory anyway, so I suppose we can just try and . . . go round it? Or we keep going east instead of south, go straight across, I guess. I know we've got problems in Sina too, but if it's that or walk onto a battlefield . . . Or . . . well, we could give up on getting to Nionia.'

Una shrugged. She wasn't looking at the maps, or at him. She gestured at Sarmatia, on the far side of the river, though there was nothing to distinguish the pale slopes from the bank on which they stood. It was as if they had reached a barrier of mirror-glass. 'Look. That's less than a mile away. And from what people say it's going to be two weeks before we can even get that far. Anything could have happened by then.'

'No – we can't just head into nothing and hope it works out,' Sulien persisted, hearing in the obstinate stresses of his own voice a replica of something she might have said.

'Oh come on, Sulien! It's what, three thousand miles? We have to get across *India* – most likely we'll be dead before we get near it! Why bother worrying about it now?'

The wind scraped through the silence that fell between them, firing tiny flecks of ice against their faces, stinging like glass-dust. Sulien shivered and grimaced, and shifted between Una and the river, making a windbreak of himself. He said in a casual voice, 'We're not going to die.'

'Rome could lose Bamaria,' explained Una after a second. 'Could lose the whole war by the time we get there. That's all I mean.'

Sulien dismissed an instinctive chill at being obliged to want Rome to lose a war.

'We could stop,' he suggested quietly. 'I'm telling everyone I'm here looking for a job – I could get one. Or we could go back west, somewhere it's not so cold.'

For a moment her face seemed to twist and quiver, and though that cleared quickly, he could see a liquid sheen in her eyes – just a thin rim of reflected light below the irises, still a long way from spilling into tears. She said fiercely, 'No. We will get there, we *will*, I promise. I'm just— I can't think that far ahead.'

All he could say was, 'All right. One thing at a time.'

Una had been wary of going back, expecting that by the time she returned, the town's authorities would be busily manifest in the damaged streets, hanging tarpaulins over the broken windows, at least; and someone would be telling people what to do if it happened again, and where to go if their houses were uninhabitable. But everything looked almost as she had left it. At the top of the street the debris from the worst-hit house had been cleared aside, perhaps by the residents themselves, though she could see the windows were still gaping, and there were no lights in any of them. At the guest house, Vituriga the landlady was up a stepladder, struggling to nail a heavy square of old carpet behind the shutters.

'Haven't the vigiles done anything?' Una asked, rather disgusted, although it was a relief not to have to worry about dodging them.

The landlady snorted expressively. 'The power's still off, too.'

'You can't sleep here tonight,' said Una, glancing around the house's dark interior.

She stepped down from the ladder and gave Una a speculative look. 'I'll have to go to my sister's,' she said heavily, plainly relishing neither that nor the prospect of refunding Una any of her money. 'So you'll be heading south now, I suppose.'

As Una said, 'Oh, but it'll be all right here by tomorrow, won't it?' she realised with an itch of anger at herself what a strange thing that was to say; how unlikely it was that a stray tourist in this bleak place would even consider staying after a night like that. 'Well, it's not so bad, is it?' she ploughed on, 'and it's a long way to Gelonus – and they're not ready for me there yet. I don't really want to go there before I have to. And I was hoping I might be able to find some of my grandfather's friends.'

'Hmm.'

And Una saw what was coming and looked down, calculating.

'Arite saw you with a young man in Sacaeum,' announced the landlady.

'Oh . . .' Una twisted her hands shyly and kept her eyes on her shoes. 'Well, yes, he's just someone from home. It's a funny thing, meeting him here . . .'

'Oh yes?' said the landlady, raising her eyebrows.

Una clenched her teeth behind a modest simper and nodded. 'It's been a long time,' she mumbled. So the immediate problem was solved, Vituriga thought the young man was the reason Una was in no hurry to leave. And of course she was right.

'I suppose he's staying in the caupona there?' Vituriga went on, reverting to melancholy contemplation of her house. 'You might try there for tonight; they'll have rooms free.'

'Oh, I don't think my mother would like that,' parried Una, though she did wonder for a moment if that would be the simplest course. But all those posters – 'Be Vigilant . . . especially if you live near a border!'

She turned from the landlady and wandered a little way down the street. A large, dishevelled family emerged from their home, dragging bags and cases and arguing miserably. The two little girls from the night before stared at Una from the window of a dilapidated car. At the far corner of the street, a group of people, most of them men, came into sight. For a second it was hard to place what was strange about them, then Una realised that they weren't encased in padded clothing like everyone else, but were all dressed in identical sets of light work clothes. Some of them had blankets wrapped around themselves like cloaks or shawls, and they were hugging themselves, bent almost double under the weight of the cold. They huddled close together as they moved, either for warmth, or against possible attack. They were slaves.

'From the factory,' said Vituriga, coming after Una. 'Nionians!'

There were around ten in the group, only one of whom looked at all as if he might have been partly Nionian, but Una could feel sudden tension quiver through the street, as if an electric circuit had just been completed. The slaves seemed aware of it, hurrying along with heads lowered, sometimes flicking around hunted glances, but one of them, a short, cropped-haired young man, was plainly too angry and too desperate to care. Beckoning insistently to the others, though they were hanging back and hissing at him to stop, he moved towards an empty house, its windows dark and glassless like the rest, and pulled at the door.

'Get out of there,' shouted a man, erupting from the house opposite and racing across the street. Una started to run at the same moment. As she reached the little group, the man dragged the young slave away from the door before hurling him backwards, staggering and slipping on the ice that glazed the street.

'What are we supposed to do?' snarled the slave through blue lips, crouching to recover the blanket that had dropped from his shoulders. 'Are we just supposed to sit there and die?'

'Don't, Batu, just leave it, please,' urged one of the women frantically.

But Batu ignored her, lurching forward, and the older man squared up to meet him, smirking grimly, for though the slave was young and well-muscled, he was shivering so fiercely that he couldn't even curl his hands into fists. The rest were in no better state.

Una moved between them as two of the others pulled Batu back.

He gasped, 'Where are we supposed to go?'

'What's happened?' said Una. She had one arm outstretched, so that her fingertips were level with, but not touching, the older man's chest, marking out the distance. He was perhaps only in his late thirties, despite the long creases in his face and his greying bristly hair. The family from the house next door to the taverna had wandered over now, and with them two other men who might have been the crease-faced one's brothers; they had drawn up beside him, glancing between themselves, unsure what to do, even a little embarrassed, but ready for trouble.

'You mind your own business, love,' spat the first man viciously. But he didn't move closer yet, or knock her hand aside.

'Same as here,' said the slave woman, meeting Una's eyes warily. 'The windows broke. There's no heat. There's nothing . . . no one's come.'

'They're escaping and they're robbing people's houses,' the man exclaimed shrilly. 'I bet they're loving this! I bet they were cheering those fucking things on last night! That one, anyway,' he added, and made another lunge, this time towards the boy who looked a little Nionian, who'd been lurking with eyes lowered at the back of the group. His brothers moved with him, and the whole knot of people started shifting, Una squeezed in the middle of it, with the boy behind her, shouting, 'Stop!'

The young woman who'd sheltered with them the night before was dancing back and forth at the back of the group calling out, 'Don't hurt her – careful! Careful, you're going to hurt her!', sounding anxious, yet self-conscious, as if she couldn't decide how serious this really was.

'Stop, stop, stop,' Una repeated, her voice descending gradually from a shout to a rhythmic whisper, keeping her eyes on the crease-faced man's. 'Come on, stop. Those bombs did enough damage. Leave it at that.'

'Yeah, *his* pals!' cried the man, bitterly, flinging a fist at the sky and pressing towards the boy again, but with less momentum this time.

Batu mumbled, 'Leave him alone.'

'He's a slave. He's already lost. He's already been punished,' said Una, louder. 'No one's staying out in this cold. Not them or anyone.'

'Factory owners should sort them out,' said one of the other men, half-heartedly.

'Whoever runs this town should have got the power running and fixed the windows; they should have set up somewhere for people to stay. But they haven't, have they? So we have to do something.'

Most of the remaining inhabitants of the street seemed to have gathered now, around twenty people. Vituriga was staring at Una, frowning. This was certainly very unlike the diffident, ingenuous girl she'd been acting for the past few days. She cursed inwardly, wishing someone else was doing this, but it was too late to go back. She called out, 'Who else doesn't have a place to stay?'

The town's grimy baths hadn't opened that day. When they found the man who ran them he was reluctant to unlock the doors at first, and even more reluctant to let them light the furnace, but these obstacles seemed almost too minor to trouble with by then, and Una marched over them with irritated ease. They dragged in blankets and mattresses; though the place was small for a public bathhouse, still it had space enough to house twice as many people. The three main chambers were below ground, and the stained walls were thick. Una had first noticed the place when driving around the town harvesting details with which to bolster the story of her imaginary grandfather, finding the school he might have gone to, the boarded-up temple where he might have prayed. She had thought of going there to kill time and escape the gnawing cold; she had not done so partly from the usual fear of being recognised, but also from a dumb dread of physical comfort.

'You're not really going to stay there with all of them?' asked Vituriga, who'd stubbornly followed Una.

'Oh, well, it isn't just the slaves; Mada and Leimeie and her little girls from up the street are going to be there as well. And I'm too tired to go looking for anywhere else now,' said Una, truthfully, in a strained version of the sweet voice she usually assumed for the landlady, hearing how sharp and wrong it sounded.

Inside, she tried to stay out of the arguments about food and who, if anyone, should provide it for the slaves. No one would die of starvation overnight, and she knew she must try to repair her camouflage, encourage them to start to forget about her. Even so, some of them obviously expected that she would at least propose something, and she found herself suggesting wearily, 'Just buy as much as we all need and claim anything back from the factory owners.'

The hypocaust warmed the chambers slowly. The slaves crouched or lay exhausted in the caldarium, their bodies pressed in a kind of bitter ecstasy to the heated floor. Una's mind caught on a spike of memory: the tropical greenhouse in Gaul, and how grateful they'd been for the warmth then. And Marcus, by the pool of waterlilies, fumblingly asking her if she thought he would ever go mad.

The foreign-looking boy sat on the floor in a niche in the tepidarium, head down, and spoke to no one. Una was sometimes conscious of words that coursed through and came apart in his mind, though she didn't understand them. His whole self was concentrated in a single, shamed wish not to be noticed. Nevertheless she watched him from across the room for a while, then crouched closer to him and whispered, 'Are you from Tokogane?'

'He doesn't speak much Latin,' said Batu. 'At least, he doesn't speak much at all.'

But the boy had understood, eyelids lifting quickly for a distrustful glance at her, lowering again at once.

'I'm so sorry,' Una said to him under her breath, feeling the scorch of stale adrenalin, seeing the street outside the Colosseum again, and herself running with blood in her hair, not fast enough.

Later she lay close to the wall, in the vestibule of the tepidarium, with the other women, warmer than she'd been for weeks. But she dreamed of the Rha at night, and it was not freezing, but melting, and she and Sulien had to cross it anyway. First she was staggering thigh-deep through wet, grainy ice-slush, and Sulien was somewhere behind her in the dark, following close, though out of sight and silent. She thought she could feel the acid bite of the cold, and she knew it would kill them both, knew it made no sense for them to have held out this long. The water burnt on her flesh, and then down her throat – for now they were, impossibly, swimming, and Sulien was thrashing forward, tugging her through the channels of black water, between the slabs of ice.

She meant to slip away as fast as possible in the morning, before anyone could renew interest in her, or ask to see her identity papers. But when she woke a bewildered team of quaestor's contractors and a pair of vigiles had already arrived, trying to account for the missing slaves and the residents of the bombed-out street.

'So who organised all this?' asked one of them, brusquely, and the mother of the two little girls pointed at Una proudly and said, '*She* did.'

When the wind let fall a single, stray floating bomb into Sacaeum it was broad daylight, and Sulien was in the back room of the little bar with the woman who ran the place, her back against the wall beside a rack of crates and her legs around his waist.

She must have been ten years older than him, more, even, and it hadn't occurred to him, at first, to find her attractive. The weather had already scuffed hard at her pale, thin skin, and left a pattern of folds around her eyes. Her lips were narrow and dry, with a disappointed droop to them, and they never quite closed over long front teeth. He'd gone back to the bar to eat; there had been only one other customer, who left before Sulien's food arrived. When he'd first noticed how the woman kept looking at him, he was afraid it was because she had recognised his face – she'd stared at him pretty hard the first time he'd been there, too – and he bent his head over his meal, wondering what on earth he should do. Even when she stared at him meaningfully and smiled – a sly tug of her long lips which changed the droop into something languid and expressive – he still wasn't certain he'd understood her, and was even a little embarrassed. But as she reached for his plate she trailed a hand along his arm and remarked, 'You're very handsome, aren't you? I'm sure you know it.'

And she grinned. He supposed she was too bored in this cold, ugly town to bother with shyness, or to care about the risk. And he was bored too, with nothing to do but wait for the river to freeze. More, it was as if, just by touching him, she'd pulled open a seam of desperation trapped under his skin for all these months. He looked up at her. Her hair was scraped back in a rough, lustreless bun, but wisps of it fell in sweet spirals around her brown, lemon-shaped eyes, and he noticed the delicacy of her long neck, the wide sweep of her cheekbones.

Oh well, he thought, and pulled her into his lap to kiss her.

'Have you got a husband's going to walk in on us?' he asked, hot against her cheek. 'Because I really don't need any more trouble.'

She laughed roughly and said, 'He's in Sarmatia.' And Sulien tried to feel at least a nominal twinge of guilt as he let her draw him through the door behind the counter before deciding there was only so much self-denial that could be expected of him at present.

She didn't ask him his name, so he didn't have to give her his false one, and she kept saying, 'You're good, you're lovely,' as if she knew him, and had no doubt at all it was true.

Sulien clutched her gratefully, gasping with something that was more like pain than anything. He said nothing himself.

The bomb landed a few streets away just as he cried out against her breast. The bottles rattled and both of them yelped, and then after blinking at each other for a second, dissolved into confused and frightened laughter.

Sulien said, 'Well, that's never happened before.'

'Fucking Nionians,' she said, hopping neatly to the ground.

Sulien felt the chill settling back into his flesh. He started buttoning his clothes. 'I'll go and look.'

'You can't go outside! There could be more of them.'

Sulien lingered, obligingly, and they waited and listened in a quiet that quickly became awkward, and Sulien began to remember the time he'd spent waiting in his rooms in Rome when the voice on the longvision had told him to, how much faster he should have moved then.

The woman shrugged, restless too. 'Well, maybe there's no harm in having a look. At least they come down slowly, don't they?'

She straightened the collar of his coat by the door. 'You be careful.'

There was nothing in the sky now but snow, pushed slantwise by the wind as it fell into the black, reeking smoke disgorging along the street. The bomb had drifted down between the houses, landing on the roof of a parked van. What was left of it was still burning, a dirty red light muffled in the smoke.

Someone shouted, uncertainly, 'Is anyone hurt?'

There was no answer. At first it seemed that no one had even been there to see the bomb fall. There were no shops or businesses on the street, just dark, narrow houses, some of which were boarded up. Sulien wasn't sure at first who had shouted, then he saw a few people, half-hidden by the smoke, emerging cautiously from a side street, either returning after scattering from the balloon's path or, like him, compelled to see what had happened.

All the windows of the nearby houses and cars were broken, and an old trirota had been crumpled and knocked against a wall. But it was strangely quiet; no alarms had sounded, no one was screaming.

A door opened, quite close to Sulien, and a woman tottered out and sat down at the roadside. Sulien bent down beside her, because anyone would have. She had broken a wrist, falling, and was scattered with little cuts from flying glass. She was pale, and giddy with shock. Nothing too bad, nothing to kill her. 'There, you're all right,' crooned Sulien, warm with relief and guilt. 'Was there anyone else inside?'

She shook her head and asked indistinctly, 'Are the vigiles coming?'

Sulien said, 'Yes, they're coming,' and looked around urgently for someone else to take over before they appeared.

Thankfully a man Sulien thought he recognised from the bar

came running up to them, asking, 'Is she all right?' and Sulien said, 'You wait with her, I'm going to see if anyone else is hurt,' before retreating with a hasty pat of the woman's hand.

Another woman was calling in through a broken window, 'Sarata, Sarata, are you in there?' Sulien glanced at her uneasily as he went on down the street. It's not so bad, he thought; nothing irreparable. He coughed as the wind flung a loop of rank smoke around him, and began to shiver again. He hunched over against a sudden gust of snow so fierce that for the next few steps he couldn't see anything clearly but his boots, scraping through the grit and ice, but something was moving a little way ahead, and as the wind dropped again, Sulien looked up.

A boy, about eight years old, was leaning against the wall, silently pulling himself along one-handed. He stopped moving, and Sulien sprang forward, into a slithering run across the icy ground to catch the boy as he buckled.

Of course, this was why he had come. Of course he was needed. He must have tricked himself out of knowing it.

The boy let out a thin, outraged, hacking cry, like a baby's.

Sulien repeated softly, 'You're all right, you're all right,' although this time it wasn't true. He silently cursed to the same rhythm, and despite everything he knew he felt a stab of undiscriminating rage at the Nionians. Some part of the van had been blown in through the window and had hit the boy in the back, knocking him to the ground and smashing the shoulder blade, dragging the bone away from its ties, the broken edges tearing at the veins and arteries beneath.

Sulien grimaced and looked around, both dreading that people were coming, and hoping for some kind of impossible help. He dragged off his coat and laid the child on it carefully, shuffling closer to a doorstep so he could prop the boy's feet off the ground. 'Where's your mother?' he asked, afraid of the answer. His teeth were starting to chatter.

The boy whimpered, 'I want her. Want my mother . . .' His eyelids drooped over huge, unfocused pupils.

Sulien closed his own eyes, detesting himself for his moment of hesitation. If the medics were good, if they understood quickly enough what was wrong, a surgeon might be able to stop the bleeding inside. But the boy would lose the arm, even if he lived.

He could see the way the broken pieces should fit together. He could see how the flesh and bone had been, just a moment before, whole and sound. However many posters there were of his face in this town, of course it made no difference. He murmured again, 'You're all right.'

The bells of an ambulance or a fire engine sang somewhere, drawing close. A woman came hurtling down the street towards him, shrieking, and almost pounced onto the boy. Trying not to look her in the face Sulien mumbled, 'Well, I . . . I don't think he's hurt so badly. I need to go and—' And he withdrew with as much disguised haste as he could.

As he turned he saw the woman from the bar, standing on the other side of the street still, watching him. Sulien swallowed, managed a sheepish smile at her and hurried past, hugging himself and thinking mechanically, 'I've got to get home.'

She caught up with him before he'd reached the next block. She was carrying his coat. 'You don't want to leave that,' she said, 'you look frozen already. And they've got him inside. He'll be fine now, won't he?'

Sulien put on the coat in silence and then muttered, 'He should be careful for a while, I think.'

They walked on without speaking for a while. Sulien didn't raise his eyes from the ground, but he could see her twisting her hands uncertainly. Then she said in a low voice, 'I'll tell that kid not to say anything.'

Sulien breathed out a helpless laugh and looked at her. She had a faintly nervous half-smile, but she looked him in the eye. That's it, he thought, we're leaving now, whatever the ice is like. She added, 'And I won't say anything.'

Sulien found nothing to say. Tiredness burrowed through him.

She asked softly, 'Do you want me to give you a lift some-where?'

Sulien sighed. 'Can you let me use your longdictor first?'

He had her drop him at the edge of Una's town, though it would probably make little difference now if she saw where Una had been staying, or the two of them together. He hadn't been into the town before, and he was dismayed to pass buildings without roofs and a blackened gap where a house should have stood. Una had given him directions to a disused temple of Magna Mater, a forlorn, squat little building, flaking boards wedged between the concrete columns. Sulien waited, shivering, in the courtyard, watching the snow erase his footprints.

Una arrived late. She braked beside him with a bad-tempered jolt and asked, '*Now* what happened?'

Sulien sighed and started loading his backpack into the car. Una climbed out to persist, 'Someone drove you here? What's going on?'

'A woman from the caupona. She's all right.'

Una pursed her lips and fixed him with a searching glower that made him feel she was on the point of knowing everything that had happened, whether or not she was reading his thoughts.

He looked away, feeling the shiftiness of it, and said, 'Don't.'

'Oh, Sulien!' she groaned, leaning against the car and casting a disgusted glance skywards. 'So much for not being noticed!'

'Well, she already had noticed me, Una, and turning her down wasn't going to make her forget. I can at least hope that wasn't what was on her mind when we were—'

Una, wincing, groaned again – partly sisterly revulsion, partly defeat.

'Anyway, she's trying to help.'

'We can't have help,' said Una, flatly now.

'She's not why we have to leave. There was a bomb in the town, and there was this kid . . .' He could not describe the boy's injuries; his throat closed as he pictured them. He could feel at his core that same raw, frantic pressure the woman from the bar had uncovered in him, and his hands starting to shake with it, more than just juddering against the cold. 'I had to,' he said, fiercely. It was almost an apology. 'I had to.'

Still leaning against the car, Una had closed her eyes, and snowflakes were settling on the lashes. She wasn't quarrelling, he realised. She turned her head slowly to look at him and smiled. 'Of course you did,' she said. 'I've been . . . getting myself noticed too.'

'Doing what?'

Una croaked a little laugh and climbed back inside the car. 'Telling people what to do.'

He got in beside her. 'You can't help yourself, can you?' he said, trying to tease.

Una rested a warning hand on his wrist and said quietly, 'Keep your hood up,' because a vigile officer was walking up to them and signalling for them not to move.

He came up on the driver's side and Una dutifully opened the window. 'You're the young lady who's been staying at Vituriga's?'

Una beamed out sweetly, pleased to see him. 'Yes, I just wanted to show my friend the temple before I go – my grandfather used to come here.'

Sulien, slumped low in the seat beside her, raised a hand in silent greeting, keeping his face in shadow. We do look different, he tried to reassure himself, feeling droplets of melting snow filtering uncomfortably through his beard to the skin beneath. As well as being a different colour, Una's hair was shorter now than in the pictures, and he'd helped her chop a slightly uneven fringe into it.

'There's not much to look at,' said the officer, glancing at the temple with the same woebegone manner which seemed to afflict everyone here when contemplating their hometown. But he wasn't threatening; he seemed a little embarrassed to be bothering them. 'Look, we just wanted to follow up some things from the other day . . .'

'Oh, I hope I didn't cause any kind of trouble!' exclaimed Una.

'I just thought it would be sensible if we all got out of the snow. It wasn't anything really.'

'No, no. Well . . .' Sulien could hear the impatience in his voice at this stupid, remote possibility he had to check, just in case. 'Could I see your identity papers?'

'Oh, of course!' Una trilled eagerly, as if she'd been offered a treat. She began searching confidently in her pockets, gradually building a look of puzzled alarm. 'Oh— I think I left them in the safe in the guest house— Oh thank goodness you stopped me! That would have been so awful! Look, I was just going to drop my friend back to Sacaeum – he's going to be late – would you mind if I do that first and bring them round straight afterwards?'

'Well— If we could just get it over with? It's only round the corner.'

Una didn't hesitate. 'Well, all right; why don't you get in? I might as well give you a lift there.'

Sulien clenched the hand the officer couldn't see into a fist, closing his eyes.

'Oh, no,' said the officer, slightly flustered, 'you just drive on, I'll meet you there in five minutes.'

'Fine,' said Una tightly, and drove away, not too fast, not yet.

They looked at each other as they rounded the first corner. Una pounded a fist against the side of the car.

'Five minutes,' repeated Sulien, breathless.

Una pushed down vengefully on the controls and the car skidded forwards, engine whining.

'It's my fault,' she remarked in a calm, matter-of-fact tone, not seeking a reply, as they broke through the last line of houses onto the sudden steppe outside.

Sulien swung round in the seat to gaze backwards along the road. 'He believed you. Maybe he won't do anything . . .' But really he expected the black vigile cars to appear on the road behind them; he was surprised that it hadn't happened sooner.

Una saw them too. She said, 'Ha,' a grim, one-syllable laugh, and forced the car faster.

The air was growing opaque with snow, but just for an instant,

Sulien thought he saw three shapes in the sky, borne low on the wind. The next moment the road between them and the vigiles was swallowed up, and Una, crouched close over the controls, pushed the car almost blindly into the whiteness.

Her face was awful, bone-hard, barely blinking – that same dead-fox look she'd had the day of Marcus' death, sitting in Sulien's kitchen, gripping the edge of the table. Rather than look at her, Sulien knelt on the seat, peering back at the headlights ploughing out of the snow and the heavy flakes, whirling like a swarm of black flies in the beams. They came close enough to fill their car with a diffused, pale-gold light which faded as Una spurred forward, out of its reach. She almost missed the turning she'd been waiting for, but swerved roughly to the left and the car skidded free for a long stretch before Una could do a thing to control it.

A van reared into visibility ahead of them, disappeared behind them, and for a few minutes, enclosed in the snow, Sulien saw no sign of the black cars, might almost have thought the vigiles had driven on south, or given up. But all those posters— Anyone could guess where they'd try to go.

The light was going, but the snow began to clear a little as the frozen Rha spread out in front of them: a broad, ash-coloured seam between the ground and the pale sky. And the vigiles' cars came plunging along the empty road behind them, accelerating now their quarry was in sight.

'It's too thin – we'll have to run. We have to leave the car,' Sulien said, his voice rising as Una showed no sign of slowing or turning onto the narrower road that ran along beside the river.

Una stared straight ahead at the ice. 'They'd just pick us off the other side. We wouldn't make it half a mile,' she said in a pragmatic voice that had nothing to do with the wild, frozen-over brightness in her eyes.

'You'll kill us! Stop!' cried Sulien, and tried to grab for the controls, but somehow they were just clutching each other's hands as Una charged the car off the road, down the bank and onto the ice.

The car shot across the frozen surface like a bead of water across the top of a hot stove and swung right round in a wide, violent arc until they were facing back towards the bank they had left behind.

The black cars stopped on the shore. The headlights flooded the ice.

Though it hadn't smashed at the first impact, Sulien could hear the ice creaking like old floorboards underneath them; he could feel it shifting, even through the body of the car.

The vigiles were climbing out now, and an oddly listless voice, flattened even more by a loudspeaker, ordered, 'Give yourselves up.'

'Come on,' panted Sulien, grabbing for the controls, but Una was already straining to move the wheels, which just spun uselessly on the spot.

Four or five men were venturing down onto the ice on foot. Somewhere in the distance behind them, a deep, unmistakable boom growled low on the steppe. The vigiles stopped moving for a moment and scanned the sky.

Sulien felt the tremor, slight but definite, running through the earth and into the ice. 'Backwards – back, reverse it!' he shouted.

Una grappled with the controls and the car whined and spurted backwards, and they both felt the *crack!* beneath them, and the car jolted down an inch or two as it passed over the break—

Una managed to drag the car the right way round, so that they were facing the Sarmatian bank again. She said, 'Get out.'

'What?'

'Get out – run to the other side. Less weight.'

'Well, *you* get out!'

'No,' said Una, without looking at him, relaxing implacably into the seat.

Without further protest, Sulien opened the door – then ran round, yanked open her own door and tried to drag her out. But Una shoved back at him, and the car swerved; Sulien was sure he could hear the swish of water under the wheels, and he was

148

heavier than her: perhaps his weight *was* the crucial difference. Panicked, he slid away on the stinging ice.

'Run!' shouted Una again from inside the car as it went careening away to the side.

He couldn't run properly on the ice, but it felt solid enough that he didn't feel in any imminent danger of falling through himself. But to his horror he saw the fissure their car had made had already widened to a dark gulf, growing rapidly as fragments broke off from either side, the damage spreading back, chasing the weight that had caused it. He loped forward, towards Sarmatia, but looking over his shoulder to keep the car in view, trying to haul it the right way with nothing but will.

Perhaps he hadn't been seen as he rolled out of the car; perhaps the vigiles still could not see him in the snow and the fading light, for they began firing, but not at him, at Una.

The darker streaks: those were where the ice was thinner, Una remembered, and she tried to watch for them now. She steered the car a little upriver, where it might be stronger, and though she was conscious of working with all her strength to reach the further bank, all the while she seemed spread beyond her body, outside the car, coursing through the flying snow, with the black water burning cold under the ice.

She heard the bullets whisk around the car as it slipped and twisted, and they seemed merely annoying, not important. She hunched down, and hoped they would not hit the tyres. Down on the right, she saw Sulien fling himself forward a few yards and then turn back, shouting something that the wind whipped away. Then the car stuck on the ice again, and Una ground her teeth as she laboured to get it moving, and with a gush of cold air a bullet pierced the back window and bored into the seat beside her.

She couldn't hear Sulien, but she could feel him as if he were still in the car with her, dragging at her, shouting 'Come *on*, please, please—'

An explosion glowed on the ice, to the north, a brief roaring column of gold and white, and she felt the shock battering through the ice. Heavy drops of water began to rain down around the car, beating on the roof.

'Get out!' screamed Sulien hoarsely from the bank, churning the air in a frantic beckoning motion. 'Run!' Though he couldn't see it from here, the ice must be rupturing, fissures racing to meet each other.

Another balloon was drifting over the river, and the vigiles had stopped firing and, like Sulien, were watching as it passed in sedate silence above the roof of the car and swept gently towards the western bank.

It touched its load to the ice, and it was almost unbearable when nothing happened. It bobbed like a toy. The wind dragged it along for a few yards, then scooped it up into the air again.

The car began to move, just sliding helplessly, jolted from its standstill by the echoing throb of the last blast. And though he thought, with complete clarity, 'There's nothing I can do,' still Sulien tried to run back towards it.

The bomb sank to the ice again, and this time it erupted, a great spout of fire and water, and for a moment he saw Una's face, looking straight at him, wild and inhuman in the fleeting light.

She wrenched at the car's controls and the car accelerated to the right as behind her the ice splintered and gaped. The vigiles had fallen back from the tracts of black water opening in the heart of the river, and Una hurled the listing car eastwards, towards the thicker ice near the edge of the Sarmatian bank; towards Sulien.

The car trundled quite slowly up onto the bank. Una got out, and stood there beside it, still.

Sulien pulled himself up the bank to her, shaking. Before he could speak, or touch her, she asked, quietly, 'Can you drive for a while?'

This was a different province, and it might take a little time before the Sarmatian cohorts could react, but of course the

Venedian vigiles must have alerted them, of course they were on their way. So Sulien just swallowed and nodded and swung into the driver's seat and set off north. He took the smaller roads when he could find them, afraid of meeting the vigiles' cars head-on.

All right, he thought, and his voice sounded shrill, even in his mind, so they know we're in Sarmatia. It's a big province; we'll be out of it soon.

He'd been living like this long enough to know what he should try to do. There was a large town, Boudinium, about ten miles off; he would try and filter through the outskirts, blend into the eastbound traffic. He would aim to put two hundred miles behind them tonight, make it to Roxelania if he could. There they'd leave the car in a city car park and make the next leg by train, or cargo-tram, if they had to.

Una had sunk low in the seat beside him, her arms wrapped round herself, and sat with her head resting against the window, silent, shrunken.

They were not safe, even without the vigiles' headlights right behind them, and he had no idea where – *if* – they could sleep tonight . . . but twenty miles from Boudinium, Sulien's heart had stopped striking so hard and fast against his ribs, and he no longer had to fight the shaking.

For the first time since he'd taken over the controls, Una spoke. 'Sulien.' Her voice was like a little trail of dust.

Sulien looked over at her.

For a long while, Una said nothing more. He could see her lips slightly parted in the half-light, as if the words would neither come nor go away. At last she whispered, 'I've been trying so hard, I swear . . .'

'I know,' he told her. 'I know.'

'I want to stop, so much.'

Sulien sucked his breath through his teeth. He had offered her that only a few days ago, but now . . .

'And we can't,' she said softly. 'We couldn't, even without this, because they'd find us, one day. Because it would always be too hard. And if we could stop, if *I* could, I feel like I'd just . . . end. Run out. Do you see? And you're the only thing— You're all I—' The sentence seemed to jam on something, and she shook her head impatiently, as if to shift it free. 'I want to see you all right. But I don't know what we should do now. I don't know how I can go on any further. Because . . . I don't want to get there, not really.' Her voice dropped again, almost to nothing. 'Not at all.'

Sulien adjusted the controls of the car, very carefully, as if the danger were still one of speed and sliding wheels. 'Look,' he said, 'today's been terrible. I know that. But you don't need to do a thing now. I will do more – I'll do everything, I promise. And we *can* make it there. And when we do, I know it won't undo— It can't undo what's happened. But it will be better than this. And you'll be able to rest.'

He looked over at her, reached out to touch her shoulder, and saw the corner of her mouth twist up as if dragged by a wire.

'I know how it sounds,' she said, 'but I don't want it to get better.'

'Una,' began Sulien, baffled and frightened, fumbling to understand, 'is it because it feels like it would be betraying Marcus, or – or forgetting him? Because you know he'd never want you to be so unhappy.'

Una made a small sound, a dry, longing break in it. 'No, he wouldn't ever want that. No, it's because . . . because it's . . .' She closed her eyes, then opened them again, a little surprised at finding a way to explain. 'In the north, where the sea's so cold, there are fishermen who think that if they fall in, it's better if they can't swim. Because it'll just drag it out – make it harder . . . when they might as well go down fast.'

Sulien thought of the terrible water they'd barely escaped, and her face, outlined in the fire as the car scythed across the ice. 'Oh, Una,' he said, squeezing her shoulder.

Una shifted a little closer to him, but her eyes were motionless and unfocused under low eyelids, so that he had to flinch from the memory of Marcus' dead face. 'I'm sorry,' she said.

Sulien said gently, desperately, 'We've come all this way . . .'

'. . . all this way,' agreed Una, a slow, limping echo from somewhere far off.

Later, Sulien found that the next three or four days had been wrung from his memory, leaving only watery tidemarks behind. He knew they had abandoned the car in Roxelania, that they must have travelled by cargo-trams or on freight-trains, while every public longvision they passed was shrilling in excitement at how two of the three outlaws were all but trapped; Rome was closing its teeth on them. He remembered shaving off his beard under a viaduct, and Una strapping a cushion under her clothes again before they entered some soot-stained town.

But he couldn't separate out one day from another, wasn't even certain how many days it was – not that he wished to, or tried to remember. It was all fused together, and his mind slid seamlessly from Una, beside him in the car that night, to a freight depot in Iaxarteum, and the two of them running along beside the tracks.

Sulien had checked the place the previous night, watching the trains lumbering east. But it had to be daylight for this; it was too cold at night, when the air blazed icily around the speeding trains, even though it was not so cold here as it had been at the Rha. They no longer cared whether they were carried north or southwards now: if they found themselves up in Scythia, they could try and cross the Sinoan border and be done with it – Rome would need to apply some pressure before the Sinoan police would make any active effort to look for them, and they might be able to bribe their way on towards Annam.

When the vigiles found them, they were crouched among the tumbled crates and discarded reels on the embankment, waiting for an endlessly long line of rusting hopper-cars to pass by. On the other side, a goods-train was dawdling on the third set of tracks, the ladders and side doors of its square, upright cars practically inviting trespass. And it seemed in no hurry to move; it would be easy to board, safe.

The train of hoppers shrieked as it began to gather speed, then

Una said, with almost nothing but exhaustion in her voice, 'They're here,' and the next moment Sulien heard dogs barking.

They said nothing more as they rose and ran down the bank towards the tracks. Up close the hopper-train seemed so much faster. It was wrapped in a sheath of dirty, blasting air and the tracks howled under the deafening weight of it. Una and Sulien, pelting along the gravel beside it, couldn't hear a thing the vigiles were shouting behind them, even if it would have made any difference. Sulien had a hand wrapped round Una's arm and was trying to drag her with him because he was faster and could reach higher, and the possible handholds were already rushing by almost too fast even for him. It had to be now, *now*, no time to judge it better.

He reached for the frame at the back of a car, grasped Una to him at the same moment and leapt.

One foot trailed in space as he clutched at the frame, trying to swing both his own weight and hers inwards while the train seemed to try to shake them off its flanks like a huge animal. He could feel Una, straining to hold on, felt her weight swing to the side as she managed to close a hand on the rail. But her feet just scraped on the ledge at the hopper's base, and he couldn't get a better hold on her, couldn't shift the arm he already had round her without letting go, couldn't free his other hand—

He knew she'd tried, he knew she hadn't let herself fall.

He felt her arms, rigid with effort, and her cold fingers, gripping the strap of his backpack, but her feet swept off the ledge and as he fought, shouting, against the force surging outside the train, he saw her face.

And she smiled at him, a very small, wry twitch of the mouth, resigned and sorry and unbearable, as the flying air plucked her away and the train snatched him onwards, under the bridge into a hurtling current of blackness and noise.

Una landed face-down in the gravel beside the tracks. Her body rang with the impact, but at a distance, the pain lost somewhere before it reached her, and she did not bother assessing how badly she was hurt. She lifted her head a little to watch the train whip past before letting it drop back onto the grit, shutting her eyes and breathing the scent of hot metal and tar and dust. Then she turned clumsily onto her back. The ground was solid and still beneath her, and as the train's violent wake subsided, the air cleared and cooled a little and a breeze from the steppe brushed soundlessly over the tracks. She could hear the dogs baying in excitement, very close now, and the men crunching over the stones. The sky was a faded blue. Una lay and breathed slowly, staring at it.

BEGGING, BORROWING, STEALING

The wet slopes of the embankment shone dark amber in the lamplight, and the Tiber sparked in the rain. Varius had built a tiny fire on the path that ran along the river, a tiny red glow in the darkness below the arches of the Cestian Bridge. This wasn't territory he could expect to have to himself for long – he could see a little encampment of people crouched around a similar fire on the opposite bank – but for now it felt safe to him, a room closed off in walls of running water.

He was surprised Delir was such a small man, scarcely taller than his own daughter, who walked beside him, next to Ziye. And Delir looked weak, and sick, dragging his whole self along like a crippled limb. Varius tried to dampen down pity without extinguishing it all together, as if Delir were one of the badly injured people he had seen at the slave-clinic. He needed to be able to work.

Delir said, 'You worked for Leo once. You sent Marcus to me. I am so sorry I didn't protect him better.'

From what Lal and Ziye had said, Varius had half-expected something like this, but he still didn't like to hear it, and didn't know quite how to reply. A little stiffly, he reached for Delir's hand. 'You protected him at the time,' he muttered.

'I understand what you want to do,' Delir said, 'and I can't blame you for it. But what right have I to take any part? When if I had not been so – so *arrogant* – to think I knew better than two empires what to do with someone who—'

Varius felt the name skirted round, excised.

Lal burst out, 'You don't *know* what would have happened. He wouldn't have let the vigiles catch him; he'd only have done it sooner if you hadn't found him.' There were tears in her eyes;

Varius thought this was not the first time she had said this. She turned a beseeching look at Varius that seemed to beg him to make Delir believe it.

Delir was murmuring, 'I could have tricked him, perhaps, given him to the vigiles. I could even have . . .' He swallowed. 'He would have been executed if they had found him. I couldn't bear to think of how it might be done. But his life was in my hands on that island. I didn't want him to suffer – I could have made sure he didn't.'

'But you'd never have done that!' exclaimed Lal, fiercely; 'you can't even say it now! What's the use of blaming yourself for not doing something you just couldn't do? You tried to make sure he couldn't hurt anyone – you gave up everything to do that. It isn't fair.'

Delir was silent, weathering this out as if Lal's outburst had been a list of further accusations, rather than a defence of him.

Ziye sat down cross-legged on the ground near him, but her face was turned towards the river.

'You saved someone dangerous,' said Varius, 'and so did I. Marcus half-killed Drusus back in Sina. I was there, and I stopped him. If I had just left him there, Drusus would have been dead a year ago.'

Delir shook his head, the gentle look on his face already insisting that it wasn't the same thing at all.

Ziye asked quietly, 'Why did you stop him?'

Varius sighed. 'There would have been no way of hiding it. Faustus wouldn't have forgiven him. Marcus might not have been executed, but at the very least he would have been disgraced. And he would never have become Emperor. And—' He hesitated, tempted to stop there, but he was committed to the whole truth now. 'I thought Marcus would never have been the same again, afterwards. He was afraid he was losing his mind. He would have been a murderer. I didn't want that to happen to him, I didn't want him to lose . . . who he was.'

'And was any of that wrong?' asked Delir.

Varius looked down into the fire, silent.

'And now you mean to do the same thing yourself,' said Delir. 'What about what it will do to you?'

Varius felt vaguely exasperated. 'It's not likely to matter much. Look, do you need a promise that you're still a good man before you'll help me? I don't think it would make much difference to you, not from me. We can't put things back the way they should have been. But perhaps we can make things better than they are. That's what I'm asking of you. You don't have to help me kill anyone.'

In a low, dubious voice Delir asked, 'How?'

'The succession,' said Varius, also dropping his voice. 'The only person who would have supported Leo or Marcus and might have a chance is Eudoxius. We left him in charge during the peace talks. He's . . . well, he's better than Drusus, anyway, and I'm pretty sure he's not much in favour now. He was at the funeral, but there's been no sign of him since; I don't think he's even in Rome. He has at least one place in the country, and I think there's another one abroad somewhere. He'll have to be ready; he needs to come back to Rome and start building support. I can't find him by myself, and I can't go near him even if I could. I can't do anything that would make Drusus suspect him. There must have been someone in your network who's got a job in government – it doesn't even have to be an important one, but someone like that could find out where he is. And they should be able to contact him too – they'd have to be willing to take some risks, but—'

'But I've seen Eudoxius on the longvision,' said Ziye, interrupting, 'and he couldn't convince Rome to give up slavery, even if he wanted to. He seemed – well, nice . . . but he's not a leader. And he's an old man.'

Varius lifted a hand and rubbed his matted hair, feeling a horrid quiver of helplessness and panic run through him. 'I know – I do know. But can you think of anyone else? I can't— I don't know what else— I don't know what else I can do—'

Delir looked at him and said sadly, 'Your life, too,' as if adding Varius' name to a mental list of thousands.

'I'm all right,' Varius said. And although taking stock of his own situation he could not see how this could be true, he meant it. He was cold and desolate and probably a little insane, but something in him remained more whole than he could account for. He said, 'I'll need an address now; I have to get a room, I suppose,' and was astonished to feel a slight twinge of reluctance.

'I can help you with that much,' said Delir heavily. 'We know people who won't ask for identity papers – won't ask too much of anything.'

'Thank you,' said Varius. 'And Eudoxius?'

Delir and Ziye looked at one another.

'There is someone,' muttered Lal, almost to herself. 'We *can* help.' She met Varius' eyes and he knew she would get him the information, even if Delir and Ziye refused.

Delir admitted, 'We had someone in Cappadocia, just an assistant to an assistant in the Governor's office, or something like that. If he's even still there . . .'

Varius took a tiny room at the bottom of a crowded block on the northern edge of the city, and tried to spend as little time as possible actually inside it. It was good to have a bed and a place out of the rain, but being penned in so close to so many other people made him nervous. He hadn't liked closed spaces ever since his time in prison; now it felt strange to be inside at all. He felt he needed to do something to make sense of his change in circumstances, should anyone be paying attention, so he tidied himself up – only a little – and acquired a case of cheap watches, jewellery and combs. He continued roaming around the city, still smelling of alcohol, making lacklustre efforts to sell his trinkets at tram-stations and outside temples, while he waited for word from Delir's contact in Cappadocia, or from Eudoxius himself.

Drusus addressed the people again after the fall of Bamaria, and Varius moved through the ecstatic crowd spread through all the Fora, trying not to listen to Drusus' speech, or to the crowd that kept chanting, *Novius, Novius* . . .

It was the first time that the possibility occurred to Varius that nothing Drusus had begun could be stopped, that killing him now might only make him, in a sense, more powerful. For once he was almost relieved that he couldn't get close enough.

On public longvision he watched the news of the thousands of bombs floating like spores across the Empire, a handful drifting as close as Egypt and Asia Minor, and he listened to people talking. Despite their number the balloon bombs had killed few and done little serious damage, but everyone shuddered at the idea of silent weapons on the wind, and they celebrated fiercely when news came that a ship carrying them had been destroyed in the Arabian Sea. The fighting was still far off, but in Rome the war felt more real now.

He was half-heartedly pestering tourists with his case of trinkets near a tram station on the Field of Mars one morning when he heard a satisfied voice saying, 'Well, I just hope they don't let them slip this time. That girl looks such a sly little bitch.' Varius looked up with immediate foreboding to see that the government news-kiosk on the corner was doing brisker business than usual, and the people clustered around it had an alert, excited look.

The advertising magazine came out that day too, so he bought both. Una and Sulien had just barely dodged arrest on the border between Venedia and Sarmatia. Varius started leafing urgently through the magazine, trying to think of something he could do if he should find their signal in it. He frowned at the page where it might have been, thinking, *Run, run*, as if he could propel some measure of strength or luck to them through the print. Later he found he'd wandered close to the temple of Isis and Serapis, and because they were the gods of his Egyptian ancestors and gods of death, he went and leaned his forehead against the temple's outer wall, praying without belief, 'Please, let these two go. Please, not them too.'

A few days later Varius was woken by insistent knocking on the door of his room. He lay still for a second of paralysed dread, long enough to realise that the sky was still black and it was very early indeed. Warily, he got up. The room was so small that he barely had to take a step to reach the door. But there was no one there when he opened it; he heard hurried footsteps receding towards the outside door. A large crate stood at his feet.

Varius dragged the box inside, crouched beside it on the floor and looked it over with nonplussed paranoia before beginning to yank it open. The box was filled with secondhand office equipment – an autoscribe with a couple of ink cartridges, a longdictor, even a bundle of pens and a pair of scissors, all carefully padded in layers of shredded paper. There was a note, unsigned, which read, 'For use in your endeavours. I regret I cannot be of further assistance.' And there was a smaller box, right at the bottom of the crate, and the box was full of money.

Varius sat on his heels, open-mouthed, staring at it, and then, for want of knowing what else to do, counted it. A hundred and fifty thousand sesterces.

He panicked a little then. It was more than he could possibly distribute around the scattered hoards where he'd stored his money, and he was afraid both to leave it there and to take it with him. He stood dithering over it for a while, despairing over every possible hiding place and course of action, before finally packing the money up again and stowing it on top of the narrow cupboard.

He knew 150,000 sesterces wasn't much to Eudoxius. There had been no indication of whether he was even willing to return to Rome. Oh, it's all right by him, so long as he doesn't have to do anything; he'll just sit in his country house and throw money at it! thought Varius, ungratefully. He made a hasty call to Delir and Ziye and by the time he reached the family's pair of cellar rooms in the Subura, after an agitated morning ploughing round the city as normal with his case, he had driven himself to a pitch of perverse resentment.

He told Delir, 'It's not money I want.'

Delir stared for a second and said, 'You stupid young man, of course you want money.'

'It's only four or five serious bribes,' said Ziye, 'and how else are you really going to get near Drusus?'

And they were discussing means of keeping it reasonably safe when Lal came running into the cellar and said, 'It's Una.'

Una lay on the vibrating floor in the volucer, her wrists and ankles chained. She had not made a sound, nor any voluntary movement, since they'd hoisted her off the gravel, just hung limp in their arms. There was gritty blood on the side of her face and lip and bruises glowed along her body. She thought some of her ribs were cracked and her wrist was broken, nothing worse, but the soldiers weren't sure how badly she was hurt, and therefore had been comparatively gentle with her, so far at least. She kept her eyes closed as the aircraft rose and roared west. She was telling herself a story, in images rather than in words, and she repeated and refined it, loading every moment of it with will, insisting that it be true.

Sulien flies through the outskirts of Iaxarteum, the sparse city landscape shuttering past him in grey and black, wind already lashing the heat from him as he clings to the frame. He knows there are only minutes before the vigiles have the train stopped, before they're there to intercept him. The train gathers speed, but then slows again as it approaches the point where the tracks diverge, fanning wide across the huge, colourless emptiness outside the town. The ground is still blurred when he looks down, but the sound of the train changes, he can feel it groan. I have to do it, I have to do it, he thinks, and lowers himself as much as he can, lets go. He rolls and bounces, comes to rest on rough dry ground. Perhaps for a moment he can't move, the breath knocked out of him; when he manages to get to his feet, perhaps, on instinct, he starts stumbling back the way he has come.

But there's another train coasting this way, and he knows he has to get aboard. It's a passenger train just out of Iaxarteum Main Station – the vigiles either haven't thought or had time to have it shut down yet. It's an older train, running on the same tracks as the freight trains, not hovering above the broad mag-netway line that cuts between the others and stretches away to the east. It'll soon be going much faster than the train of hoppers, but for now Sulien has a little more time to judge his moment. He grabs a rail or pipe, pulls himself up into the gap between the carriages, feet braced above the coupling. The buffers jump and judder below his feet, and when the train curves the gap narrows – the first time it happens, he thinks he'll be crushed, but it never closes as tight as that; it always opens out again. Another train blasts by and the freezing air sucks and pummels at him; he has to grip tight and lean in towards the train to keep his footing, but he does, he does.

He's moving so fast he can't think about anything else.

He's exposed and visible, out there on the side of the train. It won't be long before someone sees him. When the train stops between stations, out on the steppe – one of those inexplicable breathing spaces in a journey – he jumps down, shaky and sick and longing to lie down in the scratchy grass, but he ducks under the body of the train, climbs up into the underframe, wedging himself against the truss-bars, spread-eagling himself over the wheelset. He's hidden by the brake-cylinder, by the wheels themselves.

He hugs a long strut and locks his hands round his wrists, gripping. He shuts his eyes so he won't see the massive wheels turning right beside him, or the axle spinning over the juddering flow of the ground below. Sometimes stones or hard scraps of rubbish flick up from the tracks against his back; sometimes the whole structure swerves, swinging him closer to the wheels and the metal above him. It isn't so cold under here, but the dark air is terrible. He feels as if he's suffocating, and the noise drives into his skull like a chisel, but hours pass, carrying him further and further away.

It's so loud he can't think about anything else.

And now Una wanted to skip ahead to a time when Sulien had been in Nionia for some months, a year or more, picking up the language like another accent, and so much faster than he thought he could. He'd be working, helping people, as he always should have been. He would have friends – so many of them – and he'd tell them what had happened to his sister, and they would comfort him. He had been a slave, he'd so nearly been crucified, and it had seemed to rinse off him almost completely, almost at once. Only little traces, like that way of holding his wrist, had remained with him. He'd been without her for seven years, and however much he'd wanted her back, it hadn't stopped him being bafflingly happy, then and afterwards. Sometimes it had outraged her that things that had left such rough, wrong, ugly edges on her had been softened or let slip by his kindly, unreliable memory. Now, lying on the metal floor, panic flared in her at the thought that perhaps it had always demanded more effort from him than either of them had realised. But even if this was the worst of all, even if he was so much more tired now, surely she could still trust this wouldn't cripple or kill him. Given a while, he'd scrape together enough happiness to live on. He would get married, he would have children.

But it was what happened now that mattered most, and she had to see him through it, even if only like this, by willing him to do the things that would save him. She saw him stumbling away from the train in darkness, at the edge of some town, crouched against a wall, clutching his head and gasping as the dizziness wore off. Now there would be nothing to deflect what had happened. She began to think of what she would have felt and done if it had been her – and no, she couldn't bear it, she had to leave a small gap. A few minutes then, or however long was safe, until if someone was speaking to him, he'd be able to listen.

If she could, what would she tell him?

He knows what she'd tell him to do. 'I don't care what you say,' he thinks in answer.

  Don't argue, Sulien, says Una's voice in his mind.

  Sulien shakes his head, 'I'm going to get you back. I'm going to. I—' At this point, he's bound to be thinking this way.

164

Well, I'm not going to watch you do something that stupid. I'm gone, I'm sorry, I tried. We both tried, and it happened anyway. Either you get out of this now or neither of us does.

And it's fine, Sulien, really it is. It will be in the end.

'Don't believe you.'

Of course he can't believe it, not yet. But he's cold and exhausted and hungry, and he must still have enough care for himself to want to look after those things. And beneath that there must be some particle of unrecognised trust that she's right, that it's worth guarding himself for a kinder time ahead.

There's some food and water in his pack – not much, but it'll do. He's got money too, they always carried half each. It might be better if he travelled through the night, didn't waste the dark sleeping, but he's probably already at the limit of what he can do without rest. He can't walk into a guest-house tonight, even if he could find one – every town on a rail line or magnetway will be primed to watch for him, especially if he hasn't had enough luck to be carried out of Sarmatia. But if he can find any kind of shelter at all – a culvert, a bush, a bit of corrugated iron propped against a wall – his clothes and the sleeping bag will keep him alive, even if he's reached the snowy forest on the edge of Scythia rather than the deserts of the south. He has what he needs to survive, for now.

Perhaps after all it's best if he just goes to sleep. He accepts, at least, that there's nothing he can do tonight but try and keep himself out of harm's way. He walks as far he can from the tracks, finds somewhere hidden and lies down. Tomorrow he'll do whatever he can to change his appearance and hurry on. And by then his sister will be so far out of reach that it will be clear to him which way he has to go.

'Please, Sulien,' murmured Una, once more, before her grip slid from the story and she fell away from it into soft, solitary dark, where she thought *Marcus*, and fell onwards, beyond thinking anything, into sleep.

Sulien staggered across a rutted field, dragging his pack by the strap. He hadn't made it far from the tracks before he toppled into a shallow ditch and stayed there. His bones still seemed to shake and bang with the motion of the train; his eardrums blared with its noise. He did not realise at first that a sound was emptying itself out of him: a long groan, almost a howl. He swallowed it back as he felt it, in case anyone heard and came looking – he must not allow himself to stop caring for these things. He pressed his face against the ground to stifle any more noise and gagged on the black dust that lined his throat. He heaved and sobbed, almost tearlessly, for only fitful spurts of water would come, loosening the grit in his eyes.

Slowly sound returned and he could hear himself panting and spluttering into the coarse grass. He stopped.

'Una,' he said.

The dry wind came scrubbing across the field. There was nothing else, not even a train passing, no one.

'I'm sorry,' he whispered.

Almost as if she were really speaking to him, he heard Una's voice answering that, and telling him what to do, sounding more impatient than anything.

'Shut up,' he said to her, and tried to get up. And it didn't work; his limbs, even his height, felt alien and insubstantial; for an instant he was teetering somewhere unnaturally high before the ground and sky rolled horribly and he was down again, clinging on to the grasses as if he could have fallen even from here.

He thought, I wish they'd taken us both.

He did *not* wish that. He hadn't jammed himself into that hellish space above the train's wheels for so long to wish himself helpless now. He mumbled aloud, 'I'm going to get you back. I'm coming.'

First of all he had to know what had happened. Would they have shot her at once, there by the tracks? The fall itself might have killed her.

Tears came more freely at that thought, but he sat up and

dragged his pack open, his fingers slow and clumsy, and groped for the bottle of water inside. He stopped himself draining it at the last moment and used what was left to rinse as much of the grime as he could from his face and hands. He slicked his hair back from his forehead with the last of it, wishing he still had the beard or something more about himself that he could alter. He changed out of the clothes he'd be described as wearing, pulled up his hood.

It occurred to him that the air was not so cold here, and the earth was sandy under the threadbare grass, and there was a surprising salt tang in the air. Until now if he'd given any thought to his location at all, it was only with the despairing conviction that he had no idea where he was. But he couldn't have come far enough to have reached a true coast. He must be near the Hyrcanian or the Caspian Sea.

At the edge of the field a dusty road ran parallel to the tracks, towards a faint yellowish glow in the dark sky. Sulien found some longer grass and hid his pack so he wouldn't look like someone who had come far. He was grateful not to have to carry the weight as he made his way towards the light.

It took him about half an hour to reach the centre of a fishing town on the shore of the inland sea. It seemed a prosperous place, even jaunty, compared with the disappointed towns in the north, but it was still quiet, and shut down for the night. Sulien passed through a little forum crowded with empty frames of market stalls and found the small public longvision was either turned off or broken. He swung a hand hard against the edge of one of the stalls and thought for an instant of Una's arms filled with flakes of glass as the metal chimed out, dangerously loud. But though he retreated at once from the sound, a minute or two later he had forgotten why his hand hurt. He did nothing about it.

He saw a pair of vigile vans standing near the gates of the town's station and shied away.

He found another longvision a little way beyond that, in a square where there were still some shops open. Sulien lurked at a corner. A few other people coming out of the shop glanced up at the screen as they passed, but there was no sound and Sulien had to wait through a long sequence of advertisements, during which he could feel whatever noise it was he'd made alone in the field building behind his ribs again. At last the news came on, and the jubilant tone of it was obvious, even in silence.

He had been working so hard, all through that walk in the dark, to believe that she was still alive. Without thinking about it, he had expected at least a temporary relief if it were true. But he looked at the satisfied faces of the two state newscasters and he only felt sick.

There were no pictures of Una. He'd thought he was hoping for a sight of her, but instead he found he was thankful for that much; he didn't want to see her captured. There was some wobbling footage of a volucer, rising into the grey air, and a caption rolled across the screen saying they would have Una back in Rome by the following day, but there was nothing of what they were going to do to her, or when, or what was happening to her now. Perhaps if there had been sound . . .

Then there was a parade of pictures, photographs and drawings, of his own face, shaven and bearded, and he began hurrying back the way he'd come, trembling a little. He did not look like the few coppery-skinned, broad-cheekboned people he'd seen here. This wasn't a large town where faces would be more varied, or where travellers from the west might be commonplace; he wouldn't last a morning here. He had to get away at once, though he didn't think he was capable of another journey like the one that was still resounding through his body. He was tired enough to feel a black froth of dreams breaking against his eyelids whenever he blinked. He wouldn't be able to hold himself in place; he'd be shaken out of consciousness, smashed across the tracks. And even apart from that, and even if he could be sure of dodging the vigiles again, it wasn't enough now to scramble aboard a train which could be heading almost anywhere.

He passed the station again, on the far side of the street, and a fare-car stopped, dropping someone off. It lingered for a moment then moved on slowly, looking for another customer, the insignia of its provincial livery glinting dimly in the streetlight. Sulien eyed it, and an ugly spark of possibility fired in his mind. Without really believing he could be going to act on it, he started walking towards the car and tentatively, as if it were a gesture that might mean nothing, he lifted his hand.

The car stopped beside him and the driver looked out at him, tired, innocent. He asked, 'Where to?'

Sulien stared at him for a second. 'I think I got off my train at the wrong place,' he said, hearing his own voice as toneless and unnatural. 'What's the next stop?'

'Do you mean Socanda or Saramanna?'

'Yes, Saramanna. That's it,' said Sulien woodenly, and climbed into the car beside him.

The warmth of the car and the support of the seat were almost enough to put him to sleep at once, even while electricity prickled through his nerves, jolted open his eyes whenever they slipped closed. Back in Rome neither he nor Varius had known how to steal a car. Now he could see a way.

'Not from round here?' asked the man, with mild, amiable curiosity.

'Venedia.' Sulien glanced guardedly around the cab, taking in the identity documents lying on the car's console, the cap on the man's head. He had nothing he could use a weapon and there was little space to make a swing. Once they were outside the town he'd have to grab the man's head and try and slam it against the window, do it again if the first blow didn't stun him. If he struck too hard, he'd break the man's skull.

I can't, he thought, his breath beginning to come faster and deeper. Sickness tightened in his stomach. He'd once had to knock someone out before, and it had shaken him then. But this man hadn't done anything wrong, had only let someone into his car who might be about to murder him. And Sulien had committed himself as soon as he climbed inside – he couldn't let himself be deposited at whatever town they were heading for, off his course and miles away from his belongings.

But I don't want to do it; it's not fair, he pleaded inwardly. Not fair, when if he could have jumped a second earlier up onto that train— If he could have kept hold—

And what were they doing to her? How much were they going to hurt her before they were finished with her?

'Are you feeling all right?' inquired the driver, beginning to tense a little, glancing between Sulien and the road.

Sulien nodded, jerkily. He could guess how his voice would come out if he tried to speak. The car slid down towards the beach, past the rows of fishing boats and out of the town into the dark desert beyond. Sulien tried to slow his accelerating breath and failed completely. Stalling, perhaps, he began thinking about what would have to happen in the man's brain, where the blood flow would have to be interrupted. He felt himself plummet helplessly into the detail of it, everything outside of that scattering.

Now, come on, do it now. Sulien turned towards the man, saw his hand reach, slow and distant, as if controlled by a languid stranger with a remote control. Then for a moment he couldn't see past the fizz of the world dissolving and bubbling away, like limestone in acid, taking him with it.

Then it cleared and the car was swerving; the man sagging sideways against him. Sulien clutched for the controls without understanding what had happened. He didn't remember the blow, couldn't feel the after-impact of it in his muscles, but of course he'd done it—

He fought through a frightening, undignified struggle with the car as the driver tumbled into his lap until at last he managed to bring it to a standstill. He got out and looked down at what he had done.

He felt strangely diminished; something had been taken out of him.

The man was breathing steadily, but he was deeply unconscious. Rather gingerly, Sulien checked his pulse and peered into his eyes. He decided that the man would wake in about an hour, though that was probably more wishful thinking than medical judgement.

There was no blood, anywhere, not a mark on either of them.

Well, now what was he going to do?

He had to get as much use out of the car as possible before anyone knew it had been stolen, and he'd have longer if he could delay the moment when the driver reached a longdictor.

East, he thought. The vigiles knew which way he and Una had been heading, so they'd surely expect him to try and continue, not to come racing back towards Rome now. At that Una's voice spoke sharply in his mind again, saying, 'Because it's stupid,' but Sulien didn't even bother with an answer this time, just loaded the man carefully into the back and drove back to the field to collect his bag. He had a map, and now he searched it hastily for some rough idea of where he was, finding Saramanna on the northwest coast of the Hyrcanian Sea. He lifted the man's cap from where it had fallen and jammed it onto his own head, then raced eastwards into the desert.

Rounding the tip of the sea, Sulien came briefly onto a minor motorway, only two lanes wide and nearly empty, but just beyond the junction he found himself joining a straggling tailback from a vigile van parked half across the road. A couple of vigiles were checking what traffic passed through. The car hitched and choked a little, as if echoing the spasm that went through Sulien. He picked up the man's identity papers, waved them at the window as casually as he could.

The officers glanced at the car's livery and the driver's cap and didn't stop him.

Once off the motorway the rough, narrow roads were almost empty and it wasn't hard to find a long track, dwindling away through the bristly scrub. Sulien followed it away from the main road for ten miles or so before stopping.

It would take the man a while to find help from here. Sulien grimaced at the cruelty of it. He bundled the man into his sleeping bag and left him on the sand beside the road with a wad of notes tucked into his pocket.

Then he doubled back on himself, overtaking a couple of other fare-cars on the motorway, where the vigiles weren't even checking the westbound traffic. Once he was out of their sight, Sulien hurtled westwards, driving faster than he ever had before. Perhaps he'd achieved nothing but waste an hour driving out of his way, but it was at least possible that he'd set them looking for him in the wrong direction.

Once he blinked awake to find himself skidding off the road. Fortunately he'd left the motorway behind by then, and the ground was flat and solid under the wheels. He braked and sat out there in the dark – he didn't know for how long – blinking and empty, before wresting the car back onto the road.

The land heaved itself into ridges bristling with ghostly low-growing trees. The road had unravelled into irregular stripes over the humps, leading between stacks of rock. It had been hours since he'd seen another car, and probably no patch of this intractable landscape was safer or more exposed than another, but when he found a taller thicket of saxaul he edged off the road into it for what camouflage it gave him. He ate a little, then slept for what he hoped was no more than an hour. It was still dark when he woke, and he was still soaked with exhaustion, but he was clear-headed enough now to go on.

He'd driven more than five hundred miles when he reached the Caspian Sea. It was almost dawn. He skirted the suburbs of some shipbuilding city on its shore, Dahae or Vitium, he thought, not wanting to stop long enough to squint at the map again, and by the time he was five miles or so away from it along the coast, there was enough light in the sky for him to find a rocky shelf above the dark water and drive slowly up to the very edge. He gathered everything he wanted, climbed out and pushed the car down.

The splash sounded loud enough to wake the city. Sulien started away from it without looking down to see if the water had closed over the car – there was nothing he could do if it hadn't. He limped back towards the town to find a longdictor and set about contacting Varius.

'Please let me go,' said Noriko. Drusus, who had flung his arms around her mischievously as soon as she entered the dining room, pressed her closer, and danced her round in a circle, laughing. A small troupe of musicians was playing in the gallery at the other end of the hall.

Stiff in his arms, Noriko waited passively for him to stop for a second or two. She was mortifyingly conscious of being observed. Then, as he clasped her even tighter, pulling her off-balance so her breasts were crushed against his chest and his hips butted against hers, she grabbed his hands and shoved them away from her, dragging free with a little cry of outrage.

Drusus laughed again, apparently too exhilarated to be angry. His cheeks were a little flushed with wine, but he was not really drunk, just relaxed and animated. 'You can't blame me for being in a good mood.'

'Because you have arrested Noviana Una?'

'That's not her name any more,' said Drusus, with a flash of irritation. But it passed quickly. 'That,' he acknowledged cheerfully, 'and I am the first man to expand the boundaries of the Roman Empire in a hundred and forty years.' He came closer again, smiling, and stroked a finger over her cheek. 'And you are so beautiful.'

Noriko twitched her face away. 'I am your cousin's widow.'

'Come on, now,' said Drusus, 'it was a political marriage. It's been months. What difference can it really make to you now?' But he flung himself down on the couch to begin eating. 'In any case, you mustn't worry. I'm your guardian now, you're quite safe with me.'

He seemed to be acting as if Noriko were the only other person present, but as well as the musicians and the servants, there were a couple of silent young women lying beside him at the table. Noriko found their presence strangely distressing, and confusing – were they slaves, or prostitutes, or high-born concubines, or

173

were they perhaps married women whom Drusus had somehow appropriated? In a way, she supposed, it made no difference – whatever their origins, it was obvious enough why they were there. But it was as if there was an illegible footnote in the corner of a page she had to read – distracting, and a reminder of how foreign and isolated she was here. Not that she had needed it.

She was permitted a little more freedom now, and she prowled restlessly around the Palace and its grounds, trying to explore the limits of her internment, though there were usually a few of Drusus' servants and guards spying on her. But she had not been allowed to resume residence at Marcus' house in Tusculum, or even to venture beyond the Palace gates at all. And this extended leniency had not come without conditions. Drusus often wandered into her rooms now, and every few nights he summoned her to his table. He required little of her once she was there, though he liked to talk of Rome's victories and Nionia's defeats in front of her. Noriko could pretend to be indifferent or deaf, but Drusus knew she was neither; she supposed that was at least part of what he wanted from her. He could see his power reflected in her, both in her patience and in its failures.

She tried to avoid him when she could, though excuses were hard to come by as she had nothing to do except to work on her Latin. She was deeply afraid of what it would mean if she ever goaded him so much that he had her brought to him by force. Tonight, though, she had come without protest; she had to see him.

'At this rate,' said Drusus, 'the war will be won by the summer. And then we will have to discuss your position.'

He left a pause; he wanted her to ask what he meant. Noriko considered and decided she was free to say nothing. She nodded demurely.

'Of course it wouldn't be at all appropriate now; the people wouldn't stand for it,' said Drusus, giving up on the response he wanted and carrying on with the conversation regardless. 'But when we have peace, I think I could teach them to love you as their Emperor's wife. I think it would be very fitting.'

174

Noriko was not wholly surprised, although she had to contain a lurch of panic. When Drusus had taken over as regent during the peace talks in Sina, she had wondered if she might be expected to marry him rather than Marcus. She remembered what Una, left in Nionian custody for fear of what Drusus would do to her if he could, had said to her then: 'Do anything rather than let that happen . . . I'd rather be a slave again, or dead, than married to him.'

Well, if there was any way out of it, it was not to shriek now that she would never consent. Her consent had not been asked. He did not expect to need it.

'Well, what do you think?' demanded Drusus.

Noriko gazed at the edge of the table. There was no answer, and no display of feeling, that would not disadvantage her. Let her be as opaque and untranslatable to him as the women lounging beside him were to her. She said, very modestly, without raising her eyes, 'Nothing, your Majesty.'

Drusus shrugged, perhaps a little disappointed, but undismayed, and resumed eating. Noriko remained perched, decorous and strained on the couch opposite him, her hands clenched in her lap, waiting to be invited to speak again.

'Eat something,' urged Drusus after a while.

'I cannot,' Noriko said softly. Drusus looked at her. Hoping that was permission enough, she ventured, 'What is going to happen to Una, your Majesty?'

Drusus smiled, casual and fierce at once. 'About what you would expect.'

'I hope that may not be true,' replied Noriko, 'for I find I cannot help imagining the most terrible things.'

'Well, then,' said Drusus blithely, 'I wouldn't think about it.'

'I do not have that discipline; I cannot stop thinking about it,' said Noriko. 'You have made her an object of such hatred, and she has no rights to protect her from it.'

'Rights? She's getting a trial,' said Drusus, 'and that's more than she's due.' His expression had tightened a little, defensive at being challenged, or uneasy at having already conceded so much.

'I think the trial will not take long, and that there is no doubt how it will end.'

'Indeed not,' Drusus agreed, with the same unembarrassed smile.

Noriko felt dangerous indignation sticking in her throat and tried to swallow it back. She had decided before she came that it was useless to dispute the charges against Una. There was no defence she could make that was not also an accusation of him, and she must not reproach him, she must give him no reason to be angry. She was perhaps too close to it already.

She said with as much care as she could, 'But still she may have to live for some weeks yet. I cannot bear to think how that time may be filled if her keepers believe there are no restrictions on what they may do to her, even, perhaps, that they are pleasing you by abusing her.'

'She does have to be questioned, you realise,' said Drusus. 'We still need to find Varius – and her brother.'

'I know, your Majesty,' Noriko assured him, meekly, 'but surely she cannot know more of where her brother is now than the men who arrested her. If she has some poor little piece of information, and if without knowing what it may be, you – your vigiles – try to make her tell it by torture, will it not probably be useless or unrecognisable by the time they succeed, if they ever do?'

She had looked up several words that day to be sure her Latin would not fail her. Torture was one of them. It was a difficult word to smooth into the soft, light tone she was trying to maintain, but one she was careful not to avoid.

Drusus smiled again – clenched teeth briefly bared – before softening into a look of half-amused tolerance. 'What an unpleasant subject,' he said lightly. 'I'm sure her interrogators will do whatever works. I don't believe traitors should be coddled.'

'Of course I know very little of politics,' said Noriko, 'but I understand that excitement is very high just now. Perhaps while it lasts the people will not be sorry to think of her suffering. But later, if they should hear that it was worse than was . . . than was necessary, when they remember that this was a very young girl, perhaps they will feel that it was badly done. But I do not think anyone will ever blame you for restraint, or feel shamed by it, or ask why no one did more to hurt her.'

Drusus was quiet, the fingers of one hand pattering distractedly on the tabletop, the large, sleepy eyelids lowered in thought. For a moment the likeness to Marcus was sharp enough to catch and sting.

'Do you think that may be so?' Noriko asked tentatively, after a moment.

'I think it's very magnanimous of you to speak up for her like this,' answered Drusus, a mocking note in his voice. 'She was your rival, after all.'

'No.' She suppressed a sigh. She was suddenly very tired. 'No, no, it was not like that.'

'So what is it like?' Drusus leaned forward, no longer smiling. 'Why are you so concerned for a criminal?'

'I do not know if I can explain it to you,' said Noriko, helplessly. There were reasons enough that she could not mention to him – Una's warning to her, and the unselfishness of it; how they had both worked to keep Rome and Nionia from war; the fact that they were both in his power and caged now.

She searched for an acceptable reply and then murmured, 'I think it is a natural weakness in me. You would understand if I were unwilling to watch another woman being hurt at length, in front of me? If I could not stand the sight of even an animal's blood? I have met her. I know her face. Unfortunately I can still imagine it very clearly. So for me it would be as if I had to watch all the time.'

'And do you think an Emperor should be just as squeamish?'

Noriko raised her eyes from the table at last to look at him. 'I hope you may show compassion to *me*. I am asking you to think of me, not of her. You have been so kind to me; please be kind one more time.'

Drusus' eyebrows lifted, and he said, 'You didn't seem to be so impressed with me a minute ago.'

Noriko rose, briefly closing her fists as she walked around the table and knelt beside his couch. 'I regret any moment in which I have not shown you proper gratitude. I am the daughter of your enemy; you might have placed me where she is, I know that. And instead you have protected me. So I know how capable you are of kindness. I would not ask for any more from you if I could help myself. I know I cannot persuade you to spare her life. But please, let her be treated well while she is in prison. Let her at least be treated decently. Otherwise I cannot bear it— I will have no peace, I will be ill, I know it—'

She let tears trickle out of her eyes, lifting her face so he could see them. It was easy enough to cry for Una and for herself, but she fought to keep her features smooth as she wept, which was harder.

'Oh, Jove,' said Drusus, exasperated, though he bent his face closer to hers. 'Very well, I'll tell them to keep their hands off her, will that do?'

Noriko sniffed and snivelled and whispered, 'May I see her?'

'What? No. I think you should be satisfied with my word,' said Drusus.

'But I shall be so afraid they have not obeyed you. Perhaps they might think you did not mean it. Please. Unless I can see for myself that she is unhurt, it will always be on my mind, I will be always afraid . . .'

Drusus reached out gently and wiped the tears from her cheek. His face was strangely soft and wistful. Noriko froze, not even breathing. His fingertips traced their way to her mouth, slid over and between her lips.

Later, she flung herself down on her bed, letting out a stifled scream of disgust and fury into the bedclothes.

Tomoe curled up on the bed beside her, offering comfort; stealing some for herself.

'We can't stay in this place,' Noriko said to her.

*

Sulien lurched into one of the longdictor chambers down at the port and toppled onto the bench there, trying to steady himself enough to dial the code. What little rest he'd had over the last twenty-four hours had been on trams or out in the open, screened against the daylight by saxaul trees. He'd taken a room for the night in Dahae, but it had hardly been worth the risk, for he couldn't really sleep. He'd had three days to wait until the magazine came out, and the couple of hundred miles he'd covered, moving south along the coast, seemed like less, creeping along on the spot in a salt-crusted landscape that didn't change.

He was unreasonably shaken that there actually were a couple of real replies to his advertisement, but then there was Varius, grim and guarded: 'I saw your notice. You can reach me on this code.'

Just to hear his voice almost sabotaged Sulien: he gulped for air and shook, and here were more inexcusable minutes passing in which he wasn't doing anything.

It took him a few false starts, but he dialled the code and Varius answered at once. 'Yes?' he said warily, and then, as Sulien struggled and failed to answer, 'Where are you?' Sulien's voice continued to stick like a wrong key jammed in a lock.

'Not that I think anyone's listening,' said Varius quietly, 'but I'm not going to say your name. Are you still there?'

'Yes,' managed Sulien at last, 'I'm here – I'm in Issedoneum. I'm coming back. Can you help me? I have to get back.' There was a pause and Sulien shouted into it with abrupt violence, 'I'm not leaving her there! I'm not going on by myself. Don't you dare tell me that.'

Another pause. 'All right,' Varius answered, evenly.

'Sorry. Thank you for . . . oh gods, thank you for even answering. I'm sorry.'

'Are you safe for the moment?' asked Varius.

'I don't know. More or less. There's no one around just now. Yes.'

'Do you still have money?'

'Yes. Half of what we had left. But I don't know what— I think

179

I'm about two hundred miles from the border with Persia, but I don't think I can get a car again, and trains are too dangerous. I've been getting trams and walking the last few days. It's too slow.'

'Can I contact you where you are now?'

Sulien looked around unsteadily. 'Not really, it's very public. I don't want to stay in the same place for too long.'

'All right, will you be able to call me again in three hours? But don't try and keep moving – I can tell from here you need to eat and rest.'

Sulien mumbled something incoherent that was not quite assent.

Varius said gently, 'Three hours won't make any difference.'

Delir could not have owned the atlases very long, having come from Sina with almost nothing, but he had saved them from the family's flat and now his fingers moved over the thick, beautiful pages with unthinking love, searching out Issedoneum. He said, 'Yes, I have friends in Rhagae. They will help.' There was an agitated, manic haste about him that Varius hadn't seen before, but he sounded completely certain.

'Would they go across the border for him?'

Delir grimaced. 'I doubt it.'

'But they could take him across the province, to Tauris or Urmia?'

Varius had contributed most of the contents of Eudoxius' crate to Lal as well as financing more supplies, and now her forgery equipment – bottles, brushes, the autoscribe and a lumpen copy-press, and sheets of paper, plastic and metal – took over one corner of the cellar. A small array of papers and security passes in various stages of completion was spread across the desk, on top of newssheets gloating over the plans for Una's trial. Lal was leaning back from her work, kneading her sore eyes, unruly hair splayed around a pale, underslept face.

'You are doing so well with these,' Delir said, hurrying to supply praise like a fuel.

'I don't know – I need a picture of him, obviously—'

Varius stared at the newssheets on the desk and said dully, 'Why couldn't they just finish it when they found her?'

'Can't you see why?' asked Ziye. 'Drusus has built her up too much for that. They tell stories like this in the arena, they make the crowd love one fighter and hate another, but you don't work people up like that and then show them nothing, you don't say it all ended offstage. People want to see her. Then when it's over, and they've watched it all, they're all part of it; they can't place the blame on Drusus alone; they can't easily change their mind. They won't be able to say it isn't what they wanted.'

'Better for her and Sulien if they'd shot her at once,' Varius muttered.

Lal looked appalled, but it was Delir who said, 'Don't say that. Whatever the reason, she's still alive, and something may happen, we may be able to do something. There must be some hope in that.'

'I said I'd help them, so I will,' said Varius. 'If he can get himself into Persia, your friends can take him all the way across it. If he could go by magnetway for the rest of the journey . . .'

'But he needs papers for that. And I need his picture,' repeated Lal. 'I need more time to finish.'

'Do you have one of those for yourself, Lal? And could you work on Sulien's while you were travelling?'

Lal's face changed, becoming at once sombre and bright. 'Yes, I have one. I could go and meet him. Yes, I could bring him back here.'

'What, alone? No,' protested Delir instantly.

Ziye said bitterly, 'Why shouldn't she go where she chooses, if she's in the mood to go off saving people? You did.'

'Ziye,' said Lal.

'What should I say?' cried Delir. ' "Yes, I have no right to stop you, so go and get yourself arrested like that poor girl?" Please don't do this, not after everything else.'

'Don't you think I've been in worse danger than this?' replied

Lal quietly. 'And don't you remember what Una and Sulien have done for me? What's a train ride compared with that? Of course I'm going.'

Sulien wished Varius had talked for longer, that he had not been so reluctant to go into any detail. He'd given Sulien a Persian longdictor code, for once he was over the border, and said, 'One of us will bring you the rest of the way,' which had to mean he'd found Delir, and that there was more than one friend waiting for him back in Rome. But it would have been good to hear Varius actually say that; it would have made it tangible. And though he knew how hollow it would be if Varius told him Una probably hadn't been harmed, might still be saved, still he desperately wanted to hear someone say it anyway.

He thought about heading for the tracks again. Perhaps it wouldn't be such a risk here; the checks might be less stringent than further east. But even so, the closer he came to the Persian border, the more vigiles would be patrolling the line.

He walked along the cold quayside. The longdictor chambers were clustered next to a seaside amusement arcade, all shut up for the winter except for one or two brave food-stalls; beyond there were rows of moored pleasure-boats, sealed up like bobbing sarcophagi. For a moment Sulien thought wildly of stealing one of the smaller boats, but the next moment he was jeering at himself: what, and pilot it two hundred miles? But perhaps he could hide himself on board a vessel heading the right way, as Una had done for him all those years ago – there had to be ferries, even in winter. But he couldn't do the same things Una could, and in any case, how would he get to shore safely? He could hardly swim for it, not in water as cold as this must be, or wade up the beach fully dressed and expect no one to notice.

What was left that he had not already tried or thought of?

He'd pared down his belongings to nothing but the clothes he was wearing and the rolls of cash, hidden in his pockets and in his boots. Sulien began mentally to count it out: yes, it would be stretched thin, but if it had been imaginable to carry on alone, it would have been enough to carry him to Nionian or Sinoan territory . . .

If it could have taken him two or three thousand miles, surely it was enough to vault him across just a couple of hundred miles now?

He remembered Marcus at the caupona in Wolf Step: young, defenceless, no money in his pockets, but wielding an air of privilege like a weapon, scaring a pack of black marketeer thugs into a panic, giving orders and expecting them to be obeyed, refusing to explain himself . . .

I haven't done that, Sulien thought. I haven't tried being rich.

[VII]

COLLABORATION

Noriko had never seen Una free. In the Nionian quarters at the palace in Bianjing she had been a been a prisoner no one had sought or expected, someone of high but complicated status, to be treated like a guest, at least while the uncertainty lasted. Noriko remembered her dressed in silk, crouched in a chair like a bird of prey on a branch, extending a tense authority over the space she was held in. Noriko knew it would not be like that now, but that was the image in her mind as the car passed through the prison gates. Praetorians walked on either side of her, and the prisoners she passed in the yard were herded rapidly away as she approached. But they saw her, and they knew who she was, or at least recognised her as Nionian, and they had begun to jeer and spit before the guards could hurry her inside. The prison guards themselves glowered and bristled as they looked at her; no one else had even spoken to her. A Roman warship had been sunk in the Promethean Sea two days before.

A female warder shut the door of the starkly lit interview room and lugubriously pulled out a chair for her. Noriko ignored it, staring. Una was sitting waiting for her, chained by her wrists to the edge of the high metal-topped table; Noriko saw the cast on her wrist and the slumped posture first – Una's head was down, as it had been the first time Noriko had seen her, but now her lank hair had been sawn off at jaw-level, and pale brown roots showed above the fading dye. Then she looked up and Noriko saw the deep purple-black stain printed with strange neatness onto one eye like an official stamp, and the bruises and scrapes mottled across the rest of her face.

Noriko felt at once faint and electric with rage. So she had been lied to; she had humiliated herself for nothing. She wanted to sweep Una up and plough through the building like a hurricane and deposit her hundreds of miles from these barbarians' reach. She said thickly, 'You were not supposed to be hurt.'

Una smiled with one corner of her mouth and gestured at her face with an air of weary apology. 'Most of it's from when I fell off the train.'

'Most of it?'

'They wanted to know where Varius was.' Una looked down, picked with swollen fingertips at the edge of the cast, adding mildly, 'I told them the truth. He came with us as far as Germania. I don't know where he went after that.'

Noriko dropped into the chair almost involuntarily; her legs were shaking.

Una glanced up at her again. 'No one's touched me since then. Thank you.'

'You should not have to thank anyone,' said Noriko.

Una fidgeted with the cast again and laughed. 'Why do you think they put this thing on me? It's ridiculous!'

'I wish—' began Noriko, and stopped herself, conscious that she did not want the stolid wardress to hear her wishes, which were in any case self-evident and would not help.

'How are you?' asked Una quietly.

'Oh—!' Noriko parted her hands a little, at the strangeness of being asked by someone in Una's physical state, and the difficulty of answering. 'He wants to marry me.'

Una did not speak, did not repeat the warning she had given Noriko a year and a half before, but they looked at each other, and Una extended her better hand a little across the table. Noriko slid her own forward to meet it, an overlap rather than a grip.

'One day people will come to their senses,' said Noriko, hearing it come out shriller and more desperate than she had meant.

Una nodded, slowly, without any certainty, but accepting the sentiment. She asked, 'They haven't found my brother, have they?'

Noriko shook her head, and Una smiled again. She looked

almost relaxed, almost peaceful, thought Noriko, though neither of those words could be the right one.

'Listen,' said Noriko, 'Marcus had something – a hat, made of blue wool. You gave it to him, I think?'

Una tensed. 'He told you that?'

'No. I do not think he meant me to see it. But I did see it. And it was not like anything else he had. It did not look like something a prince would own. But I could tell it was important. And I could tell . . .' Una would not like to think about Noriko's life with Marcus, she thought, and hurried past the memory of it. 'It is in the coffin with him.'

No tears came into Una's eyes, but they went wide, and she trembled. 'Thank you,' she whispered.

'Time's nearly up,' announced the wardress at the door. 'One more minute.'

'Oh, this is unbearable,' Noriko exclaimed in impulsive Nionian, which made the woman's expression of aggrieved distaste deepen. She amended in Latin, 'No, a little longer – please.' She realised the woman thought she had said something obscene, and wished she had.

Una leaned forward. 'Can you come again?'

'I do not know. I doubt it. I will try.'

Una's eyes slid towards the wardress and back, and Noriko knew there was something she wanted to say without letting the woman understand.

'I don't want it to be in the arena,' she remarked, her voice almost offhand, though now there was that sharpness and tension in her face that Noriko remembered; it had scarcely shown before.

As she felt herself grow cold, Noriko tried to convince herself she had briefly fumbled the Latin, had not been concentrating hard enough. She said, 'What?'

'It's not the dogs,' said Una, 'or whatever other way they'll do it – well, of course it is that too. But all those people watching . . . I hate thinking about it.'

'The dogs?' repeated Noriko stupidly.

'If I could be alone,' said Una, in a low voice, 'if there was no one there, it would be easier.' She'd raised her hands, furtively, meaningfully, towards her throat.

And Noriko understood what she was being asked for: a drug, a blade, if she could find any way of providing it.

'That's it,' said the woman curtly. 'She'll go back to her cell now.'

'I will try to come back,' promised Noriko unsteadily.

The wardress had opened the door and guards began crowding into the room.

Noriko wanted to defy them all somehow, and as she stood up she bowed her head and said formally, 'Lady Noviana.'

Una grinned. 'I think you can call me Una now.'

Noriko let them lead her to the doorway; stopped there. 'I hope you will meet him in a better life,' she said.

Cleomenes had a good enough reason for being in the prison; he'd been spinning out an interview with a gangster he'd put away last year. Now he was loitering in the hall through which he thought the Princess would leave, making conversation with a warder and hoping no one would wonder why he didn't go away.

Between the fuss over the Imperial wedding the year before and the Roman boys dying out on the Promethean Sea he felt a mild thrill despite himself when he saw her coming, at once star-struck and slightly defensive. He found himself a little disappointed she was wearing such unexotic Roman clothes and had all that hair piled up in a large dark knot on the back of her head, though he could see the good sense in it from her perspective.

'My Lady,' he said, showing his papers, 'Commander Diodorus Cleomenes. Could I have a word?'

The Princess already looked strained and besieged among her guards. Now she froze and looked up at Cleomenes with the kind of expression he was more used to seeing on cornered shoplifters.

'It's all right, boys, I won't be a minute,' Cleomenes said to the Praetorians. He was afraid to think what might happen if this got back to his superiors, but he was hoping there was no reason these men should think to mention it to anyone. He was just a senior member of the vigiles as far they were concerned.

The Princess followed him reluctantly into an anteroom and stood looking down at her clasped hands.

'How is she?' he asked. 'What did she say?'

'I saw her so briefly,' she replied politely, looking away.

'Have they hurt her much?'

'She is fortunate to receive Roman justice,' avowed Noriko virtuously, though with what must have been a restrained lash of irony.

'Madam, we've only got a few minutes. There's plainly something you're worried about telling me. Listen' – he looked around and lowered his voice to a hiss – 'you can trust me. Didn't your husband ever tell you what happened back in '57? When they had him locked up in the Sanctuary at Tivoli? I was there. So was she.'

'How interesting,' said Noriko, through teeth that were clenched tight with evident panic.

Cleomenes lost patience. 'Damn it, woman, it's not a trick! I'm not trying to trap you! I'm taking a huge risk myself in talking to you. Will you pull yourself together and talk to me?'

Noriko's mouth dropped slightly open. She remarked, 'You cannot speak to me like that,' and then she began to laugh in a brittle, desperate way that made Cleomenes fear she'd burst into tears next.

'I can't go near her myself,' he said more gently. 'All I'm asking is how she is.'

To his relief Noriko controlled herself. 'You are concerned for her?'

'Her and others. Yes.'

Sulien knew how he needed to look, but he couldn't walk into an expensive shop dressed in travelling clothes he hadn't changed in three days and try to kit himself out like a nobleman. He would have to heave his way up through the classes in stages, a self-made man's career compressed into a single afternoon. But trying

188

to rehearse it in thought made him feel cold and faint as if with vertigo—

No, no, just start doing it, he told himself, start doing it now.

The market reminded him painfully of the one in Tolosa where they had met Marcus, and the little stall with green curtains behind which he and Una had been almost safe. Sulien shook away the association and went to work. First, he bought a secondhand set of plain, formal clothes, as good as he could find in the quarter of an hour he had allowed himself. He was half-convinced that even the contrast between the new clothes and those he was wearing would be striking and suspicious – worse, he felt as if desperation was scrawled all over him. He was taken aback when a figure at the edge of his vision turned out to be himself in a mirror, looking quite ordinary and undramatic – very pale, eyes hollow and lips tight, if you looked closely at them – but still just himself, just a man in a city, not some misshapen creature in human clothes roaming about loose. No one had demanded he explain himself –why should they?

He went on to the city baths. For the last few days he'd made do with bottles of water and packs of wipes to make himself look passably normal, but he needed to be cleaner than that now, and he needed a place to change. Hurried as his bath was, his body basked gratefully in the heat, without his permission. This didn't feel like an acceptable use of time, even though it was necessary, even though he knew he couldn't leave for Persia before tomorrow.

She's not dead, and they're not going to kill her today, he thought. Anything else can be fixed, yes, it can. But these promises to himself made his heart race and trip instead of calming him, and he tried to stop making them.

He walked out in the faintly musty new clothes with his hair combed neatly back from his forehead and tried to carry himself differently, to keep his head up. He started towards the better clothes shops up in the centre—

No, wait, not that yet. By the time he reached them he'd already need to seem like a rich man on some long business trip, and the costume he needed for that went beyond clothes. He'd seen a place in the market selling reasonably impressive luggage sets, but – this was like some stupid logic puzzle that had to be completed in the right order – they'd have to have something in them so they wouldn't feel empty when handled.

He found a set of encyclopedias in a bookshop a few streets away from the market. 'Oh, this is just what I'm looking for,' he volunteered to an indifferent assistant, stuttering a little. 'My— My father collects this kind of thing.' Was that plausible? Were they obviously not what a collector would want? 'Getting them around is the only trouble . . . Do you think someone could help me carry them down to the market near the docks? I was going to need to buy some extra cases anyway.'

So he went back to the market, chose a pair of grandiose suitcases made of burgundy leather, almost too bulky for him to carry around himself even when empty, and loaded them with the books, padding the gaps with the clothes he'd been wearing before.

They were hiring out slave workers near the docks, extra hands for loading and unloading the cargo ships and fishing boats, for building jobs up in the town, and to fetch and carry for travellers like himself. They might all be nominally for sale, though no one looked to be buying; the dealers saw Sulien coming and visibly brightened. They gestured for the slaves slouching on the low stage to stand up straight while calling to him, 'Need a porter, sir? Looking for a bodyguard while you're in town? Sir, very good value assistance for you, sir!'

Most of the slaves were men, and Sulien's age or older, with their skills and prices marked on signs hanging round their necks. But Sulien cringed at the sight of a couple of pitiful girls, fourteen at most, sitting hunched on the edge of the platform. I can't, he thought as he approached, and remembered thinking the same thing sitting beside the fare-car driver, before he'd done . . . whatever he had done. Well then.

His mind wouldn't stop keening to itself, but he strode up briskly and managed to put on a good show of studying the line of slaves. 'Yes, I need a couple of decent porters for the afternoon,' he said quietly to the nearest dealer, trying to make his voice sound firm and confident, vaguely surprised when it worked.

'Well, take your pick; they're all of them strong enough. How about this one? Very reliable.'

Sulien scanned the line again, and not just for the sake of realism. All the descriptions of him had mentioned his height. It might look less if he was one of a group of taller people, even if the others were slaves stooped under the weight of his book-filled cases.

'Hope that's not too heavy for you,' he said as he walked away with the two men he'd picked. Like a fool, as if the kind of person he was trying to be would have worried.

One of the men looked mildly unnerved; the other grinned. Sulien was both baffled and helplessly grateful. 'It won't be that far,' he added, despite scoffing despairingly at himself in his head.

'Don't you worry, sir, I'm used to it,' said the man easily.

Sulien nodded and made himself stare straight ahead until the impulse to explain that he had been a slave himself and to apologise had more or less worn off.

He led his small entourage around the better shops selling ready-made clothes – not that there was a great deal of choice here, nor that the clothes on offer were quite as well-made and fashionable as the increasingly fawning shop assistants seemed to think. Gradually, a garment at a time, he replaced almost everything he was wearing and let the assistants press expensive accessories on him – rings, and a silk neckcloth that cost almost as much as the rest of the outfit put together. Groomed and elegant now, his reflection seemed unconnected to him, like a figure painted on the glass.

The grandest guest house he could find was a large, ambitious building with marble floors in the wide entrance hall. It was not old, but it had a slightly morose air about it, and inside the paint was peeling and the air cold. Sulien affected a faint swagger as he approached the desk, the two slaves heaving his luggage and shopping behind him.

'I need a room for tonight,' he announced at the desk, wondering if there should have been some loftier, more obnoxious way of saying it.

'Do you need quarters for your slaves as well?' asked the clerk.

'They're just hired men. Had to leave my valet back in Dahae. Damned inconvenient. Food poisoning or something.'

They discussed what rooms were available, and at what price. Sulien asked for the best. He was just debating with himself when he should make his next move when the manager, probably curious, emerged from an office adjoining the lobby.

'Oh yes,' said Sulien, as if it were an afterthought, glad he still had the slaves waiting behind him providing the right background, 'I need to take the first ferry over to Tapuria tomorrow – you can sort out the tickets for me, can't you?'

'Of course, sir,' said the manager, 'I'll just need your identity papers,'

'What, just to wander over to Tapuria?' said Sulien incredulously, and sighed. 'Gods above, this ridiculous war. This provincial mentality. We're all Romans, aren't we? It's not as if I'm going anywhere serious.' He sighed again and reached for the finely tooled wallet he'd bought twenty minutes ago. How much was enough? Fifty sesterces? Better make it a hundred. He wagged the folded notes with a long-suffering air. 'Oh well, you can probably deal with it.'

'You don't have your papers on you, sir?'

'My valet usually handles that sort of thing,' said Sulien, shrugging, and slid the notes across the counter.

The manager looked pious. 'Well, I can't make any promises, sir, but we'll do our best for you.' He took the money.

Sulien wanted him to make a promise, and so for a moment disliked him intensely.

*

He arranged for the slaves to come back the following morning. He tipped them and almost everyone else who came near him extravagantly; burning through his money was beginning to give him a thin, feverish pleasure.

Left alone at last, he looked around the suite: it was slightly cold, and slightly faded, but this was by far the most comfortable space he'd been in in months. The soft carpet muffled his footsteps.

He considered the longvision, but he couldn't bear to look for news of Una now, and he couldn't turn it on for noise or distraction, knowing that such reports must be happening. He sat on the bed, staring at the blank screen, and thought of crying, but someone would come to the door soon – the manager, to tell him whether or not he had done all this for nothing, or the vigiles, come to arrest him – and he didn't want to be found in tears by any of them.

There were always sounds in the prison: shouts and doors banging, and, for Una, the busy, wounded mutter of so many other minds, like heavy rain against a window, or as if the prison were a medicine chest on board a ship, and every prisoner a bottle rattling in its drawer.

But for now, from minute to minute, the cell was quiet enough to let her rest, shoring up the stillness and solitude within herself. I will always be grateful to Noriko for this, Una thought, and then considered what that meant now – 'always'. Two, three weeks? Or perhaps longer, perhaps forever. Delir and Lal believed in Heaven, they would believe she had gone there. She thought, with a deep, hesitant thrill, of being unfolded like silk, out of her body and out of the world, pitched into an immensity in which neither she nor Marcus would be lost.

Even two weeks seemed very long indeed, her sense of time had so loosened and changed.

Sometimes she tried to think of Sulien – not of him now, but in that better time in the future, call it ten years, to be safe. His friends, his wife. She wouldn't imagine them in much detail, because these must be real people that she would never meet, not characters she was inventing; she needed to leave space for them to fill. But perhaps if she thought of him, say, coming home from work, heading from one safe place to another, only briefly alone between—

But no, it was not safe to think of him at all, because if none of it was going to happen, if he was racing away from that future instead of towards it, if right now . . . ? And how could peace and terror be wrapped up so close within each other, within this little room where she slept dreamlessly, where there was nothing to be done? She'd heard the guards talking, about the arena, or other ways it might happen – burning— Oh God, she was only human; she could not bear that much physical pain, not with people *watching*. No one was meant to be able to bear that. And Noriko wasn't going to be able to come back and save her from it, she knew that really. Why should Drusus let her?

There were people coming towards her cell – not just the usual guards, though they came in first after they unlocked the door. Una stood up, back against the wall, her shoulders raised, as Drusus walked into the room. He was wearing his uniform, the black cloth mournfully splendid, the gold at his shoulders and at his breast gleaming in the stark light.

They stood separated by the width of the cell, staring at each other.

'Everyone out,' he said.

The guards withdrew, closing but not locking the door behind them. Neither Una nor Drusus moved.

Una tilted her head slowly, studying the uniform. She asked, 'Does it make you feel brave, wearing that?'

Drusus strode across the room, seized her shoulders and knocked her back once against the wall. 'What are you? A slave? A whore, aren't you? Weren't you? It's past time you remembered what you are *for*.' He swung her round onto the bed, threw himself down on top of her. She was thinner, more weary now than that other time he'd been so close to her, struggling against her on the roof of the Palace, and this time she did not fight him. She felt like almost nothing between him and the thin mattress; she was vanishing underneath him, like bones in clay. He thought he would be glad that she was so weak, so incapable, but instead he felt as if somehow she were escaping from him, and he shook her, slammed himself against her, to try and pin her there.

'What is to stop me?' he demanded hoarsely, close to her face. 'What is to stop me now?'

Una had closed her eyes, gasping a little with the impact of his weight. She said, 'Nothing.' And then, raggedly, she began to laugh. She opened her eyes and looked into his. 'Nothing. You can do anything you want with me; you're going to kill me. And you're still afraid of me. You'll be afraid of me even after I'm dead.'

Drusus didn't mean to listen to her, or to stop; he meant to make it worse for her for laughing. But cold breathed through him and when he looked at her face it felt as if he were the one vanishing, as if she were lying on her back looking up at empty space. That strange mist of horror around her on that hot day in the garden of the Golden House a year and a half ago, that sense of being too close to something monstrous and wrong and deadly, it was here, shut in the room with him. He remembered the Sibyl's warning coming unlocked in his mind the moment before the Colosseum roof erupted inwards – and he scrambled back from Una and off the bed, was on his feet before he could think what he was doing.

'As if I could stand it with you. I don't know what Marcus ever saw in you. Ugly thing.'

Una sat up slowly, pulling her clothes straight. She had a slightly huddled, flinching posture now, her arms drawn in across her body. But she watched him, frowning, mouth a little open, and she looked strangely fascinated.

He hadn't liked her looking through him, as if he were nothing but a current of air, but this detached, inquisitive staring was no better. He didn't want to move closer to her again, but he made himself do it to strike her across the face. The blow landed more half-heartedly than he had meant, but perhaps that was just as well; better if there were no bruises on her when she appeared in front of any cameras.

Una did not react, other than to settle her gaze on a patch of wall away from him.

He had not finished yet. He reached into an inner pocket of his tunic and held up a razor blade.

Una's eyes moved over it briefly with no change in expression.

'Did you want this?' Drusus asked. 'The Princess went to some trouble, I think, trying to get hold of it. Now what reasons could she have, a lady like her, stealing such a strange thing, and all the while begging me to let her pay you another visit? I understand. She is soft-hearted. I forgive her. But you won't see her again.'

He went to the door, slapped on it once.

'Get rid of this for me, would you?' he said, handing the blade to the guard who came in response.

'Are you finished, Sir?' asked the man.

Drusus turned back to Una. 'No.'

The door was closed again.

'Have you seen the arena hounds?' he asked. 'You must have seen pictures, at least, but have you ever seen them at work? Have you thought how they came to exist? They used to set men against lions once, in the arenas. And they had tigers too – bigger than leopards, they were supposed to be, and they had different markings. I wish they could have managed to keep a few pairs alive, it must have been magnificent to see. But when they realised there were none left, so they began breeding dogs to try to make a substitute. It took years of experiments, countless failures . . . People who remembered lions wouldn't have been impressed by a single dog, would they, however large it was? But imagine ten, or twenty of them, moving like one creature, one mind between them. They're bred for pack instinct, as well as power. Of course they're so inbred now that they don't live very long; they go blind, and the size of them puts strain on the heart. But any one of them could kill you in a moment if it went for your throat. A pack of them could tear you apart in a second and there wouldn't be anything worth watching. Perhaps that's how it happens sometimes, in the provinces, with badly trained dogs, handlers who don't know what they're doing. But not here in Rome. Not in the Colosseum.'

Una sank her attention into the white paint on the rough-plastered wall, away from him.

'The hounds are released from the gates. All of them white, you can't tell them apart – you can hardly see where one begins and another ends. They surround the criminal, and first they might bite a little, their claws might gash your skin, they'll pass a few minutes that way. You'll be bleeding, but you won't be dying, not yet. Then they gather in a mass, and for a moment they'll be . . . *still*. Then it's almost like cattle stampeding: they'll run the criminal down, charge over him. They're heavy animals, and sometimes their weight breaks bones, but that won't kill you. You'll still be able to run – they will try to get you running. Then they'll close in again, and now they might start tearing, ripping pieces off you: flesh from the thighs, the hands – sometimes with a woman, they'll go for her breasts. But they know to pace it, they'll fall back, then they'll charge again. It should never take less than twenty minutes. Sometimes it can last as long as an hour.'

Soon he would be gone, and she'd never have to see him again. He would be there in the Imperial Box, where Marcus had died, but she need not look at him. As for what he was saying, well, it was not as if she hadn't known it would be terrible, but it was not happening now; so she needed only to work not to let her body betray her; not breathe faster; to keep her hands from tightening on the edge of the bed, or on each other.

'Princess Noriko has been appealing for you to be spared this,' said Drusus quietly, 'ever since I allowed her to see you, and all the more fervently since her attempts to cheat justice on your behalf were discovered. Finally I said to her, I will put it in her own hands. So, here I am. You can be executed like a Roman citizen, quickly, privately, if that's what you choose. If you co-operate with the prosecution at your trial.'

Una wanted to rest her head in her hands, or against the wall, but not while he was here. 'What do you want me to say?'

'I want you to confess that you are a traitor to Rome.'

'I won't say I helped kill Marcus,' said Una, dully. 'I can't say that.'

'You can say you are guilty of giving help and comfort to Rome's enemies. You can say you have attempted to defect to them. You can say you have conspired against the Emperor.'

Una thought of the money she had put into Varius' bag and reflected that that, at least, was true – though not the rightful Emperor, she added to herself, and then wondered wearily why she thought it worth bothering with the distinction. 'What does it matter?' she asked. 'Why do you care what I say?'

Drusus frowned, puzzled. 'I want there to be no confusion. I want people to understand what they're watching.'

Despite herself, and even expecting to be struck for it, Una found herself staring at him again, bewildered and curious. She murmured, helplessly, 'I can't seem to understand you. The way you think . . .'

Drusus shook his head, dismissing this. 'Well, you know I'm telling you the truth, don't you? You know this is a real offer. This is why I came. Don't you think it's fair?'

Una gave a raw laugh. 'Yes,' she said. 'I think it's fair.'

'And do you accept it?'

'Yes,' said Una.

Drusus gave no sign of satisfaction. He crossed the room, gripped the wrist that wore the cast and dragged her to her feet. He held her in front of him for a moment, as if uncertain what to do, then with a shudder he dropped her to the floor and left.

There, that's all right, that's done, Una thought, crawling back onto the bed and pulling the blanket over herself. It was a shame to have to concede anything to him, to let him score that final point over her, and certainly that was what she had done. But she was almost there; nothing more would be asked or taken from her.

And yet it was true: he had been afraid of her. Her chest hitched again with painful laughter. You were right not to give up, Varius! she thought.

Down at the port, Sulien watched the slaves piling his cases onto the loading racks beside the ship. Everything was slow and chaotic; the disgruntled crowd on the quay pulsed and drifted in unpredictable spasms, and no one even seemed to know what time the ferry would leave. The sky was bright, the water smooth and still. Sulien closed his eyes and breathed the cold air off the sea, trying to take some relief in being out of the guest house. He knew he should stay out of sight, yet he'd spent most of the night in the bar downstairs because he couldn't sleep, and couldn't stand the silence in his room. In the morning he'd ordered and been unable to eat an expensive breakfast. He had spent more than three thousand sesterces in one day and had only a couple of hundred left.

A man had come from the hiring stand across the dock to take the slaves back. Sulien was exasperated at the silly twinge he felt at letting them go without explaining why he'd made use of them; it was just as well the almost overwhelming temptation to talk to them was gone.

At last they were letting passengers aboard. He squared his shoulders, walked up to one of the armed border guards standing at the ramp, produced the ticket the guest house manager had handed him, and waited for disaster to crash in on him—

The man looked at the signature scrawled on the back of it and said, 'Oh, yes, sir, that's fine.'

Sulien slid a couple of notes into his hand, trying not to show how empty his wallet was now, and walked incredulously up the ramp, half believing they were just giving everyone on the quayside a laugh at how stupid he'd been before shooting him.

He locked himself into his first class cabin. It was small, and not very luxurious by Mediterranean standards, but there were a lot of faded cushions everywhere, and some lustreless fruit in a bowl beside the bed. He had twenty hours till landfall, if he got that far, if they didn't come now and break the door down. He wanted to get out of the softly sterile room almost at once, and yet he lay down on the bed, not expecting to sleep with his body simmering with panic, but not knowing what else to do with himself, where else to be.

When he opened his eyes the light had changed, and the ship was hours out to sea, the movement so smooth that he hadn't felt it begin, and couldn't feel it, even now.

Sulien wandered up to the third deck and found a lounge where a large elderly woman with dyed-black hair was trying to entertain a listless assembly of other passengers, singing terrible love songs in a strong, sombre voice. Sulien sank into a seat and stared at her until she was finished, grateful for anything to fill even part of his mind, push out what was there.

When that was over, and after trying to eat again, he went out onto the promenade deck and stood there sightlessly facing the sea. It was a long time before he realised how cold he'd grown.

At Rhages, Delir's brother-in-law drove past him twice because it didn't occur to him that the supercilious-looking young man in expensive clothes standing by a stack of leather cases could be the one he was looking for.

Varius had bought Lal as much privacy aboard the train as possible; even her meals were brought to her little single-berth compartment. Lal thought he had intended her to stay out of sight for the whole journey, except when she changed trains at Byzantium. But everyone else wandered up and down the sleeper car, groaning and chatting, dodging occasional charges of restless children; it would have made her more conspicuous, she decided, to be the one person holed up in her room. And when she was left alone for too long she felt her thoughts begin to darken and sink; there was a cold well at their centre which she dared not investigate.

In any case, a Persian woman who was travelling with her daughters in a compartment along the carriage had discovered her and, disapproving of an unmarried girl travelling by herself, she absorbed Lal into her family for the length of the journey. Lal did not much mind this, though it was a strain having to disguise how anxious she was, and when she failed, to think of explanations. She stayed as close to the truth as she could, and not only because it was easier: 'A friend of mine's ill,' she said. 'They say she's going to die. She's only young, it's not fair. And I don't know what will happen to her family.' Of course, then she had to supply a suitable illness – heart trouble, she said, vaguely – and she disguised Una and Sulien further with Persian names, a widowed mother and a home in Aspadana.

She knew the women would be kind about it: 'Your friend is in God's hands, whatever happens,' the mother assured her, clasping Lal's hands between hers, and Lal hoarded the sympathy and the promises of prayers, hoping they might add up to something that could be transferred to Una and Sulien, like investments or property.

Only ten days till Una's trial now. The journey was slower than it would have been a year ago, now that the train stopped at every provincial border for security guards to pace along its length, inside and out, checking everyone's tickets and papers again. Lal tried to be with the Persian family at these times, so her papers were handed over with theirs. Her stomach twisted every time, even though she knew it was unlikely her careful forgeries would be subjected to anything more stringent than a quick glance now.

And she was constantly afraid that someone would knock on the door while she was trying to work on Sulien's travel papers, though the movement of the train wouldn't allow her to do anything very precise.

Rain dragged at the windows as the train skimmed through Greece and Thrace. Straying a little way from the station at Byzantium while she waited for the connection, Lal glimpsed towers and domes glowing across the Bosphorus and found them dimly familiar: she'd been a little girl, coming west with her father after her mother's death. Lal thought of her mother with a pang, and with it came the thought that it was incredible that anyone lived to be old, that there were not scars and missing pieces on everyone. Lal herself had had no business surviving her illness the year before. The war was lapping around the edges of the Empire, consuming both inwards and out. And Sulien, rushing across Persia towards her – what was she bringing him to?

No, this was why she needed to keep herself occupied and around people, to keep these useless thoughts from taking hold.

She met the girls and their mother back at the station, and was soon ensconced in their compartment again, though her own was further away this time. The train slid through the tunnel beneath the strait.

Bahram left the van a short distance from the terminus at Urmia and went to the station by himself. Sulien sat with a volume of the encyclopaedias he'd bought in Issedoneum, on a mattress in the back. He'd hidden here for the past three days, shivering through the nights under piles of blankets while the van was parked outside whichever guest house Bahram was sleeping in. He had scarcely seen daylight, except when he stumbled out of the van at charging stations, or onto bare stretches of road, to empty his bladder or to walk the cramps out of his legs.

Bahram had been irritable and resentful at first, barely speaking to Sulien except to grumble about Delir calling out of the blue to insist that he take this risk. Even so, Sulien was glad he was there, even as a silent, moody presence sealed off in the cab. At least he was someone with whom there needed to be no more pretence. And at the end of the first day, when they were almost two hundred miles clear of the Caspian Sea and hadn't yet crossed a checkpoint, Bahram had, grudgingly, grown friendly enough to pat Sulien's shoulder and mutter, 'I'm sorry about all this with your sister. It might come out all right at the trial, somehow.'

Sulien had been trying to read an entry on the valves of the heart for what felt like hours; the facts were familiar, even comforting, but the words were a tortuous conveyer belt that kept returning him mysteriously back to the beginning. A week until the trial – *a week*. And it would take him at least three more days to reach Rome.

Bahram must be on his way back now, with whoever it was. Sulien climbed out of the van – it was dark, should be safe enough – and saw Bahram turning the corner of the street, and beside him was Lal.

He almost shouted her name, and the effort of swallowing it brought tears to his eyes. She saw him and charged at him, dropping her bag as she reached him, and embraced him, pulling him down into a stoop so she could wrap more of herself around him. They kissed, without thinking.

'Come on, stop that,' said Bahram, embarrassed.

Sulien broke the kiss, remembering that Bahram was Lal's uncle. Lal didn't move away from him but fastened herself to his arm, her fingers warm around his.

He couldn't speak at first. 'I'm so glad you're here,' he managed at last.

'I am too,' she said.

She took a picture of him against the side of the van, then frowned and raised the camera again, saying gently, 'Try not to think about any of it; just for this one second.'

Looking at the first picture, Sulien understood: pinned by the flash against the white panel of the van his face looked hunted and famished: a fugitive's face.

Lal climbed inside the van and began trying to clear a space in which to work. She sighed at the dim light, but Bahram produced a torch from the cab and handed it to Sulien to hold steady for her. She began to set out her disguised materials – the fluids had been decanted into perfume and lotion bottles in a make-up case and the sheets of plastic were closed inside a photograph album. Sulien remembered watching her work in her painted cabin in Holzarta and felt a small, pleasant stir of nostalgia.

'This is what your father has you doing?' asked Bahram sadly.

'Not much any more,' said Lal, in a brisk, cheerful voice, ignoring the implied disapproval. 'Someone has to.'

It was four hours before they could get a berth on a train heading back towards Byzantium. Sulien tried to give Bahram some of the expensive items from Issedoneum that he no longer needed – the rings and the neckcloth, the wallet. Bahram refused with dignity and they began a kind of reverse haggling over what he would accept (the books and one of the cases, in the end, and then only because there was no point in Sulien carrying them to Rome).

Lal, feeling sorry that she had no time to spend with her uncle, began, 'I'll try and come back when—' but in Sulien's presence she couldn't think how to finish the sentence: 'When it's all over' – what a dreadful thing to say! And how could it be over, even at the best?

'You should,' said Bahram, understanding. 'You have little cousins who'd like to see you.'

They sat leaning against each other after Bahram was gone, waiting for the train.

'Varius has money,' whispered Lal, 'a lot of money. Did he tell you?'

'He said something about it.'

'He'll help, you know that. We'll try everything. We haven't given up. We won't.' She meant this as she said it, but as soon as she finished speaking a chill went through her and made her grip Sulien's hand again.

There were two beds in the compartment, both narrow and, for Sulien, uncomfortably short, but they slept only in one, folded around each other. The next day they were never apart for more than a minute or two, and rarely not touching: their feet loosely tangled on the small strip of floor, their fingers entwined as they sat side by side, speaking little. But it was not until they were flying past the Thracian coast that Lal kissed him again.

Sulien drew her into his arms with a sigh and they sank back onto one of the little beds. Slowly, Sulien undid the fastenings of her dress, pulled it down over her shoulders. Lal felt as if her own body were a sheet of photographic film or drawing paper, on which she felt a terrible need to record him while there was still time. His skin seemed too cool, too pale. Anxiously she tried to leave tracings of warmth and colour on him with fingers and lips, until he went still—

'What is it?' whispered Lal.

'We can't.'

'Why not?'

'It's wrong,' murmured Sulien bleakly.

'No, it's not wrong,' said Lal, feeling her own breath hot against his throat, her body charged with determination and panic.

Sulien let his head fall back and closed his eyes. 'I have to get to her,' he said quietly. 'When we're in Rome I won't be able to think about anything else, Lal; I can hardly think of anything beyond that now. And if I can't do it . . . if I can't—'

And she couldn't bear how he looked, then, lying so still, with that expression on his face.

'I don't think I'll be any good to you – or anyone,' he murmured. 'And you mustn't do this because you want to help me, Lal, that's not right.'

'It isn't that,' said Lal, 'I want – I want—' Shyness and urgency silenced her and she dropped her mouth to his again, and despite what he had said his lips opened against hers and he clutched her, shifted and turned so that she was on her back.

'Well,' he said, his voice uneven, but with a flicker of a smile in it now, 'we're both still here.'

'We're both here.'

[VIII]

FIAT JUSTITIA RUAT CAELUM

'You were there,' Sulien interrupted as Cleomenes began to explain what Noriko had told him in the prison, 'you can get to Una—'

'No, Sulien,' said Cleomenes.

'You can, or you can get me in—'

'Sulien, I can't. They know I know you. *And* her. Going in there at all was pushing it – so's coming here, come to that. And what do you think we could do? Say we need to borrow her for a minute? I can't wander around wherever I like in the prison; I had authorisation to go as far as I did and no further. I can't get near her and that's that.' He paused, and then added warily and reluctantly, 'We could . . . I don't know, but I could maybe get something from her. The Princess said she was asking for some way of . . . well, killing herself.'

Sulien sat down, as speechless as if he'd been winded. He put his head into his hands. Beside him Lal laid a cold hand on his arm, Delir whispered something, a fragment of a prayer. But Ziye looked at the ground in a motion like a nod, her mouth grim, and Varius was watching him with grave, unsurprised sympathy, clearly having heard this already.

He'd been in Rome for only a few hours; there were four days left until Una's trial, and he was grateful that no one had yet tried to tell him to stop and rest. Ziye and Delir had been waiting at the cellar in the Subura. Varius had arrived shortly afterwards, Cleomenes unexpectedly with him.

Outside the cellar the dark city felt comfortably familiar, and that was jarring and awful – almost as if Rome had been waiting for them all these months, knowing they could never have got away, they would always have been forced back.

Cleomenes continued almost sheepishly: 'Seems she was worried about there being people around, watching it happen. She said she could face it better alone.'

'Alone,' Sulien heard himself repeating in a low, unfamiliar voice, somehow muffled, as if he had water in his ears. 'What do we do?' he moaned, into the black airlessness which had knotted itself around him.

He saw Varius and Cleomenes exchange a glance, and then Varius said softly, 'What she wants.'

Sulien started up, and then Lal was dragging on his arm, pulling him back, and Ziye was on her feet in a tense, ready stance. He was surprised; he hadn't exactly had the idea of hitting Varius; he didn't know what he'd been going to do. He gasped, 'No. No. Shut up.'

'Sulien,' began Varius again quietly, his expression more sincere and kind than Sulien could stand.

'No. I'm not *killing* her. She doesn't know what she wants; she's not in her right mind. She wasn't even before this, you know that, you know why. Just because *you* tried . . .'

A small acknowledging flinch pulled, very briefly, across Varius' face.

Ziye said, 'I'm sorry, but I've seen what happens when they use arenas for executions—'

'Don't,' Sulien begged her, 'don't tell me about that.'

'In that situation, wouldn't anyone want the same thing?' asked Varius.

'Not if they could get out.' His voice was coming to pieces. 'Varius, please, you said you'd help.'

Varius sighed, and looked a little less certain. 'Look— Of course, if there's any possible way. But if there's not—'

'There is! There has to be.'

'What if we lose the chance to do even this for her? What if you both end up in the Colosseum? I can't let that happen.'

Sulien swallowed, rubbed a hand through his hair. 'All right, maybe we can't get into the prison, but they've got to move her when the trial starts.' He looked at Cleomenes. 'You could find out how they're transporting her, couldn't you? And the route they'll take? If we could get the van to stop somehow, I mean, if there was an accident or a crowd of people in the street—'

'There won't just be a van; there'll be outriders on trirotas at the least, and they'll all be armed,' Cleomenes said, 'and they won't just lead the van into traffic and stand around scratching their heads.'

Lal said tentatively, 'Sulien and I were thinking on the train . . . maybe we could get vigile uniforms? I've got some vigile passes almost finished for Varius already.'

'How would that help? They'll have a team already assigned to do this; they'll all be from the same force. A uniform isn't going to stop people noticing you didn't work with them yesterday.'

'It wouldn't have to be like that,' Varius said, in a detached, neutral voice, frowning into space. Cleomenes looked at him, raised his eyebrows, and Varius spread his hands. 'I'm not saying it can work, but they – we – wouldn't have to pass ourselves off as part of the escort. In theory that shouldn't be a problem.'

Ziye said, 'But this can't be done in four days.'

'But we've got longer than that,' protested Sulien, 'we must have. Surely they won't just— They won't— Not that same day? The trial'll go on for a little while – they'll need to move her back and forth . . .'

'They'll probably keep her in the cells at the Basilica until it's over,' said Cleomenes.

'Well then, when it's over, when they take her back to the prison, or . . . or to the Colosseum . . .'

Cleomenes was silent for a while, looking down at the floor. 'All right, so somehow you stop the van,' he said quietly. 'There's a driver, a couple of guards inside it. What about them?'

'I'll kill them,' said Sulien at once, thickly.

Cleomenes nodded, as if this was what he'd expected to hear. 'Suppose you can. What would that make me if I helped you do it? They're just vigiles, they joined to try and make things a little better, like me. It's not their fault.'

Sulien, choking on a furious attempt to answer, drew a little unexpected hope when Varius broke in heatedly, 'If they're taking a nineteen-year-old girl to be torn apart by dogs, I'm not worried what happens to them either.'

'That's not fair, you know that's not what it's like – what are they supposed to do?'

'Refuse to do it,' answered Varius. 'You would, wouldn't you? Why else are you here?'

'Oh, come on – and what if they're just taking her to court?'

Sulien said fiercely, 'It's the same thing and you know it.'

Delir said, 'You can't go around killing people in the middle of the street.'

'But it's all right for them to kill my sister!' cried Sulien.

'It's not only a question of what's right or wrong; I do not think it will work,' said Delir firmly. 'There would be too much noise, and they will have guns of their own, as Cleomenes says. We must think of something else.'

Cleomenes shuffled uncomfortably on his bench. They were all silent again.

Ziye got up and began unpacking a bedroll from inside a chest. 'You'll need to sleep here, won't you?'

'What?' Sulien was startled; sleeping was such a distant consideration.

'It's late. I should get home,' announced Cleomenes.

'No,' said Sulien, panic rising again, 'please! I'm sorry if I— We can work something out if we keep going, *please*.'

'Sulien, if there's a way to do this, we're not going to have it by tomorrow,' said Varius.

'But we've hardly got anywhere,' said Sulien, feeling raw pressure building behind his eyes, and in his throat.

Ziye came close to him. 'This is enough for now, and more than you think. I don't think you know how tired you are.' She put her hands on his shoulders, her voice uncharacteristically gentle. 'You cannot make good plans or prepare yourself well in this state. You can believe me: I know something about being ready for a fight. You'll be surprised how things can come clear, if you let them.'

209

Varius left shortly after Cleomenes, promising to return the next morning, promising not to stop thinking.

Delir had a little pot of sleeping pills, new, perhaps bought specially for him. Sulien only noticed after he had accepted one how Ziye and Delir had altered what must be their usual sleeping arrangements around him. Ziye had quietly taken Lal off into the other room, leaving Sulien and Delir together, Delir taking what was probably Lal's bed. Sulien felt a flutter of guilty amusement before the pill began to work. He slid confusedly into sleep, from which he awoke in the dark, his throat raw from shouting, to find Delir crouched beside him, shaking his shoulder and lying softly, 'It's all right, it's all right.'

Tadahito's eye was caught by the machine guns, fanned out into a circle, like a sun, and fixed to the wall. They were of Nionian make and though glossy, not new. He felt slightly unnerved, and yet it was encouraging too, a reminder of the foundation upon which he had come to build. They were waiting for the King.

Beside him Kaneharu sighed softly. It had been a relief to be outside, travelling down through the mountains to Harar, after three weeks in a submarine crawling across the Indian Ocean, swaddled in such boredom that it had been hard to believe that above their heads a war was still going on. But here in Independent Ethiopia, the craters in the roads and the flocks of children picking across the rubble made it feel closer, even though these were the scars of other conflicts. And it was not only the occasional battles with the Romans or with the Nobatae or Luo that had left these scars and gouges on Harar. The kingdom had only one unshifting border, the hard line to the north where the Roman Empire cut Ethiopian lands in two. South of that line Africa might be outside the rule of any empire, but Rome's weight still lay upon it, throttling trade and deepening the famines that had raked through the horn of Africa over the past half-century.

As the princes had travelled through the city they had seen the remains of the old Roman monuments, slowly being stripped down for building materials, which were as scarce as everything else.

The palace itself was small, and built cheaply – no marble or glass trappings here – but it was new, and extravagant in shape, with its clusters of painted domes. The Princes were waiting with their retainers in a small state room overlooking a garden of dried-out roses. The King was apparently at prayers.

Tadahito suspected this might simply be the King's way of showing them he was not particularly keen to see them, but when at last the servants opened the door and Salomon the Sixth appeared, there was a distant look on his face that took a little time to fade away.

Marcus Kebede's claim of descent from the old Imperial house of Axum was, in Tadahito's view, somewhat far-fetched. The last of the dynasty had lingered on as a puppet monarchy under the Romans for centuries, but when the wave of uprisings against Roman rule in Africa had reached Ethiopia, Roman troops had taken them from the capital and probably slaughtered them; at any rate, they had never been seen again. Kebede's claim of Solomonic blood rested on stories of secret marriages and baby princes being smuggled away by nursemaids, but whatever the truth of his ancestry, he had emerged out of a cycle of civil wars twenty-one years before and assembled the splintered, petty kingdoms the Empire had left behind into Independent Ethiopia.

Now he was in his fifties, a short, bespectacled, thickset man. Around his neck hung a silver pendant, a complex lattice of diamond-shaped holes with a circle of rays flaring from the centre so that its shape – a cross – was scarcely recognisable.

He gestured to the servants who proffered little glasses of yellow honey-wine. He smiled. 'Your Highnesses, I am very glad you are here,' he said, but as the solemn, dreamy look that had lingered from his prayers faded, an uneasy combination of affability and wariness replaced it. His eyes were cool behind his small spectacles.

'I wish we were meeting in times of peace,' said Tadahito.

The King's eyes tightened dubiously, and yet he leaned forward in apparent sympathy. 'You wasted a lot of time trying to deal with the Romans and now they've turned on you – they've as good as broken you in Siam, haven't they? You cannot deal with them – they're all like this, vicious, evil. This madman they have leading them now—'

Tadahito sighed, thinking of all those months of work, of Noriko. 'Things would have been different if Leo the Younger had lived.'

'If there was anything good in him it would have perished one way or another. Goodness dies rather easily in this world, but especially in Rome,' said King Salomon, with an air of finality, and his fingers strayed briefly to the pendant round his neck.

They were both speaking Latin. Even now, more than a hundred and fifty years after the Romans had left, it was a first language for many Ethiopians – although the King prided himself on not being one of them, and spoke with a strong, unabashed accent that Tadahito found hard to understand at first. It was strange, Tadahito thought, to be discussing a mutual enemy in his own language.

'Well, we hope we can strengthen the bonds between our nations,' ventured Kaneharu, sipping cautiously at the honey-wine. They had already discovered that the sweetness masked how strong it was.

The restrained scepticism lurking in the King's expression finally surfaced. '*Bonds*,' he said. 'You sell us weapons; we pay for them. You sell them to the Luo and to the Nobatae too. This is not a special favour, not charity; it is a normal, everyday arrangement. I am not sure there is anything here that needs to be made stronger.'

'With our help you could unite your kingdom. You could take back Axum – the ancient capital,' urged Tadahito. 'And with your help we can defeat Rome.'

The King looked away. 'Your Highnesses, let us speak plainly: you are *losing*, and if your vast Empire cannot hold itself up, I do not think my poor kingdom can support you. I am sorry for you, but not so sorry I wish to fall with you.'

'May we show you what we propose?' asked Tadahito, softly. One of his retainers opened a scroll case and unrolled a folding den-ga screen on which a glowing map of the world appeared.

The King lifted his eyebrows a little and Tadahito felt suddenly embarrassed. Even in Rome they did not have these flexible screens yet; it looked both gauche and ostentatious here, as if it existed only to make a point. They could have done this just as well with paper.

He put his unease to one side and continued, 'Of course Rome's forces are fully engaged in Tokogane and in Asia. They will not interpret a small uprising in their Ethiopian territory as a serious threat; they will expect the regional government to deal with it. We would need you to commit Ethiopian troops, to disguise our presence here as long as possible, but we will arm them, and our Samurae forces will reinforce them. The submarine that brought us here is already inside the Gulf of Avalites; two more will arrive within days. From here Axum is within range of our missiles, and so are these cities on the coast of Arabia' – he indicated their positions on the illuminated map – 'and when our combined forces are poised outside Axum, we will launch them. Nothing the Romans have in the region should be adequate to defend it – or Ocelis, or Eudaemon. We will take command of the Deire Strait. We will trap Roman shipping in the Red Sea. And we will have made an incision deep into Roman territory. The Mediterranean provinces will no longer be safe from us. Egypt, Cyprus – Rome itself will not be safe.'

King Salomon watched, frowning, as the screen showed a fleet of warships and submarines moving up the Red Sea, haloes illustrating the range of their missiles blossoming around them. It looked like a game for children.

'And even if this is possible,' he asked, 'then what? A new Nionian Empire in Africa? Not here.'

'You would retain sovereignty over your kingdom, of course,' Tadahito said. 'It would be essential for us to operate within and across your borders. We would have to establish bases, for the duration of the war. But this would be a strategic arrangement, nothing more; we would take no part in any internal matters. It would not be permanent.'

The King peered at the screen again, and laughed. 'Well, of course – you would not walk up and say to my face, "Please give us your country?"'

'You have our word,' said Takanari, prompting a short roll of the eyes from the King.

'We are not in a position to make expansions into Africa,' said Tadahito. 'We want to drain resources from Rome; we want to gain time, not territory. Roman counter-attacks will come, of course, but we will defend our allies now and we will reward them later – because if we can only hold out now, we will win. We have a weapon – we call it Surijin. It is nearly perfected. We need only to stay in the war long enough to use it.'

'What's that thing they all wear?' asked Takanari later, gesturing at his chest. Many members of Salomon's court were wearing variations of the same symbol round their necks.

'You should not come here without learning something of the culture,' said Kaneharu. 'We had time enough on the boat.'

'It's a stylised cross. The method of execution.' Tadahito explained.

There was a pause and Takanari grimaced. 'They make jewellery of something like that? That's grotesque.' Crucifixion was still sometimes practised in Nionia.

'It will help us,' said Tadahito.

'Why?'

'Because it commemorates the death of their principal holy man,' said Tadahito, 'who was killed by the Romans.'

'Well if they come down the Via Didiana, there's this empty block overlooking it here. And there's a one-way street leading off it here, to the Via Atia. But I'm not sure it's busy enough round there for this to work,' murmured Varius, pushing aside the crumpled lists and half-plotted timetables to make room for the street map. 'But there's a building further along where you can get up the fire escape.'

They were in Varius' cupboard of a room, and Sulien was very thankful Varius was there, for whenever he was absent, Sulien felt an irrational grind of paranoia that perhaps he was out buying poison for Cleomenes to smuggle to Una. Or maybe it would be Ziye, or Cleomenes might do it alone, and make sure none of this went any further. Una had asked; what was there to stop them, if they thought it was right?

But Cleomenes had sent them to a supplier of vigile kit in the Horrea Galbae, and three sets of uniforms, bought with Varius' money, were folded in a bag under the table at Delir's. Sulien had been astonished that you could just walk in and order vigiles' caps and tunics as if they were any other suit of clothes. Delir did not like having them in the flat, but there was work still to be done on them; they needed brass on the collars and badges on the caps, and those were more difficult to come by. Cleomenes had brought one of his old uniforms, they'd spread the genuine insignia between them and fill the gaps with braid and military emblems from flea markets. There was a fluorescent jacket to cover the deficiencies of whichever tunic was least persuasive.

Varius tore off a fresh sheet of paper and began making yet another list, a refinement of the one before, working quickly through the points that were already established: the characteristics the site of interception must have, the items they still had to acquire, numbered schedules of action for each of them.

'What about the side street?' asked Sulien.

Varius shut his eyes as if trying to transmit himself there. 'Back walls, not many windows. There's a gate into a courtyard off the back of a caupona, where they put the bins out. That's a possibility, I suppose.'

Sulien smiled a little. 'How can you just *know* that?' he asked.

'I've been walking around a lot,' said Varius.

There were times when Sulien thought the rough beard and matted hair looked ridiculous on Varius; the careful, diligent civil servant was so evident underneath. But put him back in the office now and perhaps it would be the other way round: however you dressed him, he would remain a profoundly, comfortingly strange man.

'We need to time the journey from the Basilica to the prison and from the prison to the Colosseum,' Varius went on, 'and between all these points along the way. They'll clear the streets, so we'll do it at night when there's less traffic.'

It was the first day of Una's trial. Sulien's was beginning in his absence in some other court, but without him there it lacked all the drama howling around Una, and along with the rest of the empire, Sulien and Varius were not much interested in it. For now Varius' unreliable secondhand longvision was turned against the wall. They'd had the idea that they could work through it, not waste time tormenting themselves over how she looked and what was said about her. Cleomenes could tell them anything crucial later. But Sulien felt each minute like a small weight placed upon the last. And as it edged past noon, Varius too fell quiet, his pen slowing on the page, until they were both sitting in silence, doing nothing but watching the clock.

'This won't work,' Varius said at last, reaching out to turn the longvision round. 'We have to see it.'

For a moment they thought they had the wrong time or the wrong channel, because a man's face filled the screen and he was talking fiercely, straight to camera, and not about Una but about the war: '—on both our eastern and western borders, our soldiers are risking their lives, while our enemies in their weakness and fear snatch at what chances they can to scatter death and outrage in our provinces. And it is in this context that the seriousness of this case, this charge of treason against Rome and conspiracy against the Emperor, must be considered—'

It was the Praetorian Prefect in charge of the court, they realised.

Then they brought her in. An eager, hostile surge of noise erupted from the spectators in the gallery and the lictors moved forward, knocking their maces on the floor to quieten them.

Sulien felt his lungs tighten, as if that awful sound had somehow drawn air out of the room.

Una gave the camera a quick, self-conscious glance. Sulien, shocked when he saw her hacked-off hair, fought to stop himself from thinking how it had been done and by whom. There was something strange about her skin; for a moment he thought she was ill, then he remembered he'd seen her look like that before – the first time they'd seen each other since they were children – waxy make-up over bruises.

Her wrists and ankles were chained. As the two of them had limped eastwards from border to border, Sulien had thought that she'd begun to look older than she was. Now, between the heavyset men, she looked painfully young, younger than she'd ever seemed to him. Nevertheless, she was composed, and in a way he had expected that, he knew she wouldn't let them drag her in weeping and cowering. But this was not the exhausted, hopelessly enduring calm he'd watched soaking through her like a bleach as they drove away from the Rha into Sarmatia. She looked alert, and rather bemused. Her face quivered for a moment as she was led to a chair at the centre of the court, where she had to face the ranks of spectators directly. But as she sat down she seemed to recover herself, and then she lowered her eyes and shed any expression at all.

'I am Noviana Una,' she said, when told to give her name, laying slight but perceptible stress on the first part of it.

There was a stir in the court and a lean compact man in his fifties sprang up from his seat and cried out, 'Sir, that name was a privilege extended to her on emancipation. Her rights as a freed-woman have been revoked; she is no longer entitled to bear it. She has no right to a trial at all; only the monstrous scale of her treachery, the fact that the entire Roman people are her victims, dictate that her crimes be examined in public, rather than that she be sent straight to the beasts as she deserves.'

Sulien tried to swallow away the dryness in his throat. Varius looked sick too, and said, 'That's Hirtius.'

The name sounded dimly familiar to Sulien, he was famous for prosecuting . . . someone. He shook his head. It made no difference who he was. Convulsively he pulled the map closer, to get back to work again, for the reassurance of being active. But he couldn't look away from the longvision, or turn it off.

'We have not yet begun,' said the prefect. He asked Una, 'Do you acknowledge this confession?' An attendant had passed him a document several pages long; others were handing out copies to the panel of senators seated around him on the platform.

'Yes,' said Una, and did not speak again for the rest of the sessions that day.

Hirtius stepped forward with a rolling flex of the shoulders, a swivel of the neck, an athlete's final warm-up. In a loud, confident voice, he began to speak again: 'Prefect, senators, you will find in those pages a catalogue of crimes you might expect it would take a Spartacus a lifetime to achieve. Instead, what do you see before you? A young girl, who at first sight you might think incapable of conceiving such vicious thoughts and harbouring such depraved feelings. Perhaps your first instinct is to pity her. Yet that soft-heartedness, though most fitting to her age and sex, is alien to her nature and wasted upon her. She herself admits that in her earliest years she was infected by, and gave herself utterly to, an unnatural will to undermine, betray and destroy the security of Rome. She was a slave, and yet escape from her legal owners was not enough for her. The privilege of lawful freedom was not enough for her. So great was her desire for power, and so strong her malicious influence upon others, that she insinuated herself into the highest reaches of legitimate authority. She was a friend and supporter of Dama, the leader of that infamous group of anarchist slaves and arsonists, the tools Nionia used to cause such destruction – I will not say untold destruction, judges, for indeed it *must* be told: every loss of property and life must here be named and remembered.

'And no one here can have forgotten what came of it. The Colosseum stands barely a stone's throw from where we sit; the walls that witnessed the assassination of the late Emperor Titus and his nephew, Marcus Novius, are not yet whole. Finally, she was arrested in the act of attempting to defect to Nionia, in a time of war.'

Sulien and Varius, horridly transfixed through all this, both started as the longdictor emitted a long chirrup. After eyeing it distrustfully for another second Varius lifted the circlet as if it might carry disease and said in that same wary voice Sulien had heard in the longdictor chamber in Issedoneum, 'Yes?'

Sulien rose anxiously to his feet as he recognised Cleomenes' voice, muffled as it was on the other end of the line. 'Are you watching it?'

'Yes,' answered Varius.

Cleomenes said something Sulien couldn't make out. Varius closed his eyes and sat down heavily on the bed, bowing his head and exhaling with what Sulien recognised, after a moment's nervous confusion, as relief. He could see his shoulders sink as tension dropped away from them.

'What? What is it?'

'Thank you,' said Varius into the longdictor, before turning it off. He reached to slam off the longvision and looked up at Sulien. 'They're not sending her to the Colosseum, whatever Hirtius says. Cleomenes says the confession's part of a deal.'

Sulien couldn't feel any great relief in this himself, and found it excessive in Varius. 'Well then, what—?'

Varius sighed again, and straightened, became still. 'It would be a firing squad,' he said.

'I don't care how they want to do it,' Sulien said violently, 'it doesn't matter.'

Varius paused, then released the breath he'd taken without saying anything. He nodded.

'But this means we've got less time We would have had until the Games for the Saturnalia, if they— If it's not at the Colosseum then they won't have to wait for anything, they could finish the trial by the end of the week and then . . . and there'll only be one journey we can intercept.'

'We'll have only one chance anyway,' said Varius. 'And in another two days we'll be as ready as we're going to get.'

Sulien nodded and sat down on the bed. Sweaty, feverish weariness poured through him as the spurt of panic ebbed away. His own feelings seemed hard to follow now; Varius was right, it could hardly be bad news that the Colosseum was no longer waiting for her; he should be at least a little glad, shouldn't he? She was not sitting there in the chamber in the Basilica Noviana right at this moment, anticipating *that* death, waiting for the hounds to tear her to pieces.

At least he wouldn't have to worry about Varius buying poison any more; that was something.

It was a bright winter day. As they had hurried her first into the van, and then down the steps into the cell beneath the Basilica, she had felt the open air on her skin, warm compared with the grinding cold of those weeks in Venedia and Sarmatia. At first it had been terrible to face the people in the gallery, feeling the first brunt of their excitement and anticipating their disappointment when they realised her death would not be played out in front of them at the Colosseum. But she could see past them now. In the high windows at the back of the court the sky shone blue. Una sat in her chair and kept her eyes on it.

Her advocate was addressing the chamber. She had not known, until they took her into the court, that there would be any kind of defence at all. Hirtius had gone on speaking without a break for more than an hour.

'My client, as my colleague has said, denies none of this, and you will hear the truth from her own lips later. My task is only to remind the Prefect, the senators and the people here of her youth—' There were some groans and jeers in the gallery, and he talked on, largely unheard, without waiting for them to die down, '—and that in confessing freely she has at least not compounded her wickedness with lies. I would suggest also to the court that my noble colleague perhaps credits her with too much understanding of her actions. He spoke of sedition as an infection. I agree with him. But this girl was only one symptom, not the source of it. Perhaps we could never find any one person with whom it began, not among the fanatics led by Dama, nor even among the aggressors in Nionia. It is the contagion of our times, which we must fight and contain as best we can. How potent must it be, to infect not only slaves and outlaws but citizens too, for my colleague has already mentioned men such as Caius Varius and Delir of Aspadana. We must always be on our guard against it, citizens, in our families, in our slaves, even in ourselves. For even the love of justice and peace can be preyed upon and abused by those who love only chaos. Our Emperor's late uncle and cousin – casualties of this struggle, and of course, clear of any stain upon their character – pursued ideals that, though pure and worthy in the abstract, are, in our imperfect world, not only impossible but dangerous, all too apt to be twisted. Can we be surprised then that an uneducated slave girl, lacking the power of moral discrimination, could be corrupted altogether? Having fled from civilisation in animal terror of recapture, chance led her to a gang of criminals who rejected all authority, who exposed her to a poisonous combination of subversive ideas, dissident religion and witchcraft. Since then she has acted in selfishness, greed and ignorance, as an animal acts, but without calculation – I cannot say without malice, but it was malice only of the moment. Of course there can be no argument but that a dangerous animal or a disease must be destroyed, but Rome may show mercy to the extent of sparing this benighted girl the Colosseum, or any more protracted means of execution. Let her be swiftly extinguished and as swiftly forgotten.'

'If Rome is to show such mercy, it is right that the people should understand how great that forbearance is,' began Hirtius, rising again.

Una knew she would need to be able to absent her attention, or the trial would be unbearable; she had practised doing so. It had not occurred to her that it would also be boring. On the second day, more restless than she'd ever been inside her cell, she began to want to move just for the sake of moving. She resisted visible fidgeting as far as she could, but flexed her toes inside her shoes.

Sometimes Hirtius startled her out of her reverie by shouting at her directly, rather than addressing the Prefect: 'And then, surely, if you were not consumed with covetousness and audacity, you would have been content!' and for a few minutes afterwards she would feel her heart pounding as if she'd been about to run, and blood throbbing even in the fingertips of her chained hands.

Hirtius spent a long time questioning a vigile officer to prove that she had been at Dama's farm, then moved on to the time she and Varius had spent in Nionian custody in Sina. A minor diplomat whom she did not recognise and who avoided looking at her confirmed the Nionian Imperial family had definitely visited her, and admitted she had been seen wearing clothes they had given her. But that's in the confession, Una thought, with a pang of simple exasperation. Why do we have to bother with this? Why don't you just end it?

In her cell under the Basilica she found it difficult to lie still and let the minutes course through her, as she had done before. She paced and shook. Sometimes when she closed her eyes she saw white dogs, pouring towards her like a froth on a torrent of water, almost felt the teeth meeting in her flesh – but why? She was safe from that now; there was nothing to fear. She waited for the agitation to exhaust itself, lying down and promising herself again that it was nearly over; she allowed herself to remember Marcus' arms round her, in the bright sea at Siphnos, in bed in their apartment in Athens—

But even to picture him made her twist in anguish and start up again. Phrases from the day in court that she thought she'd been careful not to listen to in the first place stuck after all in her mind. Only as she caught herself snarling aloud, as she strode back and forth across the cell, 'Lying,' did she identify the feeling as rage.

She sat down again on the hard bed, baffled and almost amused at herself. It seemed to her that she should no longer be capable of anger. She had known the nature of what would be said, just as she knew what the outcome would be, and none of it could mean anything, not to her. Whatever happened in court, or in the world now, she could have no part in it. The last second of her life, in any sense that mattered, was already past: it had come as she lost hold of Sulien, as she fell to the gravel and the train roared on. These final days were like blank space at the bottom of a concluded letter; the trial was just a tedious matter of observing formalities to wind up what had already happened.

But electricity fizzed along her nerves, her heart bucked in her chest, the concrete floor was very cold on her bare feet. Her brain was full of noise and motion, not peace.

On the morning of the third day, the day she was due to read out the confession Hirtius had already savaged from beginning to end, she realised that not everyone in the gallery was hungry to watch her die. Una had tried not to perceive any thoughts but her own, to exclude everything from her senses except the blue sky through the windows, but as Hirtius began to speak, an outraged shout seemed to erupt in the hall, as if she herself had lost control completely and screamed what she'd only whispered to herself in her cell.

Lying—! You lying bastard!

It was so loud that for a moment she was confused that no one reacted; Hirtius talked on, there was no disapproving rustle from the gallery, no word from the Prefect; the lictors stood motionless. There had been no shout.

Una lowered her gaze from the high windows and met the eyes of a young woman, seated several rows from the front, plainly dressed, pale, silent.

The girl wanted Hirtius to choke before he could get out another word, she wanted lightning to strike him where he stood. She thought it was incredible that Una always looked so calm, no matter what they said, gazing at the far windows as if she could see something no one else could in the sky. She wanted Una to feel her staring at her.

Una thought the girl was not a slave now, but had been.

And there were others, standing at the back of the hall, waiting with the coats and bags, some of them in chauffeurs' or body-guards' livery, some indistinguishable from anyone else in that hall, except that they watched her steadily, without the hostile expectancy of the rest, but with stern, angry sympathy.

Something sharp whistled through her, more like terror than comfort; a match set to fuses laced along her bloodstream. She tried to draw her attention back into herself, or to spread it away into the air. She shivered, trying to catch her racing breath. She closed her eyes and saw red and gold sparks against black.

They would live with what they heard in this chamber. This was not, for them, a period of empty inevitability. No, nor for her either.

She grew aware of the flat glare of the cameras, like a dull pressure on her skin. She opened her eyes.

Once again they knew they had to watch, on this first session of the interrogations. This time they were gathered in Delir's rooms in the Subura, and Varius had already had them recite their tasks for the day of the attempt, twice, as if it were some kind of play. Sulien had helplessly unreal moments when he felt it would never be more than that; not just that they would fail, that something would happen to prevent them even trying.

He thought Una looked worse as the camera closed in on her: tight-lipped, breathing fast and shallowly. Her eyes were shut. He hovered close to the screen until Varius said, 'Please – we all need to see her.'

Sulien sat down and knitted his fingers into Lal's.

'There can be no doubt that Nionian agents had succeeded in recruiting a group of desperate and unprincipled outlaws and assassins to serve their purpose, namely, the overthrow of the Roman world,' concluded Hirtius. 'The only question remaining is this: should Rome choose to mitigate its just anger against her?'

Una lifted her head and looked fleetingly and searchingly at the camera.

'The prisoner will answer the charges herself,' announced the Prefect.

Una rose slowly to her feet and stared steadily into the crowd as a hissing swell of noise rose to greet her. Watching her face Varius leaned forward, frowning slightly, holding his breath.

'I am grateful for the opportunity to confess to the crimes I am accused of,' she murmured, though so quietly and indistinctly the Prefect interrupted, 'Speak up,' and the microphones flared briefly as someone adjusted the sound.

Una cleared her throat. 'I am grateful for the opportunity to confess to the crimes I am accused of,' she repeated. Her eyes were downcast now, fixed on the sheets of paper in front of her. 'I understand that though it is impossible I should be allowed to live, this court may spare me a slow death if I take that opportunity.'

Then she looked up, straight into the camera, and Varius moved towards the screen as if to catch some teetering thing about to fall, and said, '*Una, no—*'

She spoke fast, to be sure of getting it all out before she could be stopped, or before her courage could fail, but clearly: 'But all I will say is that the last act of Emperor Marcus Novius was the abolition of slavery.'

The Prefect and the two lawyers all rose at once, Hirtius shouting; the lictors crowded in around her before they even had orders what to do.

The sound from the crowd built more slowly, a confused, soft burr that swept across them like a wave, growing to a loud roar, and somewhere in the middle of it all there was a shrill cry of joy, and scattered across it, defiant sprays of applause.

'The prisoner will not continue to abuse this court,' shouted the Prefect above the noise, 'she will be returned to her cell at once.'

Una struggled fiercely as the lictors seized her, crumpled the pages of the confession and swept them into the air. 'All I have ever done has been for that!' she called out for the crowd in the gallery to hear, even if the microphones would not, and then she went still and let them take her away.

They knocked her to the floor in the cell, rougher with her than they'd been before. Una scrambled up, gasping for breath. Some terrible luminous thing was flooding through her, burning, slicing her to shreds, and soon it would resolve into terror at what she had done. Yet for a few moments more it felt like exhilaration, like wanting to leap or dance.

Varius turned his back on the longvision and her stern, radiant face, feeling a blow at his chest like the impact of a thrown rock, a booted foot. He could see it happening; however good the plan sounded every time they went over it, he did not have enough faith in it to soften or blur that vision of what the hounds would do to her. He had lost too many people to be able to stand this now; and none of their deaths had been as terrible as the one she had just chosen.

Sulien was staring at the screen, one hand over his mouth, incredulous.

The Prefect had vanished from the courtroom, leaving the clamour to rumble on until the lictors escorted him back to his seat on the platform.

'Since the prisoner's guilt is manifest and undisputed,' announced the Prefect, 'and since further interrogation is futile in the face of her recalcitrance and mendacity, this trial is at an end, and she is hereby condemned to the beasts. She will be returned to the prison in which she awaited trial—'

'No,' whispered Sulien, at last.

And the knowledge that Sulien would soon insist that this merely altered the conditions of the rescue, which would work because it had to, made Varius ache with envy and pity.

'—and thence to the Colosseum, where her execution will be publicly presented during the New Year's Games.'

Two startled-looking state newscasters appeared on the screen:

'An early end to the trial, the Prefect having judged it pointless to continue!' chattered one, in a bright, shrill tone.

'For God's sake, turn it off,' said Delir, hollowly.

Ziye gave Varius a heavy-eyed look and said, 'That stupid girl.'

Varius rubbed the space between his eyes, smiled without humour. 'We should have known she'd do that.'

Just as Varius had expected, Sulien fired up, more at their tone than what they'd said. 'No,' he started, 'no, listen – this is how we thought things were a few days ago, we've already planned for this. All right, so we can't get her coming out of the court. But the place on the Via Prenestina was better anyway, and now we've got until New Year's Day – it means we've got more time to get it perfect.' He stopped, a slow amazement brightening his face, and the resemblance to his sister sharpened, almost too close to the way she'd looked a moment before. 'Everyone heard her,' he said.

Varius meant not to answer, to keep nodding along to anything Sulien might say rather than quarrel with him, for as long as this awful time lasted. But he couldn't stop himself: 'What use is that? They'll never let anyone hear it again. It won't mean anything to most people. It isn't worth what she's paying.'

'She's not going to pay anything!' said Sulien, desperately, inevitably.

Lal was beside him. 'They can't wipe it out of people's heads. No one's ever even heard Marcus was Emperor before now! People have to see it means something.'

Varius had no heart to argue with them further. It made no difference to what he meant to do, that much was true. Perhaps they were even right. They both looked vivid and brittle, as if it would take far less than the whole weight of Rome to smash them to bits.

Delir looked miserable, and yet there was a faded version of the same brightness about him. He said, 'I am not sure it is very different from your own plan, Varius, is it? We have very few means of resistance.'

Varius could neither deny the comparison nor stand to examine it closely. He said, 'Well, it's all right, Sulien, we won't stop.'

RESTRAINTS

This was not the last night she had left, but it was the last night outside the walls of the Colosseum. They were moving her to the cells beneath in the morning. Una rose suddenly from the bed and marched to the door as if she expected to find it open, went back to the bed and sat with her arms wrapped round herself again. She had not pulled back the blankets, or closed her eyes: she didn't want to sleep. The lights had been turned out hours ago. The blackness was tight around her.

'Marcus,' she said aloud.

How long had it taken him to die? Twenty minutes, half an hour. Probably it would be no longer for her, whatever Drusus had said. It would feel longer than it really was, but still it was a very little time out of a whole life, or even a life that wasn't whole. If Marcus had undergone that, she could too.

'Marcus. Marcus,' she said again, but barely even whispering now, mouthing the words into her hands, her fingers cupping her warm breath against her face. 'I'm nearly there. I won't be long now.' She waited in the dark. 'Come and meet me. Please, if you can, if it's possible, come now. If you were here just for a second I could— I could . . .' Her eyes were clenched shut, as tight as they would go, yet the tears leaked out at the corners. 'Come on. Please. Please try. Please God, let him come. Marcus,' she repeated, louder now, rougher, almost an accusation rather than a plea.

She curled up stiffly on her side, trying to hold closed the soured wound she felt in her chest, a cold gully of poison running from her throat to her breastbone, she hoped the dogs would tear just there, and scrape it out of her quickly.

It was strange how, as she looked into the camera lens and

spoke, she had been so conscious of possessing, for a few seconds, the Empire's attention: millions watching and listening to her, and yet it had not occurred to her to think that people she knew would be among them. She thought Varius would almost certainly have seen it. It would have hurt him, and yet somehow she felt a small, selfish comfort in thinking that for those seconds they had been in a kind of contact. Lal perhaps, maybe Delir and Ziye too: they must have watched at least part of the trial. Others she remembered from the camp: Tiro, Tobias, Helena. And Noriko would know that what she had worked so hard for had been thrown away.

But she had to believe Sulien had not been near a longvision in days. He was somewhere in India by now, slumped in the back of a truck jolting down a pitted road from Methora to Palimbothra, or even out of the Empire already, entangled in a flow of Bamarian refugees in southern Sina, or in Siam, held for questioning in a cell like this one, not trusted yet, but safe.

But he would find out, in the end; he would know what she had done.

You wouldn't have the strength to do the same thing again, she thought, watching herself from a distance with a certain disgust as she sobbed and writhed on the bed.

Well, I had enough to do it once, she answered herself fiercely, and the tears stopped, though she continued to shake and gasp.

I don't regret it, she announced, breathless even in her mind. And she began to chant it to herself in silence: I don't regret it, I don't regret it, I don't regret it. She was not precisely sure what it meant, now, to regret or not. But the rhythm of it calmed her for a while.

It was a cold morning, barely grown into daylight, even though it was long past dawn. Standing on the first step of the fire escape at the rear of the block of flats, Lal was almost at Sulien's height, high enough to press her forehead against his. She wanted to kiss his lips again, but since they had stepped off the train in Rome certain ways of touching had become impossible, held in suspension.

He too had been sentenced to the hounds *in absentia*, the day after the end of Una's trial.

Lal could not think what to say to him. There was nothing he would do differently if she told him to be careful; he knew well enough what the risks were already. She didn't want to lift her hands from his shoulders.

'We need to get ready now,' he whispered at last, without moving.

Lal nodded. 'Well,' she said, 'tell her I've missed her.'

'You'll see us both in three days,' he said. 'You can tell her.'

'I know.' I love you, she thought of adding; perhaps she would always regret it if she didn't. But she did not think it would help him to hear it now. It would be a distraction; perhaps he would make a mistake and fail and it would all be her fault.

She had thought she was managing to look reasonably cheerful and confident, but clearly she wasn't, from the way he grinned at her and said, 'We're going to do it. I'll be all right.'

Lal put her hands to each side of his face, framing it, 'See you soon, then,' she said, and slung the pair of bags over her shoulder and began to run up the steps. You don't believe it, she told herself, so why aren't you trying to stop him?

But strangely, she began to feel more hopeful the further away she was from him, and by the time she reached the roof she was not sure why success had seemed so impossible.

Sulien looked around and stepped a little closer to the wall, then put on the uniform jacket over the tunic. He felt superstitiously for the bolt-cutters tucked inside it before buttoning it up, skimmed his hand lightly from the syringe in his pocket to Varius' gun in the holster at his hip. He would not have to use it, he reassured himself, though that would be more for Cleomenes' sake than his own. It was loaded, nevertheless.

He walked out onto the main street. Varius, also dressed in vigile uniform, was waiting on the corner, calmly answering a passer-by's request for directions. He'd shaved his beard the night before, and had tried briefly to salvage at least some of his hair before shearing that off too in frustration. He looked crisp and professional now – the best fit for this, really. Delir was too old and too short for the uniform, Sulien still too young. They walked together, two officers on patrol, chatting.

They passed a van parked brazenly athwart the entrance to a tiny side street. No one was much bothered by the blocked-off access, so far at least, and the van looked deserted; Ziye was hiding in the back.

'Another two minutes,' Varius said.

Sulien looked back at the deserted upper reaches of the building, where Lal was waiting. 'This is costing you so much money.'

Varius smiled. 'A return on your investment,' he said, 'or Una's, anyway.'

Up on the roof, Lal opened the first bag, looked at the heaps of bank notes inside and sighed, then gathered an experimental double handful and hurled it out above the street. She ducked out of sight, crouching at the edge to watch what happened. A few notes fluttered back around her and for a moment she was afraid too little of the cash would even reach the ground, or else that it would all tumble limply to the roadside, not into the traffic. But then a damp puff of wind caught it and she saw the money begin to drift and spread in the air like smoke. It scattered softly along the road. She rose cautiously, lifted the bag, swung it out and emptied the money into the air.

The notes speckled the street, blowing into small heaps against walls and gutters like fallen leaves, sprinkled down onto people's heads and shoulders. Pedestrians began to stoop for them at once, but at first the cars continued to stream past, oblivious. Then, as the flow of traffic stopped at a crossing, the crowd began to spill into the middle of the street, first only in one lane, then in both, and people began to get out of their cars. Another shower of money drifted down through the air. Delir, slowly circling the block in the oldest, cheapest car they'd been able to find, stopped in the middle of the road behind several other stationary vehicles, a few yards short of the side street. He got out and started gathering up notes like everyone else, picking his way along the street, away from Varius and Sulien, who had retreated a little way around the corner.

Then the first two outriders swept into the street and ran into the morass in a blaze of dying speed. For a few seconds they stood nonplussed astride their trirotas, then they began to weave between the abandoned cars. A slightly forlorn cry carried up the street to where Sulien and Varius stood: 'Return to your vehicles!'

There had been no way of knowing exactly what would happen when the money was thrown, and sometimes Sulien had only been able to imagine a riot. So far, at least, it was not like that. People cheerfully ignored each other even as they foraged alongside one another, busily scooping up the notes grazing along the paper trails the wind had laid between the cars, excited and intent, but not yet frenzied, no one seemed to have grabbed for anyone else's spoils. They paid no attention to the vigiles shouting at them to clear the street.

The second pair of outriders led the van into the street. It was a big, square-edged, lumbering vehicle which looked too large and belligerent for the transport of a single prisoner. She's there, thought Sulien, hardly able to believe it even after all this planning. She's right there.

Lal tossed a last few handfuls of cash over the barrier and raced across the roof and down the fire escape. She hurried across two streets and down an alleyway, behind a hoarding and into the empty ground of a stalled building site Varius had found, the bare skeleton of an office block awaiting the money to clothe it in brick. She pulled off the hooded coat, gloves and loose trousers she was wearing and let down the bunched-up skirt of the dress she had on underneath. She stuffed the clothes into one of the bags before stepping back out onto the street. She walked as far as the Via Tiburtina, quickly, but stepping carefully, as if the ground was slippery under her feet. She boarded a tram towards Vatican Fields and managed to sit still and gaze blandly out at the city until the tram swung past the Colosseum, when she jerked her face away from the window hard enough to startle the person sitting next to her. She could no longer dodge the knowledge that either way it was done now; they had either succeeded or failed.

Delir wandered past the prison van as it slid to an uncertain standstill, casually shedding the final package of money across the road behind it. It was far less than the bagfuls Lal had flung from the rooftop, but enough that the van was soon hemmed in by the scavengers. Traffic had begun to back up around each turning in any case as Delir slipped back into the bustling crowd and hurried back along the street towards Varius and Sulien.

They watched him slip behind Ziye's van and into the alley. He walked out briskly a few moments later, dressed like them in vigiles uniform, with the fluorescent jacket over the tunic.

'I AM ORDERING YOU TO CLEAR THE AREA,' bawled an officer, his voice vibrating with almost comical desperation.

'Now, would you say?' asked Delir quietly as he reached Varius and Sulien. 'Yes,' said Varius, 'now.'

The three of them spread out across the street. As they passed, Ziye backed her van along the pavement, opening the entrance to the side street.

Sulien spread his arms wide, standing like a fence across the way. 'I can't allow you through. Will you please go back the way you came,' he droned flatly into an oncoming current of people.

There were baffled groans. 'Make up your minds!' shouted someone.

'It's a safety procedure,' claimed Delir implacably.

A number of people ignored them and barged past, but there were enough who either stood and argued or obediently trudged back towards the van, churning the froth of people around it.

But Sulien wasn't really looking at them. It was difficult to keep his eyes away from the stranded van that held Una, but he dragged his gaze from it to the outriders. Varius and Delir were watching them too, waiting for them to wander further into the scrum. One was speaking into his radio.

A few people had begun to climb back into their cars, clutching as much money as they could carry. But it made little difference; ahead of the van a small mob was rooting for blown notes under Delir's car, which still sat, with a couple of others, obstinately in the middle of the road.

Varius and Sulien glanced at each other and continued up the packed street, leaving Delir behind. In his pocket, Sulien's fingers were tight around the vigile identity pass Lal had made for him, but the nearest officer just brandished his radio in frustration as he saw them coming and shouted, 'What the hell *is* this?'

Sulien stared flatly at the man's healthy, ordinary face, looking for some sign of consciousness of what he was helping to do.

'It's a mess, isn't it?' he made himself say, shrugging. 'We need to get you through this now.'

'You're telling me!' said the rider, irritably.

'We're going to move some of these vehicles out of the way manually,' explained Varius. 'We can't wait for these people to get in the mood to come back to their cars. It's going to get even worse before the support units can get here; the junction's blocked up ahead.'

Sulien thought Varius sounded a little too measured and deliberate for what the situation was supposed to be, but the man was still looking around incredulously at the chaos and did not seem to notice. 'I guess,' he said, anxiously.

'It just needs a few feet that way and you could get through,' Sulien said.

'Let's get the rest of your team over here,' urged Varius. 'We need more pairs of hands.'

The three of them walked over to the van. Sulien's pulse blared with each step closer; it seemed enough to shake the street. *Una, Una, I'm here, I'm here*.

Varius tapped on the window. 'We need help with this, we've got to push these cars over that way,' said the outrider to the driver inside.

'I'm Captain Soterius Ater, we're with the Nomentan Cohort,' said Varius, displaying his identity pass. 'You need to be ready to take the first turning; whoever you've got in the back needs to come and help.'

The driver was tense in his seat, but he didn't hesitate. 'Lads,' he called, banging on the dividing wall of the van, 'we've got a problem out here; come on.'

And the doors opened at the back. Sulien leant against the side of the van, light-headed, looking away. If he walked around to the rear of the van he might have seen inside, but there was no way to do it that would look natural, and it was just as well. He was not sure the pretence would hold if he saw her.

It would only have been for a second anyway; the men shut and locked the doors behind them – but Sulien had seen the set of keys at the driver's waist, where Cleomenes had said it would be.

Varius gestured the other outriders over, led them off towards the deserted cars. Four outriders and two guards. Sulien hung back, slipping round the corner of the van, hoping to be forgotten. Varius was alone in a knot of vigiles and Sulien's throat tightened to see how precarious this looked. Ahead of them Delir's fluorescent jacket glowed through the bustle. He was trying to herd people out of the way in earnest now.

Varius and the vigiles spread around a pair of cars, took hold and began to lift.

Sulien stepped forward, opened the passenger door of the van and swung up in beside the driver. The man looked at him in mild confusion and Sulien turned to face him, opening his mouth and taking a breath as if to explain, and drove the syringe through the man's sleeve into his arm.

The driver jolted in shock. Varius had made Sulien rehearse these dangerous seconds before the drug took effect, but he felt now that he had no need of practice. He had done this before, he remembered, and without a weapon of any kind. He grabbed the man's hand as it moved for his gun and forced it down, slammed the muzzle of his own weapon against the driver's ribs at the same time.

236

He whispered, 'You shut up and keep still and go to sleep, or I'll kill you.'

At last the man crumpled. Sulien had to cram him down awkwardly under the seat and climb over him, a performance that felt so conspicuous and ungainly it seemed too much to hope that everyone in the street, vigiles and civilians both, would still be too occupied with what they were doing to notice what has going on in the cab. But then he was in the driver's seat, placing his hands lightly over the controls, and the street was still full of people looking at the ground.

He had to sit and wait, sweating, while Varius and the others struggled to shift the cars. The breeze slapped a ten-sestertium note against the windscreen and Sulien watched it quiver there. Someone, reaching for it, might look inside; there was nothing to stop them.

He drove forward, swift as possible past the panting vigiles and the displaced cars.

Varius' radio crackled as soon as the van began to move. 'Ater,' said Delir, in case the vigiles around Varius were listening, 'I've got a young man unconscious here – might have been trampled.'

'All right, stand by, I'm on my way,' answered Varius, and took off as fast as he could towards Delir without breaking into a run as Sulien turned down the side street. Behind him, Ziye rolled the second van back into position, blocking the way.

Sulien stopped. The street was still as quiet and shadowed as it had been every time they'd scouted it. A little way ahead was the reason they'd chosen this point on the route to the Colosseum: a stairwell leading down to the kitchen door of an eating house for which Varius had handed over a month's rent in cash. The keys were in Sulien's pocket. There was a change of clothes for each of them waiting inside, and the main doors of the eating house opened onto a broader, busier street running at an angle to the Via Nomentana. There was a trirota standing ready at the front.

'Sulien.' Una's voice was just inches behind him, high, breathless.

He plucked the set of keys off the driver's waist and stumbled out of the van, unlocked the doors.

Una was seated on a metal bench at the back of the van, leaning forward, rigid against the restraints that held her. Her eyes were wide, her face racked with tension and shock, but her lips parted in a smile of incredulous excitement.

'You weren't meant to do this,' she said, stammering, as he climbed inside, 'you weren't meant to come.'

'That's grateful, isn't it?' said Sulien, scrambling across to her, pulling out the bolt-cutters. There were no keys for the restraints on the bunch he held; they would have had copies waiting at the Colosseum.

Una let her head drop against the wall behind her, gasping. 'Hurry,' she breathed.

Her wrists were fixed together above her head, shackled to a bar on the wall. At first, crouched on the floor of the van at Una's feet, Sulien noticed the position only with a hurried pang of indignation at the cruelty of it. He clipped through the chains that bound her feet together and tethered them to the floor easily enough, stood up to free her hands.

But he saw now that the cuffs were heavier than anything on which he'd tested the bolt-cutters. He'd expected a length of chain between them, but instead they were joined by a thick, solid block of metal an inch wide. Even before he tried he knew that he couldn't close the bolt-cutters on that, nor on the bolt that held them to the wall. And when he tried to cut through the cuffs themselves, he couldn't get the blades between the metal and the cast on her wrist.

They had known about the cast: Cleomenes had mentioned it, and they'd even seen it on the longvision. None of them had ever thought about it as an obstacle.

Una arched back awkwardly, trying to see what he was doing.

'Wait a minute,' said Sulien, absurdly, trying to find a gap between the ratchet and the plaster by holding her wrist against the wall with one hand. Una slid forward to the edge of the seat, trying to give him more room to work.

'Is that better?'

'Yes,' he said, but the points of the blades skidded uselessly on the surface of the cast, nipped at the outer edges of the cuff.

He felt Una going slack, the hopeful tension draining out of her.

'I'm doing it,' he insisted. He shifted his grip on the handles, the plastic growing slippery in his hands now, trying to stifle the growing tremble in the muscles of his wrists and fingers. He rested a knee on the bench and repositioned the blades to chew at the plaster of the cast itself. Una flinched and hissed. In desperation he put the cutters to the block between the cuffs, but succeeded only in scoring shallow grooves on the metal.

Una sighed, long and quiet. She said, 'Sulien.'

'Shut up.' He struggled on, dragging, levering, fighting the urge to pound the head of the bolt-cutters against the joint of the cuffs, like a hammer. He couldn't risk breaking them.

Una said, slowly and reluctantly, 'It's not working.'

'I can't *do* this if you keep going on at me.' He put the bolt-cutters to the other cuff and managed at last to chop through it, but that didn't free her hand; the broken ring still stood rigidly around it. He'd have to cut out a section of the ratchet and the blades had twisted slightly now, and he'd made no progress on the cuff around the cast at all.

'Sulien,' said Una again, 'there's no time.'

They'd calculated that he should have her out of the van within forty seconds, and it must have been twice, three times that by now. How could this not work, when everything else had, after he'd come so far? He took the gun from his hip and began slamming the butt of it against the bolt, loud, furious gasps coming through clenched teeth. He flung a couple of wild blows at the wall too, barely realising he was doing it.

'Stop,' Una was pleading, 'Sulien, stop it. They're coming— You've got to go.'

'Get down,' Sulien said, placing the point of the gun against the fixture.

Una shouted, 'No, don't!' But Sulien pushed her down and to

the side, trying at once to force her head as far from her chained wrists as possible, and to lower his body over her, covering her. He turned his face away and fired.

The bang seemed to come from everywhere at once. Una jerked and cried out and hot shocks of pain burst along his arm and in his side. Sulien grabbed for the cuffs to check them first, before even caring how badly he or Una might be hurt.

The plate between the cuffs was scuffed and dented, that was all.

The driver's radio fizzled in the cab: 'Castus. Please respond. Castus. Where are you?'

The bullet had shattered on the metal, sending pieces ricocheting around the van. They were both bleeding, Una from her left hand and the side of her neck. Her cast was scorched, and a flake of metal was embedded in the plaster; the skin on her other wrist was red and burnt. Sulien stood there, gazing at the damage, blankly conscious that he could have killed them both. The word 'lucky' turned over in his mind with vast, clumsy weight. The gashes to his waist and forearm were bleeding freely and burned with a bright, lively pain. He felt, suddenly, how long it had been since he had really slept.

Una said, 'You can still help me.'

He looked down at her. She stared at him, a clear look as inescapable as gravity, and he realised he was holding the gun just inches from her face.

He could not speak even to say, 'No.' He shook his head, dizzily, and backed away, shutting his eyes.

Una advised in a relentless whisper, 'Just don't think about it. And don't look at me.'

Without answering, Sulien shoved the gun back roughly into its holster and grabbed for the bolt-cutters again, sawed and levered at the cuffs. He seized both her wrists, smearing his blood and hers over the metal and plaster, and dragged, crying now, as if sheer desperation would give him the strength to pull the shackles straight out of the wall. Una's hands clenched, tried to wrest away from his. He knew he was hurting her, he didn't care—

'Please,' she said.

And his sinews gave way all at once, his hands dropped from the cuffs and he sank to his knees in front of her. He put his hands to her shoulder and her face and tried to answer. It should not have been difficult to explain something as simple and essential as the fact that he couldn't kill her, ever, and it was unconscionable that she should ask. And yet as his eyes squeezed shut on an acid swell of tears, for a second he did picture himself doing it, and it did look possible. But he could do nothing now but cling to her and shake his head, unable to say a thing.

Una was straining tight against the restraints again, trembling. She said in a rush, 'All right, all right! You don't have to. You don't have to— I'll be all right. But you can't stay now, they're coming.'

'I'll come back,' Sulien got out, finally tearing through the obstruction in his throat. 'I'll get you out of the Colosseum. I'll come back.'

Una's jaw tightened and a tremor puckered through her, but her mouth tugged into a smile, and she nodded. 'Fine. Just hurry.'

He held her quickly, then lunged across the floor to push open the doors. The van Ziye had left as a barricade at the end was shifting, unseen hands pushing it aside, and there was a shriek of sirens from somewhere – the other end of the street. But if he was fast enough . . . He felt for the keys to the kitchen in his pocket.

Una had said what she knew she had to, to get him to leave.

He wiped his eyes. After the relative dark inside the van, the pale strip of sky above the street was strangely bright and soft, dappled with shadow. He thought of Lal, who would be hurrying through the city, thinking of him.

He turned, slowly, and looked back at Una.

Una stiffened. 'Go on, run. For God's sake, Sulien.'

Sulien exhaled, and let his shoulders drop. He pulled the door of the van closed.

'I can't,' he said, quietly. 'I've left it too long. I won't get away.'

Una rose up, dragging against the cuffs, breathing hard, her face distorted and mask-like with horror. 'No.'

Sulien sat down on the bench beside her. 'It's all right.'

'At least try, please at least fucking *try*,' gasped Una. 'You have to.'

'No,' he said, and put his arms round her. 'I don't.'

Una had started crying at last. 'Sulien – the one thing I could say I'd done – back in London – I saved you.'

'Yes,' said Sulien, 'you did. So can't you see why I can't go?'

Una drew her knees up close to her body, sobbing, a despairing huddle in his arms.

'I'm sorry,' he whispered, tears filling his own eyes again.

She grew a little quieter, her face buried against his chest. They could hear the noise of vigile trirotas and cars screaming closer, and pounding feet on the cobbles outside. Unwillingly, Sulien drew the gun again and looked down at it, his other hand tightening hard on Una's shoulder. 'I should— I suppose I have to—'

'And then yourself?' asked Una, in a wrecked, accusing voice.

He nodded. It wasn't quite so hard to contemplate now.

But perhaps even now he couldn't really believe he would do it, for his hand was so heavy and sluggish, dragging the muzzle up through the resistant air towards her head, and Una just wept and shuddered against him, without urging him to hurry.

And even knowing what it would mean for them both, he was relieved when the vigiles burst in through the doors and struck the gun out of his hand before he could fire.

Varius sat with a pen and calculator in a corner of a packed cookhouse, pretending to study the files he'd spread on the table, filling columns with imaginary figures over an untouched plate of fritters. He had stuffed the vigile jacket and cap into a plastic bag and flung it into a skip, picked up the briefcase he'd hidden inside it. He'd finished changing his clothes in the bathroom of the cookhouse – it wouldn't be very strange, even if anyone noticed; he could have been getting ready for a meeting or an interview. He was longing to move, to know what had happened – but the story wouldn't have broken yet, and he had to be careful hanging around longvisions.

He set out into the city, changing direction often. He took a fare car towards West Aventine Railway Station and went inside, then walked out through another set of doors heading north, towards the centre. The air felt strange on his clean, shaved jaw and scalp; the crowd felt different as it flowed around him. He realised that though he had a false name and forged papers ready to produce if need be, this was the first time in months he had not been in any definite disguise. The vigile uniform and the tramp's haze of alcohol and dirt had both carried a story, and a warning. These bland, inexpressive business clothes said almost nothing; they were not unlike what he might have worn to work before any of this had happened. Someone tried to sell him something as he passed the Raudusculan Gate. It had been so long since that had happened that it shocked him, to have a stranger calling out, 'How about you, sir – high-quality watches!' It felt unnerving to be so unguarded, to have to trust that this was not what the vigiles would expect of him, and yet it made him carry himself differently, his head up, almost feeling as if he were just another professional hurrying briskly through an ordinary working day.

Every time he came anywhere near a public longvision, of course he had to stop and look. Advertisements, dancers, a preview of a show. Varius forced himself to stride on, grimacing – what was taking so long? Perhaps it had worked, but they were going to cover it up – perhaps they didn't want to admit they'd lost her. Then how would they account for her absence at the Colosseum? He began to think of possible answers, and tried to stop himself, superstitiously afraid of having any expectations at all. He had honed the plan into plausibility, all the while trying not to place any inward bet on the outcome. He had been afraid of pitching his hopes dangerously low, rather than too high, even so, when they were actually in the street, watching the money tumble down, he couldn't help but see it was working. The

243

vigiles hadn't recognised or challenged any of them; Sulien was in the driver's seat of the van – they were almost there.

Once he heard sirens sweeping past, but he didn't see the cars. He went south at last, to Remoria Station. Delir and Ziye had planned this stage, scattering after the attempt was made. They had agreed they must keep apart for the first few days at least; they would meet later, outside Naples. Varius already had his ticket in his pocket. He had no connections there, and it was almost as teeming with people of every colour and from every province of the Empire as Rome itself; he should not stand out.

Then he looked up at the silent longvision screen above the station concourse and saw the news. For a moment it was as if there was a dam in his mind against which the words strained, as he tried to force them to mean something else.

At first it said only that an attempt to rescue Una had been thwarted, and he tried to hope that they were already dead, that they'd both been shot, but he couldn't; he didn't mean it.

They were both in the Colosseum cells. He remembered standing in the terraces with Lal and Ziye, months before, looking across the arena towards the place where Marcus had died. He saw Una's face at the moment she'd condemned herself to die in the same place and felt a helpless flash of anger with her.

What had it been? At what point after Sulien turned the van down the side street had they failed, and was it something he might have seen and solved? He should never have agreed to help Sulien; he and Cleomenes should quietly have done whatever was necessary to get a dose of some fast-acting poison to Una. It would have been bearable to think of her dying like that, bearable at least compared to this. And Sulien would have lived. At least one of them should – it was too much that the gale that had started blowing with Leo's and Clodia's deaths and had swept off Gemella and Marcus should have both of them too.

He looked away from the screen; he mustn't be noticed staring at it. He realised he was shaking, and gripping the handle of his case

244

with convulsive force. He did not know how much might have shown on his face. He began to move.

He was supposed to go to Naples whatever happened, once his part was done. But he realised that even though he had contemplated this, as the worst that could happen, he hadn't really included it as a possibility in his plans. At least, he could not think he had truly conceived of riding out of Rome, knowingly leaving them to the dogs. In any case, he was already out of the station and hurrying down the steps.

He couldn't think of anything he could do in so little time. Was he planning only to be there to watch?

The thought almost stopped him in midstep, winded. But he supposed he would do that, if nothing else: be present, bear witness.

He went straight to the centre and took a room in a large, glossy businessmen's *mansio* overlooking the Colosseum.

[x]

ARENA HOUNDS

Makaria must have heard the volucer coming in low over the Aegean, must have known she could be the only possible reason for its approach, but she did not come to meet it. When Drusus landed in the yard behind her villa on the highest peak of the island, the only sign of life was a brood of hens, who flapped away in clumsy panic into the herb garden as the aircraft descended. A couple of bony goats bounded past too. Drusus had only visited his cousin on Siphnos once before, but he did not remember there being so much livestock so close to the house – which looked run down, greying and flaking in the bright winter sun. No slaves appeared from inside, but as they approached through the garden the leader of the heavy escort of Praetorian minders he had set around Makaria came around the corner of the house and told him everyone was down in the big olive grove in the valley.

'But Lady Novia is accompanied, I hope?' said Drusus rather sharply.

'Yes, of course, your Majesty.'

Drusus could have waited in the house while they fetched her, but he had been tense and restless enough even before being shut aboard the volucer and it was some relief to be on the move. Besides, he was curious to see how the restrictions he'd placed on Makaria were working. From the air he had seen that the streets of the few tiny villages on Siphnos looked empty, stunned into submission, and there were scarcely any boats pulled up on the beaches or moored in the little harbour. He was pleased to find as they drove across the island in one of the Praetorian cars that the houses were indeed dark and shuttered, the shops boarded up. But there were vigiles everywhere, saluting him as he passed along otherwise deserted roads.

It struck him with vague wistfulness that this little island was perhaps the safest place in the world he could be, with hardly anyone left to threaten him, and all these guards to protect him. The next moment he remembered Salvius, dead on the staircase of the palace, and the feeling changed. Who would take his side against all these armed men if they should turn on him?

A quiver wormed its way across his shoulders, and he tried to shake it off. This sense of siege was what he wanted Makaria to feel; he had no business feeling it himself, no matter what that deranged bitch of a girl had said on the longvision.

'How many people are left here now?' he asked the Praetorian driving the car, as they stopped at the edge of the grove.

'Only about four hundred,' the man said cheerfully.

There had been almost two thousand. The islanders, Makaria of course excepted, had full freedom to leave, but they had to apply for special permission to return, which would almost never be granted. A single boat came once a month with supplies from the mainland, just barely enough to keep two small grocery stores on either side of the island intermittently in stock.

But it was halfway through olive-harvesting season, and it seemed a good quarter of the remaining population had emptied into the island's largest grove armed with poles, ladders and tarpaulins. A couple of his guards went off searching for Makaria – and even here Drusus was glad to see there were both Prae-torians and vigiles standing between the trees, watching the villagers – who looked harassed and strained – and following Makaria, who was trundling over the rough ground on a battered farm-buggy, the carrier box at the back already laden with large tubs of olives.

'No, no,' she cried to a boy of about twelve who was poking half-heartedly at the branches of a tree on the edge of the field. '*Hit* it. Get the pole in there and strike downwards. Like this!' And she jumped down from the buggy, seized the stick from him and began determinedly thrashing at the tree, expertly loosening a black rain of olives onto the canvas spread below.

'I see you're keeping busy,' said Drusus.

Makaria stiffened. She handed the stick to one of the lurking Praetorians rather than back to the boy, barking, 'You're twice his size, you do something useful for a change.' She turned, brushing down faded overalls, and Drusus marvelled anew that she could be the daughter of an Emperor. And yet she looked like him, even now, lean and weathered as she was, her unkempt hair and greenish eyes almost exactly the same shade as his.

She said curtly, 'What do you want, Drusus?'

The nearest harvesters were climbing down from the trees and laying down their sticks as they noticed Drusus, glancing uncertainly from him to Makaria, whispering among themselves, unsure what was expected of them. Some of them discreetly melted away into the trees. It was possible that many were not even sure who he was; they would barely have seen him on the longvision, for he had had the island's cables cut as soon as Makaria arrived there, and no newssheets came in on the monthly boat. He had had the radio frequencies altered too, jamming broadcasts to Siphnos from across the Aegean.

'First of all, I want you to remember your position,' answered Drusus, 'and mine.' He gestured his guards towards her. The men seized her and pushed her to her knees.

There was a hastily silenced cry of alarm from somewhere among the olive trees, then the surrounding harvesters also began dropping to their knees.

Makaria sighed. 'You are welcome here, your Majesty,' she said dully, staring at the ground.

Drusus looked down at her in silence for a while. 'Very well, cousin, you can get up,' he said at last, quietly, and moved closer to her. 'I don't mean for you to have to work like a farmhand,' he murmured as she rose to her feet. 'Surely four hundred people are sufficient to do these things for you?'

'Someone needs to do it for them, Drusus,' said Makaria. 'We need every pair of hands we can get. And I won't have anyone who stays here going hungry, or good farmland going to ruin.' She reached up to strip a spray of olives by hand in one fierce tug. She

248

flung the handful into one of tubs on her buggy. 'How is your war?'

'Oh, everything's going very well,' said Drusus. He took her arm companionably and they walked together back towards the road. 'We've taken Bamaria, and we control much of the north-west of what used to be Nionian Terranova. We've had considerable success using poison gas.'

He felt Makaria's body clench and saw her lips tighten before she looked away.

'Yet it's still not over,' she said at last.

'It won't be long. They're weakening in Siam, and once we're in a position to enter their Sinoan territory, Sina will start seeing sense and then it'll be as good as over.' He paused, and then remarked, as if casually, 'That little whore Una has been on trial for treason. She was sentenced to the Colosseum a few days ago.'

They were on a stretch of sandy road overlooking the sea. Makaria took a long breath and closed her eyes for a moment, then turned her head and gazed out patiently at the blue water, saying nothing.

'Did you know?' asked Drusus, scanning her face. 'Who told you? You are not to receive information without my sanction.'

'This might teach you that you cannot always control what people know,' said Makaria.

'Who told you?'

Makaria continued to watch the horizon as if he wasn't there.

'Tell me,' demanded Drusus.

'A man from the village. He's gone now,' said Makaria, 'on the ferry. I don't know where he went, or who told him.'

Drusus grimaced. 'Then you know of these claims she made in court? We've been questioning the Praetorian who was there when Marcus died.'

'He was a good officer,' said Makaria softly. 'He helped.'

'Yes, yes, no doubt. Is it true, then, that there was a piece of paper?'

'That?' said Makaria, with a harsh, miserable snort. 'You've come all this way over some nonsense I scribbled down to comfort him when he was dying? He wasn't rational – he was in pain. I'd have said anything he wanted. I might just as well have sung him a song or told him a fairy story.'

'Where is it?'

'I have no idea. I had other things on my mind that day, or have you forgotten what it was like? Maybe I dropped it in the Colosseum, I don't know. If you haven't found it in my rooms in the Palace I'm sure it's long gone.'

Drusus had the house searched. He and Makaria sat stiffly drinking wine in the central hall, Makaria occasionally flinching and sighing while the Praetorians crashed from room to room. They opened the safe to expose jewels Makaria never wore, upended tables and chairs, emptied drawers and chests, dumped out boxes of papers from the library study and library, shook through the pages of every book. Drusus wondered uneasily about the practicality of searching the rest of the island, interrogating the villagers. Someone might know where it was; they would confess if they were frightened enough.

And yet could his men ever hope to check every inch of an island that must cover thirty square miles? Even under watch, Makaria would not have needed much help to hide something her guards hadn't known existed. And she might be telling the truth, and the paper might have been long since lost or destroyed.

'What would you do if you found it? Even if you tore it up with your own hands, would it really make any difference?' asked Makaria, exasperated. 'I wouldn't be scared of a scrap of notepaper if I were you. But if that girl's put doubts in people's head about you, I don't know what you can do to get them out.'

'The people have no doubts about me,' said Drusus.

A woman came out from one of the rooms, apparently driven into the open by the upheaval. Her long red dress was so plain that for a moment Drusus took her for a slave, but seeing him she dropped an unthinkingly aristocratic curtsey and he saw that there were tiny rubies in her ears and she wore a plain gold chain around her neck, very like one that Makaria wore herself. She was perhaps halfway between his age and Makaria's. Unbound wiry black hair hung to her shoulders, and her black eyebrows and long Greek features gave her handsome face a slightly severe cast, at odds with her actual expression, which was self-conscious and faintly apologetic. Her skin was suntanned, her body solid and robustly graceful.

'This must be Hypatia,' he said. He had had no inkling of the woman's existence until taking the throne and turning this sudden scrutiny on his cousin's life, but the Praetorians had told him that not only did Hypatia share Makaria's home now, she'd been living with her for the last ten years or more. Drusus extended a hand. 'Come and sit down.'

Hypatia obeyed, smiling apprehensively. She asked, 'Will you be staying here tonight, your Majesty?'

'I think so, yes,' said Drusus.

'Hypatia is— She manages my household and my accounts. I prefer to have a woman do it,' announced Makaria, a little abruptly. She avoided looking at her friend.

A Praetorian emerged from the aula and said, 'Would you come to the longdictor, Sir?'

Drusus came back into the room a minute later, and beamed at Makaria and Hypatia, who had remained sitting at a distance from each other, in oppressed silence. He announced, in wonder, 'It's extraordinary – we've got them both. The brother – Sulien – he as good as handed himself over. You'll never believe how they caught him.'

Now Makaria looked stricken. She tensed for a moment, as if to rise from her chair, before slumping back and biting off whatever appalled response had come to her lips. She took a grim swig of her wine while beginning to blink rapidly against tears.

Drusus felt limp and dazzled with relief and gladness, all the tension he had felt over Una's desperate posturing in front of the cameras and some pitiful scrawling of Marcus' seemed suddenly silly. He said, 'Well, the games will get the New Year off to a good start this time!'

Makaria's control broke and she stood up, banging down her

glass on the table. 'Drusus, what is wrong with you – how do you justify any of this? You must know how indefensible it is. Leo and Clodia? Salvius' wife and children? These two now – did you *want* to be a tyrant? Una and Sulien were the ones who told the vigiles where to find Dama's camp outside Rome; they did as much as anyone could to try and stop him. The boy tried to save Marcus' life, I saw it. I don't see how they could possibly be any threat to you now – and even if somehow they are, can you really believe this is right?'

Drusus frowned, and then looked from Makaria to Hypatia and stared at her, watching a dark blush spread slowly across her face.

He said softly to Makaria, 'I told you, if you had people you care for here, to be careful.'

Makaria sat down again, cowed, but still she moaned, almost to herself, 'Can't you explain it to me, just once?'

'It's necessity,' said Drusus. His expression was very open and frank.

'For whom is it necessary?' said Makaria, feeling for a moment as if she might be on the brink of some discovery, for one or both of them: 'For Rome, or for you?'

But Drusus just blinked and shook his head, looking irritable and puzzled.

Nevertheless, he let the search continue into the night. The guards were still ransacking the house when Makaria went to bed. She lay in the dark and cried quietly, remembering pressing a key into Sulien's hand in a little study in the palace, hiding him from Drusus and giving him another year and a half to live. She felt disgraced by her helplessness now; she felt disgraced even by the proximity of Drusus' blood to her own.

The bedroom door eased open and Hypatia came running barefoot across the room and dived under the covers beside her.

'What are you thinking?' whispered Makaria, wiping her eyes. 'Go back to your room – what if they find you're not there and come looking for you?'

'They've been over all the bedrooms already,' said Hypatia,

shifting closer and flinging an arm across Makaria's waist. 'They're downstairs. They won't come back.'

Makaria's body softened against Hypatia's but she said, 'You should go. You should leave on the next ferry. You heard what he said. It's not safe for you to stay with me. I can't do a thing to protect you and I couldn't stand it if he hurt you.'

'Why do you say these things when you know I won't leave you?' Hypatia reproached her, leaning over her and kissing her lips.

Makaria seized hold of her in a kind of rage, impatiently gathering up her nightdress and pulling it off. They moved fiercely and yet with terrible caution, tense with the effort of keeping quiet, while part of Makaria's mind reflected that it was one small, mildly ridiculous benefit of the constraints upon them that the secrecy and anguish renewed them as lovers; when they touched now it was earnest, dramatic, nothing of the companionable routine of ten years. Whispered declarations spouted from them when they were alone as if they were naïve, astonished girls, barely knowing the first thing about each other or themselves.

They dared not sleep beside each other, but they couldn't bring themselves to part yet. They lay there audaciously long, hearing the thuds and footsteps from below grow quieter and more intermittent.

'If he found it—' whispered Makaria.

'He never will.'

Makaria sighed. 'I'm going to free the slaves we've got left as soon as he's gone. Not that any of us here are very free now, but at least they'll be able to leave. I can't be the one to look after that piece of paper and not do that. Although I don't know what it's worth, just to keep it hidden, when I'm stuck here. Perhaps I shouldn't have told him it didn't mean anything. I should have told the truth. I'm a coward; I'm a hypocrite, I should have done everything differently. Oh, I hope Marcus can't see what's going to happen to those two – and I can't help them, I can't do anything.'

Hypatia smoothed Makaria's hair in silence for a while. At last she murmured hesitantly, afraid of making it worse, 'At least . . . at least they'll be together.'

They wouldn't let him stay in the same cell as Una, no matter how desperately he begged. The air down here felt stiffened and filthy, like a dried-out dishcloth: too thick to breathe, or to see through. Sometimes Sulien heard someone crying out and beating against a cell door and thought it was himself, and then realised dizzily that it must have been some other prisoner nearby – he was simply sitting, staring at the door, and couldn't move even to flex out the cramp in his legs. The cell was too small for him to lie at full length. There was only a bench to sleep on, and since he'd been there they'd thrown a lump of bread in through the hatch in the door only twice – or was it three times? He thought that was fair, that was all right; you did not want to go out there rested or well-fed, you wanted your reserves to give out as quickly as possible.

At first he'd shouted Una's name – he wasn't sure for how long. It was hard to keep track of time, which seemed to move in swerves and lunges and skips. There was one dull reddish light in the ceiling that blinked and flickered as the building shook, which was nearly constantly, with the pounding of feet in the stands above, the humming of machinery, fireworks, and the irregular thuds of whatever battles were going on out in the sunlight. It was as if the Colosseum were a gigantic vehicle, its hidden engine jolting and steaming, driving endlessly forward over stony ground – and yet, though he felt it through the bricks all the time, he could scarcely hear the sound from overhead, except when it stopped. The tunnels below ground seethed with their own noises: cages on wheels and trolleys carrying weapons or props rattled past the door of his cell, with guards, slaves and stagehands always shouting to each other, and tannoys keeping a continual relay of summons and instructions: 'Cleaners to corridor twelve,' or 'Medical attendants on standby at the Victory Bay,' or 'Provocateurs and katar fighters: this is your five-minute call.' Only for a few hours at night was it almost quiet, which was both a relief and somehow worse at the same time: his senses glowed with exhausted release even as he shrank in horror from the renewed capacity to think clearly.

But he did think about his life during this time. It took an effort – even now he disliked deliberately looking back; it frightened him. But he thought especially of the last four and a half years, since Una had saved him in London, and measured the worth of them, knew how glad he was he'd had them. And when he tried to imagine what this time would be like outside the Colosseum, knowing Una was alone inside, it seemed worse even than this, it really did. And when it happened, it couldn't be as bad as crucifixion, it wouldn't go on as long.

But he wanted to say these things aloud, or something else, something better – to Una; he should have said them in the van, while there was still a chance. But how could he have let it come to this, how could he have failed so totally? And where was Una that even now, in the near-silence, either she couldn't hear him calling or he couldn't hear her answer?

The smell of the place was as heavy in the air as the noise, and it throbbed and changed through the day: caustic detergent in the morning over an old unexpunged base of blood, sweat and animal excrement which swelled and bloomed as the hours passed, before slaves raced through the corridors again, dousing the floor and walls with disinfectant and subduing it.

And sometimes he could hear the dogs barking.

It could not be that he had done it for nothing, that each of them would go up to the arena separately, alone. It couldn't be like that. Nothing could be that cruel.

When they came he was as overcome with physical incredulity as if he'd had no warning, no choice. He blurted, 'No— Please—' as they took hold of him, and as useless, as undignified as it was, he would have fought them if he could. But there was no strength in him; his arms swung weakly against their grip, his legs wouldn't hold him up. They half-carried him, his feet skimming and stumbling along the floor, down a passage, up a flight of stairs. They had to jostle him past so many people as they reached the floor above – he could not take in a thing about what they were doing, only that there were so many. Then there was a new, acrid note of hot metal in the bloody daytime smell, and he turned his head to see a man, ludicrously clad in fancy-dress, with a black hood over a beaked mask, heating iron wands in a brazier. Sulien's mind, reeling, supplied the purpose of the wands: to press against the bodies – his body – to be certain it was dead. He saw the black column of a lift-shaft descending to the crowded floor, the doors towards which they were taking him, and he began to shout again for Una.

There was a downpour of sunlight as the doors opened, so bright it stunned him, and his eyelids winced shut with the blaze still printed upon the redness inside. And then the men holding him pushed and let go, and he was alone in the light. The doors were closing and he was crouched, gasping, on the platform as it began to rise. He couldn't see, he could barely make out the sides of the lift-shaft sliding past, then he was rising from the hole like an animal smoked out from a burrow into the untempered noise he'd felt through the walls. Still blindfolded in light, he could not see the crowd in the stands; the sound could almost have been the roar of the sea or wind—

And yet it could not; it was intolerably and unmistakably human.

He called out, 'Una.' He could only just hear himself under the flood of voices.

And yet he did hear her, answering, 'Sulien.'

He blinked, straining to force his eyelids open against the light. There was Una, turning, dazed, as she rose from another trapdoor on the other side of the arena, then she climbed up out of the shaft before the lift had stopped and came stumbling across the sand towards him.

Sulien staggered into a clumsy run. The floor of the arena seemed to pitch underneath them; they could barely keep their balance long enough to reach each other.

'*It's all right,*' he said, as they met.

But his vision had cleared now and he could see the thousands of people making that noise, row upon row of them rising towards the ellipse of blue sky above the walls. His gaze stuck for a moment on the rebuilt Imperial box, shockingly close, and Drusus, a calm, alert figure sitting behind a screen of bulletproof glass, watching. He could see the vanished wreckage and Marcus' body at the same time.

'Don't look at them; you don't have to see them. They're not there,' said Una, in a strange, stern, gabbling little voice, her cold hands closing hard on his arm and shoulder, fingertips boring in. 'There's just us.'

So he looked at her instead, her face grey and haggard and her eyes red, but time dissolved between them; a fast-flowing stream carried him down, back to their childhood, back even beyond the reach of his memory, coursing fast over the years apart as if they had never happened.

At some signal neither saw, with a soft breeze of indrawn breath around the stands, the crowd hushed. The gates at the end of the arena were opening.

They couldn't keep to their feet any longer, the shudders passing from one to the other as they held each other brought them down to their knees. Above them, part of the glass roof – the repairs were still not finished – was drawn over the arena, enough to bend and warm the sunlight as it passed through. The sand was hot, as if it were summer and they were by the sea.

The hounds poured out from the gates.

It was true: they were like a single creature, the spaces between them blurred by speed and a kind of bulky grace, for they moved more like a school of fish or a flock of starlings than a pack of dogs, all turning at an instant, the sun flashing white on their flanks. Their cries as they ran were unlike any baying of dogs Sulien had heard before, deep and rhythmic, almost chanting. The sand rose into a haze as they swept forward, following the curve of the arena and joining into a loop around them, a solid rampart of muscle and bone. They were larger than wolves, their massive forequarters disproportionate to the narrow waists and hips. The blunt, pale heads were almost earless, the eyes tiny, the red mouths gaping.

Sulien bent his head over Una, one hand on the back of her head, pressing her against him. He breathed out, closing his eyes. He whispered, 'It's better than being alone, isn't it?'

He could feel that she was crying. But she said, 'All right. It's better.'

The hounds plunged inwards, flinging themselves upon them.

Varius was standing in an aisle on the first level, above the first-class seats. He forced himself to watch as the hounds covered them, then turned away sharply, a sick hollow in his stomach, his fists painfully clenched, and strode quickly into one of the inner passages that circled the building. He hurried down the steps to the ground floor, to the rows of longdictors in one of the exitways. He entered the code for the vigiles.

'My name's Caius Varius Ischyrion,' he said quietly to the man who answered. 'All this time you've been searching for me and I've never left Rome. I've slept in the street outside your headquarters and you didn't find me. I'm in the Colosseum now. I've placed bombs throughout the building. You have five minutes.'

Sand filled Una's mouth. The hounds crashed over them like a wave; she and Sulien were rolled across the ground, first tangled together, then tumbling apart, grasping at each other's arms. Claws raked across her midriff, at her scalp. Hot, rotten breath puffed against her face as she choked and spat and tried to flounder closer to Sulien under the trampling feet. He was making the same flailing effort to stay beside her.

Teeth fastened on her shoulder and held fast; the dog began to pull and worry at her flesh. The sound she made was not a scream – down here, in the rising fog of sand, she had no breath, there was no time – but more a strangled groan of effort as she strained not to lose her hold on Sulien's arms, her skin tearing, her legs scraping on the sand, seeking for some purchase, until the dog shook her loose and towed her away from him.

Sulien shouted for her and she twisted and kicked reflexively, even tried to punch or scratch at the thing with her free hand, but the teeth lodged in her flesh tightened and it hurt far too much. She hung limp as the animal ran, dragging her across the sand like a toy. Four or five of the dogs came running along with the one that held her, skipping over her trailing body, snapping almost playfully at her legs. She could see the sunburnt pink skin under the white hair, and a stripe of her own blood, dabbled over the ground.

There was a ripple of laughter in the terraces, and despite every effort she could make to shut the crowd out of her consciousness, her eyes blurred with anger and misery. Her body was already gashed and torn, with pain running wild through it; her clothes were wet with blood and the horrible slaver of the things, and it had only just started, still so much of it left to go.

Then the dog let go, dropping her face-down on the sand, and ran on. She rose onto her knees, pressing a hand to her shoulder, and turned clumsily to look back. She couldn't even see Sulien under the rest of the pack. They seethed over him like water boiling in a pan.

But the distance between the two groups of hounds could not hold for long. Moving again in that eerie unison, the creatures sprang away from Sulien and rushed at her. Instinctively she put up her arms to shield herself, but they flowed past her, making that ugly, cadenced cry as they met their fellows behind her. And there was Sulien, lying curled on the ground, then rising lopsid- edly and looking for her, blood streaking his arms and his hair.

Behind her the hounds were gathered in a single mass, some of them pawing at the ground. Some muzzles and paws were stained red.

'They will try to get you running,' Drusus had said. She had believed she would not do that; there would be nothing to run towards. But she ran now, with the pack at her heels. It was such a small distance to cover, but they were so fast, and they caught her before she could reach Sulien, ran her down like a speeding car or a train. She felt the heavy clawed feet pounding over her back. She couldn't lift any part of her body more than an inch before it was slammed down again.

Sulien dragged himself onto his feet as they piled onto her. He ran forward, snatching up something from the sand almost without seeing it: a broken length of wood – the remains of some fight with javelins or staves – and struck at the heaving mob, weakly at first, and then with despairing force, stabbing down with the broken end. They parted a little as three of them turned on him, leaping up; he swung the shaft at them, sweeping it across their faces with all his strength, and incredibly, for an instant, they fell back, enough to let him wade between them towards his sister, still jabbing and hitting out.

A hound latched onto him from behind and he staggered, but for another moment remained upright. He whirled the shaft again, though he didn't connect with anything this time. Now he heard whoops of approval from the crowd, and a sigh of disappointment when the dogs brought him down. But he had fallen across Una, and he felt her arms close around his back.

An alarm hooted from above the arena and a voice over the loudspeakers interrupted, announcing something, but the hounds were crushing the breath out of them with their sheer weight and Sulien couldn't hear and didn't care what it said.

On an empty flight of stairs Varius pulled a handful of firecrackers from his pocket, lit them and flung them down onto the concrete, hurrying on before they went off. The series of reports were very loud, and though they sounded more like a burst of gunfire than like any kind of bomb, that was all it needed, and the Colosseum's passageways magnified the sound, stirred it round the walls. As he passed the archways he'd seen that the spectators were already abandoning their seats, pushing anxiously, despite the calls from the Colosseum guards for calm and order. Now there were shrieks, and people began to run.

He was dressed in his vigile uniform – of course descriptions of him wearing it had been all over the longvision and the news-sheets, and going back to retrieve the jacket from the skip had been dangerous in itself – but there was nothing else for it, not in the absurdly limited time he had. And he was pretty sure that in the growing panic people were unlikely to see anything but the uniform when they looked at him.

He left the Colosseum just as the first flock of vigile and Praetorian cars came shrieking down the Sacred Way. He crossed the Via Labicana towards the gladiators' barracks at the Ludus Magnus. Here too, trainers, slaves and gladiators were in the process of evacuation and were standing in noisy throngs outside the open doors.

'Let me through, please,' he said firmly.

Drusus rose from his chair and glanced instinctively up at the roof, alarmed and suspicious. 'What is it?' he asked the Prae-torians who were trying to draw him away. 'No, I command you to tell me what's happened.'

He had been leaning forward in his seat to watch as the lifts carried them up to the arena, his hands clenched under his chin, and yet at no point had he felt the renewal of elation he'd expected. He hadn't liked watching them run towards each other like that, and as they crumpled to their knees with their arms round each other, something twisted and tightened in his chest. He'd blinked, and turned his eyes to the gates from which the hounds would emerge, but that physical sense of unease did not diminish. Partly it was the behaviour of the audience: yes, most of them were happily cheering for the hounds, laughing when a few of the brutes dragged the girl off to one side, but there were too many who were looking touched or saddened, or who covered their eyes – chiefly women, of course – but then the boy had started trying to fight, and the burst of applause had come from men too. He'd found himself wishing for the dogs to hurry and get it over with.

'The vigiles have received a message from someone claiming to be Varius, who says he's planted explosives in the building,' said the Praetorian. 'We must get you to safety, Sir.'

Drusus looked down anxiously into the arena. Una and Sulien were now hidden under the heaving surfaces of the hounds' backs. Then the animals shifted a little and he glimpsed a body lying still and bloody underneath – he could not even make out who it was. But he knew how this went, and he knew even a lot of blood didn't necessarily mean much. Only a few minutes had passed; it was too soon for them to have died yet, unless the unrest had startled the dogs into losing control.

'It's a trick,' he said, hesitantly, for he was not certain how far he meant it. He had said so often that they were all enemies of Rome, that there was no difference between them and Dama, but his mind seemed to dazzle and catch when he tried to remember exactly how it had begun.

A stuttering boom rang loud in the corridors, and he flinched hard, remembering the last time, and that moment of awareness before the dark as the roof had shattered above him.

'You really must come, your Majesty.'

Drusus turned away towards the passage, but he said to the captain, 'Make sure they're dead.'

Ziye fastened a respiratory mask over the lower part of her face; a cap already hid her hair. People were still pushing their way out of the section of seating closest to the gladiators' gates, but the clothes she was wearing would have guarded her against questions or interference, even if the few last clusters of scared, jostling spectators had had any attention to spare. The plastic overalls were not quite the same as those the Colosseum's morgue attendants wore, but they were passably close, and in any case, impeccably official-looking. Ziye strode briskly down the aisle and climbed over the railing above the arena. She crouched for a moment on the edge and jumped down.

It was a long drop, but she landed in the arena as neatly as if she'd never left it, rolling deftly on the sand and springing back to her feet, even though her body was no longer that of a professional fighter and she felt her joints grumble in protest. Ignoring the tumult in the stands she looked up at the vault of space held within the Colosseum's walls, and even though the hounds were a milky foam covering Una and Sulien just half the length of the arena away, even though she had meant never to walk this ground again, she felt comfortable, at home.

A troop of dog-handlers had spilled out of the gates, carrying boards, goads and tranquilliser guns. They were trying to herd the hounds to safety, into the tunnel that ran beneath the Colosseum to the vivarium. They were all slaves; the dogs' lives were worth more than theirs, and they were in panicky haste. Their whistles and calls were shrill and hurried and when Ziye looked at the hounds they seemed at best only temporarily distracted from their work. For the moment she could not see Una or Sulien at all.

She heard another deep burst of sound bouncing round the loop of the walls: Lal or Delir, scattering more crackers under the feet of the crowd.

There were more shrieks, and however strict their orders must have been, several of the slaves dropped their tools and ran. Ziye ran too, through the gladiators' gate and down a ramp into the dark staging bay below. She could hear the panic and uproar roiling through the underground passages, but she couldn't see it; there were boards like those the handlers carried blocking every way except one, to channel the hounds to and from the vivarium. She'd hoped she could snatch what she wanted from a shelf or a rack on the wall, but she did not see it in her first swift glance around and there was no time for a more thorough search. Instead, when another of the handlers came fleeing down the ramp, Ziye let him pass her, then closed in and jabbed an elbow into the small of his back. He crumpled backwards and she caught him with her right arm around his neck before he could make any sound. She squeezed with forearm and bicep on the arteries on either side of the jaw, counting as she felt the strength run out of him, dragging him back to lay him down in the shadows. And for a moment, even though she regretted this blemish on her promise to cleanse herself permanently of violence, she was almost sorry the crowd in the terraces had not witnessed this. It had been a good piece of work.

The rubbish sacks stuffed with paper were still by the gates where he had left them; Varius swept them up and carried them inside. There were no vigiles – except himself, of course – in the Ludus Magnus yet. Gladiators and their managers and mistresses were still hurrying down from the barracks above. Every gate and door stood open.

He passed through the colonnade, crossed the practice ground and moved into the tunnel through which the gladiators marched down into the innards of the Colosseum.

For an instant the hounds froze, tense, their heavy paws flexing uncertainly. Then they began again to trample and scrape, but soon they stopped again and this time they skittered away, pouring and reforming like a drop of mercury, and Sulien dragged himself up, pulling Una with him, and tried to place himself between her and the dogs as the pack pivoted around them. He reached again for the broken javelin, which was half buried in the sand. It was harder to keep a grip on it; his hands were unsteady, and slippery with blood.

'Sulien – don't,' moaned Una, 'just let them do it.' And Sulien didn't know why he was trying to prolong this, but he couldn't stop. The hounds made a feint inwards, playing, perhaps, and retreated for a moment when he brandished the staff at them. He hurled himself at them, shouting, and an image flashed across his memory: Una's eyelids straining stubbornly open after he'd drugged her on the day of Marcus' death, resisting for no good reason.

There was a stabbing pain in his back that felt strange for a second, but everything hurt anyway, all of it running together like splotches of ink. The hound in the lead reared up and he struck it across the chest. Something was happening in the arena, but blood kept dripping into his eyes, and in any case, the hounds were finished playing now and came charging back in earnest, effortlessly mowing them down, knocking Una away from him again. This time the onslaught passed in a numb blur, as if they were rushing right through him.

When it was over he tried to stand again, teetered upright for an instant, then toppled down onto his knees and couldn't get his balance to rise a second time.

Una did not get up. She was lying on her back, her clothes shredded and scarlet, her eyes closed. Sulien floundered across the sand towards her, a cry bubbling out of him— But no, not yet, she was still breathing, and steadily, as if she were merely asleep. But he supposed she wouldn't wake again now.

He wiped his face and looked around, and grasped for a moment that the stands were emptying and that the dogs had drawn off. But the understanding leaked away almost as soon as he had it – it didn't matter what anyone else was doing; he could scarcely even keep his eyes open now. He was bewildered that he seemed to be fading so fast – yes, they were both covered in blood, but had either of them really lost so much, or been wounded so deeply yet? An annoying need to account for it fussed at his mind, and he frowned, fretfully turning over the only diagnosis that made any kind of sense: shock, lack of sleep and food . . . but still . . .

Of course it didn't matter. Even the pain was almost finished with now; a deep wave of dizziness was rising to swallow it. Sulien let it suck him down to the sand beside Una, he let it drag his eyes shut, thankful.

The vigiles were spreading hastily through the basements of the Colosseum, scouring through its tunnels and cluttered recesses, trying to control and order the flow of stage hands, prison guards, medics, lighting and sound technicians. Varius moved among them in the dim underground light, scanning the walls as he walked by. Naturally, after so many years, Ziye had not been able to tell him the location of the fuse box. He could probably manage even without finding it, but darkness would help him. He didn't see it as he passed between the lift-shafts on the upper floor, or at the bottom of the stairwell as he moved down to the level of the cells. But as he reached the guards' workstation, a broad booth with a glazed partition opening on one side towards the cell-block, there it was, on the outer wall.

Varius looked around. He had to wait for a second until a vigile officer further down the passage had flung open a door to a storage room and barged inside. Varius opened the panel and examined the labels above the switches with hurried care – he didn't want to take out everything. Then he flicked a firecracker into a corner and as it sounded, slammed off the switches.

Shouts of horror scattered through the blackness. Somewhere, something heavy crashed to the floor.

Varius had his torch ready in his hand. He switched it on, glanced at his watch, and went on towards the morgue.

At last, and as one, the hounds came surging away towards the handlers and the gates. Ziye flattened herself against the wall as they rushed by. She had already seized a low-slung trolley, designed for clearing away corpses and other rubbish from the arena; she tried to shield herself behind it now. She'd fought arena hounds once before, a novelty act, three of them, leaping and clawing like a triple-headed monster out of a myth, during a lean year when her troop was in Gaetulia and audiences were sparse. She was not going to do it again.

In all that empty space, the two crumpled bodies looked strangely unimportant. She could see how Sulien must have crawled his way to Una; he'd left a ploughed-up trail of reddened sand. Ziye bent and plucked out the tranquilliser dart she'd fired into his shoulder. The one that had hit Una lay in a shallow furrow in the sand beside her; it must have been knocked out of her flesh as she fell. So much the better; perhaps a little less of the drug would have entered her blood. Ziye sucked her teeth as she looked down at them, more worried about the load of sedative in the darts than any of the wounds on them. There had been no time to find out much about the tranquilliser, and it had had to be an identical dose for them both.

Well, even at the worst, it would be a better death than how the dogs would have finished them. She collected a third dart poking out of the sand a few feet away – she'd missed with her first shot – and hauled first Sulien, then Una, onto the trolley. With some difficulty she got it moving again, and it felt like a long way, dragging the thing across the sand, out in the open. But she was only taking the bodies to where they belonged. She shoved the trolley onto a scuffed square of metal near the northernmost peak of the arena's curve: the lift-shaft that ran down to the morgue.

She could see vigiles breaking from the gates into the arena now, like some new gladiatorial act; they were heading towards her. Of course, the lifts could not be operated from above; she could do nothing but wait.

There had been no other executions that morning, and the morgue staff had already fled; the room was empty. Varius crossed it in two strides, dropping the rubbish sacks, hand at once outstretched towards the button that summoned the lift. He stood, jigging slightly from foot to foot and fidgeting with the switch on the torch as he waited. Some of the single-mindedness that had kept him calm so far had begun to evaporate; he could not stop his brain from cataloguing the worst possibilities behind the doors as the lift hummed its slow way down.

The morgue lay deep below the arena; the sunlight that reached the bottom of the shaft was weak and pallid. Ziye was standing over a shadowed, motionless heap. At once, Varius turned the beam of the torch downwards, bracing himself for the inevitable shock of red. 'They're alive,' Ziye informed him crisply, steering the trolley into the room.

There was no time for anything more; they could hear rapid,

heavy footsteps along the passage. Ziye covered the bodies – it was hard to think of them as living, as Una and Sulien – with a length of plastic sheeting, and Varius retreated into the thicker shadows at the back of the room.

A vigile officer opened the door and swept the light of a torch across Ziye's masked face.

'What are you doing still in here?'

Ziye shrugged. 'Everyone's overreacting. It's like a bunker down here. I could barely hear it when it happened last time. I was going to take them to the incinerator first.' She gestured down at the trolley and the vigile officer trained his light on its load. Varius' attention was drawn to what must be Sulien's hand, emerging from the plastic, intact fingers trailing on the floor of the morgue.

'You're sure they're dead?'

Ziye snorted faintly. 'Throats torn. Too much commotion up there; the dogs don't like it.'

Varius had been edging his way silently along the back wall of the room. In the dark he had been unable to make out anything about the man until he was right behind him, except that he was about his own height and his voice sounded young. Close up he could see the insignia on the uniform, junior to the rank he had assumed himself; good. He pushed past, as if he'd only just come in through the door, and bent over the base of the trolley, lifting a corner of the sheeting and touching a bloody wrist, a throat, before the other man could get the idea of doing it himself. He thought he could feel a hidden, withdrawn life in the skin, even before he found a slow, tired pulse, felt a wisp of breath against his palm. His own heart kicked in tense sympathy.

He looked up and nodded. 'Radio it through,' he said, 'I'll handle things in here.'

The man nodded back and tramped out of the room. Varius' heart gave another guarded leap.

'Where are the bags?' hissed Ziye, looking around at once for the rubbish sacks. Varius pulled them over, opened them both.

There were handfuls of empty sacks on top of the paper that filled out each one.

Una and Sulien were so unwieldy, so awkward, as Ziye and Varius wrestled them into the sacks. It was such heavy, irritating work that it felt oddly prosaic, like packaging up some complicated piece of furniture. They struggled, panting, preoccupied only with weight, and how to work the hinges of knees and elbows. But when it was almost done, each of them folded down inside the bags, only their heads still to be covered, they seemed to become human and themselves again, and Varius, lifting Una's head to pull another of the bags down over it, looked down at her face with a sudden sting of recognition and renewed fear. He ripped a hole in the plastic near her mouth and thought nevertheless, they won't be able to breathe; we're suffocating them.

Then they piled the full sacks over them and stuffed a third bag with more of the plastic sheeting when that didn't look like enough to hide the shape of the bundles underneath. Ziye went to the door and Varius studied their work for a moment by the torchlight: a trolley heaped with anonymous plastic sacks.

'It's clear,' said Ziye.

He wheeled the trolley out of the room. He'd turned off his light; they made their way by the flickering beams of the vigiles' torches. The paper-filled sacks were so light that Ziye had to walk alongside the trolley and keep a hand on the topmost bag to keep it from falling. It was as well to have her in the lead, Varius thought; in the dark he might have lost his bearings, lost time. Once they had gained the upper floor she marched ahead, unhesitating. They moved along, a cumbersome, purposeful shadow, bumping occasionally against a heap of props or one of the vigiles, who cursed and ran on.

They reached the tunnel out to the gladiators' barracks. The flow of workers from within the Colosseum had almost given out. A few more vigiles went by, one with a pair of brown-and-white dogs which looked almost puppy-like, compared with the beasts in the arena. Varius kept the trolley close to the wall, didn't walk too fast, and forced himself not to let his gaze drift past Ziye's back towards the daylight ahead. Evidence, forensics, he repeated to himself silently, as if he might forget or fumble the words if he were asked for an explanation.

But they saw only a pair of officers out in the practice ground at the Ludus Magnus, and that at some distance, and no one asked them anything, not even when they walked the trolley out through the gates onto the street. Varius tightened his grip on the handles as his head grew light, and his skin was washed with sudden sweat, as if a fever were breaking. He glanced at Ziye, whose own skin looked pale and taut; he thought he could make out the lines of a grimace below the mask.

They turned off the Via Labicana down a broad shopping street, turned again into a quieter road almost choked with parked cars. It wasn't empty; someone was backing out of a parking space, and further down stood a little group of nervous people who might have run here from the Colosseum for shelter. But their van was there, and nothing had happened to it. Ziye opened the doors and let down the ramp and the people from the Colosseum watched, vaguely interested in this manifestation of vigile business.

Ziye began to drive as, in the back of the van, Varius was throwing the stuffed sacks aside, tearing open the plastic to see the damage.

NEW YEAR'S DAY

Perception came in bits and pieces: a sparse litter of unnecessary things, drifting in on the tide. Something tangled around his body; someone making a noise and demanding something; cold air on damp bare skin. Sulien did not even form the thought that none of this mattered; there was nothing of him left to think at all. But after a time, as the trickle of sensations crept on, he noticed himself turning his head away from the jostling, shouting person beside him, and it occurred to him that he was waking.

He whispered, 'No,' and felt his lips move and air, swelling his lungs.

'Sulien,' said Varius' voice, sounding strained and exasperated, 'come on: you have to help. I don't know what I'm doing with this.'

The cry of the hounds throbbed in the air, and he wanted to bring up his arms to cover his head, but he could not move – he was afraid of being able to move, of consciousness taking hold in his body. He did not know, or want to know, why Varius was there.

He was not exactly in pain yet, except for the immense weight of his eyelids and the aching haze in his head, but he could feel the lines of his injuries marking out the parameters of his body, like preliminary strokes of a pen.

Varius shook him again, and began urgently rattling off the names of drugs so that Sulien had the impression, at once frightening and comforting, of having slid back five years, or ten years, from the moment of dying into Catavignus' beautiful study in London, preparing for some exam . . .

. . . but his eyes tipped open, just for an instant, though he took in nothing of what he saw – and even if he'd wanted to, he could not have stopped his eyelids from dropping again at once. But the act of opening them was enough; at a stroke he lost any doubt that he was alive. Even as he collapsed back into sleep he knew, this time, that he'd wake again, and within minutes or seconds.

It was a little quieter, and he could smell antiseptic. Half-heartedly, Sulien opened his eyes. Varius was still beside him, but he was no longer shouting at him, he had turned away and was muttering feverishly, under his breath. He sounded barely sane. Sulien understood more or less where he was, that somehow Varius had got them out of the Colosseum. He didn't know how it had been done, and couldn't even begin to wonder. However it had happened, it was a mistake. He still could not think except in bewildered, aching spurts, but he was sure they would not get away; this was an extension, a repetition, of capture and death, not a true escape. The smallest touch of any other possibility stung like disinfectant on newly torn skin.

Now he was awake, of course he had to know what had happened to Una. He resented the uselessness of it, resented even the effort of lifting his head, but he looked around, and saw her lying in a mess of torn plastic sacks, patched with untidy clumps of bandages. The motion of the van shook her slightly, unresisted tremors which somehow displayed how still she was, so still that from here he couldn't see the movement of her breath.

Sulien rolled sluggishly onto his side, and realised the worst of his own wounds had been cleaned and crudely dressed. There was a clutter of medical supplies scattered around them both: bloody bundles of gauze, bottles of saline, a pair of empty syringes.

Varius was kneeling between them, bending over Una, eyes wild, teeth clenched, looking back and forth between her face and what looked like a handwritten list of instructions, as if there might be some overlooked answer somewhere.

He turned, and Sulien dropped his eyes at once, because he

could not look Varius in the face. He was heavy with bleak fury with him, and shame at it.

Varius raced through the list of drugs again: narcotics, antagonists. He was bristling with nervous energy; it was exhausting even to hear him. 'You both had the same dose of the tranquilliser; there wasn't anything we could do about that. Look, here.' He pressed an empty dart into Sulien's limp, indifferent hand. 'And we were guessing with the antidote too – but you started waking up at once. You didn't look like that, even before I gave you anything. But she— Nothing's happening. Do we give her more, or would that—? Can you do something?'

'I don't want,' began Sulien, dully. But even in his mind the words slithered away; he could not actually tell Varius how lumpishly ungrateful he felt, that he only wanted to let Una sleep, to lie down again himself.

He shifted closer to her. 'Wake up, Una,' he said, unhappily.

'How are we doing? Where are we?' shouted Varius to the front of the van, and Sulien realised he had not yet even wondered who was driving. He assumed, without thinking about it, that there were vigile cars already hounding the van along the unseen road, closing in ahead.

'We're on the Via Valeria, coming up to Carsioli,' called Ziye. Her presence, along with almost everything else, was unfathomable to Sulien. He wondered where Lal was, and was glad she wasn't here. But he was startled that they were so far out of Rome. How could the vigiles have allowed that?

Una was heavily unconscious still, and a slow, thick feeler of blood was creeping from under the bandaging at her shoulder. But her breath was already a little stronger than it had been. A second dose of the antidote would have woken her, even if Sulien hadn't been there.

'Will she be all right?' demanded Varius.

'Yes,' said Sulien, without tone, still without looking at him.

Varius nodded, but didn't display any obvious relief, just moved to the next matter with jarring swiftness. He tossed a bag

273

of clothes at Sulien. 'Get yourselves cleaned up enough to put these on,' he said, scrambling towards the seats in the front.

Sulien pulled vaguely at the contents of the bag; but for now that would have to be enough, he couldn't do anything but slump back against the side of the van, watching Una, but seeing the dogs' red mouths gaping whenever his eyelids slipped shut. He thought of asking where Varius hoped to take them, but decided it would take too much effort, even if he had truly wanted to know.

Una's eyes opened a little way and for a while remained fixed, without apparent surprise or pain, on the low ceiling. Then they turned slowly towards Sulien. Her face creased and she said, 'It hurts.'

A knot of pain that had nothing to do with what the hounds had done to him tightened and locked in Sulien's chest. 'I can't breathe,' he thought, finding it oddly funny to be panicking over that now. But the same moment he had to brace himself as the van veered sharply, and his pulse went clashing in the bites and scrapes all over him and it was too much; he couldn't stand any more of it. And it would have been over by now— It had been over . . .

Una reached out blindly, groaning, and dragged a torn sheet of the plastic sacking over her body, trying to hide or clothe herself. She looked around. 'Varius?' she croaked.

Varius turned at once, but only to give her a tense, curt look, a nod. He said, 'Get yourselves ready.'

Una was trying to sit up, her hands batting weakly at the floor of the van, clutching at Sulien, and crying out as she tried to prop herself on her left arm.

He made equally clumsy efforts to lift her. She leant against him, baffled, gasping, and said at last in a whisper, 'I don't think anyone's following us.'

Sulien didn't answer, tried to forget he'd heard. He started to prise Varius' rough dressing away from the ragged punctures in her shoulder. He could keep his attention there, and later, on the slashes on his own legs and back; he could coax the worst of the bleeding to stop, smooth down some of the pain, and he got so lost in the difficulty of it that he forgot to think of time passing, only realised when they were at last struggling, exhausted, into the clothes, how long all this had taken. More than an hour must have passed since Varius first woke him.

The clothes made no sense on their bodies; he thought, as Una, grimacing, wrenched on a dark wool coat. Baggy prison wear, bloody rags and scraps of plastic had been right for what was happening, for raw, pulpy skin and bruised bones, not costumes meant for human beings, with neat seams and soft linings. How strange he must look, as Una looked to him, with her blood-sticky hair, and her scored hands emerging from these stupidly well-made and well-chosen things. Lal, he thought – oh, he was sure it was her; she had been in charge of the clothes. Even the colours suited them; she'd have done that without even thinking about it. In spite of her efforts blood was oozing through his sleeve.

'Sulien,' began Una again, in a too-soft, too-hopeful voice.

He shut his eyes and said, 'Don't.'

But the van was slowing as it turned downhill, the road seemed rougher, quieter. And then they stopped. Varius leapt out, pulled open the doors.

The light— Again the light was too strong, white and cold and stinging above the sea. They stumbled out onto the road, heavy and off-balance, almost blind, the wind sharp through their clothes and bandages. They were on a narrow road leading down to a jetty, where a few small yachts and fishing boats were moored. A pale, pretty village rose on the hillside over the little bay.

Ziye was still inside the van. She leaned out of the window, looked at Una and Sulien, staggering and mute in the light. 'I'll see you,' she said tersely, no more, and drove away. Neither of them even thought to thank her.

But there was no one around on the road, only a woman walking a dog down on the beach, too far off to see the blood they hadn't been able to rub away or cover up. But Sulien could still hear the noise the hounds had made, booming somewhere in his skull along with the beat of his heart. When he blinked, he could almost believe he was still sprawled there on the hot sand and this—

But of course this wasn't like a dream; they were really here, limping down the jetty, and they'd be lucky not to topple together into the sea, for they could hardly stand upright, let alone walk. And still he was waiting for something to happen, for volucers to descend, vigile boats to pile out of nowhere into the little bay. Varius marched them along, almost angrily, as if he expected it too, and now he was actually herding them onto the deck of the boat moored furthest from the shore. Everything around was so quiet and blue as Sulien crumpled down on the little strip of deck behind the cockpit and Varius wrenched fiercely and inexpertly at the controls. The boat went jolting out from the harbour, over the slow waves.

Una was crouched on the bench seats by the windows, looking back at the shore. Varius forced the little yacht along as if the whole of the Roman fleet was behind them, but there was nothing, only the sound of the engine burring through the water and the air. Sulien dragged himself up to see the land already reduced to a pale line behind them, and then gone, leaving only the dark suppleness of the sea.

Abruptly, Varius turned off the engine, let go of the controls. He said, quietly, almost a question, 'It worked,' and he dropped back in the seat and lay there, breathing hard, trembling. Then he began to laugh – low, hitching spasms at first, then louder angry, delighted. He shouted, 'We did it. It worked, I got you.' He rose from the seat as if looking for something to punch, and turned to them, scarcely recognisable with triumph. 'That'll show the bastard.'

Sulien looked around at the impossible sea and tried to answer, but that seemed to dislodge something in him, and all that came were tears.

Varius stopped laughing long enough to produce a bottle of methousia from beside the helm, take a deep swig from it before pushing it firmly into Sulien's hands. He collapsed onto the bench opposite and covered his face, laughter coming more quietly now, but still unstoppable.

Una sat staring from Varius to Sulien and back, open-mouthed, mechanically rubbing Sulien's arm, still incapable of making a sound.

Drusus rose and paced about the Imperial Office, trying to allow a little time for the sense of dissatisfaction and suspicion to dissipate, but it continued to build, rising like acid to the back of his throat. 'I want to see the bodies,' he announced.

Almost as soon as the Praetorians had swept him back into the Palace, word had come through that the executions had been completed despite the interruption. It had been repeated and confirmed more than once already, and at the first hearing he had felt reassured. But that had soured quickly; he felt held in a kind of sick suspense. He had not felt easy even before the dogs had been loosed from the gates.

The four men before him looked at one another – just fleeting, expressionless glances, but Drusus suddenly wondered if he had made a mistake summoning them here together. It had seemed the most natural and efficient thing to do, and of course the duties of the vigiles and the Praetorians often intersected, but you did not want them to get too close, to start thinking of themselves as a single force.

'They've already been incinerated, your Majesty,' said Cilo.

It had been Cilo who had led the raid on Salvius' house. Drusus had appointed him Praetorian Prefect after that, hoisting him up over several ranks. The others too had all been appointed since his coronation: Arvina, the new Vigile Prefect, and Lucullus, the captain of his own personal guard. Only Thalna, the commander of public order operations, who'd been in charge of security at the Colosseum, had arrived at his job without any intervention from Drusus; his predecessor had resigned after the attack that had killed Marcus and Faustus.

Drusus scrutinised them all. Cilo was the only one to hold his head up. They all looked respectful and abashed. They had unconsciously lined themselves up, close together, in almost identical postures with their hands clasped in front of them – it would have been rather comical if he'd been in the mood for laughing. 'I wanted proof,' he said thickly.

Another slight pause while they silently negotiated which of them should speak. 'I apologise, of course, your Majesty,' said Arvina, 'but they were confirmed dead, and cremation is the usual practice after an execution.'

'Which is a matter for the Colosseum staff, in any case, your Majesty,' added Thalna, meekly.

Drusus only felt more aggrieved and distrustful, all the more so because he realised nothing they could do or say now would ease this feeling. 'And Varius? What about him, what excuse are you going to come up with now? He got away! He was able to walk into the Colosseum— He announced himself! You allowed him to threaten my life, threaten the people, disrupt everything and get away!'

'At this point we have no way of knowing if he was ever really there, Sir,' said Arvina.

'Someone certainly was!' Drusus paced with greater energy. 'Did we all hallucinate those explosions?'

Thalna said, 'We found the remains of firecrackers – they can be very loud, you know, Sir, and there's a strong echo—'

'Firecrackers,' said Drusus, his voice rising, 'all that over firecrackers? So – what? You're telling me nothing really happened today, it was all – what? A misunderstanding? What was the man trying to do?'

'Well, we know these people do have sympathisers – Dama had supporters. It might be that they were willing to settle for causing panic and disruption, not having the means to do any more.'

'And you let them get away,' Drusus repeated. But he couldn't really make himself concentrate on these hypothetical *sympathisers*; he continued in the same gulping breath, 'Sulien and Una – how do you *know*? Are you sure? Who saw them dead?'

There was a slight pause. 'The Colosseum staff had already

transported them down to the morgue,' said Thalna. 'Two vigile officers checked the bodies.'

'And I saw them myself, in the arena,' said Lucullus.

Drusus turned away, because there was nothing more to be said. But a hot sweat flushed over his skin, and he swung round, sweeping up some loose papers from the desk and hurling them forward. He shouted, 'You're *lying*, all of you! It was all a trick, I *knew* it, I said to you—! They're alive, and you know it. You don't dare to admit it! You cowards, go after them— *Find them!*'

Cilo's face remained steady, blank. 'They were confirmed dead, your Majesty.'

Drusus looked wildly around the beautiful garden painted on the walls of the Imperial Office as if for escape. He collapsed into a chair, gasping, 'You're protecting them! It's come to this: you're colluding with Rome's enemies. Each one of you I thought I could trust. I was wrong. I was wrong. I'll have you all shot for treason.'

For a moment naked consternation and outrage flashed through them and the line broke as they flinched or started forwards – but almost at once, as they caught one another's eyes, they collected themselves, and settled back into an orderly row. They stood more stiffly than before.

Cilo bowed. 'You are the Emperor.'

Drusus hunched low over the desk, staring down at his drumming fingertips. Heat continued to wash across his face; now he didn't want to see them looking at him, didn't want to think about this any more. 'Get out of my sight,' he whispered.

His head ached. His cubicularius had come in half an hour ago, harassing him with the latest in a series of increasingly irritating messages from General Turnus, who wanted to see him about some local trouble in Ethiopia, of all places. For a moment he found himself thinking, I never wanted this.

The soldiers left together. They did not speak, or look at each other again; they were eager to be out of each other's company. The Colosseum's incinerator had been lit early that morning, ready for the executions, and it was still too hot, even now, to be inspected properly. But the sliding tray that was used to push the bodies into the fire was still on its strut outside the oven, clean, ready for use. No one seemed sure who the officer who had checked the bodies had been, nor the morgue attendant who had been so diligent in collecting them.

That Una and Sulien were dead was a matter of recorded fact. Now there were certain questions to which it would not be wise to find the answers.

'We shouldn't be drinking this,' said Sulien suddenly, 'not after the drugs. It could— It could . . . You know.' He waved his hand to indicate the behaviour of chemicals for which he had forgotten the vocabulary. 'It's dangerous.'

'I really don't care,' said Una.

They were anchored within the fringe of islands along the Dalmatian coast, beside a blunt nub of rock, bare except for a patchy coating of grass and the droppings of seagulls. A song was playing on the radio. Sulien didn't want to remind himself when he'd last heard music, but still it came: almost a month ago, on board another ship, the old woman singing as the Caspian ferry glided towards Persia. Tears prickled again in his eyes before he looked around at the bottle and the scattered food, at Una and Varius, who had been nodding along gently to the music, and he thought, *and now we're having a party on a yacht*, and giggled under his breath at how preposterous it was.

But he'd worried Varius, of course, who reached out to take the bottle away, demanding, 'How dangerous? What will it do to you?'

Sulien blinked, thinking about it. 'Make us more drunk?'

Una remarked, 'I'm not drunk.'

She was sitting on the floor with her hands neatly folded in her lap, her expression grave and careful, her eyelids heavy with subtle, lopsided effort.

Sulien laughed weakly at her.

'I'm not that drunk,' she said.

'You'd better stop,' said Varius, searching for the stopper.

'No, we need some more,' protested Una, gesturing expansively. 'And you need some more.'

Varius obediently downed more of the spirit.

'But careful,' she added, struck suddenly by other considerations, 'because we've got to make it last.'

'No,' said Varius, 'there's plenty.' He pulled open a cabinet they hadn't noticed under one of the seats to display an impressive stock of bottles. 'I didn't really think we'd get here,' he admitted, 'but if we did, I knew we'd need it.'

Sulien and Una gazed at the bottles, and then began to laugh again as they caught the awe in each other's faces. 'Varius, you're a lifesaver. And I didn't even want you to save my life,' said Sulien, taking the open bottle back.

Una continued laughing, leaning against the seat with her cheek pillowed on her arm, but she looked quickly at Sulien and the amiable haze cleared for a moment, leaving anxious watchfulness behind.

'You thought of everything,' she said to Varius.

'We still may crash on the rocks,' said Varius. But he grinned, and rose to his feet to turn up the music; he reached, unexpectedly, for Una's hand. 'Here,' he said, 'can you stand?'

He pulled her up. Una didn't manage to stay on her feet for very long, but for a little while they lurched across the gently pitching floor and called it dancing.

Hours later, Una woke in the little cabin below deck. She was lying beneath the level of the water, and she could feel it, folded round the hull, softly pushing and rocking. Rain was drumming lightly on the deck. For some time after opening her eyes – she could not have said how long it lasted – she had the impression Marcus was there. She did not see or hear anything, nor did she expect to. She had no sense of anything said; it didn't occur to her to try and speak to him, or to feel anything except the ordinariness of it: his calm, matter-of-fact attention, as if he was watching her for no special reason, just having woken first, on any usual morning.

It faded, but without any new smart of loss. She lay still for a long time, feeling herself inhabit her body, stretching out warily within it. The gashes and cuts throbbed quietly and at last she pushed back the sheets, wincing a little, and considered the streaks, dots, crosses that had been scrawled over her, as if reading a letter or a book.

The hangover she must be due hadn't descended yet; her head felt clear. She sat up. It must be dawn; for the cabin was dark, yet she could make out Varius, a motionless shadow on the bed in the stern, and she saw that Sulien was no longer in the bunk opposite hers.

Shivering, she dragged one of the blankets around herself and crept up the little stairs to the upper level. She picked her way through the debris of the night before. It didn't seem like real light in the air, just a deep grey dilution of the darkness, but once she was outside, she could see a seam of blue light splitting the sky off from the slate sea, and her own breath, vanishing and coming again.

Sulien was sitting up near the bow with his legs dangling over the side, watching the curls of mist on the sea. He glanced at Una as she sat down next to him, but for some time neither of them spoke.

'It's cold,' she murmured at last.

'Not really. Not like in Sacaeum, or on the Rha.'

So she pulled the blanket tighter and they were quiet again, a layer of warmth between them where their arms touched, like cement between bricks. She was trying to decide what she should say and whether to speak at all, for the longer they sat there the more possible and tempting it seemed that they could carry on like this for ever, silent on everything that had happened during these last weeks.

But in the end he spoke first. 'We can't go on the way we were.'

She agreed quietly. 'No.'

'Except we have to, don't we?' he said, and smiled, but it was an ugly, joyless thing. He lapsed back into silence for a while. Then he asked in a low voice, 'What did they do to you in prison?'

She said, on instinct, 'Nothing,' and saw that was a mistake as his face tightened: he had started guessing what that word might cover, and it would be harder to make him believe her now. 'Well, not nothing, but nothing so bad, I promise. Noriko protected me. It was nowhere near what it could have been.' She made sure he was looking at her, stared at him. 'I'm all right.'

Sulien still looked dubious, but he met her gaze for a while and then looked away, letting it be, for now.

'I used to think about where you were,' she said, 'all the ways you might have kept going. How it would be for you, in a few years . . .'

Sulien made a low snorting sound.

'You should have tried, at least, Sulien. I told you to run. That's what I wanted – you knew that.'

'You said it was better I was there' said Sulien, remotely, 'in the Colosseum.'

Una closed her eyes, but she didn't try to stifle the memory of how it had felt, pressing out the sight of the hounds against his chest, clinging to him as the hurtling feet swept over them both. 'It was, of course it was better – for *me*, but not for you. You shouldn't have done that.'

He shifted away from her a little, still not looking at her. He stared out at a flock of seagulls, whirling and stabbing at the water. 'I don't know what you expect me to say. Are you really surprised? There's nothing surprising about it. I should have seen there might still be a chance to get you out, but I couldn't— I couldn't. And if it happened again—'

'Then it can't,' interrupted Una.

But he wasn't listening. His face suddenly contorted, and he bowed forward as if caught by an attack of seasickness. He said again, '*If it happens again . . .*'

She said more firmly, 'We can't let anything like that happen, ever again.'

Sulien gave that ugly, hopeless smile again. 'Yeah. The whole thing's been a great way of teaching us to be more careful.'

'No,' said Una, 'you're right: we can't go on as we were. It nearly killed us – it was killing us even before they caught me. He's making the whole world poisonous, and we can't live in it, and we can't get away. The only thing we can do is try to change it.'

Sulien said bleakly, 'Yes. That sounds much easier.'

'We can – *he* thinks we can. Drusus—' She hesitated, wary of returning to the subject of her time in captivity, but this concerned him too closely to keep to herself. 'Drusus came to see me in prison. You know there was a deal; that was how it happened.'

Sulien was looking at her with alarmed, almost accusatory eyes, and he had stopped breathing at Drusus' name.

She sighed. 'He just hit me a few times. And he talked about what it would be like in the Colosseum. And—' There were words she just couldn't say to him, even when she tried. '—he threw me on the bed, but he . . . he didn't— He can hardly stand to be anywhere near me. You have to know how frightened he is, Sulien: he's frightened of us both. And I know what he thinks we are. The Sibyl told him something in Delphi – I don't know exactly what, not what the words were, anyway. But he thinks it meant he would become Emperor, and that if anyone could stop him, it would be us.'

'He's mad,' said Sulien dully.

'Yes,' Una said, 'I think in a way he is.'

The boat wasn't new, and the previous owners had left a shelf-full of nautical charts and books. Varius spread out the maps on the benches and examined the books with slight apprehension. 'All right,' he said, 'I suppose I need to know a little more than how to go in a straight line before I attempt to go any further.'

Una ran her hand over a scuffed place on the seat. 'What's her name?' she asked.

'I painted it out,' said Varius, 'but it's *Ananke.*'

'I can steer,' Una said, 'and I remember a few things about

docking, I think. I mean, nothing very much, but . . . Marcus hired a boat this kind of size a couple of years ago, when we were in Athens.'

'Oh,' said Varius softly, 'yes. He talked about it.'

They were alone on the deck; Sulien had given up shortly after Varius rose and returned to bed.

Una smiled self-consciously. 'I felt a bit like a traitor,' she said, 'I mean, the places that I came from – and all the slave auctions happening every moment, and there am I with the next Emperor, on the Aegean, just . . . floating. Decadent. But it was beautiful, being there with him.'

Varius hesitated. 'Can I ask something about the day he died?' he asked carefully.

Una nodded.

But he could not quite look her in the eyes to talk of this. 'You were there with him . . . ?'

Una's face puckered for a moment. 'No. When I got there it was already too late.' Her voice twisted on itself. 'I wish more than anything—'

'I'm sorry,' said Varius, angry with himself for asking, and miserable that Marcus hadn't had that much comfort.

'You don't have to be sorry about anything – and he wasn't alone, at least. Makaria was there with him. She wrote down what he wanted to say.'

Varius succeeded in refilling the tank from the spare canisters of gas. 'I think we can get as far as Corcyra on this, by the end of the day.'

'Varius,' said Una, sitting up, her voice charged with slightly feverish excitement, 'we need to think what to do. I didn't use to think there was anything, any point, but now . . . I mean, look what you've done. Why shouldn't we be able to do more? I want to know everything you found out in Rome. We have to start to establish what's possible.'

Varius looked at her. Her face was alight with eagerness, but she looked so thin, so worn and battered. Already, where Sulien's attention had been at work, the wounds that showed were closed over, and looked many days older than they were, but her skin was chalky where it was not dappled with bruises or striped with dried blood, and he could see a broad gouge on her scalp through her ragged hair. And there was still a glaze of tears in her eyes, and dark shadows beneath them.

'Not yet,' he said, 'give yourself a little more time. Sulien needs it too.'

Una sagged and looked down, fatigue showing even more sharply in the outlines of her face. 'I know.'

The following morning the three of sat round the chart table, Varius holding Una's forearm steady, while Sulien cut the blood-stained cast from her wrist.

They took a wobbling course along the coast to Corcyra, and didn't realise how lucky they had been until the winter wind swung down from the north and raked up the sea, just as they pulled in to the first small marina they saw. They did not dare to sail at night in any case, but they were all conscious of how unprepared they were to handle a storm out on the open water.

The harbour was almost deserted, the few other yachts there tightly battened down; no one was sailing for pleasure in this weather. Una and Sulien stayed hidden below deck, shivering as the cold advanced across the bay, while Varius went out in search of fuel and food. He came back excited and agitated.

'Look at this,' he said, plunging down the steps into the cabin, extending a rain-battered newssheet, 'it doesn't make any sense. It just says there was a bomb scare – there's nothing about you being alive, nothing about searching for you. It isn't even the main story.'

'What—? Do they still think we're dead?' asked Sulien, in-credulously.

'I never even hoped for that,' said Varius. He frowned, and shook his head. 'No, they can't. It couldn't hold that long, there weren't any bodies – there are all kinds of things wrong. I knew they'd work it out; the question was when.'

'But they did think we were dead, for a while,' said Una. 'And they told Drusus.'

They stared down at the paper together. Abruptly, Varius laughed. 'I could have spent a lot less money if I'd known that was going to happen.'

'They'll still keep looking for us,' said Sulien. 'If that's what they've told him, they need to make it true. They can't ever let him find out they lied to him.'

There was another brief silence. 'But it'll be hard for them,' said Una, gently. 'Much harder – no one can help them unless they admit what they're looking for, and they can't let it spread, even within their own forces. They can't alert the border guards, they can't use longvision, or put up posters . . .'

'They can tell whoever they want that they're looking for *you*,' said Sulien to Varius. 'Maybe you'd better be the one who stays in the cabin now.'

Varius sighed. 'Then it might be wiser if—'

'—if we separate again? No,' said Una at once.

'No,' echoed Sulien, more quietly, but with dull, resigned force. He smiled, and it was still a sardonic curl of the lips, but he said, 'You're going to stop the war and bring down the Emperor. You don't dump the recruits you've got.' He lowered his head onto his arms, as if too tired to hold it up, and muttered, 'Whatever you want to do, it's going to take more than one person. And more than three.'

The wind held them at Corcyra for another two days. On the evening that it dropped they steered eastwards round the coast and waited in the bay outside Corcyra City until after midnight, then they walked up into the town, with bundles in their arms.

Sometimes Una would break into a run for a few steps, springing over puddles, testing her own body, and the cobbles beneath her feet, as if to walk on solid ground, not to pass through it or hurtle off it into the dark sky, was some startling feat of acrobatics. It was so much, after subsisting on slices of sky and space; it was almost more than she could swallow, the yellow lights of the city, heaped like corn on the hill, and the turns and openings of the streets around her.

But Sulien trudged along quietly at her side, his head down, and when he looked around it was with a tired, nearly indifferent incomprehension.

'I'll take the temple,' said Varius as they came into the forum at the top of the hill. He disappeared into the street that ran alongside the temple while Una and Sulien went on to the Basilica, lurking in the shadows of its portico.

Una looked around for witnesses or security cameras, but then put down the roll of paper and said, 'Look, this might be such a mistake. There's no getting away from it: we do this and they know we were here; they'll be able to track us.'

'Maybe not,' said Sulien, 'at least, maybe not for a while. I mean, the local vigiles think we're dead, so why would they report it to anyone in Rome? And the words aren't new. They're out there already.' But he spoke with that flat voice she was growing to hate, even when what he said was hopeful.

He unrolled the first heavy sheet of paper, but Una put a hand on his wrist, stopping him. 'Sulien. Decide if you want this. If you don't—'

'Why would I not want to stop someone who's done these things to us?' asked Sulien, with a faint hint of a mystified sneer.

'Because you don't think it'll do any good. Because you don't think it's possible.'

Sulien gazed heavily at the text on the paper, painstakingly stencilled in the waterproof paint they'd found on the boat. He shrugged. 'Oh, I don't know. Does it even matter what's possible? We can try.'

Una stared at him for a moment, then sighed and let go. 'All right, then,' she said. She bent for the can of glue and sprayed a coat of it onto the locked door of the Basilica, then stepped back as Sulien lifted the poster and pressed it into place.

The words had come out a little skewed and smudged, but they were fierce and stark, the tall black letters straight enough to read:

THE LAST ACT
OF
THE EMPEROR
MARCUS NOVIUS FAUSTUS LEO
WAS
THE ABOLITION OF SLAVERY

Tadahito could still smell the smoke as the propellors of the volucer stirred the air. The red walls of the Palace of Axum were pocked with bullet holes, but there was a small crowd on the steps waving palm fronds. Already statues had been felled and bronze eagles torn down, and one of those crosses stood before the gates, spilling a huge shadow across the steps. Unlike those he had seen back in Harar, it was made of dark wood and its lines were bare and plain. Tadahito thought it looked almost ready to be used for an execution. But the people on the steps were singing something strange and beautiful and elation suddenly swelled through him on its notes.

'Welcome home, your Majesty,' he said.

King Solomon looked at him unsmiling, as if suspecting mockery of some kind. 'It is Lord Jesus who has brought us home. And we welcome *you*.'

Tadahito gave a polite nod.

Solomon advanced towards the palace and the little crowd surged forward to try and touch him.

Kaneharu was smiling broadly. 'They will say this is when we began to win,' he said.

'You can't start thinking like that yet,' protested Takanari, 'we must be sure we have control of the coast – Missiwa and Arsinoë. We should deploy a squadron to each of them before our flotillas arrive. And we must aim to have a presence on the other side of the border before the Romans have time to react.' But he bounced

289

slightly on the balls of his feet as he spoke; it was clear he was barely managing to keep himself from leaping around and crowing like a child. The first tests and responsibilities of their adulthood had been so immense – such a weight on all of them, with the terror of disgrace as well as the fear of defeat – all three of them looked at each other, then embraced impulsively.

It was more than a thousand miles from here to the Mediterranean, and Rome was another thousand miles beyond that, but this was the first real victory they'd had, and they were closer to their sister than they had been in more than a year.

[XII]

ALEXANDRIA

From a hundred miles away they had been able to see the Pharos at Alexandria; a bright mast on the horizon, spreading into a bruise of light where it pierced the clouds. In daylight, as they neared the harbour's entrance, they could see the tower from which the light rose, with four sphinxes crouched at its base, and tall palm trees ranked along the causeway that connected it to the land. There was a strong wind sweeping across the coast and the sky was dull, but the obelisks and domes of the city cluttered densely along the shore, glinted here and there with black copper, glass and gold. The bay was crowded with freighters, ferries, military ships – far more than they'd ever seen in one place. They crept in cautiously towards the docks, as a flight of Roman volucers rasped southwards through the sky.

'I should go over your scars,' said Sulien. He hadn't done so since the storm that had pummelled them for a terrifying night as they rounded the southern tip of the Peloponnese. They'd lost an anchor, and bent a propellor on the rocks as they tried to find shelter, and the engine kept overheating. But the ship limped on, and they'd left posters at Heraklion on Crete, and at the first town they'd come to on the Libyan coast. It was ten days since they'd left Italy.

Una was at the controls of the ship. She shrank very slightly away. 'They don't hurt. It's not worth it. You've done enough.'

'You'll have them for good if I leave them much longer.'

Una raised her hand towards the pale streak that dipped out of her hair onto her forehead, the other mark at the corner of her jaw. 'You can only really see these two, and the ones on my hands. No one's going to know what they are; they could be from anything. And the rest . . . they're all right. I don't mind them.'

Sulien ran his fingers over a triple band of scars running down his own forearm without looking at them. It was true they didn't hurt any more, but he couldn't forget for a second where each of them was; the memory of every strike of claws and teeth would be carved into the tissues, no matter what he did. He couldn't imagine talking about them so casually, saying they were all right. Yet perhaps it would be unnerving to be without them, to have to look down at a body blandly denying anything had happened. He shook his sleeve down irritably and nudged Una aside to take the helm.

Ziye and Delir had been talking quietly about the conquest of Ethiopia and what the Nionians were doing in the Red Sea, but as the train slid across Palaestina towards Africa, Lal thought impatiently that she didn't care about the war at all; it was all too far off to be interesting. She surged restlessly around the little compartment, seething with nerves and uncomfortable joy. Sulien was like a continual shout in her ear, breaking into every thought; sometimes all her brain could manage was to hum his name over and over until it turned into a kind of blurred birdsong in the background of everything.

She was tempted to interrogate Ziye again for details: how Sulien and Una had looked, what they had said when they first woke in the van, even though she knew there was nothing more to be told. They had been confused and bloody, they had barely spoken, by the time they reached the coast they had been able to walk. But they were alive, they were alive, and to the disbelief of all of them, no one seemed to know it. And yet, even now it had worked, it was terrible that rescue had depended on them being hurt badly enough that it should seem possible they had been killed, and it was terrible to imagine what those days must have been like under the Colosseum. And if she'd loved him already, it was that horrified effort of imagination, which had begun the moment she realised he had been captured, that had started this almost-madness, and torn little holes in her mind out of which everything else had leaked.

They had spent a fortnight at Smyrna, hiding near the port in an otherwise empty guest-house owned by one of Delir's old contacts, and every day Lal scoured the news and the weather reports, then wandered down to the docks to look anxiously out to sea. She had never seen the little ship Varius had bought, and though she knew that really it was a yacht with cabin space and even some kind of kitchen, sometimes, when a storm slammed against the coast, she pictured them freezing aboard a tiny life-boat or clinging to a collapsing raft, or swallowed by the sea, and never found.

Varius and Delir had agreed on a means of finding each other, should they all make it as far as Alexandria, but beyond that there had been too little time in those awful, sleepless days between Sulien's arrest and the morning of the Games to make arrangements that would have let them communicate easily. Delir, Ziye and Lal had had a slower, heavier journey of it, conveying themselves overland with books and boxes from the basement in the Subura: Lal's forgery and printing equipment and Varius' money.

One day in Smyrna, walking back from the docks, she turned her head to look at a jumble of posters on a hoarding, without realising why. Then she started and clapped a hand over her mouth to muffle a yelp of shock and had to hurry on before she made herself even more conspicuous by standing and gaping at it.

It said, 'The last act of the Emperor Marcus Novius was the abolition of slavery,' and it was not the only one. Two days later, in one of the streets running off the forum, she found a rough screenprint of a girl with ragged hair, her face upheld, her ter-rified eyes fixed on some invisible peak behind the viewer. Even without the roughly printed words stacked underneath, Lal could see it was supposed to be Una, as she'd looked on the longvision at the moment when she'd chosen the arena hounds.

And then, a week later, when they thought it was safe to move on again, there was the graffiti she saw in a bathroom in the station in Ancyra, one fierce, hurried line:

They reached Alexandria in the last week of January. The air was cool, but the sun was strong, and as they descended from the train, Lal cast a distracted look at her father and saw how harshly it shadowed the lines on his face and lit up the white in his hair. And he looked smaller and slighter than ever, and yet, at the moment, almost happy. 'Really, this is the greatest of the Western cities, Lal, not Rome, not even Athens as it was,' he announced grandly. He was the only one of them to have been there before, and began talking cheerfully about the Ptolemies, about the many expansions of the Library, about whether the best place to eat in the city would still be open after twenty years.

But Lal, who usually felt a little flutter of excitement at entering any new city, couldn't listen; she felt impatient with all the towers and gardens and eating houses for being in her way.

She wanted to go straight to the Museion, because if the others were here, that was where Varius would have left instructions for finding them. But she could not go alone – women could not enter the Library unless accompanied by a man or furnished with a letter of introduction – and Ziye and Delir were intent upon finding a temporary home first, so they set off to the Jewish Quarter in search of somewhere to stay.

Lal spent the evening almost speechless with the consciousness that Sulien might be less than a mile away, and the night trying uselessly to quieten the noise he made in her mind so she could sleep.

The next morning they caught a tram across to the Museion. Alexandria was laid out in a formal lattice of streets, centred at the crossroads of two boulevards wider than any Lal had ever seen, each bearing seven loud and terrifying lanes of traffic through the heart of the city. But the Library had spilled haphazardly over its initial boundaries, and now reading rooms, book stacks, lecture theatres and printing presses were housed in buildings of many ages and styles: granite towers, halls with windows of cut alabaster, even a cluster of low bubbles of green glass. Students wandered the colonnades in dutiful groups behind their tutors, or sat sprawled on the steps outside the central hall. Its gates were framed in heavy pillars, the capitals vivid with malachite and cinnabar, and ram-headed sphinxes crouched within the portico. Inside, the ceiling of the lobby was a bright noon-blue studded with golden stars, with the gods and creatures of the constellations painted in pale, transparent lines around them. Busts of the great poets and scientists were placed around the walls, and the space was full of exclaiming tourists who wouldn't stay quiet no matter what the frowning wardens did. Heavy double doors at the top of a steep flight of steps led to the Library itself; Delir showed the false papers Lal made for him, signed a declaration promising not to damage any of the books, and led them inside.

The noise of the city dropped away with surprising abruptness, kept out by the thick walls and by the dense fortification of the books themselves. The shelves rose in ten tiers of galleries around the walls and lined alcoves and stairwells, and more books still were hidden in panelled cupboards and chests. The immense skylight above let in a soft light over the long tables that ran the length of the hall.

Delir and Ziye at once adopted a feeble and quite excessive deference to the quietness, Lal thought; they tiptoed along, unreasonably slowly. So she hurried on ahead of them, light on the balls of her feet, almost running down the colonnade past the tables, through the Greek section, past Epic, Tragedy, Comedy, upstairs into the first gallery to find Roman History. She was looking for the first set of copies of Cossus' *Rome and Nionia* on the open shelves. Varius would have left a longdictor code pencilled onto the thirtieth page of the fourth volume.

She found the alcove, the shelf, the book, and as she reached for it, someone tapped her on the shoulder; she turned, startled, and saw Una, a stack of books held one-armed against her chest. She was smiling.

Lal reminded herself just in time to stay quiet, but opened her mouth in a silent cry of delight, and embraced her.

Delir and Ziye came into the alcove behind them, and Ziye reached out and lifted Una's chin, saying nothing, and for a few moments they gazed at each other. Until then Lal had not even noticed the scars on Una's face.

'Thank you,' whispered Una, 'all of you.'

Lal's pleasure at seeing Una shifted suddenly into slight dismay, because she felt as if even normal people must be able to see how hopelessly her thoughts knotted and tangled around Sulien.

She might as well just say it, then. 'Is Sulien here?'

Una's smile faded a little, but she said, 'He's at home— I mean, where we're staying, over in Rhakotis. He'll be so happy to see you.'

Lal stifled a little twitch of disappointment and looked around, wondering if Varius had accompanied Una instead. 'But you're not allowed in on your own . . .'

'You are if you work here,' said Una. She put down the stack of books on the table and returned a volume to its place on a shelf. 'I wanted to work, and I knew you'd be coming. I can tell you how to get to our place, or I'll show you, if you can wait an hour.'

They waited for her. Lal tried to read, but she was too restless and so she crept around the upper galleries where there were fewer scholars to disturb, looking at the carvings on the pillars; she found a few abandoned sheets of notepaper and a pencil and passed a few minutes copying a face she found carved above a small window.

Sometimes she looked down and saw Una, steering a little cart of books around a lower gallery, or alone in an alcove, standing reading a book for a little while before putting it away. It should not have been surprising that she looked better now than she had at the trial, but still Lal was struck at the change. She'd gained a little weight and her hair had faded almost to its natural colour.

It was dragged into a cluster of small knots on the back of her head which disguised, in some measure, how short it had been cut. And yet it was not that, not really, nor even the altered brightness of her skin or eyes. There was an eagerness in her steps, an expectancy in the way she held herself. Lal thought of the poster in Smyrna; the desperation the artist had tried to reveal was gone, but something else, a stern force, seemed even stronger in her than it had before.

They were staying in a small holiday flat near the Canopic Docks, close to where the canal met Mareotis Lake. Lal saw an incongruous pile of ageing tourist magazines on a table near the door as Una let them in. The tiled room was almost bare. And Sulien was a long shadow coming down the steps from a little roof terrace.

Lal's flight of feeling towards him seemed to trip on something – a small dip of sorrow and doubt – but then she forgot it, for he was smiling broadly, and he pulled her into his arms. His name chimed deafeningly in her head, and tears filled her eyes.

'I missed you so much,' she whispered hoarsely.

But when he repeated the same thing to her, the doubt came back again.

Una had turned aside as they embraced, and looking back at her, Lal saw a crease of pain fading on her face . . .

But it did fade, and she asked Sulien, 'Where's Varius?'

'At the docks, worrying about the yacht.'

But Varius opened the door almost as he said it and for a few minutes the flat was brimming over with jubilant noise as every-one embraced or clasped hands, and Lal saw that her father, too, was brushing tears from his eyes. They crowded onto the terrace, into the winter sunlight bright on a jumbled rooftop terrain of washing lines and longvision aerials. Sulien sat beside her with his hand wrapped round hers, just as when they were in the cellar back in Rome, watching the last moments of Una's trial.

Too much like that, she thought, when she looked at his taut, still-smiling face.

Varius looked restless and preoccupied, and yet Lal thought he'd shed something along with the matted hair and beard, the vigile uniform. No, she thought, you would not have thought he had any reason to hide from anything.

'Do you have any family here?' she asked him, looking down across the canal towards the lake.

'Not in Alexandria. My grandparents moved to Rome when they were first married. I think I've got second cousins in Pelusium, but I've never met them.'

'Maybe you should see them,' remarked Sulien, oddly, in a low voice.

'I can't,' said Varius, a little baffled, 'of course I can't. I couldn't put them in that position.'

'When all this ends, you should see them.'

Delir said, 'The money is safe. I made you another five thousand.' He gave a modest shrug.

'Thank you,' Varius told him. 'I've got to get at least some of the money back on the boat, too; it doesn't really belong to me. I've used more than half of it now. And Eudoxius didn't give it to me for any of this.'

Una leaned back meditatively on the brick parapet, eyes closed against the sunlight. 'I don't think you should sell the boat yet,' she said. 'We might need it.'

But Lal, Delir and Ziye all looked at one another, tensing. Delir grimaced and began reluctantly, 'I don't think you have heard. I'm so sorry, but Eudoxius—'

Varius' eyes widened. 'What?'

'It was about two weeks ago. You would have been at sea. It wasn't in the news for long . . .'

Varius sat down, his face changing colour, seeming to hollow out from within. Una moved across the terrace towards him. 'Varius—'

'I did this. I killed him,' said Varius flatly, quietly.

'No, no – it said natural causes,' Lal protested.

'You think that means anything? You think they ever told the truth about what happened to Salvius?'

'Did they ever say anything about Salvius?' asked Ziye.

Varius looked up at her uncertainly, without answering.

Una said, 'If they knew he'd helped you, why would they hide it? Why would they miss the chance to keep anyone from helping you again? They'd put him on trial, seize his property. They'd make an example of him.'

'He was old,' agreed Ziye, briskly. 'He had a heart attack. It's unfortunate.'

Varius exhaled, and lowered his head in something like a nod, but he still looked bitter. 'Well, that's that. It always was a stupid idea.'

'Varius.' Sulien didn't move, and his voice was very quiet, but everyone else grew still as he spoke. 'If you still want to try and kill Drusus, I'll help you. I owe you that, I owe you – everything. But we'll never see what comes of it. It's not something you can survive. You've always known that. Is that still what you want?'

There was a silence. Una was gazing at Sulien with a helpless expression, her lips tight, but she said nothing.

Varius retracted a little under Sulien's quiet, neutral scrutiny. Eventually he answered, 'No. Of course not— Not just for the sake of it, not if all that happens is one of his generals takes over and everything carries on as it is now.'

'But we can't give up, can we?' Una asked. 'None of us want that. *Something* is possible; you've proved that. You found people who felt the same, you raised money – you *saved* us.'

Varius said slowly, 'There isn't anyone else on our side who'd have even a chance of staying in power.'

There was another pause, then Una said, 'Yes, there is.'

Night came on early. As the sun set Sulien and Lal were left alone on the roof terrace. They kissed at last, and Lal, ignoring the ache in her chest, thought, 'I have never been so happy.'

She was not blind; she could see how wan and far-off he was, the fadedness, but the fact of him there – alive, whole in her arms

– had been so hard-won. She gripped his hands, feeding love and determination into him. It wasn't the first time she'd tried to pour herself into someone else this way, and when he did that for people who were hurt or sick, it worked.

'There are these posters about you and Una in Smyrna and Ancyra,' she told him. 'Maybe they're everywhere now.'

'Our posters?' he said, confused.

'You've seen them?'

He told her what they'd done at Corcyra, Crete and in Libya, and Lal explained what she'd seen. Sulien's expression lit up with slow, incredulous excitement. 'We hoped for that – well, hardly even hoped, but— And they're different – they say different things?'

And the news left a trace of brightness in his face for a time.

'I can make better ones. We can print more of them,' said Lal, eagerly, 'hundreds of them.'

Sulien's smile remained, but it altered somehow. 'At least it'd be something to do. Really I need to work, like Una. As if Varius hasn't done enough without having to keep me as well. I did get a job last week, but I only lasted two days. I couldn't— I couldn't concentrate.'

'But Sulien, if anyone ever had an excuse for being tired—! Even if everything had gone right the first time, even if they'd never done that to you, even if you'd never been—' Her eyes blurred even to think of it and she found herself unable to name the Colosseum. 'Even if you'd never been there.'

Sulien nodded, passively.

'When we saw on the news that they'd arrested you,' she ventured, but he closed his eyes and Lal saw that perhaps it was a mistake to talk any more about those days, and yet she could not prevent herself, 'we all came right back. Varius must have already told you. We didn't even discuss it. We didn't know how to find Varius at first, but I knew he would be there, I knew . . . So my father just went back to the place in the Subura and hoped he'd call. And we had so little time, but there was nothing we could do at first and I just . . . I never stopped thinking about you.'

Sulien pressed her a little closer, but he was gazing past her at the cracked tiles on the parapet, his eyes empty, his brows contracted. For a while he hesitated.

'I could have tried to get away on my own,' he murmured, finally, 'but I didn't.'

A chilly feeling came over Lal. She gazed up at him. 'When? In the van?' She had never known precisely what had gone wrong.

'Yes. Before the vigiles came.'

Lal glanced down the steps towards the flat. She hadn't noticed how dark it was growing out here; the light was on in the kitchen now. She could just make out Una's voice among the others.

She supplied, 'You couldn't leave her.'

Sulien's voice was flat, definite. 'No.'

Lal tried to weigh the importance of this. What difference did it make – that it had happened at all, and that she knew it now? It scarcely counted as a real choice in the circumstances. Probably they would have caught him anyway, even if he'd tried to run, so it would all have turned out exactly the same.

But for him it had meant giving up everything, and he meant her to understand that had included her. Would she ever have expected or hoped for anything different, if she'd known he would have to make such a choice?

'Well, of course not,' she said bravely, trying to prevent a catch in her voice.

Absently, Sulien chafed one of her hands between his. He said, 'I wish we could just go home.'

Down in the kitchen, Delir had sketched a rough map of the Mediterranean. Una frowned down at it, trying to estimate the distances between the points she'd marked on it. She would look at the atlases in the Library tomorrow.

'How many people would we need?' she asked. Varius was leaning over the map beside her and instinctively she looked at him, even though it was as much a question for the others.

Varius grimaced dubiously. 'We'll be thankful for whatever we can get. I suppose five or six hundred would have a chance, if we could find that many.'

'Then we'll bring a thousand,' said Una. 'The more we bring, the fewer shots will be fired when we arrive – on their side or ours. Before they know who we are, or what we want, they'll know there are too many of us to fight.'

'That would mean perhaps two hundred boats,' said Varius. 'None of this is going to be cheap. Or fast.'

Una thought of a secret fleet of fishing boats, small yachts and speedboats, hidden in coves and harbours across the Mediterranean, gathering into an armada in the dark on the open sea. The excitement already flickering through her deepened and steadied into a feeling that was almost pride, almost as if it was already real.

She turned to Delir. 'You know how to do this,' she said. 'You've run a network of people; you know how to keep it hidden.'

Lal and Sulien had come down from the terrace in silence. Sulien sat down at the bottom of the steps, leaning his head against the wall, listening, annexed to the conversation while remaining outside it. Lal hesitated for a moment, but then sat beside him.

Delir sighed. 'In the Pyrenees we had certain advantages,' he said. 'Even aside from not yet having made ourselves so very interesting to the government. The people there were Vascones; they didn't consider themselves Roman. They didn't even speak Latin. They tolerated us. I don't believe there's anywhere else like that in Europe, certainly nowhere that would be helpful to us.'

'Still,' said Varius, 'small scattered groups along the coast, say no more than ten people in any one place . . . ships that stay on the move . . . That would be harder to detect than a single fixed base.'

Una remarked softly, 'I never used to think of myself as Roman.'

'Never used to?' asked Sulien, from the steps. 'Do you mean you feel more like a good Roman girl after all this?' The sarcasm had no edge, only a tired weight.

Una looked down at the scars splayed across the backs of her hands, then over at her brother. 'I don't know. There were so many Romans who came to watch us being torn apart— I don't know how I can say I'm a Roman after being a slave for all those years, and after that. But I don't know what else to call myself. I don't know any other language. We tried to get out, but it's too far and too hard. We don't even want to live anywhere else, do we? But now I think there are born citizens who don't think of themselves as Romans any more easily than I do. I think there are thousands, maybe millions of people on our side, there always were, and that even with what I can do I didn't see them. I didn't count them. And I think there will be more.'

She remembered herself, at fifteen, striding across London, gusts of chilly rage whistling through her. She could still feel the same cold, sharp air now. And she thought of the name she'd given in the courtroom in Rome, Noviana, the unchosen, double-edged addition that still tied her to Marcus. She wouldn't give up either of them now, the rage or the name.

'Nevertheless, what you're talking about would take years,' said Delir.

'But years of work have already been done,' said Una. 'It's been nine years since you began building a refuge for slaves. And it was years before that that Leo and Clodia started planning to abolish slavery. But it can't have started with them either.'

Something reared up unexpectedly in her memory: the lawyer who was supposed to put on a show of defending her saying, perhaps we could never find any one person with whom it began. A small snag of laughter, defiant and bitter, caught in her throat. 'And we couldn't stop the war from happening, and Holzarta is gone. And Marcus is gone. And Leo and Clodia.' Very briefly she hesitated. 'And Gemella,' she finished. Varius' gaze, which had been on her, veered away towards the distance in sudden pain, and Una felt a pang of guilt, but then he looked back at her and she knew he was glad she hadn't left out her name.

Una went on in a stronger voice, 'But not all of the work is gone. Not all the slaves who escaped. Not all the connections between people who might never even have talked. We can build on what's been done, whether we finish it now, or whether it's someone else, further on.'

'Your network of contacts,' began Varius to Delir.

'I think most of them just want to be left alone.'

'Well, probably, but we can ask them,' said Varius. 'If they can even give us a few sesterces to do this, it will help.'

Ziye stood up and began pacing slowly and uneasily. 'We will have to spend some of this money on weapons,' she said. She sounded perfectly calm and pragmatic, but her lips were tight. 'Or we will have to steal them, or be given them. You can talk of firing fewer shots, fine, but there will have to be guns in these people's hands. There are always ways, of course.'

'Like Dama,' said Delir, a crack in his voice.

Ziye gave him a troubled, complex look. 'Yes.'

Una opened her mouth to counter this and was taken aback when she could not speak. Dama ran ahead of her down the street outside the Colosseum, burning in the rainy air. It would always be almost within her reach to change it; he would always still be running; Marcus would always be right there, waiting for her; her hand would always be sweeping over his still face.

If she could cram all her memory of Dama into that one day, that would be simpler, and easier to bear than if she had to remember talking together, walking through the mountains towards Athabia – or worse, in Rome, when they were older, how he had stood at her door the night of Marcus' wedding to Noriko, scores – hundreds of deaths already on his hands, and she'd thrown her arms round him.

She had to recede from the conversation for a while, could only sit there, biting her lip, waiting the memory out.

Ziye muttered, 'I said I would never fight again.'

'But you can keep to that if you want to,' said Lal. 'No one *has* to fight – I mean' – she glanced around – 'do they? There's enough else to do.'

'It's not that simple. This is a promise I have already broken, at the Colosseum. Very well, I had skills and knowledge that were needed. Una and Sulien are alive because of it; it was worth it. But it is not honest to break it once because two lives are at stake and then not, when we're talking of ending a war, removing a tyrant . . . But then, what kind of promise was it in the first place, to keep unless it became inconvenient? And even suppose I make my promises all over again, it makes no difference; whatever I do now with my own hands, I will be up to my neck in what you do. And that's right; that's as it must be. But we must be very sure of what we do.' She stopped and smiled tautly. 'No, I don't think certainty is any measure. I imagine Dama must have been sure.'

'We're not Dama,' said Sulien, distantly. 'He wanted to start a war. We're trying to stop one. I say we win.'

Una grew aware of Delir's gentle, self-accusing attention. She raised her head to look at him and he reached across the table for her hand. 'My dear, I'm so sorry. I am so sorry.'

'I wish I could forget I ever knew him,' said Una in a whisper.

'Yes,' agreed Delir, bleakly. 'I wish that too.'

'Well,' Una murmured, 'we can't, ever, and I can't— I can't talk about him. So what do we do? I forgive you, if that's worth anything . . .'

Lal got up from her place on the steps. 'Look,' she said impatiently, 'we've got most of a plan – one that might not work – to make things better. It makes sense. Dama didn't have anything like that; he just hoped that if he dragged everything down and raised enough chaos, something good would grow out of it by itself. At least, I suppose that's what he hoped. And maybe it will, in the end – but it's already costing far too much, and it's slower and harder than it should ever have had to be. Nothing good that happens will be any thanks to him, so we don't have to be afraid of being part of it, or being like him. There was peace, back then. Marcus would have been Emperor; he would have abolished slavery. And now, between Dama and Drusus, I don't see that things can get much worse, whatever we do.'

There was quiet again for a while. 'And Drusus?' said Ziye.

Sulien took a breath, and somehow again drew attention to himself even before he began to speak. 'Something happened, when I was on my own in Sarmatia,' he said, softly. 'When I was trying to get home. I needed a car, and—

'I think I did something. I don't know what it meant.'

Roman air squadrons swept daily over the city towards the Red Sea, and yet the Nionian ships continued to advance northwards; Mariaba, the capital of Arabia itself, was under heavy fire. The longvision reports admitted that much, but they had grown sparse and even more blustering than before, and the rumour began to circulate that Mariaba was already fallen, and that a phalanx of Ethiopian and Nionian troops had extended up the Nubian coast as far as Ptolemais Theron.

Yet for another fortnight, Alexandria seemed to drift in a strange, serene trance. People believed the worst about Mariaba, and yet batted around jokes about the same happening to Alexandria. A few shops closed, and sometimes they saw anxious families cramming their possessions into overloaded cars and heading east or to the docks. At the Library Una spent her mornings carrying the most valuable books down to the underground stacks. These occasional symptoms of danger seemed at once frightening and foolish, unnecessary – like a quaint superstition, and even though the six of them discussed leaving and made the decision against it in the knowledge that some kind of attack was probably inevitable, still they were not immune to the general disbelief that anything bad would really happen. The weather was clear as glass; there were free concerts at the Museion. The city felt not merely normal, but distilled, more timelessly itself with every day the ships drew nearer.

Then, still early in February, Lal woke one night, because the building was trembling, to a vast trampling, rushing sound, as if the sea were rising to engulf the city. The air began to scream and tear, and the whole street churned with noise and pressure. The Nionian warships and aircraft carriers had reached the Heroopolite Gulf, and bombs and shells were hurling down onto Alexandria.

'I want to take Ptolemais back. No, I don't want it back, I want it burnt to the ground. Those people are worse than the Nionians, they're worse than— than— they're ingrates, backstabbers – they didn't even *try* to hold out, they just went over to the other side, just like the Ethiopians. They were waiting for the opportunity— I'll see that no one else dares. I'll gas the place, I'll make what happened at Okura look like a birthday party.'

Around Drusus, the generals stood in flinching silence until he at last noticed their expressions.

'Never mind!' he almost shouted, abruptly forcing a smile. 'Never mind. That's in the past. Now, let's get these bastards away from Alexandria.'

General Turnus began to say something with that unbearable patient air and Drusus put up a hand to cut him off. 'Not this feeble complaint about too few men again; surely even a thousand loyal Romans should be able to— I've already said I want conscription. Why is it taking so long?'

And yet he wasn't certain, as he said it, exactly how long it had been. It was all happening so fast, weeks' worth of events passing in days.

Noriko sat staring dully out at the gardens. She had asked for the longvision to be removed before Una and her brother were killed, and she didn't want it back now. Sakura and Tomoe picked up news from the servants, and occasionally Noriko spoke to wandering court officials from the first floor. She knew of the Nionian victories in Africa, and she wondered if her brothers were there, leading the advance. But this new phase of the war only reminded her how useless her marriage had been, and it made the memory of Marcus ache within her. She did not believe it brought any prospect of release for herself or her ladies-in-waiting. No, the more the war began to tilt against the Romans, the more vulnerable they would be.

Three days before, she had turned a corner in the passages near her apartments to find Sakura pressed up against the wall by two Praetorians. One had a hand clamped over her mouth and his other hand under her skirts, which the second man seemed to be gathering higher. They were laughing together – a casual, boyish sniggering.

Noriko, to her subsequent shame, had been able to do nothing but gasp loudly and stand there gaping in paralysed horror.

By the time she was able to move again the two men had seen her. They were still chuckling when they let Sakura go and walked off.

Sakura had stumbled forward into Noriko's arms, shaking.

She had done nothing. Her arrival had been enough, on that occasion at least, but she sensed her own flimsy privileges as Marcus' widow, Drusus' intended wife, were wearing thin. She could not protect Sakura and Tomoe any more than she had been able to protect Una. She would not be able to protect herself.

Despite this, when Drusus charged into her rooms, the first words out of his mouth were, 'Are you happy? I know you're thinking they'll fly in and kill me and you'll get to go back home. Well, I told you, *this* is your home, this is where you stay, with me, whatever happens.'

He stopped and examined her with dissatisfaction. Noriko was sitting blanketed within her own hair, which felt heavy and tangled; she was listlessly aware of a faintly sour scent rising from it, from her skin and clothes. She had not felt like bathing today. She wore no make-up. It didn't seem worth asking the others to comb out her hair.

'You're letting yourself go,' complained Drusus, anxiously. 'You need to take more care of yourself. What would your people think if they saw you like this?'

And apparently prompted by that idea, he lunged at her and started kissing her. At first Noriko merely screwed up her face and tried to twist her head away, but he went on, gathering her

308

tight against him, leaning his weight onto her until her arms were awkwardly trapped between their bodies. There was no point in even trying, she thought drearily, and then was startled at the piercing, siren-like volume of the first scream she let out. She began to writhe and flail.

Struggling with her, Drusus panted impatiently, 'It's all right!'

He didn't have enough room; he dragged her down from the couch to the floor and pinned her hands down while he man-oeuvred his hips between her thighs, then let them go to try and pull her dress open over her breasts.

Noriko clawed and twisted like a cat; the silk carpet beneath them was rucked up under her thrashing heels. She forgot Latin. She snarled and accused him and demanded help at the top of her lungs in furious Nionian. Drusus' teeth were clenched; his face above her looked at once desperate and puzzled, as if there were some misunderstanding.

Sakura and Tomoe erupted into the room and at once began to shriek and bat and kick at Drusus. Tomoe seized at his hair; they dragged him back.

Noriko scrambled out from underneath him and staggered to her feet, continuing to shout. For a moment, she detached from her own outrage and terror to see the havoc as ridiculous: Drusus trying to swipe clumsily at all three of them like a beleaguered bear, the women dancing around still battering at him, all howling in a language he couldn't understand.

Inevitably, a small crowd of Praetorians and servants ran in. Drusus straightened, but didn't let go of Noriko; he gestured the guards towards Sakura and Tomoe and gasped, 'This is private – get them out of here.'

Sakura and Tomoe burst into renewed screams and struggled as the guards took hold of them. Noriko broke away from Drusus and hurled herself unthinkingly into the brawl, pummelling with her fists, dragging at Tomoe. For a wild second there was a kind of scouring relief in fighting and screaming, in not having to pretend to be calm. But then they bundled Tomoe out of the door, and despair caught up with her again; tears filled her eyes for the first time. Regardless she elbowed blindly at Drusus' stomach as he, too easily, pulled her back.

Someone else peeped into the room: Lucius, a small, shuffling, white-headed figure, who cringed diffidently in the doorway and wrung his hands. Nevertheless, he was in the guards' way, and with Sakura still struggling between them, they stopped.

He inquired timidly, 'Is everything all right, Drusus?'

'No,' panted Noriko, grasping for the Latin, feeling she might as well say anything now. 'Your son is a monster. A rapist, a murderer—'

Drusus slapped her, affecting an air of careless authority, but he was flushing. He answered Lucius: 'It's perfectly all right, Father.' Unconsciously he ran a hand over his head to smooth his hair. 'Leave us alone, would you?'

Lucius cowered and grimaced piteously, but he looked at Noriko and murmured to Drusus, 'You've got slaves for that.'

Drusus made a scoffing sound, but his jaw was tight with discomfort. He glanced around uneasily at the large audience that was now gathered in the room and said, 'She's engaged to me. I'm the Emperor. I consider us already married. This is a personal matter between man and wife.'

'I was Marcus' wife,' Noriko wailed, ashamed and angry with herself for the tears that kept falling. 'I'll never be yours.'

'I think it's probably best if you leave her alone,' suggested Lucius softly, and Drusus stared at him with a strange helpless expression, embarrassed, resentful, desolate.

'Oh, for heaven's sake,' he muttered at last, and stalked away, summoning the guards and servants out of the room with another gesture.

Tomoe fled back into the room, dragging the doors shut behind her. The three women collapsed into a breathless, keening heap. Sakura and Noriko clutched each other; Sakura kept lapsing into odd frantic giggles, almost as if she didn't hear herself.

'We can escape,' said Tomoe, in a low taut voice.

It's impossible, Noriko thought, and had not the heart to say it out loud. She wondered, not for the first time, whether they were already past the point where the only correct, honourable course was suicide. She could not bring herself to say that either.

'We can. Lady Noviana and her brother did. Everyone says they are alive.'

Noriko lifted her face from Sakura's hair, feeling a jolt within her as if she was starting out of sleep. 'What?' she asked. 'Who says this?'

'The servants. They were slaves once. They know. They say Lord Varius saved them. They say they are raising an army.'

[XIII]

RECRUITMENT

The bombers were busy over the port again, and what remained of the colonnades that lined Alexandria's great boulevards would have been no shelter if a stray shell had hit. Still, Una and Varius kept underneath them when they could, though sometimes they had to venture into the open to skirt round a spill of rubble. The day was warm and blue and smeared with smoke, the noise of the bombers shredded the air like tissue paper. Far ahead they saw a handful of human figures racing across the empty width of the street, slightly stooped over, their shoulders raised as if it were only rain or hail falling from the sky. They might simply have been caught without shelter, or perhaps they too were part of the tiny, secret overground population of these raids: looters or fugitives exploiting the strange, dangerous freedom of the city that the bombs conferred upon them.

The little group reached the cover of the far colonnade and vanished, leaving Varius and Una completely alone on the huge thoroughfare. Even now, after almost two months of this, it was eerie that such a human, artificial place could be as bare of people as a ravine in a desert. It was as if the city had been abandoned completely to the machines striking overhead.

A drift of sparks came floating over the rooftops and something collapsed near enough to make the ground lurch. Una and Varius flattened themselves against a wall in an automatic embrace, then ran on without speaking.

By now people talked of being used to it, and it was partly true. They no longer bothered to flinch, or cover their ears. The shops would open as soon as the Nionian spiras ran out of bombs and the power came back on. But the noise got inside them, always drumming and banging in their bloodstreams, even when the sky was clear, so that they remained always half in shock. The noise seeded itself into their nerves, and kept up a rhythm of sudden pounds and shivers and skips in their bloodstreams, even when the sky was clear, so that they were in continual practice.

There was no light at the harbour any more: the tower of the Pharos was, inevitably, fallen; the causeway broken into the sea. Already the memory of it whole seemed distant and other-worldly, as if it had been decades rather than months, like a sketch of something from a time before photographs.

There was a row of mansions and luxury inns on Canopus Street; some of them remained untouched, standing alongside hillocks and dunes of rubble. There was one that looked whole from the street, except for broken windows – the ruins crouching as if in embarrassment behind its marbled front. There was a ballroom that was cracked open to the pounding sky, half the ceiling and the back wall gone, like a stage set. Inside, on the walls, streaked with water and smoke, weightless dancers still glided, disappearing into blackened plaster and smashed brick. Here and there, glass crystals from shattered lamps cast small rainbows through the crumbled masonry. The room was littered with the broken remains of dozens of red velvet chairs, though a few remained perfect, standing delicately on their gilt legs over the weeds already beginning to rise from the cracked ground.

Una and Varius scaled the remains of the building next door, climbed the crumpled railing into the walled garden. Mimosa and rhododendrons blazed around the huge reddish crater gouged among the beds. They picked their way around its rim and entered the ballroom through the gateway of felled bricks the bombs had opened up.

At once Varius began silently counting the people waiting for them. Fifteen he already knew; there were – yes, thirty new-comers. Some of them were perched nervously on the surviving gilt chairs.

This was why they had stayed: slaves were escaping through the holes smashed into Alexandria. The vigiles and the gov-ernor's office knew it was happening, but like the outbreaks of looting, it was difficult to do much about it, when so many people roaming the ruins or packed into refugee camps and the new shanty towns on the banks of Lake Mareotis had lost their papers and their homes.

'We'll make this quick,' he said, 'then we'll try and find some shelter like everyone else.'

Some of them gasped when they recognised Una's face from longvision or the posters; they crowded towards her. 'It's really true, it's you,' breathed a woman, with tears in her eyes. 'Can I . . . ?' She had already reached out a tentative hand to touch Una's.

Una smiled, and wrapped the woman in her arms. There was some applause, and even as the sky shrieked and a dusting of plaster drifted down from the remains of the ceiling, the heady mood climbed a little higher. Una, who felt, in fact, trapped and uncomfortable in the embrace, was half-ashamed of having succeeded in making it look natural. But it was needed. She was getting better at it.

Varius went through the names of the fifteen they had met before, and led them off to one side. 'You've done what we asked, some of you twice over now. Thank you. You know we've begun to place small groups of people in certain towns around the Mediterranean and Aegean. Each group begins with a single person. Their first task is to find a way to live in a strange place – that isn't an easy thing to do. But most of you have escaped slavery in the last few weeks and you've managed to survive in this city with bombs raining down on your heads. We can provide advice, and money for the first week. Later they'll need to be ready to receive the recruits we send to them, find likely places for them to work, and to live. We need more of those people.

'And it's time now to start this work in another city, in another province. We need a group of people to begin it. We know, from what you've done already, that we can trust you and that you're capable. So we're asking if any of you would undertake either of these missions.'

'Which other city?' asked one of them, a woman called Praxinoa.

'We won't spread that information beyond the ones who need it. I'm sure you can understand why. If you choose to do it—'

Praxinoa nodded.

'I'll go somewhere else,' said a man called Theon. He had been working with them for more than a month and had done more than they'd asked of him already. 'Start what's been going on here again. Yes.'

Una was in the midst of the newcomers. 'We need to know you,' she said, 'who you are, what skills you have, how far you're prepared to go.'

'—if you can trust us,' a girl finished for her, an odd tightness in her voice, at once defensive and brimming with feeling. She held herself stiffly, her fists clenched.

Una turned, letting her eyes rest on each face in turn. 'Yes,' she said, 'but I already know we can – I know each one of us here can trust each other.'

'You can trust me,' the girl said, in the same angry, half-choked voice, 'and my name's Thekla. And I want— I want to do something. But I don't think I've got any skills. Aline said you want an army and we're just . . . We're women, and—' A blush spread painfully over her face, as if the blood were spilling from a wound under the skin, '—we're from a brothel, in Rhakotis.'

Una looked at her quietly for a moment. 'It's women and older men we want most of all,' she said firmly. 'It's going to be harder for young men to join us, now there's conscription.' There was a muffled weight of anxiety in that word every time she uttered or thought it, but for now, for these people, it would mean an opportunity.

The thuds of the anti-aircraft guns at the port pulsed deep under the screams of the shells. She moved closer to Thekla. 'We've all been bought and sold; our bodies have all been used, but we're none of us going back. We are free. We're free because we are standing here in an air raid, and the vigiles can't find us.

And we're free because of the rightful Emperor's will. And we're free because in our souls we always were. And soon everyone will see it.'

They clapped again, and some of them shouted aloud, the noise drowned in the blasts in the air. Una was taken aback, even though she had been working with the words and the throb of the guns and the rhythm of the feeling in the room for it to happen; even though it had happened before. She hadn't written anything down, but she had thought and planned what needed to be said, and she read, between shifts at the Library, or when the air raids trapped her down in the vaults with the books. Usually she read histories, trying to understand how the empires had come to this point, but sometimes whatever happened to be left open on a desk: a translation of *The Prometheia*, a pile of fairy stories for children, Sappho. And sometimes, as she carried books from place to place, she could feel the patterns and flow of a voice running in her mind and pulling at her, like something once read or heard that she was trying to remember. But when she reached for it – for it was never quite within her grasp – the voice would become recognisable as her own, though altered, older, clearer, and the words were new.

'Well, I'm not that old,' said a man, 'though maybe I seem it to you. But I'll sign up for anything if it means getting out of here.'

'It will mean that, either now or later,' said Una, 'but anyone who comes with us won't be leaving danger behind. If all you want is to get out, there are simpler ways. But if you want more than that, this is what we ask of you, and it's the same we asked of the people who brought you here. Find two more like you – there are thousands out there in this city, and each of you only need to find two. They're hiding out in the camps by the lake. They're freedmen who haven't forgotten. And some of them have never been slaves. If they are angry enough, talk to them. Use your judgment: if someone might want to help, but isn't strong enough now, or if they have duties they can't leave, then don't spread the risk to them. And keep yourselves as safe as you can – mind who's listening. You don't mention our names or this movement in the first conversation. We won't meet here again. You report to a contact, who will lead you to the next meeting place. But you can find these people, and we will bring them with us. And we'll change Rome.'

She became weary and dispirited after it was over, when she and Varius were coughing as they hurried through the clouds of dust hanging over the streets. Instead of slowing her the fatigue made her stride along with unnecessary, self-punishing speed, but her eyes ached and she rubbed at them, complaining, '—and they're nearly half what we have! Only a hundred people, after all this time. And four boats!'

'But people keep coming,' said Varius, 'and in another month we'll have three hundred.'

The streets were coming back to life; people were beginning to emerge from cellars and shelters.

Una sighed. 'If only the money would go out and recruit more—'

'Why aren't you in uniform?' an elderly man suddenly demanded of Varius, stopping dead in front of them.

Varius gave a conciliatory smile. 'Too old,' he said, lightly. He was a few months short of thirty-two – for now, just outside the conscripted age range, though from the start there had been speculative gossip about whether it would be extended, and how soon.

'You're not too old to sign up,' the man cried bitterly. 'Coward!'

Una was glaring at him murderously. Varius managed another tactful grimace and steered her on before she could say anything.

'I haven't had the letter yet,' Sulien said, in response to the same question.

'And he's nearly *blind*!' blurted Lal, and they barely managed to get out of earshot of the two sneering women who'd stopped them before breaking into giggles.

'Self-righteous old cows,' Lal whispered, still laughing.

Sulien's smile dropped faster than hers. They could see the brown haze of smoke and dust to the north, over the centre of the city. He and Lal had been relatively safe in one of the shanty towns that had sprung up among the reeds beside the lake. But they knew Una and Varius would have been above ground, rallying the new volunteers. He understood why they did it, and wished they would not.

Lal looked at the smoke. 'They'll be all right,' she said, and believed it completely. It was a strange symptom of living in a bombed city: the more people were killed, the more the survivors, horrified and exhausted as they were, felt assured of their own invulnerability, or at least of their own luck. It felt quite sensible and justified to extend this glow of belief to Una and Varius, who were, after all, more weathered in matters of survival now than most people.

They walked back towards the city along a strand of the canal. The docks here and at Lake Mareotis had taken far less damage than those on the seafront. Varius' little boat was safe so far, and Varius, Sulien and Una were still living in the flat nearby. Lal and her family had moved; the guest house they had been staying in was still standing, but several houses on the same street had been razed that first night. Now they were in a house on the other side of the lake. It was small and ugly, but more space than they'd had in ages. Rents, at least, had come down.

The vigiles were trying to patrol the official camps more stringently, though many of them had been funnelled off into the army, leaving the remainder harassed and overstretched. Still, Lal and Sulien were careful there, quietly visiting people who had either joined the group already or were known to sympathise, but scattering none of the leaflets they had spread into the camps' unlicensed suburbs and the villages of tents and huts. The leaflets – deliberately printed in a watery ink on tissue-like paper that was almost guaranteed to fall apart within a fortnight – made no explicit exhortations, only repeated that Marcus had declared an end to slavery as he was dying. Lal and Sulien never put them directly into anyone's hands, just left them lying around, where they might be found and perhaps talked about. They were good for allowing existing supporters to probe friends' strength of feeling.

There were leaflets and posters everywhere these days, even in the camps: the propaganda pamphlets the Nionian aircraft dropped over the city in between the bombs, urging in surprisingly garbled, sometimes rather comical Latin that Nionia was not Egypt's enemy. And, always, the hectoring, wheedling appeals to Roman manhood to enlist at once.

Sulien was well over six foot tall, and scars aside he was visibly healthy. He knew how increasingly exposed he was in the space the city's young men were leaving behind. And though he had collected a number of different sets of identity papers from Lal, there was no way to hide *what* he was. No one would have believed he was younger than eighteen, and boys below the lower age limit were signing up anyway. If he'd let his beard grow again, he might have passed for twenty-five, but never for over thirty.

And yet he did not worry about conscription. He was vaguely baffled and sorry that he could not feel the same anxious rage that Lal and Una felt on his behalf.

'Well, they can say whatever they want,' he said to Lal now, kicking at a soggy poster that lay crumpled at the canal's edge, 'but I'm exempted on the grounds of being dead.'

A letter had already come to the flat, addressed to the occupant, instructing any men of the required age to report to a recruiting station. They had thrown it away, but Una remained pale and tight-lipped for hours, and had begun to talk about places he could go to hide. Sulien didn't know why he was unable to take it seriously. In part, and like many young men at the time, he could not imagine himself going to war, just as no one in the city really believed they could die. But then he found it hard to think about himself at all – about his own future – as something distinct.

He'd seen army convoys rolling out of the city, and the recruits in their new uniforms lined up in the forum, parading through the streets. Some looked bullish, excited by the waving crowds, others incredulous, terrified. Sulien felt a rush of sympathy for all of them – he was surprised at how strong it was, how it felt more real than almost anything.

The flat was empty when they reached it. They rarely had it to themselves, so they pulled off their clothes and climbed into bed – they had survived another air raid, and it seemed the only thing to do. The skylight window had been left closed and the room was sticky, embalmed in trapped sunlight, but Lal trembled as she lay down; tears prickled in her eyes as she kissed him. She understood her own body better now than at the beginning, and yet she could not get used to this. Every time it felt like charging headlong, enraptured, into unexplored, frightening space, even though he was so sweet and she knew there was nothing to be afraid of.

'I love you,' he murmured to her, not for the first time, and Lal, delighted, anguished, arched and pulled him down, pressed her mouth to his to stop him talking. These avowals became uncomplicated and precious in her memory when she was alone, but in the moment that they were said they racked her with contrary feelings. She was sure he was not lying, nor did she believe that he was mistaken. Sometimes she thought it was only a shadow in her own imagination. And the mere idea of losing him after everything made her gasp and cling, and drive her fingertips into his skin to pull him even closer.

Occasionally she confused her apprehension with religious guilt, which was something she could at least find words for, and Sulien became quite animated and inventive in persuading her out of it.

Sulien fell asleep for a little while afterwards. This was rare; usually they were more furtive, they made love hidden by the reeds beside the lake, or in a deserted bomb shelter, and then dressed quickly and carried on with the day's business, behaving as if it were a secret, even though everyone must know. It was for Delir's sake, chiefly, that they wished to preserve some sort of illusion that it might not be happening, even though far too much had passed for him to attempt any protest now. He would be happy if she and Sulien ever married, it occurred to Lal, and then she could not help but imagine what it would be like, if they did get married, back in Rome, some time after the war was over. If she was right to trust their plans, the end might not be so far off.

Sulien began to talk in his sleep, tormented gibberish and moans. He shook, and raised a hand, perhaps to fend something off, perhaps pleading. Lal sat uncertainly stroking his hair, distressed and hesitant. 'Sulien,' she said at last and he sat up and stared at her with awful, unrecognising eyes for far too long. Then he sighed and lay down again, saying nothing.

Lal moulded herself to his side, kissed his shoulder.

He didn't move; his eyes were shut. He might have been asleep again, except for the rhythm of his breathing.

'Was it the Colosseum?' she asked at last. She tugged unconsciously at the sheets, pulling them higher over his chest. The scars were not disfiguring, but she hated the sight of them.

Sulien frowned. 'No,' he said, dully, without opening his eyes. And then, 'I can't remember.'

Then, at the end of April, squads of soldiers began to patrol the streets, knocking on doors rounding up the young men that were left. One evening Una saw it happen, a couple of dazed, stumbling boys dragged out of a block of flats. She stopped, almost dropping her bag, staring in horror, and involuntarily caught the eye of one of the soldiers as he dragged the boys towards a covered truck. If he would just have let them walk by themselves – it was clear enough that they were too frightened and too outnumbered to run away – but he wouldn't let them keep on their feet for more than a second. He was only Sulien's age, but he was hulking with indignation, far more truly disgusted with these boys than the job demanded. He was irritated by Una's attention. *What of it?* his look growled at her. Una, who had not been so close to a soldier since the Colosseum, gripped her false identity papers in her pocket and blinked meekly before turning away, a mousy little assistant librarian hurrying home from work.

She raced back, half expecting to see the same trucks standing outside the building by the canal. She already had Sulien virtually imprisoned in the flat. He had given up even trying to get a job; he no longer came to meetings, only occasionally slunk down to the refugee camps. Otherwise he barely went outside except onto the roof terrace, or to run to the bomb shelter.

'That's it,' she said, when she'd told what she'd seen, 'we've been messing around with this long enough. You're next out to Greece.'

Varius, at least, caught the urgency at once. 'It would only take three days to get him to Naxos. He could stay with Tenos and Isione.'

'But it's happening in Greece too,' Sulien protested, 'or at least it will be soon.'

'When it happens there we'll think of something else,' said Una grimly. 'Anyway, they can't send troops out to every island.'

'They'll have the vigiles. And I'll stand out anywhere.'

'You'll live in a cave or under a bed if that's what it takes.'

Sulien laughed, even though it was clear she meant it.

Una hissed in frustration and studied him darkly, contemplating objects and stratagems she could use to injure him, endow him with a disqualifying limp, anything to make sure.

Sulien startled her by appearing to read her thoughts, as if, for a moment, he'd picked up her gift. 'What do you want to do, shoot me in the foot? They'd know. They've got court-martials for that sort of thing. That's how people get executed.'

'Sulien,' said Varius, 'you sound as if you want to go.'

'No, of course not,' Sulien said, in mild surprise.

Una stared at him. Yes, he was telling the truth, there was no active desire, just a disconcerting absence of any strong feeling.

He finished vaguely, 'But . . . it's happening to everyone. There's no point worrying about it.'

Una felt like shaking him, and instead dropped her face into her hands, kneading her eyes. She'd had little sleep lately, one late night of longdictor calls and discussions followed by another broken up by air strikes.

'There is a point in worrying, and you're letting us do it for you,' said Varius sharply. 'Can't you understand what it would mean for Una – for all of us – if they take you away? Didn't you hear how many men they lost down in Alodia? Why do you think they want so many more?'

Sulien looked stricken. 'I'm sorry – I didn't mean it like that. I'll go to Naxos. I'll try and keep my head down. It'll be all right.'

'They're not getting you,' said Una, through clenched teeth.

Sulien looked at her in sympathy. 'If it did happen,' he said, hesitating, 'I'd find a way to come back.'

'Don't talk about what you'd do *if* it happened!'

There was a short silence. Sulien said quietly, 'I have to tell Lal.'

'Do it now, then,' said Varius.

'What – tonight?' Sulien asked, taken aback.

'Those trucks were only a few streets away,' said Una. 'For God's sake, it's not as though we want soldiers finding the three of us together anyway.'

Sulien nodded reluctantly.

'They're probably checking ships up at the lock,' said Una. It was increasingly hard to avoid inspections of one kind or another when sailing out of Alexandria: so many of the docks along the coast were now little more than charred scree on blackened beaches that the traffic on the canals had come under sharper and more suspicious scrutiny. The passage of a small private yacht was no longer unremarkable.

Varius reached for the identity papers he was currently using. 'I'll take the boat around the coast. I don't think there'll be any checks if you come out through Mareia, and if there is any trouble you could go round on the Via Eleusiniana. Meet me at Taposiris and we'll go on from there. I'll go now; you follow tonight if the Nionians give us the night off, otherwise early tomorrow morning.'

Sulien's mouth twisted a little, into a distant, unhappy smile. 'All this trouble,' he muttered.

'Well, at this point we've all caused a lot of trouble to each other,' said Varius briskly, with some slight hope of flicking that expression off Sulien's face. He was not successful.

Varius left, and it struck Una suddenly that they had made a mistake; she should have gone herself. It had not occurred to her to alter the arrangement at the time; the boat was Varius', and she hadn't wanted to let Sulien out of her sight before she had to. But she would not have been seen as a possible conscript.

'Those boys I saw didn't even look eighteen,' she said. 'Perhaps they don't care any more if you're a few years over or under. And everyone says they're going to put it up to forty-five anyway.'

'They'd think it was weird, though, a girl on her own in a boat, late at night,' said Sulien. 'They might have arrested you, or followed you—' But he could manage, for Varius, some of the worry he hadn't been able to muster for himself. Aside from the conscription squads, Varius was still known to be alive, still publicly sought, although lately there had been far less room for him in the news.

Sulien called Lal, who said, impulsively, 'Let me come with you, then,' as soon as he explained.

Sulien didn't think to warn her of any difficulties, or ask if she was sure. 'Yes, come,' he said, leaning against the wall and closing his eyes. 'We'll get jobs in a bar on the beach. And if we never have enough money for rent it won't matter, we'll just sleep on the sand. It'll be summer soon.' And he drifted pleasantly for a minute or so into the idea of it: Lal wrapped around him in the warm sea, lying beside him on a carpet of pine needles. But there was an ache suffusing it all, that he felt without consciously noticing it, just as he did not notice himself failing to concentrate properly as Lal talked of what she should pack and how soon she could reach him.

It felt natural to him that the call should be interrupted by air raid sirens.

Despite their furtive operations among the ruins in other raids, there was no question of attempting to travel now. Private vehicles were banned from the roads during the attacks. At least for the rest of the night the risk of running into a conscription squad was done with; all they had to do now was survive the bombs.

The noise of the explosions paced heavily from the north towards their street, like a giant wading knee-deep through the houses, kicking up sprays of concrete and brick. They ran downstairs and up the street to the shelter, where they jostled in among fifty wan people crammed into a stark and increasingly rank-smelling concrete box beneath a junction. They picked their way through to a familiar corner of it, unrolled their blankets, claiming a strip of territory on the concrete floor, and lay down. Sometimes there were songs and jokes, and bottles of methousia passed around. But tonight people only sighed and coughed and quarrelled fitfully as the night boomed and splintered, all of them tired and frightened, but by now past the point of crying and praying for it to stop.

Sulien was close to the wall; he could feel it shiver. At first, nights in the bomb shelter – the windowless concrete, and certain elements of the smell – had reminded him unbearably of the cell under the Colosseum. Yet tonight, he felt strangely safe – or at least, calm. The shelter was so packed that there was scarcely an inch of space between himself and Una, who was lying rigidly on her side, a tense, jealous barrier between him and the rest. They didn't talk, lay coaxing sleep without expecting it to come. He glanced at her once and saw her eyes were shut, but the set of her face remained determined and angry, her teeth clenched. Then there was some vague stir further out on the floor – people rearranging themselves, making room for someone – and Una shifted closer, and now he could feel her forehead butting against his arm.

The past bulged into the present again: they were lying side by side on warm, bloody sand, he was closing his eyes. For once, the memory of the Colosseum came without the usual ripples of panic, the usual desperation. He remembered painlessness, certainty.

It should have been impossible to sleep, but he did, and dreamt of nothing.

Varius had been stopped at the lock, but the soldiers on duty there had not been particularly belligerent, but scornfully amused at the excuses he offered, along with the papers that declared his age.

'Well,' said one, tossing the plastic wallet back to him after a cursory search of the cabin, 'you have fun with your boat for the next couple of months, and then we'll see you down in Alodia.'

He'd travelled perhaps five miles down the featureless coast when the bombing started. The echoes blared around the ship, off the pale rocks, the surface of the sea. Looking back he saw the sky on fire over Alexandria, the domes and towers outlined black against sheets of flame. The perverse sense of normality that insulated the city evaporated when one saw it from a distance; it was incredible that anyone could survive even one such night, that they could have been living there so long.

Very late, two or three hours before dawn, the sky grew quiet and Una and Sulien dragged themselves, shivering, to their feet, filed up the steps of the shelter, and staggered back towards the flat. They lurched speechlessly to their beds, unable to think of anything but collapse.

The noise seemed to burst upon them just seconds after they had lain down – in reality, almost an hour later. Una was closest to the sound; the flat had only one real bedroom and she slept on a fold-out bed in the living room. She sprang up, thinking confusedly of more bombs, her head filling with the noise, but when she realised what was happening, it was even worse. Sulien had just stumbled blinking into the room, and there were soldiers outside shouting for them to open the door – which they promptly broke down anyway.

For a moment it was the train in Iaxarteum, the van in Rome

all over again. Still barely awake, Una and Sulien clutched at each other, backing away from the door. Then one of the soldiers announced something about conscription enforcement, and Sulien went still, realising that the men did not know who they were, only wanted him.

He rubbed his eyes, and put up a hand. 'Let me get dressed,' he said.

Una had understood what was happening a moment before. 'No. No,' she had been repeating, unheard by anybody. Now, making a decision, she ran forward to cling to the arm of one of the soldiers, begging in a much louder, clearer voice: 'Please! Please, just give me a minute to say goodbye to my brother.'

'Should have said that to him months ago,' the man grunted, shaking her off.

'He wanted to go before,' she whimpered tragically, 'he only stayed this long to *look after me!*' Real desperation was driving the performance almost to the edge of parody. Tears – actually of shock and fury – trickled down her cheeks. But even without such embellishments she looked pale and vulnerable enough, and somehow younger than she really was, standing there barefoot in her nightdress, her eyes dark and huge. The soldiers shifted and glanced at one another, softened a little.

'Well, go on,' the leader said gruffly. 'And get your clothes on.'

Una seized Sulien's wrist and dragged him into the bedroom, almost slamming the door shut behind them.

Sulien leant back against the door, closing his eyes for a second, then looked at her, ready to talk. But Una wiped her eyes roughly on the back of her arm, strode across the room to fling open the shutters and said, 'Get out of the window.'

Sulien stared, and sighed out an exhausted laugh. 'Don't be stupid,' he said.

Una ignored this. 'We can get across to the roof terrace opposite and climb down,' she said, a fierce, mad edge to her voice. She swept a couple of sets of identity papers and a bundle of cash into a bag and slung it on over her nightdress.

'No, we can't,' said Sulien. He pulled on a pair of trousers under the loose tunic he'd been sleeping in, pushed bare feet into his shoes. 'It's a fifty-foot drop. And they'd see. They'd shoot us.'

Una ground her teeth and leaned out of the window, trying to judge the distance. '*You* think of something else, then.'

Sulien came forward to take hold of her shoulders. 'Una,' he said, 'there isn't anything else. You're wasting the time we've got.'

Una turned, still not looking directly at him, scanning the room and raking through her brain, searching for some saving detail on which to hang an idea. But she began to shake, her breath coming in rough, angry gasps: she could find nothing.

'We'll get you out,' she promised at last, her voice strangled.

'What?' Sulien shook his head, almost exasperated with her. 'No.'

'We've got out of worse.'

'And how many times can we expect to get away with it? We've been running around under the vigiles' noses practically asking for something to happen as it is. I don't want you risking your life any more – or Varius risking his again, not over this. It's not the Colosseum. Or a cross. It's not certain death. And everyone else has to go. Why should I be any different?'

'How can you ask that?' said Una hoarsely, only just managing to restrain herself from shouting, 'when you know how worthless, how stupid this war is? You know how hard Marcus tried to stop it – how hard we're still trying. Have you forgotten who began it, and what he's done to you? Do you think you've got some kind of duty? You were a slave for sixteen years! Why can't you ever really believe that? What could you possibly owe that hasn't already been taken from you?'

Sulien hesitated. 'Of course I know all that,' he said, 'but I've got no choice, and anyway . . . However it started, I don't want Rome to *lose*. There has to be something left, something that can get better. Or what use is everything we've been working for? And they're sending other slaves.'

'And they've got no right— it shouldn't be happening! None of this should be happening!'

'But it is happening,' said Sulien.

Una opened her mouth again, but no more words came. She sat down, suddenly, on Varius' bed.

Sulien sat beside her. 'We've had bombs falling on us all night,' he said. 'We've got used to it. I don't expect I'll even notice the difference.'

'*I* will,' breathed Una, in a dazed, helpless whisper. 'I will.'

'There's Drusus' prophecy,' he murmured. 'If it's true, and if it's got anything to do with us – well, anything to do with me – then I'll be all right. I'll get back.'

Una shook her head. She said dully, 'That can't be right. Can't be how it works.'

Sulien shrugged. 'I don't know. It's something.'

Someone banged on the bedroom door. Sulien turned a little towards the noise, shifting away from her.

'Wait—' said Una.

But the soldiers shoved the door open, and Sulien rose to meet them. They gripped his arms, as if he'd been making an attempt to escape, and he let them. The leader barked, 'Come on, you. Out.'

The building settled into silence again; in other rooms, people were unstiffening in their beds, going back to sleep. As if afraid of waking them, Una crept across the floor on light, careful feet, aimlessly moving from the broken door to the roof terrace steps and back. Then she turned out the lights and lowered herself quietly to the floor in the doorway between the bedroom and living room. She sat there in the dark, slack and still, barely feeling her back aching against the jamb, in a kind of comfortless, open-eyed sleep. She didn't move until dawn began to thread through the shutters, when she crawled onto Sulien's rumpled bed, and lay staring for another hour in a continuation of the same trance. Then Lal came rushing into the flat through the broken door and found her there. She pulled Una up into her arms, crying, as she realised what had happened.

*

Varius, already sure something was wrong, called early from Taposiris, and Lal answered the longdictor in tears. He scowled and swore, hurried down to the sea and went back.

He found Lal had heaved the door up from the floor and was standing on a stool with a screwdriver, trying to reattach it to its frame, tears still running down her face. Una was sitting upright and pale at the kitchen table, still in her nightdress. She began to cry briefly when she saw Varius, but then stopped, exclaiming wildly, 'I know where he is; I know where they took him.'

'Where?' On the voyage back he had already been trying to think of some way to undo this, or at least to set his mind into the right frame for finding one.

'A training camp near somewhere called Hibis. It's in the desert, we can find out where—'

Una had spoken very little until now, had been able to give Lal only the barest outline of what had happened. But she felt a little more real with Varius there, and started to hope again that Sulien had been wrong and they could find a way to bring him back. And as she began haltingly to recount the course of the night, she felt a touch of vicarious guilt, for Lal's sake, aware that she was longing for any kind of verbal keepsake from Sulien, and that he had left none for her. For a moment Una almost convinced herself she could make something up; it seemed hardly dishonest – Sulien would have meant to say goodbye. She had no doubt he would have done so if he'd had a little more time to think.

But she was almost too sleep-starved and wretched to explain the bare truth; it was beyond her to add anything to it.

Sitting beside her at the table, Lal's face grew hot with the effort of not asking, 'Did he mention me? Didn't he say anything at all?' But in increments, it became obvious to her that if there had been anything, Una would not have kept it to herself so long.

It suddenly seemed childish and undignified to be crying, so she stopped.

Una rubbed her eyes. 'I know he cares about you,' she managed, 'it was just all so fast. And we were so tired.'

Lal nodded, reasonably.

Una insisted again, 'We can find him, we can get him out.'

Lal murmured, 'But he didn't want us to try and find him . . . ?'

Varius and Una were equally inclined to ignore what Sulien wanted. Una was due at work and refused to call in sick, despite Lal's urging that she looked it. The Library had lost one of its lecture theatres, the roof of an observatory and many windows in the raids, and far fewer students slouched in its alcoves, but the main buildings and the collections within were almost unharmed. Una roamed among the shelves, hollow-eyed, almost incapable of following an index or a request form, yet she search-ed out copies of military records and maps and deposited them furtively on a desk in front of Varius, who sat with a notepad, and a stack of poetry books to disguise what he was really working on.

But as the day went on, Sulien's prohibition, along with other things, began to corrode their sense of what was possible. There was no money – all that remained of what Eudoxius had given Varius was either spent or committed now. And the training camp, they established, was deep into the desert, connected only to a tiny oasis town by a single road that led nowhere else. There would be no cover of trees or buildings or traffic, nowhere to hide on either the approach or the departure. The dunes would be swarming with recruits on field exercises. Still, Una thought desperately, there must be some way of getting close.

But there was no way that did not carry a very strong risk of failure and death. I don't want you risking your life any more, Sulien had said, or Varius risking his again . . .

From an upper gallery she watched Varius as he sat frowning down at the pages, dark head propped on one long hand, trying to dismiss similar doubts. He looked tired and unhappy, and yet safe there in the book-lined alcove, as if the presence of so many printed words around him exerted a soft, protective force. Una wished with sudden and painful energy that it were true, and for a moment she tried to imagine how he would live if it were ever really over, if they won.

But even if she had no scruples about risking herself or Varius, even if she didn't care about the work they had begun, there was Sulien himself. He would be no likelier to survive a rescue attempt than the rest of them. There was no way to measure one danger against the other. Perhaps they would only wreck what chance of surviving the war he had.

As evening fell they walked in silence along the cratered streets back towards Rhakotis. They both knew the truth; Varius was trying to think how to say it to her, so at last Una said it herself, stiffly: 'We can't do it.'

Then she had to stop and lean against a wall splashed with recruitment posters. 'He won't come back, they'll kill him, I know they will,' she said, sobbing, 'I always— I can't— I can't *keep* anyone—'

And Varius, holding her, found himself rashly promising, I'm here, I'll stay, no matter what happens.

For those first days, despair possessed her like a physical illness. Her body ached; there was nothing on which she could concentrate; everything became unbearably sharp when lingered over. Helplessly, she saw Sulien bending over Marcus' body and then, fleeing the memory in anguish, she thought of that first autumn in Gaul, five years before: she and Marcus and Sulien, all three of them in different ways still new to each other, in a necropolis outside Tolosa, in a forest on a mountainside. And she remembered Marcus' old fears, which, at least, could never hurt him any more, and she wondered what it would take to send someone mad, if not the terrible strength of this ache to go back.

And yet it was as if she were on a long rope, a leash that, while she whimpered and struggled, kept her within certain limits. Even at her worst, crying and cowering from the future on Sulien's bed, she was aware of a very small part of herself standing back and keeping a stern, impatient watch. It was not a voice, there were no words, but it might have said: All right. You are allowed a certain amount of time for this. But then you must go on as you were.

*

332

She began to hold meetings again. During a daytime raid she and Ziye broke open a couple of trucks transporting slaves to a market. Delir and Lal travelled east to Petra and came back with twelve hundred sesterces. They settled ten supporters in Aila – Theon and Praxinoa among them – to replicate the underground recruitment campaign they had led in Alexandria. And seven hundred miles south there was a Roman offensive outside Meroë that the longvision reporters said would be decisive, and a week later no one was certain whether it had ended, and what had changed. Sulien would be heading there soon, Una thought.

Only a few of the growing band of volunteers knew where Una and Varius lived, or how to contact them directly. A man named Chaeremon, one of their first recruits in the city, was one of them, and one evening early in May he called the flat, sounding both anxious and excited. 'I've been talking to young Thekla – she's run into somebody interesting. Not trouble, as such, just more volunteers, but it worries me.'

'Someone you don't think we can trust?' asked Varius.

A short silence. 'I wouldn't exactly say that.'

They met Chaeremon at the docks on the edge of the lake and walked a couple of miles along the western shore, then into the rough paths chopped and beaten through the reed beds. It was not summer yet, but there was a soft, overripe warmth in the evening air and the lake was purring with mosquitoes. Una wondered how long it would be before disease began to run out of control. Some of the city's refugees were living on small boats in the shallow basins of the lake; on the land, lanes of duckboards lay over the increasingly marshy ground between the shelters. There were a few government-issue white tents, and many huts of thatched reed, and shacks cobbled together out of anything – plastic, sheets of wood, billowing flaps of colourful fabric. Thekla stood in a doorway of one of these, holding back a length of scarlet cloth pinned up as a curtain, looking out for them.

Inside, a hot, red light filtered through the curtain. Four people were sitting on the ground, and a woman was standing waiting.

She seemed young, from the light, agile posture of her body, the sheen of her dark skin, but her face was almost wholly obscured by a red scarf, and her arms were folded, rather combatively, against her chest.

Una frowned, certain she had never seen this girl before and yet feeling strangely as if she ought to know her. Then the stranger said, 'I've been searching for you,' and unfolded her arms, revealing that one of them ended in a battered plastic socket fixed with a pair of crude hooks. The thumb of her remaining hand was missing too.

She tilted her head a little, looking through her scarf at Varius, who started in amazement and said, 'Bupe.'

Bupe nodded, oddly formal. 'I'm glad you are alive.'

'Likewise,' said Varius, though his surprise at seeing her was not wholly pleasant. She'd been almost a corpse when she'd been dumped at the Transtiberine slave-clinic two years before, burned and filthy, her hand blown away. Her face and body had been sprayed with fire by a detonator at the Veii Arms Factory, and she'd disappeared before Sulien had even finished treating her – to join Dama, as they had discovered much later.

She turned her shrouded head to Una. 'You're Sulien's sister?'

'Yes.'

'I heard the squads have taken him.'

'Yes.'

Bupe nodded again, displacing the scarf enough to show a grimace of curt sympathy and regret. And there were edges of scars, extending from some terrible centre under the folds of cloth, but her visible eye was bright. 'We lost some of our own to them too. I'm sorry he's gone. I never thanked him for what he did for me.'

But she had. Sulien had told Una about the last minutes of his escape with Lal from Dama's compound near Rome, the burnt girl silently staring at them near the gates, then turning her blinded eye to shut out the sight of them and letting them pass.

Dama felt suddenly close, a thickening in the texture of the warm air, an alteration of the light. Una's chest grew tight, her skin prickled as if a blunt knife were running over it. She had to force herself to say his name. 'You were at Dama's farm.'

'Yes,' said Bupe levelly. 'I believed everything – almost everything – he told us then. Some of us tried to go on believing it, even after he was dead, even at the start of the war.'

Una gritted her teeth.

Bupe stared at her out of her red hood for some seconds. 'But he didn't tell us everything. And then you— What you said at your trial – no one chooses to die like that over something that isn't true. So we could have had freedom without all this. And now slaves are being sent off to fight for Rome too. I don't care how it happens now. I didn't think Rome could be any more evil than it was. But it is – it is. I hate this Emperor, I will do anything I can to stop him. Have you heard what happened in Patara?'

Varius and Una glanced at each other – they had not.

'You will soon. Of course they are trying to keep the news from spreading, but it was too big. I know – I was there. We got some women and boys out of a workshop making clothes— We burned it afterwards, just a little place. But there was a big meatpacking factory close to it, and they must have heard about what we did there. And they must have heard about you, too, because the next day they wouldn't touch the machines; they said they knew they were already free. Then when the supervisors tried to punish them, they smashed the place up. They fought their way out. And it spread – slaves from everywhere, houses and factories and everywhere. Some shops got smashed, you know. But then they all came together in the forum, hundreds of them, I don't know how many. They tried to take over the courthouse. They wanted to make the praetor say it, that they were free. You should have heard the noise we made – I was there – we frightened them, at least.'

Her voice was vivid with anger and strange satisfaction. In quick, bright, flashes Una could see it – the furious, ecstatic faces, the rush at the courthouse doors – and she was torn between exhilaration and sick certainty of what must have followed. The uprising would have been put down bloodily. The people Bupe was talking about were dead.

'Of course the vigiles came and started firing,' said Bupe, calmly, chillingly. 'Everyone must have expected that. It took a while. We got out before the worst of it. And they couldn't shoot everyone. But later there were bodies all across the forum, and the blood— It pools in the gutters, and there's the smell . . . You had to expect it, but afterwards . . . It went on, and got worse. Anywhere there was one of those posters up – any street anywhere near it, they went round all the houses and workshops and everywhere and took the slaves – all of them from some places, one or two from others, I couldn't see any pattern to it, but most of them were people who had nothing to do with it. Even their owners couldn't stop it. And they killed them. They hung some of them in the street. They even got out the crosses again and crucified them. They said the orders came straight from the Emperor. It was because of you. You can see that, can't you? Because of what you are doing. And he will do it again.'

Drusus and the men who had carried out his orders – they had murdered these people, Una thought, no one else. She had just time to think this, to cling to the thought like a rope, because there was a roaring in her ears and a cold wind seemed to fly around her, as if she were falling. She was ashamed of an impulse to look to Varius for reassurance, or for an understanding of shared guilt. But she could not have acted on it in any case, she could not move. She stood there rigidly staring.

'They hate him in Patara now,' said Bupe softly. 'Even the citizens, even the slave owners: they hate the Emperor more than they hate the Nionians. Nionia never robbed them, or made the streets smell like that. More people will come to you because of it. Many of them are looking for you.' She lifted her mutilated arms. 'There are fifty with me. Even I can hold a gun. Do you want us?'

[XIV]

COMMILITII

Noriko, daughter of the Go-natoku Emperor and wife of Marcus Novius Faustus Leo, to Diodorus Cleomenes, with polite greetings.

You told me to trust you I know this is not what you meant. But I can think of no other. In his room here I have found letters of my husband I know you were most loyal to him and help him many time. My ladies and me we are in serious increasing danger. I can not write what will certainly happen soon if we do not escape from here. But you may imagine it is very bad. We are watched and forbidden everywhere it will be very hard even to get outside but I think we can do it. But if we have nowhere to go after that we will be lost.

Here is this bracelet. Please sell it and I hope you can use the money because I am sure you will need it if you are willing to help. Perhaps for a car.

Please for my husband's sake I beg you to help us.

Please forgive my poor Latin I am writing in haste.

Noriko did not read the letter over; it was too embarrassing even to look at the frantic writing, the crumpled paper. She rolled it up despondently and hid it inside her sleeve. She had written it in bed by the dim glow of moonlight through the curtains, so as not to wake the maidservant sleeping in the little bed against the far wall. She was not allowed writing materials; even the notebooks in which she did Latin exercises had been taken away. But she was still free to wander the palace and gardens, and so, hidden in cushions and curtain hems around her bedroom, she had a secret store of hidden pens, swept off tabletops and desks when her minders were not looking. And no one had yet thought of

337

confiscating the cases of old letters in the bureau where Marcus had written some of his private correspondence.

She was not even sure what to do with the letter once she'd written it – how to get it out of the Palace, let alone as far as Cleomenes, whose address she didn't know. She had found no letters from him, though his name had been mentioned in a couple of messages from Varius, and that had been enough to confirm to her that this was someone who would not betray her. All she could think to do, for now, was keep it on her, together with the bracelet, under her sleeve, waiting for an opportunity. The bracelet had been a present from Marcus; she had thought it would be easier for Cleomenes to sell a Western piece safely and discreetly. She had not worn the bracelet since Marcus' death – or even very often before that – and yet, handling it and remembering him, she would have preferred to use one of the gifts from her family, for she had begun to feel she might see them again.

While searching, she'd found drafts of desperate letters Marcus had written to Una, before and after their marriage. Noriko had clenched her teeth and looked away.

Trunnia, the woman in charge of spying on them, must once have been a slave, and perhaps that was why she enjoyed her power over three foreign noblewomen so much now. Often, when Noriko and the others tried to talk to her, she made an irritable show of not being able to understand their accents. She complained to the other maids about their outlandish habits and histrionic moods in an audible half-whisper when Noriko, Sakura and Tomoe were in the next room. And she supervised the other servants when they went through all their belongings, after the incident with the razor.

And yet among the servants there were potential allies. By now Noriko knew who some of them were – the girl who had whispered to Tomoe that Una and Sulien were alive; the liveried functionaries who opened doors on the lower floor; a young boy they sometimes saw polishing the banisters on the stairs nearest their rooms. But it was not easy to talk to them alone for any length of time.

To her horror, Drusus summoned her to dinner once after the assault in her rooms. The page who came with the message was accompanied by a couple of baleful Praetorians, and Noriko was even more frightened now of being dragged in forcibly; she felt almost sure that once it began, the violence would surge to the height it had reached before.

'My ladies-in-waiting will come with me,' she said, when she could think of no safe way out. She didn't want to leave Sakura and Tomoe, both for their sake and her own.

'Just you,' said one of the Praetorians, grinning. 'Take them along and we'll only have to bring them back.'

Noriko recognised him with a shudder of anger and fear; he was one of the pair who had attacked Sakura. She bit her lip and acknowledged herself trapped. She was almost as afraid of being alone with the Praetorians as with Drusus, but she would not ask Sakura to go anywhere in this man's company, even without the threat.

While they waited outside she shut herself into her bedroom to dress, angrily, in the drabbest formal wear she could find. She talked briefly with Sakura and Tomoe; Tomoe suggested they lock and barricade themselves into the bath suite until she came back. Trunnia sighed and rolled her eyes, but did not try to stop them.

Noriko marched down the palace corridors, her body barbed with tension. Behind her the two guards whispered and sniggered, in that disgusting way she remembered, but they did not speak to her directly, nor touch her. She walked quickly across the glittering floor and lay down stiffly on the couch opposite Drusus, ignoring the food.

At least Drusus did not speak to her, though for long periods he stared at her, broodingly, from beneath lowered brows. There were, as usual, a couple of attractive women in evening dress lounging elegantly on the couch beside him – a young blonde who gamely kept up a stream of squeaky chatter across the otherwise silent table, and, clutched closer to Drusus, a girl about Noriko's own age, wearing a white dress, with dark, velvety eyes and heaped-up black hair. Noriko still did not know who the women were, or how Drusus procured them, but she had noticed that some of them recurred. The blonde was new, but that dark-haired one had been present more often than any of the others.

The girl never spoke, and she looked like someone. Noriko had not placed it at once, because the resemblance was to someone she'd only seen in photographs, but now, in the white gown and with her hair dressed that way, the similarity was obscene: Lady Tullia, Faustus' wife, the murderess, the one Drusus had killed. It was as if a ghost lay there, blinking and smiling at nothing across the table. Noriko's skin crept at what the likeness meant. She wanted to keep her eyes lowered and away from Drusus, but they kept being drawn back towards the other woman, fascinated despite herself. Was it only a fancy, or did she herself look a little like both of them – Tullia, and this replica of her? The dark hair and light skin, something about the chin and the mouth – was it not possible that Drusus might see it that way?

And usually Drusus did not touch the women much while Noriko was there, but this time, once he'd downed a few glasses of wine, he had the dark girl almost on her back, practically underneath him, right there in front of everyone, while the little blonde gritted her teeth and prattled on. But Noriko was sure this was for her benefit. He wanted her to watch as he ran his hand, almost clawing, from the girl's waist to her breast. And he wanted her to see that the pale skin of the girl's bare arms was striped with purplish bruises, with the fierce pressure of his fingers on her shoulder leaving no doubt how they had been made. Her mouth had a bruised, puffy look, and the upper lip was blotted with a red mark that might have been a bite. Noriko might have wondered that he was not ashamed to let her be seen in public, dressed up and marked like this, if she hadn't been certain the other woman's body was a message to her. He wanted her to imagine herself lying there, she thought, whether or not he

340

knew that was what he meant by it. He was telling her it was not over; she was not safe.

Never, since they had met over Marcus' body that first awful day, had she been in his presence without revulsion. Now it was so strong that she thought she'd be sick if she even touched the food. The room was huge, but it felt stifling, she could hardly breathe. There was a filthy texture to the air, a smell in it like the rusty stink of blood. When Drusus looked at her she wanted to writhe and struggle as if he were actually touching her again.

If there was anything that made it a little easier to endure, it was that he looked almost more worn and ill-at-ease than she felt herself. His lips were tight, the flesh under his eyes was swollen and dark; occasionally a juddering twitch ran through him. He too barely ate. He lay there pouring glass after glass of wine down his throat, without any glimmer of visible pleasure – in that, or in the bruised woman who lay beside him, silently smiling.

After that dinner, there was a partial respite. Drusus was often away: he was talking to scientists at test sites off the coast of Thule; he was addressing the troops before they left for Terranova or Ethiopia. He was hardly off the longvision these days. In his absence the restrictions surrounding Noriko eased slightly; Trunnia grew a little less thorough, left them alone for longer at a time. But the Praetorians were increasingly restless; even those who had always treated them with respect lapsed now into nonchalant rudeness. And some of them roamed around the palace like packs of feral dogs, they banged on the door when the women were locked inside, hooted and catcalled at them down corridors. Noriko kept her letter in her sleeve and waited.

The three of them spent a lot of time in the gardens. Noriko disliked them – she thought the rigid lines were artless and oppressive – but they felt safer there. No one could approach across the plains of grass and gravel without being seen, and there were places like the aviary and the bower at the bottom of the sunken lawn where it was easier to hide without appearing to

341

do so. And the air was warm now, the sky was blue and the grounds were so wide it was almost as if they were free.

On a marble bench beside a fountain, a young woman sat staring at the roses, her hands folded in her lap, doing nothing at all. Her glossy black hair hung in a girlish plait down her back and her fair skin was carefully shaded by a broad straw hat. She looked almost childlike this way, and much less like Tullia. Almost by accident, Noriko met her eyes. The girl's expression had been exactly the same every time Noriko had seen her, and each time it grew more unnerving. It was a look of sweet, serene composure, but with unfocused eyes, a doll-like, meaningless smile. Noriko could see it still in place, even from here.

'Who is that?' she asked.

Trunnia sighed, which was her usual response to anything any of them said. 'Never you mind.'

But Noriko didn't need an answer. Seeing the girl now, without Drusus, and remembering how she'd been dressed the last time she had seen her, it was suddenly clear to her that this was a slave, someone who was kept elsewhere in the palace. Another of Drusus' possessions.

To her relief, Trunnia began to complain of the heat, and as there were a few distant guards in the gardens and no realistic way the three women could climb over the walls, eventually she left them alone.

When she was gone Noriko and her ladies walked another furtive circuit of the walls, just in case there was some weak point they had not noticed before, but they were aware that even if there had been, they would not get far without help. They wandered despondently back along the avenue of umbrella pines and past the fountains. The girl was still there.

This time Noriko led the others over towards her.

It was a pretty scene, like an illustration of a sentimental song – the girl's straw hat, the flowers. But as they came closer they could see that under the shade of her hat there were still those red and purple stains on her skin – more, in fact, than before. Her smile broadened slightly in greeting as she saw them coming,

342

and then retracted to its usual state. Her lovely eyes were vacant, and not for the first time, Noriko wondered if that look of static sweetness was the effect of some drug, or a sign the girl had something wrong with her brain.

She nodded kindly in response and asked, 'What is your name?'

The girl continued to smile, as if she did not know how to do anything else. And yet her eyelids moved in a faintly ironic flicker, and she gave a slight shrug. She said, 'Amaryllis.'

Her voice was pretty, too, but there was a flat, tinny quality to it, like a recorded announcement on a longdictor line. There was something wrong with the answer itself, too, something false or withheld.

Noriko hesitated. 'Is that your real name?'

Amaryllis gave another little shrug. 'It doesn't matter.' She swung her legs slightly and added, 'Isn't it such a nice day?'

Noriko tried to think of some safe way of probing deeper. 'I saw you had bruises,' she ventured. 'I think . . . the Emperor hurt you.'

'Yes,' said Amaryllis, with solemn unconcern. She picked a flower and inspected it absently. 'He has so much on his mind.'

Perhaps she actually loves him, thought Noriko anxiously. Perhaps she'd rather do anything rather than cross him – or maybe she is too used to what he does to her. She glanced at Sakura and Tomoe.

Tomoe gave a subtle shake of the head. They knew from Noriko's agitated accounts of her evenings with Drusus who this was, and Amaryllis was far closer to Drusus than any furtive servant who'd been willing to whisper to them of escape and rebellion. To push this conversation beyond pleasantries was a new level of risk.

Sometimes, nursing her letter and longing for home, Noriko consoled herself by thinking, we can lose nothing by trying. But that was not true: forced marriage or rape was not the worst they had to fear from Drusus. Noriko remembered Una in prison, the trial, the sentence. Even now she only half-believed Una and Sulien were truly alive – perhaps they'd escaped the Colosseum

343

only as symbols, myths, while their bodies were torn to shreds, burned to ash.

'Well, I was sorry to see it,' she said, almost ready to leave it there.

'But glad it wasn't you,' said Amaryllis, her voice as pleasant and impersonal as before, the sharp point inserted and withdrawn almost too fast to be felt.

Noriko flinched, and yet the sting was the first signal of someone awake behind that inert, synthetic sweetness.

'Then I suppose you have heard that he has' – she grimaced – 'done me the honour of choosing me as his intended wife. So I am grateful to know how he behaves when there is . . . so much on his mind.'

'Yes, I know that's what he wants. I wonder if it will happen,' mused Amaryllis. 'I wonder what he will do with me if it does.'

The fixed smile no longer looked like a symptom of mental weakness to Noriko; it looked as if it had been held in place so long the muscles could no longer relax, as if it were nailed on.

'Amaryllis,' she said, aware she was mangling the foreign syllables – the name was almost impossible to pronounce – 'If I could tell you— If I knew you would not tell him about this conversation—'

'He doesn't like me to talk,' said Amaryllis mildly.

Noriko sat down beside her on the bench. 'We cannot bear it here. We are afraid all the time. We must try to leave.'

Amaryllis did not seem surprised, but she examined the three of them and looked dubious. 'All the way to Nionia?'

'Perhaps we would not need to go so far. My brother has forces in northern Africa now.'

'That's still very far,' said Amaryllis, 'and right into the war. You might be killed.'

'We might be killed here,' said Noriko grimly. 'There is someone who might help. I have written a letter to him, but we're never allowed out – and I cannot let anyone know I even have pen and paper. I don't know how to send it.'

Amaryllis shrugged again. 'I go out sometimes. He lets me go

344

shopping, or to the theatre now. He didn't let me before – he didn't like people seeing me because of who I look like. But now he's Emperor he doesn't have to care what anyone thinks. Your letter – you have it with you?' She held out her hand for it.

Noriko was unreasonably shocked. 'But then why do you ever come back? There must be some way you could run. At first we were not even allowed into the garden!' Even as she said it she knew it wasn't fair – she knew it would take more than merely stepping outside the gates. But after so long trapped in the Palace, the idea of being able to come and go seemed almost outrageous to her. For a moment she helplessly resented Amaryllis for failing to make better use of the privilege, for having it at all.

'Oh, someone always comes with me,' said Amaryllis, 'and where could I go? I don't have any money. I can't do anything. And he told me that if I ever tried to run away he'd bring me back and cut up my face. I know he'd do it. Still, I used to think he might set me free one day. Sometimes he liked to say he would.'

Her voice remained bafflingly calm and mild through this. Nonplussed, Noriko asked, 'But – you would like to get away?'

Amaryllis' face underwent a sudden change. Her eyebrows rose, her lips drew apart and stiffened; she became almost ugly with incredulity. 'I wonder what you think I am,' she said, in a thickened, alien voice.

'I am sorry,' said Noriko.

'He knows he had to tell me what he'd do to me to keep me here. Even he thinks better of me than that.'

'I'm sorry,' repeated Noriko, confused, and frightened, too, of how far she might have alienated Amaryllis. Perhaps the offer of help had been withdrawn – perhaps Amaryllis would even tell someone now.

Amaryllis' face rearranged itself gradually, a fleeting, contemptuous look at Noriko escaping through the pieces of calm as they settled back into place. She muttered to herself in an oddly lofty voice, 'What can I expect?'

Noriko hesitated again. She said, timidly, 'If you come with

345

us, perhaps – perhaps you have heard people saying that out there—?'

'Una and Sulien and Varius,' said Amaryllis instantly. 'To go and join them. Yes, that is what I want.' She held out her hand again for the letter.

Sulien was holding a gun; Una was talking to him in a hurried, desperate whisper, begging him to— And then she was lying dead on the sand, her body soaked with blood and scattered with broken glass, though he had somehow missed the moment that it happened. He was only a short distance away, but he couldn't reach her. He too was lying on the ground, and he could hardly move; he barely inched forward when he tried to pull himself close to her. And he could no longer remember why she had told him this must happen, how he could have done what she'd asked of him.

Then the morning bell shrieked and Sulien lurched out of his bunk and began inserting himself into his uniform before he was truly awake, his hands already swift and practised, even though his heart was thudding to various frequencies of shock. The dream still felt solid, bits of it stuck to the sight of this huge stark room full of men, the noise of the bell drilling through them all.

The mornings were the hardest times: when the reality of what he was becoming and where he was going was harshest, and most unfathomable. He was ten days away from passing out – this course of training lasted only a month, half the length it would have been at the start of the war. And he longed for Una and Varius and Lal, and to go back to a home that had not existed for almost a year.

But the desert air was still and cool and quiet, the dawn grew on the horizon, pink and pale gold like a camellia tree. By the time they were pounding through the second mile of the morning run his head had cleared and he began to feel a contentment that was, by now, familiar. He was in the centre of the column and even though the pressure of the summer heat was building in the air and sweat was pooling in the small of his back, he felt almost weightless, held up by the closeness of the men around him.

He knew the rest of the day would be gruelling. He would be still for barely a minute unless standing at attention, and there would be arbitrary outbursts of cruelty from the officers, because conscripts who'd had to be physically forced into the army were the lowest of all. But it would be simple. He didn't mind the heat or the physical hardship or the tight framework of the rules. He felt relieved of identity. He found that though the centurions shouted at them about focus and concentration, it wasn't true; he didn't have to concentrate, not really. The effort that was constantly demanded didn't come from the core of him, he could spare it easily, ungrudgingly. He could rest even while he struggled over obstacle courses, or lay propped on his elbows at the rifle range, anonymous amongst the other men. He had been glad when they stripped off his hair and made him look just like the rest of them.

He felt strangely guilty sometimes when he thought of Una and Varius, because he was sure that they would never understand this. They would have hated every minute of this life so much that they must be imagining him suffering far more than he was.

He didn't expect friendship; he made no effort to learn names. He watched the other recruits with strong but utterly impersonal sympathy. He hoped, if he maintained this and if he stayed quiet, that he would be able to remain anonymous and overlooked himself. He tried not to talk unless he had to, even when they were left alone in the barracks. But of course, against his intentions, the men came into gradual, separate focus. There was Pas, who slept in the bunk above him and who was especially hard to ignore as he gravitated towards Sulien whenever possible. He'd lurk nervously around him, perhaps simply in the hope of hiding behind him. There was Dorion from Terenouthis, who whispered filthy jokes when they were both on guard duty in the middle of the night. There were some who were widely disliked, like Mysthes, who seemed almost wilfully incompetent, and had attracted a number of group punishments, and Sentheus, who was loud and violent, in too-obvious imitation of the centurion in charge of them. But Sulien felt the same sad, detached compassion for these too.

Una and the others might have left Alexandria by now, but he thought they would be back sometimes to meet with the recruits they'd left behind; there was a chance they would be able to collect letters. So, like everyone else, Sulien wrote. He was vaguely amazed this was even allowed, and sorry that his words seemed so unsatisfactory – he wrote to all of them that he missed them and loved them and that the training was not too bad, and it was all true; he just couldn't find the right way of saying it. The aliases he had to use for all of them made it harder – Archias to his dear Aethra, to Berenice . . . it was as if he was writing fiction.

'Who's Berenice?' demanded Dorion, leaning against the bunk. Berenice was Lal; Sulien shook his head, saying nothing. Dorion was not deterred. 'Is she fit? What are her tits like? Reckon she'd get them out for us if she was here?'

Sulien went on writing his flat little sentences in silence, though his lips twitched towards a smile despite himself. For some time, Dorion continued noisily speculating, with increasing inventiveness, about Berenice's preferences, and openness to experimentation. But at last he gave up on her and asked, 'So you've got family back in Alex?'

'My sister,' said Sulien. He saw no reason to lie, not about this – that was part of the strange relief he felt in being here. There was little need to explain himself; the worst and hardest things could be simply omitted. All their pasts had been shrunk down to the size of playing cards or stamps or coins, things that could be casually displayed or hidden.

'You've only got a sister?'

Sulien nodded, not paying attention, but Dorion quietened and looked distressed. He lowered his eyes, and then murmured, 'Was it an air raid, or—?'

Sulien was taken aback. The information had seemed so neutral to him. He felt as if he'd tricked Dorion out of unneeded sympathy, so rather than nodding and letting the subject drop, he found himself explaining, 'No, no, my father died ages ago; I can hardly remember him.' For a moment he found himself tempted to explain that he had not even known that the old man who owned their mother was his father until after his death, but he did hold himself back from that. 'And we— Well, we didn't really grow up with my mother. We haven't seen her in a long time. But yeah, she's alive.' Without knowing he was going to, and almost under his breath, he added, 'We could even have half-brothers or sisters, I suppose.'

Dorion still looked confused and sorry. 'But back home . . . it's just you and your sister?'

'No,' said Sulien, going back to his letter, 'it's not just us.'

He did not elaborate and after a moment Dorion shrugged and grinned. 'So. Is your sister fit?'

'Shut up,' said Sulien mildly, throwing a towel at him.

'You've got a lot of scars,' said Pas one day when they were washing off the coating of dust and sweat from the assault course. Pas was also from Alexandria. He was small, dark, a year or two younger than Sulien, and almost a foot shorter; he would have looked a child except for the permanent worry lines scratched into his forehead.

Sulien glanced down at himself. He felt a small twitch of trepidation and yet here, where his body was just one of many interchangeable bodies, part of a mass of raw material, the marks on it seemed inconsequential. He said, 'Car crash.'

Pas' eyes narrowed uncertainly. He looked away and asked, 'Is that what you have those dreams about?'

Sulien's heart skipped, his pleasant sense of near-invisibility suddenly punctured. Every night he thought he was far too exhausted to dream, and he was almost always wrong. So he clenched his teeth hard when he lay down, and tried to will them to stay closed, clamped shut, even if he couldn't keep the same pressure on the images that sprouted in his mind. Until now, no one had said anything. He knew his nightly attempts to control his body had some effect – he'd learned to sleep lying rigidly on his back, as if standing at attention – so he'd hoped it was working.

Did he talk when he was dreaming? He avoided Pas' eyes, afraid to ask. 'Sorry if I wake you up or anything,' he said, as casually as he could. 'It just' – he searched for some suitably offhand explanation but couldn't find one – 'happens,' he finished lamely.

Pas shrugged. 'It's no worse than Ennius snoring,' he said. He glanced again at the patterns of blotches and claw marks on Sulien's skin. He said, 'Must have been bad.'

Sulien reached to turn off the water. He said, 'Could have been worse.'

They all had bruises from hurling themselves down onto earth or concrete or at each other; from rifle butts; from the centurions' fists. Sulien ached constantly, and lines of fire burned along his limbs, forging new muscle. He had never been able to run like this, or lift his own weight so easily, so many times. He was a better shot than he had expected to be, too – not exceptional, but good enough that he was left alone.

But Pas struggled. His small body contained a certain wiry stamina; his attention, unlike Sulien's, never wandered, and he never forgot anything he was told, but he had to work so much harder than the rest of them to keep up. His face grew more and more pinched as the end of their training approached, as their exercises came to resemble actual fighting. They charged down trenches, driving their bayonets into slumped manikins in enemy uniform; they spent a day flinging grenades from behind barricades and Pas threw as straight as anyone else, but flinched helplessly at every blast.

'I think we're all going to get killed,' he muttered to Sulien, a week short of the end, after a day of fieldcraft training; Sulien was double-checking the guy-ropes of the tent they'd just pitched on the sand.

'Oh fucking shut up,' said Dorion brightly.

'It's a statistical likelihood,' said Pas. He had a tight, defiant little grin on his face, but his hands were shaking. None of them had any doubt where they were heading: south, into Nubia, to the Alodian front.

'It is not,' said Dorion. 'You'll get something blown off on the first day and get shipped home, don't you worry. You've got all sorts of parts you can easily spare.'

As always, Dorion's voice carried; Sentheus came swaggering across from his tent. 'Is he bitching again?' he asked, prodding at Pas. 'Have we really not knocked that out of him yet?'

Dorion grimaced. 'He's bitching at us, not you, and we can handle it. Piss off, Sentheus.'

Sentheus gave a loud, flat laugh of affected incredulity. 'What?' he said. 'Are you trying to impress your little girlfriend there, Dorion? You think you can talk to me like that? You haven't been paying attention if you think you can talk to me like that.'

'You're not a fucking centurion yet,' said Dorion. 'You're still low enough to be told to piss off; now piss off.'

Sentheus pushed him hard, grabbed his arms and doubled him over, trying to force him to the ground, to drive a knee into his stomach. Dorion managed to wrench an arm free and punch at Sentheus' chest. They lurched and staggered back and forth, and Sulien could see they would knock out one of the tent-pegs or worse in a moment.

'Oh leave it,' said Justus, by the next tent. 'Save it for the Nionians.'

Without any feeling other than mild annoyance, Sulien stood up and levered the two of them apart. He shoved Sentheus to one side and more or less lifted Dorion off the ground and deposited him a few paces away. For a moment both Dorion and Sentheus dithered, panting and glowering at each other across Sulien, considering whether or not to rush at each other again. Then Sentheus slunk back – but there was Pas, who'd receded quietly to the other side of the tent. Sentheus gave him an impulsive shove that sent him tripping over the guy-ropes, then kicked at his side when he was sprawled on the sand.

Sulien crossed over to Sentheus and quickly, simply, felled him to the ground. He knew what he wanted – Sentheus to be down and to know he was beaten – and he moved with complete confidence in his ability to do it. It was almost as easy as pushing buttons on a keypad.

He hoisted Pas up, waited until Sentheus had retreated with a muttered, 'Fuck you, Archias,' and went back to setting out his kit inside the tent. But something nagged him for hours afterwards. He tried to shake it off, rather than examine it, but later, when he was crouched in a hollow in the dunes in the darkness during a simulated night raid, it occurred to him that it wasn't a feeling, it was a lack of feeling. It was the realisation that the training had worked. He feared for Pas, whose eyes were already haunted after only stabbing sandbags and throwing grenades at sand, who was not, nor ever would, be ready in the same way. And yet he envied him a little too, for not compromising, for not allowing himself to be changed. Still, it was Pas who made him realise, on the day that it was done and they were soldiers in scarlet dress uniforms waiting to parade out, that his old self wasn't lost completely.

'This is it, Shouter,' Pas said.

'What?' Sulien was baffled for a moment, then, as he realised it was some kind of nickname, he feared it was to do with his nightmares – he'd been louder than he thought.

'Dorion's been calling you that. Because you don't talk,' said Pas patiently.

Sulien was disproportionately shocked. He had wanted to make no impression, not to be noticed at all, and he'd chosen quietness as a deliberate strategy. To be noticed for being quiet hadn't occurred to him as a possibility. And as he'd felt ashamed of extracting sympathy from Dorion under what had felt like false pretences, now he felt embarrassed at having misrepresented himself to Pas – even though he knew it was ridiculous, considering his false name and history and the continuing danger of discovery. And suddenly the life that had seemed cut down and diminished ever since the Colosseum rose within this new, hardened body: he was Sulien, not Archias, nor any of these other names he'd dragged around since Marcus' death. And he looked at the man Pas had seen and thought, No, that's not what I'm like at all.

'I do talk,' he said, and after that it became true.

'Surprise coming up for you boys,' said a centurion, strolling into the barracks as they finished straightening the white sashes across their chests. Pas groaned in near-silence, imagining some last impromptu ordeal. But Sulien knew that couldn't be right, they wouldn't be spoiling these uniforms – which they would not be keeping either; the army was consuming too many men these days to keep the old rituals intact.

Dorion was already pulling at his collar. 'It's so fucking hot,' he complained, 'who's even going to see us like this?'

'Some general with nothing to do,' said Sulien.

Their shields, which they would keep, were ranked against the back wall of the barracks; pillars of transparent bulletproof ceramic, the Imperial Eagle spreading black wings across the centre of each. They were already warm from the desert heat, and they blazed glassily as the soldiers marched with them out into the sun. At the head of the phalanx, the signifer held up the standard, a silver hand in a circle of laurel, and behind him, a drummer began to play. At the centurion's signal they began to beat their rifles upright against the shields until the rhythm throbbed through the air and through their bones. They processed out – six new centuria – towards the parade ground.

Effortlessly, Sulien marched and turned, raised and lowered his shield and gun to the centurion's shouted commands. It was so automatic that his mind was free to wonder that this was really happening. He thought of Una and the others, and with every cadenced step forward it was harder to believe he would ever be able to find his way back to them. He wondered if anyone really would send word back to Alexandria if he was killed. Sometimes

353

he imagined Una still searching or waiting, years after the war was over, and the only thing that was worse was to think that no one would send him such a letter if anything happened to her. It would not even be on the news – if they found her, the vigiles would have to kill her in secret. It could have happened already.

But through even these thoughts the beat of the drum kept him steady.

They marched into three long rows and stood waiting for inspection, and Sulien noticed that a number of vehicles in Praetorian livery were standing on the concrete near the end of the column – and then he saw that Praetorian soldiers were everywhere, spread finely but at regular intervals across the perimeter of the parade ground, around the small speaker's platform, a cluster of them beside a small open car with the Eagle emblazoned on its black flanks. There were a few civilians with longvision cameras at the base of the platform, too.

Sulien thought, it can't be.

But the car began to move slowly down the line of soldiers, and Drusus was standing upright in the back, in his black uniform, his arm raised.

'Hail Caesar!' shouted the signifier, lifting the standard.

'HAIL CAESAR!' the soldiers roared in response. Sulien opened his mouth and made the shape of the words, but couldn't have given them any sound if he'd wanted to.

The car approached, and he was startled at how instinctively his hand flexed on his rifle – but of course it was unloaded, precisely as a safeguard against such impulses. They would not let the Emperor out in front of a pack of armed boys, many of them conscripts, with only a month's training behind them. There was nothing he could do. He extended his right arm in a salute with terrible amusement and anger.

Drusus drove past, and looked right at him.

Drusus felt the usual reliable pleasure as the soldiers shouted and saluted him. It should have been stronger today, when for the first time in months he'd had good news. So, although he was still suffering from lack of sleep, and a constant slight nausea his doctors couldn't seem to do anything about, he persuaded himself that it *was* better; that he could feel the swerve of history turning back the right way, and these young recruits the first witnesses of it. As always, he was glad of his uniform: it made him feel as if he were one of them – or rather, as if they were part of him, as if he contained and magnified them. But as the car carried him past the row of stiffly raised arms and impassive faces, he felt an unaccountable jolt, as if the car had passed over a split in the asphalt, and a chill within him. His skin itched – the desert flies had bitten him here and there and he had to stifle the instinct to scratch at his face. That would not have looked right.

He ascended the small stage and as he looked down the soldiers saluted again. But now he felt their cold, fixed stare as somehow accusing. It was as if their raised arms were pointing at him.

He stuttered a little as he began to speak. 'I am proud to be here with you as you enter into this most honoured brotherhood of any Empire,' he said. 'And on this day it is a special privilege to be able to tell you that thanks to the courage of your comrades in Alodia, the assault on Meroë has been repelled and the enemy is in retreat. We maintain control of the Nile; we are regaining control of the sea. The Nionian way of lawlessness and treachery cannot stand; we will extend the mantle of Roman peace across the world; we will prevail. Today, as Roman soldiers, you continue this great struggle against evil. Rome thanks you for your courage and your sacrifice.'

He squinted; the camera lenses shone in the light like the soldiers' shields.

'You all right?' muttered Pas to Sulien later, when the centuria had returned to the barracks. His eyes were at once innocently wide and searching. Sulien made a renewed effort to look normal, though he was still shaken – but at the same time he still felt this flat, disgusted amusement, and it cost a real effort not to tell Pas exactly why. He wondered if Drusus was still at the camp, and smiled sourly as he replaced his rifle in the rack. He let his fingers trail over it. There would be no forgetting who was sending him to fight. It was some relief to change out of the oppressive dress uniform, a little like cleansing himself of Drusus' nearness.

'Yeah,' he said, 'it's just . . . like you said, this is it.'

'Wasn't he *nice*?' said Dorion bitterly. 'Won't it be such an amazing fucking honour to go and *sacrifice* ourselves for him? I heard he's not even supposed to be Emperor.'

'Fuck's sake, Dorion, shut up,' hissed Sulien, looking around in alarm.

'You're the Emperor's loyal servant, are you, Shouter?' asked Dorion rather sadly.

'Will you keep your voice down? Just— Just wait till we get to Alodia before you get yourself shot, all right?' said Sulien. But he grinned a little, and after another nervous glance around the other soldiers he asked in a low voice, 'How long do you reckon he'd last if Rutilianus had him out on the assault course?'

The centurion began calling out names, dividing them into groups of twenty. 'Archias' was one of the first, and Sulien tried to will Pas and Dorion's names to be called after his. To his relief, they were.

'Infantry, ninth cohort, thirty-third Anasasian Legion,' the centurion announced when he came to their group.

There was a staggered silence, then Dorion asked, 'What, Terranova, sir?'

The others tensed: on a bad day any questioning of orders could have been disastrous, for Dorion at least. But the centurion only answered, 'Good at geography, are you, Private Dorion?'

Sulien supposed it really made no difference where they were sent, though like the rest of them, he was vaguely indignant that the future they had expected could be so suddenly exchanged for something else. And when he thought how he was being pulled even further than he'd ever expected from everyone he loved, he felt another drag of homesickness.

'The Great Ravine's in Anasasia!' said Dorion eagerly, when the centurion had gone.

'We're not going *there*,' said Pas.

'Don't be a killjoy, Pas, or we'll leave you behind,' said Sulien. And though the sadness and fear was still there, he realised to his surprise that he was also a little excited.

Drusus sat opposite General Turnus inside the car, scratching freely at the bites on his face. The cooled air was a relief on his flushed skin, and yet there was still that chill within him, a strange self-consciousness, almost as if someone on the edge of his vision were staring at him. The feeling grew stronger as they drove, until, to quell the faint panic brewing in his gut, he said cheerfully, 'They looked good – they looked ready, didn't they, Turnus? The thing is: even without the full length of training, they're all products of Roman tradition. That counts for a lot.'

General Turnus pursed his lips. 'I'm sure they will do their duty, your Majesty.'

'Really, Africa is a distraction. That's the purpose of the attacks, of course, to weaken our will. We should resist it; we should be *bold*. We should attack Nionia directly, and if it means going through Sina, then so be it.'

'Sir—! Meroë is an important victory, of course, but we remain stretched. To open yet another front; to wage war against two enemies at once—'

'We are already at war with Sina, General. They have intervened against us, in the Promethean – didn't you hear about those Nionian sailors they picked up off the wreck of the *Isonade*?'

Turnus took a careful breath. 'Sir, it was a commercial vessel, and the crew appear to have been acting on their own and for compassionate reasons; I think that to consider it an act of war—'

'Why should we not? Do you know what Junosena told me once? She said nothing happened in Sina that she didn't know about. Not that I believe her, of course, but ultimately she is responsible. Anyway, the whole Sinoan system is dried out, it's

357

ossified; you've told me this yourself. We shouldn't be frightened of it just on the grounds of size. Sina— It's run by a senile old woman.' He laughed. 'It *is* a senile old woman. They have nothing like the Onager—'

'But your Majesty, Nionia *does*. And they may be ready to use it before we are,' said Turnus. 'If we push two Empires into an alliance against us—'

'All the more reason to make a final push and finish Nionia quickly, before it reaches that point – we will take revenge for everything Mariaba and Alexandria and Aila have suffered, and what use will an alliance be to Sina then? And then we will expand to the east. It's what I said to those recruits, about the Roman peace: if we can't extend it further, then this war really will have been a failure.'

Turnus pressed his lips closed again and stared at the floor, his shoulders tense. Then he swallowed and raised his eyes to Drusus' face. 'Sir, I must advise very strongly against this course.'

Drusus stared at the general's face. Turnus' eyes were grey-green, and slightly protrusive, the skin above was pale and rucked in taut ridges. It struck Drusus that a face was just an object, no different from any other collection of angles and planes. At last he said, 'Who asked for your advice?'

Amaryllis had told them she could arrange for Cleomenes to send any reply to a woman she trusted in the Palace laundry. But two weeks had passed and though Noriko and the other women continued to linger in the garden, they had not seen Amaryllis again. Noriko had, naturally, been afraid of failure from the first – Cleomenes was bound to be reluctant to entangle himself in their trouble, even assuming he was able to help. And perhaps he would never even know his help had been sought; though Amaryllis had been confident of finding his address, and an opportunity to post the letter, she might have been wrong. And as the days passed with no sign of her, Noriko began to fear that trusting her had been a mistake. She did not think Amaryllis would actually betray her to Drusus – but she had handed over the bracelet, as well as the letter, and Amaryllis had complained of having no money with which to make an escape.

One day, when rain and thunder kept them inside, the lights went out. Noriko gave up her listless attention to her book, and Trunnia, who had been sewing, sighed and walked out of the room.

She had been gone barely a moment when someone knocked at the door. Noriko tensed, even though it was too quiet a tap to be a bored Praetorian, until a low voice outside said, 'Let me in – it's Amaryllis.'

Amaryllis fled inside. 'Ugh,' she said, 'I thought she'd never leave you alone. And the Praetorians are getting worse than ever.' She had a folded sheet of paper in her hand, already opened.

Noriko hurried with it to the window, tilting it towards what little light there was. It was not a letter, but a tourist map of the centre of Rome. An X was marked on a certain street on the far side of the Esquiline Hill. The address meant little to Noriko – it had been almost a year since she had been able to leave the palace. At the edge of the map there was a list of dates and times. Nothing else.

'He would meet us there?' whispered Tomoe.

'Only at these times.'

Cleomenes was giving them an hour, every evening for a week. Amaryllis pointed to one of the dates, only three days away. 'The Emperor will be back that night – we should be gone before then.'

Noriko and her ladies looked at each other. The idea of being gone without ever having to see Drusus again made Noriko almost dizzy.

'We have not enough time,' said Sakura faintly.

Noriko remembered plunging out of a car into the street in Tusculum, how overwhelmed and lightheaded she had felt, just to be outside the usual barriers that had always stood between her and the world. None of them really knew how to live out there. She had never even been into a shop or a market to buy food.

'No,' she said to Amaryllis, 'I think the night he returns is when we should do it.'

The first step was to evade Trunnia. Noriko rarely drank alcohol, but that evening she asked for wine as soon as she decently could, and they all sat sipping it in silence, trying not to glance at one another. Then Noriko rose casually, still carrying her glass, and as she wandered past Trunnia – as if to pick up a book on the table – she fumbled her grip on the glass and emptied it down Trunnia's front.

Trunnia sprang up, dripping and outraged, and looked down at the large red splash on her dress.

'Oh, no,' said Noriko.

'You did that on purpose!' said Trunnia.

Noriko shook her head, wide-eyed, as Tomoe tried to wipe at Trunnia with a handkerchief.

'Get off me!' Trunnia growled, jerking away from her. She stared at Noriko, her face rigid with indignation and suspicion, and Noriko gazed humbly back, wondering if Trunnia was actually going to hit her.

Trunnia finally looked away and grabbed the handkerchief from Tomoe. She swept out, irritably dabbing at herself.

Tomoe sighed with the temporary release of tension, and the three women all clasped hands for a moment. Noriko looked at herself in the mirror before hurrying out of the room. She no longer neglected her appearance, and she was dressed carefully, in sombre Roman clothes – it was a way to keep as much of her jewellery on her as was discreetly possible. Sakura and Tomoe were wearing much of the rest. She was prepared.

Now she needed either of the guards who had attacked Sakura, for preference the one who had escorted her to Drusus' table a few weeks before. She found him with three others in an ante-room on the first floor, between the private and administrative quarters of the palace.

Noriko cleared her throat. Even before she spoke, a look – sharp and greedy, and entertained – flashed between the men as if there was something at once intrinsically ridiculous and titillating about her. Though she had expected it, she flushed and tensed, and the man she was looking for grinned at his colleague. He was young, round-headed, with a rather childlike, fleshy face and stubby features.

'Can you tell me if it is true the Emperor is coming back tonight?' she asked.

One of them, a little older than the others, shrugged. 'Sorry, darling.'

'But if he is, will he want me to dine with him? I prefer to have some warning so I can prepare . . .'

'Wait and see. Patience is character-building,' said the same guard.

Noriko walked over to the Praetorian she recognised. 'I want you to come with me to look at something,' she said.

There was a pause, and a laughing catcall from one of them.

'Just for a minute,' Noriko said patiently. 'I can see something strange from a window upstairs.'

'You'd better go,' said the other guard, 'there's something *strange* out there!'

'She might get lost on her own,' said another.

The round-faced Praetorian smirked. 'As a special favour,' he said, and went with her.

Noriko led him up towards her rooms but turned away before she reached them, into a quiet gallery. She had hoped, when it came to it, she would be able to think of something natural to say, but she was speechless with embarrassment and nervousness.

'So,' he said, at last, 'what did you want to show me?'

'Really, there is nothing,' said Noriko. 'It was . . . It was a joke.'

'A joke?'

'Yes. I get so bored.' She cleared her throat again. 'And lonely,' she added. She took a breath and, rather feebly, lifted her hand to his face and let it trail down to his chest.

The gesture – the entire stratagem – seemed immensely stilted and unconvincing to her now; she had barely even managed to smile. She was trying to work herself up to something more plausible, but there was no need, for the man chuckled a little and muttered, 'I bet you do,' and pulled her against him, pressed his mouth squashily against hers.

Noriko managed to stroke his hair, but the hot, amused gasp he gave into her mouth, and his hands, immediately dragging at her clothes for any opening, made her think of the sounds he'd made as he and the other man had pulled up Sakura's skirts; she remembered Drusus' weight on her. She clenched her teeth shut against his large intruding tongue and writhed, but he either did not notice or took it for excitement, and swung her round to push her up against the wall. Noriko managed to pull her mouth free, and tried to keep it clear of his lips by pressing wincing kisses along his jaw.

She had not expected it would be quite so easy, nor that it would go so swiftly beyond her control. His hand had worked its way inside her tunic, felt for and squeezed hard on her breast—

Sakura stepped around the corner and took a picture with the camera Amaryllis had bought in Rome.

Noriko broke free. 'Now you are going to help us,' she said.

The Praetorian staggered a little and gaped at them. He grinned uncertainly.

'The Emperor will come home this evening. We would like to go down to the Praetorian garage now and have you to drive us out of the Palace,' continued Noriko, 'otherwise we will tell him what you have done and show him this.'

Amaryllis and Tomoe emerged from the landing into the gallery.

'You *bitches*,' the Praetorian said hoarsely. He hesitated for another moment, still a little dazed, then he made a lunge towards Sakura, who backed quickly away as Noriko and Tomoe closed in front of him.

'That will make things even worse for you,' said Sakura shrilly, from behind them.

'She's right,' said Noriko, 'surely we are not the only ones who know what you did to her. You thought no one would care – but *I* do. And what will people think if I begin screaming now and they find you fighting with us? Why should anyone disbelieve anything of you?'

'You must know the Emperor wants her, don't you?' said Amaryllis idly. 'He doesn't like to share with other men.'

The Praetorian panted, his face seemed swollen and red. 'You're never going to do it, you stupid bitches – you think anyone's going to believe you weren't leading me on? What's he going to do to you if he sees that picture?'

'I don't know,' said Noriko. 'Perhaps terrible things – perhaps nothing. But whatever happens to me, it will not help you. You will be dead.'

Amaryllis was leaning against a wall, her face as unfocused and serene as if in a gentle daydream. 'Before my master was Emperor, one of his guards had me once. He wouldn't listen to me,' she said pleasantly, as if talking of something as unremarkable as what she'd had for lunch. 'We were in Byzantium. My master had the others take him out into the street and shoot him.'

The Praetorian's mouth caught in an uneven snarl, his throat closing as he tried to say something.

'Of course,' said Amaryllis, 'you will never be able to come back. You've ruined your life here.'

Noriko pulled a comb from her hair. Kaneharu had given it to her before her wedding: two silver prongs supported a cluster of gold peonies with small rubies at their centres, from which tiny golden bells and pearls hung in looped chains. 'We only need you to take us a very short distance, and then I will give you this.'

'Don't give him anything,' said Amaryllis, disgusted.

'I will give you this,' repeated Noriko. It would hurt, to give away something so beautiful to such a man, but soon she would not need the comb to remind her of Kaneharu. 'So you have a chance to get away and live. But stay here and try and fight us and you will have no hope at all.'

The bright red had drained from the Praetorian's face, leaving it almost grey. He sagged. His eyes turned blankly to the floor.

'We are not waiting for you to think about it. We would like to leave now,' said Noriko firmly.

Noriko knew the Palace well; she and Amaryllis led the Praetorian through the quieter halls and stairways. There was a temptation to duck onto the servants' stairs, but there could be no possible good reason for their being there. Tomoe and Sakura navigated a different course through the Palace, to keep the camera safely away from the Praetorian, and to avoid them all being caught in a single inexplicable group. Occasionally they passed bands of guards standing sentry outside some late meeting, or singing and laughing raucously at the end of a passage, and the Praetorian would stare desperately at them, as if pleading silently for help.

'If we don't meet the others,' murmured Amaryllis to him, 'you know what will happen.'

The Praetorian kept up a chant of obscenities under his breath as they walked – 'evil bitches, pack of vicious sluts, slitty-eyed whores' – which Noriko patiently ignored, but as they stepped out into a courtyard, Amaryllis snapped suddenly, 'I don't like that,' and he fell silent.

The Praetorian garage was beneath the courtyard, and Noriko tensed as they approached the entrance, but though there were security cameras mounted on pillars around it, there were no guards here outside the Palace but within the heavily protected perimeter of the grounds.

'But there could be someone down there, so you wait here,' said Amaryllis to Noriko. She looped an arm proprietarily through the Praetorian's and marched him off while Noriko lurked in the shadows of a cedar tree beside the driveway, twisting her hands, her teeth clenched tight with anxiety.

The car emerged with Amaryllis inside it just as Sakura and Tomoe came running across the courtyard from the gardens.

'We would like to go here, please,' said Noriko, politely, as if to a chauffeur, ducking inside the car and pointing to the place on the map. The Praetorian uttered a wordless growl and jerked the car forward so suddenly the women were jolted back against the seats. They crouched low; in the back Sakura and Tomoe clung to each other.

The car swerved: he was going too fast.

'Careful, please,' breathed Noriko from the floor beside him. 'Remember your own life is in your hands.'

Lights flooded the car as they approached the Septizonium. Noriko sank lower still as the car stopped; she could not see the guards on the gate, but the lights terrified her. We will never have another chance, she thought; Drusus will say we are traitors and put us in the arena like Una and Sulien. She watched the Praetorian hold his pass to the window, and saw his face was still puffy with fury.

'Maa nante koto nanda,' moaned Sakura in the back as they rolled through the gates and down into the city.

Noriko trembled; her head pounded. She had to struggle to control her breath. For the first minute or two she was almost incapable of moving from her place on the floor, but as she felt the car turn and heard the hum of traffic around it she whispered, 'Where are we?' and cautiously lifted her head. She lifted the map and tried to study it by the cold blue glow of the streetlights. She recognised the Sacred Way, the entrance to the Via Labicana, but after that—? What if he meant to spite them by placing them on the wrong side of the city – and how would she even know the right place if he brought them there?

He turned left where she thought he should have turned right and she said, 'You are going the wrong way.'

'It's a fucking one-way system,' said the Praetorian in disbelief.

Noriko didn't know whether to believe him, and now they were off the course she had expected, she could make no more sense of the map. She glanced anxiously into the back and saw her own expression mirrored on Tomoe and Sakura's pale faces.

But Amaryllis was sitting composedly between the seats, and

that complacent smile was on her face again, as if this ride were nothing unusual.

'Go faster,' said Noriko. 'You can, surely, in a Praetorian car.'

Obediently the Praetorian began to carve through the traffic.

Noriko steadied herself against the dashboard and shut her eyes.

It took twenty minutes to get into the suburbs, and Noriko at last began to see correspondences between the streets outside and the map again: they were skirting a strip of rough parkland along a branch of the Tiber, and that looked right.

Then the Praetorian turned onto a short, pot-holed road lined with bins, between jumbled tower blocks. 'Here,' he said sullenly, slamming on the brakes and stopping the car, 'now get the fuck out and get the fuck away from me.'

Nervously, Noriko surveyed the street. It was lined with bins and parked cars. There was no one about – no sign of Cleomenes. She had almost forgotten to worry whether he would be there to meet them.

One of the cars had a door open. All its lights were off. Noriko waited, watching it, and no one stepped out. It was the only thing on the street that was even slightly out of place.

The street itself – alien territory – frightened her almost as much as the possibility Cleomenes would not be in it. Noriko was shaking again, and her fingers were numb as she felt for the door handle.

'Give me the thing,' demanded the Praetorian.

'When I have checked,' said Noriko.

'Bitch,' replied the Praetorian, without expression.

She pushed the door open and forced herself out. The dark air was surprisingly fresh, and scented – she could smell the green leaves by the riverside. A little unsteadily she hurried towards the car, and there was someone inside it after all. His hair was colourless in the dull blue light, but she could see the brightness of it. He turned.

Noriko gasped, and beckoned towards the others – a vast, wild,

366

sweeping movement. Sakura and Tomoe burst out of the car, with Amaryllis trailing more sedately behind.

Noriko held up the comb and threw it back along the street, saw it gleam and bounce in the gutter. She saw the man scramble out of the car and drop to his knees, searching for it, and then she turned away and didn't look back.

Cleomenes looked at them as they packed into the seats, startled. 'That was a Praetorian car—'

'He won't be telling anyone about this,' said Noriko. 'Thank you very much for helping us.'

'It's my job,' he said heavily. 'Or it was supposed to be.'

Noriko sagged back in the seat, almost enjoying the remaining shudders of tension as they flowed out of her. She began, stammering a little, 'Please, is it true—? Lady Noviana—?'

'Una and Sulien? Yes, they're alive,' said Cleomenes, 'and last I knew they were in Egypt with Varius and the rest. And I'm sending you to them. They might have some idea what to do with you – I know I haven't. Unless you've got something better in mind?'

'No,' said Noriko. The smile felt strange as it spread across her face; it had been so long. 'Nothing better.' And she looked at Sakura and Tomoe and as Cleomenes began to drive they flung their arms around each other and burst into stifled screams of delight and triumph.

Amaryllis alone remained silent.

'I knew he was up to something,' said Cleomenes' wife. 'Either he was mixed up in something political or it had to be an affair.' Cominia was short and plump, with soft, brown hair, large hazel eyes, a little snub nose. She laughed. 'And here he is with four girls in a den of vice. Not many wives would be so understanding.'

They were in an inn outside Centumcellae. No one had been around to see them as Cleomenes hurried them inside. 'It's got a certain reputation for privacy,' he had said grimly. Noriko understood what he meant by 'reputation' when they reached the dark, tilt-floored, stale-smelling room with the browning roses on the thin walls. Sounds of exertion carried through from the room next door.

'I shouldn't have let you get involved,' said Cleomenes. He glowered unhappily at a pornographic print on the wall. Noriko wondered if she would look excessively prudish if she took it down – everyone seemed to have been at least mildly scandalised by it, except for Amaryllis – and Alexander, Cleomenes' solemn, red-headed two-year-old who was at present trying to excavate a hole he had found in the dirty carpet. Cleomenes scooped up his son and sat down dolefully on one of the beds with the boy on his knee. 'I don't like him being in a place like this.'

'I think he's too young to get any funny ideas,' said Cominia, unrolling a pack of combs and scissors on the dusty dressing table. 'Anyway, you couldn't do this without some help.' She surveyed Noriko and made a sympathetic hissing sound through her teeth. 'I'm sorry, love – your Highness, it's gorgeous hair, but it's got to come off.'

Noriko sighed, but she'd known it was inevitable. 'We will start a new fashion when we go back home,' she said as bravely as she could, trying hard not to contemplate how common everyone at court would think they looked.

'We don't have to cut it *short*,' reasoned Tomoe, 'only to here . . . or perhaps here—?'

Cominia smiled and gave Noriko's arm an encouraging little shake. 'It's all right! I'm a professional. You're going to look lovely!'

Noriko was trying to nerve herself to go first when Amaryllis broke in, 'Do mine.'

'Well, you don't need anything quite so drastic, dear,' said Cominia.

Amaryllis' expression remained bland, but she coiled all her hair around her fist and drew it tight, as if threatening to pull it out at the roots. '*He* wanted it like this. He made me wear it like *her*. He used to— He— I want it off me.'

Cominia sat Amaryllis down in front of the dusty mirror and made a first, exploratory stroke with the scissors.

'More than that!' cried Amaryllis.

At her own insistence, and to the quiet horror of the three Nionian women, Amaryllis ended up virtually bald.

Noriko took her place in front of the mirror. She couldn't help tears coming into her eyes when Cominia gathered her hair just below her shoulder blades and cut off more than four feet. And yet, although of course she knew that so much hair was heavy, still she was amazed by the lightness when she lifted her head: she felt as if she might rise through the stained ceiling and into the night air like a balloon, and float away south over the sea.

Cominia set to work shaping and tidying what was left.

Later, they examined the jewellery. 'Some of it you might be better off hanging onto, just in case,' said Cleomenes. 'More portable than blocks of cash. But obviously you need money, and you can't go around flashing this stuff everywhere. I know a fence back in Rome – that's where I took the bracelet. Though you're never going to get what they're really worth.'

'We are very grateful to you – whatever you think is right,' said Noriko. And she laid aside an aster pendant made with sapphires, and another jewelled comb. In a lower voice she murmured to him, 'Whatever you can get for these, please keep it.'

Cleomenes let out a small, embarrassed sigh. 'I don't want you to do that. I'm Roman, and Rome should've— should've done right by you girls and it hasn't, so—'

'Please – for the risks you have taken. For your son.'

Cleomenes' pink face clashed even more extravagantly than usual with his hair. He couldn't meet her eyes, but now he nodded.

'I've got some clothes for you,' said Cominia. 'They're not very *nice* clothes, I'm afraid, and . . .' She paused, then went on, 'I'm sorry to have to say this, but it's going to be a while before you'll be able to get decent papers – if you can at all – and you're going to have to explain being Nionian somehow. I'm really sorry, but

369

it's the only way. You're going to have to pass as slaves – there are Nionian girls from out west on the market now . . .'

It was hardly worse than their long imprisonment, or the loss of their hair, but the clothes were embarrassingly skimpy and lurid, and Noriko grimaced while Amaryllis, running a hand over her stubbly head, stared at them stony-faced.

'I am sorry about this,' said Cominia again.

'No, no,' Noriko said politely, trying to mean it, 'thank you.'

They stuffed the enormous lengths of cut hair into plastic bags; Cominia went over the floor with a little hand-held vacuum cleaner to make certain there was not a strand left. 'Carpet could use it anyway,' she muttered.

And after that Cleomenes and Cominia gathered up Alexander and left them alone. 'We'll come back early tomorrow and get you down to the coast. They'll be sending a couple of boats over for you—'

'Then they really are building an army,' whispered Noriko, feeling dizzy again.

'More like a navy, from the sound of it. Mostly old men and girls,' said Cleomenes. He shrugged. 'Who knows?' he asked, with an air of vast resignation.

There were only two beds; and Noriko couldn't relax on the scratchy, faintly greasy sheets. She had never been so unguarded in her life, and she was acutely aware that all they had to protect them was a single flimsy locked door. And yet it was better than a centuria of Praetorians, and though she slept lightly and woke often, she felt safer in this squalid place than she had at any point in the last year inside the Palace.

In the morning she lifted her head and saw Amaryllis sitting on the carpet in a square of sunlight, rigidly hugging herself and rocking gently. Her face was red, and swollen with tears, and she was quivering with the sweaty tremors that follow violent nausea. She was completely silent.

Noriko slipped out of bed to kneel beside her; she touched her shoulder. 'Amaryllis,' she whispered gently.

Amaryllis flinched away a little. 'That's not my name,' she said, in a thick, angry voice. There was a long pause while Amaryllis rocked soundlessly, her mouth dragged into a kind of dreadful grin of pain. Then at last she lifted a hand to wipe at her face, which slowly relaxed.

More clearly she said, 'My name's Maralah.'

[XV]

BATTLEFIELDS

It was the first anniversary of Marcus' death. Una and Varius had both retreated into themselves over the preceding weeks, speaking less and less, except of the most routine things. They were bracing themselves, shoring themselves up against what they knew was coming.

The celebrations of remembrance were both inescapable and intolerable. There were speeches and parades, and Drusus' pious face lifted bravely up towards the sky or downcast in contemplation on every longvision. It was like the endlessly publicised preparations for Marcus' wedding with Noriko, but far worse. Una read in a newssheet that Drusus was unveiling a statue of Marcus in Rome and was incoherent with rage and grief for hours afterwards.

They were no longer living in Alexandria. They travelled around the coast from one secret group of former slaves to another, sleeping on the ship when there was no bed or floor space free. They wanted to be far away from people – and from the longvision – on the day itself, so the night before they sailed out from the coast of Crete and hid the *Ananke* beside a tiny outpost of rock in the Aegean.

In the morning the sea and sky were like blue lacquer on glass. It was a beautiful day and Una lay curled in the cabin trying not to exist until it was over.

She had never known her own birthday; she thought it fell somewhere in the first part of the year. It must be past by now, and she must be the age Marcus had been. She thought – she knew how usual a thought it was – that she would be carried further and further past him until one day she would be old, and he would always be twenty, always the same.

She shook her head, a little surprised she was thinking in such terms: it was hardly certain – or even particularly likely – that she would live to be old. And yet it was *possible*; there were hundreds of them now, ranked and waiting around the Mediterranean: she could feel the force of all those people building, like the pressure rising in the summer air. She could see their fleet on the open sea. But afterwards . . .

At last the cabin grew too hot and stifling for her to continue hiding under the bedclothes, so she went up to join Varius on the deck. He was lying in the sun with his eyes closed, yet he did not look as if he were merely sunbathing, or asleep; every line of his body was tense and his lips tight. He, too, was concentrating on enduring.

Una sat down a little distance from him, gazing down at the wavering white reflection of the *Ananke* in the blue water.

'Do you have dreams he's still alive?' she asked him after a while.

'Dreams where I see him,' murmured Varius, 'but it's always as if he's come back for a little while. I don't forget what happened.'

Una sighed. 'I do.'

Varius nodded, without opening his eyes. 'That's worse. Sometimes I still dream Gemella's alive, that it was all some kind of mistake. But not so often now.'

'How do you think about Gemella now?' asked Una, tentatively. 'Do you think she's still . . . anywhere?'

'Sometimes I'm sure she is – sometimes it's as if she's right there.' He extended a hand, fingertips stroking lightly through the space beside him, and smiled, and a surprising sweetness spread briefly across his face. But it was only for a second. 'And other times I think there's nothing; she's gone. But even then—' His face tensed, he was, she could see, reluctant to continue, but at last he said, 'Back at the Academy I was more interested in politics than philosophy, but I remember some of the philosophers used to say that every moment exists forever – that time is an illusion. And if that's true, then Gemella— Her life isn't gone. It's still happening, somewhere. And it can't be touched, or lost, and I'm still there with her, even if I – if what I am now – can't get back to her.'

Una leant her head against the gunwale; she thought of the moments in which she felt Marcus' death was for ever present, always happening, and wondered if she could ever think of the rest of his life like that.

'I only knew him for four years,' she said. 'If we win, if we ever go back to some kind of normal life, I don't want to go back to how I was – how I would have been if I'd never— if he— What if one day it's all just a— an episode? If it's as if it was someone else who loved him—?'

Varius was quiet for a while, then he opened his eyes and looked at her. 'Do you really think that could happen?' he asked.

Una let out a long breath, and felt tears run suddenly from her eyes. 'I suppose not. No.'

'I don't think there's going to be an end, Una, even if we win. There'll be enough work for ten lifetimes. You wouldn't be able to give it up if you tried.' He pulled himself up, and smiled at her. 'That's not a bad thing.'

The remains of the Great Wall of Terranova were still visible from above: a broad, crumpled stripe broken by a bright curl of the Sanga River. They were flying northwest over Enkono, or Mohavia, or whatever they were calling it now.

The sun was rising beneath them in a flattened pool of light. The ground was almost like another sky: bare, reddish, smoke-stained, huge. The air above it was thick with bullets and fire.

Sulien stood a few men back from the hatch at the rear of the volucer, trying to keep his feet as the aircraft swerved. The noise was deafening, and yet his own pulse seemed to him to be roaring almost as loud. He couldn't even guess how many Nionian fighters were in the sky with them, but it looked like thousands; from here it was almost impossible to believe that anyone was going to reach the ground alive. They were all heavy with equipment and armour; moulded plates fastened to their torsos and arms, close-fitting helmets on their heads, shields strapped awkwardly to their left sides – but such defences were pitiful against this mauling sky.

Well, this is going to be over fast, Sulien thought, trying to be wryly resigned in order to get himself past the total disbelief as the last man in front of him dropped away. And in his turn he approached the screaming threshold, and stepped out, and was lost in the clawing air.

Someone who might have been him kept count of the seconds. He pulled on the cord and for an instant he was – impossibly – falling upwards, breath shocked out of him, before the square black canopy steadied. And somewhere in those first dreadful seconds, in helpless flight between the bullets, he was shot through with blind, terrified elation. The air tore away a cry from his lips, inaudible even to himself in the blast.

He tried to steady himself, and looked down to see the colours of the landscape emerging, beneath his dangling feet: the red-ridged earth bristling with grey scrub, light cresting the dry hills.

Ten miles upriver from the ruins of the Wall the Sanga cut through dark cliffs and the city of Aregaya rose up the hillside on both sides of the canyon, the grid of blue and green roofs abrupt and unnatural against the desert. The caged river glittered under the bridges the 6th Arcansan Legion was fighting to recapture, and at least one was down already. Smoke was rising from both sides of the gorge.

Gunfire whipped a string of pendent soldiers out of the sky some way ahead and below of Sulien, their parachutes twisting and withering, and he turned his head away. He shut his eyes – but not for long; the rush of noise and sensation was even more overwhelming in the dark. Everything around him was hurtling so fast except for the earth, which came dawdling up to meet him. Oh, come on, come on, he pleaded to it. He could hardly bring himself to try to steer his descent – it was one thing to consign himself passively to the danger, but so much harder to propel himself deliberately into the fire – when every direction looked murderous.

He was coming down onto a sandy plain already spotted with craters and black parachutes, between a crooked range of dark mountains and a huddle of low hills. To the east, towards the mountains, he saw a dark mass on the earth – a dense expanse of darker brush, he thought at first, but as he floated lower he saw that it was moving. It flowed and separated, and for an instant he wondered if it was a disordered unit of enemy forces. But then further down he realised that a herd of panicked bufali were charging across the edge of the battlefield. He saw a small explosion spurt in the midst of them, scattering the nearest animals, sending the main body of them surging the other way.

The city vanished over the horizon and the ground swung up at an unnatural angle and tripped him; he fell onto his side, breathing hard, as his parachute collapsed lazily over a bulbous cactus. He'd landed in a shallow runnel between mounds of red rocks and for the moment he could see only grey bushes dotted with yellow flowers, nothing else. The terrible noise continued above him like some strange kind of weather, but down here the air was hot and still, and felt strangely undisturbed. It was as if he'd fallen out of the war.

But then bullets raked past him. He slammed his shield upright into the sandy earth and crouched behind it, breathless, frantically pulling open catches, dragging his gun free of its fastenings, trying to get out of his harness. He couldn't see where the volley had come from, but he fired back blindly, then scrambled away into the cover of a low spur of rock where he stopped for a moment and finished adjusting the rest of his kit. He was shocked to see that there were several white scuffs on the shield already, a long narrow streak left by a bullet; jagged marks of flying shrapnel that must have hit while he was still in the air.

Sulien clambered up onto flat ground, where what was left of the 33rd Anasasian Legion continued to rain gently out of the sky around him. He was relieved not to be alone any longer. He wondered if any of them knew what they were doing. A few months ago Rome had controlled both Enkono and Sorasan-myaku; now the Nionians had cut Roman reinforcement lines and stranded a section of Roman forces to the north. Sulien's cohort was supposed to be capturing a junction outside the city, enclosing Aregaya while reopening the roads to the north and east. How would they know if it was working?

He'd checked his compass, and although he might not be exactly sure of the distance, he knew Aregaya was ahead. The sun was rising over the jagged hills. He squinted through the powdery haze of churned dust thickening the air. At least he was used to sand and heat. Perhaps sending troops trained in Egypt to Terranova wasn't quite as stupid as he'd thought.

He met the eyes of another Roman soldier through the sage-brush and they converged as they crept forward, meeting in the cover of a low brake of shrubs, where they put their shields together into a narrow fence and exchanged shaky, half-sane grins. Sulien recognised the other soldier, Hanno, from his own centuria, though he didn't know him well – the lanky dark boy was from Aravacia, he thought.

'You're the decanus of your octet, aren't you?' whispered Hanno.

Sulien nodded; technically he was in command of eight men. Pas and Dorion were among them and had been in the line behind him in the volucer – by request, rather than coincidence. The theory went that close-knit octets were more effective. It didn't count for much on the battlefield even if they were with him, for nothing if he couldn't find them. Or if they were all dead.

'I can't see an officer anywhere,' said Hanno.

'We'll just have to make it a bit further north on our own,' Sulien said. He pointed, and at that moment there was a blast and a spray of red soil fifty yards or so ahead. Dreadful high screams sawed through the air for several long seconds after-wards, then stopped abruptly. Sulien gritted his teeth.

Another private came scuttling across the sand to join them. He collapsed onto his knees, shaking, his shield lying loose and useless at his side, 'Fucking mines!' he said wildly, 'they never said there'd be fucking mines! We haven't got engineers, all the tanks are over east – I suppose they want us to just fucking wade through them . . . we haven't got a fucking prayer!'

Keeping his own shield braced, Sulien gripped the other man's arm, accepting that for the present he was at least marginally in charge. 'Calm down. You have to calm down. You're all right. Get your shield up.' He gestured the newcomer into position behind himself and Hanno. With this third shield facing backwards, the three of them were relatively enclosed.

'What's your name?' asked Hanno.

'Caerellius,' answered the stranger fretfully.

'It's not mines,' said Hanno, 'they've sprayed the place with those bomblet things. I saw them falling.'

'What difference does it make?'

'We've got a chance of seeing them, at least,' said Sulien. 'And there can't be as many.'

'How do you know that?'

Sulien ignored him and rose cautiously so he could peer through his shield, first across the plain towards the hidden guns, then at the ground directly ahead of them. He had Hanno hold up both their shields, with Caerellius' horizontal across them both, raising the transparent wall to five feet and leaving him free, if more exposed, behind it.

He began hastily gathering up stones from the sand. 'All right, brace,' he said, and began flinging them over the barrier as if they were grenades, trying to place each one further ahead.

'What are you doing?' Caerellius demanded shrilly.

Sulien ducked behind the wall of shields on each impact, but nothing happened – at least, nothing immediately in front of them, though the noise never abated and the sand continued to lift in huge puffs all across the plain.

Sulien took back his own shield and moved ahead of the others. 'Single file, two shield-lengths apart,' he said, 'and try and stay in the tracks of the man in front of you. Watch your feet when you can.'

He led the way, staying as low as he could, keeping his shield raised and angled against the storm of projectiles in the air. He almost forgot to worry about the bomblets; thick, relentless gunfire was sweeping across the desert from some invisible source and shells were bursting all around them. Roman gunners in the hills behind them were offering covering fire, but down here it was all one onslaught of sound and dust. Sulien still couldn't see any enemy soldiers – there was no point in trying to shoot back.

A parachute was draped across the ground in their path and something terrible lay half underneath it, a body smashed to pieces, still in the harness. Sulien almost tripped over it. Behind him, Caerellius gagged. They could see other small columns of men advancing through the thickening dust, though the brown haze blurred them all to shadows. They made slow progress, running a few yards, then dropping behind the cover of their shields to test the ground ahead with stones. They crossed a line of shattered pylons and stopped again. Sulien could barely see through his shield now; the clear surface was dappled with opaque white scars. He was amazed it had happened so fast; they'd barely been on the ground an hour. He wondered if one more direct hit would shatter it now.

'Archias! Shouter!'

Dorion was calling to him in a muted yell across the sand from behind another cone of blackened metal. He was with Gnatho, another man from their octet, and a pair of soldiers Sulien didn't know.

Sulien almost laughed aloud in delight at seeing him alive, and the relief left him clearer and steadier than before as a faint, lingering dizziness that he hadn't even been conscious of went away. He gestured to Dorion to meet him further ahead, and a few minutes later the seven men congregated in a crater perhaps three-quarters of a mile north of where Sulien had landed.

Dorion was still smiling when he reached them, but his eyes looked glassy. 'Simalio's dead,' he said, 'as soon as he touched the ground, poor bastard.'

Sulien grimaced, shaken and yet ashamed for being relieved it wasn't anyone he knew better. 'The others?'

'Thought I saw Petreius land all right somewhere over that way, ahead of me,' said Dorion, waving an arm, 'but I never caught up with him. I don't know about the rest.'

They looked at each other, both knowing they were thinking the same thing. 'Pas—' Sulien started.

'Oh, you can't expect the kid to even *fall* straight, he's probably just . . . stuck watching the fireworks up in the mountains somewhere,' said Dorion, though his smile had vanished.

Sulien forced the thought of Pas away and they scrambled onwards towards Aregaya.

The sun had climbed beyond the horizon. Sulien began to feel as if his head were being cooked within his helmet, and he struggled with the urge to pull it off. Sweat plastered his scalp and trickled into his eyes, welled underneath the plates on his chest. He swallowed scant mouthfuls of warm water from his flask as they huddled beneath their shields in yet another crater. Once they'd scattered as a barrage of shells slammed down almost on top of them, and as Sulien plunged into the sand with his shield over his head, he was still able to marvel at the scale of what was happening around him, and how few people it had taken to cause it.

But perhaps that wasn't quite true; the actions that had led to this had begun a long time before anyone on this field was born.

He forgot both reflections almost at once, irritated and frightened that he'd let his attention wander even that much. He scrambled up painted red-brown, gritty with sweat and sand, but still unhurt, and certain their little group would not be whole when they gathered again. And he was right: Lanatus, one of the men who had joined them with Dorion, was gone, and Caerellius no longer shook or complained, just stumbled along staring emptily at the ground with wide, blank eyes.

They were approaching the foothills of the Tosutoya Mountains, dry and brittle against the sky like heaps of stained gravel.

They came to a small thread of a road, where a forlorn sign, just a little dented and tilted to one side, was still excitedly promoting something in pink and yellow Nionian characters above a corpse lying face-down in the sand. There were more bodies scattered before the barbed-wire rolls spread across the road, and tangled within it, but by now Roman rockets had broken through the line in several places. And here they finally encountered a centurion, firing from behind his shield in the shelter of a wretchedly low ridge of sand and directing a charge through the nearest breach.

'Covering fire!' he bellowed, gesturing furiously at the approaching infantrymen. He was scarcely audible over the throbbing noise of the guns and the ringing that was building within their ears. And at last they could see the main road, skimming between the rocky hills on concrete pillars and sand embankments, and the junction itself: eight lanes looping around each other, with a shadowed underpass at its centre. Sulien was distantly bewildered by how normal it looked, despite the thickets of barbed wire and the light machine-gun emplacements perched up on the flyover, and the heavy domed fortifications dug into the ground all round it. The moulded concrete barriers, though pockmarked and fallen here and there, still looked new, and almost identical to those on Roman motorways.

Sulien and his makeshift squad flung themselves down behind the ridge and began to fire up at the gun emplacements, over the heads of the Roman troops as they surged towards the gap and scrambled through. It was the first time since that first panicked moment on the ground that Sulien had fired a shot, and even now, supporting the stock of the gun against his shield, he felt he was not really trying to kill men, just adding a very little to the load of metal in the air. And part of him was comforted by that, and yet, now he could see where they were, he found he hated the gunners in their concrete shells hidden in those humps of earth. If they had been out in the same hot lethal air as the rest of them, he could have forgiven them. The ugliness and terror of the ground that lay behind them seemed to be building, pushing through him as if against a dam, trying to find a venting place. This anonymous release of fire didn't seem enough.

'Move through – get your shields up!' shouted the centurion, pointing at Sulien's group, and Sulien raised his battered shield in front of him, while the others lifted theirs above their heads. He led them forward.

Huge, jarring strikes landed on his shield as he darted through the wire, and as he'd feared, the clear ceramic finally shattered and he was knocked over into a heap of bodies. At the time Sulien felt no horror; something clamped shut in his mind. Caerellius fell over him, and Dorion, thinking he was wounded, stooped under his own shield to drag Sulien forward. 'No, I'm all right, keep going,' Sulien shouted, though he could hardly hear himself over the noise. He expected Dorion to topple over dead on top of him at any moment

But Dorion ran ahead. Sulien's shield-arm was still ringing with the shock of the strikes. He thought it was broken, until he pulled it free of the loops and realised it was only badly bruised, stinging where crumbs of the ceramic had scratched the skin. Almost without thinking, he reached out and dragged a dead soldier's shield over himself, then struggled up and ran on.

On the other side the terrain offered them a little more shelter. Sulien plunged into the relative safety of a crater between the dunes and looked back, but he never saw the centurion follow them through the wire. He saw Hanno running closer, just a few strides from the crater's edge, before bullets pierced his head and his chest at the same moment, and Sulien felt the shock light him up, like a spark to phosphorus, a strange energy that blazed through him. Unfelt tears ran from his eyes, but he felt incandescent, awake, and in no danger at all.

'Hanno,' said Dorion, in a thready voice as they huddled under the tortoiseshell of shields in the crater with the other leaderless men they had collected.

'It was that gunpost up on the right,' said Sulien fiercely, the guess becoming certainty as the words left his mouth, 'they got him. We can take that.' He pulled himself up against the crater's edge, watching the play of gunfire across the ground. 'They're sweeping back and forth. Wait till they turn it the other way—Now!'

And without hesitation he charged up out of the crater and across the ground. He saw Nionian soldiers aiming down at them from behind the barriers up on the road and shot two of them almost effortlessly; he seemed to have plenty of time in which to aim and fire. He hurled a grenade along the long trench that ran back from the rear of the gun emplacement, and felt a burst of overwhelming relief as the explosion lit the walls of the bunker from within. They leapt down into the trench as soon as the blast subsided, and Dorion ran up into the dugout, firing, but there was no sign of anyone left alive inside.

Another flow of Roman soldiers poured through the gap in the wire towards the junction. As a file of them rushed past the gunpost one of them stopped and dropped down into the trench beside Sulien, gasping, 'Archias!'

This time Sulien felt too stunned to be happy. The blazing feeling that had carried him up to the emplacement was beginning to give way to numbness. He stared at Pas, trying to drag his mouth into a joking grin. He managed, 'Where the hell've you been?'

Pas gave a ragged little smile and gestured at the chaos behind them, and said breathlessly, 'I don't know . . .'

Sulien put a hand on his shoulder and gave it a baffled little shake. Dorion emerged from the bunker, and, seeing Pas, gave a crow of triumph.

A tesserarius ran up and crouched beside the trench. 'You took this one out, lads? Good men. We're going up onto the flyover. You get over there and clear them out from underneath it.'

Sulien led them dodging over the uneven ground towards the underpass. Four or five men dashed out into the foothills on the other side of the junction, leaving the bodies of their fellows slumped beneath the pillars. Sulien's party threw another few grenades into the recesses of the underpass to make sure.

Now a heavier wave of Roman troops was coursing up the

embankment, and the concrete hollows rumbled with the weight of what was happening overhead. Then a flight of volucers swooped north over the junction, scattering the hills beyond them with fire.

'I think we've sort of got this done,' said Dorion, looking around uncertainly.

Pas frowned. 'Don't go saying things like that. Bad luck.'

'I guess . . . We need to hold this position, in case they re-form over on the other side and try to come back through,' said Sulien, trying not to look at the face of a dead Nionian soldier who was sitting slumped against one of the pillars. Privately he hoped someone would come and tell them what to do.

As they retreated a little towards the southern entrance to the underpass, a troop of thirty shieldless Nionian soldiers surged over the barrier and came charging down the embankment towards the plain, firing wildly. Sulien marvelled: they were hopelessly unprotected – they must have known it was suicidal. They were all shouting the same word—

And they were cut down in seconds. Sulien barely had time to lift his own gun before there was no one left to fire at.

'Archias!' shouted Dorion, behind him.

Pas was on the ground, blood spurting thickly from the side of his neck.

Dorion was already bending over him, trying to hold the wound closed, babbling, 'Oh, shit . . . oh, you'll be all right, you stupid little . . .'

For a second Sulien stood blankly looking down at Pas, thinking, of course this was going to happen sooner or later. Then he pulled Dorion out of the way, took hold of Pas and dragged him deeper into the shelter of the pillars. He knelt over him, grimly pressing down with his bare hands on the wound. He said, 'It's not that bad.'

The bullet had missed Pas' windpipe, but it had torn open artery and muscle, and the blood was welling up between Sulien's fingers, coating his hands red to the wrists. Pas was conscious but faint with pain and shock, his skin already paling. He stared up at Sulien, didn't try to move or speak.

Caerellius called for a medic, and then again, with more force, but no one seemed to hear.

'Oh, come on, no,' moaned Dorion, miserably raising both hands to his head.

'He's fine, it's just a fucking scratch,' Sulien said fiercely, 'go and get a medic down here. The rest of you, keep covering that entrance up ahead.' Dorion lingered, transfixed by the quantity of blood, until Sulien repeated, 'Do it now, Dorion.'

Dorion's face contorted with distress and anger, but he obeyed, picking his way over the dead soldiers.

Caerellius and Gnatho moved a little further along the underpass, their guns at the ready, but they kept glancing back over their shoulders at Sulien and Pas. At least they were in the shadows of the pillars, Sulien thought, and besides, there was nothing strange to see. He leaned down on the wound, pressing the edges together, letting his eyes close. Just stop, just stop, he thought to the blood, such a little thing to ask, for the torn fibres to close under the pressure of his hands, just enough to keep the blood inside. He'd leave the rest to the medics—

Pas shuddered a little, opened and closed his mouth before managing, 'Archias— What—?'

Above them, up on the flyover, things were going quiet.

'See,' Sulien murmured to him, as the bleeding began to slow, 'you just need a few stitches, that's all. Shame it wasn't worse, really; you're not going home yet.'

Pas blinked up at him and his forehead puckered, as if with puzzlement rather than with pain.

Dorion, looking pallid and grim, came running back with the medic, but Pas saw them coming and lifted a shaky hand to show that he was still alive. 'I think it looked worse than it was,' Sulien muttered as the medic bent over Pas, who even tried to confirm it by making a move to sit up.

Sulien let the medic get to work and drew back. He wanted to separate himself from what he'd done.

There was still the sporadic thunder of mortars up in the hills, but the fighting on the junction itself seemed to have stopped. Now Sulien remembered that the bodies he'd fallen among in the breach in the wire had still been warm, that the expression on Hanno's face had not even had time to change before he fell, that he was not certain how many people he had killed today. On one of the ramps leading up to the flyover another soldier was sitting on the crash-barrier with his head in his hands, and Sulien wanted to do that too, he wanted to drop to the ground and cry, or vomit or fall asleep. But there was this hard, bright glaze of wakefulness covering everything. He felt that he could keep hold of that, at least for now: he could stave off everything he'd seen and felt, stop it from hurting him beyond what he could stand, and for as long as he could do these things he must not stop. *Later*, he told the barrage of jagged new memories rattling through him, as he looked up at the smoke rising in the west over the captured city.

'I am trying to reach Grand Preceptor Zhu Li,' said Ziye, in Sinoan, into the longdictor.

'Is this a joke?' said the faraway crackling voice of the woman who had answered. She added cagily, as if afraid of being further taken in, 'This is a dentist's.'

'Please wait,' said Ziye. 'Would you know the longdictor code for your local magistrates' office?'

But the line went dead, though whether because the woman had broken the connection or because a cable somewhere had been severed, there was no way to be sure.

They were about a hundred miles west of Alexandria, at Tamiathis, where Delir and Ziye had taken over a small printing and copying shop. It provided a thin stream of income, and the equipment was useful to Lal, but more importantly, it was a means of money-laundering.

They were in the windowless back room now, among the reams of paper and binding machines, and Varius was on another

386

longdictor, going through the same routine as Ziye. 'I'm sorry, this must be the wrong code?'

'No Latin,' said the baffled voice on the other end of the line.

'I'm sorry,' repeated Varius, sighing, and crossed out another line of symbols on the list in front of him. 'I swear it's one of these,' he said, while the others groaned gently and Ziye's lips tightened.

A year before, Varius had spent weeks talking to Zhu Li and other officials, discussing the tortuous details for the Sinoan peace talks. He was sure that at least one of the longdictor codes must be lodged in his memory somewhere, and if only he could retrieve any one of them, a message could be passed to Jun Sen and on to Tadahito. It was painful now to think of that time, and all that had happened since, but Varius closed his eyes and tried again to will himself back into his office in the southwest tower of the Palace, with Rome spread outside the blue-tinted windows, a leather chair underneath him, and a constant burr of tense voices in the corridor outside his door. He moved his fingers over the longdictor's keys without pressing them: it was there, the right sequence, he could so nearly see it—

They were trying other routes too. At present Lal was silently rereading her last letter from Sulien, which Varius and Una had collected in Alexandria, but she had spent the afternoon calling old friends in Tianjin in an effort to trace Liuyin, the official's son who had once been in love with her. Old connections of Delir's had promised to search out possible contacts in the Sinoan Civil Service and get back to them, but they could not afford to wait; the lines were being cut. Varius tried another variation and got only static. Rome had declared war on Sina a fortnight before.

Ziye had grown increasingly tense and taciturn ever since the public declaration. She was surprised that the invasion of her country should matter so much to her now, when she had spent most of her life outside Sina and had few fond memories of it, and when she had already lived through more than a year of war, and months under Nionian bombs. Nevertheless, she winced at the news of what was happening on Sina's western borders. Maracanda and Luntai had fallen almost at once, and apparently without much effort on the Roman Army's part, despite how far they were now extended. And she now had a triple reason to worry about what people saw when they looked at her scarred face: that she could be mistaken for Nionian, that she could be recognised as Sinoan, and that she could be known as herself.

She fidgeted with the list of longdictor codes. 'I appreciate these girls need help,' she muttered, 'but the vigiles need only one good lead on them and they'll fall right on top of us.'

'Ah, we have no choice. What else can we do? Who else can they turn to?' said Delir.

'I owe Noriko whatever help I can give her; she protected me when I was in prison. What they would have done to me if not for her . . . And she was Marcus' wife.' Una spoke evenly, with almost no betrayal of feeling, except a pause after the last word. 'But she can help us too, where Tadahito's concerned. If she's with us, that means passage into Alodia or Ethiopia, or wherever Tadahito is now. It means an audience with him – we can't lose that chance.'

Noriko and the other women were being passed from one group of partisans to the next across the Mediterranean; they should be somewhere off the west coast of the Peloponnese by now. And yet there had been no acknowledgement on the news that they was missing. It was strange. For once Varius found himself wishing for hysterical headlines in the newssheets, and photographs continually splashed across the longvision. Not that he was surprised by the silence – it would have been acutely embarrassing for Drusus to admit that Marcus' widow had defected from right under his nose. But it must also be that he still hoped to find her, and was wary of alerting Nionia that she was free and in need of help. Varius was almost sure that any intelligence agency worthy of the name must have learned the truth regardless, and in that case Nionian agents must already be in Roman territory, looking for her. But certainty would have been a relief.

'Well, this is no use anyway,' said Ziye, pulling off the headset. 'I have been through all of these. Varius, you might as well admit you have forgotten this code. We should wait and see what Mouli can do, or concentrate on finding Liuyin.'

'I know Zhu Li; it would be far better to talk to him direct,' said Varius, irritated, 'and I know I can't be more than a couple of figures out. Unless it's already too late to get through . . .'

He finished dialling as he spoke, and got another dead line. He gritted his teeth and rubbed between his eyes. Lal put her head down on a stack of printer paper.

'Perhaps we should all get out of this room for a while,' suggested Delir.

It was late, but the light was only just starting to leave the sky. The air raids had grown more sporadic since June, and though Tamiathis had never been as heavily bombarded as Alexandria, Una and Lal did not get very far from the little print shop before they came to a field of rubble stretching the width of several streets. Children played stubbornly on the heaps; a few untouched palm trees were still standing here and there, and weeds were beginning to grow among the stones.

'Here,' said Lal, taking the letter from her pocket and holding it out, 'you read it.'

Una took it with slight reluctance. Sulien's letters made him seem almost more absent. The words were always like him and yet there was an opacity behind them that was not; it was unnerving to hear his voice in her head and yet be so unsure of what he was really thinking. The occasional censored lines that lay across the page like bars made it worse – it was so easy to imagine that they contained something precious, something that had been stolen from them.

This letter was very like the ones she had received herself: most of it was an impersonal chronicle of the soldiers' training – marching, hand-to-hand, weapons training – with brief glimpses of Sulien in the reassurances that strung the letter together, that it was really not so bad. Near the end there was one small flicker of life, and a detail that was new to Una: 'Dorion is trying to read over my shoulder now, making an idiot of himself and distracting me. Now he's asking me about you. I'm glad you can't hear what he's saying. Hmm . . . right, you're never meeting him.'

It ended, 'Please be careful, always. Look after yourself, and look after the others when you can. You know how Aethra and Heraius can be: try not to let them get too obsessed – not that there's much anyone can do to stop them. I do love you, Berenice.'

'I hate that stupid name. I wish I'd never chosen it,' said Lal. 'And there's been nothing since his training finished. What do I care what happened months ago in some camp? I want to know where he is *now*. All these weeks he's been fighting somewhere, and this is all we have!'

Una wished Lal would stop radiating the thought that perhaps he was dead, had been dead all this time, with such intensity – it was hard to block it out. 'No news is good news,' she said, tightly.

'Oh, Una,' cried Lal, 'you know how he was even before he went – he was only just starting to be himself again. Even if he— Even if nothing happens, what will he be like when he comes back? He's already been through enough . . . he shouldn't be out there, he just shouldn't – what will it do to him?' She flung her arms impulsively around Una and said, 'He needs us— I want him back here so much!'

Una could find nothing to say in response. She could not weakly add, 'So do I.' She couldn't explain that her own fear for Sulien had no such gradations, no details; it was a single, huge, solid block: she was afraid he would die. Only that; anything else she would think about when she saw him. But she and Lal sat together, side by side and silent, on a heap of fallen bricks, until an air raid siren started to cry out into the dark blue sky.

Sulien raced along what was left of the street. There was a tiny stir at the corner of a house ahead of him, barely a dark flicker on

390

the edge of his vision, but he registered the upward swing of the barrel of a gun and crouched behind his shield and fired. The figure darted back and Sulien launched himself into a run. Ahead of him a flight of concrete steps led up to nothing. He'd have better cover beside it; he thought he might get a clearer shot—

They had been over this ground before, they'd fought for these streets and apparently won, and yet here they were again. Sulien could picture the row of blown-out shops around the corner where the gunman was hiding, having blasted some of those buildings open himself the week before. It was only here, in the northern districts of the city, that some remnants of the Nionian forces still had any kind of foothold, and though the Romans were prising them out it was slow and repetitive and bloody. At least this was not as bad as the first time – only small-arms fire now, and not so much of it. Cerinthus and Isidorus had been hurt back in the little square a block behind them, where they'd been pinned down for almost an hour that morning, but they would live, not like poor Flaccus, blown apart by a mortar in that first assault. He had survived for several horrible minutes afterwards, out in the open where no one could get to him. Sulien thought he'd have gone mad listening to his screaming, if he hadn't had Dorion there – Dorion, who'd been shaking with dry, gagging sobs behind their shields, but at least he was someone else to concentrate on. Sulien had kept up a desperate onslaught of talk at him – babbling about Alexandria and Rome and he hardly remembered what; it didn't matter what anyone said at a time like that – until Flaccus fell silent and the volucers swept in. He didn't know what he would have done if he had been able to get close to Flaccus.

Sulien's centuria was down to forty-six men now, though most of the dead had fallen that first day, out on the plain. The octet he was leading now was a compound of two broken halves, but Pas was there, hurrying along the other side of the street with Petreius. He'd had a week's rest in the base; his wound had, of course, healed well. He had been sick the first time he'd shot an enemy whose face he could see, and Sulien had had to scoop him up off the rubble, and pull him along, muttering to him urgently, '*Later, later.*'

Now Pas and Petreius moved across the shattered paving to join him by the steps; Gavros was leading in another octet in from the east, towards the gunman's street. Sulien's radio buzzed: 'We've got the west street covered. Are you ready to go?'

'Confirm that,' said Sulien, beckoning his men. The two octets probed the entrance of the street with a couple of volleys, then they closed into a solid rampart and charged forward. Bullets rattled on the roof of shields above Sulien's head, but now the rest of the centuria were sweeping in from all points of the crossroads and the Nionian militiamen on the ground were trapped between the closing walls of the Romans' shields.

This time their intelligence was correct, and they found the weapons cache behind a false wall in a cellar. The soldiers helped themselves to ammunition, grenades and pistols, but there wasn't a suitable truck in the area to carry the heavier weapons, so they cleared out with their spoils and let a volucer bring down the building in another eruption of black smoke. The city air never seemed clear of it.

Sulien tried to feel some sort of satisfaction that the number of weapons in play had been reduced; they'd killed five men this morning but surely saved at least as many lives – *someone's* life must have been saved, maybe Dorion's, or his own, or some of the hollow-eyed women he'd seen filling buckets of water at the standpipe in Yomogiu District.

They all breathed shallowly in Aregaya, trying not to inhale the stench that enveloped the city. Everyone tried to pretend it was just the sewage that had seeped up from overwhelmed septic tanks in the east, and the uncollected rubbish in the streets. But there was that other smell laced through it, strangely mild as it entered the nostrils, before the foulness of it squeezed the back of the throat and roiled the stomach. There were bodies rotting under the rubble, and still unburied out on the plain.

They scarcely saw living civilians as they crashed in and out of deserted rooms and chased masked men from block to block.

Sulien was grateful that so many of the city's inhabitants were out of the way of their guns and grenades, but their absence seemed as quietly accusatory as the expressionless looks or forced smiles they met in the few markets and shops that were still opening. Sometimes the tidiness of a bedroom with a smashed-in door or the rows of little indoors slippers in the school they were using as a barracks were almost as bad as the terrified family they found cowering under a table and the shouting mothers carrying bloodied children to the hospital.

Sulien hoped they'd move out of the city soon.

After the raid, the remains of Sulien's centuria returned to the base. A few of the men began throwing a ball around the schoolyard while Sulien sat on the steps of the little temple at the heart of the compound, spraying a coating of silicon finish onto his battered shield.

Gracilis, one of the senior centurions of the cohort, approached Sulien. 'Private Archias?'

Sulien jumped to his feet. 'Sir.'

'You're fourth centuria, yes? The decanus of your octet?'

'Yes, sir.'

The centurion squinted at him, and rubbed wearily at the flaking sunburn on his forehead. 'How old are you?'

'Twenty-one,' Sulien said, automatically telling the truth, and then worried he'd made a mistake – he couldn't remember the right answer for 'Archias'. Some of the identity papers Lal had given him made him a year or two older or younger.

Gracilis sighed and grimaced in apparent dejection, which unsettled Sulien further. 'Right,' he said heavily, 'you can read, can't you?'

Bewildered, Sulien nodded.

'And you led an assault on a gun emplacement out at the west junction.'

'Well— I— Sort of, sir.' It was difficult to think very clearly about anything he'd done that day, though not because he'd forgotten anything. The memories were sharp and bright: he

393

remembered surging out of the crater and across the sand, hurling the grenade, and yet he felt as if he'd never had any real choice, never been any less helpless than when twirling downwards under his parachute. The battle had simply happened, like a tide, tossing around the thousands of Roman and Nionian men on the plain like pebbles. Saving Pas had been the only decision that seemed to have been his to make.

'Yes,' he finished, when he realised this vagueness wasn't adequate.

Gracilis looked irritated. 'Take command of your centuria, then.'

Sulien gaped. 'What, sir?' For a moment he really expected Gracilis to laugh or realise he'd made a mistake. 'But I've only been here a couple of weeks.'

'Somebody's got to do it,' said the centurion, with a sour smile. 'And the ninth cohort's rather short of likely candidates, as I'm sure you've noticed. Your centuria – there are only – what, forty of you left?'

'Forty-six – but there'll be replacements coming,' said Sulien, 'won't there?'

Gracilis stared at him, then blinked, revealing a great depth of fatigue. He patted Sulien bleakly on the arm. 'Congratulations, Lieutenant.'

'"Lieutenant"—!' protested Sulien.

'That'll be your formal rank; but of course you'll be acting as centurion until replacements get here,' remarked Gracilis, with another ironic twitch of an eyebrow, and walked off.

Sulien took one stride down the steps in an astounded impulse to go and tell Pas or Dorion, which almost instantly shrivelled into dread of telling anyone. Instead he sat down again and resumed applying the silicon coating as if nothing had happened, except that he buffed the shield with ferocious energy and his teeth were gritted against a surge of heat that came rushing into his face. He wondered if he could have got Gracilis to make the announcement for him – no, he supposed that must be his first job – but how was he supposed to do it? He felt idiotic even thinking about it. He wondered if they would laugh at him, and then thought that with almost half the centuria already dead it wasn't funny.

It barely mattered who was in command now – that was the point. Sulien laid down the shield on the steps. A whole centuria of raw recruits: a single shovelful of fuel, hurled into the army's engine. They were there to carry the campaign forward a little way as they were consumed, not to survive. They were half-spent already. That was why he would do.

The ball sailed over towards the temple steps and one of the boys yelled, 'Shouter!' and Sulien got up to kick it back to them, then stood watching them as they resumed play. Someone had accepted their deaths already. He didn't like the idea of taking responsibility for any group larger than an octet, and he didn't expect to be very good at it, but at least he had not, would not, do that.

He came down the steps towards the other soldiers. 'Petreius,' he said, 'tell the other decani I need to see them here. I've got some news.'

Varius heard the air-raid siren from across the city. He'd been visiting Phanias, one of the leaders of the local recruits. The Tamiathis effort needed more money, and they were struggling to cope with an unexpected influx of volunteers.

Like Varius, Phanias had never been a slave. He was a reticent, anonymous little accountant in his fifties who was invisibly seething with violent disgust at the war. He had a conscripted son in Alodia. 'It's been building ever since Patara,' he told Varius, 'but I think it's Sina too.'

'I think so too. People are getting sick of this war now.'

'It's good, I know, but it's getting hard to check everyone out properly – and harder to keep them quiet. It worries me how easily some of them are finding us.'

'Then it might be time we go out of business in Tamiathis,' said Varius. 'Tell the leaders to get their groups together. Una can come and speak to them all; she'll know if we need to worry about any of them. And we'll start moving them north over the next ten days.'

He was heading back when the sirens sounded. Ahead of him a pair of women walking together and a man carrying a briefcase quickened their pace and Varius too began to walk faster, calculating he probably did not need to look for shelter yet, could probably get back to Delir and Ziye's if he hurried.

The sky was a deep indigo tonight, veined with light where flares broke across it. There were only a few aircraft up there; compared with the long, methodical poundings Alexandria had taken, this attack felt almost offhand, a casual sweep across the city, leaving great tracts of air and ground untouched.

But it was coming close: there was a familiar shudder in the ground, and someone ran past him. Varius glanced upwards irritably, wondering whether he would do better to try to make his way back to Phanias' building or to keep going, following the few other people in the street who looked as if they knew where the nearest bomb shelter was.

He ran with the rest. He felt the air churn and twist, and shrapnel clattered on the road behind him. He ducked closer to the wall as someone started shouting, 'Get under here, under here!' and he saw there was an office block just a little way ahead with steps running up to a raised entrance; the women were already cowering underneath them. But the howling swept in towards him and the tremors drilled through his body. Oh, I don't have time for this, Varius thought crossly, before the roar overtook him, a blast of pressure slammed him to the ground, and something tore across his back as he fell.

Everything continued to boom and shake around him. There was a roar of falling bricks somewhere nearby, and he covered his head, but the collapse must have happened in the next street, for nothing else struck him. Varius lay still for another moment, breathless and dazed, waiting apprehensively for his body to make sense of what had happened to it.

He lifted his head, and the pain bit hard enough to make him gasp, but he could move, and he wasn't losing consciousness.

There was another boom, further away, and a high chorus of car and fire alarms filled the air as the bombers receded. Varius struggled to push himself up onto bruised knees, and someone came running from the office block steps to help him: the man who'd been carrying the briefcase. There was a woman, too, who slung Varius' arm over her shoulders, and between them they dragged him towards the shelter of the steps.

'I'm all right, I can stand up,' he said, feeling a little better now he was upright. Someone was screaming behind them, further along the street, and Varius looked back to see a figure lying motionless on the ground, and another figure reeling about, shrieking. The man leaned Varius against the steps, patted his shoulder, then raced off towards them. Varius watched, impressed. He couldn't bring himself to go and help, and he wondered if he was being unnecessarily feeble. He wasn't in so much pain, and didn't think he was even bleeding all that seriously.

'Someone's calling an ambulance,' the woman assured him, mopping inexpertly at his back with someone's scarf.

Varius nodded, but didn't say anything. He was fairly sure he didn't need one, and was hoping for a chance to slip away before he drew any more attention to himself. He twisted, gingerly, and put a hand to his back. Blood coated his palm and he pulled his hand away sharply. It was too dark to see anything else, even if he'd been able to look at the wounds.

The woman left him and ran after the businessman towards the fallen figure. Varius rested a little longer, trying to gather his strength to start walking. He found he was slightly dizzy after all, but he decided it was probably from the impact of the fall rather than whatever was wrong with his back, and it didn't seem to be getting worse, so he straightened, and set off back towards Phanias' house.

It couldn't be more than half a mile; he'd barely noticed the walk just minutes ago. By the time he'd turned the corner into the next street he was hobbling like an old man; the gashes like a weight strapped to his back. He could feel them flex and pull with each step, the fabric of his tunic dragging stickily at patches of drying blood. He had to stop and prop himself against a wall, panting as the torn flesh throbbed, an ugly muddle of cold and heat. Wandering off by himself seemed less than clever now, and Varius looked around for a public longdictor, though he was sure he hadn't seen one on the way out, and all he could see were shuttered shops. He swore under his breath, because this was such a stupid thing to happen, such an annoying waste of time.

He groaned and limped on, hoping no one would notice the blood, or how awkwardly he was walking – if Phanias was right and their operations here were pushing too close to the surface, then this was a dangerous place to make himself conspicuous. But it was not only that; he felt oddly embarrassed by his injuries. There was something unseemly about being out in public in this state.

Phanias' house was still there. Varius had begun to worry that it might have been hit. He rang the bell and leaned against the little portico, resisting the temptation to close his eyes. Phanias opened the door and exclaimed in shock.

'Shrapnel,' said Varius, a little shakily, 'but I think it's just . . . cuts. Not deep.'

Phanias hauled him into the small kitchen, sat him on a stool and sucked his teeth discouragingly as he inspected his back. Varius noticed the spattered trail of red blots he was leaving on the tiles and felt again, pointlessly embarrassed.

'You need a hospital.'

Varius grimaced. 'We've got a medical kit back at Delir's,' he said. 'If you can just get me back there—'

'You're all ripped up, we can't just stick a bandage on it. And whatever hit you, it's probably filthy.' Phanias poked, very squeamishly, at a point a little above the small of his back, and Varius hissed. 'And this one here looks deeper to me. You've got good papers, money, haven't you?'

Varius nodded wearily.

'Well, look, it's not all bad; make them give you a note. That'll stop anyone trying to send you off to the front line for a bit now, won't it?'

'Can you call the others for me?' asked Varius, dropping his head into his hands.

'I'll try, but you know how the longdictor lines are after these things.' Phanias searched around for something clean to use as a temporary dressing, eventually settling on an ungainly wad of torn-up bedsheets, which he fastened to Varius' back with duct tape. Then he drove him to hospital.

Tamiathis' only hospital had lost a wing in an earlier raid, and Phanias had to drive over a uneven ramp laid over a crater to reach the gates. The casualty room and the lobby outside it were crowded with hollow-eyed people, many of them, like Varius, bound in makeshift bandages. When a group of medics rushed someone on a stretcher through the doors at the far end of the room, Varius saw that the corridor beyond was lined with beds. An exhausted-looking nurse glanced him over and told him to wait.

They hadn't managed to contact the others before leaving. At least one of the longdictors in the hospital lobby was working, but there was a crowd around that too. Phanias hovered for a while, but gave up when two men broke into a loud argument over whose turn it was.

For an hour Varius hunched and shifted on a plastic chair, searching vainly for a position that was tolerable, until a couple next to him who had been eyeing him guiltily for a while offered him their seats to lie across. The man had a possible broken arm; the woman waiting with him wasn't hurt. Varius couldn't put up a convincing show of reluctance.

After that he persuaded Phanias to go home – there was nowhere for him to sit, and nothing for him to do. Varius lay on his side watching the flies lurching back and forth above him under the fluorescent light. There was a feverish, grubby heat in the room from so many bodies packed so close, but slowly, as midnight passed, the sighing crowd began to thin out and he wondered if he could make it to the longdictor now. He willed himself to stand up; he wasn't paralysed, and he knew Una and the others would be worried. There was no excuse for just lying here. But his back blazed and his head was aching too, now, and he let minute after minute pass and still he couldn't move.

Somewhere in the corridor full of beds a child began howling. There was a smeared puddle of blood by the doors to the lobby, and a sour, foetid smell swelled beneath a fading layer of antiseptic. He remembered the slave-clinic he'd run back in Rome, and began making censorious comparisons: *I* would never have let it get this bad. He regretted the thought almost at once, but it was too late, the memory had released a longing he hadn't felt in a long time. All this year he'd missed Marcus, he'd missed his parents, but strangely, he had not really missed safety and ordinary comfort, and the expectation these things would continue.

He closed his eyes. If he could lie perfectly still, he might even be able to sleep.

He was vaguely aware of people advancing across the floor, but didn't see any reason to look up until he heard Delir, standing right above him, saying, 'Oh, thank God!'

Varius prised open his eyelids and saw Una was there too, a little behind Delir, quiet and staring, still while Delir started bustling around him. Varius tried to sit up and Delir, alarmed, put out his hands to stop him. 'No, no, for heaven's sake, lie down! No one has seen you yet? Do you need a drink of water?'

He tried to look at Varius' back, and Varius was grateful for Phanias' dressing, that there was little to see.

Una closed and opened her eyes in a slow, exhausted blink, and then resumed staring at him, breathing hard, but otherwise motionless. Varius had known they would worry, but he had not imagined Delir would be so effusively relieved, or that Una would look quite so shattered. Delir even patted his head, as unselfconsciously as if Varius were a small child, prompting him to suppress a puff of touched, embarrassed laughter.

'I'll call the others; they won't sleep until they know you're safe,' said Delir, and hurried off towards the lobby.

Una dropped suddenly into a crouch beside Varius, one hand

lying alongside his on the scuffed plastic chair. 'You'll be all right,' she said at last in a low, bleak mutter.

'I know,' answered Varius softly.

A nurse called a name and a boy clutching a bloody towel to his head stood up and staggered past Una, who shifted slightly out of the way without taking her eyes off Varius.

'You may as well go back,' he said. 'it'll be a few hours yet, and I'm not . . . it's not as if I'm—'

Una shook her head – a single, emphatic jerk.

'You know it's a bad idea, being seen together somewhere like this—' he started.

'No one's paying attention,' said Una dully. 'Delir can go back.'

He'd shut his eyes, but he opened them again because he could feel her still looking at him – staring in the sad, unblinking, unapologetic way an animal might stare.

Varius a little unsettled, managed a laugh. 'Well, don't look at me like that. It's a nuisance, that's all.'

Abruptly a tear slipped down Una's face.

'Oh . . .' he said, distressed, 'oh don't—'

Una looked away, her expression unchanging. At last she bent to him and whispered, 'Lal talked to Zhu Li's office.' There was a catch in her voice, as if this were bad news. 'One of the codes you tried before, it worked.'

Varius smiled wearily. 'There. I knew it.'

'They thought she was someone playing a prank.'

'He'll listen to me. I'll talk to him tomorrow.'

'Maybe we won't be able to get through again,' Una said, almost despairingly.

Varius sighed, and let his eyes fall shut. 'We'll manage something.'

Sulien was sitting slumped on the hot asphalt in the shade of a truck, leaning against the heavy tyre. He'd been up since dawn; extracting the cohort from the school had been far more complicated and tiring than he would ever have expected. Now they were assembled at the airbase to the west of the city, waiting while the rest of the cohorts rolled in. Some of the Roman troops were stationed here in the barracks the Nionians had once used; they were still loading pallets of bags and equipment into their vehicles. Sometimes Sulien scanned the sky nervously, but the base was bristling with batteries of guns, so he supposed they could fend off anything short of a missile strike. Besides, everything had been almost uncannily quiet for days. Pas was lying nearby on a bed of packing crates. The fourth centuria sprawled wherever they could, flattened with fatigue, waiting for the signal to leave Aregaya at last.

'Lieutenant Archias,' called Gracilis, brandishing a map, and Sulien hurried over to where he stood with a pair of senior centurions from another cohort.

'Sixth Arcansan, slowing everything down . . . always the same,' Gracilis complained quietly, surveying the movement of troops and vehicles. 'No point in you sitting around looking decorative. You may as well take your centuria on ahead as far as—' He looked at the map.

'Shiomura,' supplied one of the other centurions, pronouncing the Nionian syllables accurately, though with slow, mistrustful care.

'Shiomura. Make sure the way's as clear as it looks. There's a side-road running more or less parallel, starting here' – he pointed – 'split up at the junction and cover both. But get out and come back if you encounter anything serious. We'll need to know.'

Sulien suppressed a resentful grimace. Go and see how many of you get blown up, he translated silently. He said, 'Yes, sir.'

Gracilis smiled. 'Don't look so worried, Lieutenant. All the air reports say it's empty out there. You'll only be double-checking.'

'Yes, sir.'

Gracilis nodded, and let out another quiet sigh, 'Look at that, Lieutenant,' he murmured.

Sulien followed his gaze towards a hangar on the corner of the field, and the thing emerging from it. It was a large vehicle, about the length of a train carriage, escorted by a squad of soldiers as it rolled forward slowly on the concrete and stopped, forty yards off. On its back it carried a heavy, complex structure, a miniature fortress all dark metal battlements and towers, and mounted above the mass of cylinders and rails was a long, narrow cone made up of smooth, overlapping plates. A pair of specialists swung up onto a small platform behind the cab of the vehicle, beneath the length of the cone, and began to work. Sulien was just close enough to see the panel of controls, where they seemed to be entering figures into small screens, adjusting dials. As they did so, the cone lifted smoothly from its bed, tilted and swivelled, and the round opening turned from point to point in space.

Sulien sucked in a breath, and his skin crept; there was something horrible about that movement. It was as if the thing were a living creature, sniffing the air, searching for something. He supposed it could not go off by accident, and yet it felt reckless, letting it out among so many people. He wished he hadn't seen it, that Gracilis hadn't made him look, and yet the machine was compelling, and he couldn't turn his eyes away from it. And as he watched the cone flared open, like a mouth, or a bindweed blossom, and then it opened wider still, stretching into a shallow disc, like a warning crest around a lizard's neck.

'What is that, sir?'

One of the men at the controls did something and the shallow disc contracted again to a simple bore, almost like that of an ordinary cannon.

'That,' said Gracilis, 'is an expensive piece of crap that doesn't work properly.'

'Gracilis!' one of the other centurions reproached him. 'They've fixed it – it works now.'

'So we're told,' Gracilis answered dryly.

The cone settled back into place and the specialists, apparently satisfied, climbed down from the little platform. Sulien felt the tension leave his muscles now the thing was still. The soldiers waiting on the concrete unfolded a light steel cover over the device, and a dust-coloured tarpaulin over that, and now it looked like any other military truck – and yet not quite: it was a little too large, and the base and the heavy wheels were too solid, giving away the disproportionate weight.

'It's the Onager, isn't it?' said Sulien, because they'd all heard the rumours, and Marcus and Una had told him about it too, before the war. 'Does it . . . I heard some people saying it shakes everything apart like an earthquake, but then someone else said it doesn't touch buildings or equipment, just kills everything living, even through walls.'

'Either. Both. Makes you breakfast and gives you a hand-job,' said Gracilis. 'Supposedly if you set it to the right frequency it can do anything.'

'I can't see how something can kill people and leave everything else standing,' said Sulien.

'Well, it doesn't, that's the answer, isn't it? They've got another one out in the Promethean Sea, and that's as useless as this one.'

The younger of the two other centurions glanced anxiously at him. 'I'm not sure we should be talking so openly about this.'

'Why not?' said Gracilis. 'He's about to witness this momentous event, isn't he? The final proof this thing has any business anywhere outside a laboratory.'

'Don't you listen to him,' said the other centurion merrily to Sulien, 'that's what's going to win us the war.'

[XVI]

TWO DESERTS

A tired doctor dragged a few small shreds of metal out of Varius' back and cleaned and sutured the wounds. It took a long time, and Varius was surprised and slightly unnerved not to have to pay for it. It was part of the war effort now, a nurse explained; there were too many people wounded by bombs. It was disconcerting to have to be grateful to Drusus in any way.

The following day, after trying the code over and over again, he succeeded at last in reaching Zhu Li. He mildly enjoyed the drama of telling him, yes, it really was Caius Varius, and if his voice sounded a little rough it was only because he'd been blown up by Nionian bombs the night before.

Zhu Li was gratifyingly shocked. 'Terrible! Criminal!'

Varius smiled. 'But not entirely unprovoked. And Sina's at war with Rome too now, of course.'

'Yes,' said Zhu Li with heavy regret, 'it's all a kind of madness.'

'It's as Nionia's ally you can help us now.'

With some reluctance, because it went against all his instincts now, he told Zhu Li where they were, and that Noriko was hidden in a house on the edge of the desert outside Antipyrgos. 'I know the cables are being cut, Grand Preceptor,' he said, 'but I am sure the Nionians still have means of communicating across the lines. If the Empress is willing to pass this information to them, we can arrange a time and a place to convey the Princess to their agents. All we would ask is for an audience with her brother.'

That night, after many weeks when the news programmes had been too obsessed with Roman victories in Alodia or in the Promethean Sea even to mention him, there was an hour-long longvision feature about him. It went back even beyond his childhood, delving into the lives of his parents and grandparents, trying, the sombre presenter said, to trace the beginnings of his slide from apparent respectability into treason. It never speculated where he might be now, but it spent a good ten minutes discussing his family's roots in Egypt. There were pictures of him at every stage of his life.

Varius tried to be contemptuously amused by this, but in truth found it disturbing and painful: so many of those pictures must have been confiscated from his parents. And all the time, beneath the cushiony relief of the painkillers, he could feel the ache seeping from his back and all through his body. At first he tried to believe the antibiotics he'd been given were simply taking their time, but three days later he was shivering in the heat of an Egyptian August, and the wounds remained raw and swollen around the stitches.

Una gritted her teeth. 'You're not well. And those pills aren't doing anything.'

'I can't go to a hospital – not that one, anyway,' said Varius raggedly, 'not after that thing on the longvision.'

'No one recognised you – either of us. I'm sure of it.'

'There were cameras there. If we go back someone might remember.'

He and Una were still camping out in the meagre spare space above and around the printing shop. They would have been back on the *Ananke* and heading along the coast towards Noriko by now, if not for his injuries. There was no room and no time for him to be ill.

But Delir was used to acquiring black market medicine. He began a hasty round of calls and within hours he came up with a packet of pills. And these worked fast: Varius was markedly better the following morning, and the red seams across his back finally began to fade.

After another day he was convinced he was well enough to return to the *Ananke*. The others tried to talk him out of it, but Varius insisted. Tamiathis felt as dirty and stifling to him now as

406

that hospital, and he was impatient to be out of it. At last Delir drove Varius and Una along the spit of land separating the lagoons from the open sea and they walked to the beach where the *Ananke* was hidden.

There was scarcely a breath of wind, but the salt spray cooled the air as they sailed west, rounding the curve of the delta. At first the clean, blue space was as welcome as Varius had expected, but to his annoyance he found he'd recovered less of his strength than he'd thought, and though steering alongside this unchanging stretch of beach was simple enough, still his head began to ache after a couple of hours and he had to give up the controls to Una much sooner than he expected. Even then, with little to do except keep things tidy and check the radio from time to time, he was conscious of the continual effort of adjusting his balance to the movement of the waves. He sat down and started trying to make a list of things they needed to do, but then without noticing himself do it, he laid down the pen and let his head rest against the window, and soon he was asleep on the padded seats inside the cockpit.

Una glanced at him with a small pang of worry. She turned the engine to neutral and came closer, wondering if it had been a mistake for him to leave the town, trying to search for signs of fever without touching him.

But he was simply deeply asleep, and the wounds must be healing well if he could lie so easily on his back. Relieved, Una sat down on the bench opposite and marvelled, with a rush of affection for him, that he could sleep like that, his body so straight and composed and yet unguarded, open. He had not even turned his head, or raised a hand to hide himself from the daylight – almost like a corpse laid out on a bier, although she flinched away from that thought.

He looked younger when he was asleep, and more trusting, the curve of his eyelids clear and unbroken; the anxious lines on his forehead softened to nothing. She wondered if it was possible he could ever look so peaceful when he was awake, and hoped for him that it was. But she decided that even if it was not, the usual quiet tension that he carried had its own grace too.

His hands, she thought, were beautiful: the bones of each long wrist fine-planed under sandalwood-brown skin, like the neck of a musical instrument – a viol, or a sitar. The fingers, too, were long, narrow and square-cut, the fingertips slightly flared and tilted. His right hand lay open beside him, she wanted to run her own fingers over it, she wanted to lift it and carry it to her lips—

A small start ran through her. Swiftly, carefully, she cut the thought off there and discarded it. She would not allow herself to notice it, even to be shocked. She looked away from him.

But it was not so easy to expunge the faint trembling in her body, the rawness in her throat and behind her eyes. She stalked out onto the deck and stared at the sea until it faded.

Then she lowered the anchor and began rather noisily preparing lunch, and Varius stirred and looked up at her. He gave her a drowsy smile, and Una blinked stupidly as if a shaft of light reflecting off a windowpane had flashed across her eyes. He said, 'Sorry.'

'Why?' said Una, her voice involuntarily brusque.

'Falling asleep in the middle of the day.'

'You're tired,' said Una, grimly. 'We're all tired.'

The Battle of Yokusawa scarcely happened. Roman volucers had been bombing and strafing Nionian positions in the hills above the little oasis town for two days, but when the first Roman attack units approached, they met only a few ragged remnants of the heavy resistance they had expected, and they were already retreating. Sulien's cohort never even fired their guns.

They roamed abandoned artillery positions in the scrubby hills, and later wandered down into the town they had expected to have to fight so hard for. The quiet had a flat, stale quality; it felt many days old, even before they saw or smelled the unfinished meals still lying rotting on tables. The townspeople must have hurriedly bundled what they could into cars or wagons; cupboards stood open and empty in shops and kitchens.

But nothing had been boarded up; many of the buildings were not even locked. The soldiers moved lightly at first, afraid of grenades on tripwires or mines, but there was nothing. Even the hundreds of Roman soldiers exploring the streets didn't seem enough to disturb the silence that had floated out of the desert and claimed the place, any more than shaking a corpse was enough to bring it to life. A gaunt dog limped across the street and flopped down in the shade, too weak and tired to be interested in the swarming strangers. A very young soldier crouched and patted it.

'Well, look at us, all still alive,' said Dorion, opening a cupboard in a kitchen with the mild hope of finding something alcoholic. 'I vote we do the rest of the war like this.'

'This is weird,' said Sulien, looking at the veil of sand that had already blown in over the floors. 'It's just like Shiomura.'

He had been surprised to find the roads out of Aregaya just as empty and undefended as Gracilis had said they would be, and they had seen no one at the little village on the edge of the salt flats either. But this desertion was larger, stranger. It made his skin itch with distrust.

'You can't blame them if they don't want to do another Aregaya,' replied Dorion. 'I don't either.'

Sulien grimaced and went outside, and he spent half an hour looking for Gracilis.

He found him at the town's small fire station, watching as some of the men of his century filled up a water carrier vehicle from the pump.

'Sir,' he said, 'what is this?' Confusion and unease made it come out blunter than he'd meant.

Gracilis turned, eyebrows just perceptibly raised. 'What do you mean?'

'I mean, where are the Nionians? Why didn't they try to hold us back?'

'We're getting reports that they're regrouping about twenty miles to the north-east,' said Gracilis. 'Most likely the Sixth Arcansan and some of the Novian Ironclad will swing round and try and hit their flank. We'll be advancing after them in the morning.' He smiled unhappily. The flesh beneath his eyes was sagging, greyish. Sulien wondered if he ever slept. 'I'm sure we will see them sooner than we'd like.'

'But why are they retreating?' persisted Sulien. 'They were up in the mountains – we're coming in across the plain – even if they're outnumbered, they should have been able to cut strips off us.'

'It could be they've decided to give up on Mohavia for now – pull their troops out to the north or west. Thule will matter more in the long run, even more than the capital here.'

Sulien managed not to sigh in frustration. 'But sir, what if it's not that? Are we sure they're not . . . leading us somewhere?'

Gracilis did sigh. 'Look,' he said, meeting Sulien's eyes at last, 'is that a possible interpretation of events? Yes, it is, and yes, it's occurred to me too. So what do you want me to do? Tell the Primus Pilus? I already have. But we're one cohort, and there are thousands of us down here on the ground, every one of us with our own ideas about what's going on. Our orders are clear: we are to keep chasing the Nionians. If it is a trap, well, by the time anyone listens to us, it'll be too late.' He sighed again. 'You might as well accept that.'

Sulien opened his mouth, and realised he had no way to argue. He nodded. 'Yes, sir.'

The covered bulk of the Onager had been pulled into the fire station, to hide it from the air. Sulien felt that deep shudder of aversion again. Every time he glimpsed it, or thought of it, little tendrils of panic started to creep through him. He found himself constantly daydreaming of good reasons to get his men away from the thing. If it worked, if they were going to use it, then he wanted to be elsewhere.

There were a few brief skirmishes the following day, and after that, the Nionians melted away in the desert sun like morning mist.

The heat was crushing. The red hills shimmered and crackled with it. The Roman army advanced on, into silence.

They anchored the *Ananke* in a narrow cove between steep ramparts of white scree. Una and Varius followed the twist of the valley back from the sea, looking for a way up.

'Let me see the map again,' said Varius. 'I'm not sure this is the right place.'

'It is,' said Una, and stopped, pointing up towards nothing Varius could see. She was smiling. 'There's Noriko.'

A young woman wearing sandals and loose trousers rolled up to the knee, her dark hair caught back in a rough ponytail, mounted the ridge. She saw them and came running down across the dunes, beaming.

She skidded recklessly over the last few feet of gravel and caught Una's hands. 'If I could have known when I saw you last! Or even a month ago! That we would both be free!' she cried. 'Oh, I am so happy to see you.'

Una laughed with her, though for a moment the laughter seemed to hitch its way over sobs as they both remembered, but then it steadied again.

Noriko turned to Varius, grinned, and dipped her head forward in a cheerful bow. 'Diodorus Cleomenes asked me to tell you he hopes you are doing nothing particularly stupid.'

'I don't know why he always thinks *I'm* the one who does stupid things,' Varius complained mildly. He was still marvelling at how different she was. Unprotected by screens and parasols, Noriko had, for the first time in her life, a pink daubing of sunburn across her nose and cheekbones, and there were even streaks of dark auburn scorched into her hair. 'Your Highness – I would hardly have recognised you.'

Noriko's face dropped, settled into a look of dignified resignation. 'I am very changed,' she agreed gravely.

'But not for the worse— I mean, I'm sorry—' began Varius, but by now they had reached the cliff top and were heading towards a thin, sandy road where a dusty truck was waiting.

'We will *drive* you to the house,' Noriko said proudly.

Another woman with dark, close-cropped hair was standing

beside the vehicle. 'We've both been learning,' she said diffidently. 'And it's all flat from here.'

'This is Maralah,' said Noriko, 'and she has come all this way to join you. She is very eager, very brave.'

Maralah nodded with restrained vehemence, staring at them hungrily. 'I'll do anything,' she said.

A little warily, Varius and Una climbed into the truck, and Noriko jolted them awkwardly along the road. They could see an aqueduct snaking across the landscape ahead, sharp and white against the sky in the hard light, leading off towards the thick white towers of steam from a desalination plant on the horizon.

'Is it safe for you to be out here?' asked Varius.

'We don't go into the town, or out on the fishing boat – only Maralah can,' said Noriko, 'but driving around a little here where it is so empty, yes – we think so.'

Driving, Noriko considered, was really much easier than she had once imagined. She pushed along cautiously, very careful not to go too fast. She caught her reflection in one of the mirrors above the windscreen and saw that she was frowning studiously against the bright glare. She forced her forehead smooth at once, to avoid wrinkles.

She was unsurprised Varius thought her almost unrecognisable. She was not wholly reconciled to her new appearance. She often thought of Makaria, also an Emperor's daughter, and more weatherbeaten and wild-haired than Noriko was even now, but still, part of her continued to lament that she would never truly look like a Nionian princess again, that her life would always be marked by what had happened. And yet she liked to look at herself, liked to notice the swishing shadow of her tangled hair as she ran across the sand. Sometimes the idea that the court at home would be shocked at the sight of her was perversely satisfying. Even when she was morosely convinced she looked like a peasant, she no longer feared being laughed at, or pitied. She had struggled her way out and brought Tomoe and Sakura with her and she had proof. It was like having a scar.

Evadne would not be home yet; she worked across the bay

at the desalination plant. Her little house was a square, stark white block on the cliff top, its shabbiness bleached away in the downpour of sunlight. There was a garden beside it planted with onions and melons, and a sapling date palm. Tomoe was weeding while Sakura sat in the shade of the house, a radio on the step beside her. Noriko glanced at the garden with pride, because they had worked on it every day for the past week and in even that short time they had made it larger and better. There were still limits to where they could safely go and what they could do, but they had been able to do that, and Evadne might make a little extra money selling some of the produce next year, if she was still there.

Noriko's smile faded a little, as she considered everything that might prevent that. Every morning and evening Evadne crossed the bay in a little boat, part of the secret navy, whose battered flagship Una and Varius had just sailed into the cove.

'Evadne says you're almost ready – you almost have enough people,' whispered Maralah to Una and Varius.

'More than I hoped for,' said Una. 'We still have to find out if it's enough.'

They could scarcely all fit into the little house, so they gathered in the shade outside with Sakura, listening to the radio.

'The warships responsible for the recent attacks on the Eternal City of Rome have been sunk in the Mediterranean, the Department of Information revealed today,' said a stern male voice. 'A spokesman for the Emperor praised the resilience of the citizens of Rome and urged them to remain steadfast. We will not be cowed . . .'

The mood of cheerful reunion evaporated. Una watched Varius, who was leaning against the whitewashed wall, his face set in that look of neutral attention that she knew was just as likely to indicate dread as real calm. Sometimes she could feel them both thinking the same things, even though she tried not to.

There had been rumours for weeks that Nionian ships had finally broken in the through the Strait of Gaditanum, that hovercraft were skimming north across the Petraean Peninsula, that a submarine had made it through the Pharaonic Canal. They never trusted the news until someone they knew confirmed it, but it was probably true that the ships had been destroyed – they wouldn't last long in the Mediterranean, even now. The strikes could not have been that heavy, not compared with what Alexandria had endured, but bombs were finally falling on Rome. Varius' parents were there, he hadn't seen or spoken to them in more than a year.

'Has anyone heard,' asked Varius, 'which areas of Rome . . . ?'

Tomoe looked up. 'They say Janiculum, Vatican, Aventine.'

Varius sighed.

'We can call Cleomenes,' Una murmured to him. 'He'll be able to find out about your family.'

'If he's alive himself,' said Varius flatly.

They could not call him yet; they were waiting for Delir to call with instructions from the Nionians, or for contact from the Nionian agents themselves.

'I wonder,' said Noriko in a low, reluctant voice, 'if the reason this is happening now . . . If, as long as my brother knew I was in Rome . . .'

She was guiltily hoping someone would contradict the idea, but Una only gave her a bleak look and said, 'We need to see him.'

Evadne arrived and distracted them from the longdictor and the radio, lifting the despondent atmosphere. She had been a housekeeper to a wealthy family in Sabratha, freed as she reached the end of her childbearing years, with a fairly generous gift of money, but her four children were still slaves. One girl was still serving the same family; she didn't know where the others were.

Nevertheless she was firmly, purposefully cheerful. 'I saw your yacht in the cove,' she said to Una and Varius. 'Almost time now.'

She began cooking, with Noriko helping, her eyes streaming

as she clumsily, doggedly, chopped an onion. Evadne opened a drawer and twitched aside a cloth to show a gun lying among the spoons. 'I have been teaching Maralah this too.'

Maralah nodded fiercely again. 'I know there might not be much time left,' she said, 'but I will be ready, I promise.'

'I think you're ready,' said Una, carefully. 'You matter much more than the gun.'

Maralah did not smile, she never did, but her eyes widened a little and a gratified quiver ran over her face.

'She'll be fine,' said Evadne, covering the gun again and patting Maralah's arm. She grinned at Varius. 'Look at this place: six women and just you! I should have brought Thraso and Elius, but we would all be sitting in each other's laps. How outnumbered you must feel.'

'It's tough,' agreed Varius, smiling.

They were crammed in wherever they could find space to sit down, eating the spicy vegetable stew, when at last the long-dictor sounded. Varius was closest, and snatched up the circlet. 'Is this a bad time to call?' inquired a tense, faintly accented voice.

They'd suggested the code and countersign to Zhu Li. 'Not bad, just late,' Varius replied.

'Let me speak to the Princess at once,' demanded the voice fiercely.

'We haven't kidnapped her,' said Varius, a little irritated.

He handed the longdictor to Noriko, who hastily finished her mouthful before answering in Nionian.

Una and Varius waited, tense, unable to understand what was being said. Noriko gestured for a pen and paper and Evadne seemed to rummage through every drawer and box in the tiny house, trying to find them for her.

Noriko anxiously twisted a strand of her tangled hair as she talked, until at last she switched off the longdictor and showed the set of coordinates she'd taken down. 'Here,' she said, 'to-morrow night. They say it is past a town called Pharusium and then away from the road into the desert. They will find us there;

they have a hidden volucer to take us across the lines.' Her face brightened in slow, incredulous happiness. 'My brothers are waiting,' she said softly.

'That's a long way,' said Evadne as Varius cleared a space among the dishes to unfold the map. 'The girls'll have to pass as slaves again.'

Una knew that would have to mean her too; it was better, if they had to explain themselves, that they fitted into two distinct categories. Evadne would have to accompany them into the Libyan desert; she and Varius could be business partners transporting four slave girls. She nodded. It was only one day, and they might well not be stopped at all; certainly no elaborate pretence would be required.

It was strange to think it how long it had been since she had actually been owned by anyone. She glanced at Maralah, for whom it had been just over a fortnight, the exultation and rage and numbness still raw. She could hardly believe that five years of freedom, however limited and fragile, separated them. Five years was not enough time to get used to it, she thought. Her own freedwoman's rights had been taken away, and she had been unsurprised. But in the possible world that lay beyond Drusus, beyond the end of the war . . . She caught Maralah's eye, and smiled at her.

And yet the journey ahead frightened her. Partly it was the thought of the desert itself – the heat here at its northern edge, by the sea, was at the limit of what she could stand, and it was late August, and Pharusium was more than three hundred miles further south. But it was also that Maralah was right, Evadne was right: it was almost time, and this drive into the heat was the beginning of the attempt, and they were doing it without Sulien.

'You will come back, won't you?' Maralah asked her, suddenly, quietly. 'You won't leave us – you won't go off and live in Nionia or somewhere?'

'Of course I'll come back,' Una said, taken aback. 'Well— I can't promise we won't get caught on the road, or shot down over Nubia, but if I'm alive I'll come back.'

Maralah nodded, but her eyes slid away. 'You've got friends on their side – the princess. And after everything – the arena, and everything – I could imagine you might just want to be safe.'

'I won't. We won't,' said Una, a little concerned that she had allowed herself to look too tired, too afraid or weak. She lifted her head, setting her jaw.

Varius managed to get a call through to Cleomenes. He and his family were safe, and he promised that he'd check on Varius' parents – but it might take a day or two for the answer to come back, and they couldn't wait.

Varius sat in silence by the longdictor for a while. Then he sighed and looked across the map at Una. 'Well, what do you think? Get off the road and sneak across the border, or bluff it out at the crossing?'

'Your stitches have to come out before we go anywhere,' Una said sharply.

Varius was a little startled. 'Oh. I suppose so. I hadn't thought about that.'

Una folded her lips. She had known it was more on her mind than his, and felt a small glow of annoyance with him. It was a perversely comforting, straightforward feeling. 'No. You hadn't. And they should have come out yesterday or the day before, really.'

If he'd thought of it himself, he might have asked Evadne to do it, but now it would have to be her. Delir should have come, she thought. He could have done it. Sulien should be here, and then it wouldn't need doing at all.

'Let's get it over with then,' she said impatiently.

'The light's best outside,' said Evadne as she poured boiling water over the smallest pair of scissors she had.

Una looked away for a second while Varius pulled off his tunic and sat down, and then she shook her head at herself and dragged up another stool behind him.

Noriko hovered, looking over Una's shoulder at the wounds, sombre. 'I didn't know you were hurt,' she said.

Varius looked up in an attempt at a shrug that ended in a wince, as Una made the first snip and pulled at the threads. 'It's nothing bad.'

'But that was a bomb?'

Varius nodded – then tried to hold back a growl as another thread snagged as it pulled through the skin. Una murmured 'Sorry,' and laid a concerned hand flat on his bare shoulder. She lifted it away as soon as she realised she'd done it, but a jarring charge of unwanted happiness had already run along her nerves at the contact of his skin against hers. She gritted her teeth and went back to work with even greater care, though she was already working so delicately that she had to stifle little tremors of effort in her hands.

Noriko went back inside, not wanting to disturb Una, and as she found a quicker, surer rhythm, the rest of the first line of stitches came out more easily, Varius scarcely flinched and Una relaxed slightly. Neither of them spoke. But even though she touched him as sparingly as she could, still her fingertips picked up little specks of feeling, like motes of dust drifting through a shaft of light. She could almost persuade herself it was just a chance tangle of friendship and loss and the memory of the hours he'd been missing in Tamiathis . . .

She moved the scissors to the longer, twisted seam at the base of his ribs, where the little dark knots were cruder and deeper. Varius drew a breath through his teeth and she could feel him tensing against each tug. A little blood trickled over his skin, distressing her more than even she thought was reasonable.

'It's all right,' said Varius, because she'd stopped. His voice was only a little roughened. 'You're doing fine.'

But it wasn't right, she thought. He turned his head to smile at her, and she looked back, stinging with strange helplessness, the scissors hanging loose in her hand. The sun was low in the sky now, but still raking hot gold light across the cliffs, skimming and trembling through Evadne's garden, breaking into slices of bright and dark in the fronds of the date palm, and all the light seemed to curve and gather round him, concentric to him. He was the one real, stable thing left. But he was bleeding, and another swell of chaos might carry him away from her at any moment.

'Do you want me to take over?' asked Evadne, watching from the doorway.

Una rose to her feet. 'Yes.'

'Why do we always get these jobs?' complained Dorion. 'Running out into the middle of nowhere on our own.'

'Because he asks for them,' Pas answered.

'You hate us, do you, Archias? You want us to suffer?' said Dorion dolefully. 'Sir,' he corrected himself.

'Hate you? After all I do for you?' Sulien said. And it was true, he was doing this for them: for at least a day they were away from the Onager, no longer part of the current carrying the Roman Army north. Ahead of their advance the bulk of the Nionian forces continued to melt back into the hills, leaving empty mining towns and deserted farms behind them, while small, agile assault teams goaded the Romans' western flank, prodding them eastwards, and volleys of gunfire lashed at their volucers from the mountains that divided Enkono from Sorasan-myaku. There was something up there, the air reports said, a radio post hidden among the trees, directing attacks.

Sulien had volunteered to take his men and try to find the place as soon as he heard about it. Aesius, the cohort commander, had said, 'It's not worth detaching a whole centuria.'

'Sir,' Sulien had replied grimly, 'we're *not* a whole centuria.' They were down to forty-three men now, after Astylus and Nelius had been killed in an ambush, and Merenda had been invalided back to Aregaya. Sulien still had nightmares – not unusual; now someone had to be thumped awake to stop him shouting whenever they managed to sleep – but he didn't know when he'd stopped seeing the hounds, or Una dead; his dreams were full of the same explosions and blown-off limbs as everyone else's.

But for now they were riding back a few miles towards Aregaya along the road they'd already taken, and then turning down towards the mountains. The heat-clogged air was as dense as ever, but Sulien was sitting on the outside of the truck, where the speed whipped up a little dry breeze. They passed a few bodies in a crater, untended crops withering under dry irrigation wheels, a roadside tea-house with its shutters smashed. But by the time they were a mile clear of the Onager he felt relief rise through him and the vast space around them began to feel comforting rather than intimidating. He felt both the Romans and the Nionians might forget their little group of vehicles altogether; surely there was enough bristly red ground and blue sky here to hide them from anyone's notice. There were green woods up in the mountains, above the reach of the desert. He wished there were somewhere like Holzarta waiting up there, a hiding place he could take the fourth centuria to escape.

'What's that?' said Caerellius suddenly, and Sulien stiffened, looking ahead for whatever Caerellius had seen or heard. But he could see nothing, and Caerellius just stared straight ahead, his mouth tight with disgust, his nostrils flaring.

Then Sulien caught the smell too; it washed across the little convoy and the whole centuria knew, at almost the same instant, what they were going to find on this road. It was the smell that pervaded Aregaya, but here it was stronger, more sustained, and it grew with every breath and with every turn of the wheels beneath them. They looked at each other.

'Oh, *shit*,' whispered Dorion.

They saw cars motionless on the road ahead, as if they were just running into a very long tailback of traffic, from roadworks, or an accident.

A sour eddy of the smell made Pas gag. Sulien tied a cloth around his own nose and mouth. Others were already doing the same: it was more of a ritual gesture than a practical one; it didn't really keep much of the smell out, but it was something between them and what they were approaching. The drivers of the trucks needed no command from Sulien to move faster, they accelerated, compelled by awful curiosity. They knew what they had found, and they could not go on without seeing it.

A little closer, and they could see how many cars had swerved off the road or collided; others were neatly spaced on the asphalt, their doors standing open.

Sulien shouted for the drivers to halt when he saw the first bodies. They were face down, their limbs sprawled as if they had been running back this way when they were overtaken. There were more lying in the scorched grass on either side of the road, curled up or clinging to each other. Black hair fluttered in the hot breeze.

Sulien swung down from the truck and walked a little way along the road, one hand pressed to his face, treading softly, as if afraid of breaking the silence here.

He tried to keep his eyes half focused, to skim his gaze across the road, not settling. If he looked any closer, he knew he would start to pick out the children. The sun had dried flesh to darkened leather – was that what had dragged open so many mouths, or had they died that way, lips straining for air, or screaming? They lay half-fallen from the cars from which they'd tried to scramble free, or huddled underneath them, or slumped inside. There was a pale trail of powdery residue over everything, metal and asphalt and clothing and hair.

'No one touch anything!' Sulien called out.

But no one had thought of touching anything; they picked their way among the cars silently, for as long as they could before the smell set solid like concrete and held them back. The queue of dead extended as far along the road ahead as they could see.

Sulien tried to silence the part of his mind that handled numbers, tried not to guess a figure beyond 'many', but despite himself he knew that it was thousands. And he thought he knew where they'd come from: the vehicles were loaded high with cases, bundles, unsorted heaps of cooking pots, bedding, books, and some of it had come tumbling from roof-racks across the road. The things that belonged in the empty cupboards of Aregaya.

'Maybe they did it themselves,' suggested Dorion tentatively.

'What?' asked Sulien, dully incredulous.

'I mean, the Nionians, for some kind of . . . to make it look like . . . I mean, maybe it wasn't us,' explained Dorion, stammering slightly.

Sulien blinked, and saw the red gaping mouths of the arena hounds. He saw the cross. Rage washed through him. 'You think we wouldn't do this?' he demanded. 'You think Romans wouldn't? Where the hell have you been living, Dorion? Because I wish I could go there.'

'Don't yell at me,' said Dorion, visibly shaking, 'I never fucking wanted to come here.' His voice broke, and he raised his hands to his eyes.

Sulien sighed. He was trembling too. He put his hand on Dorion's shoulder.

'What the fuck do we do?' whispered Pas.

But there was nothing they could do. There were so many dead and so few of them that they couldn't have begun to start burying them, even if they had dared to touch the poison that coated them. Sulien wanted some gesture of apology or respect, *something*, but even if he could have thought of anything, it would have turned obscene as they performed it, he knew that.

So they limped back to their trucks and carried on, rolling off the road in a long detour that took them miles further from the Roman lines than had been planned. The smell of the road chased them all the way to the mountains.

'I've never been alone in a house before,' said Maralah, standing in the doorway of the tiny white building on the cliff, the key in her hand. She looked at once fragile and dangerous, with her set, pale face and unblinking eyes.

Evadne rumpled her stubbly head fondly. 'You'll do all right. Just be careful with the stove. And don't shoot anyone unless you're sure you have to.'

Noriko hugged her, and Maralah clung to her with sudden fierceness. Then, with a long, keen look at Una, she drew inside.

Una, Noriko, Sakura and Tomoe were dressed in the flimsy, revealing clothes Cominia had provided, with cheap plastic jewellery bright at their wrists and ears. The fluttery blue sundress Una was wearing reminded her of the star-printed dress she'd worn the day of her escape, five years before. A sheer pink scarf veiled the worst of the scars on her shoulders and arms. The women eyed each other in resigned self-consciousness. Sakura kept trying to tug the little skirt she was wearing lower. Una's lips were set in a familiar, stubborn line. But she avoided looking at Varius.

The truck was oven-like from the moment they climbed into it, and the thin tar-fibre dresses melded damply to the seats and their skin almost at once.

Varius took the controls of the car first, with Evadne beside him. His back had been painful all morning, but he assumed that was the price of having the stitches out late and unanaesthetised, and he expected it to fade. They lumbered along the gravelly track from the house onto the road towards Antipyrgos, following the course of the aqueduct as it marched across the land. Broad green bands of farmland striped the desert where pipes and channels carried the water down to the fields of lentils, beans and flax.

They barely spoke as the dry air rasped past the car, sitting listless with heat. Varius felt it gnaw at the flesh of his back, pool in his joints, sting his eyes. His heart began to flutter and tug in his chest as the arches of the aqueduct repeated monotonously alongside the truck; if it hadn't been for the other traffic he would almost have wondered if they were moving at all.

'Varius,' said Una, her voice thin and taut.

'What?' Varius mumbled.

'You have to stop the car.'

Varius had been driving mindlessly, too lost in the heat and the pain to notice either. He pulled over in a sandy lay-by and dragged himself out. He felt baffled by the rush of nausea that came on as he took a few steps into the breathless air, but he swallowed down most of a bottle of water and it faded. The truck was too hot to touch, but he leant against it anyway. In the sunlight the other cars blazed like comets on the road, the air melting around them.

'Maybe we should turn back,' said Evadne, examining him, touching his forehead, 'leave you with Maralah.'

'Mmm.' He didn't have a strong opinion either way: the thought of going back to the little house and lying down in the shade was tantalising, but it would be a long, uncomfortable drive now whatever they decided.

'No,' said Una fiercely, 'you're staying with me. You're coming. They'll have doctors there.'

Varius rubbed his eyes and tried to shake himself out of his sluggishness. How could he care so little about the end to so much work and danger? 'I have to be there to see Tadahito,' he said. He climbed heavily into the passenger seat beside Evadne and closed his eyes.

There had been too little time to scout for a safe place to slip illicitly across the border between Tripolitania and Libya, and they would have lost time getting back to the main road anyway. They joined a long queue at the crossing south of Theon Limen, where ranks of stationary vehicles were stranded on the asphalt.

In the back, Tomoe passed around mirrors and cosmetics and the women began silently applying bright, heavy paint to their faces. Una joined in, painting a scarlet layer of disguise onto her lips. It was too hot to do it before the moment it was necessary.

At last they rolled up to the gate and a border guard peered at the papers Evadne handed him. From the back seat Una concentrated on him, readying herself to try to push his attention away from them if necessary, but he was bored and slow in the heat, with sweat dark under his arms and shiny on his forehead. 'Your business in Libya?' he asked.

'We've got a buyer for these girls in Garama,' said Evadne breezily.

Una and the other girls huddled sullenly together in the back, their hair falling forward over their lurid faces, but the officer only glanced in at them.

He strolled around the truck to Varius' window, still studying his papers. 'I see you're of conscription age, sir. Do you have a statement of professional or medical exemption?'

'Yes,' said Varius, hauling himself upright and fumbling for the letter from the hospital in Tamiathis. The air was thick, and heavy as sand, and just lifting his hands from his lap cost an effort. 'I have a – a short-term deferment . . .'

'He isn't well,' said Evadne, and the officer peered at Varius, grunted, and to Varius' slight dismay said, 'Yeah, all right,' before he had even seen the letter.

He waved them through and Evadne drove on into Libya.

The farmland gave out as the highway rose on great pillars, wading deep into the pale sea of rolling dunes. The road skimmed a thousand feet above the desert floor, though in places the sand had climbed up hungrily towards it, drifting in steep, crescent-shaped ridges against the columns. Tank-like sand-ploughs crawled across these hills and valleys, and scoured the road itself, guarding the viaduct from the weight and flow of the desert.

There were broad, round bays at intervals along the highway where there were shops and charging stations. Two hundred miles into the desert, they stopped for Una to take over at the controls of the truck. Though she felt beaten with the heat, she was grateful for the chance to do something. She was so conscious of Varius, shifting restlessly in his seat, shivering, and she pushed over the speed limit, passing a cargo tram convoy with a container carrying a load of camels poking their gloomy heads through the bars. But otherwise the southbound carriageway was almost empty now. Most of the traffic was coming the other way, fleeing the advancing battle lines in Nubia and Gaetulia.

The sand turned amber as the sun began its descent, the sleepy human contours of the dunes sinking and smoothing out into an empty gold plain, scattered with dark rocks like lumps of ash which rose into pointed, charred black hills in the distance.

The highway soared eastwards towards Gaetulia, and Una led the truck spiralling down a junction, through Pharusium, then onto a road that was little more than a flattened, gritty channel in the sand.

The lack of any landmarks made Una anxious, especially now the sky was darkening; the road sometimes seemed as notional as a line of longitude on a map. And she was horrified when, after thirty miles, it thinned and disappeared altogether into miles of blank sand, even though the map had told her to expect it.

She drove uncertainly for a few hundred yards, then stopped the truck and began arguing with Evadne about the compass readings.

'Well – it's more or less over there,' said Evadne, gesturing.

'More or less isn't good enough,' insisted Una. She and Varius had learned to navigate together out on the sea, but Varius was slumped in heavy-eyed stupor against the window and the courses they had plotted had always been a few degrees away from perfect. Una had never quite understood what they were doing wrong, but it hadn't mattered too much on the Mediterranean, and she had never misjudged so badly as not to recognise the island or port they were searching for when it appeared, however unexpectedly, over the horizon. But out here it would take only a small error to lead them miles from the meeting place, and she had been calculating grimly what such a mistake might cost them for hours, even before she'd noticed the sharpening edge to Varius' breath.

'Let me see,' said Noriko, taking the compass, bending over the map. She worked sums under her breath. 'We are heading a little too sharply south,' she announced, confidently. 'True north and magnetic north – they are not the same; you must adjust. I think ten more miles south-southeast, past those hills.'

Una gazed at her in surprise, and Noriko shrugged and coloured a little. She murmured, 'My tutors at home . . .'

'What it is to have a royal education,' remarked Una, and looked away, sorry for the moment of veiled spite. But she was cut by the unexpected reminder of Marcus, and the funds of startling facts and skills he'd inherited along with his name, to spend as effortlessly as money. She had first resented and then loved all the things he had known, and now she found herself thinking miserably that Noriko and Marcus could have had a good marriage – she should have been more steadfast in keeping out of their way.

I'm not whoever I would have been if I hadn't met you, Marcus' voice interrupted fiercely in her memory. I love you, I only want you . . .

She let Noriko take over the controls, sat still beside Varius in the back. *You could have done that*, she told Marcus in her mind, as Noriko guided the truck carefully across the sand. *You'd have steered us right.*

Varius' skin was scalding where her hand brushed against his. She didn't know how the ache of Marcus' absence and Varius' closeness could both be so strong, without one cancelling out the other. She tried to clear both away.

Noriko drove them past a line of the dark hills, checked the compass again and stopped. The stretch of sand between the rock clusters was no different from any other; there was no landmark for other travellers to head towards.

They sprawled out of the truck. The air was still solid with heat, but at last there was a faint, scratchy breeze, and the sun was no longer scouring at their eyes and skin. Una stalked discontentedly around the vehicle and jumped up onto a spur of rock, trying to see further into the dark.

'Where are they?' she complained.

'We're early,' said Noriko soothingly.

Varius had lurched off among the ridges to vomit. He stumbled back and crashed down onto his side on the sand. There was a steady pressure of pain at his back, but he was so relieved he could lie down, and that the nausea had receded, that he thought he felt almost well, just loaded down with exhaustion. The stars were out now, huge and close. They seemed to rock softly in the air; sometimes Varius thought he could feel them lapping against the desert and against his skin, like water.

Evadne draped a wet cloth over his forehead, but it felt as warm as blood. Tomoe and Sakura were talking somewhere nearby.

427

Then Evadne was gone and Una was kneeling beside him, pressing another bottle of water into his hand. She murmured, 'Perhaps I did something wrong, pulling the stitches out.'

Varius shook his head. 'It's the same as before.' He put a hand, gingerly, to his back. There was a well of heat there, beneath the ribs. 'I think . . . they didn't clear everything out; whatever hit me, something went deeper, there's something still in there . . .'

He closed his eyes, and so missed the look on Una's face, but he felt her hand tighten and tremble on his. For the first time it occurred to him that she was afraid he was dying, and he dragged his eyelids open to look at her in surprise. 'It's all right, I'm not that bad,' he said, and fell into confused, weightless sleep.

Noriko had changed out of the skimpy dress into the loose trousers and sleeveless tunic she'd been wearing before. She watched Varius with sympathy, but she was, for now, incapable of real worry, and confident he would soon recover. She was too happy even to fear the flight across the front. She sat cross-legged on the sand, trying to comb the sand out of her hair and gloating silently at how soon she would see her brothers, almost humming their names aloud to herself.

Una glanced at her across their heaped belongings and felt another blunt scrape of envy and loneliness.

Suddenly the comparison occurred to Noriko too. She looked across at Una and asked, 'Is your brother in Tamiathis still?'

'No,' said Una, 'he's fighting the war.'

Noriko stared. 'No,' she said, as if the statement made no sense at all, or as if Sulien ought to have been able to explain his situation to somebody and claim an exemption. She lowered her eyes, sombre now. 'Of course. I am sorry. How could he avoid it? But it seems so . . . wrong.'

'Yes, it is,' agreed Una, quietly, drawing up her knees and wrapping her arms round them.

Noriko was silent, adding up the damage to Varius' back, the bombs falling on Rome, Sulien's absence.

'I'm sorry,' she repeated, at last.

'You've had no part in any of this,' Una said.

428

'I was supposed to have a part in stopping it,' said Noriko, sighing. 'No, I know Drusus began the war. Your brother would not be in danger if not for him. But we are the danger. Or part of it, at least.' She smiled sadly at Una. 'I will do anything I can to help.'

Varius woke later to find Una was shaking his arm, whispering urgently, 'They're here.'

Varius lifted his head with a groan and saw that Evadne and the truck were already gone, and two men were striding purposefully towards them. They were dressed in the light linen robes they'd seen as they drove through Pharusium, and Varius blinked in confusion when they bowed to Noriko and addressed her in Nionian. There was nothing he thought of as Nionian about their features, and they were both dark-skinned, the older of the two darker than Varius himself. From a distance, at least, they might have been taken for African, but close up, and having heard them speak, there was something about their features that was out of place here. It took a moment for him to realise that they were probably from Goshu or Palawa – one of Nionia's southern possessions.

The older man was conferring with Noriko, Sakura and Tomoe. Sakura had begun to cry a little with excitement and the last pangs of homesickness. The other agent came and bent over Varius, studying him.

'Can you walk?' he asked suddenly, in Latin, and Varius recognised his voice: this was the agent he had spoken to on the longdictor.

Varius rubbed at his face. The fine sand crept everywhere, into their hair, nostrils, tear-ducts, the whorls of their ears. He felt as if it had worked its way under his skin.

'Yes,' he said, and he tried, clumsily, to rise.

The man frowned and heaved him unceremoniously to his feet, slung Varius' arm over his shoulders and marched him off towards a gap in the rocky hills ahead. Once he was standing, Varius didn't believe he really needed the man's support, but he managed only a vague mumble of protest as the man hauled him along. And it did seem a very long walk across the sand, with Una pacing anxiously beside him, before they reached two camouflaged desert cars waiting for them in the shadow of the rocks. The Nionian women were escorted into the car ahead, and Varius worried hazily that he and Una would be left behind after all. But the pair of vehicles stayed close together, and Varius felt his throat tense with nausea again, and he forgot to think about it.

The Nionians' cars were more agile than Evadne's battered secondhand truck and skimmed very fast across the sand until they reached a shallow crater where a team of men were dragging the sand-coloured covers off a black volucer. It was a Roman military craft, and the men were dressed in Roman uniform, and for Varius the seasick sway of the world worsened when he heard them shouting to each other in Nionian.

Noriko and her ladies-in-waiting were already inside, dwarfed by armoured tabards and helmets. Tomoe sat drooping forward and covering her face, overwhelmed, while Sakura was still laughing and crying at once, and Noriko was turned towards the window, gazing out solemnly at the empty Roman sand.

There was armour for Varius and Una too, which Varius decided was not worth the effort of putting on. He collapsed onto a seat, once again almost paralysed with fatigue. But he'd barely shut his eyes before Una was grimly lifting his head and strapping the helmet on for him. 'It won't help, if anything hits us,' he protested wearily.

She scowled and pressed the breastplate against his chest. 'It would have helped if you'd been wearing something like that in Tamiathis.' Her palm rested for a moment over his heart.

The volucer rose in a cloud of sand and for almost an hour they flew through utter emptiness, the sky black and silent, the desert rippling in the starlight below them like the bland upper surface of clouds. Then, as they approached the triple border point of Libya, Egypt and Nubia, they began to hear the grind of other machines in the sky around them, and then a low stutter of anti-aircraft fire. Specks of fire scattered like gold coins across the earth and sky.

The volucer shook and plunged, the five passengers gasping and clutching at each other as a flash of cold light broke over them. In the cockpit the pilot shouted something in urgent Nionian into his radio and banked sharply.

Una pressed against the juddering window, watching the flarings of light in the dark, wondering if Sulien were somewhere down there, on the ground.

[XVII]

SURIJIN

The palace at Axum was armoured against the summer heat in heavy stone; the hall was shadowy and cool. The Roman frescoes of fighting Olympians had already been painted over with a bright mural of people in robes advancing solemnly around the walls, their hands uplifted, their faces framed in yellow haloes. Una looked up at an arch above the heavy doors at the back of the room, where a man approached a burning tree standing on a crag against a circle of clouds. She didn't know the story, but she thought she knew what it meant. 'Please,' she thought, gazing at it, her jaw tight with anticipation, as they waited for Tadahito.

The doors opened, and the Nionian princes appeared with the Ethiopian king.

The king wore military uniform, now: white and gold, in contrast to Drusus' black. But Tadahito had never adopted it, although he'd been far closer to the front line than Drusus ever had. He was more simply dressed than when Una and Varius had seen him in Sina, but he was still elegant, the long patterned sleeves of his pale linen tunic tied back from his forearms, gold silk braid knotted over the sash at his waist. Noriko hesitated for a moment, staring at her brother across the length of the hall, conscious of her dusty clothes, her hair.

'Noriko!' said Kaneharu, his voice high and loud with simple delight, like a child's.

Then Tadahito gave a choking cry and rushed forwards to wrap her in his arms, and they staggered together, both weeping.

Una smiled for Noriko's sake, but wanly. The scenes of Sulien's safe return that were forever trying to play themselves in her imagination always chilled her – he stepped through some door, off a train, but he came stained in emptiness that stayed on her like ink after the daydream ended. It was hard work, suppressing these dangerous little plays in her head, it couldn't be sustained with one of them acted out in front of her.

Noriko stumbled from Tadahito's arms to Kaneharu, and then Takanari. Kaneharu swung her off the floor, laughing, but for a moment Tadahito sobbed, making no attempt to restrain or disguise it. Then he wiped his eyes, and looked at Una and Varius. 'Thank you,' he said, and managed to pull a temporary scrap of formality across his face. 'I know we need to talk; please allow us just a little time.'

He hurried away with his brothers and sister through the doors.

Varius looked at Una, murmured, 'It might be less than a month – it might be days, before we bring him back.'

Una smiled again, unevenly, and wondered how much rested on this meeting.

King Salomon examined Una and Varius curiously, and Varius panted, 'Your Majesty,' and bowed shallowly, afraid of losing his balance or provoking the pain skulking in his muscles.

'You are Varius Ischyrion and Noviana Una?' Salomon asked. 'You were both part of Leo the Younger's circle.'

Una could tell that this comment, where it included her, carried a subtle load of prurient disapproval, but Salomon was at least gracious enough to try to disguise it.

'He is the reason the Prince says I am too unforgiving to the Roman Empire. He says if Leo the Younger had lived he would have made it something different.'

Varius and Una glanced at each other and shifted a little closer together, the better to bear the thought of how things would have been different. But it seemed hopeful to them too, that Tadahito still talked with such regret of Marcus. Varius said, because it was simplest, 'Yes, he would.'

The King gestured him towards a chair. 'You should sit down, Varius Ischyrion. We were told you were ill. There are doctors waiting to see you.'

'Thank you,' Varius said, sitting down, still surprised and

433

ashamed at being so visibly weak, 'but I have to talk to the Prince first.'

Una watched him. 'You have to let them look at you.'

'After this.'

'You can't play around with this, Varius.'

'I'm not – just another hour. I'll be all right that long.' And he did feel better than he had on the journey across the desert. He'd slept on the volucer, once they had dodged through the thickets of gunfire above the battlefields at the borders of Nubia. He'd been given tablets that had soaked up the worst of the pain and heat. But the air seemed to be slipping through the grasp of his lungs, and it was more than twenty-four hours since he'd been able to eat anything. He knew that once he lay down he wouldn't be getting up again for a while.

The King left them, and they waited. Varius' head throbbed heavily, but even with eyes shut, he was oddly attentive to Una's footsteps, following her restless progress around the room as she paced and glared at the paintings.

At last Tadahito returned, alone. 'It has been so long since I saw either of you,' he said, 'and I am sorry you are hurt, Varius. It has been a terrible time for everyone – and both of you more than most.'

'Both empires have suffered greatly,' agreed Varius carefully, 'and now Sina is involved as well.'

'If you want asylum in Nionia – anywhere in the Nionian Empire – of course it is yours,' said Tadahito. 'And Lady Noviana, you believe your brother is somewhere in Alodia or Nobatia? I wish I could promise his safety, after you brought me back my sister— But if by any chance he falls into our hands, of course I will ensure he is looked after.'

'Thank you,' said Una. 'My brother and I did hope to ask you for asylum once. But we came here to discuss the end of the war.'

Tadahito's expression – friendly and attentive – remained oddly fixed, while his body seemed to sag with weariness. He said politely, 'I see.'

'We had agreed on so much in Bianjing,' said Varius, 'a way

434

of sharing power in Terranova and Tokogane. The wall was down. We were deliberately set on the path to war by a man who wanted both empires to destroy themselves and each other, who knew that in power Drusus would betray every effort we had made for peace. But without Drusus in the way, we believe something can be salvaged.'

'How?' said Tadahito, but it was scarcely a question, more a perfunctory courtesy. 'How can anything be recovered of that time?'

'We can remove Drusus from power,' said Una. 'We can install someone who would engage with Nionia under the same principles agreed in that treaty. We can prevent years of continued war. We are ready to do it now.'

Varius began, 'If you can be ready to declare a ceasefire—'

'I am afraid that may not be possible,' said Tadahito, delicately.

There was a slight pause as Una considered the answer and saw that it was only a tactful softening of outright denial. She asked, slowly, 'Why is it not possible?'

Tadahito smiled, but Una was struck suddenly by how tired, how almost shrunken, he looked, how he had aged more than he should have in a single year, though perhaps that was true for all of them.

'If you'd said this to me a year ago,' he said, and there was a sharp crack in his voice, 'but now it is not enough for the war to end. Too much has happened. We will accept nothing less than outright victory. I have spent more than a year of my life in this fight; I want to win.'

There was silence. Varius tried to ignore the rattle of his heartbeat, the sudden chilly dousing of sweat. He said, laboriously, 'That's understandable. But with a leader capable of repairing— Let us at least explain what we plan to do—'

'It doesn't matter to me who is on the throne,' Tadahito said, 'not now.'

Una looked from Varius' drained face to the expression of distant pity on Tadahito's and bit her lip. 'But it is not as if agreement between our nations is unimaginable – we had it once. It could end now, the loss of life – Nionian lives—'

'The war will end,' said Tadahito softly, 'and very soon. Not as you would wish, perhaps – not as any of us would wish. But it will end.'

Una stared at him, and saw an army fallen in a desert, and a dry wave passing through a city, felling walls and towers. A word, spoken in his mind, with a dull, unhappy expectation of release and rest.

Tadahito smiled again, regretfully. 'I am sorry. I respect your efforts to rid yourselves of a tyrant, but there is nothing more I can discuss with you.'

Sick as he was, Varius noticed that Una stopped breathing; that her gaze at Tadahito had grown fixed and rigid. 'Una?'

'*Surijin*,' Una said, a soft hiss.

Tadahito started sharply.

Varius blinked aching eyelids. 'What?'

'The weapon,' said Una, in a low voice, but very clearly, 'they have already used it, against the Roman Army in Tokogane. He's about to use it on Rome.'

Tadahito's eyes went wide with suspicion and shock, and he breathed, 'How can you have heard—?' He looked once round the room, as if for spies, then stared at her again, flushed with anger at himself for talking so openly. But his face relaxed into resignation almost at once. He might almost have said aloud that it was too late for it to make any difference.

Varius tried to assemble the pieces of the calm, reasonable argument that were so nearly within his reach, but he could only croak out, pleading, 'You can't—'

'Why not?' asked Tadahito, bitterly. 'Do you think your side would scruple to use such a weapon against us, if it had one? Do you know what they have done already? What else but Rome's total subjugation will keep Nionia safe now?'

Varius tried to focus his eyes on Tadahito's swimming face, then dragged himself to his feet.

'I cannot allow you to contact anyone in Rome,' said Tadahito, but Varius barely heard him; the Prince was talking somewhere miles away, and tides and earthquakes were breaking up the space between. He did hear Una, calling his name, somehow flying after him across the distance while the painted men on the walls glowed and crowded close.

Una reached him before he fell, and tried to hold him up. She sank to her knees under his weight, his head resting in her hands.

The heat that had been coursing through him for days had been suddenly extinguished; now his skin was cold. His eyes were open; he looked around, confused at finding himself on the floor. 'Una,' he said, surprisingly clearly, 'I need a longdictor. My parents— I have to get them out of Rome.'

A small group of servants had gathered round them and Tadahito came hurrying over.

'And Cleomenes – I have to—' whispered Varius, and ran out of breath.

'They are waiting for him in the infirmary. Take him there,' said Tadahito sadly. He still spoke in Latin, for the servants' sake.

Varius struggled weakly for a moment as they lifted him and then went still, unconscious at last.

Tadahito turned away, as if not to intrude any further. Still kneeling on the floor, trembling, Una called out fiercely, 'Your Highness.'

Tadahito stopped for a moment and turned his head a little, but he did not look at her.

Sulien hadn't touched the radio at his belt since they'd left the road. He would say it was broken if he had to. He didn't want to talk to any Roman soldier outside the fourth centuria, especially not anyone senior to him, or anyone who had been here longer. He kept thinking of Gracilis, whom he had liked – had he known what was just outside the city? No, no, he couldn't have done, Sulien was convinced of that. Gracilis would have said something; he would have acted differently.

But he found it made little difference to persuade himself he could see a clear patch here or there in the stain spreading from that road of corpses.

They'd left the trucks, hidden as best they could at the base of a rocky bluff in the foothills. They hardly spoke – the effort of walking through the heat provided some excuse for that, and some distraction from what they'd seen. They followed the course of a dried-up stream into the mountains, picking their way over the pale, cindery stone towards the cover of the dusty pines on the slopes above. They'd veered a long way off course and now they were lost. He hoped they could stay that way for a while. As long as it lasted they were just a small, demoralised crowd of young men wandering through the mountains, worn out, almost innocent. Sulien felt disgusted about continuing with his orders, even in this half-hearted, roundabout way. They passed a hollow in the white rock, barely deep enough to call a cave. If he'd been alone, perhaps he would have crawled inside and waited for the war to end around him. But he was not alone, and though they barely even looked at each other as they struggled up the mountainside, he was so grateful for the solid, tongue-tied presence of his men around him. And he repeated to himself – almost loudly and stubbornly enough to shut out any other thought – that they were going home one day, all of them, if he had anything to do with it.

So eventually they would have to return to their legion, and in some state that did not invite immediate execution for disobedience or desertion.

He divided them into five groups, and led an octet up a spur of rock onto a shallow ramp above the plain, dotted with pine shrubs. Looking across the flat spread of the valley towards the dark, salt-encrusted hills, it was clear enough where they were – only three or four miles from the chain of peaks marked on the map, and somewhere in there was the Nionian radio position he was supposed to take out.

And then a strange shudder passed through the desert: a long drone, just below the reach of hearing, scraping through the air. The soldiers felt the rock stir under their feet; they felt it on their skin as a faint breeze with a flat, unnatural weight behind it. Dust lifted like a tablecloth from the ground below. For a moment Sulien thought he saw a ghostly blur of light in it, then he blinked and realised the shimmering was a trick of his eyes – the wave seemed to stir the fluid in them too. He saw Minius and Asper, who were further down the slope, lurch as if the earth had turned to pitching water, and then he felt a wave of seasickness himself, and Dorion too bent over, pressing his hands to his head.

It stopped just as abruptly, but now the plain and the far hills were hidden under a curtain of hanging dust, and the nausea lingered too.

'Well,' Sulien said, blackly. 'It does work, after all.'

Pas said listlessly, 'That Onager-thing we've been dragging around.'

'Yeah,' Sulien answered, and raised his voice to call to Minius and Asper, 'Everyone all right?' And they stumbled on, all of them faintly queasy and unsteady for a while.

They knew they had just watched the infliction of a new and scarcely imaginable kind of force, and yet after what they had seen on the road, it meant little to them; Sulien felt as if the swell that had just rolled across the earth only confirmed something they had already found out. All he wondered was who was going to burn or bury all the dead that lay across Mohavia now.

They came into a steep valley of taller, denser pines, though the slopes were disfigured with craters and burnt trees where the Roman bombers had tried to smash the command station by luck. Sulien's group descended slowly, with another pair of octets spread along the slope to their left. It was very quiet, even their breathing and footsteps sounded hushed. The slash of sky above them had turned beige: the dust from the plain was muffling the air.

Sulien remembered that frozen, breathless feeling, waiting in the hidden camp at Holzarta while the Roman soldiers roamed in the woods outside. He swallowed dryly with regret and doubt.

The decanus of the second octet whistled and Sulien turned

to see him pointing urgently at the peak above them. For a moment he could see only a line of trees before his eyes suddenly adjusted and the trunk of a tall pine became the metal column of a communications tower, painted like bark and bristling with green artificial branches. It was no wonder the air patrols had been unable to spot it from the sky.

Sulien signalled his men. They'd been carrying their shields on their backs; now they all quietly transferred them to their arms and readied their guns. Sulien switched on his radio to whisper instructions, and had his group crouch among the pines while the fourth and fifth octets progressed westwards along the valley so they could gradually descend the south slope and cross to the north. If there was anything at the bottom of the valley, they should have it almost surrounded.

Sulien would have been surprised that they hadn't already met resistance, except that it was almost routine now that the Nionians were never where they expected them to be. By now they would know the Onager had been used, of course, so they might have been ordered to retreat, or they might have fled.

And Sulien was just beginning to wonder if they might be able to put the tower beyond use with grenades and leave without so much as seeing a Nionian soldier when a spray of bullets spurted from the shrubs on the slope opposite them and they had to take cover behind their shields to return fire.

Sulien could make out only four men in the shadow of the pines, huddled under their own shell of round shields. Perhaps there were a few more down in the base of the valley, but the other half of his centuria was already descending the slope behind them, converging on them from both sides. 'Tell them to stop firing!' Sulien ordered Minius, who had that much Nionian. 'Tell them to surrender; it's ten against one, for fuck's sake.'

Minius shouted that across the ravine, but there was no break in fire. Sulien could still level his gun at the men and fire, though his finger was slow on the trigger, and he couldn't bring himself to aim so deliberately as before. Nevertheless, whether it was his bullet or someone else's, one of the Nionian soldiers toppled forward, and rolled down to lie splayed on the slope, braked by a clump of sagebrush.

Another Nionian lobbed a grenade across the valley and as the Romans scattered, the remaining three broke out, running east along the incline of the valley. But one of them fell, wounded in the foot, and the Romans closed in around them, herding them down to the valley floor.

Sulien skidded down to the stubby concrete building. It was camouflaged much more crudely than Holzarta had been, with dried branches and stones piled roughly across the roof. There were two soldiers on the ground outside it, one on his back with a hole in his chest, the other crouched over him and trying vainly to hold the blood inside him, though it was now only spilling out, no longer pumping.

Dangerously, Sulien closed his eyes against the sight of them; for a moment he felt that if he blinked hard enough he could make the war go away, and transport himself back to any warm corner of the past, where he and Una and Marcus were safe. 'I'm sorry,' he said gently to the survivor, 'he's dead. Look, just put your hands up, all right? Up?' He gestured with his gun, hoping his tone would convey enough of what he meant. Minius was still some distance behind him on the slope.

The soldier's teeth were clenched with desperation. He was young, like all of them, amber-skinned, with a broad, bony face and a sparse moustache on his lip. His hair was tightly knotted back, like most Nionian soldiers, but Sulien had not seen anything like the pattern of blue lines tattooed onto his cheeks before. He looked past Sulien at the mass of Romans approaching with the three other Nionian soldiers prisoners their midst. He leapt to his feet, and suddenly there was a gun in his hand, but he was swinging up to his own head before Sulien had even fully registered it was there. Sulien had no doubt he meant to do it and yet there was a moment's incredulous hesitation before he pulled the trigger, in which Sulien read a wild, unacknowledged hope of being stopped— So he sprang forward and clubbed at the young man with his shield, knocking him to the ground and sending the gun flying. It was only then he remembered his own slowness to fire in the prison van, on the way to the Colosseum.

'Fucking hell, sir, I almost shot you,' said Asper, who'd cocked his own weapon the moment he saw the Nionian's.

'Never mind, no harm done,' said Sulien, grimly, scooping the gun out of the soldier's reach.

The boy moaned and crawled back to his comrade's body. He knelt there, covering his face and rocking gently. After a moment he bent forward and touched his forehead to the dead man's. One of the other prisoners crouched beside him and laid a hand on his back.

Sulien left an octet guarding the prisoners, and beckoned Pas and Asper to follow him. He warily pushed open the door of the station, and a shot smashed off the edge of his shield. Sulien sighed with fatigue and fired back, and was relieved to have hit the last enemy soldier in the place only with a ricochet, in the arm. After that the man mutely let them take his gun, and they pushed him outside to join the others.

A couple of electric fans were still whirring in the control room, fluttering the edges of the maps pinned to the back wall, a spatter of blood across them now. The other walls were lined with desks loaded with radio equipment. 'Don't touch anything,' Sulien said for the second time that day, wondering if this was a trap, and the whole place was rigged.

There was a door at the back of the room opening onto a tunnel dug into the hillside, where they found a generator room and a barracks with bunks for twenty people. They had two corpses, and four prisoners. Where were the others now?

They went back outside and looked uneasily at the huddled captives. 'What are we going to do with them?' asked Pas.

'Take them back,' said Sulien. 'We'll get that tower down and smash up this stuff, and then take them back with us.' He tried to sound convinced that this was a good idea, though he didn't know what would happen to them. Probably someone would sell them as slaves. But at least they would be alive.

And one day all the slaves would be free.

'Take us back with you?' repeated the tattooed soldier, in unexpected Latin, a thin, desperate note of laughter in his voice. 'Where? Where do you have to go back to now?'

One of the other prisoners hissed something, alarmed, but the soldier could not be stopped. 'Don't you know your army is gone? It doesn't matter what you do to us: we have the Surijin. Didn't you see it, out there? We've won.' He bent over the body again and moaned, 'Why are you here? Why aren't you dead out there with the rest, where you belong?'

All around him, the Roman soldiers went still, as they thought of that quiver that had raced through the earth and into their bones. Sulien felt the faint sickness twist again in his gut. He looked at his men's wide eyes. They were all looking at him.

He licked dry lips and adjusted the switches on his radio. 'Ninth cohort, fourth centuria to command,' he said, hoarsely. And said it again, and again. He turned away, because he couldn't stand the others watching him while he pleaded, 'Is anyone there?'

The radio hissed softly, like the sighing of dust on the plain.

'Tomorrow that is what we will do to Rome!' crowed the soldier on the ground, in despairing triumph. 'Then what will you do?'

Noriko said, 'But I lived in that city.'

She had been given strange new clothes. There had been no way of acquiring anything from Nionia in time, and no one had wanted her to arrive in Cynoto dressed like a young Roman matron, so Tadahito's valet had arranged for local seamstresses to make dresses out of parachute silk. The neat white costume had been made to something approximating Nionian style, though lighter and simpler than anything Noriko might have worn at home. The diamond patterns at the neckline were Ethiopian. Her hair was smoothed back over her shoulders. She did not feel she looked quite Roman or Nionian, or anything else; she and Tomoe and Sakura looked like the only inhabitants of a lonely new nation.

443

Tadahito gave her a look of fierce, scared relief and gripped her hand, exclaiming, 'Yes – as a prisoner, as a slave!'

'Not when my husband was still alive.' She supposed she had been a prisoner in a sense even then, but Marcus had been too.

Tadahito was not listening. 'We should never have sent you there.'

Noriko remembered Drusus' weight, both the physical horror of being forced down beneath him, and the daily burden of his presence in the palace. If Tadahito did what he said was already inevitable, then Drusus was only days away from death. But she thought of the quiet street where she had met Cleomenes, and the servants she had talked to in the palace, and she felt cold and breathless and lost.

'Some of the people who helped me are still there,' she said. 'They risked their lives for me. Cleomenes and Cominia. They have a little boy.'

Tadahito looked young and panicked. His hair was a little disordered, the knot at the back of his head askew. He said, 'Parts of the city may be unaffected. I'm following our father's wishes. There were children in Yuuhigawa and Aregaya too.' The sentences clattered oddly together like misaligned tiles.

'But this! So *many*, Tadahito!'

'I know,' said Tadahito miserably, 'I know – but it will save just as many lives, in the end. People die in war, Noriko; better if it brings an end to all of this. How can I let it go on and on, when we can stop it? And then we will go home.'

Noriko seemed to wheel away from herself in a moment of vertigo. She could believe that hundreds of thousands of people, millions, even, were about to die in Rome. It was this conversation she could not believe was happening. She looked at her brother. She could not think of him as so incalculably dangerous. She felt as if the decision were a ghost, a conscious and malignant being, pushing itself into the world through Tadahito as if through a door. And through her father too, through Drusus. To get away from them all, she left the room.

*

444

There had been no need to move Varius out of the palace, for the best equipment in Axum was already there. Noriko passed two doctors, one Nionian and one Ethiopian, talking in unpractised, frustrated Latin in an anteroom as she approached the door of the medical room.

Varius was grey and motionless in the bed. Una was not there. Noriko did not look at Varius at any length; she was unnerved by the crank and whir of the machine doing the breathing for him. She already knew that the surgeons had cut a tiny splinter of shrapnel and a patch of poisoned tissue out of his back. She knew that despite this, his body's systems were continuing to fail.

She walked on along the passage, peering into dusty, empty rooms that still looked like some forgotten part of the Golden House in Rome. She called quietly, 'Una?' because she could not believe Una would have gone far.

She heard a low crash somewhere over a soft mumble of machinery and hurried towards it.

A heavy door at the bottom of a small flight of stairs opened into a small laundry room. A dryer was whirring and the air was warm and crackly with dust. A bench was overturned on the floor and Una was standing over it, panting, her face running with tears.

She turned as Noriko opened the door and said wildly, 'I can't go on looking at him like that. I love him.'

She took a few helpless paces around the little room.

'I didn't know that,' said Noriko quietly.

Una sighed, and wiped uselessly at her eyes. She managed to twist her mouth for an instant into a self-mocking smile. She said, 'No, nor does he.'

Noriko was flicking through memories, searching for signs she had missed. Yes: Una's agitation as she took out the stitches. Noriko wished she had known it before; she would have been pleased and hopeful, she thought, even if Varius knew nothing about it yet. And the idea of them happy together half-convinced her that there must, somehow or other, be more hope for Varius than anyone seemed to believe. She began impulsively, 'Oh, but if he recovers—'

Una said, flatly, 'He won't recover,' and then gasped and shook again. When she could speak she said, 'I did find a longdictor, but I can't get a line to Rome or Tamiathis or anywhere. I have to try again. But I don't want— I can't— Who's going to explain this to his family?'

Noriko waited in silence while Una continued to stumble restlessly around the room. 'I don't understand how,' Una muttered, 'I always thought I'd never— And I still feel the same about Marcus—' And Marcus' name twisted more tears out of her. 'Sulien could save him— Sulien's dead, perhaps, already—'

She sat down on a crate against the wall and hugged herself, and seemed to Noriko's eyes to dwindle to perhaps a twelve-year-old's size. She was no longer sobbing or shaking, but tears still spilled heavily from her eyes, which were wide open and staring into an invisible distance. She whispered, 'What can I *do*?'

'They don't have the right medicines here. I will take Varius back to Cynoto,' said Noriko. 'He will have the best possible care.'

Una looked up at her, and her wet eyes seemed unnaturally magnified. She protested, 'But they can't move him – it's too dangerous—'

'But he is in such danger already. Surely even a small chance is worthwhile.'

Finally the tears stopped, and Una said, in a clearer voice, 'You're right.' But she slumped heavily against the wall 'Then I won't be with him,' she murmured after a long silence. 'I wasn't there when Marcus died.'

She shut her eyes and looked, for a moment, as if she would never get up again. But then she did rise, and wiped hard at her wet face again before bending to right the fallen bench, then trudged out of the little laundry.

Noriko stopped her at the door of Varius' room. 'You must come too. Please. I can't leave you alone here. I am sure it would be better for Varius if you stayed with him. And if . . . if the worst happens, then you must let me help you. I could find somewhere for you where at least you can have peace. I know you would never be happy at court in Nionia, but . . . perhaps I will not spend so much time at court now myself. There is a house in Yamagata, by a lake. It belonged to my mother's family. I have not been there in years, but it is very beautiful. Very quiet. We could stay there for a while. Please think about it before you decide. Of course I know it is not what you planned. But now—' She shuddered over the thought of what was about to happen to Rome, couldn't put it into words. 'I think it will all be over soon,' she whispered.

'It isn't over,' said Una. 'No, it won't be over.' Her voice was nearly toneless, but it had steadied. And when she looked at Noriko she even smiled. 'You're so kind. And I wish you weren't going so far away. But I promised Maralah – I promised them all. I have to go back. Whatever happens, I have to go back to my people.'

She put her arms round Noriko for a moment, and then turned and pushed open the door. Before it swung closed, Noriko saw her drop into the chair beside Varius.

Sometimes, Varius was aware of himself dying. He tried to gasp for air, horrified by the tube in his mouth, which he felt was suffocating him rather than helping him breathe. He opened his eyes and strained to keep them open, though the light stung like a slap of seawater. But he couldn't match the huge force weighing on his eyelids, his lungs, his heart, that pushed him down into the boiling dark. He recognised it from five years before, when he had bitten down on the poison outside the Palace in Rome. He made another exhausting effort – he saw Una's face – and he could remember how it had been back then, trying to find his way into death, like running your hands over a wall in the dark, searching for the door.

No, not now, he thought, trying to hold the door closed this time. No, I can't. Not without even knowing.

*

447

The dust was still sinking back to earth when they reached the plain; they drove into a brown fog of it through which leafless trees and shrubs emerged like starved prisoners turned loose across the desert. Everything was the same colour.

It can't be true, Sulien had said. Not everyone can be dead.

He'd taken Pas and Dorion with him. Back at the base in the mountains, they had given up trying to reach anyone on the Roman side with their own radios and started experimenting with the more powerful Nionian equipment. He'd left Minius in charge, still trying.

Sulien slowed the truck because it seemed that slow mounds had sprouted like knee-high molehills across the ground ahead, littering the surface of the road. He wondered for a moment how the Surijin had had that effect, and then saw the soft, grass-like clumps of hair, the hard curve of horn, and realised that the hillocks were the bodies of bufali, painted into the landscape by the dust.

He braked. 'I don't know if I can—' he began, and stopped. They hadn't spoken in a long time; it was as if he couldn't remember how. He let his head droop forwards, put up a hand to cover his shut eyes. 'Do we have to see this?' he asked in a whisper. 'Do we have to see this too?'

Neither Pas nor Dorion answered for a long time, though Dorion slung an arm round him and pressed his forehead against his shoulder.

'We've come this far,' said Pas at last, hollowly. 'And there might be someone left. Maybe in the hills.'

Sulien sighed and pushed the truck on, slowly, into the haze of dust, trying to weave around the dead bufali, though he rolled over at least one of them.

It turned out there were only a few more miles to go.

On the road to the mountains, and in the pine valley before the battle, there had been at least the constant buzz and chirp of insects. He only realised it now that even that sound was gone.

The bodies looked as if they had been modelled out of the dust that covered them, or as if they were growing out of it like roots.

It was like a preliminary burial, both kind and ruthless: blurring away pain and identity – the contours of faces and hands strangely meaningless without colour. There were a few hundred, here at the back of the convoy. No one seemed to have had time even to try to run, like the refugees on the road from Aregaya. He might have been able to guess more about how they had died if he had looked more closely, but he didn't.

Some of the trucks had crashed and overturned, of course; something had caught fire and burned itself out, leaving a faint scent of smoke in the air. But it was strange how intact so many the vehicles were. Nearer the front of the convoy, some tyres had burst and a few windscreens were cracked, but not all of them. Inside, the bodies were bare of the covering of dust. Sulien glimpsed blood through a window and at that he stopped the truck.

Pas was crying. Sulien hugged him for a while in silence then opened the door and swung himself up onto the roof of the cab. He didn't want to step down onto this ground.

He had a better view up here than he'd wanted. He turned dizzy, swayed a little. He dragged off his helmet, which now seemed pointless, let it fall, and sat down. He started to think of Gracilis, of the boys he'd watched playing pelota, but every thought tripped and interrupted itself and ended in the same moan: *I can't, I can't.*

Dorion climbed up to join him, then Pas. They huddled close to each other, the only three living things for miles.

'Round those hills . . .' suggested Dorion hopelessly. 'The other legions . . .'

Sulien shook his head. 'If there was anyone, they'd be here.'

He didn't know what he would have done, how he would have been able to go on breathing if he hadn't been able to feel somebody else doing it, if somebody's back hadn't been warm against his side. And yet he felt frightened of what the other two might say. Please, he thought, don't ask me what we should do now.

But neither of them did. Dorion said, 'And they're going to do this to Rome?' speaking quietly and weakly and with as little

449

expression as if they were talking about some successful public works project.

'He said that,' Sulien answered, in the same slow helplessly neutral tone.

'I never really thought that could happen.'

'No,' agreed Sulien. After a minute or so he added, 'I lived there.'

'In Rome? I thought you were from Alex?'

'I lived in Rome before that.' He closed his eyes. 'A while ago.'

'Well, I'm sorry,' said Dorion.

Sulien shuddered as people he knew in Rome began to crowd into his mind as if for shelter there: everyone at the clinic, everyone in his old building, Tancorix and all the singers and actors he knew through her. Tancorix and Cleomenes both had children . . . and again the line of thought cut out. He lay down on the warm metal roof, as if in imitation of all the soldiers on the ground. The dust was trying to blend them in with the rest; he could feel it settling over them; once he wiped a hand across his face and it came away filthy. He didn't feel as if they would ever move, or anyone would ever find them here.

And still some idiotic part of himself that insisted on ignoring what was around them chirped, *But this can't really happen to Rome. Something will happen to stop it.*

And then it occurred to him that when he'd been on his feet, he'd seen what he thought was the Onager, further back along the convoy. He thought, idly, it might still work, if it ever did work. *We could take it somewhere and . . .*

No, he couldn't finish that thought either.

Una would be making decisions by now, at least insisting that they move. He wished drowsily that she was there to do it. He couldn't picture her the last time he'd seen her very well, when she'd been crying and banging open windows; instead he thought of her sitting beside him on the deck of the *Ananke*, making plans in which he'd never wholly believed, and rallying escaped slaves from piles of rubble in Alexandria. He felt oddly confident she was alive, though usually remembering those he'd left behind was tangled in thoughts of air-raids and arrest and executions. He was not even afraid that she might be in Rome. It had been so long since he'd been able to write to her. What will she do with her ships and her army now? he wondered. And will even she understand about all this when I see her?

It made no sense to think he would see her ever again. He couldn't imagine what would happen next, but it would hardly be a ferry home.

His radio buzzed. For another moment he lay still, staring up at the clearing sky, and couldn't bring himself even to lift his hand to answer – but he knew it was Minius, back at the Nionian radio base, and he thought distantly: I got them out of this, at least; I didn't know I was doing it, but I saved them.

'Are you there, sir?' said Minius.

'Yes,' Sulien said dully.

'Did you find them? It's true, isn't it?'

'Yes, it's true.'

'Yes,' repeated Minius. His voice was strangely wry, helpless laughter lurking in it somewhere. 'That's what they told us. We've been trying the stuff here like you said, and we did get through to a base back in Aregaya. They're pulling out of there as fast as they can. They think there's some attack coming from the west, Sinoan troops landing at Tipaea, so—'

'They didn't have any useful ideas?' asked Sulien with a listless mixture of hope and sarcasm.

'They said the Nionians will probably find us pretty soon . . . they said no one can get to us. And we can't really get to them . . . or anyone.'

Sulien listened, unsurprised.

'They said we could die free like Romans,' said Minius, and paused. 'I think they meant before the Nionians get here.'

'What?' said Sulien, shocked into alertness, sitting upright. 'Well, we're not doing that. You can tell everyone they're fucking not to.' He stopped, suddenly frightened, 'Are you all right? No one . . . would've done it already?'

'No,' said Minius, 'no, no one's done that.'

451

'Well, good. Of course not. You're not stupid. You've got look-outs posted, haven't you? Well, move if you have to, otherwise hold out there as long as you can, and we'll be back later.' He clipped the radio back on his belt and looked, this time without turning faint or flinching, at the devastation. Something will happen to stop it, he thought again, and slid down from the roof.

'Come on,' he said.

Obediently Pas climbed down, but once on the ground he collapsed limply against the truck and leant there. 'And do what?' he asked.

'The Onager's back there. We're going to take it and show the Nionians we've got one too.'

Dorion didn't move. He looked down at Sulien from the roof of the cab, his legs dangling. 'I'm too tired for this,' he said quietly.

'What, you'd rather stay here? Get down here, Dorion. It's not as if things can get any worse.'

'They can't? Well, our side could execute us for stealing it, which I admit probably won't be a problem,' said Dorion, with a croak in his voice, his mouth skewed into a despairing little smile. 'And when the Nionians find us with it, they'll be even more pissed off with us than they would be anyway.' He drooped suddenly, and put his head into his hands. 'And what do you want to do, find a Nionian town and destroy it? I'm not going to do that, I don't care if you think they've got it coming or what-ever, I just can't. I've had enough – sounds like our whole army has. Why should we be any different?'

'No,' said Sulien, 'I'm not saying that's what we should do. I want to get their attention. That's really what these weapons do. You don't have to— You don't have to do *this*.' He gestured at the devastation around them. 'Then, perhaps if I talk to them—'

'You want to talk to the Nionians?' said Dorion, in disbelief.

'I might be able to.'

Dorion stared. 'You've really lost it, Archias,' he said pityingly, and sagged again with exhaustion. 'The thing's probably broken now anyway.'

Pas was still slumped against the truck, but his eyes were grave and steady on Sulien's face.

'Do we get to go home at the end of this?' he asked.

'I don't know,' said Sulien. 'If it works, if anyone will listen . . . I think we might be prisoners for a while, Pas, even if we're lucky. We don't know what's going on out there in the world. But the war's going to end – if we can maybe change the way it ends, we might get home one day. It's better than just waiting here or putting our guns in our mouths, isn't it?'

Pas nodded. 'Archias,' he said softly, 'Shouter . . . I'll come with you if you want, if you'll tell us first who you really are.'

'What?' Dorion muttered drearily from the top of truck, while Sulien stiffened. He returned Pas' gaze in silence.

'This should have killed me, shouldn't it?' Pas went on, putting his hand to the blotchy scar on the side of his neck. He smiled lopsidedly. 'It didn't look worse than it was. I could feel it. And it's not just me. Galeo was going to die of sunstroke. And Acilius should have lost his hand . . .'

Sulien exhaled. 'All right, Pas,' he said. 'You're right. I'm Novianus Sulien.'

'What?' yelled Dorion, shockingly loud in that wasteland of corpses and dust, and hurled himself down off the roof of the truck to stare at Sulien's face.

'Well then,' Pas said, shrugging. 'If half of what those posters said was true . . . if you could get out of the Colosseum . . .'

'*Oh blind gods!*' Dorion exclaimed, and began to shake with shrill, breathless laughter.

'Dorion,' said Pas, 'calm down.' He strode grimly to the nearest truck, leant in over the driver's corpse and tried the engine. 'It's still working,' he called.

Sulien gave Dorion's shoulder a shake. 'Come on,' he said, 'you've worked with me all this time – you know everything they said about my sister and me wasn't true. You know Drusus lies. He lied when he sent us here.'

Dorion giggled a little more. 'So you're *not* a revolutionary maniac who wants to bring down the government?'

'Well,' admitted Sulien, 'I am that a bit.'

Dorion trembled and went still. 'All right,' he said, in an almost normal voice, though his eyes were still wide and unfocused, 'fine.'

[XVIII]

ONAGER

Sulien steered the Onager away from that place as fast as he could. His heart was beating almost painfully hard, but steadily, like a bell tolling. The dust was only a soft bloom on the blue sky now. They'd had to dismantle a horrible barricade of bodies and vehicles to get the Onager free, sweating and crying as they hauled corpses away from the back wheels of trucks, then down from their cabs, so that they could climb in and back each one away. At last Sulien threaded the bulk of the carrier through the obstacles and past the stricken convoy.

Dorion sat hunched in the cab beside Sulien, sometimes shaking, rubbing his hands over his hair. 'They'll see us,' he gabbled quietly, as much to himself as to Sulien, 'they might not have seen us through the dust before, but now they will. From the air, or on the road . . . come on, Shouter, we're not going to be able to get anywhere in this thing – where are we going to go?'

'They've been pulling all their people a safe distance from that thing. They won't get back for a while,' answered Sulien, 'and even if they do see us from the air, they'll only think we're one of theirs. What else is going to be alive down here?'

Pas was driving close behind them in a smaller truck they'd scavenged from the battlefield. 'There's a city on the other side of those mountains,' he said over the radio, 'almost due east, seventy or eighty miles away.'

'It's too far,' whispered Dorion.

Sulien clenched his teeth. 'We'll have to get as close as we can.'

Dorion relaxed, just a little, when they reached a pass up into the mountains and a bird sprang up from a clump of pines. Sulien gave a shaken laugh of relief too: it was so good to see things alive again.

The weight of the Onager's carrier began to tell. Sulien had never driven anything as heavy before; it had been hard enough down on the plains and across the shallow rises of the desert, but now the effort of guiding it round these narrow mountain roads wrenched at his already tense body, spilled nervous sweat from his skin. His hands gripped and slid on the controls. How ridiculous it would be if this ended with the Roman superweapon stuck between overhanging cliffs, he thought, or sliding off down a slope of shale, or stranded on a thread of road too narrow to let them turn back.

After the murky russets and browns of the desert, the greens and silvers they were plunging into now seemed barely believable. A pale jade river in spate blasted along beside the road; a waterfall hung in white columns above a gorge. Sulien had forgotten water could move like that, so lavish and reckless. A lake gleamed blue in an urn-shaped crevasse. They passed into a thick forest, trees larger than anything Sulien had seen before, the dark-red trunks broad as tanks, the splaying roots like huge webbed feet.

The scale of it all daunted them both. Sulien went on promising Dorion that they weren't lost, that they could find their way to where they needed to be and then back to the others, but every time the road led them above the screens of trees, another immense field of domes and peaks opened ahead, against which even the Onager's bulk seemed tiny. And they hadn't even looked at its control panel yet. Even if it did work, they wouldn't know what to do; they'd press some wrong button and destroy themselves and everything around them.

Sometimes it was Dorion who reassured Sulien: 'Oh, it can't be that hard,' he said, unsteadily, dragging himself upright from the curled position he'd been lying in. 'They only needed geniuses to build the thing, not to fire it. Who did they make it for? Grunts like us.'

The roads were hushed and empty. Sometimes they saw villages of low wooden cottages among the trees, and once they passed a pair of trappers, animal skins slung over their shoulders, who looked at them in the same horror with which Dorion and Sulien looked back. But no one spoke or aimed a gun at them, and so Sulien continued to manhandle the Onager onwards. Once volucers growled above them while the three of them were clustered around a map at the roadside, and for a moment Sulien was back in the Pyrenees with Una and Marcus, and tears filled his eyes again. He wiped them away without trying to hide that he'd been crying; it was too late for shame now. The others said nothing.

They reached a thin loop of road above a sheer cliff of bare grey rock. Below them the mountains rolled down the sky to the east, and for the first time Sulien thought he could just see a soft colourless blur of level ground between two peaks. He pulled out his binoculars and stepped down from the cab. The air up here was cool and soft, a different substance from what they'd been breathing all these weeks. The sky was pale, the light just beginning to leak away. Sulien trained the binoculars on that small crescent of the true horizon, held between the mountains as if in a cup.

'It's there,' he said.

He had to turn up the magnification as far as it would go, and then he couldn't hold the binoculars steady enough to pick out any details of the city; it was just a pale grey pattern of blocks and lines. He saw the glint of the evening sunlight on the flanks of volucers circling above it like gnats, but not even a pinprick of electric light. They would be afraid, of course, of Roman bombs. It was only a hundred and thirty miles or so from Yuuhigawa, the Tokaganean capital. Sulien thought of that first night of the war, watching rockets pour down onto Yuuhigawa on that screen in Aternum, and nights with Una in the air-raid shelter in Alexandria, and he lowered the binoculars with a tremor of longing and pity.

'What's it called?' he asked Pas, who had the map.

'Tamohara,' answered Pas softly.

Sulien stared across the mountains. He wanted the land itself to offer some sign, something to assure them that this was the right place, that they were not monstrously stupid, or evil.

He didn't think they had the strength or certainty to keep going much further. 'We'll try here,' he said.

With only three of them it took a long time just to drag off the Onager's cover, and once it was clear, Dorion slumped with fatigue against the dark mass of coils and rails as if it were something as harmless as a sun-warmed brick wall.

'It might not work at all,' Sulien said, almost hopefully.

But when he climbed into the control deck and tentatively pressed a switch above the main dials, the Onager rose as if with slow curiosity from its cradle, its black mouth spreading open as if to eat – or to vomit.

The controls were not quite as simple as Dorion had hoped, but they were not completely unfathomable either. The Onager's sensors had calibrated its own elevation already; they spent some time breathlessly arguing over the map and the compass, trying to calculate that of the city. Finally Sulien entered the co-ordinates, and with a low whir like the buzz of a vast wasp, and with awful clarity of movement, the cone angled and swung towards that faint smudge on the horizon where however many thousands of people lived.

And then he turned the dials so that the Onager drew its aim a little to the side, a few degrees closer back. And over and over again he looked from the map to the dials to the mouth of the Onager, trying to be sure its empty black gaze was fixed now on one of those distant peaks that framed the city.

Sulien looked at the screen. Beside a simple model of the target drawn in lines of blue light, it blandly offered a range of possible depths and breadths and scales of impact. He knew, as he turned the dial upwards, that he was guessing what those figures meant.

The Onager's cone closed up again, narrowing to a long dark muzzle.

Sulien gently lifted his hands from the control panel, afraid a careless movement now would undo the settings or worse.

'Anyone else feel like being the one to do this?' he offered, looking at the heavy lever set into the panel.

The others glanced at each other, suddenly breathless. 'Sorry,' said Pas, stepping back.

Delicately, as if the machine might break, Sulien took hold of the handle. Under his ribs, something was twisting so hard it was about to tear in half. He thought of Rome, terrible and beautiful, crashing through history; he thought of the Colosseum and of rooms where he had mistakenly felt safe, and he thought of Marcus. He pushed the handle to the top of its groove.

The mountains screamed.

The noise of the wave of pressure that burst from the Onager's mouth was below hearing, but the treetops splintered as it ripped across the landscape and struck the far peak with a crack that throbbed through everything. Sulien felt his eardrums burst and tumbled down from the platform, wrapping his head in his arms, to join Pas and Dorion. They all cringed together on the ground, waiting for it to stop.

Then Sulien raised watering eyes long enough to see the top of the peak split and crumble, and a great column of dust spiralled up as if a volcano had erupted. The shattered rock slid away and disappeared over the new, wounded horizon.

The ground and air were still trembling with shock. Above them, birds were raising havoc in the air, their frantic calls muted by the ringing in their ears. Sulien was shaking almost too hard to find the city again through the binoculars, but before the dust spread across the distance and covered the horizon, he did see it. All he could tell was that it was still there.

'I can't hear,' Dorion mumbled.

'He can fix it,' gasped Pas, 'come on! We've got to get away from here.'

They piled into the small truck and bounced away, leaving the Onager standing on the mountainside, still staring into the distance.

*

Tadahito stared at the laurel wreath carved into the footboard of his bed. The palace at Axum, with its huge red walls, was very different from what he always pictured when he thought of Rome, but inside it was impossible to forget this had once been a governor's palace in a province of the Roman Empire. Salomon was busily trying to strip all that away and fill up the space with something new – so new as to seem raw, faintly unnerving, even, to Tadahito: a whole culture force-grown over less than two hundred years out of just a few scraps of belief and tradition the Romans had left untouched.

For months Tadahito had barely slept more than two solid hours at a time. He could coax himself asleep, but he could not stay there. Now he lay there trying, for a little while at least, not to think about the war, not to dwell on Varius and Una's horror at the end he planned for it. He reminded himself that Noriko was safe now; that this whole thing was nearly over. He would be able to resume his life, and the discussions of possible marriages the war had interrupted. But the usual hooks of tension remained lodged in his muscles and kept dragging him through dreams of ruined cities and poisoned children, and then out of sleep altogether.

So although it was long before dawn, he was already awake when his chamberlain quietly entered his room.

'What is it?' he murmured. He wondered if Varius had died.

Lord Morokata's face was blurred by the curtain, but Tadahito could see how tense his posture was. Morokata answered, 'The Romans appear to have deployed a Surijin-like device in Toko-gane.'

Tadahito sat up with a gasp, and the next moment had to suppress an impulse to let himself drop back onto the pillows in despair. They were not at the end of the war, then; the end had slipped away into a poisoned distance.

It was a moment before he could even speak. 'What was the target?'

Morokata hesitated slightly. 'It seems to have been Tomacho, in Sorasanmyaku, your Highness.'

Tadahito did not notice the hint of equivocation. There was scarcely a city in the Nionian Empire he could not have placed almost instantly on a map; he was able to measure its proximity to Yuuhigawa at once. He surged out of bed and flung a robe over his nightclothes. He asked, 'Is there anything left of it?'

'Yes,' said Morokata, 'there was an avalanche, but the city was not significantly damaged at all. It may have been a misfire.'

Dazed, Tadahito shook his head. 'How could they *miss*?'

It was dark by the time they reached the radio bunker hidden on the western slopes of the mountains. Crowded inside the radio control room, Sulien's centuria and their four Nionian prisoners sprawled on the floor or perched on desks as if in a disorderly classroom; their eyes were wide and forlorn. Asper had enlisted one of the prisoners into a game of dice. There was a mess of empty tins and packets on the floor, and a faintly gingery, meaty smell in the air: the Romans had discovered the base's rations store. Sulien suddenly noticed how hungry he was.

'What's happening?' asked Minius, as Sulien, Pas and Dorion lurched inside.

'Oh, what isn't?' Dorion said, dropping cross-legged to the floor in exhaustion.

The soldier with the tattooed face was hunched on the floor, his head down. Sulien crossed over to him. 'You,' he said, 'you speak Latin; what's your name?'

The man ignored him, but Minius said, 'He's called Hidaka; that's what the others say.'

'Hidaka. You must have been taking orders from Yuuhigawa,' said Sulien. 'Get hold of the most senior person you can there and tell them they have to talk to me.'

Hidaka said simply, miserably, 'No. I will do nothing for you.'

Sulien sighed and hoisted him forcibly to his feet. He steered him over to the banks of equipment. 'You are going to give your people information that they will want. Someone almost destroyed Tamohara a couple of hours ago; tell them it was Novianus Sulien, and tell them I have to talk to the Crown Prince.'

461

'Tamohara?' repeated one of the other prisoners nervously, and Minius started and demanded, 'It was *who*—? What happened out there?'

Hidaka stared at Sulien for a moment, then sullenly turned to the desk and lifted a headset, muttering, 'When they know you are here they will kill us all.'

'Tell them the Onager's still aimed at Tamohara and we have someone waiting to fire it again in twenty minutes if he doesn't hear from us,' said Pas.

Sulien glanced at him. 'Yes,' he agreed, 'Say that.'

'Why haven't they found where it came from yet?' asked Prince Kaneharu.

'It's dark,' said Tadahito wearily. 'There are hundreds of square miles to cover.'

'There is nothing in the region that should have been capable of doing this,' said Takanari, rubbing his eyes. 'Not *now* . . .'

Tadahito did not know how many times he had heard that phrase over the last hour; he had said it at least once himself. He was not sure what else anyone could say. Although the state room they were using as an operations centre was simmering with jittery activity, he found himself glumly suspecting its real purpose was to distract them from the fact that there was nothing they could do. They were too far away.

But just as he thought that, Morokata looked up from a long-dictor and said, 'Your Highness,' in a voice that quietened everyone.

Tadahito turned to him, swallowing down a knot of apprehension in his throat.

'We have an explanation for the situation,' said Morokata, levelly. 'A Roman general has captured one of our radio bases in the eastern Kosen Mountains. He's using our own equipment to contact Yuuhigawa. He claims the blast was a warning shot' – there was a rustle of breath sucked in or sharply expelled – 'and he says he is ready to destroy Tomacho in less than a quarter of an hour.'

462

There was a strangled silence. 'Unless what?' asked Tadahito.

Takanari was leaning forward. 'But this man is acting on his own?'

'Not that we should necessarily allow ourselves to be held to ransom in this way, but he is demanding to speak to you, Your Highness,' said Morokata. 'And apparently he is adamant that you be told his name: it is Novianus Sulien.'

'*Novianus Sulien?*' repeated Tadahito, and blinked. For a moment he almost wondered if he were truly awake. He said, 'He's not a general.'

Kaneharu's mouth was slightly open, 'Lady Noviana's brother,' he said. 'How would he be able to do this?'

'If you have one of these weapons, you don't need an army to fire it,' murmured Tadahito. 'Clearly I have no choice but to talk to him. Arrange for the signal to be relayed here. And tell them not to attack until I have finished with him.'

He found Noriko outside his rooms, wrapped in her parachute silk, her face still a little crumpled with sleep.

'It's all right,' he said to her, 'go back to bed.' He didn't mean to lie to her; he wanted to keep all this from touching her. He wanted her to be resting peacefully before a morning when the war was almost won.

'I will not be able to sleep now,' said Noriko. 'Una's brother is alive?'

'Don't run and tell her until we establish how long he's going to stay that way,' said Tadahito sourly.

Morokata appeared in the doorway. 'The line is prepared, Your Highness.'

Noriko pulled up a chair and sat down with an air of quiet obstinacy while Tadahito paced around the longdictor table, trying to work off the tension. He did not bother telling her again to go away. At last he lunged into the chair and seized the circlet. 'Novianus Sulien,' he said, 'I thought I knew something about you by reputation. I must have been mistaken.'

'That city—' Sulien's voice, bouncing across nine thousand

463

miles, was faint and scratchy. '—Tamohara – did the avalanche hit it? Or was there an earthquake or – or anything?'

'I don't understand why you are asking me this,' said Tadahito, in an icy tone that lent a certain stateliness and menace to the fact that he was, indeed, very confused.

'I could have destroyed it – Tamohara. The weapon you used in Mohavia, you call it Surijin? Ours is called the Onager.'

'I do not think it matters what names we use,' said Tadahito. 'You say you will destroy Tamohara unless what?' He considered and added, 'Perhaps you should be aware I have your sister here.'

Noriko shook her head in distress. Tadahito looked away from her.

In the Kosen bunker Sulien rocked back in his chair with shock, 'What?' he stammered, 'Una – is she—?' Tadahito's implied threat barely touched him; he was too amazed at the thought that Una was so close to the thin, stern voice in his ear, too overwhelmed by everything that had happened today. 'Then you know—?'

'Explain to me what you mean by threatening Tamohara,' insisted Tadahito.

With difficulty Sulien dragged himself back to the question. 'No, no, your Highness, the city's safe – there's no one out there. I had to make sure they'd actually pass the message on to you. Your people know where we are; they could have killed us all and you'd never have even known I was trying to talk to you.'

Tadahito closed his eyes, almost resenting the jolt of relief that resounded through him; he felt it knock away what little grasp he had on what was happening. He asked, 'And what did you wish to tell me?'

'That you don't want to fight this kind of war,' Sulien said. 'You can't. You killed almost all of us in Mohavia today, and I know why. But if you don't stop, now, then it won't end with Rome, not with both sides holding these weapons. I know Rome has at least one more, somewhere on the Promethean Sea. And that's all I know about it; when your soldiers get here they can do whatever you want to me, but that's the truth. And there could be others out there.

'Your Highness, even if you destroy Rome itself, even if you split the Empire into pieces, you won't be safe.'

Tadahito said nothing.

'My sister has a plan to end the war,' said Sulien. 'All this year we have been working for that – my sister and Varius and— All of us.'

'I know she has a plan,' said Tadahito, carefully expressionless.

'Then please, at least listen to her. *Please*. I know you've seen battle, your Highness, but you haven't seen what these weapons do. You can't have seen as many bodies as I have today. Please, don't do it to Rome – just *please*—' He stumbled to a halt. He had no more to say. He waited in silence, aware of the weight of the fourth centuria's gaze.

Then Tadahito broke the connection.

'You don't know what you should do,' said Noriko. She was standing looking down at him while Tadahito leant over the desk and put his head into his hands.

'I must talk to Father,' he said, in an exhausted moan, and was relieved only his sister was there to hear him sound like that.

'*I* will tell you what to do. Cancel the attack. Let Una do what she says she can. Give them a little time to try. And bring her brother here. You already promised her you would look after him.'

'How can I give up our plans now?' asked Tadahito. 'Isn't it already too late? If they have a weapon like that – if we don't strike again, they will respond to what we did in Enkono.'

'Then we must bring the war to a peaceful end as soon as possible.' Noriko laid a hand on his back and bent down so that their faces were almost level. 'Look up,' she said, and he did, and met her eyes. 'If I can come here from Rome and make you listen to me, if you do this when I tell you it is right, then Marcus and I did not marry for nothing. And it was something more than a waste that I have been so far from home for so long.'

Varius' room was dark except for the chilly glow from the machines beside him. Una was still in the chair by the bed, with her head pillowed on her folded arms, resting on the mattress.

Tadahito touched her shoulder. 'Una,' he said quietly, because that was what his sister called her now.

Una woke with a blurred little cry of shock and looked at once to Varius' face before blinking up at Tadahito.

He said, 'I've just been talking to your brother.'

'You've sold us out, haven't you? That's what this is – you're not who you said you were; you've been working with them the whole time. And we're going to rot in some prisoner-of-war camp while you swan off with them and—' Asper's power of speculation failed and he finished, 'You're not even fucking Roman!'

Sulien sagged, too tired to brace himself against how much this hurt.

'You just fucking dare say that again—!' said Pas, furious.

'He's a convicted *traitor*! Didn't you ever watch longvision back home?'

'We'd all be dead if it wasn't for him,' said Caerellius. 'Whatever his real name is.'

'Oh yeah, that's what he says,' Asper muttered.

Six or seven of them rose to their feet, anger washing dangerously between them. Sulien tried, impossibly, to look them all in the eyes at once. He said, 'The war's going to end. You're all going to live. Everyone's coming home.'

'Throw down your weapons!' shouted a voice outside. A battalion of Nionian soldiers had reached the base.

'Do as they say,' said Sulien, dropping his own. 'Line up in your octets. File out.'

Slowly he led them outside into the dark, his hands raised. The flanks of the valley were lined with soldiers pointing guns.

'Where is Novianus Sulien?' someone called.

'I'm here,' Sulien answered, and behind him, Dorion whispered, with mock-cheeriness, 'So, you'll be on your way, then.'

Sulien turned his head. 'It's not for long. I swear it's not for long now. And the Prince promised me everyone would be treated well.'

'Oh, well,' said Dorion, 'if he *promised*—' The sarcasm wasn't as scathing as it might have been, Dorion was handling it lightly, just cuffing at Sulien with it. But still Sulien hated the abandoned, let-down look on his face.

'I don't want to leave any of you behind. Listen,' he said urgently, watching a Nionian captain making his way down towards him, 'you can come with me.' He looked past Dorion to Pas. 'The three of us—'

Dorion glanced from Sulien to the others and back and a little shudder went through him, but he said curtly, 'No, I'm staying with them.' His chin was raised, his shoulders squared.

'All right,' Sulien said, 'look after everyone, then.'

Pas asked slowly, 'You really reckon you can stop all this?'

'If you can, you'd better get on with it,' said Dorion, shaking again, though now he was managing to smile. 'You go with him, Pas, if they'll let you.'

The captain approached, already glaring at Sulien in obvious distrust. He beckoned him tersely out of the line. Sulien dragged Pas with him and said, 'I need him to come with me.'

The captain scowled and shouted something into his radio without answering Sulien. He gestured impatiently to his men and with commands and shoves, the Nionian soldiers began ushering Sulien's centuria away up the hillside. Dorion looked back over his shoulder. Sulien's throat tightened.

Pas lurked at Sulien's side, apprehensive.

'These are all your men?' the captain asked as a squad of Nionians pushed into the base behind them.

'Forty-three of us,' said Sulien, 'and four of your men.'

'Forty-three,' repeated the captain, shaking his head in disbelief.

One of the Nionian soldiers called out from the doorway of the base.

'Come back inside,' said the captain. 'They are calling again from Axum.'

Sulien beckoned to Pas, afraid he'd be swept off with the rest if he were left alone, and they followed the captain back inside the command centre. Tadahito would hardly be calling back to announce that he had changed his mind and was going to have the whole centuria shot, or that he would destroy Rome today after all; nevertheless, those were Sulien's first thoughts, and his pulse continued to bang painfully even after he'd dismissed them. Gingerly, he lifted the headset.

'Sulien!' Una almost screamed into the longdictor.

And Sulien dropped into the seat, with a long, worn-out laugh. He heard it sound less than sane, and couldn't immediately stop. 'There you are,' he said, as if he'd been looking for her all this time and her absence had been surprising and unreasonable. 'There you are.'

'I didn't know—'

Now he could hear that she could barely speak, something was choking her.

'The weapon,' she managed, 'I didn't know you were there.'

'I'm glad you didn't know,' he said. 'Are you all right? Is everyone safe? Is Lal with you?' And he pushed back the chilly awareness of how long it had been since he had thought of Lal.

Una said, 'Varius—' and her voice twisted away, agonised.

Sulien leant his head against the back of the chair and shut his eyes. He asked, slowly, 'Has he been arrested?' and because she was trying to answer and still failing, he supplied, even more softly, 'Is Varius dead?'

'No,' said Una, 'no, he's here, but he—'

'Listen,' interrupted Sulien fiercely, 'he's going be fine. Whatever's happened, he just has to hold out another couple of days. Tell him he has to. Tell him I'm coming.'

ANANKE

'There's my sister,' said Sulien, leaning close to the volucer window as it descended.

Pas was sitting opposite him. He'd been quiet through the fifty hours of this long, sudden journey; Sulien, on the other hand, had scarcely stopped talking – he couldn't stop himself. Pas had listened, solemnly, and Sulien was grateful for that, and glad Pas had guessed who he was. All these months he'd been in the army he had been content to get by without a past, but now, as they flew back towards it, from the Kosen Mountains to the coast of Hyouden, the relief and the fear of what he'd find kept boiling over out of him into words. He chattered feverishly about Varius, and the three times he'd saved Sulien's life, and how typical it would be of him if he wouldn't give someone else a chance, wouldn't wait long enough for Sulien to help him now.

Then they'd stopped again, for hours, at a Sinoan military base on the edge of the Arctic Sea, where no one spoke enough Latin to tell them why, and Sulien, distraught at the delay, paced and ground his teeth and explained to Pas how he hadn't been in time to save Marcus, and how he couldn't stand it if he were too late now, not after everything, it just couldn't happen. And he rushed through a jumbled account of how he and Una had met Marcus in the flea-market in Gaul, five years before. And how neither of them had liked him much until what had happened in Wolf Step on the way to Holzarta, and then . . .

But when Marcus died, he and Sulien had been half-estranged, only part of the way back towards friendship, and it was *his* fault, and now there was nothing he could ever do to put it right.

Sometimes, though, something he said – about Drusus, or Marcus, or how he'd never said a proper goodbye to Lal, who was so sweet – would lead him back towards the war, and then he stopped, and he and Pas would look at each other in silence. The war crumpled language, and yet Sulien felt a faint, scared flicker of regret that they were leaving it.

Una was waiting on the steps above the courtyard, her hair whipped about by the downblast from the wings. Her face was upturned, her body rigid with urgency and tension. But Sulien released a breath and, just for a moment, let himself sink comfortably into the seat. She would not look like that if Varius had just died.

Flinching a little at the sight of the huge, ugly cross standing for some unfathomable reason outside the palace gates, he jumped down onto the paving before the volucer was fully settled on the ground and ran up the steps to Una. She did not take a step towards him; she remained fixed in place, waiting, too gripped with expectation to move, but as he reached her at last she lifted her arms with a stifled cry.

Her bones seemed to click and grate when he put his arms around her, as if over these last months they had been shaken or dragged a little out of true, but she held onto him with almost bruising strength, then pulled back and stared at him, speechless but dry-eyed, while Sulien was crying again a little, barely noticing it.

'Varius,' he said, and Una led him into the palace at a run.

Something had changed, and it worried Varius that he couldn't make out what it was. His throat felt scraped and sore – something had been pulled out of it. There was still a stripe of pain along his back. His lips were cracked and dry. There was a reason for these things, almost in reach, but there was something else that was more urgent, something harder to understand, and yet simpler, *better* . . .

He drew in a soft, easy breath, and the air felt clear and rich as music as it filled his lungs. And then it occurred to him that the last thing he had known was that that he had been battering out his strength against the vast weight piled on him, and now it was gone. He seemed to float incredulously above the place where it had held him down.

He might almost have thought he had died, that this was what it was like, except that when he moved, he could still feel the residue of pain, diffused through his muscles. And someone was holding his hand, and had been for a long time. Varius rediscovered the light pressure of cool fingers folded round his with drowsy happiness. He remembered, dimly, how hard he'd had to work for each heartbeat; it had been so good to feel that someone was there.

He opened his eyes, and saw Una standing over him with a tall, tired, sunbeaten young soldier in a dusty uniform beside her. Both of them were staring at him as if he were doing something remarkable.

Varius smiled vaguely at them both and found his eyelids sliding shut again.

Then he realised who he'd seen, and without quite being able to open his eyes again, he smiled more broadly and said, 'You're alive.'

They both laughed. Sulien said, 'Well, you were the idiot who forgot how to breathe.'

'I'm sorry,' Varius said peaceably, and they laughed again, though when he lifted his eyelids again he saw how Una's smile kept falling apart.

'Don't say sorry,' she said, 'just don't do that again, ever—'

It was Una's hand holding his, of course. Varius was not at all surprised by this, and yet he stared at her with calm wonder, hardly knowing why, until at last she blinked nervously and looked away. He tightened his own fingers on hers.

His jaw was rough with stubble, snagging on the pillow when he turned his head. 'What day is it?' he asked, and then lifted his head sharply, horrified. 'Rome—'

'It hasn't happened,' said Una quickly. 'Sulien stopped it. Sulien and Noriko.'

'How?' asked Varius, and looked back to Sulien. The burst of shocked energy had been too sudden, and exhaustion welled back as it lagged away. He croaked, 'How are you here?'

And they began telling him, and Varius was frustrated when he realised there was nothing he could do to keep himself from falling asleep before he had understood anything after Sulien began, 'We were in the desert . . .'

Una and Sulien went into one of the anterooms further down the passage. Except for the small laundry room that Una had run to three days before, there was nowhere more private to go; there was a bedroom for her somewhere in the palace, but she had never let anyone show her the way there and didn't know where it was.

She tried to say something, but it collapsed into a sigh and she sagged against a wall and let herself slide down it until she was sitting on the polished floor. Sulien ignored the bloated velvet furniture and sat down cross-legged in front of her. They did nothing but look at each other with rickety smiles that ached and shouldn't have lasted, but somehow held up.

Sulien said, 'You look more tired than him *or* me.' Una's hair was matted, her skin dull. There were bruise-coloured bulges under her eyes.

'You haven't looked in a mirror yet then,' said Una. Her nose twitched with a tired pretence of disapproval. 'And you need a bath.'

'You're hardly one to talk, you know.'

Una exhaled a silent laugh, and then slumped even more heavily. She rubbed a hand over her face and resumed gazing at him, the ripple of the smile gone now, only the tiredness and sadness clear as glass beneath. 'Oh, Sulien—' was all she could say for a long time. And then, very quietly, 'I wish you'd never had to go.'

'But I did have to, didn't I?' Sulien closed his eyes as every spurt of gunfire and blood, the scream of the Onager and the fields of the dead jarred through him. And he thought of his last sight of his men, being marched away along the valley, and took a heavy breath full of his promise to bring them all home. And he looked at Una and could tell she had felt at least some of this; she was leaning towards him, her eyes wide and black and, for her, unusually soft. 'I wish it had never happened,' he said, with a little thump of his fist against the marble floor, 'of course I wish that. But since it did, I don't think I'm sorry I was there.'

But he could not quite say he was certain he was not sorry. And Una did not look as if she could agree, but she nodded.

He changed the subject. 'How many people have you got now?'

Una smiled again, a cracked little fragment of a thing at first, but it built, steadied. She answered, 'Two thousand and seventeen.'

Sulien grinned back. 'Well,' he said, 'that sounds like enough.'

The sun was setting in flags of red and blue cloud above the roofs of Axum. In the palace courtyard the volucer's wings were already turning, stirring up a warm breeze.

'You are sure you refuse my help?' Tadahito said. He'd offered money, weapons, even aircraft.

Una said carefully, 'You have helped us as much as we could ever ask, and we're grateful. But we can't take anything like that from you. If we let you pay for what we're trying to do, Nionia would own it – we'd be fighting the war for you. We can't do that. It has to be Roman.'

Tadahito looked unhappy, afraid he was making a mistake, and aware his part in this leave-taking was awkward. The Surijin's cry hung silently in the air. Sulien and Pas were just as uneasy – they were fastidiously courteous and thankful, but they avoided looking at him when they could. They were still both dressed in their uniform, among the Nionian soldiers and the standing guard around the courtyard. There was still the memory of what they'd seen; there was still the threat.

You have a week, Tadahito had said. That's all I can promise you, or Rome. By then events will have moved on and I will have to respond.

There was no time for the rest they all needed. Well, we'll rest on the volucer, thought Una; we'll rest after this is done. Only a day had passed since Sulien's return, and Varius should have spent at least another day in bed – at least, aside from a few experimental walks up and down the corridor, Sulien had been able to convince him to stay there, until it was absolutely necessary to leave.

Still, just to see him on his feet, or making hurried calls, to Delir, Evadne, Theon and Praxinoa, made her dazed with relief, even if he still swayed sometimes, or subtly propped himself against columns or furniture. She kept herself out of his thoughts, but she could feel the course of them, moving with a clear, busy strength his body hadn't quite regained yet. But it wasn't enough; she kept wanting to touch him to be sure he was really there, and struggled not to extend any accidental brush of their hands.

Now he was leaning against the courtyard wall. Una, exasperated at herself for needing to do it, was rationing how often she allowed herself to look at him, but she was keenly aware of how he was standing, the exact placing of his right hand on the dark red stone.

She did not quite allow herself to notice that it was harder than ever to keep the blare of feeling turned down low because she was more hopeful, less guilty. It amazed her that he and everyone else could not hear it.

Noriko was standing with Tomoe and Sakura, her face as clear and serene as if the war were already over. Una smiled at her, sadly, because despite all the difficulty of bringing her here, she was sorry that Noriko could not come back with them across Nubia, and into the fight that was coming. They reached for each other's hands.

'Good luck,' said Noriko.

'I'll write to you.'

Noriko smiled. 'That's not enough,' she said. 'When this is over, come and visit me.'

Lal set up a line of bottles out on the sand at the furthest extent of the headlights, crouched just in front of the car's wheels, and commenced shooting. They had one gun between the three of them, and either she or Delir would be carrying it – Ziye had made it clear it would not be her. Delir, who had turned out to be a reasonable shot himself, flinched whenever Lal fired a round, but he was equally unhappy at the idea of her being unarmed.

'You can't see what you're doing in this light,' he said for want of a better reason to tell her to stop, despite the fact that she had hit three of the bottles already.

'It'll be dark on the night too,' Ziye remarked.

'I don't like doing it either,' muttered Lal irritably. It was true; the gun frightened her. But the very act of forcing her fingers steady so that she could squeeze the trigger and the kick of the weapon as she fired relieved some of the dark twists of pressure within her.

They had been waiting for more than an hour on this empty stretch of road and she was seething with impatience and excitement, and yet, though she could hardly understand the feeling, she was afraid of meeting Sulien too, even after all these red-raw months of missing him. There was part of her that wished she could simply take the knowledge he was safe and escape with it somewhere, into peace. I won't be able to bear it, she thought. The story Varius had told Delir of Sulien's return was too much, the wonder of it inflating the heated spaces in her brain already full of him. She wished his arrival could be more ordinary, to leave her a little more space to think and breathe. If she looked at him and saw that those blank patches in his gaze at her and in his letters had grown—

I want to think about guns and ships and identity papers and the paintings I'm going to do when all this is over, she thought sullenly, exploding a fourth bottle.

'It's a pity you don't like it, really,' mused Ziye, watching her calmly from her perch on a camp-stool by the car. 'You're good at it.'

'You're good at beating people up with your bare hands, but you don't like doing it either,' said Lal.

'Not any more,' Ziye agreed equably.

475

'I can see them!' Delir cried.

Lal sprang to her feet. Four people were coming up the track: Una, Varius, a slight, dark boy she didn't know in Roman uniform, and— And there was Sulien, and her heart surged up, carved a trail of light through her like a firework. The weight of hundreds or thousands of bloody injuries even he could not repair fell away from her imagination; he was whole, perfect, and he looked overjoyed to see her.

He strode ahead of the others towards her and for an instant she thought, *Don't*—

But then he took hold of her and swept her into a kiss, and he tasted of bruised sand and hot sky, and she forgot what had been worrying her. She loved him; all she had needed was for him to come back, for all six of them to be together. She laughed.

She had always found it difficult to picture him in uniform with his hair cropped; the thought of it had felt like a disfigurement; she was startled now at how natural it looked in reality.

'This is Berenice,' Sulien said to the other soldier, but before she had time to scowl at the name, he finished, 'Lal, this is Pas.'

Delir patted Pas on the shoulder. He looked shy and overwhelmed in the midst of the noisy reunion happening around him. Delir was indignant when he heard how ill Varius had been, and shook his head in reproof. 'I should have gone instead; I knew you weren't well enough,' he muttered.

'I think I'd had it, wherever I was,' said Varius cheerfully. 'Hadn't I, Sulien?'

Even with so much of her attention hopelessly tangled around Sulien, Lal noticed at once the look that spilled from Una when Varius' back was turned. She was startled. Were the others tactfully pretending they didn't see, or—? No, they really did not.

As they climbed into the car she twitched an eyebrow at Una. Una was silently horrified. Lal impressed herself with her own restraint in saying nothing.

It was almost dawn by the time they reached Tamiathis.

'If I could just tell my mother I'm safe,' murmured Pas,

hesitantly. 'She's only forty miles away. I can't believe that— I can't believe I'm here.'

'Not yet,' said Una at once, 'you can't explain how you got here.'

'It'll be just a few more days,' said Delir kindly.

Varius was stupefied, helpless with tiredness by now, and Ziye summarily assigned him Lal's bed above the printing shop. She pulled down the shutters and produced piles of blankets and bedrolls.

'A few more days!' repeated Lal, dizzily, flinging herself down beside Una and hugging her. Sulien was in the storeroom with Pas. The separation chafed a little but with the warmth of his lips still stamped on hers it was bearable for now. There would be time for them later.

'You're not even frightened,' said Una, wondering. Her voice sounded fragile in the dark.

'No,' said Lal, resolutely, and turned onto her side to face Una. 'You can't be – not now?'

Una stared up at the ceiling. 'I've promised so many people so much,' she said.

'Well then,' said Lal, 'I'll promise you it's going to happen, I can feel it.'

But she woke less than an hour later, heart and breath jarred by Sulien's voice raised in a hoarse shout from the next room, and the sound of a short, tangled struggle.

Una was awake too, lying tense beside her. Lal gave a small moan of distress and started up.

'Wait,' whispered Una.

On the other side of the door they could hear a low rumble of conversation: Sulien and Pas were talking. Even from here, she could hear Sulien's breath steadying, growing quieter. Every now and then the names of people and cities she didn't know floated through: Hanno, Gracilis, Aregaya.

Una could not stop thinking about everything that had to be done and everything that could go wrong, and yet here she was, in the printing shop stockroom, baffled at having nothing immediate to do.

Twenty longdictor calls had been made, in a code agreed months ago. She felt at once that the real meaning was being shouted out all the way to Rome, and that she could not understand it herself. Those simple conversations with a few trusted people: how could they really be confirming that hundreds of others were beginning to move?

Yet over the nine months since they had begun, she had at some point looked every one of these two thousand and seventeen people in the face. The thought smoothed her over with pride even while it made her shiver: What am I doing to these people? she thought incredulously – as good as murdering them, perhaps? Sometimes the sight of Sulien and Varius, the closeness of death just freshly washed off them both, stopped her breathing, leaving her frozen at the very thought of it.

Sulien was standing over Varius now, examining the charts of the Mediterranean and Aegean and trying to take in the finished contours of plans that had been barely formed when he'd left. Varius was going over the routes, humming quietly under his breath – not really a song, only a soft accompaniment to thinking. They'd tried to let him sleep longer than the rest of them, but he'd risen, groaning, and lurched downstairs into the stockroom when he heard them moving about. 'Perhaps you should stay out of it,' Una felt compelled to say to him, 'meet us in Rome when it's done.'

Varius turned an incredulous, aggrieved look at her. 'After all this?' he said, flatly.

'Two days ago you were *dying*, Varius.'

'He isn't now,' Sulien pointed out.

'And when I woke up,' said Varius, 'everything had changed and I'd missed it. I'm not having that again, not now of all times.' But he smiled then, with painful sweetness. 'I'll be there with you.'

Sulien said, 'We all know what we're in for, Una, and we're

all volunteers. We didn't have even one cohort like that out in Mohavia.'

'So I need to get round to Sabratha and pick up the *Ananke*,' said Varius firmly, turning his attention back to the charts. The little ship was still in the cove by Evadne's house.

'We could do without it,' Una suggested. 'We can fit in with Phanias, or with Bupe in the *Carmenta*.'

'But that wasn't the plan,' objected Varius, startled, and then stopped, considering it. He looked saddened.

Una smiled. 'We need every ship we have,' she corrected herself.

Sulien said, 'I'll come with you, Varius. I can keep an eye on you. You can't drive four hundred miles and then sail a boat another two hundred miles, not alone.'

'I was thinking you'd come, Una – you know the boat best,' said Varius.

Una hesitated. It was ridiculous that the choice should feel so loaded: it was only one day to be without either or both of them.

Then Lal came in, having overheard the last part of the conversation, and settled it by appealing to Sulien, 'Don't leave again yet.'

'We'll meet you tomorrow outside Heraklion,' Una told Sulien.

The small white house on the cliff was locked and empty. Una turned to face the bare sea. Somewhere beyond the horizon a fishing boat was already carrying Maralah and Evadne towards Rome.

She drew in a breath full of salt air and forgot to let it out; her body locked around it, teeth clamped tight.

'After all this time,' murmured Varius beside her, 'I can't believe we're really doing this.'

'I feel –' began Una, so low she could barely hear herself. But a colder breeze scythed off the sea and cut off whatever the rest of the sentence had been, and she shivered.

'It will be all right,' said Varius almost as quietly. His hand

479

knocked against hers, which was screwed into a fist, until it loosened and their fingers hooked around each other.

They steered the little inflatable dinghy out into the cove and climbed up onto the *Ananke*'s deck. Una caught Varius running an affectionate hand over the roof of the cabin, smiling as if he'd come home.

She sat down on one of the cockpit benches and smiled too. 'You used to say this boat didn't belong to you – she was just a resource for the cause, don't you remember?'

'Well,' conceded Varius, 'things are different now.' And he stroked the *Ananke* again as if to console her, and looked at the sky. 'It's still light,' he said. 'We might as well take her up the coast – less to do tomorrow.'

Una groaned quietly. She had driven all the way along the coast of Egypt from Tamiathis, refusing to let Varius take over even briefly. But she dragged herself up and reached towards the controls.

Varius pushed her lightly away. 'I'll do it, Una.'

She looked at him anxiously, but his face was alert and he looked perfectly steady as he took the helm. She sank back onto the seat and a little of the tension in her body flowed out into the dark water beneath the bow as he steered the *Ananke* out onto the sea. Sometimes, after drooping closed, her eyelids would spring open in indeterminate panic, then as she found him still there at the helm, a shadowy figure as the dark settled around the ship, she would let her head drop back against the seat again, reassured.

But they were both so sodden with tiredness when at last they dropped anchor that Una felt they would leave an inky trail of it behind them as they climbed down into the cabin. Varius looked down at Una, standing by the bottom of the steps, and he wanted to say good night, or to promise her again that it would be all right, but with a defeated sigh at the sheer impossibility of speech, he embraced her instead.

Una put off the moment of lifting her head from his shoulder another moment, and then another, and then it seemed, to both of them, too tiring to move apart at all. Her eyelids had fallen shut again. They were almost asleep there on their feet, almost asleep as they sank down onto the same bed, and lay still.

A question, a wisp of doubt, rustled quietly in Varius' mind as he stretched himself out on top of the tangled covers, but they were both so exhausted; all these hunted months had been so hard, and they had travelled so many miles together in this little boat, gone to bed night after night only a few feet apart in this cabin, so what did it matter if they fell asleep like this now? They were no longer holding one another, just lying side by side, and Una was already so still, her breath soft and even, and Varius himself was so close to the boundary of sleep himself he could hardly tell whether or not he'd crossed it yet. The sea lifted the *Ananke* and let it down, the rhythm steady, and sometimes Varius could feel a dream beginning to brim up out of the deeper wells of sleep: that they were no longer floating on the surface of the sea but underneath it, suspended together between the seabed and the air, safely breathing the water, hidden.

Una too felt she was so nearly asleep the difference barely mattered; there was just one tense thread holding her to consciousness, and she lay waiting for it to break. This is all that I want, she told herself, feeling his pulse echo softly in her own flesh, almost overcoming the ache there. I don't need anything else, just to lie here like this.

Whenever his eyes drifted open, Varius could see the surface of the water outside, dimly reflected on the ceiling above them – a net of light, trembling and breaking – and he was surprised that it had grown no brighter. He felt as if hours had passed, and yet it seemed natural that the night had stalled here, as if nothing would change again now, and they would always be floating here, always on the point of sleep.

Una shifted slightly, bringing up her hand so that it fell across his arm, her fingertips weightless on the edge of his chest.

Then, as if only by chance, as if they were lying passively in the flow of a current that lifted and turned them towards each

481

other, their faces came together on the pillow. Their lips brushed together and caught.

Una sighed, and settled herself even closer, her slow, sleepy fingers stroking his arms, tracing over his closed eyes. Varius let his lips part and close against hers as if he was whispering in his sleep. And still it seemed to him that this was as separate from their real lives as a dream they would forget on waking, that they'd slipped out of the world. A faint shiver went through him when he felt her hand come to rest lightly on his waist under his tunic, but it was not enough to shock him back to himself, to make him ask what they were doing.

It was almost difficult to touch him, to push away the fabric over his skin when the boundaries of her own body were turning as vague as clouds. It was such a relief to kiss him; Una felt it was like letting out a held breath and gasping down air. It was so strong it made her blurred and soft, and she imagined she needed to soak up only a little more of it and then she would be able to stop. If he did not let her go, if he kept kissing her, just a little longer, that would be enough for the rest of her life.

Varius' hands copied hers, nudging fastenings open, and under her clothes he felt the warm patterns of claw- and toothmarks threaded and banded across her body; his fingers discovered a spool of fine ridges that ran down across her shoulder to her breast. He held her tighter, so sorry and so glad they were there, the living hum of her body ringing softly through the smooth and marked skin alike. He bent his lips to the scars, feeling he could lay down small protective wards, like plates of invisible armour, little seals of resolve that he would never let it happen again. And he remembered holding her face between his hands the day the wounds had been made, the urgency, the jolt of recognition.

And at that the illusion or pretence that they were only dreaming or not themselves vanished and he was fully awake and incredulous, and bewildered, and angry with himself – with both of them. And he startled into a confused struggle where his intentions seemed to tangle and double back on themselves, so that when he meant to let go of her he clutched her more fiercely instead, rolled her underneath him, pulling aside her clothes and his own. And she met him with just as much panicked, grasping force: kissing harder, teeth and fingernails out, hands closing on each other's hair. Whatever he was trying to say kept getting crushed breathlessly between them.

But at last he remembered how to stop, and he dragged himself clear. He sat up and knelt there on the bed in the dark, gasping. The *Ananke* rose and fell, and he wished everything would keep still for a minute so that he could think.

Una was still, naked on the bed beside him. Then she raised herself so that they were kneeling face to face, staring, though it was too dark to see more than each other's shadowed outline, the faint liquid glint of each other's eyes.

'Una,' he said, in a whisper, and his voice sounded questioning, lost.

Tentatively, Una laid her face against the join of his neck and shoulder. He felt her sigh again, her breath skimming like a feather across his chest. Varius closed his arms around her, feeling a baffling prickle of tears in his eyes. And he thought that it was too late now anyway, and, surprised at how lovely a thought that was, he gathered her even closer, lifting her into his lap. They both trembled again as her legs parted around him, moving now with the slow rock of the sea, and when they fell together onto the bed again he found tears on her face too, tasted the salt on his lips.

Varius woke and the cabin was full of light. He turned his head at once to look at Una because he had not forgotten for a moment. It was the memory, the excitement that had woken him. Una had moved a little away from him as they slept and was not touching him, though both her hands were extended across the covers towards him. He couldn't see her face; it was hidden under her hair.

He wanted to pull her back into his arms, but he was afraid of waking her, afraid to see regret flicker into focus on her face.

He worried: because it was too ingrained a mental habit to stop now, almost deliberately trying to distract himself from the happiness buzzing and singing through him like a radio playing too loud. Almost two years after Gemella's death he'd tried to love someone else, and he remembered how miserable he had made himself with guilt and stirred-up grief. Una might feel that now, and there would be nothing he could do to change it.

But he didn't feel that himself. He found he could think of Gemella, even with Una lying there beside him – not quite without pain, but without any sense of betrayal, and without disrupting the flow of happiness that kept thrumming through him, louder and louder no matter what he thought about.

It was strange he could be so sure of something it had not occurred to him to want before.

He lay there, anxious, smiling, waiting for her to open her eyes.

NOVIANA, NOVIANUS

The sky was as clear as they'd hoped, the breeze just strong enough to grind the black surface of the water to a fine glittering grain, like coal powder. A little ahead, the *Carmenta*'s lights led the way. The *Ananke* and the short trail of smaller boats that had joined them as they passed Milos sailed dark.

In the western distance, towards Paros, a few red sparks shone, detached as stars. Even Una was uncertain at first whether they had anything to do with the small, jumbled assembly of fishing boats and motor dinghies creeping north among the Cyclades. But the distant vessels wandered eastwards, and closer together, and a white light flashed briefly in greeting. Pas, perched on the *Ananke*'s prow, raised an arm, but Una had already seen it. It meant that around those seeds of light a flotilla was growing.

Then the *Ananke* sailed around the flank of Polyaigos and into the vanguard of a long advancing line of ships. Una's hands tightened painfully on the ship's controls. She felt little spikes of joy hammering in her chest. Suddenly it was just as she had imagined it: a rebel navy gathering at the heart of the Empire, ships full of free, stubborn men and women, sailing towards Siphnos.

Behind the island's steep wooded slopes, another hundred ships were closing in.

Una steered as close to a beach on the western shore as she dared, drawing up alongside the *Carmenta*, whose lights winked out. Sulien was close beside her in the cockpit; Varius was at the anchor in the stern – he and Una were keeping a shy, cagey distance from each other just now. Lal and Ziye were crouched on the deck of an old fishing boat that had had no name, until

Chaeremon had named it *Alexandria*. Una could see them, just twenty feet across the water.

Varius dropped the anchor into the shallows and they waited. It was too late – in the night, and the war, and the gradual desertion of the island – for there to be any glint of electric lights showing now. Siphnos was blindfolded, while out on the sea the ships drew in towards it.

Then a light flashed three times, high on the island's north peak, then another, much closer, just above the beach.

Una and Sulien looked at each other, and their breathing fell into rapid step. Scouts had already scaled the northeastern slopes, then: the first wave of fighters should be ringed around the little port that was Siphnos' largest town.

Varius was the first to climb down over the side into the water. It was autumn now, and he gasped at the chill. Una and Sulien dropped after him and ploughed through the dark water up to the beach. Underwater, Varius and Una managed a cold and fumbling clasp of hands. Ziye waded to shore hand-in-hand with Lal while Delir helped to drag a dinghy up onto the sand, not daring to let the motors sound yet.

More than three hundred others came with them, mismatched weapons held high above the water as they stumbled on rocks and hurdled the low waves onto the beach. Their names banged in Una's head.

Bupe's party had splashed onto the beach ahead of them. Thirty of them were crouched here on the sand, checking weapons, shaking water from their boots. Another twenty of the freed slaves who'd once fought for Dama would be landing at the western harbour.

Bupe glanced at Una. 'Sure that's all you want?'

Una was armed only with a wooden staff that had once been a rake. Many here tonight had spades, or lengths of pipe, or bread-knives, rather than guns. Ziye had nothing at all. But even so they outnumbered the vigils, and they should still outgun them, provided they could keep reinforcements away from the island for long enough.

'I'll get by,' she said.

Bupe adjusted the grip of her prosthesis on her rifle with practised skill using fingers and teeth. The hooks had been customised to fit the stock. Her head was bare tonight, revealing the soft, rather childlike features untouched by the crumpled patch of bleached scar tissue.

'Well then,' she said, 'time to try.'

They surged up the beach, through the dark olive groves, and on up the hill towards Makaria's house.

There were fewer guards now; the youngest and strongest had been channelled away into the war. The invaders poured through the streets of Siphnos' villages, seeking out those who were left. The island's emigrants had given them a rough description of a large house that had been requisitioned for barracks for the vigiles, and it wasn't hard to find – there were few that size left that weren't boarded up.

They easily overwhelmed the single officer standing guard outside and flooded in. A few excited gunshots peppered windows and ceilings, but not flesh; there was no need; they had surrounded the sleeping vigiles before any of them could reach their own weapons. Now they set to work sorting and tying their prisoners into manageable roomfuls of trussed bundles, and settled in to wait.

In a guard post outside gates of Makaria's villa, one of the three Praetorians on the night shift reached instinctively for the button on the desk, and alarms began to shriek through the house and grounds, just as he realised that neither the twelve men stationed here, nor all the vigiles in the barracks, would possibly be enough. The others ran outside, though he could not begin to imagine what they planned to do. The sound of gunfire rattled the windows as he started to dial the longdictor code for the base in Athens, and as it connected, a gang forced their way through the door and crowded inside the little room. He dragged off the longdictor circlet and drew his pistol, but froze as a slim black girl with one bright eye and a gun in her truncated hands pushed in between the others, sauntering with casual grace.

Gazing down the barrel of her gun, Bupe began to talk. 'I've been practising a long time,' she said, in a quiet, conversational voice. She had said this before, to people like him – security guards and night-watchmen and sometimes frightened slave-owners in their nightclothes, 'but I'm still a terrible shot. You can see how I have . . . disadvantages.' A bullet slammed into the plaster beside him. 'There, you see? I was trying to hit you then. I was angry. But maybe that was unfair. I should give you a chance.'

She swung the gun, without any appearance of attending to where it was pointing. The Praetorian let his own gun fall.

'Call the mainland again,' said Bupe, 'say some drunk kids from Seriphos tried to land on the beach, but you've seen them off. Make it sound good. Convince me.'

As Una had expected, her staff never connected with anything but air, but the mass of people bristled and snarled and heaved at the villa's gates. From inside a handful of bullets punctured the crowd, and there were screams of pain and rage, and they pushed and slammed with greater ferocity against the bars.

But no one had yet been killed here, she was sure of it.

'Drop your weapons and you won't be hurt.' Through the loudspeaker, Varius' voice was calm, implacable. 'That is a promise. You cannot fight us and win.'

Silence stretched between both sides, pulled tight, then the pressure against the gates built, steadier and heavier, as more people piled into the back of the crowd. For a moment Una was flattened painfully against the steel, and panic started to swell as her lungs constricted. Then the gates gave and the crowd swept into the garden.

There were ten men, all backing away towards the villa, their hands raised, their guns scattered across the gravel drive in front of them.

'There could be others,' Una said. 'Check every room.'

The company spilled around the building, circling it like wolves. They were ready to hold anyone else out while they pushed for a way in. They beat at the doors, broke windows.

Inside, Sulien and Pas charged up the stairs.

Makaria elbowed her way out of bed after a breathless fight with her sheets. Once on her feet, she stood looking around in the dark, trembling at the howl of the alarm and the jolts of worse sounds, yet almost affronted by the absence of someone to explain them to her. Then, gathering herself, she flung open her door and raced across the landing looking for Hypatia.

Halfway between their rooms, Hypatia met her, gasping, 'Is it the Nionians?'

'It can't be,' said Makaria. 'What would they want with us?' But a gunshot boomed inside the house, and she remembered the besieged room in the Golden House where Marcus' body had lain, Salvius' corpse sprawled on the stairs. She knew so little of the progress of the war; if Nionia has taken Rome, she thought, with creaking slowness because it remained so nearly unthinkable, perhaps they would come to finish off the last of the Novii.

If that was so, it was useless to think of escape for herself. She could not help but shrink in Hypatia's arms for a moment, overpowered by the warmth of her skin, the scent of her hair – but no, she should concentrate on what might be possible for Hypatia while there was still time.

But someone was already thundering up the stairs and Hypatia was dragging her back towards the bedroom they had once shared, hissing, 'Lock the door!'

'I should go and meet them,' said Makaria dully, thinking again of Salvius, the fallen gun by his hand.

'No!'

Makaria straightened. 'Go back to your room: barricade yourself in there until things quieten down—'

But Hypatia wrestled her inside the bedroom and locked the door herself. Someone called out on the landing, 'Lady Novia!' It was – or at least it sounded like – a Roman voice. Makaria grimaced, and she and Hypatia searched each other's eyes. The bewilderment was too much more to bear.

Footsteps tramped closer and a fist thumped on the door. 'Lady Novia, open the door. It's me – it's Sulien.'

Makaria tried to breathe. She knew it couldn't be Sulien, and she could not imagine any motive anyone could have for pretending. Pinned between these impossibilities, she could not move. It was Hypatia who finally, and seemingly out of sheer curiosity, went back and opened the door.

If she hadn't already heard him speak, Makaria might not have recognised him in the uniform and with the cropped hair, but that voice, along with the height— She took a step back towards a seat that wasn't there, just managed not to fall. She croaked, 'But you—? The arena— You're alive—?'

Sulien grinned crookedly. 'People keep saying that to me lately,' he said.

Makaria stared at him, for another moment, feeling almost devastated with shock. But then, almost before she felt the pleasure to support it, an answering grin began pulling at her own lips. She ventured, 'And your sister . . . ?'

'She's outside,' said Sulien, and Makaria gave a little snort of amazed laughter. 'You've got to get your shoes on and come, now; there's no time for anything else. There are clothes for you on the boat.'

Makaria turned as readily towards her dressing room as if she'd expected this, primed with eagerness to escape. But she did ask, 'Where are you taking me?'

'Where are you taking *us*?' corrected Hypatia.

Sulien smiled again. 'Rome, of course.'

The boats were already beginning to scatter. Bupe's fifty fighters would occupy Siphnos for another day, keeping the news of the raid locked up with the Praetorians and vigiles. And even if they failed, and volucers did sweep in, it would be impossible to pick Makaria off the face of the Aegean. The three fastest vessels they had were waiting along the string of islands leading north from Seriphos, and each one would carry her a little closer to Athens.

Makaria managed another dazed smile at Sulien as he helped push the dinghy off the sand. 'See you tomorrow, then,' she said thinly.

'It's already today,' answered Sulien, and Makaria trembled a little beside Hypatia, but the air was damp and she was only wearing a linen nightdress, so it might have been only the cold.

It was too dark to see them climbing on board the *Alexandria*, but he watched the silhouette of the ship as she began to move, and saw its wake when it brushed the sand at his feet.

He heard Una calling his name, her voice sharp with concern. Lal was sitting on a stone, breathing hard and shivering. Ziye was bent over her and Una standing with a hand on her shoulder. Sulien strode across to them in alarm, though he saw almost at once that Lal wasn't hurt.

'She killed one of them,' Ziye explained.

Sulien crouched in front of her. Her hands were freezing when he gathered them into his.

Lal announced in a crumpled voice, 'He was in the room in the dark— We were climbing in— He was against the wall—'

'Someone thought he'd make a last stand,' explained Ziye, like a translator. 'Nearly took her with him.' She added, with subtle but evident pride, 'She was so fast.'

'Then you had to, Lal,' murmured Sulien. 'You had to.'

'I don't want my father to know—'

'You think he'd rather you were dead? He'll just be happy you're safe.'

Lal nodded jerkily, but her eyes remained wide and glassy. 'I know, I know, but I . . .' She looked at Una. 'Am I the only one?' she asked. 'Did anyone else—? Did you—?'

Una said, 'If you did, I did, Lal – I brought you here. And I was afraid far worse might happen.'

Lal's cold fingers seemed to steady a little in Sulien's hands. She said, 'The way he looked—'

'I know,' said Sulien. For a moment he thought of telling her that he didn't know how many people he'd killed in Mohavia, and then decided there was nothing in that fact to comfort anyone. He rocked her against him, in silence.

'We have to move,' said Una, at last.

Lal let Sulien lead her onto the *Ananke* and fell heavily asleep, with Sulien curled around her on the narrow bunk. Una collapsed on the one opposite.

Varius took the first turn at the helm. The moon and sky were brighter now, a paring of lemon-peel against the blue. The other boats slid away around him. The solitude between these bouts of communal effort was strange, bracing. He breathed in the quiet, and let his mind shuttle back and forth across this point in time, and found every thought entwined around Una, lying just a few feet below him in the dark.

Long before his time was up, Una crept up onto the deck and wrapped her arms round him. She turned her face to his chest and found bare skin at his collarbone, pressed her lips there. He was, even now, surprised that she should be so eager to touch him, and somehow even more surprised by the feel of her breath on his skin, hungrily inhaling. He took her face in his hands and kissed her with much more ungentle force than he thought he'd meant, and for a moment entirely forgot about the controls of the boat as she pushed him into the pilot's chair and surged over him. He gasped through his teeth against her cheekbone and struggled to be content with only kissing her, the inhibiting presence of the others below deck, the miles of distance to cover, and their clothes, all in the way.

A wave caught the *Ananke* broadside, making it lurch. Varius struggled to his feet and reached in alarm to steady it and they laughed under their breath and, grudgingly, subsided. Standing beside him at the wheel, Una took his left hand and seemed absorbed in lifting and turning it over.

Even now it was hard to keep his eyes on the sea. He gazed at her. Her lips were reddened from kissing him; she was tracing her thumb over the last joint of his forefinger with great care, as if it required delicate and painstaking study.

Varius suffered another pang of disbelief that this was or ought to be happening. Sobering, or at least trying to, he began, 'Una—'

'Shh,' Una said, lowering her lips thoughtfully to the place she'd been stroking.

'I'm too old for you,' he started.

Una raised her eyebrows, unimpressed. 'There's no point saying something you just want me to talk you out of.'

Varius stifled a little spurt of caught-out laughter. 'Humour me.'

Una sighed. 'I feel older than I am,' she offered.

'But so do I.'

'All right then,' said Una, patiently, 'how old do you feel?'

Varius considered. 'Fifty,' he decided at last, hesitantly, and then felt embarrassed. Was that really true? He had always felt older, even as a child, and after Gemella's death and the terrible weeks that had followed he had grown used to the idea that he was inwardly ageing faster than most people. But it had never occurred to him to come up with a number, and now, with Una looking at him with amused exasperation, he found himself wondering if the idea wasn't rather silly.

'Well, I feel fifty-five,' said Una. 'No, sixty. So that makes you an indiscretion I'm having.'

Varius laughed and freed his hand to pull her closer to him.

An hour and a half later Sulien rose carefully from Lal's side for his shift. He was surprised to find Una and Varius both awake and on deck, but Una's neutral look of innocent calm was so good he would not have suspected anything had Varius matched it. But Varius did not, quite – there was something subtly shifty about his expression and strained in his voice when he spoke. And Sulien was suddenly almost sure they had been holding hands as he came in – which was nothing unusual in itself, although now he thought of it, the frequency with which he'd

493

seen them join hands was unusual for each of them – and he'd caught Varius in the nervous act of letting go.

Sulien stopped in the cockpit doorway and looked them over. Una's look of casual composure suddenly faltered badly. Her bottom lip folded under her teeth, her eyes flickered over Varius and trailed sheepishly away.

Sulien folded his arms. 'You're a pair of sneaky bastards,' he said.

Rome had changed. Makaria was most appalled by the sight of the Forum, little more than a field of rubble now, and the Cestian Bridge had been smashed into the Tiber. One of the towers of the Golden House itself had been gouged open, and a third of the Septizonium, the band of gates that shielded the main entrance, was gone. But there were also shiny new growths of marble and steel, though none she saw was complete: the huge shell of a new basilica, rising three times as high as the Temple of Apollo which had been demolished to make way for it; two unjoined uprights of a triumphal arch to mark the conquest of Bamaria. But when Makaria descended, dazed, from the Athens–Rome Express, the first thing she saw – the first thing any traveller to Rome arriving at Vatican Fields would see – was a great cage of scaffolding rising from the forecourt, a massive human shape forming within it, one arm raised in greeting. The statue's face was not yet recognisable but Makaria cringed, certain whose it was intended to be.

But work on all these new monuments had been abandoned: the basilica gaped rooflessly into the rain, and there was not a single slave up among the pigeons in the scaffolding around the colossus.

It was only early afternoon. Hypatia had not, in the end, been able to accompany her further than Athens, for there were no identity papers for her. After an hour of waiting, Makaria had been handed her own finished set of documents and, dressed in the well-made but nondescript clothes she'd been given aboard the *Alexandria*, she was bundled onto a train with a slightly embarrassed man who explained that he would be travelling as her husband.

No one who checked her tickets or sat opposite her had looked twice at her. It was more than a year since she had appeared in public, and she had never been as fascinating to the cameras or producers of Imperial memorabilia as other members of her famous family.

A woman called Evadne drove her to a flat in a bombed street off the Via Nomentana, where she was encouraged to sleep. Makaria managed to doze from time to time, but it wasn't easy; she was aware of people gathering in the outer room, talking in lowered but urgent voices. She lay staring at the damp-stained ceiling, missing Hypatia, her heartbeat stammering at the scale of what they expected from her. And yet at the same time she felt oddly irrelevant to all this activity focused upon her. She'd been passed all this way across the Aegean to Athens, and then to Rome; she was like a weapon, or a coin, or a key in these people's hands, something potentially powerful, but in itself inert.

After a few hours someone knocked quietly on the door and when Makaria called an apprehensive greeting, Una stepped inside.

The city was quiet, and darker than Makaria had ever known it. Cleared of the usual soup of electric light, the sky was shocking with stars. Makaria felt she had forgotten they were up there, over Rome too.

They walked quietly, swiftly: at first just a small procession little more than twenty-strong. Then, from doorways and side roads, people began to fall in beside them, until there were hundreds of them, striding through the wet streets.

'You're certain he's in there?' whispered Makaria.

Beside her, Una nodded, and Makaria's breath twisted on itself again. 'Even if— Even if— How can you be sure what will happen? You think people are going to listen to me, but I— I—'

Una looked at her sharply, her face stern. 'We raised an army for you; for months we've been risking our lives to bring you here. You have to be strong enough to get through tonight. You owe us that.'

Sulien was more sympathetic. 'You'll be fine, Madam; we're all here with you.'

'But how are we going to get inside?' Makaria protested helplessly.

Una smiled then. 'We're already inside.'

They reached the Appian Way. Beside them reared the dark Colosseum, erasing a band of sky, biting away the stars. Una and Sulien both slowed as they passed it; Sulien seemed to hunch, as if trying to disguise his height. Makaria saw them look at each other and at Varius as they left it behind.

Then the road turned at the base of the hill and they looked up at the shattered wall of the Septizonium. Unexpectedly, a messy spill of loud music and laughter came splashing down the slope from it.

Una stopped, and the rest of the column fell still too.

'Go on alone,' she said to Makaria. 'Tell them.'

Makaria stepped forward, her lips tight, as if into icy water.

One of the guard stations at the gates had been destroyed, and the rubble was still piled beside the driveway. In the one that remained a shrill, panicky party seemed to be going on. A Praetorian stumbled out towards her and said, 'Clear off, lady.' He was not even pretending not to be drunk.

'I am Lady Novia Faustina,' said Makaria. 'I have been away a long time, but I have come home now. I need to see my cousin.'

The guard blinked, and he strained to focus on her face. 'Your Highness,' he said, 'I beg your pardon.' And he frowned, worried. 'Are you— Are you meant to be here?'

'Yes,' replied Makaria simply. 'I am.'

The Praetorian reached in silence for his radio. 'Sir,' he said, 'sir!'

It took a while for any answer to come – the music inside was too loud. Then, abruptly, it stopped, and the Praetorian sergeant came tramping out, and a dozen other guards came with him or wandered over from further inside the Palace precinct.

'It's Lady Novia, sir,' said the first Praetorian.

'I need to come in and see my cousin,' Makaria repeated softly, to all of them. 'With my friends.'

In turn, the sergeant lifted his radio.

'Yes,' said Makaria, 'tell the other Praetorians I have arrived. And they need do nothing – except that I would be grateful if someone could arrange for General Turnus to come to the Palace at once.'

The sergeant shifted uncertainly. 'We can't,' he said. 'We can't do that without authorisation.'

'I am giving it to you,' said Makaria. And she raised her arm, hoping its trembling was contained within her sleeve. The column of silent, grim-faced people advanced behind her.

The Praetorians stiffened. 'What is this?' demanded the captain.

And on the other side of the gates, from within the Palace itself, streams of people came pouring towards them and gathered into an assembly as stern and numerous as that on Makaria's side: the Palace's servants – the slaves Marcus had freed.

The Praetorians looked back and forth between them, confounded. Some of them had raised their weapons, but didn't know where to aim them.

'We are coming inside,' said Makaria, 'to save Rome. Look at what these few bombs have done to it already. And they are nothing to what is coming, in three days' time. But you don't have to be afraid. You only need to open the gates.'

Drusus was down in the prison cells under the Palace.

He tried not to think of it that way: these were not cells any more. He had had some of the walls hastily knocked through and the heavy doors removed to make enough room for offices, strategy rooms, salons and a bedroom. He'd had beautiful furniture and paintings moved down from above. But there were still raw seams of brick where the dividing walls had been taken down, and those that remained were still coated in the old scratched, stark white paint. A subtle but smothering scent of masonry dust padded every room, with other damper, sharper smells layered underneath it. And there was never any daylight.

He'd moved underground after the first bombs had struck Rome. When he was above ground now, he felt dizzy with terror, but down here the weight of the Palace seemed to crush him, and he could never forget what these rooms had been. He felt as if the prisoners had imprinted themselves on the air, recorded their voices in the brick. And if so, then his own frantic ghost was one of them – two years ago they had thrown him in here, after he'd tried and failed to kill Una with his own hands. Oh, if he'd just been a little faster, or more decisive, if he'd managed to smash her head hard enough just once against the stones. He tried not to remember, but he could still feel the placing of the locked door, and Varius staring at him from the outside – and Varius *was* outside, somewhere – they were all outside. Sometimes he felt he'd locked himself in that awful day.

He would have to leave the Palace, leave Rome, settle somewhere safer. And yet it would look so wrong, it would be an admission of— of—

He wouldn't think it. But if he left, he knew he would lose something.

He scratched the insect bites on his face, and bloodied his fingernails. His body was thrumming with tiredness, but it was still too early to go to bed, and in any case, every time he shut his eyes the lids sprang open as if in shock and his heartbeat kicked out in his chest, proving he would not be able to sleep, not yet. He needed to relax first, he thought. He was not going to try and work any more tonight. He tried to watch an old longvision play, but he felt unable to follow most of it, and such small tensions in the story that he did take in – lies and misunderstandings – made his chest grow painfully tight. But it was a long time before he could bring himself to turn it off, because in the quiet he could hear strange echoes sounding from within the Palace, or rumblings from within the earth beyond the walls. And his own breathing sounded so startlingly loud down here, and sometimes seemed to be coming from somewhere outside him, as if someone were standing close beside him all the time, panting for breath.

He rang for a servant, and no one answered. Drusus did not notice at first, because he couldn't think of anything he actually wanted, and rapidly forgot having sounded the bell. He wasn't hungry; he didn't want a woman. He even had to force the wine in his cup down his throat. The night before he'd tried filling the place with officers and popular gladiators and girls, and they'd laughed and chattered to each other while the music bounced thinly off the walls and he sat in silence among them wishing they would leave.

But he wanted someone to come. He rang again.

Tulliola, too, must have spent a night down here, before— Where, on these cracked tiles still there under his silk Bactrian rugs, had she dropped to the floor? Had she cried and battered the door, the way he had?

He had been thinking more and more about Tulliola lately. It had got worse since Amaryllis and Noriko had disappeared, and the physical vividness of some of the memories astonished him – the smoothness of her hair in its coil; the warmth of her lips as he'd pushed the pin into her heart . . .

He scratched at his face again, and he realised suddenly how many times his calls had gone unanswered. He took some relief in the itch of indignation. He rose from the chair in which he'd been slumped and went into the corridor to look for a servant.

Then he heard footsteps, coursing towards the stairs, and part of him knew immediately who they were and what was going to happen. He'd been waiting for it for years. But he didn't try to run until he saw them.

He saw Varius first and, too late, he tried to think where the nearest gun was – back beside the chair he had left, probably out of reach, but perhaps—

And before he could even turn, he saw Sulien, his face rigid with sadness and disgust. And beside him was Una. The names

Drusus had tried to strip from them breathed in his ears: Noviana, Novianus.

The newly come, no Novian but one. The newer branch of Novian stem. No Novian but another comes to ruin you. Save yourself from that, if you think you can.

'I knew they lied to me,' he said, on his breath, 'I knew— I knew you weren't dead.'

And yet, if wraiths composed of crematoria smoke from beneath the Colosseum had crept in under the door, it could not have been more terrible to face them.

He knew at once that the mass of people accompanying them were slaves. He was not even surprised to see faces he recognised among them, faces he'd seen hovering about his table or disappearing into passageways. For a fraction of a second the worst, most incomprehensible thing of all was the bald accusation of the Roman Army uniform Sulien was wearing.

Then he did run, and they surged after him like a pack of hounds across the Colosseum's floor, and he just made it inside the room he had left and closed the door. And in the moment he managed to hold it shut he thought he felt Una's poisonous presence inside his head, watching his thoughts, and if he could have let go of the door he would have beaten and clawed at his skull to get it out, as it built and pushed, like this deadly human weight against the door.

He couldn't lock the door in time and he screamed as they smashed inside, lifted him like a wave, slammed him into the chair. Their hands loaded onto him, held him there.

A woman with dark hair shorn close to the skull and Tulliola's face hurled herself at him, howling, her voice splintering into sobs as her fist slammed into his throat, her nails ripped at his face. Then he recognised her, remembered her calm blank face on the pillow beneath him, and he began to gasp, 'Please, please—'

He couldn't bear to die like this, torn to pieces in this cell, that face distorted in rage before him— No, he couldn't die, the Sibyl had promised—

'Maralah,' said a low, clear voice – Varius? 'We need him to live.'

Even though he couldn't guess what they meant to do to him instead, for a second relief thrilled through the anguish; yes, anything but dying, at any cost he wanted to live.

Tulliola-Amaryllis turned sobbing into the arms of an older, fawn-skinned woman, who pulled her away from him.

And then he could see all the way to the back of the room, and his cousin, Makaria, standing in the doorway. Her body was turned away, almost hidden by the door jamb, and she looked at him sidelong over her shoulder, as if she hated to watch at all, but had to.

Your cousin against you, afterwards . . . Why had he thought the Sibyl, or the voice of the spirit speaking through her, meant the danger was Marcus? Even when she'd as good as promised him Marcus would die?

He shouted Makaria's name in rage and despair, and Makaria's face buckled, but she didn't move. And hands gripped his head and held it still as he looked from Una to Sulien and shrieked, 'What are you going to do, then – what are you doing to me?'

Were they already doing it?

Sulien looked as if he could barely stand to come any closer, but step by slow step he advanced through the cramped mass of people towards the chair. And when he stopped in front of Drusus, he shut his eyes, both as if concentrating and as if to shield himself from something unbearable, and to Drusus' terrified amazement a tear even pushed its way from beneath the lid. But Una's eyes remained fixed on him as she crept up to Sulien's side. Somewhere he heard dogs barking in a low chanted rhythm, pounding along with his heartbeat.

Una leant closer to him and Sulien placed his hands reluctantly on Drusus' shoulder, stroked his face.

'Please,' begged Drusus – and suddenly he remembered a story about his family that he'd never wanted to hear, of revenge for a crucified child, and a witch, stalking into the room of one of his ancestors, the Novian curse.

Then he forgot it. The arena hounds swept in, louder, closer, until they must be in the room already. And then he saw that they were – the noise was coming from under the skin, from behind the faces of the furious slaves, and in another second those claws and booming red mouths would be upon him.

In the end, it was simpler than they had expected it to be. Sulien mumbled, 'Let him go,' and stepped away.

'Wait,' said Una. There was one more thing to do. She reached out, wincing, and slid the ring of office from Drusus' finger.

Whimpering, Drusus scrambled back from them into the corner behind the chair and curled there, shaking and struggling and shouting.

They left him there and went out into the corridor, where Evadne stood smoothing Maralah's hair. There was no need even to lock the door.

'That was what it was always for—?' said Sulien, his voice roughened and thick, 'That's what we were for, to do that to him?'

Una had dropped with a shudder into Varius' arms, resting there with her eyes shut, as if she'd just crawled out of freezing water. She reached for Sulien's shoulder, and whispered, 'It's over now.'

'I could have killed him and not even hesitated,' Sulien said. 'This is worse.'

'No,' cried Maralah bitterly, 'no, it's far better than he deserves.'

'It was already there,' said Una, slowly. 'You could see that, couldn't you? He was doing it to himself. All we did was . . . finish it.'

'Rome will be safe,' said Makaria, though her face looked pinched and pale. 'The war will end. Remember that, if it's difficult to bear.'

Sulien nodded and muttered unevenly, 'Let's get away from him.'

*

They climbed up into the Palace, and up the marble stairs where Salvius' body had fallen. They met only a very few officials on the way to the Imperial Office, not simply because it was late, but because most of the Palace's administrative staff had moved out after the bombs had struck the tower and Septizonium. They looked startled to see Makaria, but she smiled reassuringly, and they subsided.

Inside the painted garden, Makaria stood for a moment, looking around at the walls, the heavy desk. She trailed a hand across its surface as she walked to the chair behind it and sat down.

She'd never had this view of the room before. She looked at Una, Sulien and Varius across it. Varius was smiling – a slight, sad sideways tug of the mouth – to see her there. 'Of course, you and everyone who has been part of this will have freedom, and full citizenship, and every charge against you will be stricken,' she said. 'What else can I do to reward you now?'

'I think you know what we want you to do,' said Una, her expression as hard as it had been outside the Palace gates. But then it softened into a half-smile with sheer fatigue. 'But you can't do it tonight. We will have to talk later.'

Makaria shifted a little in her seat, uneasily. 'I was thinking about your futures – in terms of money, for example.'

'There are more than two thousand of us,' said Sulien. 'A lot of them need money, I'm sure. But I just want my pay from the army. And my men – the thirty-third Anasasian, ninth cohort, fourth centuria, all that's left of it – they're in Nionian custody, I want them home. And I want my real name to be in the records.' He smiled bleakly, remembering. 'I'm not even sure why I want that, but I do. And I'd like to use a longdictor, if you don't mind. But I don't want anything more from the Palace, not this time.'

'It's late,' said Varius. 'Turnus will be arriving soon. We'll be going.'

'Already?' Makaria felt rather panicked.

Una nodded. 'It's up to you now.' She was still carrying the

Imperial ring. She leant across the desk and dropped it into Makaria's palm.

But in the doorway Varius turned back, hesitating.

'Can I ask you something?' he asked, quietly. 'You were with Marcus when—?'

The ache of it washed through Makaria, hurting, but somehow flooding out the anxiety of being here, in this seat, in this room. She settled more deeply into the chair and nodded.

Varius' voice dropped still further. 'Did he suffer?'

Makaria inhaled a long breath, bracing against the memory, and against the fear of the answer she saw on Varius' face. She wished she need not tell the truth, but she answered slowly, 'At first, yes. Yes, he did. But I think he looked . . . peaceful when it was ending.'

Pain dragged across Varius' face, pulling his eyelids closed for a second, but he nodded. 'I'm glad you were with him,' he said.

Alone, Makaria twisted the ring on her finger, feeling the gold warm on her skin, and tried to make the room soften and accept her in the same way. She breathed deeply, and remembered Sina, and an old woman seated on a throne.

In the outer office, Sulien requisitioned a longdictor.

'It's done,' he told Lal. She was still in the flat on the Via Nomentana. Maralah and Evadne were on their way there now.

Her voice still sounded thin and frail, but she said, 'Then we're safe. All of us. And you're home.'

Sulien considered the words with surprise, tried to sound them in his mind as something more than the name of a wish. And he could not quite succeed; it had been too long. But he did smile, naturally and without bitterness, for the first time since he'd entered the Palace.

Yet he couldn't bring himself to leave Una and Varius and go back to her. He needed to stay with the people who had been there with him under the Palace.

They knew, of course, that Makaria could have arranged a car to take them across the city, but all the others dispersing from the Palace gates into the dark were on foot, and none of them wanted to step into a Praetorian car anyway. So they walked, tired as they were, across the Aventine, each of them feeling the Palace and the frantic man in its cells recede, like the heat of a fire behind them.

Una placed her arm across Sulien's back.

There was no reaction at first when Varius knocked on the door of the small house. It was after midnight, and if the sleeping couple above woke it was probably to hope the drunks banging at the door would go away. At last, and with slight awkwardness, Varius called up at the windows, 'Mother, it's me.'

Lights erupted from the house. Even from outside they could hear the stairs rumble with sprinting footsteps. Two shattered, delighted people hurtled through the door and engulfed Varius in their arms.

General Turnus stared at the gold ring on Makaria's finger. It looked as if it fit there – and he did not know it was only because her right hand lay in a fist on the desk, the thumb curled close against the band, propping it in place.

'I'm sure you know that, very rarely, this unfortunate illness does occur in my family,' Makaria said. 'The last case was decades ago. Obviously my poor cousin cannot continue to govern in that condition, but treatments are so much better now. We may hope he will soon make a full recovery. Tomorrow I will be calling a session of the Senate to explain that, in the meantime, and in the interests of stability, I will be acting as his Regent. I will need to deliver an address on longvision, too.'

Turnus tapped his fingers on his side of the desk. 'Madam,' he said with wary courtesy, 'it's very surprising to see you here. Could you tell me how you got here?'

Makaria sat very straight and still in the chair, 'Well,' she said, 'clearly I could not have done so without help.'

There was a long silence. 'The army may not stand for this,' Turnus told her. 'The people may not stand for it.'

Makaria smiled. 'The army is a long way from home,' she said,

'Our soldiers are tired. I think you will agree with me, General – too much has been asked of them. The people want them home. And I am going to bring them back.'

[XXI]

PANTHEON

Even in November, Rome still had these warm, burnished days when its colonnades and bomb craters were wrapped in gold light, only a faint chill underneath it, and a blue depth to the shadows. Drusus was sitting on a marble bench in the garden of Lucius' house on the Caelian Hill, a set of watercolours on a table beside him and a heavy block of paper in his lap. He was painting the two umbrella pines that spread above the lawn.

'How are you, cousin?' Makaria asked politely.

'I'm well enough,' answered Drusus, in a level, mildly ironic voice.

There was still that red blur of roughened, angry skin over his cheekbones, spreading down onto his neck, fingernail scratches over non-existent insect bites. But otherwise he looked the same as he always had, perhaps even a little healthier – the hollow places under his eyes had smoothed away and the scratches aside, his skin looked fresh. He was dressed immaculately, though not in his military uniform now, his hair was glossy, and his expression seemed clear and alert. Makaria found she'd been preparing herself for something different, something like the dull-eyed twitchiness under which Lucius had taken cover for so long. She remembered his speech outside the Colosseum on the day he'd taken the throne, and his wounded face. He looked quite ready to do it again. She shivered.

Lucius was standing watching from the terrace now. Makaria could see his anxious, watchful bearing from here.

'And are you—? Are you keeping busy?' she asked.

'Oh yes,' said Drusus, 'I have to keep busy.'

'But not *too* busy, Drusus – you do need to rest.'

'Yes,' Drusus agreed, the slight edge of mockery in his voice

507

dropping away. 'I've been so tired. It has been so hard . . .' He looked at her quickly, a dubious, wary look. In a furtive whisper, as if afraid of being overheard, he asked, 'Am I still Emperor?'

'Of course you are,' Makaria said. 'You always will be.'

'Yes,' said Drusus, and his voice sounded soothed, but his eyes swung to the shadows among the laurels, widening as if he'd seen something move, and he stiffened. He went on, 'Yes, always, until I die; and that won't be until I'm old, the Sibyl promised me that . . .' But then he started to his feet, shuddering, raising his hands as if to protect himself, and turned to her and begged in a shrill, rising voice: 'Talk to me about something else – talk to me about anything else!'

Makaria also rose to her feet, unnerved. 'What is it?'

Drusus panted; his eyes were screwed shut, as if in a terror of seeing. 'When I think about – about that— That's when they come back. I have to rest – I have to try not to think about it, but I can't always help it. I can't help it! Help me—!'

Makaria tried to answer, but Lucius was already hurrying across the garden towards his son. 'It's all right, Drusus,' he said, 'they're going away again, aren't they? There, look at the trees instead.'

'I shouldn't be like this,' Drusus gasped, frustrated tears leaking helplessly from his eyes.

'Your picture, Drusus,' urged Lucius gently, 'you've almost finished it. It's beautiful.'

Warily, Drusus looked at the paper. It was true, Makaria noticed suddenly – it was a conventional enough little view of the pines, but far more proficient than she would have expected of him, and with a dark clarity about it that kept her eyes on it.

'I didn't know you were so good at this,' she said.

'I've been having lessons,' said Drusus hollowly, but sounding a little calmer.

There were strange shapes in the painted canopies of the trees, and streaks of white, threads of red, that matched nothing she could see in the garden.

'He hears things, of course,' Lucius told her later. 'Dogs

508

barking, he says. And people too, talking behind his back. Salvius. Tullia. But somehow it's worse when he starts reminding himself he's the Emperor, and wanting to be back in the Golden House, or on the longvision. Any time he starts thinking about *power* – that's what does it. I never did know why anybody should want it so much. I don't know how *you* bear it, Makaria. As long as one can keep his mind off that, he's better, he's almost . . .' He sighed.

Lucius was obviously tired, and for a moment Makaria thought he looked older too, but then thought she could just as well have said he looked the opposite. He was standing straighter than usual, and the scared, self-pitying haze across his expression had gone. His lined face had a sad, resolute set she'd never seen on it before. 'I'll look after him,' he said.

Civilian clothes still felt strange, sometimes constricting, sometimes alarmingly soft and unstructured around him. And the choice—! Lal thought the variety available woefully depleted, but it bewildered Sulien; he'd come back to Rome with nothing but his uniform, and now he couldn't remember the basis for deciding between one tunic and another, either in the shops or when he got up for work in the morning. But he liked the feel of his hair growing out, warm and reassuring on the nape of his neck and over the tops of his ears.

He had the day off from the clinic so he'd been round at the Demobilisation Office again, nagging them about the fourth centuria. Yes, they were still at the Roman base on the coast of Tupia; no, there were no reports that any of them was sick or hurt. Sulien remained amazed it could all take so long, even though, as he was disapprovingly reminded, the fourth centuria was receiving preferential treatment and most servicemen would not be home for months yet. Pas was back in Alexandria now, but they talked on the longdictor, arguing over where the reunion should be.

Sometimes he still had dreams. Sometimes he still found

himself murmuring aloud, in his new flat on the Field of Mars, 'I want to go home.'

There was a fresh wind blowing up on the Janiculum Hill, stirring Lal's hair and chafing fresh blood into her cheeks. And as usual she was underdressed for the chill, so Sulien folded his new coat around her as they walked, fastening her to him.

The warmth of her felt so familiar and right against his side, but for a moment when she turned her bright face up towards his, he felt that instead of meeting their gazes slid past or through each other, towards different distances. And he couldn't think of anything to say to her.

Then it passed, as it always did, and she looked so beautiful today, he thought, her eyes greener than anything could be.

He asked, 'Did Docilina knock her paintwater over herself again today?' A family out in Tivoli had engaged Lal to teach their young daughter to paint and draw.

Lal grimaced pityingly. 'That poor little girl. I do need the money, or I'd refuse to keep coming in to torture her. That would be the kindest thing. I'd tell her parents drawing never really made a woman more marriageable.'

'Oh, it might,' said Sulien, and grinned at her. 'Would you marry me?'

He'd wondered if she was expecting it, but from the expression, apparently not. Her lips parted and trembled; she breathed, 'Sulien—' and clung to him, her face pressed so hard against his chest that for a little while the ache between them disappeared.

Then she wrenched herself back, and panted, 'No, I can't— We can't.'

Sulien felt dully disappointed. The loneliness that was always whistling through the city came gusting over the brow of the Janiculum Hill with the wind, yet the feeling seemed older, staler than it should have. He thought with glum dread of having to go back to his empty flat, and said, 'Oh.'

Lal wiped at her eyes. 'I know why you asked me. You want it all back – everything you would have had. And you *would* have loved me, I think, if there hadn't been the Colosseum, and the war—'

'I do love you,' he interrupted, startled, 'how could I not love you, after everything?'

'You think you should.' Lal managed, briefly, to laugh. 'And quite right too.' She reached up to stroke his face. 'I wish it was as easy as that.'

Sulien dawdled on the way home, afraid of the silence there, but, to his relief, Una was waiting for him, come from the Palatine Library, where she was working. She and Varius were trying to get a flat close to him, perhaps even in the same building, but it had taken them longer to find the money. Varius was working with Delir now, who had started importing confectionery from Persia and Cappadocia. Sweet things were scarce in Rome.

'She said no,' Sulien told her.

Una's face dropped, but there was a trace of something other than dismay in it – lack of surprise, even almost relief, maybe. She shook her head at the question he hadn't spoken. 'I hoped I was wrong,' she murmured, 'but I was afraid if you did marry you might both regret it. I'm sorry.'

Sulien thought of what Lal had said, and then remembered his old, ransacked flat, just across the river – his scrambling effort to salvage something from it that last day. Suddenly the feeling choked him that there must have been some way he could have kept more. He began, 'I should have—'

'No, no,' interrupted Una, softly, 'don't.'

Sulien sighed. 'What about you and Varius?'

'Delir has him interviewing people. He says he knows in another few months he'll be sick of the sight of sweets, but it's peaceful for now. And then, if we can save a little money—'

'I mean,' said Sulien, 'are you going to marry him?'

Una made a face. 'Not you too. His parents never stop asking us that.' But she smiled, and lowered her eyes, briefly shy. She confessed, 'I think so.'

They poured wine, and sat by the window.

'I've been thinking,' said Sulien, 'I have to wait here until my men are back, but then I think I might go home – I mean, back to London. I thought . . . I could try and find our mother.' His voice jolted awkwardly over the last word, because it felt unnatural when he spoke it.

Una stiffened. She became very still in the chair.

'You still don't want to see her?' asked Sulien.

Una's lips had gone white. 'I can't,' she said, her voice hurried and hoarse. 'She sold us. I can't.'

'Well,' he said, 'you don't have to, but I think I do.'

Una nodded slowly.

'She might have had other children,' said Sulien. 'They'd still only be little kids, I guess, but I want to see them. And we must have cousins, somewhere – there must be someone.'

There was a pause. 'You won't *stay*?' Una said, hesitantly.

He looked at her in surprise. 'My job's here. You're here. Why would you ever think I wouldn't come back?'

There was a long pause as they both remembered the hounds tearing at them on the sand of the Colosseum, and thought of Drusus in the house on the Caelian Hill. 'Your accent hasn't changed back,' said Una, finally.

'Hasn't it?' He never noticed until she told him. 'Where do I sound like I'm from, then?'

Una smiled at him with affection and regret. 'Everywhere.'

The longdictor flashed after Una left, and Sulien reached readily to lift the circlet, feeling lucky. The quiet hadn't had enough time to take real hold. He thought it might be Pas.

'What do you mean by being in Rome for six weeks and not telling me?' Tancorix demanded.

Sulien laughed, and dropped happily into the chair beside the longdictor to listen to her. 'I'm sorry.'

'You were supposed to be dead, you know, in the Colosseum – do you know how much I cried? Then there were all these rumours you were in Africa or on the moon or somewhere impossible – and then it's all over the news that you're alive and well and cleared of all charges, and I would have thought that was the kind of thing you might have mentioned.'

'I am sorry,' repeated Sulien, guilty and touched, 'there's been so much to deal with – with the army and getting my job back and finding somewhere to live . . .'

'I can imagine,' said Tancorix, softening. 'Well, no, I mean, of course I can't. Tell me, then.'

'There's too much,' he said, 'You'll have to come round.'

'I can't yet,' she said, 'I've got a rehearsal. But I could to-morrow, or if you're up after midnight I might be able to drop round—'

'Yes,' said Sulien, 'Do that.'

'Tell me something first,' she said.

Sulien thought of how long it had been since he had carried Una's unconscious body out of Tancorix's sight, everything she didn't know. 'I'm thinking of going to London,' he answered, instead of any of it.

There was a pause. 'Sometimes I've thought of going back there,' she admitted.

He couldn't speak again at once, thinking of it all. He could hear her listening to the crack in the silence. She asked, at last, 'Are you all right?'

Sulien opened his eyes, breathed out. He said, 'Not yet.'

Una and Makaria met again in the Imperial Office.

'Did you see my broadcast?' asked Makaria.

Una nodded. 'You were very good,' she muttered. Makaria had explained she would be taking only some modest title such as Imperial Protectress. She claimed she shrank from the very idea of anything grander.

Makaria smiled. 'It wasn't true. I would like ceremonies and processions and to call myself Empress. I wouldn't have expected it of myself. It seems it does run in the family.'

The crumpled scrap of notepaper that was Marcus' will lay on the desk between them.

'I had the first family to leave Siphnos take it with them,'

Makaria said quietly. 'I asked them to send it to friends of theirs in Spalatum. Hypatia collected it on her way here.'

Una stared at it. 'When will this be enacted?' she asked. 'When will all the slaves be free?'

And there was a silence, of exactly the length and weight she'd been dreading. 'I think the time is coming,' said Makaria cautiously, at last.

Una repeated more urgently, 'When?'

Makaria looked down, turned her hand gently back and forth so that the light ran around the boss of the ring. 'Una. I haven't forgotten who put this into my hand,' she said, 'but I have the end of a war to manage. There are cities to rebuild. The Empire's as poor and tired and angry as it's ever been, and a good number of Romans think I should be shot for daring to sit here. There are men in the Senate who could probably arrange it. What good am I to you or anyone if they convince the people I'm trying to ruin Rome and drag me out of here?'

'There will always be an excuse,' said Una stubbornly. 'There won't ever be a right time.'

Makaria sighed. 'I will be introducing certain rights,' she said, 'and restrictions, on age, and standards of treatment, and length of service—'

'Length of service!' cried Una, 'then you're talking about years – *decades* – long enough for it to matter when people who are enslaved now get to old age.'

She fell back in the chair and looked at the sheet of paper on the desk to avoid Makaria's face.

'I can only do what's possible,' said Makaria, 'in the world as it is.'

There was another silence. Una said, 'It will happen much sooner than that.' But her voice sounded humiliatingly small, and there was a warning pressure of tears behind her eyes. She couldn't stop herself from thinking blackly, *then it has all been for nothing*. Marcus' straining words and his collapsing handwriting were unbearable to look at.

Varius had said, months ago, on the anniversary of Marcus' death, that there would be enough work for ten lifetimes.

Makaria was looking at her with sad compassion. Una straightened.

'I raised two thousand people in nine months,' she said. 'What do you think I can do in five years, or ten?'

'You're still very young,' said Makaria, gently. 'You're working in the Palatine Library?'

'For now,' Una replied distantly.

'I thought perhaps you might be interested to know that the academies will be opening to female scholars soon: Athens and Byzantium and Alexandria.'

'Good,' said Una, her voice still listless at first, then with more strength, 'good. I could visit perhaps, for a while. But not for too long. I'm not going away, your Highness. We're not going away.' She stood up and reached for the sheet of paper. She met Makaria's eyes. 'This is ours,' she said. 'And this will happen. There will be so many of us that you and Rome will have to listen to us. You'll do it then.' And as she turned towards the door she finished, under her breath, 'Or I'll do it myself.'

Una walked back through the city towards the Field of Mars. At first she felt bruised and angry, and shaken by the memory of her own words. The folded paper in her pocket scorched her. And perhaps she had gone too far, claimed too much.

But the cool ancient light enveloped Rome, and as she walked, it poured over her, until it seemed to flow into her bloodstream, smoothing her breath, slowing her footsteps, turning everything gold. She could almost hear the light, whispering and singing on the stones, feel the current of it moving through the streets, carrying her home.

Bombed and bruised, Rome seemed somehow even older than before. A few skeletal marble columns were still standing in what had been the Forum. The Colosseum's roof and a slice of the wall were gone altogether.

And there was the statue of Marcus in Trajan's Forum. Una

had dreaded seeing it, but now she made herself stop and face it, and she saw that even if it had been made under Drusus, even if it had been meant as a piece of propaganda, the artist was a true artist and had worked sincerely. It was almost too lifelike: Marcus' expression was grave, and faintly nervous, and hopeful. Una smiled at him, and let tears fill her eyes. The word *Emperor* had been added to his name on the pedestal.

The bombs had not touched the Pantheon. It crouched on the ground, dark and stolidly menacing, and it amazed her, suddenly, that anything built by human beings could last so long.

Una drifted through the doors, and inside, the dark mass of the dome seemed weightless around the pillar of sky that stood within it. The circle of open air in the oculus forced the eye towards it and through it, so Una looked up because she had to. Above her, swallows shot past.

[CHARACTER LIST]

(All characters *named* in the text. All dates are in AUC – e.g, 2757 = 2004 AD.)

A

Acilius – a Roman soldier.

Albus – one of **Salvius'** sons-in-law.

Alexander – **Cleomenes'** and **Cominia's** young son.

'Amaryllis' – a name for a slave-girl owned by **Drusus**.

Arite – a woman living in a small town in east Venedia.

Arria – **Sulien's** upstairs neighbour in Transtiberina.

Arvina – the Vigile Prefect.

Asper – a Roman soldier.

B

Bahram – **Delir's** brother-in-law, **Lal's** uncle.

Bassus – **Tancorix's** lover.

Batu – a slave from a factory in east Venedia.

Bupe – a former slave from Veii Imperial Arms factory, after-wards a follower of **Dama**.

C

Caerellius – a Roman soldier.

Calliope – a friend of **Tancorix's**.

Castus – a vigile officer.

Cilo – the Praetorian Prefect.

Cleomenes – a vigile commander, married to **Cominia**.

Clodia Aurelia – mother of **Marcus**, wife of **Leo**, supporter of the abolition of slavery. Murdered in 2757 along with her husband.

Cominia – a hairdresser, married to **Cleomenes**.

D

Dama – a former slave, crucified for murder in 2753, but taken down from the cross alive by **Delir**. Instrumental in establishing the slave-refuge in the Pyrenees. Involved in the rescue of **Marcus** from the Galenian Sanctuary in 2757. Afterwards a revolutionary responsible for numerous arson attacks, assassinations, and the bombing of the Colosseum in 2761.

Daw, Lord – Lord of Bamashu (Bamaria).

Decimus – **Salvius'** youngest child.

Delir – a former merchant from Persia, subsequently a fugitive. Established a slave refuge camp in the Holzarta gorge in the Pyrenees, after rescuing the slave **Dama** from crucifixion. Later, having learned of his protégé's involvement in the bombings and arson attacks of 2760, he tracked the fugitive Dama to Holzarta and accompanied him into exile and voluntary imprisonment on a remote island. Returned to Rome after Dama escaped.

Dorion – a Roman soldier.

Drusilla Terentia – divorced wife of **Lucius**, mother of **Drusus**.

Drusus – see **Novii**.

E

Eudoxius – a Senator.

Evadne – a freedwoman living on the eastern edge of the coast of Tripolitania.

F

Faustus – see **Novii**.

Flaccus – a Roman soldier.

Fulvus – one of Salvius' sons-in-law.

G

Galeo – a Roman soldier.

Gemella – wife of **Varius**, poisoned in mistake for **Marcus** by **Tulliola** in 2757.

Glycon – Faustus' *cubicularius*, or private secretary.
Gnatho – a Roman soldier.
Go-natoku – Regnal name of the current Nionian Emperor.
Gracilis – a Roman Centurion of the 33rd Anasasian Legion.

H

Hanno – a Roman soldier.
Hidaka – a Nionian soldier from Tokogane.
Hirtius – a Roman lawyer.
Hypatia – a friend of Makaria living on Siphnos.

I

Isione – An abolitionist living on Naxos.

J

Jun Shen, also (to the Romans) **Junosena** – Dowager Empress of Sina.

K

Kaneharu – a Nionian prince, half-brother of **Tadahito** and full brother to **Noriko**. Son of the **Go-natoku Emperor**.
Kato-no-Masaru, also (to the Romans) **Masarus Cato** –Lord of Tokogane, assassinated during the peace talks in Bianjing in 2760.
Kebede, Marcus – King of Independent Ethiopia, regnal name **Salomon VI**.

L

Lal – daughter of **Delir**, formerly a fugitive, living in Rome.
Lanatus – a Roman soldier.
Leimeie – a woman living in a small town in east Venedia.
Leo – see **Novii**.
Liuyin – son of an official, living in Jiangning.
Lucius –see **Novii**.
Lucullus – the captain of the Emperor's personal escort.
Lysander – a slave belonging to **Salvius'** family.

M

Mada – a woman living in a small town in east Venedia.

Magnus –Salvius' son-in-law, married to **Salvia Prima**

Makaria – see **Novii**.

Marcus – see **Novii**.

Marcus Kebede see **Kebede** and **Salomon VI**.

Minius – a Roman soldier.

Morokata – a Nionian Lord.

N

Noriko – eldest daughter of the Go-natoku Emperor, wife of **Marcus**.

Novii, The – the Roman Imperial family.

Novia Faustina, nicknamed **Makaria** – only child of **Faustus**.

Drusus Novius Faustus – son of **Lucius** and **Drusilla Terentia**, cousin of **Makaria** and **Marcus**.

Lucius Novius Faustus – brother of **Faustus** and **Leo**, father of **Drusus**, uncle of **Marcus** and **Makaria**. Suffers from the 'Novian curse' – excluded from succession.

Marcus Novius Faustus Leo – son of **Leo** and **Clodia**, nephew of **Faustus** and **Lucius**, cousin of **Makaria** and **Drusus**. Heir Apparent to the Roman throne. Married to **Noriko**.

Tertius Novius Faustus Leo – Youngest brother of **Faustus** and **Lucius**, father of **Marcus**. Heir presumptive to the Roman throne, supporter of the abolition of slavery, murdered along with his wife **Clodia Aurelia** in 2757.

Titus Novius Faustus Augustus – Emperor of Rome.

P

Pas – a Roman soldier.

Petreius – a Roman soldier.

Phanias – an accountant with abolitionist sympathies in Tamiathis.

Philia – a slave belonging to **Salvius'** family.

Praxinoa – a former slave living in Alexandria.

Psyche – a slave belonging to **Salvius'** family.

Q

Quentin, **Memmius**, an advisor to Faustus.

S

Sakura – a lady-in-waiting attending **Noriko**.

Salomon VI – regnal name of the King of Independent Ethiopia (Marcus **Kebede**).

Salvia Prima – Salvius' daughter.

Salvilla – Salvius' youngest daughter.

Salvius – General of the Legions of the Roman Empire.

Sibyl, **The** – the Pythia at Delphi.

Sulien – brother of **Una**. A former slave with healing abilities born in London. Sentenced to crucifixion for rape in 2757, but rescued by Una and later exonerated by the testimony of **Tancorix**.

T

Tadahito, also (to the Romans) **Tadasius** – The Nionian Crown Prince, eldest son of the **Go-natoku Emperor**.

Takanari – a Nionian prince, half-brother of **Noriko** and **Tadahito**, and son of the **Go-natoku Emperor**.

Tancorix – the daughter of the London family that owned **Sulien**. Formerly married to Epimachus, disgraced by admission of an affair with a slave. Now living as a singer in Rome with her daughter, **Xanthe**.

Tenos – an abolitionist living on Naxos.

Thalna – the Commander of Public Order Operations in Rome.

Thekla – a slave in Alexandria.

Theon – a former slave living in Alexandria.

Tomoe – a lady-in-waiting attending **Noriko**.

Tulliola (Tullia Marciana) Former wife of **Faustus**. Arrested for involvement in the pro-slavery conspiracy that killed **Leo**,

Clodia and **Gemella**. Died in custody, apparently by suicide, in 2757 (actually murdered by Drusus).

Turnus – a Roman General.

U

Ulpia – nurse to **Lucius**.

Una – sister of **Sulien**. A former slave with strange abilities born in London.

V

Varius, Caius – friend and senior advisor to **Marcus**. Former director of a free clinic for slaves in Transtiberine Rome. Former private secretary to **Leo**, widower of **Gemella**. Charged with murder and treason in 2757, but later exonerated.

Vituriga – a landlady at a taverna in eastern Venedia.

Vonones – a Roman military scientist.

X

Xanthe – Daughter of **Tancorix**.

Z

Zhu Li – the Grand Preceptor in Bianjing, Sina.

Ziye – a former gladiatrix of Sinoan origin. Escaped to the Holzarta refuge camp in 2754. Freedom granted by **Marcus**, living with **Delir** and **Lal** in Rome.

[A SHORT HISTORY OF THE ROMAN EMPIRE]

933 TO 2700 AUC
(180–1947 CE)

'To heal, as far as it was possible, the wounds inflicted by the hand
of tyranny, was the pleasing, but melancholy task of Pertinax'
(*Decline and Fall of the Roman Empire*, Edward Gibbon)

CE	AUC	
180	933	Death of **Marcus Aurelius**. His son Lucius Aelius Aurelius **Commodus** succeeds as Emperor.
192	945	Commodus' bloody and extravagant reign leaves Rome impoverished and riddled with corruption. He is murdered by a group of conspirators including his chamberlain, concubine and Laetus, the head of the Praetorian Guard (the urban army whose formal function was to protect the Emperor). The conspirators claim that Commodus died of apoplexy, and install as Emperor 66-year-old Publius Helvius **Pertinax**, the son of a freedman who had risen through merit to become a General, a Senator and minister of justice.

HELVIAN IMPERIAL DYNASTY

192–204	945–957	Early in Pertinax's reign, Laetus, disgruntled by Pertinax's independence, encourages a plot by the Praetorian Guard to assassinate him. The plot is discovered* and Laetus banished.

---

* This is where my history of the Roman Empire departs from the usual one. In
reality, the plot was successful. The talented and conscientious Pertinax (who
planned many of the reforms indicated here) was murdered after only eighty-six days

Pertinax disbands almost all of the Praetorian Guard, hand-picking the remainder for loyalty. At the same time he increases the powers and numbers of the Vigiles to create a counterweight police force, reasoning that any future conspiracy against the Emperor in one body will be detected and exposed by the other.

Pertinax remits Commodus' oppressive taxes. He halves the expenses of the Imperial household, grants tax-breaks to farmers and lifts restrictions on commerce.

He taxes the urban aristocracy more heavily, but the cities benefit from the wealth generated by the farms, and he restores to the Senate some of the authority it had lost.

204	957	**Death of Pertinax** After the disastrous succession of Commodus, Pertinax was reluctant to name his young son Publius Helvius Pertinax II, '**Venedicus**', as Caesar and heir to the Empire until just before his death. The senate approve the succession.
204–220	957–973	Pertinax II continues his father's economic reforms, gradually rebuilding the Empire's finances. When the economy permits it he restructures the army, detaching the legions from the frontier garrisons to create a mobile

in office and the Praetorians auctioned the throne to the highest bidder. Didius Julianus bought the title of Emperor, but was deposed and executed shortly afterwards by Septimius Severus, who returned to Rome from Pannonia to avenge Pertinax.

Severus corrected many of the problems facing Rome and at the time his reign could be viewed as a success. But he stripped the Senate of authority and allowed corruption and indiscipline to flourish in the army, whose power undermined the stability of the Empire. Gibbon says of Severus: '*Posterity, who experienced the fatal effects of his maxims, justly considered him the principal author of the decline of the Roman Empire.*'

		force. He ties pay to the rate of inflation, stabilising the income of the soldiers and rendering them less susceptible to bribery, whilst attracting a higher standard of recruit.
225	978	Ardashir, the Persian king, kills the last king of Parthia and creates the Sassanian Persian Empire, with Zoroastrianism as its state religion.
238	991	Renewed attacks from Germanic tribes along the Rhine and Danube. The revitalised army resists and pushes the barbarians back. To deal more fully with the threat, and despite protests from Roman Britons, Pertinax II pulls the legions out of Britain and leads a massive force into Germany and Sarmatia.
230–240	983–993	Ardashir invades India, and Roman territory in Syria. In 240, his son Shapur succeeds to the Persian throne.
238–242	973–978	Pertinax II completes the conquest of Germany and Venedia, pushing up into Fennia and Gothia.
242–256	978–992	Skirmishes with Persia over Armenia. Roman recapture of Syria.
256	992	Death of Pertinax II, accession of Lucius Helvius Pertinax **Sarmaticus**. Rome's victories over the Eastern European tribes continue into Sarmatia and Alania.
260–265	996–1009	Still feeling the elation of their German victory, Roman troops, augmented by huge numbers of German barbarians and with support from Palmyra, attack and conquer Shapur's Persian Empire.
265–291	1009–1044	Occasional Persian uprisings and fluctuating borders in Roman Persia, but Rome's grip remains generally firm.

291–313	1044–1066	Under Sarmaticus' adopted son Gaius Flavius **Sulpicianus**, Rome loses Persia and Mesopotamia.
313–345	1066–1098	Marcus Flavius Sulpicianus **Cruentus** reconquers Persia and Mesopotamia. Slaughter and enslavement of thousands of Persians. Persecution of Christians, Zoroastrians and Jews throughout Empire. Invasion and conquest of Arabia. Cruentus exports the Roman religion, or a Roman interpretation of local deities, to the enlarged Eastern Empire.
347–447	1100–1200	From here on it will be convenient to summarise the major gains, losses and technological advances of each century.

SECOND FLAVIAN DYNASTY 1066–1234 AUC

Reconquest of Britain, with Hibernia and Caledonia. There has been a revival of Celtic culture, but a sustained British nostalgia for Roman rule makes victory fairly easy. Sporadic incursions by Huns, but they are either repelled or absorbed by Rome, resulting in gradual, unsystematic Roman expansion into Scythia.

447–547	1200–1300	**ACILIAN DYNASTY 1234–1618 AUC**

Continued conquests of territory in Scythia. Expansion through Persian territory into India. Lengthy wars to secure it. Romanisation of Indian Gods.

547–647	1300–1400	Quelling more uprisings and rebellions in India and resulting instability in the region keep the military fully occupied – no expansion.

647–747	1400–1500	Attempted expansion into Sina (China) unsuccessful, and there are continuing problems in Syria, Persia and India.
747–847	1500–1600	Border disputes with Sina. India and Persia subside into uneasy peace, but tensions will flare up at any sign of weakness in the Empire for centuries to come. By this time the once-significant Christian sect has more or less died out of existence. Active persecution of Jews and Zoroastrians has ceased, although they are still denied full citizenship.
847–947	1600–1700	CORDIAN DYNASTY 1618–1836 AUC Libya and other Roman states in North Africa attempt to devolve peacefully from the Empire, but Africa is essential to feeding the Roman world. Heightened military presence there.
947–1047	1700–1800	Song Dynasty unifies and stabilises Sina. Rome is initially concerned about Sina's growing power, but the Emperor feels that Rome is now unassailable, reattempted conquest of Sina would be costly and futile, and that therefore there is no need to jeopardise profitable trade with Sina. Relations remain cordial – especially since Sina supports Roman rule in India.
1047–1147	1800–1900	BLANDIAN DYNASTY 1836–2176 AUC The Romans defend the Song against the Jurchen uprising. Rome introduces various Sinoan innovations, such as paper money, banking, Romanised versions of certain fashions in clothing – and gunpowder.

1147–1247	1900–2000	Quicker to see the military application of the new discovery than its Sinoan inventors, Rome sides with Sina against the Mongols, saving the Song Dynasty. First Roman contact with Nionia (Japan), and Rome welcomes the new source of coveted oriental goods, but has little political interest as yet in the chain of islands, which is riven with internal divisions and wars.
1247–1347	2000–2100	Armed with cannons, Rome invades Ethiopia. Sina watches this new phase of expansion with concern. The Nionian Emperor Go-Daigo visits Rome, learns about Roman exploration and conquest, and brings the secret of gunpowder back to Nionia.
1347–1447	2100–2200	Go-Daigo leads the Kemmu Restoration, using firearms against the powerful Hojo regency. The new firepower helps him to see off opposition from his erstwhile ally, Ashikaga Takauji. He restores the powers of the Emperor and unites Nionia. Continued exploration/conquest of interior Africa runs into difficulty when Roman African states unexpectedly turn against Rome. Roman explorers return from an attempt to circumnavigate the globe with news of a brief landing on a huge new landmass in the West. They call it Terra Nova, but this is no time for a military adventure there. Plague in Europe and in parts of Sina. The Emperor Blandius **Postumus** dies suddenly and there is a struggle for power unprecedented in over a thousand years.

1447–1547	2200–2300	The first electrostatic machine.

After a succession of short-lived Emperors, the Senate votes Sextus Vincius **Sacerdos** into power.

VINCIAN DYNASTY 2204–2509 AUC

Sacerdos is still trying to secure his position when Nionia invades Corea and attacks Sinoan territory. Sina appeals to Rome for help, but the call comes at exactly the wrong time. Rome is struggling to survive in the face of its internal rifts, African entanglements, renewed Indo-Persian problems and the decimating effects of plague. The Empire is in no position to assist.

Sina battles Nionia alone but concedes large tracts of territory. Roman relations with both Sina and Nionia are damaged.

Rome tries to repair the damage of the last century. In an attempt to rebuild Roman solidarity, Sacerdos extends full citizenship to all free inhabitants of the Empire, regardless of nationality or religion, withholding only the right to hold office from freedmen.

1547–1647	2300–2400	Meanwhile, Nionia is still in the ascendant.

Nionian explorers sight the Southern island continent and call it Goshu.

When Nionia begins to colonise Goshu, Rome becomes seriously alarmed. Nionia is beginning to look like a serious rival to the Empire. Rome puts pressure on Nionia to cease expanding and urges Sina to do the same, but since becoming a buffer state between Rome and Nionia, Sina has become increasingly introspective, and the Sinoan government refuses to get involved.

Rome completes the conquest of Africa. More experiments in electricity and magnetics.

Rome at last begins a serious invasion of central and southern Terranova, spreading cautiously into Mexica, Maia, and inland into Aravacia.

Nionia follows suit, entering Terranova in the far north. Rome is more uneasy than ever and begins seriously to debate war but for the moment, and to the dissatisfaction of many, does nothing; there is still a huge amount of land, with its own peoples to contend with, between the two powers.

1647–1747	2400–2500	Nionia pushes south, until Rome's fears that she is not only allowing her rival to claim valuable territory but that her existing Terranovan provinces are under threat become intolerable. Conflict is now inevitable and is to dominate the next century.

The two armies sweep towards each other across the country – the Romans pushing north from the south-eastern coast of the northern continent , each trying to cajole or force the indigenous peoples to side with them.

The ensuing sequence of wars, although they vary in intensity and are divided by short, unsuccessful peace agreements, is brutal and often chaotic, with naval battles in the Atlantic and around Nionia itself. Tracts of land change hands several times, at vast cost in Roman, Nionian, and Terranovan lives. The Camian peninsula in Mexica is of particular importance since for Rome to allow the Nionians to claim it would amount to their being permanently flanked.

The Emperor Vincius **Arcadius** dies in suspicious circumstances and his brother, **Nasennius**, seizes power.

The Roman military and economy has been damaged. During a brief lull in the Roman–Nionian conflict, in the final years of the 25th Century, the first African Uprising takes place in the province of Lundae in Africa.

The first – very slow and inefficient – electrically powered vehicles to run on magnetic rails.

| 1747–1847 | 2500–2600 | Madness first appears in the Novian family. |

The Africans are temporarily subdued.

The ensuing sequence of wars, although they vary in intensity andIn the second African Uprising of 2503, a poorly equipped Roman legion is massacred near Musitania (Mosi-oa-Tunya) Falls. Nasennius is widely blamed for the disaster.

Oppius Novius, Nasennius' nephew by marriage, gains in popularity in the Senate.

After an outbreak of smallpox in Rome, Nasennius commits suicide leaving no children. Oppius Novius takes power.

NOVIAN DYNASTY 2509 AUC – PRESENT

Rome secures Northern half of Africa. Southern Africa claims independence. Although bringing the conflict to an end and holding onto Northern territory are significant successes for Rome, this is the first serious loss of territory for the Empire in centuries. Cracks appear elsewhere in the Empire: there is conflict in Terranova, and old tensions in India stir again.

In 2512, Oppius' brother Servius succumbs to family madness.

Oppius works to rebuild international stability. He succeeds in reversing Roman fortunes in Terranova, where the Romans advance north. His task is eased by new technology such as longscript – a method of transmitting codes through electric pulses invented in 2511. This allows direct government of overseas territory. Longscript lines are laid under the Atlantic, and through Africa. Thirty years later come longdictors. Rome will be able to respond far more swiftly to any future unrest.

There are accelerated attempts to find a reliable form of air-travel.

Rome's military might is, just, superior to Nionia's, but it looks as though it will be impossible ever to expel the Nionians from the Terranova altogether. Therefore, Rome finally comes to grudging terms with Nionia and northern Terranova is divided between the two Empires. Under the Mixigana Treaty, a huge wall is built across the continent to separate them. Trade between Nionia and Rome resumes, but there is a persistent distrust and rivalry.

Rome develops new high explosives. Nionia seems always on the verge of catching up with Roman technology.

Rome begins to expand through Southern Terranova.

Rome works to improve the network of roads, whilst simultaneously building a vast system of magnetways throughout the Empire.

1847–1947	2600–2700	Development of flight using circling wings powered by engines – the first volucer. Continued colonisation of North and South Terranova. The arms race with Nionia goes on.

[ACKNOWLEDGEMENTS]

Many thanks are owed –

To Jo Fletcher, Gillian Redfearn, Charlie Panayiotou, Jon Wood, Genevieve Pegg and all at Orion and Gollancz.

To St John Donald and Ariella Feiner, and especially Simon Trewin for his 'evil plan.'

To Robert Low for suggesting the name of the 'Onager' (and giving me an idea that led to that of the 'Surijin').

To Tomoko Abe and members of the Livejournal group *Linguaphiles*, for help with Japanese names.

To Maisie Tomlinson and Andrew Sturdy for advice about boats and navigation.

And to RJ Ellory, Ronni Phillips, Anne Perry, Jared Shurin, Roz Kaveney, Camille Lofters, for being generally wonderful.